JOHN GRIMES
TRAMP CAPTAIN

Books by A. Bertram Chandler

John Grimes (series)
The Road to the Rim (1967)
To Prime the Pump (1971)
The Hard Way Up (1972)
Spartan Planet (1968)
The Inheritors (1972)
The Broken Cycle (1975)
The Big Black Mark (1975)
The Far Traveller (1977)
Star Courier (1977)
To Keep the Ship (1978)
Matilda's Stepchildren (1979)
Star Loot (1980)
The Anarch Lords (1981)
The Last Amazon (1984)
The Wild Ones (1984)
Catch the Star Winds (1969)
Into the Alternate Universe (1964)
Contraband from Other-Space (1967)
The Rim Gods (1969)
The Dark Dimensions (1971)
Alternate Orbits (1971)
The Gateway to Never (1972)
The Way Back (1976)

Derek Calver (series)
The Rim of Space (1961)
The Ship from Outside (1963)

Christopher Wilkinson (series)
The Coils of Time (1964)
The Alternate Martians (1965)

Empress (series)
Empress of Outer Space (1965)
Space Mercenaries (1965)
Nebula Alert (1967)

Other Novels
Bring Back Yesterday (1961)
Rendezvous on a Lost World (1961)
The Hamelin Plague (1963)
Beyond the Galactic Rim (1963)
Glory Planet (1964)
The Deep Reaches of Space (1964)
The Sea Beasts (1971)
The Bitter Pill (1974)
Kelly Country (1983)
To Rule the Refugees (1983)
Frontier of the Dark (1984)
Find the Lady (1984)

Short Fiction
Up to the Sky in Ships (1982)
From Sea to Shining Star (1990)

JOHN GRIMES
TRAMP CAPTAIN

TO KEEP THE SHIP

MATILDA'S STEPCHILDREN

STAR LOOT

THE ANARCH LORDS

A. Bertram Chandler

This is a work of fiction. All the characters and events portrayed in these novels are either fictitious or are used fictitiously.

First SFBC Science Fiction Printing: January 2003.

Published by arrangement with the author's estate, via JABberwocky Literary Agency,
P.O. Box 4558
Sunnyside, NY 11104-0558

Visit The SFBC at http://www.sfbc.com

ISBN 0-7394-3119-6

Printed in the United States of America.

Contents

To Keep the Ship

One

There is a tide in the affairs of men that, taken at the flood, leads on to fortune. But tides have a habit of ebbing—and Grimes's personal tide had ebbed. He wasn't quite on the rocks but he was most definitely stranded and would remain so until he could raise the wherewithal to pay his steadily mounting port dues and various fines and legal expenses. Meanwhile his beloved *Little Sister* was under arrest, with a writ firmly glued to her outer airlock door, and her owner-master had been obliged to seek paid employment. He was long used to three square meals a day with sips and nibbles in between and there is usually a charge for such sustenance. He could have solved all his financial problems by selling the ship—only a deep-space-going pinnace but valuable nonetheless; even as scrap she would have fetched a not so small fortune—but he was stubborn. He could have shipped out as Third Mate of the Interstellar Transport Commission's *Epsilon Draconis*—one of her officers had been involved in a serious ground-car accident when returning to the spaceport after a rather wild party—but did not elect to do so. Firstly, he had been too long in Command to relish the idea of signing on as a junior officer. Secondly, as long as he was the owner of *Little Sister* he wanted to stay where he could keep an eye on her. A spaceship entirely constructed of an isotope of gold is too precious an artifact to be left in the full charge of strangers.

The trouble had started when Far Traveler Couriers (the plural was unjustified but it sounded better), wholly owned and operated by one John Grimes, fairly recently a full Commander in the Interstellar Federation's Survey Service, more recently Master of the Baroness d'Estang's spaceyacht *The Far Traveler*, had contracted to carry a pair of *lerrigans* from Pangst, their native world, to the interplanetary zoo in New Syrtis, capital city of Bronsonia, all charges to be paid on safe delivery of the beasts. Grimes liked most animals and although he was not especially fond of small, quarrelsome dogs was prepared to be friendly with the larger canines.

The *lerrigans* were handsome enough brutes, not unlike a Terran Pekingese dog in appearance, but with zebra-patterned fur and of considerably greater dimensions, being about the size of full grown Alsatians. Grimes, inspecting them before shipment, had been favorably impressed, especially when the animals grinned happily at him. (Human beings are all too liable to misread the facial expressions of members of other species.) He did not anticipate any trouble during the voyage. A supply of canned food was shipped with the animals and, according to the literature that he had been given, they were omnivorous and would appreciate the variation of their diet by occasional scraps from the captain's table. The instructions were very definite on one point. On no account were the beasts to be let out of their cages.

During this short stay on Pangst, Grimes could not spare the time to visit the library to read up on the habits of his living freight. The consignor had not told him much, saying, "Just keep to the book, Captain, and you'll not go wrong." And when it came to books, Grimes thought, he had access to the entire *Encyclopedia Galactica* through *Little Sister*'s memory bank; there would be time enough to learn what he needed to know once he was off planet and on trajectory for Bronsonia. As a matter of fact there was a *lerrigan* entry—a very brief one sandwiched between a long article on "Lerner, Peter Frederick," who for most of his long life, had been an obscure politician on New Maine and another long article on "Lervinsky, Ivan Vladimir," at one time Secretary of the Reformed Communist Party of New Georgia. *Lerrigans*, Grimes discovered (as though he didn't know already) were pseudo-canines native to Pangst.

Pseudo or not, he thought, they were just dogs—big dogs and friendly. They watched him as he went about his business in the cabin of the pinnace. They whined—a most melodious whine—ingratiatingly. They were effusively grateful when he pushed their dishes of food, at the prescribed intervals, through the spring traps in the heavy metal mesh of their cages. They cooperated intelligently when he pulled out the trays at the base of their prisons to dispose of the soiled bedding and to replace it with fresh. They answered to the names that he had given them—Boy for the male and Girl for the female.

To hell with the instructions, he thought. They should be given the opportunity to get some exercise. What harm could it do? They couldn't possibly run away. *Little Sister* herself was cage enough.

So he let the *lerrigans* out of their boxes. They were ecstatically grateful, whining so musically that Grimes thought that there should have been words to their song. They put their front paws on his shoulders and licked his face. Grimes would have resented such attentions from the pair of *real* dogs but the breath of these animals was oddly fragrant—intoxicating, almost. They accompanied him as he went about such duties as he was obliged to carry out in this almost fully automated ship, watching him as he checked the position in the chart tank, as he made his routine inspection of the mini-Mannschenn and the inertial drive, as he punched the menu for his evening meal on the keyboard of the autochef. He had learned by watching their reactions to the leftovers of previous meals what human foods they liked so included a double serving of steak, rare. *(Little Sister*'s tissue-culture vats were well stocked.)

Dinner over, he lit his foul pipe and sat in an easy chair to watch and listen to a program of Carinthian light opera on his playmaster. This art form—if art form it could be called—was too corny for cultured tastes, but Grimes, when he was in what he called his simple spaceman mood, liked it. He was oddly content as he sprawled there, flanked by the two faithful (as he was already thinking of them) animals. He was more content than he ever had been on the occasions when he had carried human passengers.

Finally he decided to turn in. He considered briefly returning the *lerrigans* to their cages, then decided against it. He did, however, make sure that the doors to the engine space and to the tiny control room were shut. The animals could not possibly do any harm in the main cabin. They could return to sleep in their boxes if they so desired but he would be quite happy if they stretched out on the deck beside his bunk. He stripped, dimmed the cabin lights and then stretched out on the resilient mattress. He was asleep almost at once.

He dreamed, vividly.

He had not thought about Maggie Lazenby for some quite considerable time but he was dreaming about her now. In the dream she was naked, just as he was in reality, and her body was pressed to his and she was kissing him. Her breath was intoxicatingly fragrant. He felt himself stiffening, knew in some remote corner of his mind that this was only a dream and that he would very soon be achieving a lonely climax. But it was a long time since he had had a woman and the dream was a good one. What if his bedsheet were semen-stained? The ship's laundry facilities were better than merely adequate.

It was the knowledge that the lovemaking was only imaginary that saved him. He thrust upward into the dream Maggie's receptive body—and he felt teeth. He screamed, desperately rolled away from under the furry succubi. Scrabbling claws scored his back and the fangs that, had he not fully awoken in time, would have castrated him bit deeply into his right buttock. "Lights!" he yelled, and responsive to his command, the illumination of the cabin came on at full strength. The abrupt transition from near darkness to harsh effulgence dazed the *lerrigans*—not for long but for long enough. Grimes reached for the secret locker that, during a visit to Electra, he had caused to be installed under his bunk. The panel that was its door was sensitive only to the pattern of his fingerprints. It flew open and he grabbed what was in the little cupboard, a Minetti automatic pistol. He had thought that he might, one day, require this weapon for protection against some homicidally inclined human passenger—

couriers very often have odd customers—but never dreamed that it would be used against animals.

He thought all this later, when he was cleaning up the mess after treating his wounds. At this moment his main concern was the preservation of his life. He was in an awkward position, crouched by the side of his bunk, pistol in hand, his back to the snarling beasts. He brought his right hand around so that the weapon was pointing behind him, pressed the firing stud. The Minetti jumped in his grasp as the full clip of fifty rounds was discharged, spraying the area to his rear with the tiny but deadly flechettes.

Then he turned. The *lerrigans* were dead, very dead, their green blood soaking into the rich, purple carpet. The male, Grimes noticed with disgust, still had an enormous erection and the female, her haunches upraised, was obviously receptive.

He threw up, adding to the mess on the carpet, then went to the medical cabinet to spray his bites and scratches with antiseptic coagulant.

Little Sister possessed the capability to carry frozen cargo. Grimes, after he was partially recovered, dragged the bodies of the two animals into a refrigerated chamber. They would not now be of any great use to the New Syrtis Zoo but a skilled taxidermist might be able to pretty up the corpses well enough to render them suitable for exhibition in a museum. As for himself, he did not now expect the red carpet to be rolled out for him on his arrival at New Syrtis.

But he did not anticipate the very serious trouble that he had gotten himself into.

Two

The Director of the New Syrtis Zoo was not pleased. (Grimes had not really expected that he would be.) He took prompt steps to ensure that the freight on the *lerrigans* was not paid and then, after an exchange of Carlottigrams with the consignors on Pangst, brought suit against Grimes for breach of contract, gross negligence and the wanton destruction of protected fauna.

Grimes went to see the Planetary Secretary of the Astronauts' Guild, of which body he was a dues-paying member. Captain Wendover, the secretary, was sympathetic.

He said, "You realize, of course, Captain, that we cannot represent you in your capacity as a shipowner, although we are bound to do so in your capacity as a shipmaster. From what you have told me it was as a shipmaster you acted, and as a shipmaster you got into trouble." He paused, looking at Grimes over his wide desk, an elderly, soberly clad gentleman who had more the appearance of a minister of one of the more puritanical religions than a spaceman. "Now, you say that you were given literature regarding the care and feed-of the animals before your departure from Pangst. In this was there any mention of . . . er . . . sexual peculiarities?"

"No, Captain. Here. You can read for yourself."

"Thank you, Captain. H'm. But the instructions do insist that the beasts are to be confined to their cages. On the other hand—and our lawyers when the case is brought to court will stress the point—there is no reason given for this injunction." Wendover was oddly embarrassed as he continued. "I have to ask you a personal question, Captain. At the time when the brutes attacked you, were you . . . er . . . masturbating? I can imagine what it must be like in a ship such as yours, with no company, no female company especially. . . ."

Grimes's prominent ears reddened. "No. I was not. Not consciously. But I was having a remarkably vivid erotic dream. . . ."

"That adds up," said Wendover. "Before I got this job I was Master in Cluster Lines. Their ships maintain a fairly regular service to and from Pangst. After what happened aboard *Cluster Queen* the company has refused to carry *lerrigans*. . . ."

"So Cluster Line personnel didn't keep to the book any more than I did," said Grimes.

"They didn't, Captain. Of course, *lerrigans* are, to a certain degree, telepaths. They hate being confined to cages. They . . . broadcast the desire to be let out, to be given the run of the ship, to be petted and cuddled. And spacemen are fond of animals more often than not. Normally there would be no risk—were it not for the *lerrigans'* peculiar sexual makeup. They are stimulated sexually when other animals in their vicinity are stimulated sexually. The Cluster Line ships carry mixed crews. There are always . . . liaisons between male and female officers." Then, disapprovingly, "Even, at times, between males and males and females and females. Be that as it may, you can imagine the effect upon already erotically inclined telepathic beasts. . . ."

He pursed his lips disapprovingly.

"All right," said Grimes. "They were stimulated while I was dreaming. They even . . . joined in the dream. But why did they attack me?"

"Because," said Wendover, "to them the killing of another life form, a sexually stimulated life form, is essential before they, themselves, can copulate. Don't ask me why, or how. I'm only a spaceman, not a xenobiologist. All that I know is that I was Master of *Cluster Queen* when I was awakened—when the whole ship was awakened—by the screams from the Third Officer's cabin. When we burst in it was too late. He was dying, shockingly mutilated. His companion, the Purser, was a little luckier. The plastic surgeons were able to rebuild her right breast but psychologically she must have been scarred for life. But what sticks in my memory, even now, is those two obscene, blood spattered beasts unconcernedly doing what they were doing in the corner. I don't think that they knew it when the Chief Engineer battered in the head of first one and then the other with a heavy wrench. . . ."

Remembering his own experience Grimes felt sick.

"Of course," Wendover went on, "they—the consignors and the consignees—will claim that after the *Cluster Queen* affair, and one or two others, not as bad but bad enough, the odd behavior of the *lerrigans* under certain conditions must have been common knowledge among spacemen. Among *merchant* spacemen, yes. But your background, I understand, is Federation Survey Service and I don't suppose that you have, in your ship's library, a copy of Deitweller's *The Carriage Of Exotic Flora And Fauna. . . .*"

"I haven't," admitted Grimes. "I relied upon the *Encyclopedia Galactica.* If I specialized in the carriage of obscure, dead politicians that book would be very useful."

"Ha, ha." Captain Wendover permitted himself a dry chuckle. "And now, Captain Grimes, you must excuse me. There's the problem of compensation for the Third Officer of *Epsilon Draconis*—he had to get himself involved in a rather nasty accident last night. So if you call in here tomorrow morning I'll have our legal eagles—Pendlebury, Worrigan and Pendlebury—here to talk things over with you."

"And when should the case come up, Captain?" asked Grimes.

"I'm a spaceman, not a lawyer, Captain. But as you should know the legal gentry are never in a hurry."

"But my ship's under arrest and the airlock door's been sealed. The only money I have is the Letter of Credit in my notecase and I have to eat and pay my hotel bill. . . ."

"H'm. I could get you away as Third Officer in the *Epilectic Dragon*—but that would mean that you would not be present in court when the case comes up. Legally that would be in order—I think. After all, your ship is a fine security. . . ."

"I'd sooner stick around," said Grimes. "*If* my ship's going to be sold to pay my bills and fines I want to be among those present."

"Would you be interested in a ship-keeping job, Captain? *Bronson Star's* in parking orbit—it's cheaper than paying port dues—and old Captain Pinner's screaming for a relief. He recently retired out of Trans-Galactic Clippers and he's used to the social life of his passenger ships. But *Bronson Star* would suit you. You're used to being all by yourself in space."

"Not all the time," said Grimes. "But I need the money."

"So does old Captain Pinner. But he decided that he needed company more."

Three

Bronson Star was the flagship (the only ship) of the Interstellar Shipping Corporation of Bronsonia. She had started her working life as the Interstellar Transport Commission's *Epsilon Argo.* When obsolescent she had been put up for sale—at a time when the Bronsonians were complaining that the standard of the services provided by the major shipping lines to and from their planet was extremely poor. A group of businessmen decided that Bronsonia should have an interstellar merchant fleet of its very own and the sale of shares in this enterprise provided initial working capital. But it had not been an economically viable enterprise. On voyages out of Bronsonia *Bronson Star* barely broke even. On voyages back to her home world, with almost empty holds, she operated at a dead loss.

So the Interstellar Shipping Corporation of Bronsonia swallowed its pride and decommissioned its pet white elephant, having her placed in parking orbit about the planet. There she would remain until such time as a purchaser was found for her. Nonetheless she was too expensive a hunk of hardware to be left entirely unattended; apart from anything else, Lloyd's of London refused to insure her unless she were in the charge of a qualified ship-keeping officer.

The first of these had been the elderly but company-loving Captain Pinner—a typical big passenger shipmaster, Grimes had thought during the comprehensive handing over. The second of these was Grimes. He hoped, as he saw Captain Pinner into the airlock from which he would board the waiting shuttle, that this job would suit him very nicely until his complicated affairs were sorted out. He had quite comfortable living quarters and the life-support systems were working smoothly. The auxiliary hydrogen fusion power generator supplied more than enough current for the requirements of only one man. There was a late model autochef—not nearly so sophisticated as the one aboard *Little Sister* but adequate—and the farm deck had been well maintained; there would be no need to fall back on the algae from the air-purification and sewage-conversion system for nutriment.

After only a week Grimes found that the job was getting him down. He was used to loneliness, especially during his voyages in *Little Sister,* but aboard his own ship there had always been a sense of purpose; he had been going somewhere. Here, in *Bronson Star,* he was going nowhere. As the ship was in an equatorial synchronous orbit this was obvious. She was hanging almost directly over a chain of islands that looked like a sea serpent swimming from east to west—a wedge-shaped head trailed by a string of diminishing wedges. At first he had rather liked the appearance of it but soon was pleased rather than otherwise whenever it was obscured by cloud. That stupid, mythological beast was going nowhere, just as *Bronson Star* was.

Yet time passed. There were his twice daily radio calls to Aerospace Control and, now and again, one to Captain Wendover, the Guild Secretary. Wendover could only tell him that it would be quite some time before the *lerrigan* case came up. He exercised regularly in the ship's gymnasium, an essential routine to one living in Free Fall conditions. He was able to adjust the controls of the autochef so that it would produce meals exactly to his taste; fortunately there was a good supply of spices and other seasonings. He refrained from tinkering with other essential machinery; as long as it was working well he preferred to leave it severely alone. The playmaster in the captain's dayroom was an old model and must have come with the ship when she was purchased from the Commission but it was satisfactorily operational. The trouble there was that few of the TriVi programs broadcast from the stations on Bronsonia appealed to Grimes and the same could be said of the majority of the spools in the ship's library. Somebody must have had a passion for the Trust In God school of playwriting (as Grimes irreverently referred to it). He would have preferred pornography.

The days—the weeks—went by.

Grimes considered making further modifications to the autochef so that it could supply him with liquor; even an old model such as this could have produced a passable vodka. Yet he held back. In the final analysis alcohol is no substitute for human company but makes the addict unfit for such.

Four

But Grimes got his human company.

He was awakened in the small hours of the morning by the shrilling of the radar alarm. His first thought was that this must be a meteor on a collision course. By the time that he had sealed himself into his spacesuit—even though, to alleviate boredom, he had been carrying out daily emergency drills, the operation took many seconds—he was thinking that the hunk of cosmic debris should have struck by now. A merchant ship's radar does not operate at the same extremely long ranges as the installations aboard fighting vessels. Too, the alarm kept on sounding, which indicated that whatever had set it off was still in close vicinity to *Bronson Star.*

He left his quarters, made for the control room. He went at once to the radar screen. Yes, there was something out there all right, something big. Its range, a mere one kilometer, was neither opening nor closing; its azimuth was not changing. The shuttle from Port Bronson? wondered Grimes. Possibly—but surely Aerospace Control would have warned him that it was coming out to him. He was about to go to the transceiver to call the duty officer at the spaceport when his attention was diverted by a sharp tapping noise, audible even through his helmet. He opened the visor to hear better and to locate the source of the sound. It was coming from one of the viewports.

There was something—no, *somebody*—outside. He could see a helmeted head and, through the transparent faceplate, a pale face. He kicked himself away from the transceiver, fetched up against the viewport rather harder than he had intended. He stared into the eyes of the intruder. It was a woman staring back at him. Her wide mouth moved. She seemed annoyed that he made no reply to what she was saying. He nudged with his chin the on-off button that actuated his own suit radio.

"Help!" she said. "Help! This is urgent. Orbital met. station *Beta*. Explosion. Atmosphere lost. . . ."

One of the orbital met. stations? What the hell was it doing *here?*

"Don't just stand there! Open your airlock door and let us in! Some fool forgot to maintain our suit air bottles. . . ."

"Opening up," said Grimes, pushing himself away from the port and toward the auxiliary machinery control panel. He jabbed a gloved forefinger at the requisite buttons, saw the illuminated PUMP OPERATING sign come on, then PUMP STOPPED, then OUTER DOOR OPEN. The call to Aerospace Control, he decided, could wait until he had the survivors safely on board. He left the control room, hurrying as well as he could in the restrictive space armor, made his way to the head of the axial shaft. Fortunately the elevator cage was already at Captain's Flat level so he did not have to wait for it. Within two minutes he was in the airlock vestibule, watching the illuminated signs over the inner door. At last the OUTER DOOR OPEN was replaced by OUTER DOOR CLOSED. The needle of the airlock pressure gauge began to creep upward from Zero, finally stopped. Before Grimes could thumb the local control button—which, of course, was duplicated inside the chamber—the door began to open. Before it had done so fully a spacesuited figure shuffled through, careful not to break the contact of magnetic soles with the deck.

It was the woman, Grimes realized, with whom he had already talked. He realized, too, that she was holding a heavy pistol of unfamiliar make and that it was pointed at his belly.

Her voice, through his helmet phones, was coldly vicious.

"Don't try anything or I'll blow your guts through your backbone!"

She was followed by three other spacesuited figures. They, too, were armed.

"Take us up to the control room," ordered the woman.

Grimes had no option but to obey.

Only two of the intruders accompanied Grimes into the elevator cage, riding forward (there would be no "up" or "down" until the ship was accelerating) to Control. They told Grimes, menacing him with their weapons, to sit down. He did so, in the chair by the NST transceiver, thinking that he might, given half an opportunity, try to get out a call to Aerospace Control. But the woman anticipated this, fastening his seat belt so that it confined his arms as well as his body.

She asked, "Is this atmosphere breathable?"

He said, "Yes."

"Then why the hell are you wearing a spacesuit?"

"I was awakened by the radar alarm. I thought that it might be a meteor and that the ship might be holed."

"The alarm? It's not sounding now."

It wasn't. The craft that had set it off must now be drifting away from *Bronson Star*, Grimes thought.

"And the air is good, you say? There's just one way of finding out."

But her hands went not to her own helmet but to Grimes's, twisted, lifted. "Thank you," said Grimes, not overly sarcastically. The ship's atmosphere was better than that inside his suit.

"He hasn't died," said the woman, "so it must be all right."

She took off her own headpiece. Her companion followed suit. Grimes looked at the skyjackers curiously. The woman's face was thin, with fine bone structure, with eyes so deep a blue as to be almost black. Her glossy brown hair was swept back to a coil at the nape of her neck. Her mouth was wide, full lipped, palely pink in contrast to the deep tan of her skin. The man could have sat as a model for one of the more decadent Roman emperors. Greasy black ringlets framed a fleshy face, with jutting nose over a petulant mouth.

She said, "We are taking your ship. If you cooperate you will live."

"For the time being," said the man nastily.

Grimes said nothing.

"Has the cat got your tongue?" she asked.

He decided that he had better say something. In any case he wanted to find out what this was all about.

"Cooperate?" he queried. "How?"

"You know this ship," she said. "We don't. Furthermore—I'll be frank—our navigator got himself killed when we took over the met. satellite. . . ." She laughed. "We're all of us spacepersons, of a sort—but met. wallahs. Orbital flights only, apart from Hodge. . . ."

"Hodge?"

"You'll meet him. He's served as engineer in deep-space ships. He's checking up now. . . ."

A voice came from the intercom speaker. "Hodge to Lania. Main hydrogen fusion power generator operating. Inertial and Mannschenn Drives on Stand By. She's all yours. You'd better get her the hell out of here before the Aerospace Control boys realize that Station *Beta*'s not where she's supposed to be."

"Take her away," ordered Lania, addressing Grimes, making a threatening gesture with her gun hand. Her companions also displayed their weapons menacingly.

"If I'm dead," said Grimes reasonably, "I shan't be able to take this ship anywhere."

"If you're dead," she said, "you're dead. Period. It's quite permanent, you know. Are you going to play along or not?"

"I'll play," muttered Grimes. "But you have to release me first."

"Cover him, Paul," she said to her companion, handing him her own pistol.

She unsnapped the catch of Grimes's seat belt, standing to one side so as to leave a clear field of fire for the guns. Then she stepped smartly back and retrieved her own weapon.

"I have to sit in the command chair," said Grimes.

"Then sit in the command chair. We'll be sitting behind you. We're not such fools as to remain standing while you're sitting trajectory."

"Where do you want to go?" asked Grimes.

"Just get us out of here, fast, the way she's heading now. Mannschenn Drive as soon as you can so that we can't be picked up by Aerospace Control's radar. We'll set trajectory properly later."

Grimes went through the familiar routine. He almost enjoyed it, this awakening of a slumbering ship, this breaking out and away from that deadly dull parking orbit. He would have enjoyed it had he not been acting under duress. There was the arhythmic cacophony of the inertial drive and with the acceleration, blessed gravity again after the weeks of Free Fall. The ship was now headed, he saw, looking up through the transparency of the forward viewport, for the bright star that was the major luminary of the constellation called, by the Bronsonians, the Hobbit. He did not suppose that any world revolving about that primary would be the destination but it was as good a target star as any for the time being.

He cut the inertial drive. Would the sudden return to weightless conditions give him the opportunity to do something, anything? From behind him he heard the tense whisper, "Watch it, Grimes! Watch it. We have you covered." He sighed, audibly. He said, "Stand by Mannschenn Drive, for temporal disorientation."

There was the almost inaudible humming, a vibration rather than a sound, as the gyroscopes began to spin, a low hum that gradually heightened its pitch to a thin, high whine. As always, Grimes visualized that complexity of gleaming rotors, spinning, tumbling, precessing, warping the Continuum about the ship and all aboard her. Perspective was distorted and colors sagged down the spectrum. There was the usual dizziness, the faint nausea—and then inside the ship all was normal once more but outside, seen through the viewports the stars were no longer hard, diamond-sharp points of light but writhing, iridescent nebulosities. Still in view, just abaft the beam, was Bronsonia, no longer a sphere but a sluggishly pulsating ellipsoid.

Grimes restarted the inertial drive and it dwindled to invisibility.

Five

Hodge and his companion came up to Control.

They were spacesuited still but with the faceplates of their helmets open, their heavy gauntlets tucked into their belts. Hodge was a little man with coarse, dark hair growing low on his forehead, with muddy brown eyes under thick brows, a bulbous nose and a mouth that was little more than a wrinkle in the deeply tanned skin of his face over a receding chin. *The Last of the Neanderthalers,* thought Grimes. He remembered them—his mind was a junk room littered with scraps of unrelated knowledge—reading somewhere that Neanderthal Man had been a technician superior to the more conventionally human Cro-Magnards.

The person with Hodge was also of less than average height. The lustrous hair that framed her face was golden with a reddish tint. Unusual for a blonde, she was brown-eyed. Her face was not quite chubby, her nose was slightly uptilted, her scarlet-lipped mouth was generous. Grimes thought—even now he could regard an attractive woman with interest—*A lovely dollop of trollop.* And what was she doing in this galley?

Hodge growled, "It's all systems Go."

"All systems have gone," commented Lania. "Or didn't you notice? And what about the life-support systems, Susie? That's your department."

"We'll not starve," replied the small blonde. Her voice, a rich contralto, was not the childish soprano that Grimes had expected. "We may not live like kings . . ." and why, Grimes wondered, should Hodge laugh, should the other male skyjacker scowl? ". . . but we'll not go hungry or thirsty or asphyxiate."

"After all," contributed Grimes, *"I* didn't."

"Shut up, you!" snapped Lania. She addressed the others, "I suggest, Paul, that we continue on this trajectory until we've gotten ourselves organized. We have to arrange accommodation for ourselves to begin with. So, Hodge, I'd like you to fit a lock on the door of the Third Officer's cabin that can be operated only from the outside. *Captain* Grimes . . ." so she knew his name . . . "will shift his things—such things as we allow him to keep, that is—to that accommodation. Paul and I will occupy the Master's suite. You, Hodge, should be happy in the Chief Engineer's quarters. And you, Susie, can take up residence in the Purser's cabin. So, Grimes, get moving!"

Grimes didn't like it; somehow he resented this demotion accommodation-wise even more than the seizure of the ship. It was many a long year since he had occupied a junior officer's cabin. But there was no arguing with the pistols that were pointing at him.

He unsnapped the buckle of his seat belt, rose from his chair and walked slowly to the hatch that gave access to the deck below Control. The others followed him but the engineer, Hodge, did not accompany them into the accommodation that Grimes had come to regard as a sort of home.

Clothing he would need, thought Grimes, and toilet gear, and pipe and tobacco. And, if he were to be incarcerated, reading matter; from a very early age he had been addicted to the printed word.

"Take off your spacesuit, Grimes," ordered Lania. "Leave it here."

"But. . . ."

"Do as I say. Do you think that we want you escaping and clambering around the outside of the ship?"

Grimes had donned the protective garment hastily when the alarm sounded, had not taken time to put on the longjohns that were the usual underwear with space armor. Although he had always regarded the fantastically persistent nudity taboo as absurd, he was reluctant to disrobe; nakedness on a sunny beach among fellow nudists is altogether different from being unclothed surrounded by hostile, fully dressed, armed strangers. But he had no option but to do as he was told. He stripped. Lania looked at him coldly, almost contemptuously. Susie regarded him with frank appraisal. He felt his prominent ears reddening with embarrassment. The flush spread to his face, down over his body.

He asked, with what dignity he could muster, "Can I dress now?"

"Your watch," demanded Lania. "You'll know *nothing,* not even the time, except when we require your services."

He loosened the wrist strap, dropped the instrument on top of the discarded spacesuit.

Lania said, "Susie, get a shirt and shorts out of his wardrobe. Make sure that there's nothing in the pockets."

The other woman obeyed, handing the garments to Grimes. He dressed hastily.

"Toilet gear?" he asked.

"Permitted," said Lania. "Get it out of the bathroom for him, Susie."

"My pipe. . . . Tobacco. . . ."

"Yes. You can get that rubbish out of here; neither of us smokes. But no lighter or matches or whatever you use for ignition."

"But. . . ."

"You heard me. Fire is a weapon."

Grimes decided not to argue. He said, "If I'm to be imprisoned for most of this voyage I'd like some books."

"We haven't spared your life, Grimes, so that you can catch up on your back reading."

Susie intervened. "He won't be navigating *all* the time. Let him have something to keep his mind occupied."

"Oh, all right. Give him his bedtime stories."

Grimes took two volumes from the bookcase, both of them novels left by his predecessor and which he had never gotten around to reading.

"All right," snapped Lania. "Enough. Get him out of here."

Clutching his pitifully few possessions he left what were no longer his own quarters, was hustled down a deck to the officers' flat. The Third Officer's cabin had been prepared for his occupancy. Hodge had found a combination padlock in the engine-room stores, had welded a hasp and staple to the door and its frame. The main consideration, however, had been security rather than comfort. There was no bed linen on the bunk and the deckhead light tube was defective. The chair by the desk looked decidedly rickety. The settee cushion cover was torn. The only touch of color was a ship-chandler's calendar, useless for telling the date save on its planet of origin, depicting in startling, three-dimensional color a young lady proudly displaying her supernormal mammary development.

"Stay here until we want you," ordered Lania.

When the door shut after her, when Grimes heard the sharp click of the padlock snapping shut, he knew that all he could do was just that.

He made a thorough search of his new quarters. The toilet facilities, he was relieved to find, were operational although very cramped after the ones that he had become accustomed to. In one of the desk drawers were a few tattered magazines; evidently the Third Mate of *Bronson Star*—whoever he was and whatever he was doing now—had been a devotee of Hard Downbeat. Grimes permitted himself a sneer; he had never understood how that derivation from the ancient Portuguese *fado* had achieved such popularity. Then, in another drawer, he found a treasure—a rechargeable electric lighter. He pressed the stud and the ignition element at the end of the little cylinder glowed into incandescence. He made no attempt to fight temptation; after all he had become accustomed, over the years, to starting his day with a cup of coffee and a pipe of tobacco. This day had started some considerable time ago and it didn't look as though there were going to be any coffee but his pipe would be better than nothing. It was an aid to thinking.

He went through to the tiny bathroom, made sure that the exhaust fan was functioning, then lit up. He started to think about his predicament. He realized, with something of a shock, that there was something that he should have brought with him into what was to be his prison cell. This was a solidograph of Maggie Lazenby, a very special one, made on her home world, Arcadia. This planet being blessed with a subtropical climate almost from pole to pole, its inhabitants went about naked most of the time and would no more have dreamed of wearing a costume on the beach than under the shower in the bathroom. . . . The solidograph was in one of the drawers of the wardrobe; Grimes had placed it there rather than have it drifting around, with the possibility of damage, while the ship was in free fall. Perhaps, he thought, it would stay there. Perhaps Lania and Paul would not find it. He hated the idea of that fat slob holding that three-dimensional portrait of the naked Maggie in his greasy hands. . . .

Perhaps if he asked. . . .

But if he did Lania and Paul would know of its existence.

He decided that he might as well have a shower, freshen up. He stripped, stood in the little cubicle to be sprayed with hot water and detergent. He applied depilatory cream to his face, rinsed, then dried off under the warm air blast.

Naked, he padded through into the cabin just as the outer door opened, admitting Susie. Hodge, carrying the inevitable pistol, was behind her. Once again Grimes was at a disadvantage but, somehow, did not feel the same embarrassment that he had felt before. Susie smiled sweetly. Hodge grinned, displaying strong, yellow teeth, aimed his pistol where it would do maximum if not immediately lethal damage.

Susie said, "You're wanted in Control. You can come as you are if you wish."

He said briefly, "I'll dress."

As he pulled on his shorts and shirt he noticed that she and Hodge were no longer wearing spacesuits but were in a uniform that was strange to him. They must have brought a change of clothing with them from the meteorological satellite—but the devices on the shoulder boards of their shirts had no connection with Bronsonian meteorology or meteorology in general. Silver stars? Common enough, perhaps; people were wearing stars as marks of rank long, long before the first clumsy rocket soared out and away from old Earth. But golden crowns? There was no monarchy on Bronsonia. Surely, thought Grimes, these people could not be refugees from the Waverley Royal Mail. . . .

Then, with Susie and Hodge bringing up the rear, he made his way to the control room.

Six

Lania and Paul were also wearing the strange uniform although theirs was black and not, as in the case of Susie and Hodge, slate grey, but they wore long trousers and not shorts and high-necked blouses rather than shirts. And Paul's shoulder boards bore veritable clusters of silver stars under the golden crowns and although Lania's were not so profusely star-spangled each one carried a not-so-minor constellation.

"Be seated, Grimes," ordered Lania.

Sullenly Grimes complied.

"Now," she went on, "we'll find out if you can navigate. I'll tell you where I want you to take this rustbucket. . . ."

Grimes said nothing but he must have looked as though he were thinking.

"Be careful, Grimes. If the thought has flickered across your tiny mind that you can turn the ship around and head back for Bronsonia, forget it. We may not be navigators—but even we would be aware of such a large alteration of trajectory. And even if we should somehow fail to notice what you did we would know as soon as we got there. And then. . . ."

She jerked her pistol suggestively.

You're enjoying this, thought Grimes. *You female-chauvinist bitch. . . .*

"Where to?" he asked.

"In future," she told him, "please address me as Highness."

He stared at her. She was quite serious although he noticed Susie and Hodge exchange a sardonic glance. Her . . . husband? lover? did not seem to find what she had said at all out of the ordinary, however, merely maintained his pose of superior boredom.

"Where to, Highness?" repeated Grimes.

"Porlock."

"I shall have to take a fix, Highness, and then I have to set up the chart and identify the Porlock sun. . . ."

"We have you along, Grimes, just to handle such sordid details."

He got up from his chair, went to the Carlotti transceiver. He wondered briefly if he would be able to push out a message over the interstellar communications system but realized, almost at once, that this would be impossible. Somebody—Hodge, presumably—had removed vital components. The equipment was now a receiver only, although capable of direction finding. He returned to the chart tank, ran up a dead-reckoning trajectory from Bronsonia, noted which three Carlotti Beacon stations in relatively nearby space were most advantageously situated with reference to the ship. He took his bearings, saw that the three filaments of luminescence intersected very close indeed to his estimated position. (If they had not done so there would have been something somewhere seriously wrong.) He set up an extrapolated trajectory from the fix.

Now, Porlock. . . .

A navigator he might be but he had no idea as to where in the universe *it* might be although he recalled the circumstances of its naming, the story being one of the legends of the Survey Service. One of the old-time Commodores, a man whose name was Coleridge and who claimed descent from that poet, had been interrupted while he was doing something important by a call from the control room of his ship to tell him that the sun which the vessel was approaching had at least one habitable planet in orbit. Accounts varied as to what the "something important" was. The one generally accepted was that he was on the point of beating down the stubborn resistance of one of the female scientists carried on the exploratory expedition. Another was that he, following in the footsteps of his illustrious ancestor, was in the throes of composing a piece of poetry that would ensure for him literary immortality. In either case—or in any of the other hypothetical cases—Porlock was the obvious name for the body responsible for the interruption.

Porlock. . . .

The ship's navigational data bank flashed the coordinates onto the screen almost immediately. Grimes had to reduce the scale of the chart tank so as to include the Porlock sun. He discovered then that there was no convenient target star. The first adjustment of trajectory, therefore, must be made on instruments only. This was no more than a minor inconvenience.

Resuming his command seat, he shut down inertial and Mannschenn drives while the others watched him intently, their pistols ready. He turned the ship on her axes around the directional gyroscopes. He restarted the inertial drive and then the space-time-twisting Mannschenn. Sometimes, on such occasions, there were flashes of déjà vu to accompany the spatial and temporal disorientation—but this time (as far as Grimes was concerned) there was only the discomfort of mild nausea. The chilling thought came to him that perhaps he had no future.

But he knew that he must continue to cooperate until such time—if ever—as he had a chance, however faint, to escape.

Lania got up from her chair to look into the chart tank, then stared out and up through the viewports at the stars, mere vague nebulosities as seen in the warped continuum engendered by the ever-precessing rotors of the Drive. She looked away hastily, back into the tank.

She said accusingly, "That . . . that extrapolated trajectory or whatever you call it misses the Porlock sun by light years!"

"Allowance for galactic drift," he told her.

"Haven't you forgotten something?" she asked coldly.

It took him some little time to realize what she was driving at. Then, "Allowance for galactic drift, Highness," he said, hating himself for according her that title.

"Hodge and Susie," she ordered, "take him back to his kennel." Then, "Oh, before you tear yourself away from us, Grimes, what is our estimated time of arrival?"

"At our present precession rate and at an acceleration of one gravity just thirty standard days, Highness."

She made no acknowledgment, voiced neither approval nor disapproval, saying only, "Take him back to his kennel."

Seven

Grimes missed his watch. And there was no bulkhead clock in the Third Officer's cabin; her original owners, the Interstellar Transport Commission, were parsimonious in some respects, considering that only departmental heads were entitled to certain "luxuries."

But time would pass whether or not he possessed the mechanical means of recording its passage. One way of passing time is to sit and think. Grimes went through to the bathroom to do his sitting and thinking; he could smoke his pipe in there without its becoming obvious to anybody entering the cabin that he had found the means of lighting the thing.

He sat and he thought.

He thought about the skyjackers. The man called Paul was wearing the most gold and silver braid so, presumably, was the leader. But Lania, with fewer stars and smaller crowns on her shoulder boards, was the one giving all the orders—leader *de facto* if not *de jure.* The situation, perhaps, was analogous to that obtaining when a rather ineffectual Captain is overshadowed by a tough, dynamic First Lieutenant or Chief Mate or whatever.

Hodge? Just another engineer, no matter where he came from or whose badges he was wearing.

Susie? Her like could be found in many spaceships, both naval and mercantile. She was no more (and no less) than a spacefaring hotel manager.

All four of the skyjackers, it seemed, had been in the employ of the Bronsonian Meteorological Service, crewpersons aboard Station *Beta.* How big a crew did those artificial satellites carry? Grimes didn't know. But there must have been a mutiny, during which one of the skyjackers, the navigator of the party, had been killed. Somebody else—possibly the captain, with the muzzle of a pistol pressing into the back of his neck—had driven *Beta* out of her circumpolar orbit into one intersecting that of *Bronson Star.*

And this "Highness" business. . . .

Grimes had known Highnesses and Excellencies and the like and was prepared to admit that Lania and Paul did have about them something of that aura which distinguishes members of hereditary aristocracy from the common herd. He knew what it was, of course. It was no more than plain arrogance; if you have it drummed into you from birth on that you are better than those in whose veins blue blood does not flow you will end up really believing it.

But what had a Highness been doing as a crewwoman aboard an orbital spacecraft? A met. observatory owned by a planet state whose elected ruler bore the proud title of First People's Minister, not First Peoples' Minister. . . . Grimes allowed himself a break to enjoy the semantic subtlety.

He heard the cabin door open, voices.

(Didn't these people ever knock?)

He got up, knocked his pipe out into the toilet bowl (the one operational only during acceleration), flushed. He put the pipe into his pocket, came through into the cabin.

Susie said brightly, "Oh, there you are. Making room for breakfast?"

Hodge, behind her, grinned.

"Breakfast?" queried Grimes, looking at the tray that she set down on his desk. He was hungry, but a bowl of stew, however savory, did not seem right, somehow, for the first meal of the day.

"Or lunch, or dinner. Take your pick. But it has to be something that you can eat out of a soft, plastic bowl with a soft, plastic spoon. Her Highness's orders."

"Her Highness?"

"That's what we all have to call her now. And Paul, of course, is His Highness."

"But Bronsonia's a sort of republic."

"And where we came from wasn't. Or, to be more exact, where our parents came from."

"Porlock?" wondered Grimes. "But Porlock's a republic too—unless it's changed since I did my last Recent Galactic History course."

"May as well tell him, Susie," said Hodge. "He can listen while he's eating. I've more important things to do than play at being your armed escort."

"All right," said the girl. "Get dug into your tucker and listen. Our parents were refugees from Dunlevin. You may recall from your history courses that Dunlevin *was* a monarchy. Paul's father *was* the Crown Prince; he was one of the few members of the royal family who got away in the royal yacht. Lania's parents were the Duke and Duchess of Barstow, who also escaped. Hodge's father was an officer in the Royal Dunlevin Navy. My father was too, Paymaster Commander of the yacht.

"Wallis, who *should* have been our navigator on this caper, was the son of Commodore Wallis, a loyalist officer. As a matter of fact he—young Wallis, that is—was Third Mate of this ship before he entered the met. service. . . ."

Grimes worked his way through the plate of stew while she was talking. It wasn't too bad, although he, had he been cooking, would have programmed the autochef to be more generous with the seasonings. And the mug of coffee that came with the meal was deficient in sweetening.

Susie's story was interesting. He remembered, now, reading about the revolution on Dunlevin. The ruling house on that planet had not been at all popular and, as Dunlevin was of little strategic importance, had not been propped up by Federation weaponry. Even so the Popular Front had not enjoyed a walkover, mainly because the Royalists had been given support—arms and "volunteers"—by the Duchy of Waldegren. The Interstellar Federation, albeit reluctantly, had imposed a blockade on Dunlevin. The Federation did not like the Popular Front but liked Waldegren even less. And it was Federation presence that prevented too enthusiastic a massacre when the last Royalist stronghold fell; shiploads of refugees made their escape under the guns of the blockading Survey Service fleet.

Some of those refugees, obviously, had found haven on Bronsonia.

"So," said Grimes after he had swallowed the last spoonful, "you people hope to mount a counterrevolution. . . . I'm sorry to be a wet blanket—but you haven't the hope of a snowball in hell. This rustbucket isn't a warship, you know. Or hadn't you noticed?"

"Any ship," she told him sweetly, "is a potential troop transport. And any merchant vessel is a potential auxiliary cruiser. It's rather a pity, Grimes, that we shall be leaving you on Porlock. We could have used your Survey Service expertise."

He said, "I'm not a mercenary."

She said, "But certain episodes in your past career indicate that you're willing to fight on the right side."

He said, "The *right* side isn't necessarily the right side."

"Ha. Ha bloody ha. If you've ever lived under a left-wing tyranny you'd be talking differently."

"Have you ever lived under a left-wing tyranny, Susie?"

"No. But we know how things are on Dunlevin."

"Do you?"

"Yes!" she snapped. "Have you finished your meal?" She snatched the tray off the desk. "We'll leave you now. You'll be told when you're required again."

"There should be at least a once-daily check of position," said Grimes.

"You people," she told him scornfully, "are always trying to kid us, those of us who aren't members of the Grand Lodge of Navigators, that you're indispensible."

And with those parting words she left him.

Eight

The voyage wore on.

It was a voyage such as Grimes had never experienced before, such as he hoped that he would never experience again. He was able to keep track of the passage of objective time only because, at irregular intervals, he was taken up to the control room to check the ship's position. Finally he had target sun, the Porlock primary, and knew, with a combination of relief and apprehension, that the passage was almost over. Until Lania was able to replace him with a navigator who was one of her own people he was safe. Once his services were no longer required would he be set free on Porlock? And if he were, how would he make his way back from that planet to Bronsonia? And would he find *Little Sister* still there? Would she have been sold to pay his various debts and fines?

The only one of the skyjackers who was at all friendly was Susie. Paul was becoming more and more the Crown Prince—the King, rather—and Lania a sort of hybrid, a cross between Queen and Grand Vizier. And Hodge, Grimes felt, was taking sadistic delight in the spectacle of a space captain at the receiving end of orders.

Susie's friendliness was due, partly, to missionary zeal. But whom was she trying to convince—herself or Grimes? He judged that she was beginning to regret having become involved in this enterprise, that she was realizing, although she would hate to admit it, that she had far more in common with Grimes, the apolitical outsider, than with her dedicated companions.

Meanwhile she soon discovered that he was smoking in the cabin that was also his prison. Not only did she turn a blind eye—or insensitive nose—but actually brought him more tobacco from the ship's stores when his own ran out. And she gave him a chess set, and reading matter. Most of this latter consisted of propaganda magazines; it seemed that there was quite a colony of refugees from Dunlevin on Bronsonia.

Grimes rather doubted that the accounts of life on Dunlevin, as printed in these journals, were altogether accurate. He did know, from his reading of recent history during his Survey Service days, that life on that world had been far from pleasant for the common people during the monarchy. They must have welcomed the transition of power from kings to commissars. And were the commissars as bad as the kings had been? Grimes doubted it. Dunlevin aristocracy and royalty were descended from the notorious Free Brotherhood, pirates who, as a prelude to the erection of a facade of respectability, had taken over a newly colonized planet, virtually enslaving its inhabitants.

He argued with Susie during his meal times. It passed the time although it was all rather pointless; neither of them possessed first-hand knowledge of conditions on Dunlevin.

He asked her, "Why should you, an attractive girl who had a secure and reasonably happy future on Bronsonia—where you were born—throw away everything to play a part in this—*your* word, Susie—caper?"

She was frank with him.

"Partly," she admitted, "because of the way that I was brought up. Father—even though he manages a restaurant—is still very much the Royal Dunlevin Navy officer. Mother—customers refer to her as the Duchess—is still the aristocrat. They believe, sincerely, that it is my duty to help to restore the House of Carling to the throne and to destroy the socialist usurpers. . . ."

"While they stay put in their hash house, raking in the profits."

"They're no longer young, Captain. And they have contributed, substantially, to the Restoration Fund."

"And so," said Grimes, "when Their Royal Highnesses raise a tattered banner and beat a battered drum your parents are proud and happy to see their darling daughter falling into step, risking *her* neck. . . ."

"They are proud. Of course they're proud."

"But how come there're so few of you? Just Paul and Lania and Hodge and yourself—and whoever it was that got himself killed in the met. satellite?"

"Because we were the only ones able to be in the right place at the right time to seize this ship. And it took lots of undercover organizing to get us all aboard *Beta* at the same time. But on Porlock. . . ."

"That's enough yapping," grumbled Hodge. "Come on, Susie. I've work to do, even if some other people haven't."

Nine

Grimes brought *Bronson Star* down to Porlock.

He sat in the control room, with Their Royal Highnesses and Susie in other chairs so situated that they could cover him with their pistols without risk of shooting each other. He told them that if they did kill him they, in all probability, would die too. Lania told him that even she knew enough to use the inertial drive to reverse the vessel's fall. He said that the NST transceiver should be used to request permission from Aerospace Control to make entry. She told him that this was not only unnecessary but impossible since the Aerospace Controllers were on strike—a stoppage, thought Grimes, conveniently timed to coincide with *Bronson Star*'s planetfall. Doubtless a coded message had been sent to somebody by means of the Carlotti Deep Space radio.

In any case the landing was not to be made at Port Coleridge. Grimes had been supplied with charts and told that he was to set the ship down at the point indicated at precisely 2000 local time for that locality. (Porlock, like many worlds with a period of rotation less than that of Earth, found it convenient to adopt a twenty-hour day.) The set-down site, ringed in red on the map, was in one of the deserts that occupied most of the land space of the southern continent of this world. It was, Grimes estimated, at least five hundred Porlock miles (one thousand kilometers) from the nearest town. Noisy as the inertial drive inevitably is, the midnight landing should go unheard in any center of population.

Grimes always enjoyed ship handling and, in spite of the circumstances, he found pleasure in this test of his skill. There was no Aerospace Control to keep him informed as to what the wind was doing at the various levels of the atmosphere. Even if *Bronson Star* had been equipped with sounding rockets he would not have been allowed to use them. But there was a beacon, a bright red light visible only from above, that he was able to pick up from a great altitude; fortunately it was a cloudless night.

That ruddy spark, as soon as he had it in the stern-vision screen, allowed him to estimate drift, which was easily compensated for by lateral thrust although requiring frequent adjustment. Grimes quite forgot that he was acting under duress except when Paul, superciliously obnoxious, remarked that professional spacemen always seem to suffer from the delusion that their ships are made of glass.

The beacon light grew brighter and brighter, so much so that Grimes was obliged to reduce the brilliance of the screen. He watched the radar altimeter and when there were only one hundred and fifty meters to go allowed the target to drift away from the center of the bull's-eye sight.

"Watch it, Grimes!" ordered Lania sharply. "Watch your aim!"

He said, "I'm looking after your property, or somebody's property, Highness. Those laser beacons are quite expensive, you know . . ."

"You're not paying for it!" she snapped but refrained from any further interference.

One hundred. . . . Fifty. . . . Grimes increased vertical thrust to slow the rate of descent. *Forty. . . . Thirty. . . . Bronson Star* was drifting down like a huge balloon with barely negative buoyancy. *Five. . . . Four. . . . Three. . . . Two. . . . One. . . .*

And they were down, with hardly a jar. Grimes stopped the drive and the ship sighed as she adjusted her great weight within the cradle of her tripedal landing gear. The clinometer indicated that she was only a fraction of a degree off the vertical.

Grimes felt for his pipe then remembered that he had left it in his cabin. In any case Their Royal Highnesses would not have tolerated smoking in their presence.

He said, "We're here."

"A blinding glimpse of the obvious, Grimes," said Lania.

"They're waiting for us, Highness," said Susie.

"It would be strange if they were not, girl. Mortdale is a good organizer."

Grimes asked, "May I ring off the engines, Highness?"

"No. Leave everything on Stand By. We just might have to—what is the expression?—get upstairs in a hurry. So remain at your controls."

Without leaving his chair Grimes was able to look out through the wide viewports. There was activity outside the ship—dark shapes in the darkness, flashing lights, the occasional flashing reflection from bright metal.

"Susie," ordered Lania, "go down to the airlock to receive General Mortdale. You should recognize him from his photographs and you have the password."

"Yes, Highness."

Susie vanished down the hatch.

Grimes started to ask, "Shall I be . . . ?"

"Speak when you're spoken to," he was told.

* * *

Eventually Susie returned.

She was accompanied by three men, clad in drab, insignialess coveralls. Their leader—Mortdale?—was small, compact, terrier-like, with a stubble of gray hair and a close-cropped moustache. Grimes had known officers like him in the Federation Survey Service Marines, had never cared for them. Terriers—stupidly pugnacious at best, vicious at worst—were not his favorite dogs. The other two were taller than their leader. One had yellow hair, the other was bald but they could almost have been twins. Looking at their hard, reckless faces Grimes categorized them as bad bastards.

Mortdale drew himself to attention, so sharply that Grimes was surprised not to hear vertebrae cracking. "Highness!" he snapped.

"General," acknowledged Paul with a languid nod of his head.

"May I present Major Briggs and Captain Polanski?"

The two men bowed stiffly.

"Captain Polanski, I suppose," said Paul, "is the spaceman who will be taking over from our unwilling . . . chauffeur."

"No, Highness. The captain is a member of my staff."

"Then may I suggest, General, that you get your qualified spaceman aboard as soon as possible? There are the holds to convert into troop accommodation, the stores and the weapons to load, the troops to embark. This work must be supervised."

"It can be supervised by an army officer, Highness," said Mortdale.

"What about the man you were supposed to have for us?" demanded Lania sharply.

"Him?" The general's voice was contemptuous. "He backed out. There was some star tramp here short of an officer and so he got himself signed on as Third Mate without letting me know. By this time he's halfway to Ultimo."

"I would have expected you to exercise better control over your people, General Mortdale," said Lania coldly. "Thanks to your negligence the success of the operation has been jeopardized. The work of conversion, the loading, the embarkation must inevitably be delayed. It will not be long before the planetary authorities realize that something odd is going on out here in the desert."

"The World Manager and his ministers are sympathetic to our cause, Highness. They hope for a favorable trade agreement with the new government on Dunlevin. . . ."

"And who gave *you* the authority to negotiate such deals?" demanded Paul hotly. "Who. . . ."

Lania silenced him with an imperious wave of her hand.

"And as I have already said, Highness," went on the general, "my officers can oversee the work at least as well as any spaceman. As for the lift-off and the navigation to Dunlevin . . ." Grimes realized that Mortdale's rather mad, yellow eyes were staring directly at him . . . *"he,* whoever he is, got you here. He must be competent. He can take us away from here."

"He will do as he's told," said Lania, "if he values his health."

Grimes said, "I understood that I was to be released on this world. Highness."

"Did you?" Then, to Mortdale, "Have your officers put him back in his kennel until we need him again. Susie will show them where it is."

Ten

Locked in his cabin once more Grimes stretched out on his bunk. He had never felt so helpless before in his entire life. He listened to the sounds that told him of the work in progress—hammerings, occasional muffled shouts, the rattle of ground vehicles being driven up the loading ramp to the cargo port. He could visualize what was being done; among the courses that he had sat through during his Survey Service career was one dealing with the conversion of commercial vessels to military purposes. If he'd been doing the job, he thought, he would have utilized inflatable troop-deck fittings—but that presupposed the availability of the necessary materials. Failing that, tiers of bunks could be knocked up from timber or fabricated from metal.

He wondered which technique was being used. Although this was not his ship—he had been little more than a caretaker and now was a prisoner—he still felt responsible for her. And, at brief intervals, when handling a lift-off or set-down or when adjusting trajectory, he would be, after a fashion, in actual command.

Susie came in briefly, escorted by one of Mortdale's men. She brought him a packet of sandwiches and a plastic mug of coffee. She said little, was obviously reluctant to speak in front of the stranger.

Grimes enjoyed the light meal; it took a lot to put him off his food. He enjoyed the pipe afterward. While smoking it he tried to think things out. He would have to play along, he decided. Even though he owed no loyalty to the Royal House of Dunlevin he owed none to the Council of Commissars who were that planet's present rulers. Voluntarily he would serve neither. Under duress he would do what he was told until—and that would, indeed, be the sunny Friday—a chance presented itself for him to make his escape.

And meanwhile—what was happening back on Bronsonia? Had his case been brought before the court yet? And if so, how had it gone? Had he lost his ship—*his* ship—the golden *Little Sister*? His worries about his legal affairs did, at least, help to take his mind off his present predicament.

And then, telling himself that there was nothing that he could do about anything at this present moment, he allowed himself to drift into a troubled sleep.

* * *

The period of his incarceration passed slowly.

Susie, always accompanied by an armed man, brought him his meals at what seemed to be regular intervals. He asked her how the work of conversion into a troop transport was going. She answered him shortly on each occasion, non-commitally, obviously inhibited by the presence of her escort.

Then, at last, she was able to tell him that lift-off would be as soon as he got himself up to Control. Grimes welcomed this intelligence. Given recreational facilities he did not object to a period of idleness but with no playmaster and no reading matter apart from those two novels (which he had finished long since and that were not worth reading) and the propaganda magazines he was becoming bored.

Paul and Lania were in the control room, as was General Mortdale. The soldier was still wearing his drab coveralls but shoulder straps, bearing the now familiar silver stars and golden crown insignia, had been added.

"Take her up," ordered Lania.

"Where to?" asked Grimes. "Or need I ask? Highness."

She looked at him coldly. "As you said, need you ask? And now, what are you waiting for?"

Grimes said, "First I have to do some checking. Highness."

He looked out of the ports. He saw nothing but darkness. This was to be a midnight lift-off just as it had been a midnight set-down. A glance at the chronometer and a minor conversion calculation confirmed this. He walked to the big panel presenting information regarding the current state of the ship, noted from the indicators that her mass had been considerably increased but not to the extent to place any undue strain upon the inertial drive. He wished that he knew the makeup of this extra weight—how many men, how many armed vehicles, what weapons, what stores? But the question was an academic one. All life-support systems were functioning. Airlock doors were closed.

"Take your time, Grimes," said Lania sarcastically.

"Take your time, Captain," said Mortdale, without irony. "Make sure that everything is as it should be." To Lania he remarked, "A good commander takes nothing for granted, Highness."

"There's one thing that he can take for granted," snapped the Crown Princess. "And that's that he'll get his head blown off if he attempts anything that he shouldn't. All right, Grimes, get us away from here."

Grimes strapped himself into the command chair. He said into the intercom microphone, "All hands stand by for lift-off. Secure all."

"All has been secured," said the general.

The inertial drive muttered irritably and then commenced its arhythmic hammering. The noise, thanks to sonic insulation, was not too loud in either the control room or the accommodation. Grimes wondered if anybody had thought to insulate the cargo holds, which were now troop decks. He rather hoped that this had not been done. It would make him a little happier to know that Paul's and Lania's loyal soldiers would be experiencing a thoroughly uncomfortable passage.

Bronson Star heaved her clumsy bulk off the gibber plain, clawed for the sky. She lifted complainingly. Grimes doubted that the weight of her cargo, animate and inanimate, had been properly distributed. But the Commission's Epsilon Class star tramps were sturdy workhorses and could stand considerable abuse.

She groaned and grumbled into the black, star-spangled sky. As on the occasion of her landing there was no communication with Aerospace Control. Grimes wondered what report, what complaints would be made by the captain of the big airliner, a dirigible ablaze with lights, that passed within ten kilometers of the climbing spaceship; even though *Bronson Star* was not exhibiting the regulation illuminations, she would have shown up as an enormous blip on the aircraft's radar screen.

She drove through the last, tenuous wisps of atmosphere, out and up, through the Van Allens, established herself in orbit. Grimes was busy, as was the computer, presenting him with the coordinates of the target star. There was Free Fall when the inertial drive was shut off, centrifugal effects while the directional gyroscopes when the Mannschenn Drive propagated its artificial, turned the ship about her axes, temporal disorientation warped continuum about the vessel. Inertial drive again, and a comfortable one-gravity acceleration. . . .

"Back to your kennel, Grimes," said Lania.

Eleven

Grimes could not help worrying.

Even though he felt nothing but dislike for Paul and Lania and their people—with one possible exception—he still felt responsible for them. He was not the only spaceman aboard the ship—the original skyjackers must have received some sort of training before being employed in orbital vehicles and Hodge had served in deep-space vessels—but he was the only master astronaut. During the voyage from Bronsonia to Porlock he had not been overly concerned; the life-support systems had been required to serve the needs of only five persons. But now. . . . It is axiomatic that the more people there are aboard a ship the more things there are that can go wrong. *Somebody* should be making rounds at regular intervals. *Somebody* should be seeing to it that the departmental heads—Hodge and Susie?—were doing their jobs efficiently. *Somebody* should be inspecting the troop decks to ensure that conditions were reasonably hygienic. In Grimes's experience even marines, for all their spit and polish, could not be trusted to maintain a high standard of personal cleanliness. And these soldiers that the ship was carrying were not marines, were only irregulars although, presumably, General Mortdale had been an officer in the army of Dunlevin prior to the revolution.

Then—*to hell with them,* thought Grimes. After all he was not legally responsible for anything. His name was not on the Register as Master of this ship; he had been employed only as a glorified watchman. He wanted to stay alive himself, of course, but could hardly care less what happened to his captors. He would be able to tell, he thought, if there were a dangerous buildup of carbon dioxide in the atmosphere or if the water-purification system were not functioning properly. If he suspected that things were going wrong he would tell Susie when she brought him his food.

One of the worst features of his incarceration was never knowing, except on the occasions when he was brought up to Control for navigation, what the time was. Sometimes it seemed only minutes between meals, sometimes far too many hours. He was never sure when he should be sleeping or reading—not that there was anything worth reading—or exercising. (He tried to keep himself in reasonably good condition by push-ups and sit-ups and toe-touchings, all that he could manage in his cramped quarters.)

He was having a shower. (It was one way of passing the time.) He washed his shirt and shorts, hung them to dry in the warm air blast. He stepped through from the little bathroom into the not much larger cabin just as the door opened and Susie stepped in. He glimpsed Hodge in the alleyway outside as the door shut. He heard the click of the padlock closing.

He was conscious of his nakedness but he had no towel to wrap about himself and he was damned if he was going to put on his wet shorts and shirt for anybody.

"Come in," he said sarcastically. "Don't mind the way I'm dressed. This is Liberty Hall; you can spit on the mat and call the cat a bastard."

Then he realized that she was in a very distressed state, her face white, her mouth trembling. Her shirt was ripped, exposing her right breast. She was holding her shorts, the waistband of which had been ripped, up with one hand.

"What happened, Susie?" he demanded.

She stared at him wildly then whispered, "Hodge thought that I'd be safe here as long as nobody else knows. . . ."

"But what happened?"

She tried to pull herself together. "A party, in the officers' mess. . . . That band of heroes. . . ." A spark of humor was showing through. "All for one and one for all. . . . The trouble was that I was supposed to be the one. . . ."

"But surely the general. . . ."

"His officers can do no wrong."

"Or Paul, and Lania. . . ."

"Lania's never forgiven me for having been Paul's lover. . . . And Paul? He's well under *her* thumb. . . ."

Then she screamed, tried to hide herself behind Grimes. He was acutely conscious of that bare breast pressing against the naked skin of his back. The door opened. It was Hodge again.

He grunted, "Grimes's tucker time, ain't it? Here's sandwiches an' a bottle o' plonk. Enough for both of you."

"And what about . . . *them?"* whispered Susie.

"They're happy enough now. They got those hen sergeants up. The last I saw of the party they certainly weren't missing *you.* But you're safer out of sight for a while." He leered, but somehow not offensively. He thrust the burdened tray into Grimes's hands, saying, "Candy is dandy but liquor is quicker."

He turned and left, shutting the door decisively behind him.

Grimes put the laden tray down on the desk. Susie sat down on the narrow bunk. She pulled a packet of cigarillos from the breast pocket of her shirt—the side that was not torn—put one of the slim, brown cylinders in her mouth with a hand that had almost stopped trembling, puffed it into ignition. She extended the pack to Grimes. "Smoke, Captain?"

"Thank you."

He lit up.

She regarded him through the eddying fumes. She managed a slight smile. She said, "If anybody had told me, while I was a stewardess in the Met. Service, that I'd feel safe locked up in a dogbox with a hairy-arsed space captain I'd have called him a bloody liar."

"Mphm." Grimes put an exploratory hand to his smooth buttocks. "I'm not hairy," he said.

"A figure of speech."

She got up from the bunk, brushed past Grimes to get to the desk. She unscrewed the plastic cap—large enough to be used as a cup—of the bottle, filled it. She said, "I have to admit that General Mortdale's senior mess sergeant can *do* things with an autochef. Here. Try it."

Grimes sipped cautiously. This was his first alcoholic drink for a very long time. It was a fortified wine, not too sweet, with a not unpleasant flavor and aroma that he could not identify. He sipped again, with less caution.

Susie took the cup from him, raised it to her own lips. "To a glorious restoration," she said. She drank. "And death and destruction to the enemies of our gracious prince and his princess." She drank again. "And may they always be successful in protecting the tender bodies of their loyal female subjects from their brutal and licentious soldiery!"

"They haven't had much success so far," said Grimes nastily.

"And don't I bloody well know it, John! (You don't mind, do you?)" She refilled the cup. "I'm neither a virgin nor a prude—but I do draw the line at pack rape. And I do think that Their High and Mightinesses should take a damn sight more interest in what their gallant soldiers get up to. This effort tonight wasn't the first time, you know. I've been fighting those bastards off ever since they came aboard on Porlock, knowing all the time that the only one to whom I could look to help was Hodge."

"Then why did you go to the party?"

"Lania—*Her Highness*—told me that as the catering officer of this noble vessel I must be there to see that the pongoes didn't starve or die of thirst. . . ."

"You're in no danger of doing the latter," said Grimes.

"Sorry, John." She took a swig from the refilled cup, then handed it to him. "But as I was saying—I do draw the line at pack rape. And at being beaten up for foreplay. Look!" She stripped off her torn shirt, stepped out of her shirt, peeled down her minimal underwear. She pointed at a dark bruise on the pale skin of her upper right thigh, at another on her round belly, another one just below the prominent pink nipple of her left breast.

Suddenly Grimes felt a flood of sympathy. Until now he had not really believed the girl's story, had been asking himself how much of the girl's distress was genuine, how much mere play acting. But those bruises were real enough.

He said with feeling, "The bastards! I wish. . . ."

She laughed shakily. "You wish that you had the authority to throw them into the brig, or even out of the airlock without a spacesuit! I wish it too. But it makes me a little happier to think that the bloody general and his bloody colonels and majors got nowhere with me, whereas you. . . ."

The invitation was unmistakable. Grimes looked at her. Those bruises may have been ugly but they somehow accentuated the sexuality of her abundant nakedness. Her eyes were wide, staring at his own nudity. He felt himself responding. Her scarlet mouth, with its smeared lip pigment, was wide, inviting—but the thought of the mouths of the drunken soldiers crushed to hers almost put him off. He put the cup down on the desk, stooped to pick up her torn shirt, used it to wipe her face.

She laughed shakily, "Gods! You're a fastidious bastard, John! But I don't blame you. I like you for it. And I'm clean where it counts."

He dropped the ripped garment, pulled her to him. If he had not enjoyed an alcoholic drink for a long time it was even longer since he had enjoyed a woman. And then, unbidden, the memory of how his sexuality had initiated the chain of circumstances culminating in his present predicament rose to the surface of his mind. If it had not been for that erotic dream and those obscene animals. . . . His erection began to die.

But he was determined to take what was being offered to him. The woman in the dream, he reasoned, had been darkly auburn, with deeply sun-bronzed skin. . . . The actual woman in his arms was blonde, pale-skinned, ample, not slender.

They kissed—and his first contact of sensitive membranes drove the horrible memories back into the pit from which they had risen. She was not only a woman but a new woman, a new—to him—kind of woman. There was a resilient softness such as he had never experienced before; all of his past loves had tended to be small breasted, slender limbed.

She fell backward onto the bunk, pulling him with her. He was on her, in her. The coupling was fast—too fast—explosive, mutually unsatisfying. She squirmed from under him, got to her feet, smiled down at him. She said, "You'll have to do better next time, John." She refilled the wine cup, brought it to him. They shared the liquor and a cigarillo, saying little. Then, stretched beside him, gently and unhurriedly, her mouth and hands skillful, she brought him to a fresh arousal.

The second time was better, much better. They made love unhurriedly, experimentally, inventively, deferring the climax again and again. At last they could hold out no longer. Then, simultaneously (it seemed) they fell into a deep, exhausted sleep.

They awoke. Grimes was hungry. The sandwiches were inclined to be stale now but there was some wine left to wash them down. After the meal, such as it was, Susie went through to the bathroom. Grimes heard the shower running and then, above the sound of descending water, the noise of somebody making a fuss of opening the padlock outside the door.

Hodge came in. He grinned at Grimes, said cheerfully, *"Their* party's over. They're sleeping it off. An' how was *your* party, Grimes?"

Grimes said, "Thank you for the wine."

"Is that all you're thanking me for?" The engineer was looking pointedly at the obviously fresh stains on the mattress cover. "Oh, Susie!"

"Yes?" came her voice from the bathroom.

"I brought you a fresh uniform from your cabin. The one that you were wearing when I saw you last looked a bit tattered. It's probably worse now." He put the bundle of clothing on the bunk then called, "I'll wait outside till you're dressed."

He left the cabin. Susie came out from the bathroom. She looked rather sluttish with her hair still wet from the shower—but, thought Grimes, none the worse for that.

She slowly put on the fresh shirt, saying, "Dear Hodge . . . I don't know what I'd have done without him. . . ." She noticed Grimes's jealous expression, laughed. "He's my half brother. Father played around a bit in his younger days."

"Mphm," grunted Grimes.

She stepped into her shorts. She was one of those women, thought Grimes, who looked better naked. Dressed, she was just another plump girl.

He went into the bathroom. The shorts and shirt that he had hung up to dry were damp again; Susie had not thought to shift them to where they would be safe from her splashings. But he put them on. They would dry out on his body soon enough.

When he reentered the cabin Susie was talking with Hodge. They turned to face Grimes. Susie said, "Are you with us, John?"

"What do you mean?" he asked.

"From now on we're looking after ourselves. We've decided that Paul and Lania have forfeited all claims to our loyalty."

"Why did you join up with them in the first place?" asked Grimes.

"We didn't know what they'd be like once they started to rise to what they think are their rightful positions. We didn't know what their supporters—if that mob from Porlock are any sample—were really like. But we know now.

"Oh, we'll play along for the time being. We have to. But we'll watch how the cards fall. If we see a chance to take a trick or two for ourselves we grab it.

"And you, John?"

He said, "If I were being paid I'd be only the hired help. But as I'm not being paid I'm not even that. All that I want is to get back to Bronsonia and my own ship."

"Stick with us," she told him, "and you might do just that."

Twelve

Grimes said, “I don’t see how I can refuse to land on Dunlevin. But surely there will be some opposition. I can’t imagine a convenient Aerospace Controllers’ strike, such as there was on Porlock; on highly regimented, socialist planets you just don’t strike if you know what’s good for your health. . . .”

Susie and Hodge sat side by side on the settee, watching him as he ate his meal from the tray on the desk, listening to him as he talked between mouthfuls.

Grimes went on, “All that I know about Dunlevin is from those propaganda magazines that you brought me, Susie. They can hardly be classed as pilot books. They don’t tell me what artificial satellites are in orbit about Dunlevin. There must be some. Are they armed? After the way in which the Duchy of Waldegren attempted to intervene in the civil war I should be very surprised if they aren’t. Are they manned?”

He took and chewed another mouthful, swallowed.

“And talking of that—I’ve been meaning to ask for some time—just why does Bronsonia have manned meteorological satellites while almost every other world makes do with fully automated stations in orbit?”

“The Jobs For Humans movement was very powerful on Bronsonia,” said Hodge. “It still is, come to that. But there were some jobs that the humans didn’t find all that attractive. That’s why the met. stations are manned by almost unemployables . . .”

“Speak for yourself,” snapped Susie.

“. . . and misfits, such as ourselves and Their Sublime Highnesses.”

“Mphm. But to return to Dunlevin. . . . Almost certainly orbital forts, probably manned. A continuous long-range radar watch. Mass Proximity Indicators? No. When you’re sitting on, or in relatively close orbit about, something with the mass of a planet that mass is the only mass that registers. So, as long as we’re making our approach under interstellar drive were undetected—but once we break through into the normal continuum people are liable to start throwing bricks at us. . . .”

"Anybody would think," said Susie, "that you *want* to make a successful landing on Dunlevin."

"It's an interesting problem," admitted Grimes. "Too, as you've said, we have to play along—and to play along we have to stay alive. So I'll land this bloody ship for Paul and Lania. Presumably they, as soon as we're down, will be marching down the ramp at the head of their glorious army of liberation to be welcomed with open arms by the grateful peasantry. They hope. And *I* hope that they leave only a small guard detail on board. . . ."

"Coping with them should be no problem," said Susie.

It should not be, thought Grimes. Presumably the girl, with access to the ship's medicine chest, should be able to drug the soldiers' food or drink.

"There's still the problem of getting through the Dunlevin screen in one piece," said Hodge. "But suppose we do, and suppose that we're able to seize the ship—we've got it made. A navigator, an engineer and a catering officer. There's nowhere in the galaxy we can't go."

The door was flung open. One of Mortdale's aides—it was Major Briggs, Grimes realized—stood in the opening. He glared at Grimes and at Hodge, reserved an especially venomous look for Susie.

He snarled, "Fraternizing with the prisoner, are you? The general will hear of this."

Hodge made an ostentatious display of his pistol, said, "Their Highnesses' orders have always been that the prisoner is to take his meals under guard."

"Guards," snapped Briggs, "should remain standing, not sprawl all over whatever seating is available."

"I'm a spaceman," growled Hodge. "Not a soldier."

"Do not belabor the obvious, Mr. Hodge. And now, Captain Grimes, if you've quite finished your Lucullan repast would you mind accompanying me to Control?" He made an imperative gesture with his pistol. "Up!"

Grimes wiped his mouth, deliberately slowly, with the paper napkin, then got to his feet. He preceded the major up the spiral staircase to the control room.

Lania, Paul and General Mortdale were awaiting him there, sitting at ease in the command chair and the two seats flanking it. Grimes, with Briggs at his side, stood before them. Nobody told him to sit; he decided that for him to do so would only cause unpleasantness.

Lania asked, "Have you given any thought to the problem of an unobserved landing on Dunlevin, Grimes? After all, you are—or were—a naval officer rather than a merchant spaceman. You must have made a study of strategy and tactics."

Mortdale interrupted. "As I have already said, Highness, space-borne invasions are the concern of the officers commanding the troops as well as of those commanding the transports. What do you know about the Gunderson Gambit, Captain Grimes?"

"Only what I have read, General. As a matter of fact I was thinking that it might be applied in this case. . . . If this were a warship—which she's not—I'd consider that attempting to take out the orbital forts would be less risky."

"This Gunderson Gambit . . ." asked Paul, "Is it risky?"

"Less risky, I think," said Grimes, "than trying to slip past the forts unobserved in normal space-time."

"It has been tried—the Gunderson Gambit, I mean?" asked Lania.

"By Commodore Gunderson, during the investment of Tallis. It worked for him."

"But it didn't work, General, for Captain Tanner during the first Waldegren campaign, or for Captain Lake at the Battle of Kahbil."

"It could work for Captain Grimes at the Battle of Bacon Bay," said Mortdale.

"Bacon Bay?" asked Grimes. The name reminded him of something, some historical military disaster.

"Yes, Captain. According to our Intelligence that will be the best place for a landing. The majority of the population is disaffected."

"But this Gunderson Gambit?" demanded Lania. "It's all very well for you military technicians to enjoy an entertaining—to yourselves—discussion but please remember that the ultimate decision rests with. . . ." The unspoken word "me" might just as well have been said aloud. She looked at her consort. "With His Highness," she finished.

Paul squirmed in his seat. Already, thought Grimes, the man was scared shitless.

"You explain, Captain," ordered Mortdale. "You're the spaceman."

"As you know, Highness," said Grimes to Lania, "the interstellar drive propagates a temporal precession field. Normally it is shut down before a close approach is made to a planetary body. . . ."

"The Van Allens?" murmured the woman. "I recall that when we got away from Bronsonia we did not proceed under Mannschenn Drive until we were clear of the Van Allen Belts."

"There is no actual risk involved, these days, in running the Van Allens with the drive in operation. It's not usually done because crew and passengers—passengers especially—can be scared by the brush discharges from every metal projection. Come to that, there is no actual danger, physical danger, that is, if you run right through a planet or even a sun; relative to a ship proceeding under Mannschenn Drive such bodies exist in an alternate universe. Of course, if the drive went on the blink at just the wrong place at the wrong time it would be just too bad for the ship and her people—and for the inhabitants of a populated world if a spaceship suddenly materialized somewhere under the surface. And as for suns—such an accident might trigger off a nova. There's only one way of finding out for sure and nobody's keen on trying it."

"Fascinating as these horror stories are," said Lania coldly, "I shall be obliged if you will come to the point."

"Very well, Highness. The Gunderson Gambit involves running in as close as you dare under Mannschenn Drive and then . . . materializing. If you've miscalculated very badly you break through into the normal continuum below the surface of the planet. The result is a Big Bang with the ship at Ground Zero. There's also a Big Bang if you materialize at anything below stratospheric level. But where can you say that a planet's atmosphere ends? If the sudden mixture of ship's matter and planetary matter occurs at an altitude where the planetary matter is no more than a few stray molecules and atoms of assorted gases you should suffer only a few casualties, with luck not even fatal ones. There should be no great damage to the ship's structure or to her machinery. The major risk will be a descent of at least six hundred kilometers with your inertial drive making enough racket to awaken even the sleepiest sentries."

"We didn't wake any sentries on Porlock," said Lania.

"On Porlock, Highness," said Mortdale, "nobody was on the alert for an armed invasion. Furthermore, the authorities were turning a blind eye and a deaf ear to our coming and going." He turned to Grimes. "But the people on the world on which your Commodore Gunderson was landing were, presumably, expecting trouble. What did *he* do?"

"He modified his ship while he was still outside the range of planet- and satellite-based radar, then made a powered, stern-first approach. He shut down his Mannschenn Drive at superstratospheric altitude, then fell free, using his inertial drive, initially, only to maintain attitude. Finally, only seconds before impact, he slammed on full vertical thrust *and* fired his auxiliary reaction drive. It worked—for the commodore. But this ship—a merchantman, not a warship—doesn't run to auxiliary rockets."

"But even without reaction drive," stated rather than asked Mortdale, "you can do it."

"The last part, General, yes. At least, I'll try. But the powered, stern-first approach is out.

"Why, Captain Grimes?"

"To begin with, it would mean that our entry into the atmosphere, even with the inertial drive shut down for the final free fall, would be at far too high a velocity. As I've already said, we don't have braking rockets to use before set-down. And we don't have the heat shields that a warship has. We'd hit the ground as a blob of molten metal.

"Our approach will have to be a normal one apart from our shutting down

Mannschenn Drive within the Van Allens. We have to swing on the gyros, of course, so that we fall stern first to the target area. If anybody happens to be watching they'll see us appear suddenly on their radar screens—and they'll see, too, that we're just falling. There'll be panic stations—even if they assume that we're a meteorite and not a spaceship. At best—as far as we're concerned—there'll be an evacuation of the strike area. At worst there'll be an attempt to destroy the hunk cosmos debris—if they *are* fooled—before it strikes. And we don't run to antimissile laser or antimissile missiles."

The general grinned, quite amicably. "It is refreshing to discuss strategy and tactics with a man of your training, Captain. Most of my own officers are somewhat amateurish. But our main problem is one of a silent approach. We have our sympathizers, of course, on Dunlevin, a royalist underground. As soon as you can give me a firm ETA, a Carlottigram will be sent from this ship, allegedly emanating from a passenger aboard *Alpha Puppis,* to an elderly lady living in the capital city, Dunrobin. Innocent birthday greetings unless you have the key to the code. . . . We have people in the planet-based radar stations and also, in the fortress satellites. There will be brief—very brief—breakdowns, failures to observe what is showing on the screens, at just the right—for us—time. . . ."

"Aren't they taking a great risk, those radar operators?" asked Grimes.

"They will be well rewarded," said Lania.

If they're lucky, thought Grimes. *If they're bloody lucky.*

"But can they be trusted?" asked Paul. "Can they be trusted?"

"You should never have gotten into this," Lania told him, "if you haven't the guts to see it through."

Grimes wondered how long Paul would last if the counterrevolution were successful but told himself, as he looked at the flabby prince, that he could hardly care less.

All that he wanted to do was to get down onto Dunlevin in one piece and then, as soon as possible, to leave in the same intact state.

Thirteen

As the voyage drew to its conclusion Grimes was required more and more frequently in Control. Few were the opportunities when he could discuss with Susie and Hodge their plan of campaign after a landing had been made—*if* a landing was made—and fewer still were the opportunities to have the girl to himself. Their sessions of lovemaking were brief, infrequent but torrid. He knew—and she knew—that what was between them could not last, not even if they survived the landing, not even if they succeeded in making their escape from Dunlevin. The transitory nature of their relationship made it all the more intense.

They had time to talk, sometimes, after their couplings. Once Grimes said to her, "You told me, some time ago, that Lania hates you because you were once Paul's lover. I just can't see how a girl like you could fall for a fat slob like him. . . ."

She laughed, a little ruefully. She said, "He wasn't always so fat. And back on Bronsonia—at least to the refugees and their children, such as myself—he was the Prince, the Prince Charming. Many native Bronsonians thought of him that way as well." She laughed again. "I believe you're jealous, John. . . ."

He laughed, but without real humor. "Perhaps I am."

And then Hodge, outside the cabin, made his usual major production of unlocking the door.

On another occasion they were talking of less personal matters.

He asked her, "What do you know of Bacon Bay, Susie?"

"About as much as you," she told him. "It's on the west coast of New Ireland. I suppose it was named after some personality among the original colonists. . . ."

He said, "There was a Bacon Bay—no, not Bacon Bay but a name very similar—back on Earth. I remember it from a history lesson years ago, when I was just a school kid. One of the American presidents made a landing there in support of a counterrevolution. . . ."

"And what happened?"

"It came unstuck."

She said, "I have a sort of presentiment that this one will. It's just as well, I think, that we won't be sticking around to find out just what does happen. . . ."

For a change Hodge was watching Grimes eat while Susie kept guard outside.

He said, "I've been helping the general's artificers with the hovertanks. Nasty, vicious little three-man jobs. . . . One driver, two gunners. . . . You're an expert on military matters, Grimes; perhaps you could tell me why Mortdale is going to use ground forces instead of a fleet of armed pinnaces? After all, we could have loaded quite a few aboard this ship. . . ."

"A lot depends," said Grimes, "upon what arms he was able to purchase on Porlock. Quite possibly the Porlockers didn't have any military aircraft to spare."

"Those tanks," said Hodge, "were manufactured in the Duchy of Waldegren."

"And so what? They could still be Porlockian surplus army equipment. But tanks instead of aircraft for the invasion? It makes sense. Aircraft—or spacecraft operating inside or outside an atmosphere—are fine for blowing the hell out of the enemy's military installations and/or centers of population—but they're also fine targets themselves. And if you want to take *and hold,* without causing overmuch damage, you need infantry. And tanks are sort of mechanized infantry."

"They can take and hold as much as they like," said Hodge, "as long as they don't hold *us*."

"This looks like being the last time, John," said Susie. "The last time, that is, on this leg of the voyage. I hope that it's not the last time, period."

"I do, too."

"That's up to us, the three of us," she said.

He looked suspiciously at her naked belly. It seemed a little plumper than usual.

She laughed. "By the three of us I meant you, Hodge and myself. Don't worry about any other possible meaning to my words. I'm taking my shots."

"Just as well," said Grimes. "I've enough worries already."

"You worried? I've heard that when you were in the Survey Service you were notorious for your good luck."

"If my luck had held," he said, "I shouldn't be here now."

"You bastard!" she said, and Grimes had to talk hard and fast before she would allow him to continue with the lovemaking.

When they were finished he said, "But, after all, I have been lucky. This time with you. . . ."

She said, "You don't deserve it."

Fourteen

Bronson Star passed through Dunlevin's Van Allens, the natural screen of particles held about the planet by its magnetic field. The transit should have been made in nanoseconds of subjective time—but, with the Mannschenn Drive still in operation seemed to occupy an eternity. Grimes had read and had been told of the weird effects that might be expected, had warned the others—but reading about something in a book is altogether different from experiencing it in actuality.

There were the brush discharges from projections, crackling arcs between points. But a brush discharge should not look like a slowly burgeoning flower of multicolored flame; an arc, to a human observer in normal space-time, flares into instant existence, it is not a tendril of blinding incandescence slowly writhing from one terminal to the other. It crackles; it does not make a noise like a snake writhing with impossible slowness through dead leaves.

Grimes was surprised when his hand moved at quite normal speed. He stopped the Mannschenn Drive. The thin, high whine of the ever-precessing rotors deepened in tone to an almost inaudible hum, ceased. Ahead, as seen through the transparent dome of the control room, the writhing nebulosity that had been Dunlevin solidified to a great crescent, bright against the blackness of space. But Grimes's first concern was swinging the ship. He activated the directional gyroscopes, heard the initial rumble as they started, felt the tugs and pressures of centrifugal force.

He was aware that the transition to the normal continuum had not been without effects. There had been brief, intensely bright sparks in the air of the control room to tell of the forced matings of molecule with gaseous molecule. There was the acridity of ozone. An alarm buzzer was sounding. Grimes managed a hasty glance at the console, saw that the warning noise and the flashing red light signified the failure of nothing immediately important; for some reason one of the farm-deck pumps was malfunctioning. It would have to wait for attention.

Nothing—apart from a brief, burning pain in his right foot—seemed to be wrong with his own body. Had it been his heart, or his brain, the result could have been—would have been—disastrous. He watched the stern-vision screen, saw the night hemisphere of Dunlevin swing into view.

The general—he, alone, had lived on the planet, had fought on the losing side in the civil war—gave Grimes his instructions. He said, "That major concentration of city lights is Dunrobin. The one to the right of it, the smaller one, is Dunrovin. . . . Below it, on your screen, is Dunsackin. . . ."

The piratical ancestors of the exiled royalty and aristocracy, thought Grimes, had displayed a rather juvenile sense of humor when they renamed the planet and its major cities. He knew, having studied the charts, that Dunrobin was now Freedonia, Dunrovin changed to Libertad and Dunsackin to Marxville. . . . A pile of shit by any name still stinks, he told himself sourly.

"Try to fall," ordered Mortdale, "midway between Dunrovin and Dunsackin. Before too long we shall pick up a laser beacon, like the one that you homed on when you landed on Porlock."

"If it is there," said Lania—for the benefit, thought Grimes, of the pale, trembling Paul. Then, just to show impartiality in her distribution of psychological discomfort, "You needn't be so fussy about avoiding the thing this time, Grimes. You can't make an omelet without breaking eggs—or a counterrevolution without breaking beacons."

Ha, thought Grimes. *Ha, bloody ha! And we'll soon see who has the last laugh!*

But he could no longer afford the luxury of indulging in sardonic thoughts. The ship was falling like a stone, a meteorite. Soon she would be leaving a trail in the night sky like one. As long as that was the only indication of her arrival she might be taken for a natural phenomenon but if the flaring descent were accompanied by the hammering of inertial drive it would be a dead giveaway. He must use the drive now while the vessel was still in a near vacuum, incapable of conducting sound.

He applied lateral thrust, brought the bull's eye of the stern vision screen exactly midway between the lights of the two cities, held it there. As on past occasions he was forgetting that he was a prisoner acting under duress, at gunpoint. He was beginning to enjoy himself. He had a job to do, one demanding all his skills.

Bronson Star fell.

Her skin was heating up but not—yet—dangerously so. She was maintaining her attitude—so far, but once she was in the denser atmospheric levels she would be liable to topple. In a properly manned ship Grimes would have had officers watching instruments such as the radar altimeter, the clinometer, external pressure gauge and all the rest of them while he concentrated on the actual pilotage. Now he was a one-man band. All that his companions in the control room were good for was pointing their pistols at him.

Bronson Star fell.

The air inside the ship was becoming uncomfortably warm and the viewports were increasingly obscured by upsweeping incandescence. But the stern-vision screen was clear—and in it, quite suddenly, appeared a tiny, red-glowing spark, a little off-center.

Inertial drive again, lateral thrust, sustained, fighting inertia. . . . The ship responded sluggishly but she did respond, at last. Grimes was sweating but it was not only from psychological strain. It was no longer warm in the control room; it was hot and becoming hotter.

"You'll burn us all up!" screamed Paul.

"Be quiet, damn you!" snarled Lania.

Bronson Star fell.

The radar altimeter read-out on the stern vision screen was a flickering of numerals almost too rapid to follow. The beacon light was still only a spark but one of eye-searing intensity—or was the smarting of Grimes's eyes due only to the salt perspiration that was dripping into them?

Bronson Star started to topple.

Lateral thrust again. The ship groaned in every member as she slowly came back to the vertical relative to the planetary surface.

Grimes realized that somebody else had come into the control room.

"General!" shouted a voice—that of Major Briggs? "General! The men are roasting down there! They'll be in no state to fight even if they're still alive when we land!"

The troop decks, converted cargo holds, would not be as well insulated as was the accommodation, thought Grimes. They must be ovens. . . .

"General! You must stop before we're all incinerated!"

"Captain Grimes," ordered Mortdale at last, "you may put the brakes on."

Easier said than done, thought Grimes. But to slow down at this altitude would be safer than carrying out the original plan. He could apply vertical thrust gradually—but, even so, it must sound to those in the countryside below the ship as though all the hammers of hell were beating in the sky. And what of the planet's defenses? Were military technicians sitting tensely, their fingers poised over buttons?

Had they already pushed those buttons?

In the screen the figures presented by the radar altimeter were no longer an almost unreadable flicker. The rate of descent was slowing yet there was not—nor would there be for a long time—any appreciable drop in temperature. But the thermometer had ceased to rise and only an occasional veil of incandescent gases obscured the viewports.

Grimes increased vertical thrust. The ship complained, trembled. Loose fittings rattled loudly. Relative to the surface below her *Bronson Star* was now almost stationary.

"Drop her again!" ordered Mortdale.

That made sense. It might possibly fool a computer; it almost certainly would fool a human gunlayer.

The hammering of the inertial drive abruptly ceased. Again the ship fell—but there was no burgeoning flower or flame in the sky above her, where she had been.

A suspicion was growing in Grimes's mind. This landing—apart from the problems of ship handling—was all too easy. Intelligence works both ways, and there are double agents. But he said nothing. If the general knew his job—and what had he been in the old Royal Army? a second lieutenant?—he would be smelling a rat by now.

The altimeter was unwinding fast again and, in the screen, that solitary beacon was blindingly bright.

1,000 . . . 900 . . . 800 . . .700 . . .

Vertical thrust again. No matter who else might want *Bronson Star* in one piece Grimes most certainly did.

600 . . . 550 . . .

Still too fast, thought Grimes.

500 . . . 450 . . .

He increased vertical thrust.

430 . . . 410 . . . 390 . . .

"Get us *down!*" snarled Lania. "Get us down, damn you!"

Free fall again, briefly. Then full vertical thrust. Again *Bronson Star* shook herself like a wet dog as the inertial drive hammered frenziedly.

10 . . . 5 . . . 3 . . . 1 . . .

It was not one of Grimes's better landings. The ship sat down hard and heavily with a bone-jarring jolt. Had the great vanes of her tripedal landing gear not been equal to the strain she would surely have toppled, become a wreck. The shock absorbers did not gently sigh; they *screamed.*

"Airlocks open!" ordered Mortdale. "Ramps out!" Then, to Paul, "You, Your Highness, will lead the invasion. A hovertank, in which you will ride, carries your personal standard."

"I should stay here, in headquarters," said Paul weakly.

"You must show your flag, Highness. And your face."

"It is just as well," said Lania, "that his flag doesn't match his face. We don't want to surrender before we've started."

"Somebody has to keep guard over Grimes to make sure that he doesn't try anything," persisted Paul.

"It won't be you," said Lania.

"Major Briggs has his orders," said the general.

Fifteen

Grimes was hustled down to his quarters by Briggs and two sergeants, locked in. He sat glumly on the settee, smoking his pipe, trying to visualize what was happening. Sonic insulation muffled interior noises but he could faintly hear shouts, mechanical whinings and clankings. The little hovertanks would be streaming down the ramps, followed by the heavier tracked vehicles. He strained his ears for the sound of gunfire, of exploding missiles, heard nothing but the diminishing bustle of disembarkation. It seemed that the landing was unopposed.

Then there was silence save for the murmurings of the ship's own life processes. The air flowing in through the ventilation ducts was cooler now, bore alien scents, some identifiable, some not. The smell of the seashore predominated; a brininess, the tang of stranded seaweed. This was to be expected; *Bronson Star* had landed just above the high-water mark on the beach at Bacon Bay. Hodge was flushing out the ship's stale atmosphere with the fresh, sea air.

Grimes's sweat-soaked clothing dried on his body. He would have liked to have stripped, showered and laundered his garments but knew that he must maintain himself in a state of instant readiness. Were Susie and Hodge playing their parts? he wondered. Had the girl served drugged food and drink to Briggs and his sergeants? Had the engineer readied the ship for immediate lift-off?

The door opened and Susie stood there. As on a past occasion her clothing was in disarray, her shirt torn, her ample breasts exposed.

She swore, "That bald-headed bastard Briggs! The sergeants went out like a light—but not him! Two mugs of coffee with enough dope to put a regiment to sleep and still he stayed on his feet! Hodge had to put a dent in his sconce with a wrench while he was trying to strangle me." She grinned viciously, "But whoever finds him where we left him—either Lania or the Free People's Army—will treat him much more roughly!"

Grimes brushed past her, ran up the spiral staircase to Control; it was faster than waiting for the elevator. Before sitting in the command seat he looked out through the viewports, towards the glow on the horizon that marked the city lights of Dunrovin—the royalist army's first objective. Then, between ship and city, an impossible sun suddenly rose, blinding despite the automatic polarization of the ports. Grimes ran to his chair, did not bother to strap himself in. He knew that he must get the ship up before the shock wave hit.

The inertial drive was already on Stand By. It commenced its metallic stammer at the first touch of Grimes's fingers on the controls. He did not—as he should have done, as in normal circumstances he would have done—nurse the innies up gradually to maximum thrust; he demanded full power at once and miraculously got it.

Nonetheless the initial lift-off was painfully slow.

Bronson Star groaned, shuddered. She climbed into the night sky like a grossly fat old woman reluctantly clambering upstairs to bed, wheezing and palpitating. Then the shock wave hit her, slamming her sidewise—but also upward. Grimes struggled with his controls, maintaining attitude. When the ship was once again upright he saw that she was making better speed, was climbing fast and faster.

Only then was Grimes able to check that all was ready—or had been ready—for lift-off. The airlock doors were all sealed, he saw; that was the most important thing. Life-support systems were functioning.

Susie—he had quite forgotten that she was in the control room with him—called out. "John! The radar! Somebody's after us!"

He heaved himself out of his chair, went to the screen tank of the all-around radar. Yes, there were intruders, six tiny sparks, astern but closing. He had no quarrel with them but it was reasonable to assume that they had a quarrel with him.

Perhaps—perhaps!—he would be able to talk his way to freedom.

He went to the NST transceiver, switched on. At once a strange voice came from the speaker, "Free People's Air Force to unidentified spacecraft. . . ." Obviously whoever was talking had been doing so for some time. "Free People's Air Force to unidentified spacecraft. . . . Free People's. . . ."

"*Bronson Star here,*" said Grimes.

"Land at once, *Bronson Star*. Resistance is useless. Your army and your leaders have been destroyed. Land at once, or we open fire."

And why all the talking? wondered Grimes. Why had not the spaceship been fired upon already? Why should people quite willing to wipe out an army with a nuclear landmine be reluctant to destroy a spaceship? Of course, he reasoned, *Bronson Star* would be a most welcome addition to the Dunlevin merchant service, but . . . Surely if *they* couldn't have her they would see to it that nobody else did.

He looked at the stern vision screen—and laughed.

The shock waves had not only given the ship a welcome boost; it had pushed her into a position directly above one of the cities. Which one he neither knew nor cared. He wondered if its people knew that they were, in effect, his hostages.

He told Susie, "Take over the NST. Keep 'em talking. I have to make sure that we stayed relatively put. . . ."

Back in his command chair he used lateral thrust to keep the city lights coincident with the bull's eye of the screen. He watched the altimeter figures steadily climbing. He heard Susie saying into the microphone, "We are neutrals." We were skyjacked by Prince Paul and General Mortdale. We were forced, at gunpoint, to bring them and their soldiers here. . . ."

"You must return for questioning. No harm will come to you if you are innocent. . . ."

"You have no jurisdiction over a Bronsonian spaceship. . . ."

"When she is in our airspace we have. Return to the surface at once."

"Ask them," said Grimes, "'*Straight down?*'"

Susie did so. She laughed. Grimes laughed—then remembered that he still had to get past the orbital forts. No matter what his position would be relative to Dunlevin's surface a cloud of radioactive dust and gases above the stratosphere would be little worry to anybody at ground level.

Sixteen

He had hoped that the royalist invaders would create enough of a diversion to distract attention from *Bronson Star*'s getaway. He had strongly suspected that the landing would not be a great surprise to the rulers of Dunlevin; he had not anticipated that the invading force, in its entirety, would be wiped out by nuclear blast. (Surely there could have been no survivors.) He had envisaged a nasty little battle but with fatal casualties deliberately kept to a minimum so that there could be a show trial afterward with public humiliation of Paul, Lania and their adherents. But military and political leaders do not always see eye to eye—and the military have always been prone to use steam hammers to squash gnats.

Meanwhile—how trigger happy were the crews of the fortress satellites? Would they shoot first and ask questions afterward or would they try to talk *Bronson Star* into surrender? (Their Air Force colleagues had given up the chase saying, before they turned away, "You've had your chance. You'll never get past the forts.") Did the satellite crews know about the Gunderson Gambit? It was supposed to be a closely guarded secret of the Federation Survey Service—but Mortdale knew (had known) about it. And if Mortdale had known. . . .

"Susie," he asked urgently, "was the general ever in the Marines? The Federation Survey Service Marines, that is. . . ."

"Why do you ask, John? He's dead now. What does it matter what he was."

Cold-blooded little bitch! thought Grimes angrily. The general, with all his faults, had been more of Grimes's breed of cat than Paul and Lania or, come to that, Susie and Hodge.

"This is important," he said. "Was he ever in the Marines?"

"Yes," she admitted sulkily. "Quite a few of the refugees, the military types, entered Federation service. He got as high as colonel, I believe. . . ."

And as a colonel, thought Grimes, he'd have had access to all manner of classified information. He hoped that there were no ex-colonels of Marines in the satellites. It was extremely unlikely that there would be.

He said, "Put the radar on long range. See if you can pick up any of the orbital forts."

She said, "There're all sorts of bloody blips—some opening, some closing. They could be *anything.*"

"They probably are," said Grimes.

Then again a strange voice came from the transceiver. *"Fortress Castro* to *Bronson Star.* This is your last chance. Inject yourself into closed orbit and prepare to receive our boarding party—or we open fire!"

"You can't!" cried Susie to Grimes.

"I have to," he said. "Look at the gauges. You wouldn't be able to breathe what's outside the ship but it's still more atmosphere than vacuum. I can't risk the Gunderson Gambit—yet."

He had anticipated this very situation, reasoned that a show of compliance would be the only way to avoid instant destruction. Already he had thrown the problem into the lap of the computer; all that he had to do now was switch over from manual to automatic control.

"Inject into orbit!" came the voice of *Fortress Castro.* "We are tracking you. Inject into orbit—or. . . ."

"Tell them that we're injecting," said Grimes to Susie.

He threw the switch, heard and felt the arhythmic hammering of the drive as *Bronson Star* was pushed away from her outward and upward trajectory. He hoped that *Fortress Castro*'s commander was relying more upon the evidence presented by his computer than the display in his radar tank. It would be some time before the ship's alteration of course would be visually obvious.

He got up from the command chair, went to his own radar. That large blip must be the orbital fort, that tiny spark moving away from it, toward the center of the screen, the vehicle carrying the boarding party. He turned his attention from the tank to the board with the array of telltale gauges; the dial at which he looked registered particle contact rather than actual pressure. Outside the ship there was vacuum to all practical intents and purposes—the practical intents and purposes of air-breathing organisms. But the sudden—it would have to be sudden—propagation of a temporal precession field would mean the catastrophic, intimate intermingling of those sparsely scattered atoms and molecules, those charged particles, with all matter, living and inanimate, within the ship.

At this distance from the planet the risk was still too great.

Grimes stared into the radar tank. Would *Bronson Star* reach apogee before the shuttle caught her? Would he be justified in using thrust to drive the ship to a higher altitude in a shorter time? He decided against this. *Fortress Castro*'s computer would at once notify the shuttle's commander—and that vehicle was close enough now to use its light weaponry, automatic guns firing armor-piercing bullets that would pierce the shell of the unarmored *Bronson Star* with contemptuous ease, crippling her but not destroying.

"What the hell's going on up there?" came Hodge's voice from the intercom.

"We are temporarily in orbit," said Grimes. "I shall initiate Mannschenn Drive as soon as possible."

"I hope," said Susie—who, as a spaceperson of sorts, was beginning to get some grasp of the situation—"that it will be soon enough."

"Shuttle to *Bronson Star*," came a fresh voice from the NST transceiver. "Have your after airlock ready to receive boarders."

"Willco," said Susie, looking at Grimes, her eyebrows raised in unspoken query.

He grinned at her with a confidence that he did not feel.

The ship's computer, pre-programmed, took over. Grimes had forgotten to instruct it to sound any sort of warning before starting the Mannschenn Drive. He heard the hum of the rotors as they commenced to spin, the faint murmur that rapidly rose to a high-pitched whine. He saw colors sag down the spectrum, the warped perspective. And it was as though the control room had been invaded by a swarm of tiny, luminous bees, each miniscule but intense flare the funeral pyre of a cancelled-out atom. But there was no damage done—not to Susie, not to himself, not to the ship. And not, he hoped, to Hodge.

The pyrotechnic display abruptly ceased.

Grimes pulled his vile pipe out of his pocket, filled and lit it, looked up and out of the familiar—comforting now rather than frightening—blackness with the writhing, iridescent nebulosities that, in normal space-time, were the stars.

He said, "As soon as the mass proximity indicator shows that there's nothing dangerously close we'll set trajectory. And then . . . Bronsonia, here we come!"

"Not so fast," said Susie, her voice oddly cold. "Not so fast. *You* have only a few fines to pay on Bronsonia. Hodge and I face life imprisonment or rehabilitation. And that—need I tell you?—is just another word for personality wiping."

Seventeen

Bronson Star broke away from Dunlevin without further incident. She was bound, at first, for nowhere in particular. Her inertial drive was running only to provide a comfortable half-standard gravity, her Mannschenn Drive was in operation only to make it virtually impossible for any Dunlevin warships—the Free People's Navy did, Grimes knew, possess two obsolescent frigates—to intercept her.

Grimes, Hodge and Susie sat around the table in the wardroom. There was coffee—not very good. There was a bottle of some unnamed liqueur that had been distilled by the late General Mortdale's senior mess sergeant. Grimes, sipping the smooth, potent and palatable fluid, rather hoped that the noncommissioned officer had survived the Bacon Bay debacle; as he had been one of the two men left with Major Briggs to keep guard on the ship this was possible. The drugged soldiers had been dumped from the airlock, onto the beach, shortly prior to lift-off.

Grimes raised his glass in a toast. "Here's to Sergeant Whoever-He-Is. Here's to his continuing good health."

Susie said, a little sourly, "He was a good cook and even better at persuading the autochef to produce liquor. But I can't help feeling a bit sorry that we didn't kill the pongoes before we threw them out."

"Too many people died," said Grimes. "I rather hope that Briggs and the two sergeants didn't."

"And if they didn't," said Susie, "and if they were taken prisoner, they'll sing. They'll sing like a male voice trio—or, if the Free People's Secret Police is as bad as the Royalist Underground makes out, like a soprano trio."

"So," asked Grimes, "what?" He lifted and lit his pipe then continued. "Nobody on Dunlevin thinks that *Bronson Star* lifted off all by her little self. They know that she must have had a crew."

"And now," said Susie, "they know who was in the crew. The Underground will know—and what the Underground knows the royalist refugee enclaves on Bronsonia, Porlock and a few other planets will soon know."

"With your share of the salvage money you should be able to buy protection," said Grimes. "That's why I think we should return to Bronsonia as soon as possible. We—the three of us—won this ship back from Paul and Lania and their mob. Even though I was, at the time of the original seizure, employed by *Bronson Star*'s owners, I was, legally, neither master nor crew member. My name was on neither the Articles nor the Register. The salvage claim should stick."

"And you want your share," said Susie, "to pay your fines and port dues so that you can get your own little ship back."

"Of course," agreed Grimes.

"I see your point, John. But you're not a known criminal. Hodge and I are. There was the first skyjacking, remember. The met. satellite. Captain Walvis will not have forgotten how I massaged the back of his neck with a pistol muzzle while he broke out of orbit to intercept *Bronson Star*."

"You could claim," said Grimes, "that you acted under duress."

"Ha! And even if the court believed it, there'd still be the Dunlevin royalists out for revenge."

"We could go out to the Rim," contributed Hodge. "Change the ship's name, our own names. Set up shop as a one-ship tramp company."

"You've been reading too many space stories, Hodge," said Grimes. "That's the sort of thing that people do in fiction, never in fact. Known space is festooned with red tape. All—and I mean *all*—data concerning every merchant ship is fed into the memory banks of the Master Registry back on Earth—and those banks are instantly accessible to every port authority on every planet—on every planet that runs to a spaceport, that is. And those that don't haven't been discovered or settled yet."

"Surely we could *buy* false ship's papers and personal papers," said Hodge.

"Who from?" asked Grimes. "And, more importantly, what with?"

Susie laughed. "Mortdale brought the royalist war chest aboard at Porlock. Folding money, in good Federation credit bills. The accumulation of contributions from refugees such as my revered parents. . . . I haven't made a proper count yet—but there's plenty. Even if we can't—as you say—have the ship's identity changed we can pay to have ourselves . . . transmogrified? Is that the right word? But you know what I mean."

"But where?" said Grimes, more to himself than to the others. "But where? It can't be too far away; I want to get *Bronson Star* back to where she came from before there's too much of a hue and cry. Probably already the Survey Service has been ordered to keep its eyes skinned for us—and if they find us where we shouldn't be they'll be claiming the salvage money."

"Looking after yourself, Grimes," commented Hodge rather nastily.

Susie sprang to his defense. "And why shouldn't he? Nobody else is."

"*I* looked after him," grumbled the engineer. "If it hadn't been for me he'd never have gotten off Dunlevin."

"If it hadn't been for him," said Susie, "we'd never have gotten off Dunlevin. We'd be undergoing interrogation by the Secret Police right now."

"We're all in this," said Grimes. "But our ways have to part." He looked at Susie regretfully, and she at him in the same way. "I must get you to some world where you can use your ill-gotten gains to buy yourselves new lives. Then I must get myself back to Bronsonia to look after my own affairs."

"Without an engineer?" asked Hodge.

"I've covered quite a few light years in *Little Sister* without one. Of course, her engines are designed so as to require minimal maintenance. But the ones in this ship should hold out for the voyage from. . . . From? From wherever it is to Bronsonia. And if they don't . . . I'll just have to yell for help on the Carlotti—if that hasn't broken down, too."

"You could just drop us off somewhere in one of the boats," said Susie but looked relieved when Grimes refused to consider this expedient.

"We'll sleep on it," he said at last after several minutes more of fruitless discussion. He raised no objection when Susie accompanied him to the captain's quarters which, with the feeling that he was once more putting himself in his rightful place, he had reclaimed.

Eighteen

Grimes got to sleep at last. (Susie had been demanding.)

He slept, cradled against her warm, ample resilience—and he dreamed. The noise of *Bronson Star*'s engines—the subdued, arhythmic beat of the inertial drive, the thin, high whine of the ever-precessing Mannschenn rotors—wove itself into his dream. (Most dreams are based on memories and he had spent so much of his life aboard ships.)

He was back on board his first command, the little Survey Service courier *Adder*. He was entertaining a guest in his cabin, the humanoid but nonhuman envoy from Joognaan. Joognaan was not an important world, either commercially or strategically; had it been, the envoy would have traveled in far greater style than he was doing now, aboard a ship that had been referred to slightingly, more than once, as an interstellar mail van.

Balaarsulimaam—that was the envoy's name—had made his way to Earth in a variety of carriers. First there had been the star tramp that had dropped down to Joognaan for a small shipment of artifacts and a few casks of *talaagra*—a somewhat bitter wine that was prized, although not excessively so, by gourmets on one or two planets. His voyage—from world to world, in ship after ship—had been a sort of three-dimensional zigzag. On Earth he had seen the Minister for Galactic Trade but had been unable to interest that gentleman in his wares. The Federation government had not—by its own lights—been ungenerous, however. It had given Balaarsulimaam passage to Lindisfarne in the Survey Service transport *Jules Verne* and from Lindisfarne on in the courier *Adder*, Lieutenant John Grimes commanding.

He had been a lonely little being, this Balaarsulimaam. In spite of indoctrination Survey Service officers did not like having aliens aboard their ships. In *Adder* there was a further complication—with the exception of Grimes none of the courier's people liked cats. The Joognaanards are cat-like—or kangaroo-like. Just as the mythical Centaur was half man and half horse, so the inhabitants of Joognaan are half cat and half kangaroo. They have only four limbs, however.

Grimes was less xenophobic than most and was something of a cat lover. He made Balaarsulimaam welcome in his quarters. He enjoyed talking with him over drinks and felt no repugnance when his guest lapped rather than sipped from his glass.

It was one such social occasion that he was reliving now in his dream.

He was saying, "I'm rather surprised, Balaarsulimaam, that you couldn't interest any of the importers back on Earth in your wine. After all—the major restaurants pride themselves on being able to serve foods and drinks from every world known to man. . . ."

The Joognaanard's pink tongue dipped into the wide-rimmed drinking vessel that Grimes had provided for him, worked busily. He slurped, then sighed.

"Captain," he said, "the business with our wine is like the business of Scottish whisky. What I am drinking now—and I thank you for your hospitality—does not come from Scotland. It comes from Rob Roy, a planet of the Empire of Waverley. I have enjoyed the real Scottish whisky on Earth. I am enjoying this. I am not a Scottishman and I cannot tell the difference. Can you?"

"I am not a Scotsman," said Grimes. "I can't."

"And Rob Roy is much closer to your Lindisfarne than is Scotland. The freight, therefore, is much less. The whisky, therefore, is much less costly. So it is with our *talaagra*. There is a wine that they make on Austral, which is close to Earth. Even I can hardly detect the difference between it and our wine. And it must come only a short way and so is charged little freight."

"I see," said Grimes.

"But it was not only wine that I was trying to sell. It was a service—a service that people would have to come to Joognaan to avail themselves of. Our doctors—I have learned from captains of starships who have come in with injured crew members—are very clever. They have the—how do you say?—the technical—no, technique to regrow, in a short time, injured members that have had to be removed."

"So do ours," said Grimes. "But regrowing is a long process. Most people prefer to shop around for replacements in a body bank."

"There was a young lady . . ." went on Balaarsulimaam. "She was, I think, a purser in one of the ships. Unwisely she had not gone to her cabin when the ship was landing. She was concerned about the safety of certain heavy cases in one of the storeplaces. A case fell on her, crushing her face and the upper part of her body. We remade her."

"But that could have been done on Earth," said Grimes. "On almost any of our worlds."

"But we—our doctors—remodeled her. Aboard the ship was a representation of some female entertainer, a thin woman. The girl had been fat, like Susie. . . ."

(With that last sentence Grimes, even in his sleep, realized that fantasy was mingling with actual memory.)

"We remade her so that she looked almost the twin of the entertainer."

"Body sculpture is practiced on most worlds," said Grimes.

"But it is a long process and very expensive. With our doctors it is not long, and it is not expensive. All that I asked your government was that a proper spaceport be constructed on Joognaan and that we be allowed to advertise on Earth and other planets. We have credits, from the sale of our pottery and our wine—enough for the advertising but not enough for a spaceport. I think that, at first, your Minister showed sympathy—but his advisers, the representatives of the Terran doctors, did persuade him that our way was not safe. It was all, somebody said to me in confidence, a matter of invested interests."

Grimes refrained from correcting the alien. His meaning was clear enough. Members of any profession are jealous of their mystiques.

"But I will show to you, Captain, what can be done. . . ."

Balaarsulimaam waved his three-fingered hand. The door to the day cabin opened. A woman stood there. She was quite naked. Her slender body was familiar, as it should have been, even to the mole over the small, firm left breast. But, incongruous above Maggie Lazenby's slim, smooth shoulders was the plump face of Susie.

Grimes woke up with a start.

He slid out of the wide bunk without waking the girl and made his way to Control, ordered the computer to start doing its sums.

A call at Joognaan wouldn't be too great a detour.

Nineteen

"It's a good solution to your problems," said Grimes with as much conviction as he could muster. "Balaarsulimaam will help. He assured me, before he left *Adder,* that he would be at my service if ever I returned to his world."

"Shipboard friendships," said Susie, "are woven from even flimsier threads than shipboard love affairs."

Grimes didn't like the way that she was looking at him as she said this and didn't like the way that Hodge chuckled.

He went on, "In any case, you can pay. . . ."

"As long as it's not too much," said Hodge grudgingly. "But just what do you have in mind?"

"A complete change of physical characteristics for Susie and yourself—even, to be on the safe side, to fingerprints and retinal patterns. One beauty of the Joognaan technique is that it doesn't take anything like as long as the body sculpture on human planets—so I'll stay around until I'm sure that the two of you will be all right, hoping that no odd star tramp blows in to find *Bronson Star* sitting there. An All Ships broadcast must have gone out, asking everybody to keep their eyes skinned for us, as soon as we vanished from Bronsonia.

"When I'm happy—and when you're happy, of course—I lift off, leaving you on Joognaan. You stay there—you'll have no option—until the next tramp drops in. Then you buy passage in her to wherever she's going next. Your story will be that you're clones, that the Joognaanards, after they'd performed regenerative surgery on one or two spacepersons, retained cell cultures for their own experimental purposes. Balaarsulimaam will fix you up with the necessary papers."

"Nobody likes clones," stated Hodge dogmatically.

"Not when they know that they're clones," said Grimes. "Come to that, clones with money are no more unpopular than anybody else."

"A complete making over. . . ." said Susie thoughtfully. "Tell me, John, is the process painful?"

"I've been told that it's not."

She kneaded the flesh of her right thigh, below the hem of her shorts, with pudgy fingers. "Of course, it could be worth a little discomfort. I am just a bit overweight. . . ."

"I like you the way that you are," said Grimes gallantly—then wondered why he should remember that slim woman in his dream.

"And Hodge," she went on, "is no Adonis. . . ."

"I like me the way that I am," growled the engineer. "But I'm willing to sacrifice my beauty in return for safety."

"So it's decided, agreed upon," said Grimes.

"I don't altogether like it," muttered Susie. "And you haven't told us about your end of it. What story will you have to account for the long time it took you between Dunlevin and Bronsonia? How will you account for your being alone in *Bronson Star*? Everybody in Dunlevin will know by now that you weren't alone when you lifted off. Apart from anything else *I* handled the conversations with the Air Force and with the orbital fort."

"My story will be," said Grimes, "that the pair of you decided to take your chances in one of the ship's boats—and one of the boats will, of course, be missing from its bay by the time that I make planetfall at Bronsonia. After your escape the Mannschenn Drive broke down. It took me—all by myself, with no engineer to do the work—a long time to fix it. . . ."

"You couldn't fix a Mannschenn Drive," said Hodge.

"I have done so," Grimes told him. "Once. In *Little Sister.* I admit that she has only a glorified mini-Mannschenn, but even so. . . . Anyhow, I'd like you to fill me in on what sort of breakdown could be fixed by one man, not overly skilled."

"All right," said Hodge. "Your Mannschenn Drive breaks down. You bust a gut repairing it. Why, as a typical, bone-idle, spaceman branch officer don't you yell for help on the Carlotti?"

"Because," said Grimes, "I'm a money-hungry bastard. I don't want to have to split—or even lose entirely—the salvage money."

"And what about the auto-log?" asked Hodge. "That will carry a complete record of all use of main and auxiliary engines from Bronsonia on. It will show one set-down and lift-off too many."

"It won't," said Grimes, "after you've wiped it for me. A short circuit or whatever. I leave the sordid, technical details to you."

"You're a cunning bugger, Grimes," said Hodge with reluctant admiration.

"I try to be," said Grimes smugly.

Twenty

At that time there was no spaceport on Joognaan; nor was there Aerospace Control. Some ships—those that maintained the pretense of a service, albeit an extremely irregular one—announced their arrival with a display of pyrotechnics, even if such fireworks were only sounding rockets fired from superstratospheric levels to the surface to give some indication of wind directions and velocities. But there would be warning enough for the natives as soon as *Bronson Star* was well within the atmosphere; the clangor of her inertial drive would give ample notice of her coming.

Grimes was obliged to rely heavily on his memories of his one previous visit to the planet; there was very little data concerning Joognaan in *Bronson Star*'s memory banks. But he was sure that he would be able to manage after making a rough visual survey from orbit. All that he had to identify was the one city of any size situated on a coastal plain, on the southern shore of a wide estuary and with a high mountain range to the eastward. The usual landing place for visiting starships was to the south of the city in a wide clearing, an obviously artificial field set in a forest. From this a broad road ran to the big town.

The old ship dropped through the morning air, through the sparse scattering of high-altitude clouds that had not been thick enough to obscure her objective. Susie sat with Grimes in the control room. There was little that she could do to help as it was not necessary to man the NST radio. She spent most of the time staring out through the wide viewports, exclaiming now and again as something caught her attention.

"Those must be ships down there. . . . The sort of ships that sail on the sea, I mean. . . . And there's a railway. . . ."

"Early industrial culture," said Grimes. "They're still a long way behind us in engineering. . . ." But not in the medical sciences."

The clearing in the dark forest was showing up well in the stern vision screen. Grimes stepped up the magnification. There were no other spaceships in, which was all to the good. He reduced the scale again so that he could see something of the white road between city and clearing. There were a few moving black dots on it. So somebody was coming out to meet the ship. There would certainly be at least one linguist in the party, possibly Balaarsulimaam himself.

He concentrated on his pilotage, keeping the black circle that had been painted at the center of the landing field coincident with the bull's eye of the stern vision screen. He was having to make frequent applications of lateral thrust and the ship lurched as she fell through clear air turbulence. But at least, he thought, this time he wasn't bringing *Bronson Star* in with the evil, black eyes of at least three pistol muzzles looking at him.

He watched the presentation of radar altimeter readings, gradually slowed the rate of descent. At the finish the big ship was almost hovering, drifting down like a feather. Her vanes kissed the apron with the slightest of tremors rather than a jar.

She was down.

"We're here," said Grimes unnecessarily. He rang off the engines. He released himself from the command chair, went to the auxiliary control board and opened both inner and outer doors of the after airlock, extruded the ramp. He set the fans to work to flush out the ship with the fresh, forest air of Joognaan.

"Tell Hodge to join me at the airlock," he told Susie. "And you come along too."

He looked out from a viewport at the white road that ran between the somber trees like a parting in dark hair. The steam-driven cars of the Joognaanards did not have far to come. There would have been time for him, however, to change into a decent uniform if he had had a decent uniform to change into—but most of his possessions were still aboard *Little Sister,* back on Bronsonia. The hapless Paul had left finery in the captain's cabin wardrobe but Grimes would sooner have gone naked than worn it.

He stood at the foot of the ramp with Hodge and Susie a little behind him. He looked along the wide avenue as the three vehicles, puffing loudly and pouring smoke and steam from their tall funnels, approached. Shafts of morning sun smote through gaps in the trees and were reflected from bright, polished brasswork, shone on glossy scarlet and emerald paintwork. One of them blew its whistle in greeting, a loud, cheerful tootle.

The high-wheeled, canopied, gaily painted cars trundled onto the apron. They stopped. Their passengers clambered out, six of them altogether. They hopped rather than walked toward the visitors. Were it not for their rather flat faces they would have looked like black-and-white furred, bushy-tailed kangaroos.

They came to a halt before the three humans, stood staring at them. The humans looked at the natives. Which of them was Balaarsulimaam? Grimes wondered. All the Joognaanards looked the same to him. Was Balaarsulimaam one of the party? Unless things had changed he must be; during those drinking and talking sessions aboard *Adder* Balaarsulimaam had divulged that he always greeted visiting space captains, had expressed doubts that his deputy, nowhere near as accomplished a linguist, would be able to cope during his absence.

One of the natives spoke. "Greetings, Captain Grimes. Have you come to have your ears diminished after all? The offer of our services still holds good."

Yes, remembered Grimes, Balaarsulimaam had made that offer. He remembered, too, that there was a patch of black fur, an almost perfect six-pointed star, on the envoy's forehead. None of those with him were similarly marked; there were black patches aplenty but all of them irregular.

"Greetings, Balaarsulimaam," he said.

"Or have you come for trade, Captain Grimes? I see that it is a merchant vessel that you now command. I fear that we have little wine in our warehouses; the ship *Star Romany* was here only six rotations since. We have artifacts, should you desire them."

"You have already reminded me that you once offered your services."

"To give them will be our pleasure. When we have finished your ears will be as the tender petals of the *wurlilaya*."

"Thank you," said Grimes. "But it is not my ears that I wish fixed. It is this young lady, and her companion."

"But they are not injured."

"Do you recall telling me about that purser who was badly injured? How, at her request, you remade her in the image of a female entertainer? That is what I want done—to the lady. And the man I also want changed."

Balaarsulimaam made the transition from old friend and shipmate to businessbeing. "How will you pay, Captain Grimes, for operations of such magnitude? What goods have you to barter? Were it merely a matter of your ears there would be no charge—but for this other I fear that there must be."

"We have no goods for barter," said Grimes, "but I remember that you told me that your people will now accept money in lieu. We can pay in Federation credits."

"That is good. We endeavor to save an amount sufficient for the purchase of a Carlotti transmitting and receiving station. May we come aboard to discuss terms?" Then, in what was obviously an attempt at humor, "I hope that you have remembered my taste in potable spirits."

"I remember," Grimes told him, "but I'm afraid that we have no whisky, Scotch or otherwise. But what we do have in the way of spirits is quite drinkable."

He led the way up the ramp.

Twenty-one

Balaarsulimaam was the only one of the party with any real command of standard English; the others just squatted on their haunches around the wardroom, lapping the brandy that was a fast-diminishing monument to Mortdale's mess sergeant, noisily nibbling sweet biscuits, conversing now and again among themselves in voices that reminded Grimes of a convocation of Siamese cats.

Balaarsulimaam himself did not talk much at first; he was interested in the brief and edited account of Grimes's adventures since they had last seen each other. He was told of the Bacon Bay fiasco; the version given him was something of a whitewash job on Susie and Hodge. According to it they had acted under duress as much as Grimes himself had done and were anxious to escape only from the vengeance of the royalist underground rather than from the processes of Bronsonian law.

Balaarsulimaam listened with apparent sympathy, although it was impossible for a Terran to discern any expression on that black-and-white furred face. Then he said that it would be possible for the biotechnicians to operate on Hodge and Susie and that their board and lodging until the next ship dropped in—probably in about thirty days—would present no problems. He promised to do his best to maintain the clone fiction should the visiting tramp master ask too many questions—although it had to be explained to him what a clone was.

It was then that Grimes began to have serious doubts about Joognaan biological expertise—after all, the level of technology on the planet was not high; at this moment of time the proud apex of mechanical evolution was still the steam engine. And yet he had believed, when he had been told it, the story of the injured purser of the star tramp who had not only been healed but remodeled to her own specifications.

Balaarsulimaam named the price.

It was high—but nowhere nearly as high as a body-sculpture job on Earth would have been.

Grimes looked at Susie; she knew to the last Federation Credit how much folding money had been brought aboard at Porlock by General Mortdale. Susie looked back at Grimes. She nodded.

"All right," said Grimes.

"You will be pleased by what we shall do," said Balaarsulimaam.

"I hope so. I bloody well hope so, for that money," growled Hodge.

Susie glared at him.

"Then, tomorrow in the morning, I will call for you. You, Miss Susie, and you, Mr. Hodge, will bring with you representations of what you wish that your new appearances will be. Flat pictures will do, although if you have—what do you call them?"

"Solidographs," supplied Grimes.

"Yes. They will be better."

"Where would I get a solidograph from?" demanded Hodge.

"I'll find something for you," said Susie.

After the Joognaanards had left, Grimes and Susie went for a stroll in the forest. This was definitely an Earth-type—a very Earth-type apart from the dominant species—planet, a fine example of parallel evolution. To Grimes—who was no botanist—the trees were just trees, the bushes just bushes, the flowers just flowers. There were flying insects—great, gaudy butterflies, other things like tiny, arthropodal bats. An animal that scurried rapidly up a tree at their approach could have been a Terran squirrel, had it not been for its long, rabbit-like ears.

They came to a pool in a clearing; the water looked very inviting. Grimes remembered that Balaarsulimaam had told him that Joognaan possessed no dangerous carnivores, no predators that would attack animals larger than themselves—and the indigenous humanoids were the biggest life form. Did that sweeping statement apply to aquatic fauna?

While he was pondering Susie stripped.

She entered the pool with a loud splash, called, "Come on in! The water's fine!"

She struck out for the opposite bank, her pale body gleaming enticingly under the clear water. Grimes threw off his shirt, stepped out of his shorts and underwear, kicked off his sandals and followed her.

Yes, he thought, the water was fine. And this natural exercise, after the artificial calisthenics aboard the ship, was good. He met Susie in mid-pool. They clung to each other, kissed as they went under. They broke apart, surfaced. She made for a bank where sunlight struck down through the surrounding trees, brightly illumining an area of smooth, brightly green grass. She clambered out, fell to her knees and then rolled over on to her back, legs wide spread.

Grimes joined her, dropped beside her, kissed her again. She was ready, he knew, as he was ready. He mounted her, his chest pillowed on her ample breasts. Her legs came up and over to imprison the lower portion of his body. The sun was warm on his back, her skin was hot below his.

She said sleepily, "This was the best. . . ."

And almost the last time, thought Grimes. Even if he stayed on Joognaan for a few days after the bodychange Susie would no longer be Susie. Even her personality would be changing—slowly or not so slowly. Minds may—may?—be supreme but they are, inevitably, conditioned by the bodies that they inhabit.

She said, "I know what you're thinking, John."

"What?" he asked almost guiltily.

"That this is almost the last time for us. But it needn't be. Why shouldn't you change your physical identity too? You can lift *Bronson Star* from where she is now, land her again somewhere where she won't be seen by any incoming spaceships. She'll be a treasure house of metals and machinery for these people. And *you*. . . . You just sit tight with Hodge and myself, just another phoney clone, waiting for the next star tramp to drop in."

Grimes said, "I have to stay me. I have to earn a living the only way that I know how. If I change my identity the Master Astronaut's certificate, issued to John Grimes, is no longer valid. . . ."

She told him, "There'll be plenty of money left—even after we've paid for the body change and our board and lodging here and our passages to wherever. . . ."

Grimes said, "But I have my responsibilities, Susie."

"To the cheese-paring owners of that rustbucket you were baby-sitting? Forget about them. They'll do well enough out of the insurance."

They probably would, thought Grimes. After a suitable lapse of time somebody in far-away London would toll the *Lutine* bell and Lloyd's, admitting that *Bronson Star* was Missing, Presumed Lost, would pay out. And *Little Sister* would be sold to somebody not worthy of her, somebody who, in all probability, would regard her as marketable precious metal rather than a ship.

He said, "I'm sorry. Really sorry. But I have to adhere to my original plan."

She smiled in a rather odd manner.

She whispered, "We'll see about that."

He expected that she would sleep with him again that night and exert all her charm upon him to try to make him change his mind.

But she did not.

Twenty-two

Baarsulimaam called for them quite early the next morning. Grimes was awakened by the alarm that Hodge had set up to give warning of anybody or anything approaching the ship. He hurried up to the control room, looked out and down and saw the steam car standing there and a native getting out from the driver's seat. He opened inner and outer doors by remote control then took the elevator down to the stern. He reached the head of the ramp just as Baarsulimaam was coming up it.

"A good morning to you, Captain Grimes. Forgive my early coming but there was something that I should have told you yesterday. Your friends must not break their fast before the operation."

"Susie won't like that," said Grimes. "But come aboard, Baarsulimaam. Perhaps you will join me in coffee and toast after I have awakened her and Hodge."

"It will be my pleasure."

Baarsulimaam waited in Grimes's day cabin while he called Susie and Hodge. The girl was not at all pleased with the instructions that Grimes passed on to her, said. "I suppose that you'll want to stuff yourself as usual. Well, you can cook your own bloody breakfast."

"I'll do just that," Grimes told her.

Hodge, when he was awakened and told the news, growled, "I suppose I'm allowed to go to the crapper. . . ."

"That, I should imagine," said Grimes, "will be not only allowable but essential."

He went back to his own quarters, made a hasty toilet, dressed and then took the native down to the wardroom. He made coffee and a big tray of toast, found jams and savory spreads—more legacies from the ill-fated royalist expeditionary force. He and Baarsulimaam quite enjoyed the makeshift meal, even when, at the finish of it, they were being watched sulkily by Susie.

The four of them went down to the waiting steam car. Grimes felt a little guilty about leaving the ship unattended but, with the outer airlock door closed and set to open only if the correct code were pushed on the Watchman, as the special button was called, she was safe enough. Susie and Hodge clambered into the back seats of the vehicle, tried to adjust themselves comfortably on a bench that had not been designed for human bodies. Grimes got in beside Balaarsulimaam in the front. It was not the first time that he had ridden in one of these steam cars but, as on that long ago past occasion, he was impressed by the simplicity of the controls. Steam gauge, water gauge, oil fuel gauge. . . . Three wheel valves, one of which radiated heat in spite of the insulation around it. . . . A steering wheel. . . . A lanyard for the whistle. . . . A reversing lever. . . .

The native fed steam into the reciprocating engine, which started at once. He threw the gear lever, which had been in neutral, into reverse, backed away from the ship, turning. Once headed in the right direction he started off along the avenue, soon reaching a good speed.

It was a pleasant enough drive. The sun was just up and bright shafts of light, made visible by the lingering nocturnal mistiness, were striking through the tall, fir-like trees. Once or twice small animals scurried across the road ahead of the car, too fast for the humans to get a good look at them—not that Susie or Hodge were in a mood to be interested in the local zoology. They were both unfed and apprehensive, sitting in glum silence.

Beyond the forest were the fields and beyond the fields was the city. The low shrubs, with their dark-blue foliage, each laden with ripening yellow fruit, stood ranged in military precision, row after row of them. In comparison—not that comparison was necessary—the city was a jumble, a scattering on the outskirts, a huddle toward the center, of what Grimes had thought of when he first saw them as red-brick igloos. He still thought of them that way. Very few of them were higher than one story; the Joognaanards used ramps rather than staircases and a very large structure is needed to accommodate such a means of ascent from level to level.

Trees and bushes grew in profusion between the domes and even on the domes themselves although the roads were kept well cleared of encroaching vegetation. There was little traffic abroad—the Joognaanards are not early risers—but such few pedestrians as were about, such few drivers and passengers of steam cars who were already going about their various businesses, looked curiously at the three Terrans in Balaarsulimaam's vehicle—but not ill-manneredly so.

They came at last to a large dome almost in the center of the city, one of those standing around a wide, circular plaza. Glistening white letters, looking like the trail left by a drunken snail, shone above its arched doorway.

"The Institution of Medical Science," said Balaarsulimaam proudly. "We go inside. They expect us."

"I don't like this," whispered Hodge.

"It's all right," Susie told him. "If they don't fix us the way we want they don't get paid."

Grimes helped Susie down out of the car. She was carrying a small bag, he noticed. Toilet gear? A nightdress? He did not think, remembering what he had been told of the Joognaan body-changing technique, that she would be needing either.

Balaarsulimaam hopped rather than walked through the archway. Susie and Grimes followed. Hodge brought up the rear. It was dark inside the building but would have been darker without the glowing mantles of the gas lamps. There was an odd, musty smell but the odor was neither dead nor unhealthy. There was the sound of water running somewhere in the inner recesses of the dome.

The native led them unhesitatingly through the maze of corridors, bringing them at last to a room that was surprisingly brightly lit, a large compartment in which was not the profusion of equipment that Grimes, in spite of what he had been told about the Joognaan process, had been expecting. There were two long, deep bathtubs that looked like something out of a Terran museum of bygone household furniture and fittings. There was a low table by each tub. Three white-furred Joognaanards were awaiting the . . . patients? customers? The larger of the trio said something in a mewling voice to Balaarsulimaam, who translated.

"Miss Susie, Mr. Hodge. . . . You are to remove your clothing and get into the baths."

"What's in them?" demanded Hodge.

"It will not harm you, only change you. It is a . . . dissolvent fluid. A nutriment. . . ."

Grimes looked into the tub nearest to himself. Its contents looked innocuous enough, could have been no more than cold consomme, exuded that musty odor which, somehow, signified life rather than decay.

He turned away. Hodge, he saw, had already stripped. He was an excessively hairy man and without his clothing looked more like an ape than ever. Susie was obviously reluctant to disrobe.

"Get a move on!" growled Hodge. "Let's get this over with. What're you so suddenly coy about? Nobody else is wearing a stitch but Grimes—an' he's seen you often enough."

"But they've got fur!" she protested. Then—nastily—"And so have you!"

Nonetheless she stripped, handing her clothing to Grimes.

The head doctor spoke again and again Balaarsulimaam translated.

"Each of you will place the . . . image that you wish to resemble on the table by your bath. You will look at the image, think hard about it. The thought intensifiers—there is one for each of you—will intensify your thoughts, will help you to control the cells of your body." He turned to Grimes. "In your little ship, the *Adder,* you had an officer who communicated with others like himself by thought. He used the brain of some animal as an intensifier. This is almost the same."

Almost, Grimes thought. But the dog's brain amplifiers of the psionic communication officers were not housed in living bodies but in glass tanks.

"The images, if you are pleased."

Susie took her bag back from Grimes, took from it two solidographs, transparent cubes encasing human figures. Somehow he did not want to look at the one that was to be her model, felt that it would somehow be an invasion of privacy. (She was holding it, too, so that he could not get a good look at it.)

She said, "This is what Hodge will turn into. From frog into prince." She turned the solidograph so that Grimes could see it properly. "It was lucky that I had this with me."

Grimes recognized the handsome young man who was depicted in the cube. He was the hero of a popular TriVi series back on Bronsonia which he had watched on occasion.

Balaarsulimaam took the solidographs from Susie, looked at them curiously and then set them down carefully, one to each of the tables. The head doctor handed to him two flexible tubes. These he passed on to the man and the woman.

He said, "These you must hold in your mouths. All of your bodies, even your heads, must be under. These are . . . are. . . ?"

"Snorkels," supplied Hodge impatiently. "All right, let's get it over with. And I bloody well hope that it's warmer in than out!"

He took one end of his tube in his mouth, clambered into his bath. He arranged the pipe so that it was dangling over the side. Carefully he lowered his hairy body into the fluid, lay there, completely submerged.

"Must I?" muttered Susie. She shrugged, sending a ripple down the well-filled skin of her entire body. She put the end of the snorkel between her full lips, stepped into the tub. *Like Aphrodite rising from the foam,* thought Grimes. *In reverse. And if she'd been painted by Rubens. . . .*

She went down like a full moon setting into a wine-dark sea. Her body displaced more liquid than that of Hodge. There was an overflow over the rim of the tub; it fell to the stone floor with an odd, somehow ominous slurping noise.

Grimes walked to the bath, looked down. Already there was a cloudiness, the beginnings of effervescence among the hairs of her head and those at the base of her round belly.

He felt sickened and more than a little afraid. What had he talked her into? He heard the doctor saying something in his mewing voice.

Balaarsulimaam took his arm, exerted gentle pressure to try to turn him away from the sight of what was happening to this woman with whom he had made love.

He said, "Better not to stay, Captain. You are too . . . involved. Your thoughts might interfere."

"But. . . ."

"Better that you return to your ship. Your friends are in good hands."

Grimes allowed himself to be led out of the operating chamber. At the door he paused, looked back for the last time. There were the two baths, looking ominously like stone coffins, each with the table beside it, each with the squatting, black-and-white furred telepath (telesculptor?) staring fixedly at his faintly gleaming solidograph cube.

"It will not be long," said Balaarsulimaam. "You are not to worry."

Grimes allowed himself to be convinced.

Twenty-three

It was very lonely aboard *Bronson Star*.

Balaarsulimaam had come aboard briefly after running Grimes back to the ship, had stayed only for one cup of coffee and then, pleading pressure of business, had returned to the city.

Grimes decided to pass the day with a general spring clean. He started in his own quarters. He decided to clear all the clothing left by Paul and Lania out of his wardrobe and to stow it in the Third Officer's cabin. Not for the first time, while he was so engaged, he made a search for possessions that he had left behind on the occasion of his eviction—his watch, a gold everlasting pen that was a souvenir of *The Far Traveler,* a pocket computer from the same ship, the solidograph of Maggie Lazenby—but without happy result. Paul and Lania must have done something with these things—and Paul and Lania would not be answering any questions any more.

The control room was next to receive his attentions. He checked all the instruments, dusted and polished. He thought of sabotaging the auto-log himself but decided that it would be better to leave this to Hodge; the engineer would be able to make it look like an accident.

Conscious of a good morning's work behind him he went down to the galley, programmed the autochef to cook him a chicken curry lunch. It was palatable enough but had a rather odd flavor. He wondered just what local bird—or reptile?—had made its contribution to the tissue-culture vats when these had been replenished on Porlock.

He smoked a quiet pipe and then went to the farm deck. He had to give Susie full marks for maintenance, he thought. (And what was happening to Susie now? Was that once firmly fleshed body no more than a skeleton submerged in that murky, soupy solution?) Everything was spotlessly clean. The hydroponic tanks were healthily flourishing indoor vegetable plots, the tissue culture and yeast vats, every polishable part and fitting gleaming, could have been scientific equipment in a well-endowed, well-run laboratory rather than an essential component of the ecology of a down-at-heels star tramp. The observation ports of the algae tanks were crystal clear, inside as well as outside. Obviously the aquatic worms that, Susie had told him, she had managed to obtain on Porlock were doing their job. He watched one of the sluglike things browsing on the surface of the glass. He wondered if the same creatures could be used to clean the inside of the Joognaanards' body-sculpture baths. There must, he thought, be some . . . *sludge* left over. . . .

He tried hard to switch his train of thought onto a more cheerful track.

He continued his downward progress, through the holds that had, briefly, been troop decks, that still held their tiers of wooden-framed bunks. Some of the fittings were broken—probably due to his violent maneuvers when coming in to land on Dunlevin. He wondered what value all this timber would have on Bronsonia. Would the cost of it be included in the salvage award? If any?

The engine compartments were next. Hodge, Grimes decided, was not as house-proud as Susie. The only things polished were things that had to be polished, the faces of gauges and the like. There was a thin film of oil over everything else. But there was no untidiness and everything seemed to be in perfect order.

Everything, Grimes hoped, would continue that way; the last leg of his voyage must be made without an engineer.

His inspection ended, he stood at the open airlock door, looking out at the somber forest, staring along the white road that led to the city. There were no vehicles on it.

He returned to his quarters and tried to pass the time watching the playmaster. He could not find a spool in the ship's not very extensive library that was capable of holding his attention.

He had an early dinner and rather too much to drink and then retired.

His sleep was nightmare haunted; absurdly fat skeletons chased him through his dreams.

The next morning Balaarsulimaam came out to the ship.

Before Grimes could ask the question he answered it. "All goes well, Captain. The rebuilding process has begun."

"And there are no problems?"

"There are no problems." Balaarsulimaam made the high-pitched whinny that passed for a laugh among his people. "Perhaps when you see your friends you will consent to have your ears diminished. That will be without charge."

"No thank you," said Grimes.

Grimes escorted the native up to his quarters, got out bottle, ice and glasses.

"How soon," he asked, "before Susie and Hodge are able to resume a normal life?" He was painfully aware from the burning of his prominent ears that he was blushing. "I would like a little time with her before I lift off. . . ."

"I did guess how it is with you and the young lady. *We,* unlike you Terrans, do have only one sexual mate during our lifetime and so do not suffer from the problems that seem always to afflict your people. From what I learned during my voyage to Earth I am of the opinon that you flit from female to female like a *carnidal* from *bilaan* to *bilaan. . . ."*

"I'm sorry that you don't approve," said Grimes stiffly.

"I neither approve nor not approve. But do not worry. You shall sip once more from the sugared cup."

Twenty-four

Grimes did not anticipate that Susie and Hodge would be returning to the ship at night. Had he known, he would have stayed up to welcome them—or he would have made sure, before retiring, that the radar alarm was switched on. As a matter of fact he did remember that he had failed to actuate this warning device but he was already in bed, and drowsy. On this planet, he told himself, there was no need to take precautions against nocturnal attack. Furthermore the airlock door was closed and only the three humans knew the code that would open it from the outside. The last that Balaarsulimaam had told him was that he would be allowed to see the girl and the engineer the following day. He fell asleep wondering what she would look like, which star of the Bronsonian entertainment screens she would have remodeled herself to resemble.

He fell asleep without having to work hard at it.

He did not dream—although at first he thought that it was a dream that he had awakened to.

The light in his bedroom came on.

He opened his eyes, blinked muzzily and then stared at the woman who stood just inside the doorway. She was quite naked, slim, fine featured, auburn haired. There was a beauty spot, a mole, over her small, firm left breast. This minor blemish seemed unusually distinct.

He was dreaming. He *knew* that he was dreaming. Maggie Lazenby could not possibly be here, on this world.

(But she might be, he thought. She just might be. Perhaps a Survey Service ship, with herself among the officers, had landed. Perhaps he had slept through the cacaphony of its descent.)

Maggie (Maggie?) walked slowly into the cabin. She seemed to have lost the grace with which she usually moved and the smile that curved her wide mouth was not quite right.

(This *is* a dream, Grimes thought, oddly relieved.)

The scent of her, the muskiness of a sexually aroused human female, was *wrong,* wrong yet familiar. And her skin was too pale.

(But I don't want to wake up just yet, he thought.)

She came to his bed, stooped to plant a kiss (it tasted wrong) on his mouth. Her erect nipples brushed his bare chest. She straightened, turned slowly around until she faced him again. (Maggie would have pirouetted.)

She asked, "What do you think of the new *me,* John?"

He gasped, "Susie!"

"On stage live, in person, singing and dancing." She stared down at his face. "Aren't you *pleased?"*

He said weakly, "It's a surprise. . . ."

"But aren't you *pleased?"*

He was not. He realized then that, however much he might philander, his essential loyalties lay to one woman only—and Susie most certainly was not she.

"Aren't you *pleased?"*

Suddenly anger supplanted all other emotions. He growled, "So that's where my solidograph of Maggie went. *You* stole it. . . ."

"I did not. Lania threw it out after she caught Paul leering at it."

"You must have known that I valued it. You should have given it to me."

"And had her looking at us from the top of your desk every time that we made love? With you making odious comparisons and me knowing that you were doing just that? If it's any consolation to you, I used her as my model only because there was nothing else around—unless you count that tawdry calendar in the Third Mate's cabin. In any case, whose bright idea was it that I should have a body change?"

"But you aren't Maggie. . . ."

"I know bloody well I'm not. And Hodge isn't Trevor Carradine, but he looks like him and that'll be good enough for me. This was to have been a sort of thank-you-for-everything, farewell session, John—but you've ruined it." She snatched the sheet from off his body. "Look at you! When I came in you were making a tent but *now*. . . . Like one of those slime-eating slugs in the algae tanks. . . ."

"But. . . ."

"You've said enough, John. I'll go where I'm appreciated. Hodge has been trying hard to get some place with me ever since they dragged us out of their tubs and rinsed us off."

"But. . . ."

"But we have the same father? So bloody what? Some planets get all hot and bothered about incest, some don't. And in any case we're starting afresh with brand new identities.

"So this is good-bye, John. Hodge is wiping the autolog for you now and all that I have to do is to pick up the money from the safe in my office. We'll leave you to your sweet dreams of Maggie—what a name!—and you can get off this world and back to your precious *Little Sister* as soon as you like.

"Good-bye."

As she turned to go Grimes jumped out of the bed, caught her by the slim shoulders, pulled her back to him. His erection grew again. No matter what or whom she looked like, no matter how much weight she had shed, she felt like Susie. She did not struggle as he forced her round to face him, as he pressed his mouth to hers. With the full frontal contact there was only the faintest hint of the girl that she had been—but it was enough.

As long as he kept his eyes closed.

He took her brutally on the disordered bed and she did not resist. She was there too and she made him fully aware of it.

When he was fully spent and she sated, she slithered from under him, tottered rather than walked to the door. She turned, supporting herself with one long, slim arm on the door frame.

She said, "All right. This *is* good-bye. I'm glad that it was with a bang and not with a whimper—and I'm sorry that you aren't staying here to take your chances with us. . . . You still could. . . ."

He said, "I'm sorry that you can't come back to Bronsonia with me. I could use a purser aboard my own ship, when I get her back. . . ."

She said, "You just used a purser. Oh, well. Good-bye, good luck and all that. And give my love to *Little Sister*."

He said, regretting the words as soon as he had uttered them, "And give mine to your half brother."

She called him a nasty, sarcastic bastard and then was gone.

Twenty-five

He did not expect to see her again but she came out to the ship, accompanied by Balaarsulimaam and three other Joognaanards, before he lifted off for the voyage back to Bronsonia. She was dressed in one of Lania's black uniforms; her own clothing would not have fit her now. She was carrying a large parcel wrapped in a square of gaudily patterned cloth.

The natives, too, were bearing gifts—baskets of fruit, bottles of *talaagra.*

Balaarsulimaam said, "It has been good to see you again, Captain Grimes. And worry not, your friends will be in good hands. And if ever you should wish your ears remodeled. . . ."

"Thank you," said Grimes. "I'll remember. And I hope that when I come here again I shall be able to enjoy a longer stay."

After handshaking, the natives tactfully hopped out of the day cabin, leaving him alone with Susie.

She grinned rather lopsidedly. She said, handing him the parcel, "Here's something to remember me by, John. No, don't open it now." She kissed him, rather clumsily; that package was between them. "Good-bye. Or *au revoir?* I'll see you out on the Rim Worlds, perhaps. Who knows?"

She turned and left him. He heard the whine of the elevator as it carried his visitors down to the airlock. He went up to Control, watched from a viewport Susie and the others walking to the waiting steam car and then standing alongside it. She waved. He waved back although it was doubtful that she would be able to see the salute.

He busied himself with last-minute preparations, sealing the ship and satisfying himself that all life-support systems were fully operational. No pilot lights, he noted, glowed on the otherwise featureless cube of the autolog. So Hodge (he hoped) had kept his promise, so there would be no record of the deviation. He took the command seat, strapped himself in. The inertial drive grumbled into life at his first touch on the controls. She drove up, slowly at first and then faster and faster. It was a lift-off without incident, with everything functioning smoothly.

So it went on and, after this smooth departure, *Bronson Star* was, before long, on trajectory for her home world. Grimes made sure that all alarms were functioning and then went down to his quarters. He uncorked one of the bottles of gift wine, poured himself a glass. After he had finished it he poured another, but let it stand untouched on the coffee table while he unwrapped Susie's present. There were two solidographs in the parcel. One was that of Maggie Lazenby. The other. . . .

No, it was not a solidograph.

It was a squat bottle of clear glass, filled with some transparent fluid. Suspended in it was a tiny, naked woman, full-bodied, with blonde hair and pale skin, a miniature Susie. And she was—somehow—alive. (Or were her movements due only to the way in which the container was being turned around in his hands?) A rather horrid thought came to him. Susie, while immersed in the body-sculpture bath, had lost surplus tissue. And what had happened to those unwanted cells?

But, he rationalized, this was, after all, a quite precious gift. Men have treasured locks of hair from the heads of their lovers. (And locks of hair from other parts of their bodies.) Men have gone into battle wearing their ladies' favors, articles of intimate feminine apparel still carrying the body scents of their original owners. This present, after all, was the same in principle but to a far greater degree.

He put the bottle down on the table. It vibrated in harmony with the vibrations of the inertial drive. It looked as though the tiny Susie were performing a belly dance.

And was this altogether due to the vibrations?

It must be, he thought, although the only way to be sure would be to break the bottle and to remove its living or preserved contents for examination. And he had no intention of doing that. He did not wish to have a piece of decomposing female flesh on his hands and the thought of feeding what was, after all, a piece of Susie into the ship's waste disposal and conversion system was somehow abhorrent.

He raised his glass in salute to the tiny Susie, drank. He raised it again to the solidograph of Maggie. He was sorry that neither of them was aboard to keep him company on this voyage. He had never been especially lonely in *Little Sister* but she was only a small vessel. In *Bronson Star,* a relatively big ship, there were far too many empty spaces.

The voyage wore on.

Grimes rehearsed, time and time again, the edited version of the story of *Bronson Star*'s voyagings that he would submit to the authorities, wrote the first, second and subsequent drafts of his report. He prepared the Number Two boat for ejection; he was sorry that he did not have the materials at hand to manufacture a time bomb, but the possibility of such a small craft being picked up and found empty was very slight. He admired Hodge's thoroughness regarding a simulated breakdown of the Mannschenn Drive. Essential wiring had been ripped out, had been replaced with patched lengths of cable, installed with scant regard for appearance, obviously the work of a ham-handed amateur mechanic.

Meanwhile he enjoyed his meals, was inclined to drink rather too much (he had found the mess sergeant's formula for the perversion of the autochef), exercised religiously to keep his weight down and set up war games in the chart tank to exercise his mind.

The solidograph and the pseudo-solidograph he did not stow away in a convenient drawer; the representations of the two women stood on his desk, facing each other. He often wondered what they would say to each other if ever they met in actuality.

Twenty-six

All would have been well had the Mannschenn Drive not broken down in actuality; that makeshift wiring installed by Hodge had been rather too makeshift. Grimes was not in his quarters when it happened; he was in the control room with the Battle of Wittenhaven set up in the chart tank, trying to make it come out differently from the way that it had in historical fact.

He suddenly realized that Commodore van der Bergen's squadron, as represented by red sparks in the screen, was in full retreat instead of closing in for the kill. Testily he manipulated the controls but the knurled knobs seemed to have a will of their own, were turning the wrong way under his fingers.

The Manschenn Drive, he thought. *"The governor. . . ."*

Obviously it had ceased to function and equally obviously the temporal precession field was building up to a dangerous level. There should have been an automatic cut-off of power to the drive but the fail-safe device had just . . . failed. (It usually did; there were so many paradoxes involved that even a simple on-off switch would do the wrong thing.)

Grimes hoped that the remote controls were still operable. He fought his way to the command chair; it seemed to him that he was having to climb up a deck tilted at a forty-five-degree angle, that he was almost having to swim through an atmosphere congealed to the consistency of treacle. (Illusion it may have been but he was sweating profusely.) The command chair, with the essential ship-handling controls set in its wide arms, seemed to recede to a remote distance, to dwindle, as he struggled toward it. And then, with a bone-bruising collision, he was falling over it.

He stabbed, almost blindly, with a stiffened index finger, hoping that he was hitting the right button. It was like spearing a fish at the bottom of a clear stream and trying to allow for refraction.

The thin, high Mannschenn whine deepened in pitch from the almost supersonic to the normally sonic, deepened further still to a low humming, ceased. With an almost audible snap, perspective and color resumed normality. Outside the viewports the stars were once again hard, multi-hued points of light in the interstellar blackness.

He wasted no time looking out at them. He hurried from the control room, took the elevator down to the engine compartments. (Now that he was alone in the ship the cage was always where he wanted it.) Blue smoke still lingered in the Mannschenn Drive room, in spite of the forced ventilation. There was a stink of burned insulation. The cause of the trouble was obvious enough. The protective coating of one of the wires installed by Hodge had chafed through and the wire itself had been melted by the arc between it and sharp-edged metal. The power supply to the governor had been cut. In theory this should have resulted in a loss of power to the complexity of ever-precessing gyroscopes but Hodge had done his best to convey the impression of a rewiring job having been done by somebody without much of a clue as to what he was doing.

Grimes found a length of wire in the spares locker. He removed the two ends of burned cable, substituted the replacement. He went to the local control switchboard and—wondering if he were doing the right thing—switched on. He heard the low hum as the rotors began to spin, heard the noise rise in pitch. The green indicator light at which he was staring took on the appearance of a luminous fire opal, seemed to expand to the likeness of some great, blazing planet toward which he was plunging.

Then, suddenly, it was no more than a little, innocuous emerald light.

He turned to look briefly (very briefly), to stare too long at those tumbling, ever-precessing, always-on-the-verge-of-vanishing rotors is to court disaster. All seemed to be well.

He returned to the control room to check the ship's position by means of Carlotti bearings and then to make the necessary adjustment of trajectory.

He told himself, *I could do with a drink.*

He went down to his day cabin.

He noticed the smell at once; it was the same mustiness that he had sniffed in the . . . operating theatre back on Joognaan. He looked at his desk top. The solidograph of Maggie still stood there but the bottle in which the likeness of Susie had been suspended was now no more than a scattering of jagged shards. Fluid had dripped from the deck on to the carpet, staining it badly. Among the broken glass was a formless pink blob.

He felt a stab of regret.

So this, he thought, was the last of Susie. It was a great pity that she had not given him a conventional solidograph; such a portrait would have survived the breakage of its container. He sighed audibly—and it seemed to him that the wide mouth of the miniature Maggie, standing proudly in her transparent cube, was curved in a derisive smile.

He looked closely at the mess on the desk, being careful not to touch it. He did not know what the fluid in the bottle had been or what effect it would have on the skin of his fingers. He prodded the fleshy blob cautiously with a pen from the rack, turned it over. Yes, there was the hair where hair should have been, and that little streak of scarlet must have been the mouth and those two, tiny pink spots the nipples. . . . Perhaps if he put it into another container it would regain its shape. . . . But in what fluid? Distilled water? Alcohol?

He could imagine it—her?—suspended in a medium that would become murkier and murkier, with parts of her dropping off perhaps. . . .

It was a horrid thought.

He went through to his bathroom to collect a generous handful of tissues, returned to gingerly pick up the amorphous blob of . . . flesh? pseudo-flesh? and then carried it to the toilet bowl. Oddly, he felt no sentimental regrets as he flushed it away. It was too ugly, was no more than an obscene mess. The broken glass he disposed of down the inorganic waste chute.

When he was finished he noticed dark moisture on the carpet under the closed door of his grog locker. He investigated. The remaining bottles of the wine from Joognaan had shattered. He felt a surge of relief. Until this moment the frightening suspicion had lurked in the back of his mind that when the temporal precession field intensified the homunculus had somehow become really alive, had burst out of its glass prison from the inside. But it had been the painfully high pitch of the sound emanating from the Drive that had done the damage; Joognaanard glassware, all too obviously, was not as tough as that normally supplied to spaceships.

Twenty-seven

After that near disaster with the Mannschenn Drive Grimes instituted a routine of daily inspections. There were so many things to go wrong in a ship that was long past her youth and with only himself, a not very good mechanic, to fix them. He spent much time on the farm deck; its flora did more than provide him with food. They purified and regenerated the atmosphere that he breathed, cycled and recycled the water that he drank and washed in.

He noticed that the population of aquatic worms in the algae vats was diminishing. This was no real cause for concern; their only function was to keep the inner surfaces of the observation ports clean. Still, he missed them. They were, like himself, motile organisms. They were company of a sort.

And then, one ship's day, he glimpsed through a now merely translucent inspection port something swimming. It looked too large to be one of the sluglike things and its color was wrong. Perhaps, thought Grimes, the aquatic worms had mutated; this was unlikely, however, they were exposed to a no greater level of radiation in the ship than in their natural environment. Or—this was more likely—the worms brought aboard on Porlock had been a larval form. What would the adults be like? There had been a suggestion of fins or other appendages about the creature that he had briefly seen.

He spent more and more time on the farm deck. Quite often now he was catching brief glimpses of these new swimmers. He wanted a better look at them. He knew that biochemists in really big ships, the ones, naval or mercantile, that carried a multiplicity of technicians on their books, had a technique for cleaning inspection ports from the inside and that this method was also used by catering officers in smaller vessels. The tank tops had little, removable hatches directly above the side inspection ports. There was a squeegee with a handle of just the right length that could be manipulated from the outside.

He finally found a squeegee. It didn't look as though it had been used for a long time. Then, from the engine-room stores, he brought up a small shifting spanner. The nuts holding down the hatch lid were very tight; finally, at the cost of barked knuckles, he removed them. He lifted the hinged cover. He realized then why biochemists and catering officers did not relish the port cleaning job, preferring to employ some lowly organism such as the aquatic worms to do it for them. The stench that gusted out from the opening was almost palpable.

Grimes retched, retreated with more haste than dignity. Before he carried on with the job he would have to find or improvise a breathing mask. He recalled having seen a facepiece with attached air bottle and piping in the engine-room stores.

He was about to go to fetch it when an alarm bell sounded so, instead of making his way aft, he hurried back up to Control.

It was not a real emergency.

The mass proximity indicator had picked up a target at a range of one thousand kilometers. A ship, thought Grimes, peering into the blackness of the three-dimensional screen at the tiny, bright spark. He watched it, set up extrapolated trajectories. The stranger would pass, he estimated, within fifty kilometers of *Bronson Star*. There was no danger of collision, not that two ships running under interstellar drive could ever collide unless their temporal precession rates were exactly synchronized.

Grimes switched on the Carlotti transceiver. Presumably *Bronson Star* was showing up in the other vessel's MPI screen. Almost immediately a voice came from the speaker.

"*Doberman* calling passing vessel, *Doberman* calling passing vessel. What ship, please? What ship? Come in, please. Come in."

He was tempted to talk to the Dog Star liner but refrained. He would adhere to his original intention, not to use the Carlotti for transmission until just prior to arrival at Bronsonia. His story would be that he had feared pursuit by units of the Dunlevin Navy and had been reluctant to betray his position. If he now exchanged greetings with *Doberman* it would be known that he was approaching Bronsonia from Joognaan, not from Dunlevin.

"*Doberman* calling passing vessel. . . ."

What if he replied, wondered Grimes, using a false name for his ship? It had been so long, too long, since he had talked with anybody. His vocal chords must be atrophying. . . . But the apparently harmless deceit could lead, just possibly, to too many complications.

"*Doberman* calling passing vessel. . . ." Then, in an obvious aside to some superior, "Probably some poverty-stricken tramp, sir. . . . Too poor or too lousy to afford MPI. . . ."

Then the reply in a much fainter voice, "Or somebody who doesn't want his whereabouts known."

"Not very likely, sir. There aren't any pirates around these days."

"Aren't there, Mr. Tibbs? What about Shaara rogue queens? I heard that the famous Commander Grimes had a set-to with one not long since."

"Grimes! As you know, sir, I've a commission in the Reserve. . . ."

"I know it all right, Tibbs! At times you seem to think that you're First Lieutenant of a Constellation Class cruiser rather than Second Mate of a star tramp!"

"Let me finish, sir. I did most of my last drill attached to Lindisfarne Base and people still talked about Grimes, even though it's some time since he resigned his commission. Some of the things he got away with. . . . He was little better than a pirate himself!"

"So, just as I've been telling you, there *are* pirates. . . . But our unknown friend's not attempting to close us. Can't be either a Shaara rogue queen or the notorious Grimes. . . ."

There is nothing more frustrating than listening to a conversation about oneself and being unable to speak up in self-defense. Bad-temperedly Grimes switched off the Carlotti. Then he became aware that the aroma from the farm deck was being distributed throughout the ship by the ventilation system. He thought wrily, *It's not only my name that stinks.*

He hurried down to the engine-room stores, found a breathing mask and returned to the farm deck. He used the squeegee to clean off the inspection port—a job rather more awkward than he had anticipated—and then replaced the little hatch. He peered intently through the now-transparent glass but saw nothing—neither the original aquatic worms nor their successors.

Perhaps, he thought, the adults could not adapt to life in a ship's algae vat as well as the larval form. Perhaps they had died. Perhaps their decomposition had contributed to that horrendous stink, much worse than could be expected from the normal processing of sewage and organic garbage.

He hoped that the air-conditioning system would not take too long about cleansing the foul taint from *Bronson Star*'s atmosphere.

Twenty-eight

For a while after his cleaning of the inspection port Grimes avoided the farm deck; in spite of the valiant efforts of the extractor fans the stink lingered. It was one of those smells the mere memory of which can trigger off a retching fit. It had penetrated even the breathing mask that Grimes had worn.

He relied upon the control room instrumentation to keep him well informed as to the well-being of tissue cultures, yeasts, algae and the plants in the hydroponic tanks. He seemed to have no immediate cause for worry but he knew that he would have to procure fresh supplies of meat and vegetables; the ready-use cold store that was an adjunct to the autochef was running low. And there were one or two recipes that he wished to program involving fresh tomatoes. Susie, putting the hydroponic tanks into full commission during the brief stay on Porlock, had planted a few vines; she, Grimes recalled, had expressed her great liking for that fruit. Some must be ready now for the plucking.

He had sealed the farm deck off from the rest of the ship. Entering the compartment he had the breathing mask ready to slip on in an instant but it was not required. The air still held a very faint hint of the original stink but it could be ignored.

Grimes went at once to the tank with the tomato vines. There were some fruit but they were small, green, inedible. This was strange. He was sure that he had seen, the last time that he had visited the farm deck, a fine crop that was already yellow, that must surely ripen to scarlet luciousness within a very few days.

Perhaps they had fallen and rotted—but there was no trace of skin or pips on the loosely packed fibers that formed an artificial soil. Yet he could see from the vines that fruit had been there on the stems.

Odd, he thought. *Very odd. . . .*

He made a round of the hydroponic tanks. He discovered no further anomalies. He went to look at the yeast vats. These were covered only with wire mesh. Over one of the vats the fine netting was torn. Had it always been so? Grimes could not remember. Was this old or recent damage? He did not know. The surface of the spongy mass inside the vat looked undisturbed—but the yeast used as a food source in spaceships is a remarkably fast growing organism.

There had been, he remembered, a certain carelessness regarding the airlock door while the ship had been on Joognaan. Something might well have gotten aboard there. A hungry animal would very soon find its way to a source of food. So it—whatever it was—liked tomatoes and, for lack of anything tastier, could feed on yeast. Apart from the fruit it had not touched any of the tank-grown vegetation which indicated that it was more carnivore than herbivore; yeast is a good meat substitute.

Grimes did not begrudge the animal an occasional meal; with only himself aboard the ship there was food aplenty. But animals running loose in human habitations are apt to foul and to destroy far more than they eat. He continued his investigations. He discovered that it—the filthy beast!—had defecated in the tray in which otherwise promising lettuces had been growing.

He had been looking forward to a green salad.

Poisoned bait? he asked himself.

No.

The thing had not been house trained and could hardly be blamed for its use of the lettuce bed as a latrine. In any case (a) there were probably no poisons on board and (b) even if there were they would probably be ineffective against a Joognaanard life form.

A trap?

Yes.

He went down to the engine-room workshop. He found a metal tool box with hinged lid, removed its contents, washed it in hot, soapy water to remove all taint of oil, made sure that the hinges worked freely. The lid had a snap catch so that the box could be opened only from the outside.

The trap would be a simple one; just a metal rod to prop up the lid, the bait—but what bait?—secured to the bottom of the upright. A sharp tug on this should bring the lid slamming down.

He thought—judging from the size of the droppings—that the box would be big enough. If it were not the stowaway would at least get a nasty headache.

Grimes was no electrician but thought that he would be able to fix a cord to the lid that, snapping tight when it fell, would switch on the alarm which, when not being so misused, was supposed to indicate that the pump maintaining the flow of macerated garbage and sewage into the algae vats had stopped.

After all that work he felt ready for his dinner. He treated himself to steak, rare, with French-fried potatoes (these latter actually no more than processed and molded starch) and a bottle of the mess sergeant's rough red. He would have had grilled tomatoes with the meal if it, whatever it was, had not gotten to the vines first.

He saved a piece of bloody steak to bait the trap, took it down to the farm deck to set everything up.

He was no sooner back in his own quarters than he heard the alarm bell ringing in the control room.

Twenty-nine

He hurried down to the farm deck. He jumped out of the elevator cage, ran through the open doorway of the food production compartment. He saw things—small, active animals—milling around the sprung trap. He caught only a glimpse of them, received a confused impression of pale skin and waving limbs as they scattered at his approach, scurrying to hide behind and under tanks and vats.

He approached the tool box cautiously. The lid had not fallen all the way down; whatever had displaced the upright was caught half in, half out. The hindquarters of the hapless little beast were no more than a bloody mess with most of the flesh ripped from the fragile bones. By the looks of what was left it had been a quadruped of some kind.

Grimes conquered his revulsion, opened the lid. What was inside was undamaged. He knew what it was even before he lifted it out carefully and turned it over. He looked down in horror at the contorted features of a dead, miniature Susie. At last he put the mutilated body, all of it, back into the box, shut and secured the lid. He carried the container out of the farm deck and then up to his quarters, making sure that all doors were closed behind him. He put the box on his desk then poured himself a stiff drink and sat down to think things over.

He remembered how he had flushed that original homunculus down his toilet, thinking that it was dead. Its flesh would have been macerated together with sewage and other organic garbage before being pumped into the algae vats. He remembered, then, how he had told Balaarsulimaam about clones. This information must have been passed on to the Joognaanard body sculptors who, making use of it, incorporating it with their own techniques, had produced, to Susie's instructions, what was, in effect, a mini-clone. (That name would do as well as any.) He did not think that Susie's motivations had been malicious. She could not have anticipated that the bottle would be broken, that its contents would be disposed of as they had been.

One thing was certain; he must not dispose of the remains of this Susie as he had disposed of the remains of the original one. There would have to be a proper spaceman's funeral, the ejection out through the airlock of the body.

But that would have to wait. Before any mass is ejected from an interstellar ship the drive must be stopped; failure to observe this precaution almost inevitably leads to disaster. Nobody has yet returned to tell what it is like to fall into a self-generated black hole. So the most sensible thing to do, thought Grimes, would be to wait until he had disposed of all the mini-Susies and then to consign the accumulation of cadavers to space in one operation.

He told himself disgustedly, *You're a cold-blooded bastard, Grimes!*

But even though he had liked the original Susie, even loved her in his fashion, he felt no affection for her . . . progeny? Yes, that word would have to do. He remembered the high-pitched, vicious chitterings that he had heard when he interrupted that macabre feast. He did not have to open the lid of the tool box to see again the tattered ruin of what had been a shapely rump and pair of legs. For all their human appearance these clones—mini-clones? pseudo-clones?—were only mindless but dangerous carnivores.

Too, he had to look after himself.

He would have his story to tell when finally he returned to Bronsonia—a story concocted as much for the protection of Susie and Hodge as for his own benefit. And would that tale hold water if *Bronson Star*, returned to her rightful owners, were found to be infested with tiny humanoids, each one the image of a woman wanted by the authorities for the crime of skyjacking?

There would be questions, very awkward questions, asked.

So. . . .

How to disinfect the ship in the time remaining to him before planetfall?

Poison would have been one answer—*if* he had been able to lay his hands on any. But even if he had there would have been the possibility—the probabality—that the things would die in inaccessible places.

Traps?

He had tried the idea once and hadn't liked the end results.

Starvation?

The things were meat eaters. They had disposed of the aquatic worms in the algae tanks. They had helped themselves from one of the yeast vats. They had at least half eaten one of their own number.

Suppose, he thought, he cleaned out the yeast vats; these, with only a wire-mesh cover to protect their contents, were far too accessible. The tissue-culture and algae vats were safe enough from depredation, however. The hydroponic tanks? There was food there if the homunculi could adapt to a vegetarian diet. Already they had eaten the tomatoes. (*And befouled the lettuces* . . . thought Grimes sourly.) So the "market garden" would have to go. Life-support systems would continue to function nonetheless. The algae were quite capable of purifying water and regenerating atmosphere—especially when there was only one man (one man and an unknown number of mini-women) to maintain. And there was an ample supply of assorted meats. Several kilograms of those, just to be on the safe side, could be transferred from the growing vats to the galley cold stores.

And then. . . .

Possibly cannibalism would bring about a reduction of numbers, although indications were that this did not occur unless the victim was already dead. But the process might take too long.

Grimes visualized a trail of scraps of meat—not large pieces, only enough to stimulate the appetite—leading from the farm deck, down the spiral staircase around the axial shaft to the boat bay. Inside the boat would be the real bait. When the little horrors were feeding, Grimes would seal the boat bay, shut down the Mannschenn Drive, eject the boat (which had to be gotten rid of in any case as corroboration of his fictional account of the voyage) and then resume passage.

There was very little chance that the boat would ever be picked up.

If it were, of course, it would be discovered that it came from *Bronson Star* and the salvagers would be puzzled by the tiny but apparently human corpses.

But then—if it ever happened—Grimes would be a long, long way from Bronsonia. He might even be dead of old age.

In any case it was nothing to worry about. But the immediate situation most certainly was.

Thirty

Before commencing operations on the farm deck, Grimes armed himself, belting on one of the projectile pistols left behind by the Dunlevin royalists. He hoped that he would not be obliged to use it; there would be far too great a risk of shattering vital equipment. A shotgun would have been a far better weapon in these circumstances but he possessed neither the tools nor the expertise to modify the pistols or their ammunition.

The first job was to empty the yeast vats, using the scoop that had been designed for that purpose. He shoveled the musty-smelling stuff into whatever containers he could muster—buckets, plastic boxes from which he had emptied small stores, a couple of big mixing bowls from the galley. These he carried out to the waiting elevator cage for transport down to the after airlock.

It was hard enough work for one not accustomed to it and it took longer than it should have done. He *knew* that he was being watched and he paused frequently to look around, hand on the butt of the holstered pistol, every time that he caught a flicker of movement out of the corner of his eye.

But at last the job was finished and he rode down and aft surrounded by tottering stacks of boxes, buckets and basins. He carried the containers into the airlock chamber, getting himself thoroughly smeared with yeast in the process. He realized, belatedly, that the work would have been far less heavy if he had thought to reduce acceleration.

He returned to the farm deck. *They* must have heard him coming. They boiled out of the yeast vats, where they had been scrabbling for the last scraps of sustenance, just as he came through the door. Most of them bolted for cover but two of them ran straight for him. They were tiny, naked, unarmed—but he was afraid of them. He pulled the pistol, fired. The reports were thunderous, reverberating from metal surfaces. The leading assailant was . . . splattered. The second one came on. Grimes fired again, and again. He saw an arm torn from the doll-like figure—but still it came on.

It jumped. Its sharp little teeth closed on his right wrist. He screamed, dropped the gun, and with his left hand caught the pseudo-clone about its waist, felt his fingers sink into the soft flesh. It chittered shrilly. He pulled, felt his own skin and flesh rip as he dragged the vicious little being away from him. He threw it down to the deck, stamped on it, feeling and hearing the splintering of bones.

He avoided looking at the mess as he stooped to recover his pistol.

He glared around but saw no indications of further attack.

Grimes retreated from the farm deck, making sure that the door was tightly shut after him and could be opened only from the outside. Nursing his bleeding wrist he made his way to the ship's dispensary where he treated what was, after all, only a minor flesh wound with antibiotic spray and newskin dressing.

Then, back in his quarters, he put on a spacesuit. He felt that he would need armor to protect him when he continued his work. He returned to the scene of the incident, thinking that the first job would be to dispose of the bodies. But there were no bodies. Not a trace remained of them—no bones, not even the faintest smear of blood on the deck. Cautiously, alert for further assaults, he went to the yeast vats. The interior of these seemed to have been, quite literally, licked clean.

So they had been hungry, he thought. The little swine would be hungrier yet before he was finished with them. . . .

He cleared the hydroponic tanks of all their vegetation and turned off the irrigation/nutrition system lest fresh growth develop from some overlooked rootlet. He took the plants down to the after airlock where he stowed them with the containers of yeast. Finally he opened one of the tissue-culture vats to take from it what meat he would require for the remainder of the voyage. He feared that the smell of the raw beef would be too much for the homunculi, that they would emerge from their hiding places in a mass attack. Very faintly through his helmet he could hear their high-pitched squealings. He worked by touch rather than by sight, endeavoring to keep the entire farm deck under observation, ready to drop the sharp-edged scoop and to draw his pistol at the first sign of trouble.

But he saw nothing and finally withdrew from the farm deck, with his dripping load, without being molested.

Thirty-one

Just how human were the mini-Susies? wondered Grimes as he—in spite of everything—enjoyed his dinner of rare roast beef. What was their psychological makeup—if they had one? As he chewed the almost raw meat he thought about cannibalism, remembered what he had read about that deplorable practice. It was said to be an addictive vice, that a taste for long pig, once acquired, drove its possessor to gruesome lengths to keep it satisfied. There had been cannibals living in countries on Old Earth in which there had been no shortage of meat from the lower animals but who had still devoured their own kind to gratify their obscene appetites. That family living in a remote part of Scotland, for example, who finally had been hunted down and executed by one of the Stuart kings. . . .

Inevitably the homunculi would reduce their numbers by cannibalism until there would be a solitary survivor. But how many of them were there? How long would the auto-extermination program take? Grimes did not want to delay his arrival back at Bronsonia for too many days, if at all. He wanted to get back to that world as soon as possible, while there was still a chance of saving *Little Sister* from the auctioneer's gavel.

So he would have to continue with his original plan of luring the things into the boat that would also be a trap, the boat that he would then eject to explain the absence of Hodge and Susie from the ship. But what if they—those who still survived—had developed such a taste for human—he supposed that it was human—flesh that they scorned tank-grown beef? But, he reasoned, once their numbers had diminished it would be less easy for them to catch and kill each other. They would be continually ravenous. A hungry man will enjoy food that normally he would sneer at.

In any case, Grimes didn't want to go near the farm deck again until he absolutely had to.

* * *

He passed the time pottering.

He stopped the Mannschenn Drive briefly so that he could eject the garbage, the yeast and the vegetation, from the airlock. He took his time about resetting trajectory. He carried out maintenance on the ship's boats, even the one that he intended to sacrifice; after all, something might happen to necessitate a hasty abandonment of ship. He set up a pistol range in one of the holds and experimented with the small arms ammunition, trying to make bullets that would disintegrate as soon as leaving the muzzle, the fragments spreading like shot. One hand gun was ruined when this breakup occurred too soon. He gave the idea away. There would be far too great a risk of a weapon hopelessly jammed just when he most needed it.

He set up and baited his trap.

He cut one piece of raw meat from the cold store into very small pieces, hardly more than crumbs, laid a trail from the door to the farm deck down to the bay in which No. 1 Boat sat in readiness; he had decided on using this lifecraft as it was the nearest. A larger piece of meat he put in the boat itself. Unfortunately *Bronson Star* was deficient in the telltale devices common in larger ships such as passenger liners. There was no closed-circuit TV to give control-room coverage of every compartment. Grimes would have to open the farm deck door and then take the elevator down to boat bay level. He hoped that he would be able to lurk there unobserved, hidden by a convenient curve in the lateral alleyway, until his victims were all in the bay if not in the boat itself. Then, using local controls, he would close the door. This accomplished he would have to hurry back to Control to shut down the Mannschenn Drive. After this the outer door of the boat bay could be opened and atmosphere, boat and mini-Susies ejected explosively.

He decided against wearing space armor; it hampered his movements too much. He wore a belt with holstered pistol, however. He sat and smoked for a while, waiting for the pieces of meat to thaw properly, to start exuding their effluvium. He looked at the solidograph of Maggie.

He thought ironically, *Soon you'll have no competition. . . .*

He looked at the tool box still standing on the desk, his first attempt at a trap. He had quite forgotten to do anything about it and its grisly contents. It would have to wait now.

Reluctantly he got up from his chair and went to the elevator, descended to the farm deck. He pushed the button on the bulkhead that would open the door and, not waiting to watch, ran straight back into the elevator cage. He dropped to the forward boat bay deck, took station so that he could keep watch on the access to No. 1 Boat. His pistol was drawn and ready.

He strained his ears to try to detect some sound other than the thin, high whine of the Mannschenn, the clatter of the innies. He was expecting to hear the shrill chitterings that he had heard before; surely *they* would be quarreling over the scraps of meat as they came down the spiral staircase. Perhaps they were all dead and he had gone to all this trouble for nothing. Perhaps. . . .

But there was somebody—no, something—coming. Something that was not thinly squealing but was making a low, moaning sound. There was the heavy padding—padding, not scuttering—of bare feet on the treads of the stairway.

It—no, *she*—came into view.

She was as he remembered her, although a little less plump. She was chewing as she moaned to herself and a trickle of blood ran from her mouth down her chin. There were half-healed scratches on her shoulders and breasts. She stooped to pick up another meat fragment, thrust it between her full lips.

"Susie!" cried Grimes.

She straightened, stared at him. There was no sign of recognition on her face although, he was sure, there was intelligence behind the brown eyes.

"Susie!"

She growled, deep in her throat, sprang for him, clawed hands outstretched. He brought his gun up but it was too late. She knocked it from his grasp. She threw her arms about him in a bearlike hug and her open mouth, with its already bloodstained teeth, went for his throat.

It was not the first time that Grimes had been in intimate contact with a naked woman but it was the first time that he had been on the defensive. His head jerked back from those snapping teeth even as her long, ragged nails tore through the thin fabric of his shirt and deeply scored his sides. He brought his fists up to try to pummel her sensitive breasts but she was holding him too closely. But he managed to get his right hand open, found a taut nipple, squeezed.

She screamed, with rage as well as pain.

He squeezed harder, twisted.

He had room now to fight, brought his left knee up between her thighs, felt the warm moistness that, in other circumstances, would have been sexually stimulating—that was, he realized with a mixture of shame and horror, sexually stimulating. Again he brought his knee up, harder.

She broke away.

He dived for the gun but she was on him again, the weight of her on his back, forcing his face down onto the hard deck. With a superhuman effort he rolled over, reversing their positions, fought his way free of her.

Again he tried for the pistol which had been kicked, during their struggles, almost to the open door of the boat bay. She recovered fast and hit him again, a thunderbolt of feminine flesh that should have been soft and desirable but that was horrifying. He was knocked into the boat bay, fell heavily, winding himself.

He heard the thud as she fetched up against the bulkhead outside. When he scrambled to his feet the door was closing, was almost shut. He got his fingers onto the edge of the sliding panel but hastily snatched them back before they were amputated.

She must, he thought, inadvertently have pressed the local control button. Or was it so inadvertent? How much of the original Susie's own knowledge was in the brain of this replica? (Did it have a brain? He was almost sure that it did.)

He would wait, he decided, until he felt stronger, hoping that the pseudo-Susie would wander elsewhere, would not know what the pistol was for and would leave it where it had last fallen. It was not edible; she almost certainly would not touch it. And, he told himself, it would be easier to deal with this single, large opponent than with a horde of tiny horrors. (And was there a limit to its growth? Would it double in size if it ate him, Grimes? Or was its augmentation the result of a steady diet of its fellow clones?)

What was it doing now? Did it know enough? Did it remember enough to push the right button to open the door again? (But surely no cells from Susie's brain had been used in the manufacture of the original devil doll.) Were its fingers, even now, poking, intelligently or unintelligently, at the array of buttons on the bulkhead?

They were.

Grimes heard the evacuation pump start, drawing the atmosphere from the boat bay into the body of the ship. The controls for this pump were not duplicated inside the bay; the only ones that were were those for opening and closing the door. And the door, Grimes remembered, could not be opened from inside when a pressure differential existed.

He tried, of course, but it was useless.

Unless he sealed himself in the boat, and that hastily, he would not be able to breathe.

He was caught in the very trap that he had devised for the mini-Susies.

Thirty-two

Grimes activated the boat's life-support systems.

Bitterly regretting not having put on his spacesuit when he made the attempt to trap and dispose of the mini-Susies—or, as it had turned out, the life-size pseudo-Susie—he searched the boat's stores for anything, anything at all, that could be used as breathing apparatus. But he was not desperate enough to venture out into the vacuum of the boat bay with a plastic bag over his head—especially since there was little of any use that he could do once he was there.

Meanwhile, he reflected, he could survive in his prison almost indefinitely, breathing recycled air, drinking recycled water, eating processed algae that had proliferated on a diet of his own body wastes. And while he was existing drably *Bronson Star* would continue her voyage—to Bronsonia, past Bronsonia, dropping through the warped dimensions until such time as her Mannschenn Drive ceased to function. If this happened during Grimes's lifetime he would be able to eject from the ship and make his way to the nearest inhabited planet—*if* he was able to fix his position, *if* the boat's mini-Mannschenn didn't break down, if, if, *if*. . . .

But he could always yell for help on the lifeboat's Carlotti transceiver and, possibly, there would be somebody within range.

And, he thought, I can yell for help *now.*

He. switched on the Carlotti, watched the Mobius strip antenna begin to rotate. It would have to be a broadcast message, of course; a beamed transmission would have given him far greater range but unless he knew the exact azimuth of the target he would only be wasting time.

He said into the microphone, "Mayday, Mayday, Mayday. *Bronson Star* requires immediate assistance. Mutiny on board." And that, he thought, would tie in with the story that he intended to tell to the authorities on Bronsonia. "Master trapped in boat bay. Mayday, Mayday, Mayday."

He waited for a reply. Surely, he thought, that Dog Star liner, *Doberman,* would still be within range.

He repeated the call.

Again he waited.

He was about to call for the third time when a voice came from the speaker of the transceiver—faint, distorted but intelligible.

"FSS *Explorer* to *Bronson Star.* Your signal received. What are your coordinates, please?"

Explorer. . . . A sister ship to one of Grimes's earlier commands, *Seeker.* Survey Service. . . . A great pity that it wasn't *Doberman,* thought Grimes. Was he still on the Service's wanted list? But the old adage held true: Beggars can't be choosers.

He said, "I am holed up in my Number One boat. I am on trajectory from . . ." he caught himself just in time . . . "Dunlevin to Bronsonia. Not having access to the ship's control room I am unable to fix my position."

That last was true enough. With the boat still inboard the larger vessel it was impossible to obtain accurate bearings of any Carlotti beacons in the vicinity.

"*Explorer* to *Bronson Star.* Broadcast a steady note for precisely one minute, then return to receive mode. Over."

Grimes made the necessary adjustments to the transceiver, broadcast his beacon call for sixty seconds, switched back to Receive.

"*Explorer* to *Bronson Star.* We are homing on you. We have you now in our MPI tank. We estimate rendezvous thirty-seven hours and nineteen minutes from now. Can you hold out?"

"Yes," replied Grimes.

"How many mutineers are there?"

"One."

"Armed?"

"Yes," said Grimes after a moment's hesitation. It could be true. The pseudo-Susie had access to all the ship's firearms, including the pistol that Grimes had dropped.

"And you are Captain Grimes—lately Commander Grimes of this Service?"

"Yes."

There was a brief laugh. "Don't worry. We have no orders to arrest you. Confidentially, Commander Delamere didn't exactly cover himself with glory when *he* tried it on Botany Bay—and your late employer, the Baroness d'Estang, was able to pull quite a few strings on your behalf. We know that you were in charge of *Bronson Star* when she was skyjacked. What happened next?"

Grimes grunted irritably. He would just imagine those bastards in *Explorer's* control room flapping their big, ugly ears as he told his story, gloating over his misfortunes. *So,* they would be saying, *Grimes's famous luck is really running out now, isn't it?*

He said, telling the truth at first, "I was forced, at gunpoint, to navigate *Bronson*

Star to Porlock. There we picked up a bunch of mercenaries and counterrevolutionaries. Then I took the ship from Porlock to Dunlevin. As you may already have heard the invasion didn't come as a surprise to the present government of Dunlevin. Two of the royalists—a ship's engineer and a catering officer—had stayed on board with me and they helped me to escape. But the three of us failed to see eye to eye about where to go next. I, of course, wanted to return the ship to her rightful owners. The other two had some crazy idea of running out to the Rim Worlds and setting up shop as a one-ship star tramp company. They pulled guns on me and ordered me to deviate from trajectory. . . ." *And that's the answer,* he thought, *to the question of why I'm approaching Bronsonia from a slightly wrong direction.* "Cutting a long story short, there was a fight. Hodge was killed. After the funeral I adjusted trajectory and resumed passage. I thought that Susie—the catering officer—wouldn't cause any more trouble. But she did." He paused for thought. "She's quite mad, I think. Running around the ship stark naked. There was a bit of a struggle. . . ."

He paused again, heard faintly, "Who said that Grimes's luck was running out? I wouldn't complain if I had to wrestle with naked ladies!"

"Somehow," he went on, "I was pushed into the boat bay. She shut me in and started the exhaust pump. All that I could do was scramble into the boat before I asphyxiated."

A fresh voice came through the transceiver speaker, an authorative one. "Commander Grimes, this is Commander Perkins here, captain of *Explorer.* I have one or two questions that I'd like to ask. . . ."

Grimes had known Perkins slightly—an unimaginative man, a stickler for regulations. He hoped that the questions would not be awkward ones.

"Tell me, Commander, why you did not break Carlotti silence until now? Surely *Bronson Star*'s owners would be entitled to learn that their ship was on her way back to their planet."

"I feared," said Grimes, "that units of the Dunlevin Navy might be in pursuit. I did not wish my exact whereabouts to be known."

"The Dunlevin Navy . . ." sneered Perkins. "Two more or less armed converted star tramps and a deep-space tug. . . ."

"But armed," said Grimes. "*Bronson Star* is not."

"Also," went on Perkins, "the government of Dunlevin has already lodged complaint with the Federation that you, during your escape from that world, threatened to destroy one of their cities. Surely you realized, Commander, that that was tantamount to piracy."

"I merely pointed out," said Grimes, "that if their air force shot me down I should fall onto a major center of population."

"Nonetheless, you disregarded orders given you by the legal authorities of Dunlevin."

"I was acting," said Grimes stiffly, "in my owners' interests."

"That," Perkins told him, "will have to be argued out in the courts." His manner seemed to soften. "Strictly between ourselves, I don't think that Dunlevin's pitiful squeals will get much sympathy on Earth. Meanwhile, you can hang on, can't you, until we reach you?"

"I shan't exactly live like a king," said Grimes. "But I shall live."

Thirty-three

Grimes had time to think things over while *Explorer* sped to her rendezvous with *Bronson Star*. In some ways it was better that his rescuers should be Survey Service personnel rather than merchant spacemen. The average tramp captain, in these circumstances, would be looking out for his owner's interests—and his own. He would calculate just how much his deviation had cost, erring on the generous side, and then send in the bill. He might even claim that he was entitled to a share of the *Bronson Star* salvage money. But *Explorer*'s people—even though the vessel was more of a survey ship proper than a warship—would merely be performing their normal functions as galactic policemen.

But as a galactic police Commander Perkins would be far too nosey. He would want to place the mutineer, the pseudo-Susie, under arrest aboard his own ship. In addition to the medical officer aboard that vessel there would be assorted scientists, inevitably a biologist or two. It would not take these people long to discover that Susie was not human. Awkward—very awkward—questions would be asked. And if the right answers were elicited then not only Grimes would be in the cactus but Hodge and the real Susie, probably still waiting on Joognaan for a ship off planet, would not escape the long arm of the law.

He would just have to play the cards the way that they fell, decided Grimes. Possibly, as *de facto* master of *Bronson Star*, he might be able to ride a high horse, asserting that Susie was, after all, *his* mutineer and must be placed in restraint aboard *his* ship, to be delivered by *him* to the authorities on Bronsonia. Perkins had been a little junior to Grimes when the latter had still been a Survey Service officer. Just possibly he might be able to assert his no longer existent seniority.

He slept.

There was little else to do.

He made an unsatisfactory meal from the boat's stock of preserved foodstuffs; the algae in their tanks, reanimated when he actuated the life-support systems, had not yet proliferated sufficiently to be a source of nourishment.

He had occasional conversations with Commander Perkins and his officers, discussing the boarding procedure, telling them as much as he could about the layout of the ship. He told them the code for opening the outer airlock door; he did not want them to burn their way in, causing needless damage. He was assured that *Explorer*'s engineers would be able to synchronize temporal precession rates and was told that when the two vessels were almost alongside each other a transship tunnel, airlock to airlock, would be used by the boarding party.

He slept some more, ate some more, talked some more.

The time passed.

At last *Explorer* was alongside *Bronson Star.*

With temporal precession rates synchronized a switch was made to NST radio which, both in the boat and aboard the Survey Service ship, was tuned to the frequency of the boarding party's helmet transceivers. Perkins was sending his people aboard *Bronson Star* suited up, in full battle order. Any sort of scrimmage—as Grimes knew too well—aboard a spaceship is liable to result in sudden and disastrous loss of atmosphere. . . .

"Tunnel extending . . ." Grimes heard over his transceiver.

"Contact. . . . Tunnel end locked. . . . Tunnel end sealed. . . ."

Not long now . . . thought Grimes.

A fresh voice came from the speaker of the NST transceiver. "*Bronson Star*'s airlock door opening. . . ." Then there was an indignant gasp. "What the hell's this? A bloody booby trap?"

I should have warned them . . . Grimes told himself.

The officer in charge of the boarders went on, obviously to Perkins, "Sir, the mutineer has tried to block off the airlock with all manner of garbage! We shall have to *dig* our way in!"

Oh, well, thought Grimes, *that saves* me *the bother of explaining.*

"I think, sir, that we should have the gunnery officer here before we start burrowing through this mess. There could be bombs. . . ."

Grimes broke in. "There aren't any bombs aboard this ship, or even materials for making them."

Perkins said, "Commander Grimes should know, Mr. Tamworth. Get on with the boarding."

"All right for him to talk," came a barely audible whisper. *"He* doesn't have to stumble through shit. . . ."

There was a feminine laugh, oddly familiar. *Susie?* thought Grimes, staring around in momentary panic. But that was impossible. Susie may have laughed quite frequently but, so far as Grimes knew, the pseudo-clone was quite incapable of laughter. There was the sound again. It came from the speaker of the transceiver. *Explorer,* as a scientific research rather than a fighting vessel, would almost certainly carry female personnel on her books and those ladies must be listening in.

Some would-be humorist was singing softly,

"Down in the sewer, shoveling up manure,

That's where the spaceman does his bit!

"You can hear those shovels ring, ting-a-ling-a-ting-a-ling,

When you're down in the sewer shoveling. . . ."

"Mr. Tamworth! This is no occasion for buffoonery! Keep your men under proper control!"

"Sir." Then, still in a sulky voice, "Airlock chamber sufficiently cleared. Access to inner door. Inner door opening. . . ."

"Proceed straight to the boat bay, Mr. Tamworth, to release Commander Grimes. Use your weapons only in self-defense."

"Sir." A long pause, then, "No sign of opposition. We are proceeding to boat bay level by elevator, which is functioning quite normally."

"You are *what?* Don't you realize that you and your people could be trapped in the cage? Get out *at once* and use the spiral stairway!"

"Sir."

"Commander Grimes, Commander Perkins here. Mr. Tamworth and his people should soon be with you."

"So I have gathered, Commander Perkins."

Finally Tamworth came back on the air. "Ontside Number 1 Boat Bay. We have encountered no opposition. Am bleeding atmosphere back into the bay." A pause. "Have found one pistol on the deck outside the compartment. A Franzetti-Colt, caliber 10 millimeter. . . ." Another pause. "Pressures equalized. Am opening door."

Grimes let himself out of the boat, stepped down to the deck just as his spacesuited rescuers came in through the doorway. In the lead was a tall man with the twin gold stripes of a lieutenant on the shoulders of his spacesuit. Immediately behind him was another figure, not quite so tall, wearing commander's insignia.

This one lifted the faceplate of her helmet.

"Surprise, surprise!" she said.

"Maggie!" gasped Grimes.

Thirty-four

"Maggie!" Then, "What are you doing *here?"* he demanded.

"I'm one of the scientific officers aboard *Explorer,"* she told him.

"You might have told me that you were there," he said.

She said, "I thought it better if we didn't see each other again, John, if we didn't speak to each other, even. If Bill hadn't been so against it I'd probably not have come across to you. . . ."

"Bill?"

"Commander Perkins." Her wide mouth opened and curved, displaying very white teeth, but he sensed that she was smiling with rather than at him. "But at the last minute I insisted on accompanying the boarding party. I just couldn't resist the temptation of finding out, at first hand, what sort of mess you've got yourself into now."

"And talking of messes," said Lieutenant Tamworth, who had opened his own faceplate, "may I suggest, Commander Lazenby, that we get this one sorted out?" He handed the weapon that he had picked up from the deck to Grimes. "Your pistol, Commander?" Grimes took it. "And now, will you lead the way? This is, after all, your ship."

Lead the way? Grimes asked himself. *Where to?* Where would the pseudo-Susie be hiding? If she were hiding. . . . Where would she be lurking to pounce out on them?

The farm deck, he thought.

He climbed the spiral staircase that ran around the axial shaft, Maggie immediately after him, then the lieutenant, then four ratings, alert for the first sign of attack, pistols cocked and ready.

The farm deck was as he had left it. The boarders looked curiously at the havoc wrought by Grimes himself—the hydroponic tanks stripped of all their vegetation, the emptied yeast vats.

Tamworth said, "So this is where all that garbage in your airlock came from. . . . You said that she was mad. She must have been. . . ."

"She probably still is," said Maggie. "And, therefore, her actions will be unpredictable."

Grimes wondered why she—it—had not yet attacked, said nothing.

They continued their ascent, searching every compartment as they climbed. Storerooms, galley, pantry, the wardroom. As they looked into the Third Officer's cabin Grimes remembered his torrid sessions there with the real Susie, wondered what acid comment Maggie would make if she knew what he was thinking. But she was no more his keeper than he was hers.

They came at last to the Master's quarters.

Grimes was first into his day cabin, brought up and aimed his pistol. But the pale, naked figure sitting hunched over the desk was motionless.

"Is that her?" demanded Tamworth.

"It is," said Grimes. "If she attacks, shoot to kill."

One of the men muttered something about a wicked waste.

Grimes approached the . . . thing cautiously. It did not stir. He stretched out his left hand to touch a bare shoulder. The skin was cold, clammy. He grasped the flaccid flesh, squeezed. There was no response.

He muttered, "She's dead. . . ."

"I'm the nearest thing here to a doctor," said Maggie briskly. "Get back all of you—and you, John. Let the dog see the rabbit. . . ."

She got her gloved hands under the armpits of the seated figure, lifted and pulled until it was sprawled back in the chair. It fell into an odd, boneless posture. Grimes was reminded of how the homunculus that was the start of all the trouble had looked among the shards of its broken bottle.

"Cardiac arrest, I'd say," stated Maggie. "I can't see any wounds. But I'd like to make a more thorough examination. Meanwhile, Mr. Tamworth, why don't you and your men make a check of the control room to make sure that all is in order? And you, Commander Grimes, stay here with me, please. I may need a little help."

Tamworth and his men left willingly enough; in that obscene posture the dead pseudo-Susie was not a pretty sight.

"Shut the door, John," ordered Maggie. "Better lock it."

While he was doing so she picked up the solidograph of herself from the desk, looked at it. She said, "I'm pleased that you kept this. . . . But I don't think that Bill would be happy if he knew that you have it."

"Damn Bill!" swore Grimes.

"He's a nice bloke," said Maggie. "And he's in love with me. Which is just as well. It means that he'll accept *my* story of what's been happening here without question. You've been up to something, John, something very odd. That thing in your chair is not human. I imagine that you don't want it taken aboard *Explorer* for a proper examination."

"I don't," said Grimes.

"Then talk. It's all right; I've accidentally on purpose switched off my helmet radio. You can spill all the beans you want without anybody but myself being privy to your guilty secrets."

Grimes picked up his pipe from where he had left it on the desk, filled and lit it. He noticed that the lid of the box that he had used as a trap was open, that the mangled remains of the first mini-Susie to be killed were gone from it. He looked at the open, sharp-toothed mouth of the life-sized simulacrum, shuddered.

"You haven't changed," commented Maggie. "You can't think, you can't talk without that foul incinerator of yours. One thing about Bill—he's a non-smoker. . . ."

"Must you keep dragging that bastard Perkins up?"

"Why not? At least he's human. And it looks to me as though you've been passing your lonely days and nights with some sort of obscene sex doll, something that you picked up on some foul world whose people cater to the tastes of woman-starved spacemen. What happened? Did she—no, *it*—get out of control? Did you hide in the lifeboat to escape a fate worse than death?"

"Damn it, no!" shouted Grimes.

"Then tell."

Grimes told.

He had to keep it short. Back aboard *Explorer* Commander Perkins must be getting anxious when he heard no reports directly from Maggie, might even order Tamworth and his men to break into the Master's quarters.

Maggie interrupted once.

"Yes, John, I've heard of Joognaan, but I've never been there. And so Susie had herself remodeled. I can't say that I blame her if she looked like *that*. What was she like after the job was done?"

"Not bad," said Grimes noncommittally, then went on.

He finished, "Those surplus cells from the original Susie must have been changed, somehow, when the Joognaanards made me the girl in the bottle that was Susie's parting gift. They can't have died when the bottle was broken. They reassembled, somehow, in the algae tank, devoured those aquatic worms. And then, after I let them out, the horde of tiny copies of the original thrived on the yeast. And when I tried to starve them they reunited by absorption, or ingestion, and grew. . . ."

"If she'd eaten you," said Maggie, "she'd have been a giantess. But what killed her?"

Somebody was hammering on the door; either Lieutenant Tamworth was acting on his own initiative or had been ordered by his captain to ensure that Maggie Lazenby was safe.

Maggie nudged the on-off button of her helmet transceiver with her chin. "Commander Lazenby here," she said. "I'm afraid that my radio switch is defective. Unless I keep it pressed all the time it goes off. Yes, I've almost finished the examination. . . . Damn!" This latter was for the benefit of her listeners just before she switched off again.

The hammering ceased.

She said, "Poor Bill. He probably thinks that we're enjoying ourselves. But I don't think that I could with that *thing* staring at me with its dead eyes. . . . Talking of dead eyes—why did she die?"

"I can guess," said Grimes. "We know that she had a very odd metabolism. Perhaps *dead* meat was poison to her. The beef that I used as bait perhaps wasn't quite dead enough to have a lethal effect—after all, whatever comes from the tissue-culture vats is alive, after a fashion, until it's cooked. But the thing in the box—she must have eaten it—was *very* dead . . ."

She switched on the helmet transceiver again.

"Commander Lazenby here. Commander Grimes has fixed that switch for me. The woman, the mutineer, is dead. Cardiac arrest. She must have had a weak heart and the exertion and the excitement were too much for her. . . . No, Bill, I don't think that we should bring the body aboard *Explorer*. Commander Grimes has admitted that she was his mistress and still feels a sentimental regard for her. He wants to bury his own dead. . . ." She addressed Grimes. "So it's good-bye once again, John. I'm pleased that we were able to help you. We can't stay with you much longer; we have a schedule to keep. . . ." She nudged the switch again with her chin, laughed. "You never were a very good electrician, John, were you?"

She put her spacesuited arms about him, hugged him. "Good luck, John. And good luck to your friends, to Hodge and the real Susie. You know, I'm just a little jealous of her. And good luck to you? Yes—although you still have more than your fair share of it. If *I* hadn't been aboard *Explorer,* if *I* hadn't carried out the examination of this corpse that so obviously isn't a human body, all three of you would have been in the cactus. . . ."

"Good-bye, Maggie," he said. "And good luck to you, too. . . ."

He managed to kiss her through the open faceplate of her helmet. When at last he withdrew his mouth from hers, audibly, her chin inadvertently nudged the switch.

He heard, very faintly, Perkins's voice from her helmet phones, "What was that? What was that noise?"

Maggie laughed softly, released him.

He let her out of the day cabin, said good-bye again, and good-bye and thanks to Lieutenant Tamworth. The boarding party declined his offer to see them down to the airlock. Before he went up to Control he looked at the solidograph on his desk and then at the bloated corpse sprawled in his chair. He would have to get rid of it as soon as possible; the sweet stench of decay, although faint, was already evident.

The control room NST transceiver was on. He listened to the voices of Tamworth and his men as they pushed all the garbage back into *Bronson Star*'s airlock. This was not essential; as the two ships were sharing a temporal precession field transfer of mass from one to the other would have no effect. This must be, he thought, spite on the part of Commander Perkins. *Let Grimes clear up his own mess,* he must be thinking.

He looked out through the viewports at the survey ship. He could see into her control room. Maggie was not there, although Perkins was.

Perkins spoke over the NST. "You can have your ship back now, Commander."

"Thank you for your help, Commander."

"I'm rather surprised that you needed it, Grimes. You should be an expert on handling mutinies by now."

The last connection between the two ships was broken and *Explorer* faded, diminished and vanished.

Thirty-five

The first task that Grimes set himself was to rid the ship of all traces of the Joognaanard clones. After he had shut down the Mannschenn Drive he ejected the vegetable rubbish from the airlock, and then the body of the pseudo-Susie. The corpse, when he lugged it from his day cabin to the waiting elevator cage, seemed to be no more than a bag of skin filled with some soft jelly; it was indeed fortunate that it had not been taken aboard *Explorer* for an autopsy. Then he made a thorough search of the farm deck just in case any of the little pseudo-Susies remained, either alive or dead. He found nothing.

The distasteful but essential jobs completed he took a very long, very hot shower. He decided then to establish Carlotti contact with Bronsonia. *Explorer* must already have made her report to Lindisfarne Base and, even though intelligence flows very sluggishly through official channels, sooner or later the authorities on Bronsonia would learn that *Bronson Star* was on the way back to her home world.

He sent three Carlottigrams—one to Aerospace Control, one to *Bronson Star*'s owners, the third to Captain Wendover, Bronsonian Secretary of the Astronauts' Guild. In all three messages he gave his ETA in Galactic Standard date and time, adding the promise, "Full report follows." The signal to Wendover also contained a query as to the well-being or otherwise of *Little Sister* and a request that the Guild Secretary initiate proceedings regarding the *Bronson Star* salvage claim.

While he was awaiting the acknowledgments Grimes set about rewriting his report. In the original version Hodge and Susie had escaped from the ship in one of the lifeboats rather than face trial on Bronsonia. In the revised edition they had forced Grimes at gunpoint to deviate from trajectory on the passage from Dunlevin to Bronsonia. There had been a fight during which Hodge had been killed. Susie had promised to be a good girl but then, driven mad by the fear of what would happen to her when she was turned over to the Bronsonian police, had tried once again to seize the ship.

Luckily Grimes had switched on the lifeboat's log-recorder when he told his story—fictitious insofar as the latter part of it was concerned—to Commander Perkins; all that he had to do was make a transcript of his side of the conversations with *Explorer.* Luckily, too, Hodge and Susie had left almost all their personal possessions on board when they disembarked on Joognaan. Should there be a really thorough investigation all the evidence would indicate that the man and the girl had been with Grimes aboard *Bronson Star* until their respective deaths. And the boarding party from the Survey Service ship had seen a female body; only Maggie knew that it was not a truly human one—and Grimes could trust her not to talk.

The acknowledgments finally came in.

Bronson Star's owners were laconic, telling Grimes only to take up parking orbit as instructed by Aerospace Control. Aerospace Control started off by warmly congratulating Grimes on his escape and said that the full report was eagerly awaited. Wendover, too, started with congratulations.

The message went on: "Regret inform you *lerrigan* case decided in consignees' favor. Your *Bronson Star* salary garnisheed to pay court costs. Heavy damages still outstanding, also accumulated port dues and charges incurred by *Little Sister.* Have succeeded delaying forced sale of your vessel to date. Preliminary enquiries indicate no certainty of success *Bronson Star* salvage claim despite *San Demetrio* precedent. Guild lawyers awaiting your full report."

Things might be worse, thought Grimes. *Little Sister* was not yet sold—but would he, could he ever get her back? *If* he got the salvage award before the financial situation became too desperate all would be well.

If. . . .

Meanwhile, the only people who looked like coming well out of the mess were Susie and Hodge, with their changes of identity and with the money that should have gone to finance the counterrevolution on Dunlevin. If he'd had any sense, thought Grimes, he'd have insisted on taking his share of it.

It was too late now for that.

He would just have to play the cards the way that they fell.

Thirty-six

Bronson Star was once again in orbit about Bronsonia.

As before, she was hanging almost directly over that chain of islands that looked like a sea serpent swimming from east to west. But Grimes would not be aboard to admire the view for much longer. The shuttle was here with his relief and the hydroponics technician who would be making good the damage done in the farm deck allegedly by a demented Susie but actually by Grimes himself.

He handled the airlock controls from the control room, waited there for old Captain Pinner who had been the ship-keeper before Grimes got the job.

Pinner, still spacesuited but with his faceplate open and with his gauntlets tucked into his belt, pulled himself through the hatch.

"Welcome aboard, Captain," said Grimes.

"Can't say that I'm glad to be here, Captain," grumbled Pinner. "But they want you down in New Syrtis as soon as possible if not before, and I was the only one they could find at short notice to take over."

The two men shook hands.

Pinner went on, "I wish we had time for a proper talk, Captain. I'd like to hear your story about all that's been happening. . . ."

"I've left you a copy of my report," Grimes told him.

A voice came from the NST transceiver, that of the shuttle's captain. "Are you ready to transfer, Captain Grimes?"

"I'll be with you in five minutes," Grimes told him.

He went down to his quarters accompanied by Pinner. His bag was already packed but he had a quick look around to make sure that he had missed nothing. The old man helped him on with his spacesuit then said, with a chuckle, "You can find your own way to the airlock I think, Captain. I'll get back up to Control. The best of luck to you—with the salvage claim and everything else."

"Thank you," said Grimes. "Be good."

He made his way aft, using the spiral staircase. He paused briefly at the farm deck, watched the hydroponics technician, who had discarded his spacesuit, working among the tanks, planting the new seedlings that he had brought up from Bronsonia. He was unaware of Grimes's presence and Grimes did not disturb him at his work.

He continued aft. He was not sure if he was glad or sorry to be leaving this old ship. Not all his memories of her would be bad and, if all went well, she might prove to be his financial salvation.

Outside the airlock's inner door he sealed his faceplate, pulled on his gauntlets. He told Pinner and the shuttle captain that he was about to let himself out, asked Pinner to close the outer door after him. Pinner replied rather testily that he had been a spaceman long enough to know his airlock drill and the shuttle captain growled, "I thought that I was going to have to come aboard to get you, the time you've taken! A bloody long five minutes!"

Even this airlock chamber held memories, Grimes thought. Maggie had passed through it. (And would he ever see her again?) He recalled the body of the pseudo-Susie when he had placed it there prior to ejection. At the finish, the very finish, it could almost have been that of the original woman and Grimes had felt like a murderer disposing of the evidence of his crime.

Pressure dropped rapidly as the air was pumped into the main body of the ship. The outer door opened. The shuttle hung there, a mere twenty meters distant, a dark torpedo shape in the shadow of the ship, her own open airlock door a glowing green circle in the blackness.

Grimes positioned himself carefully, jumped.

He fell slowly through nothingness, jerked himself around so that he would make a feet-first landing. His aim was good and he did not have to use his suit-propulsion unit. As soon as he was in the chamber the outer door closed and he felt rather than heard the vibration as the shuttle's inertial drive started up.

The shuttle captain was an overly plump, surly young man.

He grumbled, "Up and down, up and down, like a bleeding yo-yo. Two trips when one shoulda done. I told them that. Lemme wait, I said, until the gardener's done his planting. Make just one round trip of it. But no. Not them. *They* want you in some sort of a bleeding hurry. . . ."

"Who are *they?*" asked Grimes mildly.

"Marston—he's manager of the Corporation. The police. Oh—just about every bastard. . . ."

"I suppose," said Grimes, "that Mr. Marston's glad to get his ship back. . . ."

The shuttle captain laughed sardonically. "Pleased? Take it from me, Captain, that pleased he is not. He'd sooner have the insurance than the ship. . . .

But excuse me. I want to get this spaceborne junk heap down to New Syrtis in one piece. . . ."

Grimes tried to relax in the co-pilot's chair. (The shuttle carried no co-pilot; in fact her captain was her only crew.) He never felt happy as a passenger. His companion's handling of the controls, he thought, reminded him of that mythical monkey who, walloping the keyboard of a typewriter for an infinitude of time, would finish up writing all the plays of William Shakespeare. He transferred his attention to the viewports. New Syrtis was in view now—white spires and domes set amid green parks with the spaceport itself a few kilometers to the north. He borrowed the control cab binoculars, made out a spark of bright gold glowing in the morning sun on the dark grey of the spaceport apron.

Little Sister. . . .

"Looking for your ship, Captain? I wouldn't mind buying her myself, if I had the money. . . . But Marston's been sniffing around her. In fact he was counting on the *Bronson Star* insurance money to buy her. . . ."

The shuttle was losing altitude fast, driving down in what was practically a controlled drive. *Little Sister* and the other ships in port—an Epsilon Class tramp, decided Grimes, and something a little larger—were now visible to the naked eye.

"One thing for sure," said the shuttle captain, "Marston would sooner see you shot than getting a medal. . . ."

"Mphm."

"Mind you, he's not broke. He can afford better legal eagles than the Guild can. He'll fight your salvage claim tooth and nail. . . ."

"Mphm."

"You'da done better for everybody if you'd taken that decrepit old bitch out to the Rim or some place and changed her name. . . ."

"Not very legal," said Grimes.

"Being legal'll get you no place," said the shuttle captain. "Stand by for the bump. We're almost there. . . ."

The shuttle sat down in the corner of the spaceport reserved for small craft of her kind with a bone-shaking crash.

"Thanks for the ride," said Grimes.

"It's what I'm paid for," said the shuttle captain sourly.

Thirty-seven

There was a reception committee awaiting Grimes.

Marston was there—a skinny, sour-faced beanpole of a man who looked down at Grimes with an expression of great distaste. There was the New Syrtis Port Captain who, with Captain Wendover, seemed inclined to accord Grimes a hero's welcome. There was a high-ranking police officer. There were men and women hung around with all manner of recording equipment, obviously representatives of the media.

"Captain Grimes," called one of them, a rather fat and unattractive girl, "welcome back to Bronsonia! Do you have any message for us?"

"Captain Grimes," said Wendover firmly, "will be saying nothing to anybody until he has conferred with the Guild's lawyers."

The newshen transferred her attention to Marston. "Mr. Marston, aren't you pleased to have your ship back?"

Marston tried to ignore her.

"Mr. Marston, wouldn't you rather have had the insurance money?"

Marston turned to the police officer. "Chief Constable, are you to permit me to be harried?"

"Mr. Marston," said the policeman, "these ladies and gentlemen are taxpayers, just as you are supposed to be." He turned to Grimes. "I have a copy of your report, Captain. I understand that you have urgent personal business to discuss with Captain Wendover and so I will defer my own interrogation until later. You understand, of course, that you will not be allowed to leave this planet until such time as the Police Department has completed its inquiries."

"Captain Grimes," called the fat girl, "say something to us!"

"Can I?" Grimes asked Wendover.

"Captain Grimes!" One of the other girls was aiming her recorder at him. "What happened to Prince Paul?"

Wendover had a firm hold on Grimes's arm, was obviously preparing to hustle him off. He whispered, "Tell them something—just to keep them quiet! But be careful."

"Is there any damage to the ship, Grimes?" demanded Marston.

"Only minor," replied Grimes curtly. He turned to face the reporters. He said, "I'm glad to be back. I'm gladder still to be back in one piece. I. . . ."

"That will do, Captain," said Wendover.

"I'd like a few words with Grimes," said Marston.

"Captain Grimes," said Wendover, "must discuss his business affairs with the Guild's legal counsel before he talks to anybody else."

"That is his right," said the Chief Constable, who obviously did not like Marston.

"I'd like to change," said Grimes. He was still wearing his spacesuit and wanted to get into the comfortable tunic and slacks that were in the bag that he was carrying.

"In my office," said Wendover.

"Do not forget," Marston said, "that the spacesuit is the property of the Interstellar Shipping Corporation of Bronsonia."

"Surely, Mr. Marston," said the fat girl, "you can afford to let the captain have a souvenir of his adventurous voyage."

The shipowner snarled wordlessly.

"Come on, Captain," said Wendover. "This way. My car."

"What was all that about?" asked Grimes during the drive to the city.

"Marston's in none too happy a financial situation," said Wendover. "Oh, he's not broke. He could still afford to buy your *Little Sister,* for example, unless the bidding were forced up to some absurd level. I happen to know that he'd like to have something like her so that he could get the hell off the planet in a hurry if—when—his financial affairs come really unstuck."

"He's not a spaceman," said Grimes.

"There are one or two drunken bums on our books," said Wendover, "whom we wouldn't recommend even for a ship-keeping job. Marston would be prepared to employ one of them as yachtmaster if he absolutely had to. And then, assuming that he did make it to some other world, that solid gold ship of yours would give him the capital to make a fresh start."

"Mphm."

The car sped through the streets of New Syrtis, came to a stop outside the dome that housed the offices of the Astronauts' Guild. The robochauffeur announced, "Gentlemen, you are here."

"We're here," said Wendover unnecessarily.

"So I see," said Grimes.

* * *

He changed out of his spacesuit in the office washroom, rejoined Wendover and the two lawyers who had been waiting for him in the Secretary's office. The four men drew coffee from the dispenser, sat around the table to talk.

One of the legal gentlemen was fat, the other was fatter. One was bald but bearded, the other practiced facial depilation but had long, silvery hair plaited in a pigtail which was adorned with a jaunty little bow of tartan silk; a not-uncommon fashion but one which Grimes had never liked.

The pigtail wearer, a Mr. McCrimmon, seemed to be the senior of the pair. He said, "Let us not beat about the bush. Let us drive to the essentials. I understand, Captain Grimes, that you are desperately in need of money and that you hope that a successful salvage claim in respect of *Bronson Star* will enable you to pay your various debts and resume possession of your own ship."

"Your understanding is correct," said Grimes.

"Then I am afraid that I have bad news for you. A claim for salvage on your behalf might, eventually, be successful but it will be a bitter, long drawn out battle. Captain Wendover has already suggested that we cite the *San Demetrio* precedent but, since you did not actually abandon ship and then return to her, this may not be a valid analogy. . . . "

"San Demetrio?" asked Grimes.

"It was an interesting case," said McCrimmon, speaking as though it had been heard only yesterday. "Very interesting. The officer—who was the major beneficiary—and his crew were, indubitably, morally entitled to pecuniary reward and, as it turned out, also legally entitled. If they had not abandoned ship this would not have been so.

"You are familiar with Terran history, Captain Grimes? You will know of the Second Planetary War, which occurred from 1939 to 1945, Old Reckoning? Much of it was fought at sea and convoys of merchant vessels were harried by surface, submarine and aerial raiders. One such convoy, escorted only by an auxiliary cruiser, a not very heavily armed converted passenger liner, was attacked by a surface raider, a battleship. The auxiliary cruiser put up a valiant but hopeless fight which, however, gave the ships of the convoy a chance to scatter as darkness was falling. One of the merchantmen—an oil tanker, loaded with the highly volatile fuel used by the aircraft of those days—was hit and badly damaged, actually set on fire. Her crew abandoned ship. Miraculously the vessel's cargo failed to explode.

"Some little time later the Second Officer, who was in charge of one of the lifeboats, decided to reboard. He and his men succeeded in extinguishing the flames and eventually, despite the fact that almost all navigational equipment had been destroyed, brought *San Demetrio* to port.

"The officer and his boat's crew were, of course, members of *San Demetrio*'s crew. They had all signed the Articles of Agreement. Had they not abandoned ship, had they stayed on board to fight the fires and make the necessary repairs, they would not have been entitled to salvage money. They would merely have been carrying out the duties—admittedly in somewhat abnormal circumstances—that they had signed on for. No doubt the ship's owners would have made some kind of *ex gratia* payment but there would have been no legal entitlement to reward.

"It was argued, however, that as soon as they had abandoned what was, in effect, a huge, floating bomb the original agreement was no longer valid. Their legal status was that of any outsiders who might have happened to board the vessel to endeavor to save her and her cargo."

"I think," said Grimes slowly, "that I see what you're driving at. But, as far as *Bronson Star* is concerned, was I crew in the legal sense? I was employed by Mr. Marston's outfit but only as a glorified caretaker. I had signed no Articles of Agreement. My name was not on the Register as Master."

"A good point, Captain Grimes, and one that Captain Wendover has already raised and one that we shall argue. You must realize, however, that it will be many weeks before a decision is reached by the courts."

"And meanwhile," said Grimes bitterly, "I have to eat."

"You are a rich man, Captain," said McCrimmon. "Even only as scrap, your ship, constructed as she is from a precious metal, is worth a not so small fortune. My partner and I are willing to handle the sale for you—on a commission basis, of course. . ."

"I don't want to sell," said Grimes.

"You may have to," Wendover told him, not without sympathy.

"You will have to," said McCrimmon bluntly. But he, not a spaceman, would never be able to appreciate the odd affection, the love, even, that can develop between captains and their ships.

"Think it over, Captain," went on McCrimmon. "Not that it will be necessary. The *lerrigan* consignees are already taking legal action for the recovery of the monies that you owe them."

"Well, gentlemen," said Wendover, "we have enjoyed—if that is the word—our preliminary meeting. And now, Captain Grimes, I must take you to see the Port Captain. The Chief Constable will also be present, in his official capacity. But I am sure that you have nothing to fear from them. You used force, as you were legally entitled to do, to recapture the vessel of which you were legally in charge."

"And after I've seen everybody," asked Grimes, "shall I be entitled to go aboard *Little Sister*?"

"I'm afraid not. She's been sealed, as you know. She's security against your many debts. But I've booked you into the Astronaut's Arms. It's not a bad pub and it's handy to the spaceport."

Thirty-eight

He sat in his almost comfortable, definitely characterless hotel room. He was smoking his pipe, sipping a large pink gin, his second one. (The first he had gulped.) He looked at the solidograph of Maggie Lazenby standing on the chest of drawers. Maggie had wished him luck. He needed it.

Of course, he admitted, the situation wasn't altogether desperate. Presumably he would be allowed to sell the ship piecemeal, her fittings before the vessel herself. The autochef, for example, should fetch quite a few credits. . . .

But. . . .

He looked at the naked figurine in its transparent cube. It would be as though, he thought, he were starving and were carving hunks off Maggie to sustain his own life. A breast one day, an arm the next. . . . Then a buttock. . . . So it would be with *Little Sister.* She was a masterpiece of interior design and the subtraction of any fitting would ruin her internal symmetry.

The telephone chimed.

Grimes looked at the screen, saw the face of the hotel's receptionist. He got up, switched the instrument to reception from his end.

"Captain Grimes," said the girl, "there is a lady here to see you. May I send her up?"

A lady? he wondered. Susie's mother, perhaps. . . . What could he tell her? Dare he risk telling her that her daughter was, so far as he knew, alive, well and rich?

The almost pretty face of the receptionist was replaced by that of the unattractive fat girl who had tried to interview him at the spaceport.

"Captain Grimes—this is Wendy Wayne here. Of the *Bronson Star.*" She laughed, displaying teeth that would have been better hidden. "No. Not your *Bronson Star.* The weekly paper."

"I don't feel like an interview," said Grimes.

She said, "It's not an interview I want. I've a proposition."

Grimes refrained from saying something ill-mannered.

She laughed again. "Don't worry, Captain, I've no designs on your body beautiful. I already have a lover—and *she* wouldn't approve. . . ."

"Mphm."

"Strictly business, Captain. Can I come up?"

"Yes," said Grimes.

"You've seen the *Bronson Star*, of course," she said.

"I have," admitted Grimes. (There had been a tattered copy of that scurrilous weekly aboard the other *Bronson Star*, the ship.)

"As you know, we like sensational stories, preferably told in the first person. Ghosted, of course. . . ."

I Was a Sex Slave on Waldegren, remembered Grimes.

"Our readers like them too."

They would, thought Grimes.

"Your story will be sensational. There must have been some sex. That Lania, for example. . . . She had quite a reputation, you know. And that other girl, Susie. . . . With those two aboard a ship *anything* might happen!"

"It did," conceded Grimes.

"And your own name's not entirely unknown, even on this back of beyond planet. Even our media carried the news of that mutiny aboard *Discovery.* And now you're news—NEWS!—again. Unluckily we're not allowed to publish anything about the Dunlevin affair before the full inquiry's been held; too many interplanetary ramifications. That's why the wolf pack didn't really tear you apart when you landed at the spaceport today.

"But. . . ."

"There are other tales you could tell. The full story of the *Discovery* mutiny. What you did when you were captain of the Baroness d'Estang's spaceyacht. How you came to set up shop as a shipowner in that fantastic *Little Sister.* And weren't you captured by a Shaara rogue queen on one voyage?

"So. . . ."

"So?" asked Grimes.

"As I've said, we can't publish your story of the Dunlevin adventure until we get a clearance. But we'll titillate the appetites of our readers with your earlier adventures. *On The Planet Of The Cat Women. . . . Space Chauffeur To The Baroness. . . . How My Crew Stabbed Me In The Back. . . . I Was A Shaara Slave. . . .*"

"Mphm."

"We're willing to pay, of course."

"How much?" he asked sharply.

She told him.

He borrowed her notebook and stylus from her. He did his sums. There were the damages claimed and won by the New Syrtis Zoo, the court costs. To add to them there were the accumulated port dues and other charges. Then there was the estimated expense of putting *Little Sister* back in commission. The total came to considerably more than Wendy Wayne's offer. But there was his shipkeeping pay, which had been garnisheed. The subtraction of this did improve the situation but not enough.

He said, "I shall want more than that."

She said, "You're a greedy bastard."

"I want to keep my ship," he told her. "I don't want her sold from under me."

"My nose fair bleeds for you," she said.

He was tempted to throw this fat, insolent wench out of his room but restrained himself. After all, she represented the only chance he had to get himself off the financial rocks.

He asked, "Do you want my story—or stories—or don't you?"

"I do," she said. "My paper does. But we aren't prepared to give our right arms and a couple of legs for them. There are other stories, you know, that we can get for a damn' sight less." She took the notebook back from him, squinted at the figures that he had written down. "No," she said. "Repeat, underscore and capitalize NO."

"Your paper could put me on contract," he said. "As a sort of roving correspondent. . . ."

"Ha!" she snorted. "Ha, bloody ha! And what hold would we have on you once you lifted off this mudball?"

He said, "There's the salvage award, you know. That could be a security."

"If and when you get it. *If* being the operative word. Marston's got legal eagles who'll tear that fat slob McCrimmon to shreds. But. . . . Pour me another gin, will you?"

He did so.

"Roving correspondent . . ." she muttered thoughtfully after the first noisy gulp. "Yes. But not *you,* buster. You'll just be the chauffeur, working off the good money we've paid to get your precious ship out of hock. . . ."

"And would *you* be the *Bronson Star*'s roving correspondent?" asked Grimes, his heart sinking. There are some prices too high to pay.

"Not with *you* in the same spacegoing sardine can I wouldn't!" she said. "Not for all the folding money in El Dorado. Apart from anything else, you're the wrong sex. But we've been thinking of doing an exposé on the state of affairs on New Venusberg and our Fenella Pruin is the girl to do it. And when Fenella does an exposé she often has to get out in one helluva hurry—and the schedules of passenger liners don't always fit in with her hasty departures. It cost the paper a packet to get her out of jail on Waldegren."

"The *Bronson Star* must be rich," commented Grimes.

"We're not short of a credit," she said. "Of course, most of our dirt, the really dirty dirt, is syndicated throughout the galaxy."

She finished her gin, got to her feet.

"You'll be hearing from us, Grimes. I think we can use you."

She left him with the empty gin bottle for company but he decided that he neither wanted nor needed another drink. The renewal of hope was heady wine enough. He raised his glass, in which only a few drops remained, in a toast to the solidograph of Maggie. She had wished him luck and it looked as though her wish were coming true.

But what would this Fenella Pruin be like?

He shrugged. He would cross that bridge when he came to it.

Meanwhile—and this was all that really mattered—he was keeping his ship.

Matilda's Stepchildren

One

Fenella Pruin did not like Grimes.

Grimes did not like Fenella Pruin.

Their *de jure* relationship was that of charterer's representative and Owner/Master of the vessel under charter. Their *de facto* relationship was that of employer and servant. Grimes, bound by the terms of the charter party did as he was told and Miss Pruin did the telling. He did not like it. She, most obviously, did.

It was a charter that he would never have accepted had he not been so desperately in need of money. But he had been grounded on Bronsonia with port dues mounting steadily, with heavy fines still to pay and with the salvage award in respect of the obsolescent, renamed Epsilon Class freighter *Bronson Star* still being haggled over by the lawyers. The other *Bronson Star,* a newspaper, had come to his financial rescue. This *Bronson Star* was a sensational rag which also owned trivi stations and the like. Although its sales on its home planet were not small it derived the bulk of its considerable income from syndicated material. It had earned, over the years, a reputation as the galaxy's premier muckraker. It employed a highly efficient team of scavengers; the material that they gathered was, after processing, syndicated to every world with a human population and to quite a few planets whose inhabitants, although non-human, enjoyed salacity.

Chief of the muckrakers was Fenella Pruin. Normally she followed her long nose to savoury (in a perverted sense of the word) dirt by taking passage to likely places in regular spaceliners. But now and again she had found it impossible to get away, at extremely short notice, from worlds upon which she had endeared herself to prominent citizens by her snooping. On occasion she has been considerably roughed up. Twice she had been jailed on trumped up charges and her extrication from prison had been expensive to her employers back on Bronsonia. (She hadn't been murdered yet—but, Grimes often thought during the voyage, there has to be a first time for everything.)

So *The Bronson Star* had chartered Grimes' deep space pinnace *Little Sister.*

They were, to a certain extent, killing two birds with one stone. Not only would their Miss Pruin be taken to where she wished to go—and whisked away therefrom as soon as things got sticky—but Grimes' own name would help to sell the material garnered by the notorious news hen. He, too, had achieved a certain notoriety which might well be of value to others if not to himself.

Miss Pruin was travelling under a *nom de guerre.* According to the documentation provided by her employers—and they had done a very thorough job—she was Prunella Fenn, a spinster schoolteacher whose life had been changed when her loving pupils gave her, as birthday present, a ticket in the annual super lottery, the Bronson Bonanza. Fantastically she had won the astronomical first prize. According to news items in specially printed isues of *The Bronson Star*—which had been placed aboard *Little Sister* before lift off—the sudden influx of great wealth had gone to the fictitious Miss Fenn's head. She had started to make up for lost time. From prim schoolmarm she had made the transition to good time girl. Finding Bronsonia too dull for her—and that wouldn't have been hard, thought Grimes sourly, as he read the spurious press reports so as to acquaint himself with his passenger's cover story—she had charted *Little Sister* for a galactic tour, with a first stop at New Venusberg.

He looked at the photographs accompanying some of the newspaper articles. There was one of himself among them. *The famous Captain John Grimes . . .* he read. That photographer had made him look all pipe and ears. *The famous Captain John Grimes, hero of the* Discovery *mutiny and of the* Bronson Star *affair, whose fabulous golden spaceyacht* Little Sister *has been chartered by lucky lady Prunella Fenn . . .*

Then there was lucky lady Prunella Fenn herself, labelled "the golden schoolmarm." The photographer had flattered *her.* (Probably it had been more than his job was worth to do otherwise). The portrait was of a slim, darkhaired (before making changes to her appearance Fenella Pruin had been carroty) with slightly protrusive (another attempt at disguise) front teeth, with rather too much nose (although that organ was thin and almost aristocratic) and rather too little chin. She looked like an intelligent ferret, although a quite attractive one. She looked far more attractive in the photograph than she was in actuality.

She interrupted his studies by yelling in her shrill soprano, "Grimes, what about a drink? After all the money I've paid to charter this tub of yours I'm entitled to some pretense of service!"

All the money you've *paid?* thought Grimes resentfully. Nonetheless he got up from his seat, went aft into the tiny galley, busied himself with bottles and glasses. He did not have to ask her what she wished. Her taste in potables never changed. He put a small ice cube into a large glass which he filled with brandy. He decided that it would be bad manners—not that *she* ever worried about manners—to let her drink alone. His choice was pink gin—heavy on the liquor, very easy on the ice. Normally he drank very little alcohol while in space but Fenella Pruin—correction: Prunella Fenn—was driving him to it.

She was curled up in an inflatable easy chair in front of the playmaster. She had brought a large supply of her own spools with her. Her tastes ran to what Grimes thought of as boring porn. In the screen an actor and actress made up to resemble (vaguely) Hindu deities had gotten themselves into an intricate tangle of organs and slowly writhing limbs. The really boring part was the commentary, couched in allegedly poetic language.

She took her drink from him without thanks, downed half of it in one gulp. Grimes sipped from his, but not slowly. She swallowed the rest of her brandy, indicated that she needed a refill. He got one for her. In the screen the heterosexual lovers were replaced by two naked, teen-aged girls. The accompanying commentary was no improvement on what had gone before.

Emboldened by gin Grimes asked, "Don't you think that we might have some of my spools for a change? I've some good adventure stories . . ."

"No," she said. "I'm paying and I'm entitled to watch the entertainment that *I* like."

"I suppose," said Grimes, "that it is an acceptable substitute for the real thing."

She turned away from the playmaster to look at him. Her eyes, magnified by black-rimmed spectacles that she wore, seemed enormous. Her wide, scarlet mouth distracted his attention from her sharp nose. Viewed through an alcoholic haze she was beginning to look definitely attractive.

She said, "I thought you'd never get around to it. Here I've been, cooped up in this flying sardine can, with an allegedly virile, rough and tough spaceman, and nothing, but nothing, has happened to me. Yet." She grinned. "My bunk or yours?"

"Mine," said Grimes.

She unfolded herself from her chair, all two metres of her. She touched the sealseams at the shoulders of her gown. It fell around her feet. Under it she was wearing nothing. As so often is the case with slender women her figure looked much fuller when she was naked than when clothed. Grimes got out of his shorts and shirt with fumbling haste. By the time that he was stripped she was already stretched out on his bunk on the starboard side of the cabin. He joined her.

And at the touch of her flesh all his desire faded.

She pushed him off her and he fell to the deck.

She got off the bunk and stood over him, sneering.

"A big, tough spaceman! And just because those obscene animals you carried in this ship on your last voyage tried to castrate you you're acting like a pussy-panicked pansy!"

She knew about *that,* thought Grimes. His killing of the beasts, valuable cargo, had landed him in a fine mess of financial and legal problems, had led to his being grounded on Bronsonia and his accepting the job of shipkeeping aboard *Bronson Star.* But she didn't know of his traumatic experiences aboard the skyjacked freighter on her return voyage. That was his secret, his alone, and always would be.

She snarled wordlessly, went back to her chair, resumed her interrupted viewing of the pornographic programme. She did not bother to dress. Her hand, Grimes noticed, was resting on her lap, her fingers moving. But if she did not wish privacy he most certainly did.

He got unsteadily to his feet, arranged the folding screens that would shut off his bunk and a little space around it from the rest of the cabin.

Then he tried, miserably, to sleep.

Two

Little Sister came to New Venusberg.

Grimes had heard, of course, of the fabulous pleasure planet but this was his first time there. Oddly enough it was also Fenella Pruin's first time on this world. The General Manager of Bronson Star Enterprises, however, had spent a few days on New Venusberg as part of a Trans-Galactic Clippers cruise. Although on holiday he had kept his eyes skinned and his ears flapping. He had gained the impression that there was something unsavoury—something even more unsavoury than was to be expected in a holiday resort of this nature—going on. He had decided that an investigation might well pay off and that Fenella Pruin would be ideally qualified to make it. She was known, of course, by her name and the likenesses of her that accompanied her syndicated material but it was unlikely that anybody would penetrate her disguise or her cover story. To the Venusbergers she would be no more—and no less—than a fortuituously rich bitch, ripe for the plucking.

Little Sister came to New Venusberg.

Grimes was not sorry that the voyage was over. Neither, she told him, was she. She sat with him in the control cab as he eased the pinnace down to Port Aphrodite. Among her many other faults she was a back seat driver. She took him to task for evincing interest in the chalk giantess that, viewed from the air, was a huge advertisement for the major entertainment for sale on New Venusberg. Cut out from the green turf she was, although the two white hillocks that were her breasts, the oval blue ponds that were her eyes must have been artificial. There was golden hair on the head and above the jointure of the thighs (a flowering creeper, Grimes later discovered) and her nipples (marked by a sort of lichen) were pink.

"If you were as interested in me as you seem to be in that thing," said Ms Pruin, "you might be some use."

"I'm getting my bearings," said Grimes.

"If you can't see the spaceport apron and the marker beacons from here," she said, "you should have your eyes examined. Come to that, you've other organs that need attention."

Grimes made a major production of filling and lighting his pipe.

"Must you smoke that vile thing, stinking the ship out?"

Since she herself smoked thin, black cheroots that had the cloying scent of cheap incense Grimes considered her censure unjustified and said so. A snarling match ensued, terminated by a voice from Port Aphrodite Aerospace Control.

"Control to *Little Sister*. May I remind you that your berth is marked by the three scarlet flashers? It is not, repeat not, between the White Lady's legs." There was a tolerant chuckle from the speaker of the NST transceiver. "Of course, Captain, I realise that you're in a hurry, but even so . . ."

"Little Sister to Control," said Grimes. "Just admiring your scenery."

"You'll find much more to admire once you're down," Control told him.

"And if you can do any more than just admire it," whispered Fenella Pruin viciously, "I, for one, shall be surprised."

"Shut up!" almost shouted Grimes.

"What was that, *Little Sister*?" demanded Aerospace Control.

"I was just talking to my passenger," said Grimes.

He applied lateral thrust, bringing the golden pinnace directly over the triangle of beacons, vividly bright in spite of the brilliance of the morning sun. He wondered, not for the first time, why Port Captains love to berth incoming vessels in a cramped huddle when there are hectares of spaceport apron vacant. But there was no ground level wind and *Little Sister* would fit in easily between what looked like one of the bigger TG Clippers and what was obviously a Shaara vessel; they were the only spacefaring people whose ships were almost featureless cones with a domed top.

Fenella Pruin asked, "Shaara? *Here*?"

"Why not?"

"But they're arthropods."

"And they have their vices. Almost human ones. Alcoholism. Gambling. Voyeurism . . ."

"You'd know, of course."

Grimes did know. Not so long before he and his then passenger, the attractive Tamara Haverstock, had been captured by a Shaara Rogue Queen, held prisoner, in humiliating circumstances, aboard the arthropod's ship.

All he said, however, was, "Let me get on with the piloting, will you?"

Little Sister fell slowly, but not too slowly. Grimes dropped her neatly between the two towering hulks. (He could have come down almost to ground level well clear of them and then made a lateral final approach but he couldn't resist showing off.) He saw duty officers watching from control room viewports, waved to them nonchalantly.

The underskids kissed the concrete.

The inertial drive—a clangorous cacophony to those outside but reduced by sonic insulation to a mere, irritable grumble inside the hull—fell silent as Grimes switched it off.

"We're here," he said unnecessarily.

"Do you expect me to give you a medal?" she asked.

The port officials came out to *Little Sister,* riding in a large, purple, gold-trimmed ground car. Normally junior officers of the departments concerned would have completed the clearing inwards formalities—initiated by Carlotti deep space radio fourteen days prior to arrival—but although space yachts were not uncommon visitors to New Venusberg golden ones most certainly were. What she lacked in size *Little Sister* made up for in intrinsic value.

So there was the Chief Collector of Customs in person, accompanied by two micro-skirted, transparently shirted junior customs officers. There was the Port Doctor; there was no need for him actually to sight the clean Bill of Health from Bronsonia—a formality usually carried out by Customs—but Grimes was being given VIP treatment. There was the Port Captain—and his visit was purely social.

Grimes produced refreshments. (The last batch of Scotch that he had cajoled out of the autochef would almost have passed for the real thing and as he had decanted it into bottles with genuine labels he did not think that anybody would know the difference.) He, Prunella Fenn (he must remember always to call her that) and the three men sat around one table in the main cabin while the two Customs girls went through the ship's papers at another.

The Port Captain divided his attention between the ersatz Scotch and Grimes' passenger. He was a big, florid man with a cockatoo crest of white hair, with protuberant, slightly bloodshot (to begin with) blue eyes, a ruddy, bulbous nose and a paunch that his elaborately goldbraided white uniform could not minimise. He looked more like the doorman of a brothel than a spaceman, thought Grimes. (But the Port Captain on a world such as Venusberg was little more than the doorman of a brothel.)

The Port Doctor—even though he, too, was dressed in gold-trimmed white—looked like an undertaker. He did not divide his attention but was interested only in the whisky. He picked up the bottle, studied the label, put it down again. He lifted his glass, sipped, raised his heavy black eyebrows, then sipped again. He was the first person ready for a refill.

The Collector of Customs was interested most of all in the financial side of things. What was the actual value of *Little Sister*? What was the possibility of various solid gold fittings being stolen and sold ashore during her stay in Port Aphrodite? What security arrangements was Grimes implementing?

Unwisely Grimes said that he was prepared to use arms, if necessary, to protect his property and was sternly told that the ship's laser and projectile pistols must be placed under Customs seal and that the two laser cannon—Shaara weapons that had been fitted while *Little Sister* was temporarily under the command of the Rogue Queen—must be dismantled.

But Grimes was not to worry, the Collector told him. A guard would be on duty at his ramp throughout. (Grimes did worry. He knew who would have to pay for that guard. According to the charter party the charterers would pay all *normal* port charges and the wages of an armed guard could be—almost certainly would be—argued not to be a normal port charge.)

Finally Prunella Fenn got a little unsteadily to her feet.

"I'm off," she announced. "Jock's going to show me a good time . . ."

Jock? wondered Grimes.

The Port Captain levered himself upright, his hands on the table.

"I'm ready, Prue, soon as you are."

"I'm ready, Jock."

As they left the cabin he already had his arm about her slender waist, his meaty hand on her hip.

The Port Doctor raised his thick eyebrows. The Collector of Customs grinned.

"Well, Captain," he said, "I'd best be off myself. Ingrid and Yuri will put your pistols under seal. As for your cannon—as long as you remove the crystals and put them in bond with the hand guns that will be sufficient. I'll arrange for the Customs guard." He grinned again. "And enjoy your stay. The only thing that's not tolerated here is gunplay."

He left the cabin far more steadily than the Port Captain had done although he had imbibed at least as much.

Grimes excused himself to the doctor, went out of the ship. Using the recessed rungs in the shell plating he clambered up to where the cannon were mounted above the control cab. He removed the crystals. Back inside the hull he handed these to the two Customs girls, who put them into the locker allocated for the purpose together with the pistols. They sealed the door with an adhesive wafer, told him that although it looked flimsy it was not and could be removed only with a special tool.

They accepted a drink—after all, thought Grimes, they had earned theirs, they had been doing all the work—and then left.

"Have ye any more o' that quite tolerable whisky, Captain?" asked the Port Doctor.

Three

"That lass o' yours made a big hit with Jock . . ." said the doctor.

"She's no lass of mine," said Grimes.

"Just the two o' ye in a wee ship like this? An' it's not as though she's unattractive . . ."

"You don't know her," said Grimes, "like I do."

"She's no' one o' the Sisterhood, is she? She didn't impress me as being that way. But a rich bitch . . . She must be a rich bitch to charter a ship to run her about the galaxy. An' a rich bitch is what Jock's been a-huntin' for these many years. We were shipmates in the Waverley Royal Mail, in their passenger ships, before we came out to this sink of iniquity. He was rich-bitch-chasing then—although, to give him credit, he'd prefer one not so rich but with a modicum of looks to one with all the money in the universe but a face like the arse of a Wongril ape an' a figure like a haggis. He was too picky an' choosey. That was his downfall. But that's aye the way in passenger ships; it's no' the ones ye oblige that make the trouble but the ones ye don't . . .

"Still, it's the bawbies that Jock's after more than hot pussy. An' although there's no shortage o' hot pussy on New Venusberg the best of it has no bawbies attached. But ye mean to tell me that ye weren't interested in Prunella's bawbies?" He drained his glass, held it out for a refill. "Ah, but ye wouldn't be, would ye? A man who owns a solid gold spaceship, e'en though she's only a wee boat, 'll not be short of a bawbie."

"She's not a wee boat," said Grimes stiffly. "She's a pinnace. A deep-space-going pinnace. And she happens to be built of an isotope of gold only because her original owner, the Baroness d'Estang, liked it that way."

"An' ye bought her from yon Baroness? Then ye're no' sae badly fixed yerself."

The thickness of the doctor's Waverley accent, Grimes decided, was in direct ratio to the amount of whisky imbibed. The more Scotch that went in the more that came out.

He said, "I didn't buy her. She was a sort of parting gift. In lieu of back and separation pay."

"An' ye let a woman like that slip through yer fingers? Still, I suppose she was ugly as sin an' old enough to be Methuselah's granny."

"She was neither. She just happened to prefer a villainous bastard called Drongo Kane to me."

"Kane? Ye ken Drongo Kane? We hae dealings wi' the mon, though he's no' been here himself for a while. There's a wee laddy called Aloysius Dreeble, skipper o' *Willy Willy,* who comes the no'. She's owned by Able Enterprises. Get it? Kane . . . Able . . . Och, whatever ye say about Kane ye must admit that the mon has a fine, pawky wit."

"Mphm."

"But *Willy Willy* . . . An odd name for a ship . . . Would ye ken if he has a girlfriend called Wilhelmina or some such?"

"Willy Willy," said Grimes, "is the Australian name for a small, local whirlwind. But what cargo does this *Willy Willy* bring here?"

"Passengers most o' the while."

"So Kane's in the tourist racket now."

"Whyfor should *ye* be sneering? Ye're in the tourist racket yerself, cartin' rich bitches hither an' yon atween the stars. An' talkin' o' rich bitches—just how rich is *your* rich bitch?"

Grimes remembered that he was bound by the charter party to give the charterer's representative all possible support. Now would be as good a time as any, he thought, to run her cover story up to the masthead and see if anybody saluted. He would show this drunken quack the specially printed issues of *The Bronson Star.* No doubt the Port doctor would pass the fictitious information on to his crony, the Port Captain. Then soon it would be common knowledge all over New Venusberg.

He got a little unsteadily to his feet.

"I've some newspapers here," he said. "*She* doesn't know that I've got them. They're rather amusing reading . . . A fascinating transition story . . . Miss Goody Goody into Good Time Girl?"

He got the papers out of a filing cabinet, made room on the table to spread them out, indicated the relevant paragraphs with his forefinger. The Port Doctor was not too drunk to read. He chuckled.

"Ah, weel, a big prize . . . An' so long as she stays clear o' the gamblin' she'll have a few credits left when ye lift off from here. 0' course, she may be payin' for the services o' the local studs, an' they don't come cheap. She'll no' be gettin' much in the way o' service from Jock—I'm his doctor an I should know . . ." He looked up, blinking, at Grimes. "An' are ye sure, Captain, that ye weren't obligin' her? For love or money?"

Grimes made a major production of not replying.

The Port Doctor laughed. "So ye're an officer an' a gentleman an' ye're no' tellin'." He added, far too shrewdly for Grimes' comfort, "Perhaps the way it was ye'd rather not." He poured the last of the bottle into his glass. "An' now, would ye be havin' soberups in yer medicine chest? Ye can prescribe for the both of us an' then I'll take ye tae see the sights."

The soberup capsules worked as advertised.

Grimes changed into informal civilian clothing. The evening might turn out to be a wild one and if he were going to make a public spectacle of himself he would prefer not to do so in uniform. The Port Doctor, it seemed, was not troubled by such scruples; he did not, as Grimes expected that he would, go first to his office for a change of attire.

The two men passed through *Little Sister*'s airlock. It was evening already. (Where had the day gone?) Outside the pinnace the air was warm, redolent with a heavy scent that might have been that of flowers but which Grimes suspected was artificial. The spaceport lights—except around an Epsilon Class freighter where cargo discharge was in progress—were of low intensity. The floodlights of the passenger liners had been turned on but at no more than a fraction of their normal power so that the big ships had the similitude of faintly luminous, shimmering, insubstantial towers. Music was coming from concealed speakers, drifting on the lazy breeze, a melodious throbbing and wailing of guitars. Romance, with a capital R, was in the air. It was as meretricious as all hell.

"Sing me a song of the islands . . ." muttered Grimes sardonically.

"What?"

"This atmosphere . . . So phonily Hawaiian . . ."

The doctor laughed. "I see what you mean. Or hear what you mean. I'd prefer the pipes meself."

"Mphm?"

They walked slowly across the apron to the entrance of the spaceport subway station, an orifice in the side of a single storeyed building the curves of which were more than merely suggestive, that did more than hint at open thighs. And as for the doorway itself. . . . Only on a world like this, thought Grimes, could one find such an architectural perversion. *Labia majora* . . . *Labia minora* . . . Even an overhanging clitoris . . . A dark, ferny growth to simulate pubic hair . . .

"Doesn't this make you feel like a pygmy gynaecologist?" asked Grimes as they passed throgh the pornographic portal, stepped on to the downward moving stairway.

"I got a nice fee for helping to design it," said the doctor.

Grimes looked with interest at the advertisements on either side of the escalator, each one of them a window on to various aspects of this world, each one of them a colourful, three-dimensional moving picture. WINE & DINE AT ASTARTE'S KITCHEN—EVERY DISH A PROVEN APHRODISIAC . . . And with partners like that at the dinner table, thought Grimes, what need for artificial stimuli? (But perhaps in his case there was. The psychic trauma sustained aboard *Bronson Star* and aboard *Little Sister* herself had yet to heal.) GIRLS! GIRLS! GIRLS! AT KATY'S KATHOUSE! Katy's Kathouse? Cats . . . Some of those wenches so lavishly displaying their charms looked like Morrowvians. That tied in. Drongo Kane had trade connections with this world and, quite possibly, had been recruiting on Morrowvia before he finally blotted his copybook on the planet of the cat people. But some of the other women . . . The escalator carried him on down before he could have a proper look. CAVALIER ESCORT SERVICE . . . This, obviously, was aimed at the female tourists. The escorts were tall, virile young men, impeccably clad in archaic formal finery, the fronts of their tight trousers suggestively bulging. Another display—IF YOU'RE TIRED OF ALL THE OTHER LADIES HAVE A WHIRL WITH LADY LUCK! After many a century the roulette wheel was still the universally recognised symbol for games of chance.

"Lady Luck," said the doctor. "That's where we're going."

"You're the doctor," said Grimes. (He did not care much for gambling but, for the time being, the sort of games that were much more to his liking seemed to be out.) "But I was thinking that, for a start, I'd like a change from my own cooking."

"Not to worry, Captain. Lady Luck feeds her patrons at no extra charge; she makes her profits on the tables and machines. Mind you, she's not made much out of me. Over a year I usually show a small profit myself."

They were on the station platform now, looking at the animated holograms adorning the walls. They were joined by three men, obviously spacers, officers from one of the ships in port. They knew the doctor, engaged him in conversation. Grimes—details of the Outward Clearance of *Epsilon Puppis* were of no great interest to him—studied the advertisements. Just when he had come to the conclusion that when you have seen one explicit amatory exhibition you've seen them all a single bullet-shaped car slid silently in, came to a stop. Bullet-shaped? There was intentional phallic symbolism in its design.

"This is ours," said the doctor.

He and Grimes boarded the vehicle, leaving the others on the platform. They were probably bound for the Kathouse or some similar establishment, thought Grimes, not without a twinge of envy.

As soon as the passengers were seated the car started off.

No matter what it looked like its motion was that of a bullet.

Four

Lady Luck was only two stops from Port Aphrodite.

Again there was an escalator ride, this time up to ground level. Again there was the display of explicit advertising, holograms that Grimes had already seen and one or two new ones. He was intrigued by the advertisement for the Church of the Ultimate Experience. What did it have to offer? A Black Mass? Through the swirling, coruscating mists that filled the frame he could just see, or thought that he could see, what looked like a naked woman spreadeagled on an altar with an inverted crucifix in the background.

He and the doctor stepped off the moving staircase into a brightly lit foyer. There were mobiles composed of huge, luminous dice cubes suspended from the shallow dome of the ceiling. There were almost garish murals depicting court cards not only from Terran packs but from those used by other races in the galaxy addicted to their own forms of gambling. Grimes saw the Golden Hive, analogous to the human card player's Ace, and the Queen Mother, and the Princess, and the Drone, and the Worker-Technician. So the Shaara frequented this establishment. Gambling was one vice that they held in common with Man.

"When you've finished admiring the Art Gallery, Captain," said the Port Doctor, "we'll go in. There's a small charge at the door. Did you bring any money with you?"

"Yes," said Grimes. "I suppose that they'll take Federation credits . . ."

"They'll take anything as long as it's legal tender on its planet of origin. I'm not being mean, you understand, in asking you to pay us in. It's just that I've always found that if somebody else treats me it always starts my winning streak for the night."

"Mphm. But what about me?"

"For you there's beginner's luck."

"Mphm." Grimes was unconvinced but allowed himself to be led to the tall blonde standing at the door. She was the first decorously clad female he had seen since landing at Port Aphrodite. It made a change. (There was no change from the Cr50 bill that he tendered.) She was severely attired in an ankle length black skirt, in a long-sleeved, high-collared white blouse with a black string tie. There was a black bow in her hair. She smiled with professional warmth and wished the two men luck.

"What first?" asked the doctor. "Two up? That's your national game, isn't it?"

"Tucker," said Grimes.

"Tucker? What sort of game is that?" Comprehension dawned. "Oh, it's *food* you mean. But we didn't come here to eat."

"I did," said Grimes. He thought, *I may as well try to get my fifty credits worth.*

"Oh, all right. This way."

The doctor led Grimes through the huge room, past the roulette tables with the croupiers in their archaic black and white uniforms and the players dressed in everything from stiffly formal to wildly informal attire, pausing only to stop a robot servitor trundling by with a tray of drinks. He took a whisky for himself, sipped and remarked condescendingly, "Not as good as yours, Captain." Grimes helped himself to gin.

They continued through a smaller but still large chamber in which the Two Up school was in progress. Grimes wondered what coins were being used: they looked to be the same size as antique Australian pennies. He was tempted to linger but one effect that soberup capsules always had on him was to stimulate his appetite. There were card rooms and others for dice, and others in which brightly coloured sparks chased each other around enormous screens. Most, although not all, of the gamblers were human.

At last they came to the buffet. There were long tables loaded with the kind of food that looks like advertisements for itself, that sometimes—but not always—tastes as good as it looks. There was a towering drinks dispenser with a control panel that would not have looked out of place on the bridge of a Nova Class battlewagon.

The doctor made straight for this and, with the ease of long practice, pushed the buttons for a treble whisky. Grimes picked up a plate and browsed. Was that caviare? It was. It probably had not come all the way from the Caspian Sea on Earth—from Atlantia? or New Maine?—but it was edible. And those things like thin, pallid worms weren't at all bad . . . And neither was the pork fruit salad, although this was at its best only on Caribbea, the world to which that strange organism, neither animal nor vegetable, was native.

Munching happily, he watched a tall, slim Shaara princess indulging her taste for alcoholic sweetmeats. He had seen a party of Shaara at one of the roulette tables, doubtless she was of their number. He had always rather liked the bee people, still did—with reservations. (He would never forget what he had suffered at the hands—claws? talons?—of that Rogue Queen.) He said to her affably, "They don't starve us here, Highness."

She turned to look at him with her huge, faceted eyes. The voice that came from the jewelled box strapped to her thorax was a pleasant soprano.

"Indeed they do not, sir. And no matter what my Queen Captain may say or do, I believe in getting value for my money."

Her Queen Captain . . . So she must be one of the officers from the Shaara ship in port.

"Are you on a cruise?" Grimes asked.

"Yes." If she had been endowed with a mouth instead of mandibles she would have smiled. "The ship is a hive with more queens than workers. And are you a spaceman, sir? You have the appearance."

"Yes, Highness. I am master of the little ship berthed between you and the TG wagon."

Her eyes glared at him like multiple lasers. "So your ship is *Little Sister.* So you are the man Grimes."

What had he said wrong?

"You are Grimes. My hive sisters were the Queen Captain and her officers in the ship *Baroom.* We have heard only rumours of what happened but we believe that you destroyed that vessel."

After what they did to Tamara and myself, and to lots of other people, thought Grimes, *they had it coming to them.*

But he said nothing and she said nothing more. They stood there, glaring at each other, astronauts both, with much in common professionally but culturally a universe apart. (But was there such a difference? Terran adventurers, both before and after the dawn of the Space Age, have behaved as reprehensibly as did that Rogue Queen.)

The princess turned her back to him and walked stiffly away, her iridescent wings quivering with rage.

Grimes moved on, in the other direction. The acrimonious encounter had spoiled his appetite. He wandered through a door other than the one by which he had entered, found himself in a room full of game machines.

He had always liked such contraptions.

He liked to match wits with computers in simulated space battles but he looked in vain for such entertainment here. The names shining—some softly, some garishly—above the glowing screens made it obvious that the devices had been manufactured for use on New Venusberg, possibly had been made on the pleasure planet. LOVE MARATHON . . . WHIP THE LADY . . . CHAIN ME TIGHT . . . And in the screens themselves, although none of the machines was fully activated, there were hints of pale, sinuously writhing limbs, of rounded breasts and buttocks.

CHASE ME AND . . .

The broadly hinting label appealed to Grimes. To play the game, he discovered, would cost him only a single one credit coin. He went to a change maker, inserted a twenty credit bill into the slot. Silver coins rattled into the receptacle. But they were not coins, only tokens, each bearing on both sides Lady Luck's stylised roulette wheel. Presumably they could be spent only in this establishment.

Grimes pocketed all the metal discs but one, went back to the machine of his choice. There were no manual controls. There was a sort of padded hood into which he was to insert his head with eyepieces that looked into a replica of the overhead screen. This depicted only what looked like the back view of a naked woman regarded through a heavy mist. He withdrew, located the coin slot, inserted the token then put his head back into the hood.

The screen came alive.

There was a naked woman—slender, but not too much so—with her back to him. She was standing in a forest glade, her pale skin in vivid contrast to the dark foliage of trees and bushes. Grimes was naked too; he could feel the air cool on his skin, the grass damp under his feet. Suddenly this female whose face he had yet to see became the most desirable object in all the universe. He would creep up on her, throw her to the ground and . . .

He must have made some slight, betraying noise.

She turned her head, looked back at him over her smooth shoulder. Her face, framed by long, golden hair, was more than merely pretty, her eyes a wide, startled blue, her mouth a wide, scarlet gash. Her expression combined fear and invitation.

She ran.

Grimes ran.

She was fast and Grimes, he realised, was badly out of condition. But those creamy buttocks, those long thighs, fantastically beautiful in motion, drew him like a powerful magnet.

She ran.

Grimes ran.

He was gaining on her.

He would catch her when she blundered into that bush with the great, purple blossoms.

At the very last moment she changed direction, veering sharply to the right. Grimes was not able to check himself. The shrub, as well as blossoms, bore very sharp thorns.

He extricated himself, cursing. He could feel the blood trickling down his lacerated skin. And she was standing there, legs apart, hands on hips, laughing.

There was only one thing to do to her . . .

But she evaded his clutching hands as she turned, running again, flitting between the trees like a pale wraith. He was after her, losing ground at first then gaining until he stumbled over a tree root; the pain in his bare foot was excruciating. She paused then, looking back, laughing again. Her teeth were very white against the scarlet of her lips.

She let him almost reach her, then was off again.

And they were out of the wood.

Ahead there was a low hill and on its summit there was a building—a temple? White, it was, with pillars, bright against the somehow ominous dark blue sky. Grimes *knew* that he must catch her before she reached this sanctuary.

He would have done so had it not been for the swamp between hill and forest. She knew the path across it, leaping gracefully from grassy hummock to grassy hummock. He did not. He was knee-deep, thigh-deep in stinking ooze before he realised that he must keep to those patches of longer, darker grass, as she was doing.

But she wanted to be caught.

She waited for him on solid ground, laughing still, legs wide-spread, small, pink-nippled breasts provocative.

She waited for him until he had almost gained solidity then turned again, running up the hill. Grimes pursued, his heart thudding, his lungs pumping. He actually got a hold on the long, golden hair floating behind her—and it came away in his hand. Beneath the wig was golden hair again, but short.

She vanished into the colonnade.

Stupidly Grimes stood there.

Should he follow?

Should he withdraw his head from the hood?

Later he wished that he had done so at this juncture.

They boiled out of the temple, the women, vicious, naked, sharp in tooth and claw. Jane Pentecost he recognised, and the Princess Marlene. There were Una Freeman and Maya, Mavis and Maggie Lazenby. And Michelle d'Estang and fat Susie. And the obnoxious Fenella Pruin as she had been when she derided him after his failure, and Tamara Haverstock . . .

He turned, pounded down the hill.

He could hear them after him, their surprisingly heavy feet, their shrill, hateful screams. He reached the edge of the swamp. He made a leap to the first little hummock, landed on it, stood there teetering for long, long seconds before jumping for the next.

He missed it.

And they were on him.

Their sharp teeth, their long fingernails were tearing his skin and the flesh beneath it. Their discordant laughter was loud in his ears. There was screaming, too—and loudest of all was his own.

The screen went blank, but he remained crouching there, his forehead pressed into the padding of the hood. His clothing was soaked in perspiration—and worse.

The screen went blank—but the hateful female laughter persisted.

Slowly he withdrew his head, looked around.

Fenella Pruin was there, the embarrassed looking Port Captain by her side. With a visible effort she stopped laughing.

"Grimes, Grimes . . . What an imagination you have! But do I *really* look like that in your eyes? A sort of nudist Dracula's daughter?"

"You watched in the monitor screen . . ." half asked, half stated Grimes.

"Of course. It's what it's for, isn't it?"

"But you didn't see . . . me . . ."

"But we did, Grimes. We did—although you're far better looking and far better endowed in your perverted imagination than you are in actuality. And we saw what happened to you. Proper bloody it was, too." She turned to her escort. "Why don't you see if you can do any better, Jock? Go on, be a sport. I'll pay."

"No," said the Port Captain. *"No."*

"Goodnight," said Grimes.

Acutely and miserably aware of the state of his clothing he turned away from them, slunk through the gambling halls and down to the subway station. He did not have long to wait for a car back to Port Aphrodite.

The Customs guard at his airlock was far too cheerful.

"You look like you've had a fine night on the tiles, Captain!" he laughed.

"It was interesting," said Grimes shortly as he retreated into his own little sanctuary.

Five

He stripped off his soiled clothing, had a long, hot shower. Cleansed, he was beginning to feel better. And hungry. He went into the little galley and assembled a thick, multitiered sandwich, opened a can of cold beer. He carried these refreshments to his part of the main cabin, put them down on the deck by his bunk. He stretched out and then, his body disposed like that of an ancient Roman banqueter, munched and gulped. He almost finished the sandwich but was suddenly asleep before all the beer was gone.

He dreamed, re-enacting the game—but this time he caught the girl before she reached the temple. This time her hair did not come away in his hand. He turned her around, threw her to the ground, fell heavily upon her. His right knee prised her thighs apart. He . . .

The loud ringing of a bell jerked him back to reality.

Action Stations!

Then he realised where he was and that the noise was being made by somebody seeking admission to *Little Sister*. He got out of his bunk, reached for and shrugged into a light robe. The bell went on ringing, in short, irritable bursts.

He went aft to the airlock, operated the local controls. Prunella Fenn stood there, glaring at him. "You keep a tight ship," she snarled sardonically. "Are you afraid that the wild, wild women will come and get you?" She brushed past him, looked down at the remnants of his supper. "Didn't I hear somewhere that your Survey Service nickname was Gutsy Grimes?" She stooped to pick up the can of now-flat beer, sniffed it disdainfully. "I could do with a drink myself—but not this gnat's piss. Fix me one, will you? A large brandy on one, small rock."

"I wasn't expecting you back," said Grimes.

"Surely you weren't expecting me to spend all night with that fat, boring slob? But the drink, Grimes. Now."

He went to the galley, poured a generous measure of brandy over one ice cube. She snatched it from him without thanks.

He said, "I'll rig the privacy screen."

"Don't bother," she told him. "I want to talk."

She gulped from her glass, put it down on the table and started to undress. There was nothing at all sensual about the display, not the merest hint of invitation. There were bruises, Grimes noted clinically, on the pale skin of her upper thighs. She saw what he was looking at, laughed shortly.

"There are times when a girl has to suffer to get a story. Or to get a lead . . ."

She picked up the glass again, sat down on her bed, facing him.

She said, "I think that I shall be able to blow the lid off two very unsavoury rackets. Soon I shall have the makings of a couple or three stories that will have readers and viewers all over the galaxy literally *drooling.* There's white slavery—that's been a sure seller for centuries. The others are even better . . ."

"Better?" echoed Grimes.

"You can bet your boots it is. Why do you think that the Shaara come here?"

"For the gambling?" hazarded Grimes.

"More than that. You told me yourself that the Shaara—or some of them—are voyeurs."

"Nothing especially sensational in that. You're a voyeur yourself. *You* watched what was happening to me in that damned machine."

"But that wasn't for real, was it? Anyhow, *you* should know what the Shaara are capable of. Didn't you and that postmistress wench have a rough time when you were prisoners of that Rogue Queen? The Shaara like to humiliate, torture even, other intelligent beings—but such practices are frowned upon on their own planets. *Here* they can indulge their vices. Money—enough money—can buy anything."

"I can't quite believe that even on New Venusberg human beings could make a profit from allowing their fellow men and women to be tortured."

"Grow up, Grimes! I've heard that you're something of an amateur historian—so you should know the extent of the evil of which humanity is capable. But you spacemen, for all your phoney machismo, lead very sheltered lives, know almost nothing about the *real* universe. There's a lot more to it than the clean, empty spaces between the stars!

"Anyhow, this commercialised sadism ties in with the white slave racket. Innocent little bitches—yes, and innocent little puppies—recruited on backward planets (and some not so backward) and brought here to make their fortunes (they think!) on fabulous Venusberg. An old friend of yours, Drongo Kane, is in the business up to his eyebrows . . ."

"That bastard!" growled Grimes.

"Jock told me that one of the ships Kane *owns—Willy Willy—*is due in shortly from a world called New Alice . . . I sort of gained the impression that he wasn't supposed to talk about it—but you know what men are like. When they're trying to make a girl they tend to boast, to show how big they are, how important. But there's only one way of being big that counts."

"Mphm."

"Where is New Alice? What sort of world is it?"

"I haven't a clue."

"You're the expert. Or supposed to be. You were hired as such."

"I still haven't a clue," growled Grimes. He got up from his bunk and padded to the playmaster, set the controls so that it was hooked up to the memory bank of the ship's computer. He hit the question mark symbol on the keyboard, then typed NEW ALICE.

The reply appeared in glowing letters in the screen: NO DATA.

Fenella Pruin laughed. "That thing is as useless as you are."

Grimes' prominent ears flushed angrily. He said, "This memory bank, especially insofar as navigational data is concerned, is as good as anything in a battleship."

"So *you* say." She yawned, not bothering to hide her gaping mouth with her hand. "Another drink, then I'll be ready for a spot of shut-eye. And don't *you* come mauling me. I've had enough of that for one night."

He refilled her glass. She downed its contents in one gulp; some of the amber spirit dribbled down her chin and on to her breasts. Grimes felt no desire to lick it off. She stretched out on her bunk, not bothering to cover herself. Grimes stretched out on his, operated the switch at its head that dimmed the cabin lights.

She went to sleep almost at once, snoring not unmusically.

He found it hard to get off again. Two names kept flashing before his mind's eye like an advertising sign: DRONGO KANE. NEW ALICE.

He already knew far too much about Kane—but where the hell was New Alice?

Six

Even after a late and disturbed night Grimes was inclined to be an early riser. He did not always greet the dawn with a song, however; this was such a non-choral occasion. He ungummed his eyelids, looked up blearily at the golden deckhead. He had omitted to close various doors before retiring and the morning sunlight was streaming through the control cab viewports, was reflected from burnished metal. He groaned softly. He slowly pushed the bed cover down from his body, swung his feet to the deck. He looked across to Fenella Pruin's bunk. She was still sleeping, her right forearm covering her eyes and most of her face. The rest of her was uncovered. If Grimes had been feeling stronger he would have been sexually stirred by the sight of her naked body, as it was he felt only disgust. In her sluttish posture, with the dark bruises on the skin of her inner thighs, she looked *used.* And used, moreover, by that fat slob of a Port Captain.

He padded aft to the little galley, switched on the coffee maker. After a second or so he was able to draw a steaming mug of the dark fluid. He added sugar, stirred. He sipped cautiously. He felt a little stronger. He allowed the coffee to cool slightly, then gulped and swallowed.

"Must you make that disgusting noise at this jesusless hour?"

He looked around. Fenella Pruin was sitting up in her bed, glaring at him.

"And you might put something on," she added. "Your hairy arse isn't the sort of sight that I like to wake up to."

Grimes muttered something about pots and kettles.

She ignored this. "And what's that you're drinking? Don't you ever stop stuffing yourself?"

"Coffee."

"Why didn't you say so before? Well, you can bring me some. With cream. And sugar. You know how I like it."

Grimes did know. More than once during the voyage from Bronsonia he had wondered if he were owner-master or cabin steward; the Pruin had been determined to get her—or her employer's—money's worth. He made coffee to her requirements, brought it to her. As he handed her the mug he was strongly tempted to slop some of the scalding fluid over her uncovered breasts. She snatched it from him ungraciously and a few drops were spattered on to her stomach.

"You clumsy oaf!" she snarled.

He did not feel obliged to apologise. He left her mopping her belly with the bed cover and went to the minuscule bathroom. After he had showered and depilated and all the rest of it he walked back to his side of the main cabin, ignoring the way in which she glowered at him. He took a brightly patterned civilian shirt from its hanger in his locker, hesitated between a pair of orange shorts and a kilt in the astronauts' tartan, gold, blue and silver on black. He decided on the shorts; he was never really happy in a kilt.

"A sight for sore eyes," she remarked sourly. "You're making mine sore. Going some place?"

"Probably. Do you want breakfast?"

"Two four minute hen's eggs, with buttered toast. Orange juice. Coffee."

There was no *please*.

"We're out of fresh eggs but the autochef can do you scrambled eggs or an omelette."

"Why are we out of fresh eggs?"

"Because I haven't ordered any stores yet."

"Why not? In my girlish innocence I assumed that the service in a chartered spaceship would be slightly superior to that in an Epsilon Class tramp."

"If your friend the Port Captain and the others hadn't been underfoot all day yesterday . . ."

"If *you* hadn't made such a pig of yourself every breakfast time there'd have been some eggs left."

The bells rang. Somebody was outside the ship seeking admission.

"See who it is!" she snapped.

Grimes went to the airlock, opened both doors. The Port Captain was there. His face was still florid but it was an unhealthy looking flush. His gorgeous uniform looked sleazy. More than ever he looked like the doorman of a brothel rather than a spaceman.

"Morning," he grunted. "Miss Fenn on board?"

"Where else, Captain McKillick? But come aboard. This is Liberty Hall, you can spit on the mat and call the cat a bastard."

"You can't come aboard until I'm presentable," called Fenella Pruin.

"Miss Fenn's not dressed yet," said Grimes.

"That doesn't worry me," said the Port Captain, managing a faint leer. "I don't suppose that it worries you either."

"It doesn't," said Grimes.

"You can say that again!" came the voice from within *Little Sister*. "Whoever perpetuates that myth about big, strong, virile spacemen wouldn't know if a big black dog was up him!"

Grimes' prominent ears reddened. The Port Captain superimposed an angry flush on his normally ruddy complexion. (After all he was—or had been—a spaceman himself.)

But he said, "I like a woman with a little fire in her."

"Mphm," grunted Grimes.

"Last night for example . . ."

"Mphm?"

"Never kiss and tell, eh, Captain? I can take a hint. But that dance she did at the Kathouse put the professionals to shame. In fact Katie told her that she'd give her a job if she ever wanted one. It was the business with the bottle and the two wine glasses that really impressed her, though . . ."

Grimes active imagination treated him to a series of lubricious mind pictures.

"When you've quite finished gossiping like a couple of old women you can come in," called Fenella Pruin.

Not only had she made herself presentable but had actually tidied up the main cabin. Inflatable chairs were set around the collapsible table, on which stood the golden coffee pot and its accessories. She was wearing an ankle length dress of patterned spidersilk, grey on grey, under which it was obvious that she was naked. From the neck down there was nothing at all wrong with her.

"Good morning, Jock," she said with spurious sweetness. "Coffee?"

"Thank you, Prue."

"Breakfast?" asked Grimes, whose belly was rumbling.

"I've had mine. Such as it was."

"Well, I'm having mine. Miss Fenn?"

"You mentioned omelets earlier . . . Something savoury if your autochef can manage it."

Grimes went into the galley to initiate the process of cookery. He could overhear the conversation.

"Last night—or early this morning—I asked Captain Grimes about that world you told me about. New Alice. He didn't know a thing, of course. Nor did his computer."

The Port Captain laughed. "Hardly surprising. It's one of Drongo Kane's secrets. My guess is that it's a Lost Colony that he's keeping to himself."

"A fine, profitable source of slave labour. Or white slave labour."

"Not that, Prue. The girls are paid. They aren't *slaves*."

"But they are exploited. I noticed last night that they were in great demand.

Of course some men would find those oddly shaped legs of theirs very attractive . . . Do you suppose that they're mutants? Like those wenches from Heffner with two pairs of breasts . . ."

"Just a stroll down mammary lane," said Grimes, bringing in the omelets.

"Ha," said Fenella Pruin. "Ha, bloody ha! I am rolling on the deck in paroxysms of uncontrolled mirth."

"Ha," growled Grimes. "Ha, bloody ha."

"Give me my breakfast and stop the bloody clowning."

"Actually," said the Port Captain, adopting the role of peacemaker, "it was rather neat. Mammary lane, I mean. Our genes or chromosomes or whatever—I'm only a spaceman, not a biologist—must hold the memories of all the stages of evolution through which we, as a race, have passed . . ."

"Thanks for the mammary," said Grimes.

"You get on my tits," snarled the Pruin.

"But these females with the odd legs," Grimes persisted, "what sort of hair do they have?"

"Just hair," the Port Captain told him. "Reddish brown mostly, in the usual places."

"Mphm." Grimes admitted that he had been adding two and two to make five. He had been more than half way to the assumption that there was no such world as New Alice, that Drongo Kane was recruiting on Morrowvia. But the description of the exotic wenches in Katy's Kathouse didn't fit. Morrowvian women were perfectly formed, although their hair was like a cat's fur and could be any of the feline colourations, even to tortoiseshell.

Meanwhile Fenella Pruin had wolfed her omelet. She got to her feet, saying, "I'm ready for the road, Jock. Oh, Grimes, fix your front door so that it lets *me* in. I'm not sure what time I shall be back."

"I have to record your voice pattern."

"Then do it."

After she had spoken into the microphone she said to Grimes, "Why don't you have a look at Katy's Kathouse? You seemed interested enough."

Somehow it was more of an order than a suggestion. She was sniffing out something, something that stank, and he was appointed apprentice bloodhound.

Seven

It was too early in the day, he thought, to go cathouse crawling. Surely there must be some way of occupying the time on this planet during daylight hours. There was a pile of brochures on board, left by the boarding party; neither he nor Fenella Pruin had gotten around to studying these. He found them under her bunk. He leafed through them. Most of them advertised after-dark attractions but a few catered for those not sleeping off the previous night's debauchery.

New Bali Beach . . . ?

It looked promising. His wardrobe did not include swimming trunks but, if the photographs of the seaside resort were to be believed, such attire would not be necessary. But money would be. Those waterside cafés, with beautiful, naked people sitting under gaily coloured umbrellas sipping their long drinks and nibbling their exotic foods, looked extremely expensive. Most of the advance monies given to him by *The Bronson Star* had gone to pay his outstanding debts on Bronsonia. Fenella Pruin had plenty of money with her—there was a huge wad of currency in *Little Sister*'s safe—but there would be a most distressing scene if he helped himself to a small loan. She would have to give him some sooner or later; if she wanted him to assist her in her muckraking she would have to pay his expenses. But he doubted if she would be willing to treat him to a day at the seaside.

He decided to take his lunch with him.

In the galley he constructed a pile of thick sandwiches; the ham that he had purchased back on Bronsonia wasn't at all bad and there was a cheese with character. He decanted chilled wine into an insulated flask. He put the food and the drink into a shoulder bag.

He decided to call the Port Doctor before leaving the ship, got through without trouble on *Little Sister*'s NST radio to the spaceport switchboard. An attractive redhead told him that Dr MacLaren was free and would take his call. Then MacLaren scowled at him from the little screen.

"Oh, it's *you,* Captain Grimes. Where the hell did you get to last night?"

"I couldn't find you, so I went back to the ship."

"You didn't look very hard. And I *needed* you, man. A combination of your beginner's luck and my system and we'd have cleaned up. As it was . . ."

"Mphm."

"Well, what can I do for you?"

"I was thinking of going out to New Bali for the day."

"I'm not stopping you."

"I thought that you might know something about the place."

"I went there once and didn't like it. Is that all?"

So the Good Doctor, thought Grimes, was blaming him for his previous night's losses. Subsidised by Grimes, he would be convinced, he would have been able to ride out the bad run and would have won a fortune on the ensuing good one. It was just too bad—but Grimes still had most of *his* money in his pocket.

"I'll be seeing you," said Grimes, terminating the conversation.

He left the ship, exchanged a few words with the bored Customs guard, then walked to the subway station. There were few signs of life about the spaceport. The liners, like huge, lazy beasts, were drowsing in the warm sunlight and somnolence would also be the order of the day inside the great, shining hulls. Grimes felt virtuous.

In bright daylight the entrance to the station looked very tawdry. That tawdriness was somehow passed on to the advertisements on either side of the escalator and on the platform. He found one that was not a depiction of fleshly delights but a map of the railway system. He discovered that he would have to take a Number 9 car.

He did not have long to wait for it. He was the only passenger. He reflected that there was one great advantage of public transport; nobody had to worry about whether or not it was making a profit. To pass the time on the journey he read the paper that he had obtained from the automatic dispenser, a neatly folded packet of news sheets. lt should have been free; there were far more advertisements than news items.

Spacemanlike, he turned first to the shipping information. He noted that *Little Sister,* Captain John Grimes, Far Traveller Couriers, with passengers, was in port. *Passengers?* He supposed that "passenger" would have looked rather absurd. And *Broorooroo,* Queen-Captain Shrim, Shaara Interstellar Transport, was in. And *Taiping,* Trans-Galactic Clippers, Captain Pavel. And . . .

But who was due?

Delta Geminorum, Captain Yamamoto, Interstellar Transport Commission, passengers and general cargo. *Empress of Scotia,* Captain Sir Hector Macdonald, Waverley Royal Mail, cruise. *Rim Wyvern,* Captain Engels, Rim Runners, bulk fluids.

And *Willy Willy,* Captain Dreeble, Able Enterprises, passengers.

So . . .

He turned to the social columns.

He learned that the charming Miss Prunella Fenn, of Bronsonia, was being escorted around the night spots by Port Captain Jock McKillick and that Queen-Commissioner Thrum, from Shreell, was still enjoying her holiday on New Venusberg. The photograph of Fenella Pruin made her look almost beautiful.

There was a crossword puzzle. The answer to every clue was either obscene or anatomical or both. Grimes, who was fond of word games, was able to solve it without too much mental strain. After all, that ancient Nilotic peasant with his Spanish uncle engaged in non-productive intercourse was obvious enough . . .

The car arrived at his station. He disembarked. There was the usual platform with the usual advertising, the usual escalator.

He emerged on to a wide promenade, paved with some veined, polished stone. Landward were buildings, shops mainly, few higher than one storey, their wide windows agleam with the merchandise on display. Further inland was a tower—a hotel?—that was a huge and unashamed phallic symbol. On the other side of the wide walkway was the beach—dazzling white sand, gaudy sun umbrellas, sprawling human and humanoid bodies ranging in colour from pink to the darkest brown. It was all very nice but it was nothing like Bali as he remembered that island, even though the trees that cast their shade over the walk were not dissimilar to Terran palms.

He stood there for a few moments taking his bearings. He watched a trio approaching him. There was a man, uglily obese, with his skin burned to an ugly pink, naked save for the straps of the cameras and recorders slung about his torso. There were two girls, tall, slim brunettes, each clothed in golden tan, with golden chains about their waists, with golden anklets and bracelets, with jewels gleaming between their breasts, in their navels and in their pubic hair. Before they reached him they turned to look into the window of a jeweller's shop. They went inside. Grimes wondered how the tourist was going to pay for more ornaments for his mercenary girlfriends, came to the conclusion that one of those camera cases must really be a money pouch.

More naked pedestrians passed him. The outworlders were easy to spot, even though some of them, male and female, were quite well made. They, apart from their cameras and money pouches, were . . . naked. Although splendidly nude the local boys and girls were all dressed up like Christmas trees.

He walked across the promenade. Next to the wide steps down to the beach was one of those expensive looking cafés. There was a showcase outside with representations—wax or plastic?—of the various edibles and potables on sale, together with prices. Grimes congratulated himself on his foresight; having brought his lunch with him he would not have to beggar himself by paying a minor monarch's ransom for a ham sandwich. But he did hire a beach umbrella. The price he paid for a few hours' use of the thing could have purchased at least two similar articles on most worlds. He kicked off his sandals, picked them up and walked towards the sea. Some of the supine or prone ladies turned their heads to follow his progress but soon lost interest. Perhaps, he thought, there had been some mutation on New Venusberg resulting in X-ray vision so that these wenches could ascertain at a glance how much money was in his slim wallet . . .

A few metres from the water's edge he drove the ferrule of his umbrella into the sand then opened it. He stripped, enjoying the feel of the sunlight on his bare skin; as he always made daily use of *Little Sister*'s ultra violet lamp there would be no risk of sunburn. Putting his shoulder bag and clothing in the shade of the parasol he walked down to the sea. There was almost no wind and the incoming waves were mere ripples. He waded out until he was chest-deep and then let himself fall forward. He struck out with arms and legs, but lazily, making deliberately slow progress through the slightly too warm water. He turned so that he was swimming parallel to the shore so that he could keep an eye on his possessions. He did not think that there was any danger of theft but it would be rather embarrassing if he were obliged to return to his ship naked and penniless.

He began to feel thirsty.

He waded out from the sea, back to the bright umbrella. He opened his bag, took out the insulated flask. The wine was delicious. He unwrapped a sandwich. That was good too. He noticed that people around him were looking at him disdainfully—the elegant, bejewelled girls who had already made assessment of his comparative poverty, the muscular, deeply tanned, well endowed young men. He heard them talking to the tourists whom they were with, the plump matrons and the pot-bellied males. He heard laughter that had a derisive edge to it.

Fuck 'em, he thought. There was no law that said that he must spend his hard-earned money on this clip joint of a planet. He wiped his mouth with the back of his hand and then, to compound the deliberate coarseness, the back of his hand on his right buttock. He stretched out on his back, using his bag for a pillow. After smoking a soothing pipe he surrendered himself to the drowsy warmth, slid into unconsciousness.

He was not asleep for long.

He was awakened by a steady droning noise coming from overhead. He opened his eyes, looked up. It was a party of Shaara flying over the beach, two princesses and three drones, their wings an iridescent blur in the sunlight. One of them swooped low, her huge-faceted eyes staring down at Grimes. Then the party veered inland, making a descent at the beachside café.

"Even *they* can afford to buy a drink," Grimes heard one of the girls in his vicinity say to her portly male companion. The tourist muttered in reply that spacebums should be confined to their ships.

Fuck 'em, thought Grimes again.

He was just dozing off when the Shaara came back over him. He woke up with an unplesant start when the soft containers that had held some sticky, sickly smelling confection, that were no more than three quarters empty, spattered down on to his naked body.

He scrambled to his feet, cursing. He would have thrown something at the retreating Shaara if they had not been already out of range. He glared around at the grinning faces of the other sunbathers. Then, with what dignity he could muster, he walked into the sea to wash off the slimy mess.

When he came out of the water a darkly tanned, heavily muscled young man, naked save for a white brassard with BP in black, carrying a shoulder bag, strode up to him. He pointed sternly to the scum on the surface of the water, the shreds of plastic, and demanded, "Did *you* do that?"

"I was bombed," said Grimes.

"Inebriation, no matter how induced is no excuse for pollution," said the beach patrolman.

"I was bombed, I'm telling you."

"I heard you the first time. The fine will be one hundred Federation credits, or the equivalent, if paid on the spot. Otherwise you will have to appear in court."

"But these people," argued Grimes, with a sweeping gesture of his arm, "can tell you . . ."

"He made a mess all over himself," said one of the girls, "and then went to wash it off in our clean sea."

"The Shaara . . ." insisted Grimes.

"Come off it, fellow. Whoever heard of one of *them* going into the water? But I haven't got all day to waste on you. Are you paying up—if you *can* pay—or are you coming with me to be charged?"

Grimes paid up.

Then he dressed and returned to *Little Sister.*

Eight

He spent the remaining daylight hours catching up with his housekeeping. He called the Port Aphrodite provedores and ordered a few items of consumable stores, including the fresh hen's eggs that his passenger had been pining for. These were delivered almost at once. When he signed the bill he wondered if those cackleberries came from the fabulous goose but they were neither large nor aureately shelled.

When everything had been stowed away he cleaned up, then dialled a simple but satisfying meal on the autochef—rare steak and onions with French fried potatoes, a hot, crisp roll with cheese and salad. Presumably refreshments would be available at Katy's Kathouse but he could not be sure if it would be free, or included in the price of admission. He suspected that it would be hellishly expensive—but if it did happen to be gratis he could always find room for a substantial supper.

He attired himself in semi-formal evening wear—ruffled white shirt, sharply creased black trousers, highly polished, calf-length black boots. Normally he did not much care for dressing up; his assumption of the modest finery was, perhaps, a reaction to the humiliation of the afternoon.

He let himself out of the ship, passed the time of day briefly with the Customs guard, walked slowly across the spaceport apron to the subway station. The evening was warm. The sky was dark and clear and in it floated an advertising balloon, spotlit from below, that was a quite explicit depiction of a naked woman. She was, thought Grimes, definitely pneumatic . . . In the soft lighting the station entrance was once again erotic rather than blatantly pornographic. It promised more, much more, than could ever be attained on a highly commercialised pleasure planet such as this.

Other pleasure seekers were abroad, proceeding in the same direction as himself—passengers from the cruise liners, spacemen and -women. He rode down on the escalator behind a fat man and two plump, no-longer-young ladies. He could not help overhearing their conversation.

"You really should have come out to the beach with us, William. Laugh? I thought I'd die! There was this man, a spacer. No, not from our ship, but a penny pincher all the same. You know the type. Lording it aboard their tin cans in their pretty uniforms and generous as hell with their entertainment allowance grog but too mean to spend a cent when they get ashore. He'd actually brought his lunch with him. In a *bag!* And then there he was, soaking up the sun—that was free!—when these Shaara flew over. They zoomed in to that rather nice eatery and ordered the sort of sweet, sticky muck that they like. And then they collected up all the *soggy* containers and took off and *bombed* the man. You should have seen his face! And I thought that his big, flapping ears were going to burst into flame . . ."

"People like that shouldn't go to places that they can't afford," said the man. "Oh, well. It taught him a lesson."

"He was taught a lesson, all right. He went down to the sea to wash himself off. Then the beach patrol came on the scene and fined him on the spot for polluting the ocean. When he pulled the money out of his wallet you'd have thought he was bleeding to death . . ."

"Spacemen," sneered the male tourist. "They're all the same. They spend practically all of their lives in their little, artificial worlds and just don't know how to behave themselves on the surface of a decent planet."

They reached the bottom of the escalator. Grimes followed the party of tourists on to the platform. The plump, improbable blonde, still chattering to her companions, turned to look at the advertisements on the wall and came face to face with the subject of her funny story. She froze in mid-sentence. She blushed spectacularly—her face, her neck, her shoulders, the overly full breasts that were revealed rather than concealed by the translucency of her dress. Her small mouth, which had been open, opened still wider.

Grimes looked at her coldly. He said politely, "I can set your mind at rest, madam. I could well afford that fine. I am the owner as well as the captain of *Little Sister.* You must have noticed her . . ."

"The *golden* ship," she whispered.

"Yes. The golden ship. As I have said, I could afford the fine. I just resented having to pay it in those circumstances."

(That last was true enough.)

He turned on his heel, walked away along the platform, his little triumph already turning sour. Was an eccentric billionaire—as that foolish, snobbish woman must now be regarding him—any better than a rough, poverty stricken spaceman?

The car came in. Grimes was one of the first to board. He noticed that the woman and her friends sat as far away from him as possible. He was among the first out at the Katy's Kathouse station. The plump blonde and the other two also disembarked but stayed well behind him.

The foyer of the Kathouse was at the head of the escalator. Grimes had been expecting something highly erotic but he was disappointed. Black-draped walls, a black ceiling . . . Faint, flickering light from tall, white candles . . . Vases of white flowers—natural? artificial?—that looked like lilies . . . A faint murmur of funereal organ music . . .

Was this the right place?

There was a pay booth by a black curtained doorway, manned by a cadaverous individual clad in rusty black with the merest hint of white at wrists and throat. Grimes approached this gentleman.

"Three hundred credits," croaked the doorkeeper.

"Does that include refreshments?" asked Grimes.

"Of course," he heard the plump lady whispering somewhere behind him, "the very rich are *mean* . . . That's how they get to be rich."

"Do you take us for a charitable institution?" the man asked rudely.

Grimes paid up, passed through the curtain.

Inside there was more darkness—but soft, rosy, caressing. A girl materialised before Grimes, her face and blonde hair pallidly luminous above her severe, chin to ankle black dress.

"A table, sir? For one?" Her voice was pleasant, her accent Carinthian. "Please to follow."

The lighting flared briefly and rosily and she was naked before him. Yes, she was Carinthian all right. Face and body had the Siamese cat sleekness that was the rule rather than the exception among the women of Carinthia. The lights dimmed and she was fully clothed again. A good trick, thought Grimes. He wondered how it was done. Some special quality of the fabric from which her dress was made and something fancy in the way of radiation? He let her lead him between the tables. The lights flared again. Of those seated some were briefly nude and some were not—the professional companions, probably, and the customers.

She brought him to a small table for two, ignited the black candle in its white holder of convoluted plastic with a flick of a long fingernail. Grimes was amused by the symbolism; there was only one thing that the candle holder could possibly represent.

He sat down in the chair that she pulled out for him, looked at the menu and the wine list under the transparency of the table top.

"A drink, sir? Something to eat?"

It was just as well, he thought, that he had dined before coming ashore. Katy was not as generous as Lady Luck; probably her overheads were higher and her profits less certain. Twenty credits for a cheese sandwich—and that was one of the least expensive items. Twenty five credits for a small bottle of locally brewed beer . . .

"Just a beer," he said. "The Venuswasser."

"May I order for myself, sir? I am required to eat and drink with you."

At whose expense? wondered Grimes. It was a question to which the answer was obvious. *And champagne,* he thought. *And caviar.* But what did it matter? He would put the bite on his charterer for whatever he paid; after all she had as good as ordered him to come here. And if his immediate funds ran out he could always use his First Galactic Bank credit card.

The candle holder, he saw, was also a microphone. The girl spoke softly into the folds of the vaginal orifice. She ordered his beer first. She ordered champagne—imported, of course. (Grimes thought sourly that probably only the label on the bottle would be imported.) She ordered steak. She slipped several notches in Grimes' estimation; he always held that the only possible tipple with red meat was a red wine.

She smiled at him as the revealing lights flared up again. He was prepared to forgive her for her taste in wine. Her pink nippled breasts were just right, neither too small nor too large.

"May I have a cigarette?" she asked.

"I'm sorry. I don't use them."

She spoke again into the microphone, adding a pack of Virginia Slims to the original order—another imported and therefore expensive luxury.

Then she said, "Shouldn't we get better acquainted? I'm Tanya."

"Good to know you, Tanya. I'm John."

"You're a spacer, John, aren't you?"

"I have that misfortune."

She laughed prettily. "Stop kidding. I've known quite a few spacers. I prefer them to tourists. But they're all the same. They like women—but their real mistresses are their ships . . ."

"Mphm . . ."

A waitress appeared with the order. A black, half mask with attached pointed ears gave her a vaguely feline appearance; otherwise she was naked. Her figure was lumpy. She would have to do something about it if ever she were to graduate to hostess grade.

Tanya dismissed the girl curtly, cutting short her attempt to be pleasant to Grimes. She moved away ungracefully, resentment glowering from her bobbing buttocks. Grimes regretted being stuck with the Carinthian woman as his companion for the evening; all too obviously—at least insofar as her own sex was concerned—she was not one of those legendary whores with a heart of gold.

While he sipped his beer—it wasn't bad although it had a rather odd flavour—he watched her eat and drink. He thought: And they call *me* Gutsy! He listened to the sensuous throb of the music that came from the concealed speakers. He looked around at the other tables. To judge from the overloud laughter, the attempts to sing in time to the background melody, inhibitions were being shed. He felt like shedding a few himself. That beer was deceptively strong. Was alcohol the only intoxicant in its composition?

Rosy spotlights set in the ceiling came on, their beams directed on to the stage at one end of the big room, creating an ellipse of relatively bright illumination. The music was suddenly much louder. The tune was oddly familiar although at first he could not identify it. The tempo was subtly wrong, the rhythm distorted. Then he recognised it. Anger accompanied recognition. Although he prided himself of having shed his regional chauvinism long since he resented the misuse of that good old national song as a dancehall melody.

The girls pranced on to the stage. Pranced? No, he decided, that was not quite the right word. Hopped? Perhaps, perhaps . . . Yet that word was not adequate to describe the animal grace with which the women moved. They were small-breasted, their legs were heavily muscled. Their navels were abnormally deep. It was those lower thighs that interested Grimes most. (He had always been a leg man rather than a titman.) There was something distinctly odd about the jointure—odd, but somehow familiar.

A stout woman strode on to the stage when the music stopped. Her ample breasts were almost spilling out of the low cut black dress that was a second skin over her too ample figure. Her face was chalky white under the flaming red hair, her mouth small despite the great slash of lipstick that unsuccessfully tried to create an illusion of generosity.

"Katy . . ." volunteered Tanya around a mouthful of steak.

"Who's for the kangaroo hunt?" bellowed Katy. "Pay yer money at the door to the dressing room! Only a thousand credits an' cheap at half the price! No extra charge for hire of costumes!"

"Kangaroo hunt?" Grimes asked Tanya.

"One of the specialties of the house," she told him, with a slight sneer. "Nature red in tooth and claw and all that." She looked him over. "No. I don't think that *you'd* go for games of that sort . . ."

But there was no shortage of volunteers. Men—tourists and spacers—were getting up from their tables, walking to the door to which Katy had gestured with her plump arm. They paid their money to the girl at the cash desk, went inside. On the stage the dancers were huddled together. They looked frightened but there was more than fear on their faces. Anticipation? Excitement?

There was music again—electronic yet disturbingly primeval and, to Grimes at least, evocative. He recognised the eery whispering of didgerydoos, the rhythmic clicking of singing sticks, the ominous, soughing bellow of bull roarers.

The first of the hunters came out from the dressing room. He was naked and the skin of his body had been painted black and that of his face in a ferocious design of white, red and yellow. He was carrying a spear. Grimes stared; surely it was not a real one. He was relieved to see that it was not. The shaft terminated not in a blade but a ball.

One by one the other intrepid hunters emerged. A few actually looked like real savages but most of them like what they really were, fat, soft men in fancy undress. Some were obviously embarrassed, a few were obviously eagerly looking forward to the hunt.

A tourist woman yelled, "If you could only see yourself, Wilberforce! I'll treasure this memory to my dying day!"

Katy called to her, "There'll be photographs on sale after the hunt, dearie!" Then, "All right you great black hunters! You've been told the rules! Go to it!"

The lights dimmed. The bodies of the naked women, still on the stage, were faintly luminous as were the painted faces of the hunters. The weird music continued and added to it there was a distant howling, no doubt the idea of whoever was playing the synthesiser as to what dingoes should sound like. The girls were shuffling nervously, uttering little, animal squeals.

A chill breeze blew through the vast room. Something made Grimes look up towards the ceiling. It now had the appearance of a black, clear sky with a scattering of bright stars. Only one constellation was recognisable and that only to Terrans—the Southern Cross.

The women were squealing more loudly now, jumping from the stage. They were crouching as they hopped, their hands held up to their breasts like forepaws. They scattered, bounding between the tables. One of them brushed by Grimes. Given a tail, he thought, she could have passed for a big, albino kangaroo.

The hunted were familiar with the terrain, the hunters were not. They blundered into tables, oversetting drinks. Some were deliberately tripped by the outstretched legs of friends or wives or mistresses. But the quarries would have to allow themselves to be run down eventually. That was their job. That was what they were being paid for.

The first "kill" was not far from where Grimes was sitting. The huntsman, running with his spear extended before him, just flicked his victim on the buttocks with the end of his weapon. She screamed—and it was a real scream. She fell face down, her body twitching.

The hunter yelled in triumph, pounced on to her, roughly turned her over, spreading her legs. He coupled with her brutally and briefly. He rolled off her, got unsteadily to his feet. Grimes stared disgustedly into the man's face. Even under the thick paint he thought that he could read shame. The man muttered something, shambled slowly towards the dressing room.

Grimes looked down at the girl, sprawling supine on the floor. She looked up at him. He was shocked by her expression, by the hopelessness of it. He wanted to say something comforting, to do something. He was half way out of his chair when Tanya stopped him.

"Don't waste sympathy on the little bitch," she said harshly. "She's making a damn sight better living here than she would be on her own lousy planet."

"And where is that?" asked Grimes.

"How should I know? There're girls here from all over the galaxy. None of us was pressganged."

"Mphm?"

"Of course not. Oh, I admit that getting back to Carinthia after I've made my pile won't be as easy as I thought it would be. Making my pile's the trouble. By the time I've paid the nominal—ha, ha!—rent for my room and bought a few rags and crusts there's not much left of my retaining fee. If it weren't for the generosity of tourists . . . And spacers . . ."

"Mphm."

"I'm being frank with you, John. If I take you up to my room I shall expect a present."

"I'm sorry," lied Grimes. "I have to be back aboard my ship soon. But if you can tell me anything about these girls there'll be a present for you."

"Cash on the nail," she said.

He went into a brief but intense session of mental arithmetic. There would be the bill for the meal and a tip for the waitress. Luckily he did not have to worry about paying his fare back to the spaceport. He extracted notes from his wallet, passed them to her.

"Is that all?" She shrugged. "Better than nothing, I suppose. Well, all I know about the big-bummed, flat-chested bitches is that they were brought here in Captain Dreeble's ship, the *Willy Willy.* They're under contract to Able Enterprises. Able Enterprises owns a big chunk of this Kathouse. Satisfied?"

"What language do they speak?"

"A sort of standard English. With an accent—rather like yours."

The lights were up again now. The last of the hunted girls had picked herself up from the floor and vanished from the room. The music was no longer eery but merely brassily strident. The stage was occupied by a giggling gaggle of tourist women, dancing lasciviously, tripping over the clothing that they were discarding. They were joined by a group of the hunters, still blackly and greasily naked.

Grimes waited for a while to see if anybody would be doing anything with a bottle and two wine glasses—but that must be, he decided, a party trick peculiar to Fenella Pruin. He asked Tanya to call for the bill. She did so. She scowled at him when he tipped the little waitress.

He said a not very warm goodnight to Tanya.

She said a not very warm goodnight to him.

There was no suggestion from either side that they should meet again.

He returned to his ship.

Nine

"And how did you find the Kathouse?" asked Fenella Pruin, regarding Grimes rather blearily over the breakfast table. Before he had time to reply she said, "These are bloody awful eggs. Where did you get them? Did you steal them out of a mud snake's nest?"

Grimes ignored this latter, answering only the first question.

"Expensive," he said. "You owe me . . ."

"I owe *you?* Come off it, buster!"

"I was helping you in your investigations . . ."

"You were having a bloody good time." She regarded him steadily, accorded him a derisive sneer. "Or were you? With your peculiar problem . . ."

"The fact remains," said Grimes, trying to ignore the burning of his ears, "that I had to pay my admission into the Kathouse. Then I was stuck with a bill for an expensive dinner . . ."

"For you and which floosie?"

"And then I purchased some information."

"Then spill it."

"What about my expenses?"

"You're a mercenary bastard, aren't you? All right. Let me have a detailed account, in writing, and I'll think about it. Get me some more coffee, will you? Then talk."

Grimes fetched more coffee.

He said, "In some ways the evening was disappointing. I didn't see anybody doing anything with a bottle and two wine glasses . . ."

She glared at him, snarled. "You don't have to believe everything that you hear—especially from that fat slob Jock McKillick! But did you see the specialty of the house, the kangaroo hunt?"

"Yes."

"Kangaroos are Australian animals, aren't they? You're an Australian. Was the hunt authentic?"

"Kangaroos aren't hunted. They're protected fauna."

"But they must have been hunted once. Centuries ago."

"I wasn't around then. Oh, all right, all right. I suppose that the hunt was an attempt to reconstruct a very ancient, long since dead nomadic culture. Of course, if I'd been stage managing it I'd have given the hunters woomeras and boomerangs . . ."

"What's a woomera? Some sort of weapon, I suppose."

"A spear thrower."

She laughed. "I can just imagine it. Lethal missiles mowing down Katy's customers . . ."

"It would be newsworthy," said Grimes. "Well, anyhow there was the weird music. As far as I know the Australian aboriginals didn't hunt to music—but those sounds did contribute to the atmosphere. The most convincing part of the hunt was the kangaroos themselves. Those girls with their odd legs . . . And it seems quite definite that they come from a world called New Alice and that they're brought here in Drongo Kane's ship, *Willy Willy.* The master is Aloysius Dreeble, who used to be Kane's mate in *Southerly Buster.*"

"And they come from New Alice. Anything Australian about that name?"

"Yes. Alice Springs is a city in Central Australia. It's referred to usually just as Alice or the Alice."

"And not for the first time—where the hell *is* New Alice? Nobody seems to know. Not even you."

"One person will know," said Grimes. "Captain Aloysius Dreeble. And his ship is due in very shortly."

"How do you know?"

"I read the papers," said Grimes smugly.

Ten

Willy Willy was not coming into Port Aphrodite. There was another spaceport on New Venusberg used only by vessels bringing cargoes of an objectionable nature, the bulkies and others. Presumably *Willy Willy* must be one of those others. It had not been hard to discover her arrival date and time. It has been easy enough to find out where Port Vulcan was situated. It was on Vulcan Island, the location for New Venusberg's industries—apart from the tourist industry, of course. There was a regular air service to and from the industrial complex but it was rarely, if ever, used by tourists. Holiday makers had better (or worse) things to do with their time than the inspection of automated factories.

Fenella Pruin said that it might excite suspicion if she and Grimes proceeded to Port Vulcan by a scheduled flight to watch *Willy Willy*'s arrival. It would be quite in character, however, if she, playing the role of a bored rich bitch, hired a camperfly for a few days for a leisurely drift around the scenic beauties of the pleasure planet. The camperflies were smallish aircraft with sleeping accommodation and cooking and toilet facilities. They were hybrid machines with helium gas cells incorporated in their thick wings and above their fuselages, slow but airworthy, suitable for handling by amateur pilots. They were so buoyant that it was quite impossible for them to come down hard. The girl in the Uflyit office was only mildly interested when Grimes produced his Master Astronaut's Certificate of Competency as proof that he was a capable pilot. She was much more interested in seeing that Fenella Pruin paid the quite enormous but returnable deposit.

It was a fine morning when Grimes and his passenger lifted off from Port Aphrodite. He had spent most of the previous day accustoming himself to the controls of the rented aircraft and then had retired early. Fenella Pruin had spent the day and most of the night with Captain McKillick. McKillick, looking very much the worse for wear, came to the Uflyit landing field, on the outskirts of the spaceport apron, to see them off.

He glared at Grimes from bloodshot cycs.

He said, "You know that I could have taken a few days leave, Prue, to pilot you around . . ."

She said, "And leave Grimes, here, to carry on boozing and wenching at my expense? Not bloody likely. I'm making him earn his keep."

"But he doesn't have the local knowledge that I have."

"He can read a chart. And it isn't as though we're going anywhere in particular. We shall just be bumbling around."

The Port Captain turned on Grimes.

"Look after her," he threatened with a touching show of devotion, "or I'll have your guts for a necktie when you get back!"

"Mphm," Grimes grunted.

He stood to one side and watched McKillick try to enfold the girl in a loving embrace. She did not cooperate; the wet kiss that should have plastered itself over her mouth landed on her ear.

She broke away, saying, "I'll be seeing you, Jock. If you can't be good, be careful."

She clambered into the cabin of the tubby aircraft.

"Be seeing you, Captain," said Grimes.

"Be seeing you, Captain," replied McKillick with a distinct lack of enthusiasm.

The two men did not shake hands.

Grimes boarded and went forward, sat down beside Fenella Pruin. The aircraft was designed for easy handling with minimal controls. Trying to make it look even easier than it actually was Grimes went through the take-off procedure. The electric motors whined and the camperfly rose at a steep angle, obedient to Grimes' touch. He did not set course at once for Vulcan Island but circled the spaceport as he ascended, looking down at the ships both great and small, at his own *Little Sister* goldenly agleam in her berth between the huge TG liner and the big Shaara vessel. There was some activity around the latter. He wondered briefly what the bee people were doing; they seemed to be hauling something bulky out of a cargo airlock.

After his second circuit Fenella Pruin demanded irritably, "What are you playing at, Grimes? Trying to disappear up your own fundamental orifice?"

He told her, "We don't want to be seen heading for Vulcan Island."

"At the moment we aren't heading *anywhere.*"

Grimes sighed resignedly and then, ignoring the compass, steered for a tall conical peak to the westward. The Mons Veneris Park would be as good an apparent destination as any; once he was out of sight from Port Aphrodite he would bring the camperfly around to a north easterly course. There was ample time to waste; allowing for two nocturnal set-downs they should be at Port Vulcan a good three hours prior to Aloysius Dreeble's ETA.

•

She said (couldn't she ever stop talking?), "You aren't such a bright businessman, you know."

"I know," he said. He thought, *If I were I wouldn't be obliged to carry people like you around.*

"If you were," she went on, "you'd do the same as the Shaara. Carry a blimp on board for this sort of outing."

"Where would I stow the bloody thing?" he snarled.

"Even you," she sneered, "might have more sense than to carry it with the gas cells inflated. But I suppose it would be beneath your precious dignity to learn anything from the Shaara."

"Why the sudden interest in those bloody bumblebees?" he demanded.

"It's just that we're being followed," she told him.

The pilot's cab of the camperfly was a transparent bubble set above fuselage top level, affording all-round vision. Grimes looked aft. Yes, there was something astern, coming up on them slowly. He could not be sure but it did look like a Shaara blimp. It had to be a Shaara blimp. As far as he knew there were no aircraft of that type native to New Venusberg.

"Are you going to let them pass us?" she asked.

He said, "I've no option. This camperfly is designed for comfort, not for speed."

"But a bloody gasbag . . ."

"Gasbag it may be but it's not starved for horsepower. Or workerpower, or whatever term the Shaara use."

"Don't be so bloody pedantic."

The camperfly flew on, still heading for the Mons Veneris. The blimp gained steadily on its parallel course, a little to starboard, flying at the same altitude as the humans' aircraft. Grimes studied it through the binoculars that were included in the rented equipment. He could see the arthropod crew in the open car under the envelope—a mixed bunch of drones and princesses he decided. Was *his* princess, the one with whom he had exchanged words in Lady Luck's establishment, among them? he wondered. She might be. And so what? Presumably the ban on the carrying of weapons on this world applied to all visitors, not only to human beings. And what could unarmed Shaara do to him?

They could get in his hair, that was what.

The blimp was abeam of the camperfly now, matching speed, blocking Grimes' turn on to the north easterly course. Its crew were watching him through their big, faceted eyes. Sunlight was reflected dazzlingly from the jewels that adorned the dark brown, velvety fur of their bodies.

But ships of the air are not like surface vehicles; they have freedom to move in three dimensions. Grimes made a rude, two fingered gesture to the watching Shaara, put the camperfly into a shallow dive as he turned to starboard. It was the easiest maneuver to carry out in these circumstances; it also turned out to be a foolish one.

The camperfly was directly under the airship when Grimes realised this. For the second time during his stay on New Venusberg he was bombed by the Shaara. A shower of missiles fell from the blimp's car, clattering on to the transparent canopy of the cab, thudding on to the tough plastic containing the wing and fuselage gas cells. The camperfly staggered, heeled over dangerously. The heavy object that had landed on the starboard wing tip and stayed there fell off but not before Grimes had seen what it was, one of those large earthenware containers referred to as honeypots, a jar in which the Shaara had carried semi-fluid refreshment to sustain them during their trip.

"What the bloody hell?" screamed Fenella Pruin.

"Somebody up there doesn't like us," muttered Grimes.

But there was no damage to the camperfly. Although some of the jetsam had been heavy none of it had been sharp. A container of some kind had shattered on top of the bubble canopy and overhead vision was obscured by a red, syrupy mess. Through it, dimly, Grimes could see the blimp. It was now little more than a dot in the sky. After that dumping of weight it had gone up fast.

"And just what was all that about?" demanded the girl.

"The Shaara—these particular Shaara—have it in for me."

"And so I'm liable to suffer for your misdeeds."

"I'm here too."

"More's the pity. Anyhow, what do you intend doing about it?"

"We just carry on," said Grimes, "until it's time to land for the night."

"And get bombed again."

"I don't think so," he said. "My guess—for what it's worth—is that the Shaara are keeping an eye on me. A surveillance mission only. But that princess, seizing a heaven sent opportunity to be nasty, just gathered up everything dumpable in the car and dropped it on us. Just petty spite."

"It could have been serious."

"It wasn't."

"The surveillance—if your theory is correct—is. I don't want to be snooped on."

"The biter bit," said Grimes.

"Oh, shut up!" Then, after a pause, "And what are you *doing* about it?"

"I'll think of something," said Grimes with a confidence that he did not feel.

The Shaara blimp kept them company throughout the day. Grimes could not outrun it. The arthropods, however, took no further hostile action; presumably they had nothing else that they could afford to jettison. But it was not a happy flight for Grimes and his companion; they were continually and uncomfortably aware of hostile eyes looking down on them.

As already planned they came in to Camp Diana in the afternoon. Before they landed the Shaara airship sheered off, vanishing beyond a range of low, wooded hills to the northward. Perhaps it was returning to the spaceport, as Fenella Pruin suggested. Grimes did not think so. He feared that they would be seeing more of the arthropods before arrival at Vulcan Island.

Camp Diana was situated on the south bank of the narrow river. There was a little hill overlooking the broad meadow upon which camperflies and pneumatic tents were arranged in orderly lines and upon this eminence was a silver statue of the divine huntress, bow in hand. The artist had depicted a lady who, despite her archaic armament, looked to be more versed in bedroom venery than the outdoor sport for which the same word is used. She did not have at all the appearance of a virgin goddess. By the water's edge was the hunting lodge, so called. It was a large, white building of vaguely classical architecture. On its roof was a mast with a windsock that was hanging limply in the calm, warm air. There was, too, a squat control tower and from this Grimes received his landing instructions.

He set down in a vacant space in one of the lines of camperflies, making an almost vertical descent. He watched from the cab a young woman walking out to the aircraft, looked at her appreciatively. She was dressed in filmy *chiton* that left one breast bare and that revealed most of her long, slender legs. The effect of her pseudo-Grecian attire, however, was slighly marred by a very modern looking shoulder bag. (She had to have something, thought Grimes cynically, in which she stowed the money, camping fees and the like, that she collected from the customers.)

She waited at the door of the camperfly for Grimes and Fenella Pruin to emerge. She said, her voice high and silvery, "Welcome to Camp Diana." Then, "For how long do you intend to stay, sir and miss?"

"Only for the night," Grimes told her.

"Only for the night, sir? But you will miss tomorrow's hunt. Perhaps you will reconsider. This evening you will have ample time for arbalest instruction at the range in the lodge basement . . ."

"What the hell's an arbalest?" demanded Fenella Pruin.

"A crossbow," said Grimes. "Its great advantage over the longbow is that little training is required before a bowman is reasonably competent."

"But *weapons,*" persisted Fenella. "After all the fuss you had with the Customs at Port Aphrodite I got the impression that weapons were banned on this world."

"They are, miss," the girl told her. "But for a deer hunt bows must be used—longbows for the few capable of employing them, arbalests for those who must learn archery in a hurry. They are hired from the lodge and during the hunt strict supervision is exercised." She smiled. "In the extremely unlikely event of any of our guests not returning his bow before leaving the camp he will find it of little use save as a souvenir. After all, it is not a concealed weapon. It is not the sort of thing that one can carry into a cathouse or gambling den unnoticed. In fact if a bow is carried anywhere save in the precincts of a hunting camp such as this it will at once excite the interest of the authorities." She took time off to recover her breath then continued, "Have I persuaded you to stay for the hunt, sir?"

"I'm afraid not," said Grimes. "But I should like to get in some arbalest practice this evening."

"What the hell for?" demanded Fenella Pruin.

"We might enjoy a longer stay here next time we drop in."

"Oh, well, if that's your idea of a pleasant evening, go ahead. I'm not stopping you. But you pay for your own tuition; I'm not subsidizing your fun. It's bad enough having to shell out for camping fees. How much do I owe for one night?" she asked the girl. *"What?* Oh, well, this *is* a hunting camp. You're the predator and we're the prey . . ."

She went back into the camperfly for money. Grimes looked at the girl. She looked at him. Two pairs of eyebrows were raised simultaneously.

Grimes asked, "What time are these arbalest lessons?"

"Any time you like," she said. "Do you plan on shooting her—accidentally, of course?"

"Mphm," grunted Grimes noncommitally.

Grimes demanded money.

Fenella Pruin asked, "What for? For an arbalest lesson? Your Survey Service gunnery courses can't have cost all that much!"

"I may want to grease a palm or two," he said.

She looked at him. She said slowly, "I think I can guess why. But I'm not asking. I don't want to know anything about it. I refuse to accept responsibility for any illegality of which you may be guilty."

"Unfortunately," said Grimes, "as master I cannot do likewise as far as you are concerned."

"Here's your money," she said, concluding the conversation. She peeled notes of large denominations off the large roll that she produced from her bag.

Grimes counted what she gave him. It should be enough, more than enough. He left the camperfly, walked in the late-afternoon sunlight to the lodge.

* * *

He found his way to the practice range with no trouble. Apart from the attendant on duty, a young lady got up to conform to somebody's idea of what a well dressed Amazon should wear—leather straps, brass buckles, an extremely short kilt of some transparent material—the practice range was deserted. She looked at Grimes and smiled invitingly.

"Archery instruction, sir? Or . . ."

"Archery instruction, please."

The smile faded slightly.

"Longbow or arbalest, sir?"

"Arbalest, please."

"Have you used such a weapon before?"

"No."

"In that case, sir, you will require the stimulator if you are to acquire a modicum of skill in the minimum time. It was programmed by Hiroshi Hayashi, for many years the undisputed crossbow champion of all Venusberg." She added, after a slight pause, "There will be an extra charge, of course."

"Of course," agreed Grimes.

He was led to a long counter of polished wood. Beyond this, at a distance of about forty metres, was a large target with a bullseye and concentric rings. From under the bar the girl produced a crossbow, put the end of it on the floor and one slim foot into the stirrup, grasped the wire bowstring with both hands—it was suitably padded in the two places necessary—and pulled. There was a click as the sear engaged. She lifted the weapon, put it back on the counter and then inserted a steel quarrel into the slot.Then, with the butt of the arbalest set firmly on her right shoulder, she took casual aim and pulled the trigger. The bowstring twanged musically and the target thudded as the metal bolt sank deep into the bullseye.

It all looked very easy.

"And now you, sir. Cock, load and fire."

It had all looked very easy when she did it but Grimes was amazed at the effort required to bend those steel arms. He was red in the face and perspiring when finally the thing was cocked. He loaded. He brought the butt to his shoulder. The weapon was too heavy and the balance was all wrong. He tried to steady the primitive sights on to the target but could not hold the crossbow steady. He pulled the trigger at last when his foresight flickered across the bullseye. He missed, of course, not even putting the quarrel on to the quite large target.

The girl *tsked* sympathetically. She brought from its under the counter stowage a featureless helmet of some light metal. She set it firmly on Grimes' head.

"Now, sir, cock, load and fire."

It had all looked very easy when she did it. It was surprisingly easy when he did it—this time. It was as though something—somebody—had control of his brain, was telling his muscles exactly what they should do. (This stimulator, he thought, must use a very similar technique to that employed by that obscene game machine in Lady Luck's games machines room.) He pulled up the bowspring until it engaged with an amazing lack of effort. He raised the arbalest to his shoulder, sighted carelessly, fired. He was well on the target this time although missing the bullseye by a few millimetres. He cocked, reloaded, fired again. A bull. Cock, reload, fire . . . Another bull. And another. Dislodged quarrels fell to the stone floor with a clatter.

This was not, thought Grimes, the quickfiring weapon that a longbow was. Even with his induced skills reloading took too much time.

He asked, "Could I learn to use a longbow the same way?"

"Yes, sir. But it takes much longer. You, obviously, are accustomed to handling projectile firearms employing a chemical propellant. This technique is merely enhancing the skills that you already possess . . ."

And a crossbow, thought Grimes, would be easier to fire from the open door of an aircraft. He would stay with it.

At the girl's suggestion he switched to moving targets, two dimensional representations of animals that had to be Terran deer, their ancestral stock no doubt imported from Earth. These ran rapidly from left to right, from right to left, bobbed up suddenly.

He scored well after a shaky start.

She said, "You will bring back game from tomorrow's hunt, sir."

"I shan't be at tomorrow's hunt."

"The day after, perhaps . . . I must warn you that unless you practice continuously the induced skills fade."

"Could I take two of these arbalests back to my camperfly so that I and my companion can get in some practice?"

"It is not allowed, sir. Our weapons may be used only under strict supervision."

"You must have occasional outworld tourists," suggested Grimes, "who want to keep these beautiful crossbows as souvenirs . . ."

"They are expensive," said the girl bluntly. At least she wasn't wasting time by being coy.

"How much?" asked Grimes, equally bluntly.

"Five hundred credits each. And I must warn you that if you are seen carrying one anywhere but within the bounds of a camp such as this you will be liable to arrest and prosecution. And if you say that you bought it you will not be believed. We have an understanding with the police forces. You will be charged with theft as well as carrying an unauthorised weapon."

"You're certainly frank," said Grimes, looking at the girl not without approval. He had his notecase out, was checking its contents. "Now I'm going to be frank. I haven't enough on me to pay for the arbalests *and* the tuition. And my . . . er . . . friend keeps very tight pursestrings . . ." He tried to look like a gigolo. "Perhaps . . ."

"How much have you got?"

"One thousand, five hundred and seventy five . . ."

She grinned. "Near enough."

He should have tried to beat her down, thought Grimes. But it wasn't his money. It wasn't even Fenella Pruin's money. *The Bronson Star* could well afford it.

Shortly thereafter, with the dissembled arbalests and a supply of quarrels in a carrying case that the girl had thrown in with the purchase, he made his way through the warm dusk to the camperfly.

Fenella Pruin, although reluctantly approving this acquisition of weaponry, was not at all pleased when he insisted that she learn how to cock and load a crossbow.

These were not quick-firing weapons—but if things came to a crunch they would have to do.

Eleven

The next morning, after a light breakfast that Grimes prepared from the camperfly's consumable stores, they lifted from Camp Diana. A bored duty officer in the control tower asked them where they were bound and was told that they were just cruising. (On most worlds they would have been obliged to submit a flight plan before departure but New Venusberg concerned itself only about the ability of tourists to pay for their pleasure.) The flight controller told them to have a happy day. Grimes thanked him—and wondered if the day would be a happy one. He hoped that it would be.

He flew with the rising sun broad on the starboard bow, its brilliance reduced to a tolerable level by the self-polarising glass of the cockpit canopy. Dazzle was cut down but so, inevitably, was visibility. But he was sure that attack, if there were to be an attack, would come from out of the sun.

It did.

At first the Shaara blimp was no more than a sunspot, but a rapidly expanding one. Grimes put the controls on automatic, said to Fenella Pruin, "This is it. Are you ready?"

"Yes," she said. "But I forbid you to open fire unless they start dropping things again . . ."

"They'll have spent the night," Grimes told her, "gathering big stones with sharp edges."

"You don't *know* . . ."

"I don't *know—but* would you like to bet that they haven't?"

She made no reply and he began to remove the nuts—which he had already loosened to hand tightness only—holding the rear panel of the canopy in place. Unfortunately there was no room for the segment of curved glass inside the cockpit but Grimes had foreseen this, had ready some light but very strong line that, passed through the bolt holes of the removed panel and those in an adjacent one, held it more or less securely. The thing tended to flap in the wind of the camperfly's passage; if the cord frayed through it would be just too bad.

Meanwhile the blimp was no longer a sunspot; it was eclipsing the sun. The

Shaara were on a collision course but Grimes was sure that they would lift before there was actual contact. They did so, and by this time Grimes was half way out of the bubble canopy and on to the smooth, resilient top of the gas cell that covered the fuselage. He held one of the arbalests, already cocked and loaded, ready for action. The other one Fenella Pruin would pass to him as soon as he needed it.

He edged out to starboard, putting a cautious foot on to the root of the stubby wing on that side. He withdrew hastily, back to the protection of the canopy. Even at the camperfly's low air speed there was too much wind; he would never be able to take steady aim and, furthermore, would run the serious risk of losing his balance and falling. It was a long way down and the terrain over which they were now flying was rocky. (Even had it been soft sand he would never have survived such a plunge.)

So he would have to follow the Pruin's orders (but what right had *she* to order *him*?) after all. He would not be able to open fire until fired upon. His missiles going up would pass the Shaara missiles coming down.

The blimp had reduced speed as it gained altitude and then, to Grimes' surprise, sheered off to port.

"You've gone to all this trouble for nothing," sneered Fenella Pruin. "They aren't going to attack us. Why should they? And how am I going to justify the purchase of these two bloody crossbows to my paper?"

"Wait!" snapped Grimes.

The blimp was astern of them now, but it was turning. It was coming up on them slowly, on the same course as themselves but higher. When the Shaara started dropping things they would have to make very little allowance for deflection. Their tactics were ideal assuming that the bombing target was unarmed. Grimes hastily put the arbalest behind his back. If they saw the glint of metal they would suspect that he had a weapon of some kind.

The camperfly flew on steadily.

The blimp crept up on it.

It would be, thought Grimes, just within the extreme range of his arbalest. But was that bloody Fenella Pruin telepathic?

"Wait!" she ordered sharply. "Let them make the first move!"

"It may be the last as far as we're concerned," he replied but kept the crossbow concealed.

The fat nose of the blimp was directly above the camperfly's stubby tail. Sunlight was reflected dazzlingly from the jewels worn by the princesses and drones in the car, from their faceted eyes. They must be wondering what Grimes was doing standing out on the fuselage. They would soon find out.

The obese airship slowly overflew the chubby hybrid aircraft. The car was coming directly overhead. Grimes saw spindly, arthropoidal limbs, holding things, extending outward from the gondola. The first missiles were released. He did not watch their descent but whipped the arbalest up from behind his back and fired, aiming for the rear of the car where the engine driving the pusher airscrew was situated. He missed, but the quarrel drove into and through the envelope. He heard, behind him, at least one rock crashing on to the cockpit canopy, felt the camperfly lurch dangerously as others hit the wings. But there was no time to assess damage. He passed the discharged arbalest back to Fenella Pruin, grabbed the loaded one that she put into his hand. He brought the butt to his shoulder and fired just as another shower of big stones came down. The blimp was still within range; it should not have been, that first act of jettison should have sent it climbing almost like a rocket.

Grimes realised why as his second bolt sped towards its intended target. The first one must have hit some weak spot, a juncture of gas cells. Tattered fabric flapped about a widening rent in the envelope. The airship was dropping by the stern. Unless Grimes took avoiding action, and fast, it would fall on to the camperfly.

Fantastically the hybrid aircraft was looking after itself. It swung around to starboard at the same time as it heeled over in that direction and the sinking blimp dropped slowly astern of it, just missing its tail. Grimes realised almost at once the reason for the alteration of course; the gas cell in the starboard wing had been holed and the automatic pilot had been unable to cope with the change in trim. And Grimes himself would be unable to cope until matters of far greater urgency had been resolved.

Two of the Shaara, a princess and a drone, had bailed out from their crippled vehicle. They were making for the almost as crippled camperfly. Grimes did not have to be psychic to know that they were in a bad temper. Probably they were unarmed but they would be able to inflict considerable damage with their sharp talons.

He retreated inside the canopy.

Fenella Pruin was still struggling to reload the first arbalest. He snatched it from her and, the training session not yet faded from his mind, cocked the thing without difficulty. He watched the two Shaara, their wings an iridescent blue, flying in. There was not sufficient slipstream from the slow camperfly seriously to interfere with their landing. Using all their limbs they scuttled forward to where Grimes, crossbow in hand, awaited them. They came erect on their rear legs before they reached him.

The princess said, her voice from the artificial speech box strapped to her thorax viciously strident, "You have a weapon. On this world it is not legal."

"Neither is dropping rocks on people," Grimes told her.

"You broke the law. We are entitled to protect ourselves against lawbreakers."

"Try it!" he said, levelling the arbalest.

But would he dare to use it? So far action had been taken, by both sides, against ships only. Intentions and results had been damage to property, not to life and limb. If he killed the princess or the drone, or both of them, the other Shaara would lay formal complaint to the Venusberg authorities and then Grimes would be in the cactus. The Shaara pulled more Gs on this world than he did. He did not know what the penalty was for the crime of murder but he did not doubt that it would be extremely unpleasant.

Yet without the weapon he would be no match for the multi-limbed, sharp clawed arthropod. Perhaps (he hoped) the threat of its use would be sufficient to deter the Shaara from unarmed attack.

They approached him slowly, menacingly, their clawed feet clinging to the taut fabric of the upper fuselage gas cell. Grimes' finger tightened on the trigger of the arbalest.

Behind him something hissed loudly.

A stream of white foam shot over his shoulder, played over the head of the princess and then over that of her companion, blinding them. Fortuitously the camperfly lurched heavily at this moment. The princess screeched wordlessly, lost her balance and fell overside. She was in no danger; her wings opened at once and she was airborne but flying aimlessly, all sense of direction lost. The drone still stood there, trying to clear the viscous foam from his eyes. Grimes took a cautious step aft towards him, pushed hard with the crossbow held in his right hand. The drone staggered but the claws of his feet retained their grip. Grimes jabbed again, and again. He was afraid of injuring the male Shaara but was anxious to be rid of him.

Then a metal cylinder, thrown with force and accuracy from somewhere behind him, struck the drone on the thorax. He staggered, lost his footing, fell to join his aimlessly flying mistress.

Grimes turned cautiously to make his way back to the control cab. Fenella Pruin was standing in the opening made by the removed panel, grinning happily.

"If *they* can dump used food containers and the like," she said, *"I* can dump used fire extinguishers."

"If they complain," he said, "we're still in trouble."

"Nobody was killed," she told him. "That wouldn't have been so if you'd used the crossbow."

Grimes reluctantly agreed with her and then went to the pilot's seat to try to bring the camperfly back under control.

He was obliged to valve gas from the port wing to compensate for the loss of lift from the starboard one. The camperfly was still airworthy but with the reduction of buoyancy there was a corresponding reduction of speed. The necessary calculations would have to wait, however, until the canopy panel was replaced. Grimes felt much happier when the control cab was once again completely enclosed, affording protection against an incursion of vengeful Shaara.

The cockpit resealed, he took his place at the controls, studied the chart on the desk before him.

He said, "We'll make Camp Persephone all right, although a bit later than intended. There are sure to be repair facilities there and a supply of helium. We'll get the starboard wing patched up and both wing gas cells refilled."

"How will you account for the hole in the starboard wing?"

He grinned at her. "I'm just a spaceman. You're the writer. Use your imagination."

She grinned back. "I'll just soft pedal the truth a little. We happened to be flying directly under a Shaara blimp when, quite by chance, the thing dumped ballast. We don't want to have to lay any charges. The less the law knows about our activities here, the better."

To tell the truth, although not necessarily the whole truth, is usually safer than to tell a lie.

Twelve

Camp Persephone was hot springs and fumaroles, dominated by a spectacular geyser, spouting with clockwork regularity every thirteen and a half minutes. There was a huge hotel complex for those wishing to make an extended stay and a big camperfly park with the usual facilities, including a repair shop. To this Grimes went almost immediately after landing, taking with him what he hoped would be an adequate supply of *The Bronson Star*'s money.

The manager was just shutting up shop.

He was oilily courteous, however.

"Repairs to your camperfly, sir, at this time of the evening? My staff have all left for the night and I was on the point of leaving . . . But I have no doubt, sir, that we shall be able to make an arrangement, a mutually satisfactory arrangement . . ."

"It is a matter of some urgency," said Grimes.

"Of course, sir." He coughed delicately. "Forgive me for my impertinence but now and again—very rarely, but now and again—we have tourists who are not your sort of people, who demand services and then who are unable or unwilling to give recompense in return . . ."

"So you want to see the colour of my money," said Grimes crudely.

"Ha, ha. You have a ready wit, sir . . ."

"And ready cash." Grimes brought out and opened his notecase.

"What is the trouble with your camperfly, sir?"

"The starboard wing gas cell was holed. I was obliged to valve gas from the port wing to compensate."

"An unusual accident, sir, perhaps you were flying too low and fouled a tree top or some other obstacle . . ."

"Perhaps," said Grimes.

He walked with the manager through the sulphur-tainted evening air along the lines of parked camperflies. He took the man into the aircraft, up to the canopied cockpit, shone a torch on to the jagged rent in the wing fabric. He said, "The . . . er . . . obstacle is still inside the wing."

"But were you flying *upside down,* sir?"

"I was trying to loop the loop," said Grimes.

The manager stared at him, then said, "The most peculiar accidents do happen, I know. If you will wait here, sir, until I recall my staff. . . But, if you will forgive my impertinence, first a small deposit before I do so . . ."

Grimes paid up. After all, it wasn't his money.

The repair job did not take long. The piece of jagged rock was removed from the punctured gas cell. The repair shop manager was sorely puzzled but Grimes stuck to his looping the loop story. Improbable as it was it was better than the one suggested by Fenella Pruin. Disposable ballast carried by airships is never of a character likely to damage anything or anybody underneath . . .

The repairmen worked well and efficiently. The damaged cell was removed and replaced, and inflated before the renewal of wing fabric. The gas cell in the port wing was reinflated and tested. When everything was done Grimes paid the balance of the charges and was relieved to find that when he had asked Fenella Pruin for the money he had slightly overestimated. He made a light meal of cheese and biscuits, then went in search of his passenger so that he could report that the next day's journey would be as planned. She would be in the hotel, he thought, probably eating far better than he had done. But she must have fed by now. Hadn't she said something about paying a visit to The Inferno later in the evening?

So, with wallet much lighter but not empty, he left the camperfly and walked towards the Hotel Pluto, a fantastic appearing building whose architect had taken stalagmites as his inspiration, whose irregular spires, floodlit, were whitely luminous against the night sky. Off to the right the geyser—also floodlit but in rainbow colours—momentarily distracted his attention from the man-made extravagance.

He reached the grotto-like entrance to the hotel, passed into a cavernous foyer where artificial stalactites and stalagmites dominated the decor. There were luminous signs—one of which, by an ascending spiral escalator, read Elysian Fields Restaurant and another, over what looked like a mere hole in the floor, The Inferno.

By the hole was the inevitable pay booth, a construction looking like a huge dog kennel made from rough, rock slabs. The attendant wore a ferocious dog mask and nothing else. But, so far as Grimes could remember, Cerberus had been a male dog and not a bitch. (And, in any case, the idea of Hell as an inferno was a Christian invention and bore little resemblance to the Greek Hades.)

He paid his not inconsiderable sop to Cerberus. He asked if there would be any ferry fees as an additional charge and was told that there would not be, although as soon as the proposed artificial Styx was flowing there would be fares collected by Charon.

Grimes thanked the girl. He wondered if her face were as attractive as her voice and body. He went to look dubiously into the hole. There was no staircase, either static or mobile. It was just a chute of black, polished stone, plunging downwards at a steep angle.

Rather dubiously Grimes sat down on the rim with his legs in the hole, then pushed off. At first his descent was almost free fall, through utter darkness. The acridity of sulphurous gases stung his nostrils. Then he felt that the angle of the chute was less steep, was tending to the horizontal. His speed was checked by a screen of curtains that clung like cobwebs. Beyond them there was light again—ruddy, flickering, but to eyes that had become accustomed to the darkness bright enough.

He had come to a halt on a smooth floor of rock, or artificial rock. He got to his feet, looked around. Slowly swirling luminously crimson mist restricted visiblity but he could dimly see stalactites and stalagmites—or, more probably, plastic representations of dribbles of molten lava that had solidified on reaching the ground, like candle drippings on a giant scale. The air was hot and steamy. There was music. It was vaguely familiar in spite of the distortions. *Night On Bald Mountain?* Grimes couldn't be sure but he thought that it was that.

A demon materialised beside him. Gleaming white horns—probably artificial but not necessarily so; unscrupulous genetic engineers are capable of many amusing perversions—protruded jauntily from her cap of tightly curled black hair. Grimes allowed his regard to shift downward. Her body was human enough except for the feet, which were cloven hooves. Shoes? Perhaps. But if they were her pedal extremities must have been exceedingly small to get into them.

"May I serve you, sir?" Her voice was a pleasant contralto. He could not place the accent.

"I'm looking for a lady . . ."

"There are many unattached ladies here, sir."

"A tourist. A Miss Fenn. Prunella Fenn."

"She is not known to me, sir. But probably she will be in the Lake of Fire. If you will follow me . . ."

She turned away from him. He saw that a scaly tail, terminating in a conventional arrowhead, sprouted jauntily from the cleft of her naked buttocks. He could not resist the temptation of catching hold of it, giving it a playful tug. The root of it came away from her body, snapped back when he released his hold. She looked back with a smile that was wearily tolerant rather than pleasant; having her tail pulled must have been an occupational hazard of her employment.

"Artificial caudal appendages may be purchased here. They are ideal for fancy dress parties and the like. But come with me, please."

He followed her through the acrid yet sweet mists to a small, pallidly glimmering pavilion where she handed him over to another woman attired—horns, hooves and tail—as she was. This lady told him to remove his clothing, then asked for a fee, not a small one, in return for a locker key which was on a chain so that it could be hung about the neck. She asked Grimes if he wished to buy or hire horns and a tail. He did not so wish even though he was assured that these embellishments would enhance his manly beauty. Before he stowed and locked his possessions away the first girl intimated that she was expecting a tip. Grimes gave her a ten credit bill; there was nothing of smaller denomination in his notecase. He thought that it was too much. She, obviously, did not.

Nonetheless she condescended to lead him from the pavilion to the edge of the Lake of Fire. Streamers of mist wavering above the surface of the sullenly glowing water had the semblance of tongues of flame. And there were real flames, yellow and not red, out there in the distance, seemingly floating on the surface, like a star cluster dimly glimpsed through the fire mist of some inchoate nebula.

"Your lady is out there," said the guide, pointing. "If she's here, that is."

"Do I have to swim?" asked Grimes.

"Only if you wish to."

Grimes tested the temperature of the water at the lake verge with a cautious toe. It was little more than comfortably warm. He waded out towards the glimmering lights. As he disturbed the surface it flashed brightly scarlet, illuminating the mist that swirled about him. It was like walking through fire—but a fire that had no power to burn.

He waded on. The bottom shelved gently; still the water was only half way up to his knees. He thought at first that the lambent flames were receding from him as he headed towards them but this was only some trick of refraction. Quite suddenly—by which time the water was up to his knees—he was among them. He looked down with some bewilderment at the naked men and women obviously sitting on the lake bottom each with a tray, on which was a burning candle, floating before him or her. The trays bore more than candles. There were bottles, glasses, dishes of solid refreshments.

And where was Fenella Pruin?

He looked to right and left but could not see her. But he heard her unmistakable voice, off somewhere to the right. She was complaining loudly to somebody, "Isn't it time that they put on the next show? I can't stay here much longer. I want to get some sleep tonight as I shall be leaving early in the morning—if my fool of a pilot has had my camperfly repaired, that is . . ."

He waded slowly towards her, rippling the water. Somebody called to him irritably, "Hey, you! Don't rock the boat!"

He reduced his speed. He had no wish to spill people's drinks. He apologised when he trod on a bare leg under the water, smilingly refused the invitation to sit down and keep its owner, a plump tourist lady, company.

He found Fenella Pruin. She was with a grossly fat man who could almost have been twin brother to Captain McKillick, who had stuck on to his bald head a pair of patently artificial horns. Before them was a large, floating tray laden with good things.

The big toe of Grimes' right foot made contact with Miss Pruin's naked hip.

"Who the hell . . . ?" she began.

"It's your fool of a pilot," said Grimes.

"Oh. You." She looked up at him. "What do you want?"

"The camperfly's airworthy again. We shall be able to lift off tomorrow morning as planned."

"It's a pity that you have to leave, Prue," sighed the fat man. "Just when . . ."

Grimes looked down at his obese, pallid nudity. First McKillick, he thought, and now this overweight slob. And he must have some skin disease; if a cross between a Terran leopard and a hippopotamus were possible he could have been it.

"Sit down, Grimes," snarled the Pruin. "Since you're here you can watch the second show and then see me back to the camperfly."

"But, Prue . . ." The fat man's voice was childishly plaintive.

"Sorry, Clarrie. But I'm paying Grimes, here, good money to look after me—and I like getting my money's worth."

"So do I," muttered her companion.

Grimes lowered his body into the warm water on the other side of Fenella Pruin from Clarrie. If whatever caused that ugly, mottled skin was catching he didn't want to catch it. Almost immediately one of the attendant demons appeared; this one was towing, by her tail, a little, flatbottomed barge. From it she took a tray, with a candle, set it before Grimes, ignited the wick with a flick of her long finger nails. By its light Grimes read the menu and the wine list printed on the surface of the tray. Unless the Pruin came to his rescue he would not be able to afford much. Beer would be the cheapest drink. (Here it was called Teufelwasser.) But how, naked as he was, could he pay for it?

He found out. Having set the bottle and glass on his tray the girl took a stamp and pressed it on his right upper arm. It left, in indelible ink, a record of what he had ordered and received. Presumably there would be a reckoning in the pavilion when he retrieved his effects. He looked at the sulking, mottled Clarrie. He felt almost sorry for the man; his skin bore the record of his evening's outlay on the ungrateful Pruin.

Grimes sipped his beer—it wasn't bad—and looked around. The mists were clearing and he could see that the audience was seated in a great circle with a low island in its centre. This was flat, bare of vegetation. Suddenly, appearing from the mouth of a concealed tunnel, a horde of fearsome looking demons appeared, Neanderthalers with cloven hooves, horns and tails, with leathery wings. Moving in time to the music they set up their horrifying apparatus—a rack, a brazier from which protruded the handles of branding irons, a wheel from the rim of which protruded vicious, dull-gleaming spikes. At a wave from a taloned hand the brazier came to glowing life.

From overhead came a rumble of thunder, culminating in a supernal *crack* while artificial lightning flared dazzlingly. Spiralling down from the high roof of the cavern, wings outspread, came more demons. (Those wings, thought Grimes, were all wrong aerodynamically; they were not moving and, in any case, did not have the area to support anything as large as a man, let alone a man burdened with a struggling woman. Miniaturised, personal inertial drive units? Probably. The continuous grumble of thunder, combined with the strident music, was loud enough to drown the arhythmic beat of such machinery.)

Dark-furred demons with pallidly gleaming eyes and tusks and horns . . . Shrieking, damned women, their opulent flesh whitely naked, fighting but with utter hopelessness. One of them was flung roughly on to the rack, her wrists and ankles strapped. Another was made fast to the wheel. ("Watch those spikes," whispered Fenella Pruin. "They aren't sharp and they withdraw into the rim.") Two more were chained to St Andrew's crosses.

"You must let me take you to the real thing, Prue," muttered the fat man. "This is *tame* . . ."

"Shut up!" she snapped.

And this, thought Grimes, looked real enough. With two husky demons manning the capstan the screaming girl on the rack was being elongated so that she looked more like a writhing, white snake than a human being, as was her sister on the wheel. Irons, whitely incandescent at first, slowly dulling to red, were being applied to the bodies of the crucified victims. There was an audible sizzling and the sweet/acrid stench of burning meat.

Grimes watched in horrified fascination. Towards the end he found it hard to fight down his rising nausea—and hated himself when he became aware that something else was rising too.

At last the show was almost over.

The girls were released from the rack, wheel and crosses, flung on to the ground where the demons, each of whom was more than adequately endowed, fell upon them. These withdrew at last, leaving the victims of the pack rape sprawled on the smooth rock.

The woman who had been on the rack was the first to recover. She sat up, stripped from her arms the stretched simulacra of her natural limbs and then, from her legs, what looked now only like ludicrously long hip-length stockings.

The victim of the wheel followed suit. Meanwhile, solicitously, two demons with damp white towels were cleaning the simulated burn-marks from the bodies of the other two girls.

The demons and the damned bowed to the audience, acknowledged the applause.

"Phoney," muttered the fat man. "Phoney as all hell. I know a place . . ."

"I'm sure you do, Clarrie." Fenella Pruin got to her feet, looked down at Grimes. "If you've quite finished your beer we'll get back to the camperfly."

They waded ashore, retrieved their clothing from the pavilion. The woman in charge raised her eyebrows at the solitary price stamp on Grimes' skin, accepted his money and handed him a wad of cloth impregnated with some fluid with which to remove the mark. Grimes dressed. Prunella Fenn dressed. They walked to the golden, spiral escalator that carried them back to ground level.

She said, "A pity we have to be at Port Vulcan. Otherwise I'd have taken Clarrie up on his offer. He's stinking rich—*really* stinking rich—you know and has the entré to all sorts of places that the ordinary rich, like I'm supposed to be, can't afford . . ."

"You wouldn't," said Grimes.

"I would. Too right I would. But I'll find a way yet . . ."

They left the hotel, made their way to the camperfly park. Back in the aircraft they retired for what was left of the night.

Grimes was acutely aware that she was sleeping, probably naked, on the other side of the curtain dividing the cabin. Almost he got off his bunk to go to join her; that crudely sadistic and pornographic entertainment had stimulated him. Then he remembered what had happened (what had not happened) with her before and desire ebbed.

He tried to sleep and at last succeeded.

Thirteen

The flight from Camp Persephone to Port Vulcan was uneventful.

An early start was made, with Grimes, after a mug of strong coffee, feeling reasonably competent and his passenger still snoring not unmusically in her bunk. Grimes set course at once for Vulcan Island. Soon he was flying over the sea, looking down with interest at the waterborne traffic—a huge tanker (and what was she carrying? he wondered), a large, white-painted cruiser liner, a fleet of big trawlers.

Vulcan Island showed up on schedule, a dark smudge of smoke on the far horizon under which there was the glint of metal, the reflection of the morning sunlight from storage tanks, separator towers and the like. By this time Fenella Pruin was up and dressed, sitting beside Grimes as he maintained his course.

Grimes called Aerospace Control.

"Camperfly Able Zulu Steven Four Eight, pilot John Grimes, passenger Prunella Fenn, requesting permission to land."

"Vulcan Control to Able Zulu Seven Four Eight. I have you in my screen. You'll not be in time for today's tour of the dolly factory. You should have come in last night."

"Are there any entertainments that we can take in?" asked Grimes.

"Not until tomorrow. But come in if you want to. There'll be a berth for you at the airport."

Grimes looked at the Vulcan Island chart. Airport and spaceport were well away from each other. He measured off the distance—four kilometres. If there were no transport available the distance would not be too far to walk. But there might be, he thought, another problem. Very often ports frequented only by non-passenger-carrying vessels were sealed areas, with gates and guards and all the rest of it. But he had made plans for such a contingency. Aboard the camperfly were two suits of uniform-like coveralls, two hard hats (the design of this plastic safety headwear seemed to be standardised throughout the Galaxy) and, most important of all, two clipboards. Also there was a pair of wirecutters.

He homed on the airport radio beacon.

He came in low, flying over the low, sprawling factory buildings, only one of which exhibited a splash of incongruous colour, a huge, pinkly naked, yellow-haired woman-shaped balloon floating above it. Perhaps it was not so incongruous after all. This must be the dolly factory mentioned by Vulcan Control.

The airport was an almost featureless square of grey concrete. There were three big passenger carriers in, inertial drive jobs. Tucked away in a corner were the camperflies, a half dozen of them. As instructed Grimes made his landing close by these hybrid aircraft.

A bored official sauntered out from the administration tower, waited for Grimes and Fenella Pruin to step down from the camperfly to the apron. He was mainly interested in collecting dues and charges.

Fenella Pruin asked, "What can we *do* here?"

"There's the conducted tour of the dolly factory, of course." The man leered. "Most of the fun is testing the dollies; they come in two sexes, you know. Apart from that there's Vulcan City. The shopping's not bad, they tell me. You save a few cents by buying your souvenirs here instead of at the mainland clipjoint shops."

"Could we just sort of wander around?" asked the girl.

"Sure. But outside Vulcan City there's little to see. The spaceport and the factories are out of bounds unless you have a pass."

"Shopping, darling?" suggested Miss Pruin, aiming a too bright smile at Grimes.

"I guess so," he grumbled.

"Don't spend all your money in the same shop," advised the official. "And if it's dollies you want remember that you can have them made exactly to your specifications, while you wait, in the factory . . ."

He sauntered away.

Back in the camperfly Fenella got out a large shopping bag. Into it Grimes put the coveralls, the hard hats, the clipboards and the wire cutters. There was also a Vulcan Island street map which he folded and tucked into his pocket. They left their aircraft with Grimes cariying the bag, trying to make it appear that it was empty. There was transport from the airport to Vulcan City, a subway system. After the all-pervading drabness at ground level the brightly coloured advertisements lining the escalator were a pleasant relief.

There was colour, too, in Vulcan City but it was shabby, tawdry by daylight. The main street was busy enough however, with off duty shift workers staggering, so it seemed, from bar to bar. Grimes and Fenella Pruin looked into one of these, an establishment calling itself The Pink Pussy Cat. To raucous music a girl was dancing on the bar. She was not a very good dancer and her figure should have been decently concealed. Obviously she was a reject from one of the mainland places of entertainment. Grimes briefly wondered how long it would be before—what was her name?—before Tanya finished up here.

There were shops, some of which had window displays of ingenious mechanical toys, little dolls that stripped in time to the tinkling melodies from the music boxes on the polished tops of which they danced, other dolls that fled before horrendous monsters that snatched their clothing from them as they ran round and around their circular tracks. The sort of toys, thought Grimes, that one would buy as presents for kinky parents, never for well-brought-up children . . .

Fenella Pruin looked at her watch. "I hate to interrupt your perverted windowshopping, Grimes, but isn't it time that we were getting to the spaceport? It's almost 1400 now and *Willy Willy*'s due in just over an hour."

He put down the shopping bag, consulted the street map. It was not far from where they were now to the spaceport perimeter. The way was through a heavily industrialised area in which pedestrians, especially pedestrians dressed for leisure and pleasure, would be conspicuous. Fortunately there was a comfort station not far from where they were standing and even more fortunately it was not being used by anybody but themselves. Fenella took the shopping bag into one of the cubicles while Grimes studied the advertising matter decorating an aphrodisiac dispenser. After a minute or so she emerged, looking, in coveralls and hard hat, like a very ordinary female technician. Luckily she had thought to leave the camperfly wearing plain shoes rather than the golden sandals that she usually affected.

Grimes took the bag, retired to a cubicle. It did not take him long to change.

They walked briskly away from the city, along a wide street on either side of which were the drab grey walls of factories. Occasional heavy trucks, proceeding in both directions, passed them. The few people on foot were attired as they were. Nobody paid any attention to them although Grimes wished that the shopping bag, a somewhat gaudy affair, looked a little less like what it actually was and more like a tool bag.

At the end of the long, straight road they came to a high, wire mesh fence. Through it they could see the spaceport control tower and the lofty hulls of two big freighters. To their left a high wall made direct contact with the fence but to their right was a narrow alley. They walked into this. It was, so far as Grimes could determine, just a ribbon of waste space; there were no indications that it had ever been used for any purpose.

Somebody might look into it, however. Fenella Pruin stood so that her body shielded Grimes from view while he busied himself with the wire cutters. He had little trouble in clipping a square panel out of the mesh, freeing three sides only. He bent it inwards, stooped and passed through. Fenella followed him. He forced it back into place; unless somebody looked at the fence closely this evidence of a break-in would never be noticed.

Close by their entry point was a sort of minor junkyard. There was a battered looking wardroom bar unit, complete with counter, bottle racks, sink and refrigerator. There were autochefs, one large and one small, that obviously would never cook another meal. There was a playmaster with its screen smashed in. There were engineroom bits and pieces, all showing signs of extreme wear, that Grimes could not identify. (But he was never an engineer.)

He put the wire cutters back into the shopping bag, took out the two clipboards. He satisfied himself that both he and the girl sported an array of styluses in the breast pockets of their coveralls. Then he hid the bag beneath the counter of the bar unit.

They walked slowly away from the dump, clipboards in hand, trying to look busy. Fenella Pruin was using a stylus to make marks on the topmost form on her board. They headed, but not too purposefully, towards the triangle of bright, scarlet beacons marking *Willy Willy*'s berth. They were joined briefly by a man dressed as they were, although his coveralls were yellow and not grey. He said cheerfully, "I suppose you're hopin' to get first look at Cap'n Dreeble's cargo . . ."

"As a matter of fact," Grimes told him, "we're checking the arrangements for the next shipment of bulk Scotch."

"No reason why you shouldn't admire the scenery while you're doing it. *I* never miss a *Willy Willy* landing. All those odd little bitches . . . But they've *got* something that our women haven't."

"Indeed?" asked Fenella Pruin coldly.

The man looked at her and grinned. "Jealous, huh? *You* haven't got a pair of legs like *them* . . ."

Grimes and Fenella Pruin changed direction, heading towards one of the warehouses. The man continued on towards *Willy Willy*'s berth.

"You took a risk," said Fenella to Grimes.

"How?"

"How do you know that *he's* not involved in the import of bulk spirits?"

"Because stencilled on his back were the words PORT VULCAN ELECTRONIC MAINTENANCE DIVISION.

He looked up at the hazy sky.

He could hear *Willy Willy* now, the distant grumble of her inertial drive, but could not yet see her. The noise was growing louder. Yes, there she was . . . A high, gleaming speck in the soft, overhead blue. Aloysius Dreeble was coming in fast. When Grimes had last tangled with him, many years ago, he had been mate of Drongo Kane's *Southerly Buster* and a good shiphandler. There was no reason to suppose that now, as master, he had lost any of his skill.

His landing technique was one that Grimes had employed himself, a controlled fall and then application of vertical thrust at almost the last moment. It was spectacular but safe enough—so long as the inertial drive did not decide to go on the blink when urgently required.

Grimes could see *Willy Willy* clearly now.

She was a typical Epsilon Class tramp, one of those sturdy workhorses of the Interstellar Transport Commission frequently disposed of, when obsolescent, to private owners. She dropped like the proverbial stone towards her berth, only a little clear of the two bulk carriers. Suddenly the mutter of her inertial drive rose to a cacophonous roar and she slowed, drifting down the last few metres more like a huge balloon than an enormously heavy spaceship. As she touched, in the exact centre of the triangle marked by the beacons, her drive was cut. She rocked a little in the tripedal landing gear formed by her vanes and then was quiet and still.

Vehicles were making towards her and a large number of spaceport workers. Grimes and Fenella Pruin joined these; had they not done so they would have formed a very conspicuous minority. The after airlock door opened and the ramp was extended. Up this walked the usual boarding party—Customs, Port Health, Immigration. At the foot of the ramp stood uniformed guards, tough-looking, khakiclad men and women, stunguns out and ready. Herded by crewmen the passengers disembarked.

They were women, naked women, with the same anatomical peculiarities as the girls who had been the quarries of the kangaroo hunt in Katy's Kathouse. Most of them allowed themselves to be pushed into the waiting vans without any show of resistance. Two of them, however, broke away. They bounded over the spaceport apron, their hands held pawlike over their small breasts, not running anywhere in particular but just running . . . This was what the crowd had been waiting for. At least three dozen men took up the chase, yapping like dogs. It was all very funny—if you happened to be a sadist with simple tastes.

The port officials, with *Willy Willy*'s captain, had come ashore to watch the fun. Grimes looked at Dreeble. He thought, not for the first time, how well some people match their names—or how well their names match them. He was as weedy as ever, his features were strong on nose but deficient in chin. A few strands of black hair were plastered over the pallid baldness of his head.

Grimes looked at Dreeble—and, quite by chance, Dreeble looked at Grimes. He broke off his conversation with the Port Captain. He said, incredulously, "You!"

Grimes said nothing.

"You. Grimes. I'd recognise those ugly ears of yours anywhere. What the hell are you doing here?"

"Is there any law that says that I must be elsewhere?" countered Grimes.

The officer in charge of the guard was taking interest.

He asked, “Do you know this man, Captain Dreeble?”

“I did, once.”

“Well, *I* don’t. You! Do you have a spaceport pass?”

“I must have left it in my other clothes,” said Grimes, after making a show of searching his pockets.

“Yeah? Captain Dreeble, who is this man? Who is that with him?”

“Her I don’t know. He’s Grimes. When I tangled with him last he was a two and a half ringer in the Survey Service but I did hear that he’d been emptied out. But he’s up to no good.”

“I’ll take them in,” said the officer, raising his stungun. “Are you coming quietly?”

Grimes would have done but Fenella Pruin endeared herself to the authorities by throwing her clipboard at Aloysius Dreeble before making a break for it. Grimes, paralysed but not unconscious, heard the shout of joy, the chorus of yapping as the hunters were given another woman to chase.

They caught her at last.

Fourteen

They were dragged into a small office in the spaceport's administration block. Grimes was groggy, hardly able to stand, after the stungun blast. Fenella Pruin had been roughed up considerably by her initial captors. She had been stripped and would have been raped had the guards not intervened in time. Many women would have been cowed, humiliated, on the verge of collapse. She was not. She stood there in the ripped clothing that she had been allowed to resume, almost literally spitting with fury.

She screamed at the fat man in civilian clothes sitting behind the big desk, "I'll sue! I'll make this lousy spaceport pay and pay and pay for what was done to me!"

The fat man raised his eyebrows and smiled. "You will sue? But you are a trespasser. As such you have no rights." He turned to the master of *Willy Willy.* "Captain Dreeble, do you know these people?"

"I know the man, Colonel Dietrich. He is John Grimes. The last time I met him he was captain of the Federation Survey Service's *Seeker.* This woman I don't know."

"And what are you doing here on New Venusberg, Mr. Grimes?"

Grimes found it hard to talk; he still had not regained full control of his faculties. At last he croaked, "I am ownermaster of *Little Sister,* at present berthed at Port Aphrodite."

"And you, Miss?"

"I am Captain Grimes' passenger. His charterer, rather. And people who can afford to charter spaceships are not to be trifled with. Especially not on this money-hungry mud ball!"

"Your name, please?"

"Prunella Fenn, a citizen of Bronsonia. Our ambassador here will be told of what has happened to me!"

"Bronsonia has no ambassador on New Venusberg, Miss Fenn. I doubt if such a minor colony has representation on any other world."

"The Federation High Commissioner represents us."

"And will the Federation High Commissioner bother his arse about a pair of trespassers? Trespassers, moreover, who went to the trouble of disguising themselves. Trespassers who did not enter the spaceport through the gate; the records have been scanned and nobody of your appearance was seen to enter. In any case you have no identity badges. A search of the perimeter fence has been initiated; we shall soon know how you did get in."

"And much good will it do you!" sneered Fenella Pruin.

"And much good it will do *you,"* replied the colonel mildly. He picked up an elongated sheet of paper that had been protruded through a slot in the surface of his desk. "Ah, the print-out from Port Aphrodite . . . You get quite a write-up, Captain Grimes. Always getting into trouble in the Survey Service, finally resigning after the *Discovery* mutiny. Yachtmaster for the Baroness d'Estang. Ownermaster of *Little Sister,* which used to be the deep space pinnace carried by the Baroness's Yacht. Quite an expensive little ship, your *Little Sister.* It says here that she's constructed from an isotope of gold . . . You should have no trouble in paying your fine . . .

"And now, Miss Fenn . . . Winner of the Bronson Bonanza Lottery. Blowing your winnings on a galactic tour, with first stop New Venusberg . . .

"But why, *why,* WHY should you and Grimes be trespassing on the Port Vulcan landing field?"

Aloysius Dreeble was looking hard at Fenella Pruin. He said, "I think that I may have the answer, Colonel. May I use your telephone?"

"Of course, Captain."

"What number has been allocated to my ship?"

"Seven six three," volunteered one of the uniformed officers.

Dreeble went to the colonel's desk, punched the number on the panel of the handset, picked up the instrument. *"Willy Willy?* Captain here. Get me the Chief Officer, please." There was a short delay. "Oh, Mr Pelkin . . . Will you go up to my day cabin and look in my bookcase . . . You'll find a bundle of old copies of *Star Scandals,* you know, that magazine they put out on New Maine . . . Will you bring them across to Colonel Dietrich's office?"

"Star Scandals?" murmured the colonel thoughtfully.

"Star Scandals!" said Fenella Pruin scornfully. "Does somebody here have some take-away food to wrap up?"

"Only crumpet," leered Dreeble.

She glared at him.

"You always seem to be getting into trouble, Captain Grimes, don't you," said the colonel, making conversation. "Weren't you involved in that *Bronson Star* affair?"

"Bronson Star . . ." repeated Dreeble. "Of course. Syndication . . ."

"I demand that we be released, with apologies!" snapped Fenella Pruin. "Are we to be held here while this disreputable tramp skipper paws through his cheap pornography?"

"There are writers as well as readers!" retorted Dreeble. "And some publications are more disreputable than any tramp ship could ever be!"

Dreeble's mate, a chubby, sullen young man, came in.

He said to his captain, "Your reading matter, sir."

"Put it on the colonel's desk, Mr Pelkin."

The spaceman dropped the bundle of gaudily covered magazines on to the polished surface. Dreeble started to sort through them.

"Ah, here we are! *Sex Slaves of Salacia.* By Fenella Pruin. Syndicated from *The Bronson Star* . . . And there's a picture of the distinguished authoress, Colonel."

Dietrich looked from the photograph to Fenella Pruin, then back again. "There *is* a resemblance . . ." he murmured. "And Fenella Pruin's from Bronsonia, as is Prunella Fenn . . ."

"I always read Fenella Pruin's pieces," said Dreeble. "In fact I am—or was—quite an admirer of hers. She's been in jail at least once, you know. I remember the article she did on the experience. *I Was A Prisoner Of The Prince Of Potsdam.* Kinky that prince was. Very kinky. Potsdam's one of the Waldegren planets, you know."

"I know," said Dietrich. "I've relatives living there."

"They'll have records on Potsdam, colonel. Fingerprints, retinal patterns, bone structure, the lot. Unless Miss Pruin—or her employers—went to the expense of a complete body sculpture job something is bound to match."

"If Miss Fenn *is* Miss Pruin," said Dietrich.

"Which of course, I am not," said that lady. "You'd better release us before you make further fools of yourselves."

"Captain Dreeble," said Grimes, sufficiently recovered to shove his oar in, "would be pleased and flattered to have as a passenger his favourite author. Do you think that I'd charter *my* ship to such a notorious woman?"

"You'd do anything for money, Grimes," said Dreeble. "For all your airs and graces you're no better than Drongo Kane or myself. What sort of rake-off did you get from the Dog Star Line for interfering with our quite legitimate enterprises on Morrowvia?"

"You should know that officers of the Federation Survey Service don't take rake-offs, Dreeble."

"And is that why you're not in the Service now?"

"Gentlemen, gentlemen," admonished Dietrich. "This is my office, not a spaceman's bar." He turned to a woman officer. "Take Miss Fenn—or Miss Pruin—away and record all, and I mean *all,* her personal data." Then, to one of his male assistants. "Send a Carlottigram to the governor of the Leipzig Jail on

New Potsdam, over my name, requesting all available information on Fenella Pruin . . ."

She tried to put up a struggle but stunguns flashed. She was carried out.

"And now, Captain Grimes," said Dietrich, "I must invite you to accept our hospitality until this little matter has been cleared up."

Grimes shrugged. A token resistance would do him no good and would please only the obnoxious Dreeble. He let himself be led out of the office and to a cell. This had a heavily barred door, a hard bed, a water faucet, a drainage hole in the corner for body wastes and a single overhead light strip. It was not luxurious accommodation.

After he was locked in a guard pushed a bundle of magazines through the bars.

"With Captain Dreeble's compliments," he said, grinning.

Grimes wondered if Fenella Pruin would ever be writing about the star scandal in which she and he were now involved.

Fifteen

Inevitably Dreeble came to gloat.

He stood well back from the grille as though afraid that Grimes would reach out through the bars to grab his throat. He smirked greasily. He said, "You've had it, Grimes. You've really had it. It's a bloody pity that Drongo Kane's not here. He'd be enjoying this as much as I am."

Grimes said nothing.

"But I'm sorry about the Pruin bitch. She can really write, you know. I'll miss her pieces in Star Scandals and the other sexzines."

"So will plenty of others," said Grimes. "Including her employers back on Bronsonia. She's a valuable piece of property. But they know where she is. They'll soon buy her out of jail. They've done it before."

"I know. I've read her stories. But *The Bronson Star* will be told that she's missing, presumed dead, when they start making enquiries. It'll be a sad story. Shall I tell it to you?"

"Go ahead, if it amuses you."

"It's you that I want to amuse, Grimes. Well, she left Port Aphrodite in a hired camperfly. Correct? Piloted by yourself. And on a flight over the sea the thing just vanished. Pilot error? Pilot incompetence? Your guess is as good as mine."

Grimes laughed scornfully. "It's a known fact that we came in to the Vulcan Island airport. And the camperfly's still there."

"Is it?" Dreeble made an elaborate production of consulting his watch. "For your information, it should be lifting off about now. The good Colonel Dietrich has some talented people in his employ—masters of disguise and all that. So you and the fair Fenella, carrying your packaged purchases—lots of tourists do shopping in Vulcan City—will have boarded the camperfly. You have decided not to stay the night after all. You will tell Aerospace Control that you are bound for Delphi to consult the Oracle. (It's a pity that you didn't do that before you came here!)

"So you lift. So you wamble off to the west'ard. Out of sight of land a police launch will be waiting. By this time your impersonators will have unpacked their parcels. In two of them are miniaturised, personal inertial drive units. The pseudo Grimes and the make-believe Fenella bail out, landing on the deck of the launch. The camperfly flies on. And that's where the third parcel comes in. Or goes off."

"A bomb?" asked Grimes.

"How did you guess? Anyhow, when you don't arrive at Delphi enquiries will be made and, eventually, a search initiated. A few shreds and splinters of wreckage may be found. But no Grimes. No Fenella Pruin. I imagine that she'll get quite nice obituaries in the rags she wrote for—but nobody is going to miss *you."*

"You missed your vocation, Dreeble," said Grimes. "You should have been a fiction writer. Do you really expect me to believe all this crap?"

"But you haven't heard the best of it yet, Grimes. As soon as your identities were established—the authorities on New Potsdam were very prompt and co-operative—the colonel made a full report to the New Venusberg committee of management. The Committee doesn't like snoopers. Too, most of its members are sadistic bastards. They decided that the punishment should fit the crime. You came here to find things out. Well, the pair of you are going to do just that. The hard way. My big regret is that Fenella Pruin will not survive to write about her experiences."

"If you're short of reading matter," Grimes told him, "you can always write your own. You'd be a good hand at pornographic fantasy."

"Fantasy, Grimes?"

"What else? This is a civilised planet. Decadent as all hell but still civilised. An Associate Member of the Interstellar Federation—and both Miss Pruin and I are citizens of the Federation. The only crime that we've committed is the minor one of trespass. I've no doubt that the very worst we can expect is a heavy fine followed by deportation.

"And Miss Pruin will get a story of sorts. There was that very nasty hunting down and gang rape of some of your passengers; I didn't notice *you* doing anything to protect them. I'll get my charter money. Oh, on your way out you might ask the colonel just how long he intends to keep me in this cell. I can afford bail, you know."

"Bail, Grimes? They might accept a pound of flesh, but nothing less. You're in a jam, the very last jam of your career, and don't forget it."

"Fuck off, Dreeble," said Grimes tiredly. "Go and make up some more sensational fiction."

"Isn't there a saying, Grimes, that truth is stranger than fiction?" retorted Dreeble as he walked away.

Sixteen

Grimes was fed at regular intervals—filling but savourless sludge. He was allowed toilet requisites—a towel, a washcloth, soap, depilatory cream. He was given a change of underclothing. But the guards who brought him these things refused to answer his questions, ignored his demands for an interview with Colonel Dietrich, a telephone call to the Federation High Commissioner. He could not find out what had happened to Fenella Pruin. Much as he disliked her he felt responsible for her. He realised that he was worrying more about her safety than his own.

And what if Dreeble's wild story were not fiction?

But it had to be.

Fenella Pruin was a famous journalist, known throughout the galaxy. He, as a shipmaster and a shipowner, was a person of some consequence and possessed some slight measure of fame himself. They couldn't just vanish. There would be enquiries made—and not only by people outside New Venusberg. Captain McKillick, for example. The Port Captain must already be wondering what had happened to his new inamorata . . .

But the faked camperfly disaster . . .

That would answer all questions, especially when identifiable wreckage was found.

And then one morning they came for Grimes. (He didn't know that it was morning until he was hustled out of the prison to a waiting van; his watch had been taken from him shortly after his arrest.) He was taken to the airport. The vehicle pulled up right alongside a big, inertial drive atmosphere transport; no bystander would be able to see who or what was transferred from car to aircraft. He was thrown into an unfurnished, padded cell, locked in.

Sitting there on the deck—it was comfortable enough—he could do nothing but wait and worry. Perhaps, he thought, he was just being given the bum's rush from Vulcan Island. Perhaps he was being taken back to Port Aphrodite where he would be put aboard *Little Sister* and told to get off the planet and never come back. As long as Fenella Pruin was with him he would do just that, and thankfully.

He felt rather than heard—the padding of the cell was effective sonic insulation—the aircraft coming to life. The resilient material was depressed under the weight of his body as the transport lifted. He sensed a turn, then forward motion. He settled down to endure what he hoped would be only a short voyage. He sorely missed his pipe but it, with other possessions, had been confiscated. He was uncomfortably aware of the fullness of his bladder. He looked in some desperation around the cell. At last, by the dim illumination of the overhead light, he found a panel in the deck covering that lifted up and away. There was a drainhole under it.

Well, that was one pressing problem solved.

But there were others—many others.

He would cross these bridges when he came to them.

He drifted off into an uneasy sleep.

There was nothing else to do.

He woke up when the transport came in to a landing.

The door was flung open. Two burly, black uniformed guards dragged him out into the alleyway; one of them snapped handcuffs on to his wrists. He was pulled roughly to the open door beyond which was the ramp, then on to the gangway. He expected to see the familiar environs of Port Aphrodite but he was disappointed. This was an airport of sorts, not a spaceport, little more than a landing field in a valley ringed by high, barren crags. The time was late evening. The sky overhead was dark with a scattering of the brighter stars already visible. The lights at ground level were sparse and dim with an ominous ruddy quality.

Another small party was descending the gangway ahead of Grimes and his captors. Another prisoner with two guards . . . The back view of this person looked familiar.

"Fenella!" shouted Grimes.

She turned before the guards could restrain her. "Grimes!" Then, "How many bloody times must I tell you that the name, on this world, is Prunella Fenn?"

So she had retained her sense of humour.

"Shut up, you!" One of Grimes' escorts cuffed the side of his head viciously. Then, to his companions further down the ramp, "Get the Pruin bitch away from here, Pete, before she can yap to her space chauffeur!"

"Grimes!" she yelled before she could be silenced, "have you got word to the High Commissioner?"

"No!" There was another blow, this time on the mouth. "No! Have you?"

She tried to reply but she was effectively silenced. Grimes had to stand there, in the grip of his guards, while she was dragged away, struggling, into the ominous dusk. He thought that she was taken to the lighted entrance of a tunnel. He assumed that he would be taken in the same direction but he was not, although it was also a tunnel into which he was pulled and prodded.

There was an underground railway with little, open cars running through dimly lit caverns. There was, at last, a platform beyond which were huge, steel doors that opened, but only enough to permit the ingress of one man, when one of the guards pressed a concealed button in the rock face. Grimes' handcuffs were unlocked and removed and he was literally thrown through the gap. He landed heavily on the rough floor, grazing his hands, tearing his clothing and skinning his knees. He scrambled to his feet, turned. The doorway had already closed.

He looked around. He was in a big chamber, more artificial than natural, like a ship's airlock on a gigantic scale. A door like the one through which he had been thrown was opening. So, he thought, he was supposed to pass through it. What was on the other side? Nothing pleasant, he was sure, but he would surely starve if he stayed here. Perhaps there would he food and water at the end of the rocky tunnel that was now revealed. Perhaps there would not be—but he had to find out.

He limped into the tunnel. The inner doors shut silently behind him. He was committed now. Under his thin-soled shoes the floor was smooth, possibly worn so by the passage of many feet, but the walls were rough. Light came from glowtubes set in the overhead.

Grimes sniffed. He could smell food. He listened. He could hear voices. He plodded on until he came to a right-angled bend. Beyond this the tunnel extended for only another thirty metres or so, then expanded into a huge cave. There were people there, many people, men and women, some clad in rags and some completely naked. Most of them were gathered around a long trough set against one of the walls. From this drifted savoury smelling steam. Grimes followed his nose, joined the crowd. People, he saw, were dipping stone mugs into the stew. He wondered where he might obtain one of these utensils.

A big, shaggy-haired, heavily bearded man shouldered his way out of the mob. He was clad in the remains of some uniform; two gold bands gleamed on his surviving shoulderboard. Walking closely behind him were four women. Two of them, judging by the growths on head and body that were more like feline fur than human hair, were Morrowvians. The others, small-breasted and with heavy thighs and oddly jointed legs, could have been members of the same race as *Willy Willy*'s passengers.

The big man looked down at Grimes. "I haven't seen you before."

"I just got here," Grimes told him.

"You're a spacer, aren't you? You've got the look."

"Yes."

"So'm I. Second mate—or ex-second mate—of the not-so-good ship *Suchan.* And may the Odd Gods of the Galaxy rot Captain Bejlik's cotton socks. And his feet. And his knees. And his . . ."

"Where do I find a mug?" asked Grimes, eyeing and sniffing enviously the vessels held by the spaceman and his companions.

"Haven't they been feeding you?"

"Only prison mush. And the last time was some hours ago."

"We'll soon fix that. Darleen!" One of the heavy-haunched women stepped forward. "Give your pannikin to our friend here. You can soon find another one for yourself."

"I couldn't . . ." began Grimes.

"You will. This mayn't be Liberty Hall an' if you speak unkindly to *my* cats I'll knock your teeth in—but never let it be said that Jimmy O'Brien turned a deaf ear to the appeal of a fellow spaceman. The two of us are the only two spacers here now since Komatsu bought it . . . Are you any good with long range weapons, by the way? We need another expert for the team."

Grimes accepted the thick mug from the girl's hands. He could see chunks of meat and vegetables floating in the thick stew. It tasted as good as it looked and smelled.

After a satisfying gulp he said, "This is all very confusing, Mr. O'Brien . . ."

"Call me Jimmy."

"All right. Jimmy. But there are some things that I must find out. First of all, has a woman called Prunella Fenn—or Fenella Pruin—been brought here?"

"No. You're the only newcomer we've had for days. Is she your girlfriend?"

"I'm responsible for her. Secondly, what *is* this place?"

"A barracks, you might call it."

"A slave barracks?"

"No. For gladiators."

For gladiators . . .

Grimes was not at all happy as he accompanied Jimmy O'Brien, the four women tailing along behind, across the floor of the huge cave. There was a lavish scattering of huge mattresses, most of which were occupied by groups of people eating and talking in low voices. Many of them turned to eye Grimes appraisingly as he walked slowly past.

"They're weighing you up," said O'Brien cheerfully. "They might be coming against you in the arena. They're wondering what you're good at." Then, "Here's our pad."

He motioned Grimes to sit down, then joined him. The four women waited until the men were comfortably settled before seating themselves.

O'Brien took a noisy gulp of stew then said, "Since it looks like you're one of us we'd better get to know each other. These . . ." he motioned towards the two Morrowvians, "are my pussies, Miala and Leeuni." (Miala's hair was white, in vivid contrast to her brown skin, while Leeuni's was tortoiseshell.) Keep your paws off them. And these, Darleen and Shirl, were Komatsu's girls." (They were horse-faced, but pleasantly so, and smiled at him diffidently.) "They're yours now. While you last. Or while they last.

"As I've already told you I am—or was—a spacer. My crime—if you call it that—was helping Miala to stow away aboard my ship. Miala's crime was stowing away. The Old Man—bad cess to him!—turned us in. Leeuni is a murderess—although the pimp she did in wasn't much loss.

"Shirl and Darleen were performers in some clipjoint called Katy's Kathouse. One of the so-called entertainments there is the kangaroo hunt. They were two of the kangaroos. The hunt finishes with the hunters raping the hunted. Well, the girls here didn't like being raped. Darleen kneed some fat slob of a tourist in the balls and Shirl just about bit the ear off another one. Katy—as far as she's concerned the customer is always right as long as he has a full wallet—took a very dim view.

"And now, what's your heartrending story? For a start, what do they call you?"

"My name is Grimes. John Grimes. I've a ship of my own—*Little Sister*. I'm on charter to *The Bronson Star*—it's a newspaper on a world called Bronsonia. I'm supposed to be looking after one of their star reporters—Fenella Pruin . . ."

"Fenella Pruin? I thought the name was familiar the first time you mentioned it. Doesn't she write for Star Scandals? And Grimes? Weren't you slung out of the Survey Service for mutiny?"

"I was mutinied against. And I resigned from the Service. Anyhow, Fenella Pruin hoped to uncover some interesting muck here. She and I were trespassing on the Vulcan Island spaceport to watch *Willy Willy* come in. The master, Aloysius Dreeble, recognised me and after we were arrested was also able to identify Fenella Pruin . . ."

"But do you come from New Alice, John Grimes?" asked one of the girls—Darleen, or Shirl? they could have been identical twins—in a puzzled voice with a peculiarly flat accent. "You talk like us."

"I'm Australian," said Grimes after a moment's thought.

"Australian! But Australia is where our ancestors came from!"

"Never mind old home week," said O'Brien. "Carry on, Grimes."

"That's all. They slung me in jail. I suppose that they did the same to Fenella Pruin. I saw her again, briefly, after the transport that brought us from Vulcan Island landed here. But she was taken somewhere before I could speak to her . . ."

"The Colosseum isn't the only attraction in these parts," said O'Brien slowly. "I've heard rumours—but only rumours—of something called the Snuff Palace . . ."

"But how do I get out of here? How do I find her?"

"You don't. That answers both questions. All you can hope to do is survive. It's not so bad being pitted against animals in the arena; you don't mind killing them so much to save yourself from being killed. But haven't you noticed how everybody here keeps themselves to themselves? There's a reason, a very good reason. We don't make friends outside our own teams. That was Komatsu's trouble. After he joined up with us he met a girl in one of the other groups, a woman of his own race. He got to know her. And then—I still think that it was intentional—our team was matched against hers. He was a long range fighter. She was too. When it came to the crunch he just stood there looking at her with that killing disc, a thing like a circular saw that you throw, in his hand. He just stood there. She was similarly armed and didn't hesitate. She threw her disc and just about took his head off. Then she snatched the short sword from her team leader and before he could stop her cut her own throat . . ."

"You mean this actually happened?" demanded Grimes.

"Of course it happened. Worse things happen here. But now—to business. You may be captain aboard your ship but I'm captain of this team. I'm one of the two short range fighters; my weapon's an axe. Darleen's the other one; she uses a club. Then Miala and Leeuni have long, sharp spears. Medium range, you might say. Shirl's long range—with a boomerang. I hope that you'll be able to make your contribution."

"An arbalest," said Grimes. "Is that allowed?"

"An arbalest? What's that?"

"A crossbow."

"I've seen bows and arrows used here. There are probably crossbows in the armoury. *They* keep a stock of just about every weapon known to civilised—or uncivilised—man. If you ask for a broken bottle they'll give you one. But no firearms, of course. Even so—a crossbow . . . You really can use one?"

"Yes," said Grimes, hoping that the tuition had not worn off.

Then O'Brien said that it was time that he got some shuteye. He removed his ragged uniform, sprawled out on the mattress between the naked Miala and Leeuni. It became obvious that the three of them had no intention of going to sleep at once.

Grimes asked, rather embarrassedly, "Where do I go?"

"You will stay here," Darleen (or was it Shirl?) told him. "There is room on the pad for all of us."

"No, I mean where do I go for . . .To wash and so on . . ."

"Come," said both girls as one.

They led him across the floor of the huge cave to a smaller one. In this were the toilet facilities, adequate in all respects save privacy. And those blasted girls refused to leave him and while he was enthroned, seated over the long trough through which rushed a stream of water, he was treated to the spectacle of two ladies who were more than just good friends taking a hot shower together. He wanted a shower himself; in the Vulcan jail he had been unable to enjoy anything better than cold sponge baths. He stripped, walked to one of the open stalls. Shirl (or was it Darleen?) accompanied him. The other New Alice girl took his discarded coveralls and underclothing to another stall to give them a much needed laundering.

He realised that in an odd sort of way he was enjoying himself. It was a long time since he had taken a shower with an attractive woman and much longer still since he had done so with one who washed him with such solicitude, working the spray of liquid detergent up to a soft lather with her gentle hands. He knew, as his own hands strayed, that she was his for the taking—but not here, not here. It was too public. Perhaps, if he survived, he would exhibit the same unconcern for an audience as those two lesbian ladies, as that heterosexual couple two shower stalls away.

And perhaps that trauma engendered by his horrid experiences aboard *Bronson Star* would be healed.

Just off the steam-filled ablutions cave there was a drying room in which a blast of hot air dried both their bodies and Grimes' clothing. To the girls' surprise and disappointment he resumed his garments. They took him back to the pad. O'Brien and his two women were sleeping soundly. It was not long before Grimes was following suit with Darleen on one side of him, Shirl on the other.

Seventeen

Reveille was a vastly over-amplified trumpet call.

The gladiators—Grimes estimated their number to be about two hundred—were given time to make their morning toilet before another trumpet call announced breakfast. Ablutions facilities were adequate, there being more than one minor cavern for this purpose. Breakfast was stew again—but this time of fish, not meat. It was savoury enough.

"What happens now?" Grimes asked O'Brien.

"We just wait."

"Don't we get any time to practice with our weapons?"

"The only practice we get is in the arena. But when there's anybody new in a team—such as you—there are usually a few sort of breaking-in bouts against animals before you're pitted against fellow humans. Too, usually just one death is enough to satisfy the audience—although that depends a great deal on the supply of new gladiators." He laughed. "Most times it's a new member of a team who gets himself killed."

Cheerful bastard, thought Grimes.

"We'll look after you," said Shirl (or Darleen).

Grimes wished that he had pipe and tobacco to soothe his nerves. He looked around the cave. Nobody was smoking—and certainly there must be others like himself, craving the solace of nicotine. Perhaps this was part of the technique—a gladiator deprived of pipe, cigarettes or whatever must be a bad-tempered one. He said as much.

O'Brien laughed. "You should know by this time that smoking shortens the wind and all sorts of other horrid things. A non-smoking gladiator is a *fit* gladiator."

"Fit for what?" demanded Grimes.

"You want to survive, don't you?"

"I'd want to even more if I knew that there was some chance of getting out of here."

Again there was a deafening trumpet call, followed by a harsh voice. "Denton's team and Smith's team report to the armory! Denton's team and Smith's team report to the armory!"

Not far from O'Brien's pad a huge man got to his feet, followed by another smaller and more agile, followed by four slight women. Their faces were expressionless. They divested themselves of what little they were wearing, left the rags scattered on their mattress.

"Denton's a boxer," volunteered O'Brien. "He wears a horrid spiked affair on his arm called a *cestus.* The other fellow, Mallory, plays around with a net and trident. Two of the girls use lariats, the other two throw javelins. A nasty combination. I hope that we never come up against them . . ."

Denton, followed by his people, was walking slowly to the far end of the cave. His back was almost as hairy as the front of him. He slouched like some ungainly ape.

"And Smith?" asked Grimes, indicating the other team some distance away.

"Rapier, and his sidekick fancies himself with the sabre. The two medium range men use long spears and the two girls are archers. But not crossbows."

"And how long will the fight take?"

"We shall know when the survivors come back—unless they've all been taken to hospital. That happens quite often. Then we just have to wait for the next announcement."

"But why couldn't you—*we*—just refuse to go out and kill or be killed?"

"That's been tried," said O'Brien. "But it's not recommended. After just one warning the cave is flooded with a particularly nasty gas. It makes you vomit your guts up and feel as though you're being flayed alive. Needless to say the sit-down strikers aren't at all popular with the others . . ."

They sat on their big mattress and waited. All through the cave people were sitting on mattresses and waiting. Which team had drawn first blood? Was the crowd in a merciful mood? How many survivors would there be?

"I hope you're good with the arbalest," said O'Brien after a long silence.

"I've used one recently," said Grimes.

"At one of those fancy hunting camps, I suppose. Did you hit anything?"

"It wasn't at a hunting camp—but I did hit the target."

"What was it?"

"A Shaara blimp."

"A bloody big target," commented O'Brien glumly. "Anybody could hit anything that big as long as it was within range . . ." Then, "A Shaara blimp! You must have been fighting them. There'll be Shaara in the audience, you know. If any of us get injured it'll be thumbs down for sure."

"Do you want me to resign from your team?" asked Grimes.

"It's too late now. *They* had you under full observation from the moment you entered the barracks. *They* know who was mug enough to take you under his wing."

"And he's an Australian," put in either Darleen or Shirl. *"We* want him with us."

"And shall I stand to attention while you all sing Waltzing Matilda?" asked O'Brien.

There was another long silence.

At last voices were heard from the far end of the cave. Grimes, with the others, turned to look. Denton had come back. He was limping badly. A deep slash on his face gleamed redly under the newly applied syntheskin. There was another gash on his right thigh. Two of his women followed him. They, too, had been wounded but not seriously enough to put them in hospital. And the other three team members?

"Dead . . ." Grimes heard Denton growl in answer to a question. "But we did for Smith and his bastards. All of them."

The trumpet brayed.

Then—"O'Brien's team to the armory! O'Brien's team to the armory!"

"So it's only animals for us," muttered O'Brien. "I hope that they're nice, little, tame ones!"

"So do I," said Grimes.

"But they won't be," O'Brien told him.

Eighteen

O'Brien removed his rags of uniform, folding the clothing neatly before putting it down on the mattress.

"Get undressed," he ordered Grimes.

"Why?"

"It's the rule."

"We're issued with armour, I suppose?" asked Grimes as he shrugged out of his coveralls, assisted unnecessarily by Shirl and Darleen.

"Armour?" O'Brien laughed harshly. "Not on your sweet Nelly. The customers pay to see naked flesh, to see it torn and bleeding. But come on, all of you. Let's get the show on the road."

Following the big man they walked through the cave. Heads turned to follow their progress. Some expressions were sympathetic. Most said, all too clearly, *Thank the Odd Gods that it's not us. This time.*

There was a small, metal door in the rock wall which opened when they were almost up to it, which closed after them. They walked along a short tunnel, came to a brightly lit recess which, fantastically, seemed to be a shop, although the shopkeeper behind the wide counter was dressed as a Roman soldier, the only anachronisms in his attire being the wrist companion and the holstered stungun.

He smiled greasily at the gladiators.

"And what can I do you for today, Mr. O'Brien? Your usual battleaxe, I suppose? And for the ladies? Spears and boomerangs and a *nulla nulla*?" Behind him an assistant was taking the lethal tools down from racks. Grimes stared. There was indeed a remarkably comprehensive collection of weaponry. He was pleased to see that there were crossbows very similar to the ones that he had already used. "And for the new gentleman? I assume that he'll be wanting a long range weapon—unless you're changing the make-up of your team." He addressed Grimes directly. "We have a nice line in *shuriken,* sir. There's been no demand for them since Mr. Komatsu and Miss Tanaka—er—left us."

"An arbalest," said Grimes. "And a dozen quarrels." He added, "Please." To antagonise this fat slob, who would be quite capable of issuing sub-standard weaponry, would be foolish.

"An arbalest we can do you, sir. But not a dozen quarrels. Two only is the rule. Of course, you can use them more than once—if you can get them back, just as Miss Shirley can do with her boomerangs . . ."

The assistant took an arbalest down from the rack, held it up for Grimes' inspection.

"To your satisfaction, sir?" asked the pseudo-centurion. "Good. Then let us not keep the customers waiting—*your* customers, that is. Your props will be waiting for you in the arena. And the best of luck, Mr. O'Brien. We shall be watching on our trivi."

"Thank you," O'Brien said before moving on. Then, when the party was out of earshot beyond a bend in the tunnel, "That two-faced bastard! But we have to be polite to him . . . My dream is to have him out on the sand against me one day . . ."

They came to the last door. They stepped through it into hot air, into dazzling sunlight reflected from white, freshly raked sand. Trumpets blared martial music, accompanied by drums and cymbals. There was some applause but it was bored rather than enthusiastic.

Grimes, squinting against the harsh light, looked around him. There were the tiers of canopied seats ringing the huge arena. O'Brien's team, he thought, would not be playing before a capacity house; nonetheless only about a third of the seating was unoccupied. Some members of the audience were dressed for the occasion in rather phoney looking togas and gowns. There was a royal box under a very elaborate canopy, the human occupants of which were clad in imperial purple. The non-human ones were (but of course) Shaara.

"Our weapons," said O'Brien, walking towards where these had been set down on the sand.

There was the wicked-looking battleaxe, the two long spears, the steel arbalest with two short quarrels. There were a nobbly wooden club and two boomerangs, but these cruciform and not of the familiar crescent shape. *An arbalest and boomerangs,* thought Grimes, *and that royal box within range . . .* But the air shimmered above the fence dividing the lower tier of seats from the arena. It must be, he decided, a forcefield.

The music ceased.

An amplified voice announced, "And now, for our second event, Battler O'Brien and his team versus the sand rays of Sere! May the best beings win!"

O'Brien had picked up and was hefting the long-handled axe, the women had their own weapons in hand. Grimes loaded the arbalest. He wished that he had a pouch of some kind for the spare quarrel.

"Sand rays," muttered O'Brien. "Do you know them, Grimes? They skim over the surface, not quite flying. All teeth and leathery wings. There'll be six of the bastards. Aim for the single eye. Your crossbow will be better against 'em than Shirl's boomerangs . . ."

Would it be? Grimes wondered. Far too little effort had been required to cock the arbalest. It would not have anything like the range of the weapons that he had acquired at Camp Diana.

Again the trumpets brayed.

At the far end of the arena gates opened. In the darkness beyond them Grimes saw something stirring, a shadowy undulation. The gladiators waited tensely. "Try not to move," whispered O'Brien. "Movement attracts them." The audience waited impatiently. "Send Battler O'Brien in to chase them out!" screamed a woman. "He's just standing there doing nothing—and we're paying for it!"

"I'd like to send *you* in, you fat bitch!" O'Brien muttered.

The trumpets brayed again.

"You, O'Brien!" roared a voice from the speakers. "Jump up and down! Dance!"

"Get stuffed," O'Brien said. Probably he was heard; directional microphones must be trained on the team.

"O'Brien! Hear this! Unless you *do* something it's you and your people for the Snuff Palace—for one performance only!"

O'Brien brandished his battleaxe; the sunlight was reflected dazzlingly from the broad, polished blade. It was enough. The sandrays came out of the pen in line ahead, moving fast, the tips of their wings skimming the sand, throwing up a white, glittering spray. They were fearsome beasts, their huge, open mouths rimmed with long, sharp yellow teeth. In the centres of their domed heads balefully gleamed their single golden eyes.

Clear of the pen their formation opened up. Grimes selected his target, took aim. The range, he thought, was still too great but it was closing rapidly. Out of the corner of his eye he saw Shirl throw her first boomerang but did not see what result she achieved. At least she had not aimed at the sand ray that he regarded as his . . .

"Shoot!" O'Brien, was yelling. "Shoot, damn you!"

Grimes, before he pulled the trigger, elevated the arbalest slightly. As he had suspected this was a relatively weak weapon; the trajectory of the quarrel was far from flat. But instinctively—or luckily—he had corrected accordingly. He saw the bolt hit, stooped to fumble for the remaining one in the sand. And then he had to reload.

By this time the sand rays—four of them—were among the gladiators. A huge wing knocked Grimes sprawling. He heard one of the girls scream, O'Brien roaring. He got to his feet, still clutching the arbalest. Miala pushed him over as she danced by, brandishing her long spear. Again he tried to get up but Darleen was standing over him, legs astride. Her heavy club smashed into the open mouth of a sand ray coming in for the kill, splintering sword-like teeth but snatched from her hand by those remaining. The huge, fast-moving body swept her away from Grimes, passed over him in a wave of evil smelling darkness. The long, barbed tail flicked his chest, tearing the skin, drawing blood.

He got once again to his feet.

He ignored the melee over to his right; he got the impression that O'Brien, Miala and Leeuni were well able to take care of themselves. He ran towards where the ray had the struggling Darleen on the ground, worrying her like a terrier with a rat. She was still alive, her long legs, all that could be seen of her, were kicking frantically. Shirl was sprawled on the back of the beast, her arms around the domed head, the fingers of both eyes clawing at the single eye. The tail was arching up, up, over and forward, its spiked tip stabbing viciously down. Blood was running from the girl's back and buttocks.

Grimes ran around to the front of the fight. He raised his crossbow. At this range he could not miss. Shirl saw him, withdrew her hands. He fired. The steel bolt drove through the tough, glassy membrane protecting the eye, into the brain beneath. The wings flailed in a brief flurry of sand and then were still. Shirl joined Grimes to pull Darleen from under the ray's head. Her body was a mass of blood, her own and the green ichor from the animal's wounds.

But she could still grin up at them.

"I knocked most of the bastard's teeth out," she whispered, "but he could still give me a nasty suck . . ."

But what of the others?

The fight was almost over. Only one ray still survived and Miala and Leeuni were leaning on their long spears, watching O'Brien finish it off. Its tail was gone, and one wing. It was floundering around in a circle on the greenstained sand, whining almost supersonically. With a dazzling display of axemanship the big man was hacking off the other wing, piece by piece, working in from tip to root. The crowd, to judge from the applause, was loving the brutal spectacle.

It sickened Grimes.

He took the long spear from Leeuni's unresisting hand, awaited his chance and then drove the sharp point into the sand ray's eye.

The death flurry was both short and unspectacular. O'Brien lowered his axe, stood there glaring madly at Grimes.

He howled, "What did you do that for?"

"I was putting the beast out of its misery."

"You had no right. It was mine. Mine!"

Axe upraised again the maddened O'Brien charged at Grimes, who brought up the spear to defend himself. The blade of the weapon, still sharp, sheared off the head of the spear and, on the second swing lopped short the shaft with which he was trying to hold off his berserk assailant.

It was Darleen who saved Grimes' life. Or Shirl. Or both of them. A thin slab of sand ray's wing, flung by Shirl with force and accuracy, struck the descending blade of the axe, deflecting it. And Darleen, coming up behind O'Brien, hit him, hard, on the back of the head with her *nulla nulla.*

He gasped, staggered.

Darleen hit him again.

He stumbled, sagged. He dropped the battleaxe then followed it to the sand. His hands made scrabbling motions.

The crowd was roaring, screaming. Grimes looked towards the royal box. A tall, portly man, wearing a purple toga and with something golden on his bald head, had both arms extended before him, was making a gesture that Grimes had no trouble in interpreting, with which he had no intention of complying.

Darleen, on the point of collapse herself but still holding her club, asked doubtfully, "Shall I?"

"No," said Grimes. *"No."*

The amplified voice came from the speakers. "Grimes! The verdict is thumbs down!"

"No!" he shouted defiantly.

"Darleen! Shirl! The verdict is thumbs down!"

"No!" they called.

Grimes heard movement behind him, turned to see the advancing guards in their archaic helmets and breastplates, their metallic kilts. Their pistols were modern enough.

Luckily they were only stunguns, Grimes thought as the blast hit him.

Before he lost consciousness he wondered if this were so lucky.

Nineteen

He woke up.

He heard screaming, thought fuzzily that he was still in the throes of some nightmare.

He opened his eyes, looked up at a low, white ceiling, featureless save for a light strip. He felt around himself with investigatory hands. He seemed to be on a resilient bed. He was alone.

But who was screaming?

He raised himself on his elbows, looked around. Before him was a blank white wall. To his right there was a similar view. To his left the wall was broken by an alcove in which were toilet facilities. But the noise—it had subsided now to a low whimpering—was coming from behind him. He drew up his knees, swung himself around on the bed and looked with sick horror at the fourth wall.

At first he thought that it was a window, one looking into an operating theatre. Then he realised that it was a big trivi screen. Under the too bright lights was a table, its white covering spattered with blood. Strapped to it, supine, spread-eagled, was a naked girl. Stooping over the table was a white-gowned, white-capped, white-masked surgeon. His gloves gleamed redly and wetly. A similarly clad woman stood a little back from him, holding a tray of glittering instruments. In the background were the tiers of seats with the avidly watching audience. Inevitably there were Shaara among them.

There was no anaesthetist.

The surgeon deepened and lengthened the abdominal incision, tossed the bloody scalpel back on to the instruments tray. He took from this retractors, used them to pull the lips of the horrible wound apart. There was a pattering of applause from the audience. Then, plunging his hands deep into the victim's body, he started to pull *things* out . . .

The screaming was dreadful.

Grimes just made it to the toilet alcove, vomited into the bowl. He stayed there, his hands clamped over his ears, shutting out most but not all of the noise. He heard, faintly, hand-clapping and cries of, "Encore! Encore!"

At last there was silence. He uncovered his ears and found that it was indeed so. He looked cautiously into the room. The big screen was blank, dead. He walked slowly towards it, fearing that it would come alive with some fresh scene of horror. He could find no controls; obviously it could not be turned off from this side. So his sadistic jailors, any time that they felt like it, could treat him to a preview of what might be his own eventual fate.

He wondered when they would be getting around to Shirl and Darleen. And himself. He wondered if they had already disposed of Fenella Pruin. She had not been the girl on the operating table; of that he was sure. He supposed glumly that he and the New Alice women would be given time to recover fully from the wounds that they had sustained in the arena; a torture victim who dies too soon deprives the spectators of the entertainment for which they have paid. He looked down at the transparent syntheskin dressing on his chest. The gash inflicted by the sand ray's tail seemed to be healing nicely. Too nicely.

Of course he could refuse to eat—when and if he got fed. (In spite of his recent nausea his belly was grumbling.) But what if he did? With modern techniques of compulsory feeding the hunger strike had long since ceased to be an effective protest weapon.

Out of the corner of his eye he saw a flicker of movement.

A hatch had opened at floor level and a tray had been pushed through on to the polished surface. The little door closed with an audible click. It fitted so perfectly that only a very close inspection of the wall revealed its existence.

But Grimes did not make this examination until later. He was more interested in the bowl, with a spoon beside it, sitting on the tray. Everything was made of what seemed to be compressed paper; there was nothing that could be used as a weapon, either against his jailors (if they ever showed themselves) or as an instrument for suicide.

The food, too—it was a thick stew—could well have been made of cardboard itself. But it seemed to be nourishing enough.

Unfortunately Grimes could not keep it down for long.

He was treated to an after dinner show—this time of a man being slowly roasted over a bed of glowing coals, embers that flared fitfully when fed by the drippings of fatty fluids.

Twenty

Time passed.

How much time Grimes did not know, although he did try to keep some track of it. He assumed that he was being fed at regular intervals, assumed, too, that he was being given three meals a day. The trays, bowls and spoons were made of a material that could be torn up and flushed away. He saved the spoons, laying out a row of them in the toilet alcove.

He tried to keep fit by exercising, by doing push-ups, situps and toe-touchings. He was far from sure that this was wise—the better the condition in which he maintained himself the longer it would take him to die under torture. But he could not abandon hope. Not for the first time in his life he thought that the immortal Mr Micawber must be among his ancestors. Something might—just might—turn up.

The worst feature of this period of incarceration was that he was beginning to look forward to the sadistic trivi shows. He tried to excuse himself by telling the censor in his mind that he watched so as to be assured that neither Fenella Pruin, Darleen or Shirl was one of the screaming victims. This was partly so—but he knew that he had, now and again in the past, enjoyed films in which were picturesque scenes of the maltreatment of naked women. These had only been make-believe sadism—or had they?—but this was the real thing.

It was when he became sexually stimulated that he really hated himself.

Then one night—if it was night—he was awakened by the notes of a bugle call, *reveille,* from the wall screen. (It made a change from the usual piercing screams.) He looked at the wall but there was no picture, only an ominous, ruddy glow.

A quite pleasant male voice said, "We have been observing you, Grimes."

"Surprise! Surprise!" he muttered sardonically.

"We have been observing you, Grimes," repeated the voice. "We have decided that you are promising raw material." (Grimes remembered a torture session that he had been unable to watch to a finish, that of a man being skinned alive.) "It may not surprise you to learn that many of our executioners are recruited from among the prisoners. You will be given the opportunity to join their number."

"Like hell I would!" almost shouted Grimes.

"The standard reaction," remarked the voice. "But you would be surprised to learn how many of our torturers have been recruited as you will be. After all, it boils down to a simple choice, that between being the killer or the killed. During your career in the Survey Service—and subsequently—that is a choice that you must have made, quite unconsciously, many and many a time. But when you made that choice in the past the death that you escaped would have been a relatively painless one. This time the death that you escape would have been extremely painful."

"The answer is NO!" shouted Grimes.

"Are you sure? As I have already said, we have watched you. We have observed that you were physically stimulated by many of the more picturesque punishments meted out to members of the opposite sex. You really hate women, Grimes, don't you? Soon, very soon, you will be given the opportunity to *do* something about it. And I warn you that if you fail to give satisfaction, if you refuse to take up the torturer's tools or if you accord the subjects the privilege of a too quick release, you will be given instruction in the techniques required for the infliction of a long-protracted passing—instruction from which you will not benefit as you will not survive it."

The red glow in the screen contracted to a single bright point, an evil star, then winked out.

And what would he do, Grimes asked himself, when it came to the crunch? What could he do? If failure to comply would mean only a quick death the choice would be a simple one—but he remembered vividly, too vividly, that wretch who had been skinned alive and that other one slowly roasting over the sizzling coals.

Then they came for him.

The four guards hustled him through what seemed like miles of corridors, cuffing him when he hesitated, prodding his naked back with the hard muzzles of their stunguns. They brought him into a large room, a sort of theatre in the round with the tiered seats already occupied by the audience. Over these the lighting was dim but Grimes could see men and women—and the inevitable Shaara. The stage was brightly lit by a single light sphere hanging above it. It was a set, and the other members of the cast were ready and waiting. There was a rack. There were two St. Andrew's crosses. There was a box, a sort of oven, glowing redly, from which protruded the wooden-handled ends of the hot irons. There was a table with an array of knives, large and small, straight and curved, gleaming evilly.

On the rack was Fenella Pruin. She looked at him. He looked at her. She was trying hard not to show her fear but it would have been impossible for one in her situation not to be hopelessly afraid. Strapped to one cross was Darleen, to the other was Shirl. Grimes remembered the show that he had watched with Fenella, the make-believe torturings of the women on the rack and the crucifixes. He remembered the fat man who had wanted to take her to see the real thing. He wondered if that swine were among these ghoulish spectators.

An amplified voice was speaking.

"Gentlebeings, the stars of the entertainment that we are about to witness are already known to each other. The man making his debut as an apprentice torturer is an offplanet spy who was apprehended by our security forces. He is being given the opportunity to redeem himself. The lady on the rack is his fellow agent. She will be punished for her crimes against society. The two ladies draped so attractively on their crosses abetted the man in his defiance of authority. Perhaps some of you were present on that occasion in the Colosseum. They will leam that it is unwise to transfer allegiances. Unfortunately for them it will be the last lesson of their lives . . ."

"Cut the cackle!" screamed Fenella Pruin defiantly.

"I would order you gagged," the unseen announcer went on, "but that would disappoint our customers, to whom shrieks and pitiful pleas for mercy are the universe's finest music.

"And now, Grimes, may I remind you that the show must go on? And soon, very soon. If there is too much hesitation on your part one of our experienced tormentors will usurp your star role and yours, although in an almost as important part, will be for one performance only.

"You see your working tools. The rack, the hot irons, the knives. You can use them in any order you please. Your original accomplice has stretched the truth so often that it would, perhaps, be an act of poetic justice if you stretched *her.* Or you might prefer to make a start on your more recent acquaintances, working on the principle of last in, first out. May I make a suggestion. Perhaps, during your early training in the use of various weapons, you became an expert knife thrower? And the young ladies come from a world whose inhabitants are experts in the use of thrown weapons . . . They would appreciate being despatched that way. But do not make it too fast, Grimes. You know what the consequences to you will be if you do. Just try to lop off an ear here, a nipple there. Aiming between their legs you could slice their labia quite painfully . . ."

Or I could use a knife on myself, thought Grimes. *But that wouldn't be any help to the women. Or I could kill one of them bejore the stunguns got me. But which one?*

Shirl was staring hard at him. She seemed to be trying to tell him something. She looked from him to the knives on the table, then up to the bright overhead light, screwing up her eyes exaggeratedly, then back to him. Grimes was no telepath but perhaps she was. Perhaps she was an unusually strong transmitter. There were glimmerings, only glimmerings, in his mind. Throwing weapons . . . Nocturnal vision, so often possessed by those of Terran but non-human ancestry, such as the Morrowvians . . . (He did not *know* what was the racial origin of the people of New Alice but he had his suspicions.)

There was a chance, he decided.

There was a chance for a quick death for the four of them—and a chance that they would not go to the grave unaccompanied.

But what of his own nocturnal vision? A sudden plunge into almost darkness would leave him as blind as the proverbial bat, and without the bat's sonar. But he had been trained to work in the dark, by feel, when necessary. As long as he had directions and distances fixed firmly in his mind . . .

"We are waiting, Grimes," said the voice. "Make up your mind. The choice is simple—torturer or torturee. And by being noble you won't help your lady friends. Perhaps a countdown will help you. Ten . . . Nine . . ."

Grimes walked slowly to the table, picked up a short knife in his left hand. Then he went to the electric brazier, pulled a hot iron out of the box. Its tip was incandescent.

"A knife *and* an iron . . ." remarked the announcer. "This should be interesting. Which will he use first, I wonder? The knife, I imagine . . ."

Grimes moved to the centre of the stage. He was not quite directly beneath the overhead light, now (except for the ruddily glowing brazier) the only source of illumination in the theatre. And he was, he prayed to all the Odd Gods of the Galaxy, correctly sited for his next move.

Suddenly he threw the heavy iron upwards as hard as he could, transferring the knife to his right hand as soon as he had done so and running towards Shirl. The whirling, white-hot bar hit the glaring lamp, fortuitously the incandescent end first. Perhaps the plastic globe would not have broken had this not been so—but break it did.

There was darkness—complete insofar as Grimes and the members of the audience and the guards were concerned. Grimes had misjudged slightly, made heavy contact with Shirl's naked body a fraction of a second before he anticipated it. He heard the *ough* as the air was driven from her lungs. Both his hands went up to her left wrist, found the strap securing it to the arm of the cross. He slashed, felt the soft leather or plastic or whatever it was fall away. (That knife was *sharp.)* Then her right wrist . . . (At least one stungun was in operation now, to judge from the vicious buzzing, but the shooting was wild.) Then her right ankle. (She emitted a little scream as he inadvertently nicked her skin.) Then her left . . .

Freed from the cross she fell against him, then pushed away, saying, "Look after Darleen . . ."

He stumbled towards the other crucifix. He almost missed it, found it only by tripping over Darleen's right foot. Even though he fell he did not lose his hold on the knife. He scrambled to his feet, went to work on the girl's bonds. Meanwhile Shirl, to whom the glow from the brazier afforded adequate illumination, must have made her way to the table with the knives. There was no more buzzing of misaimed stunguns. There were shouts, screams. Somebody was yelling, "Lights! Lights!"

Darleen was released. Without a word she ran to join Shirl. Perhaps there were now no knives left to throw but there were still the hot irons and, in the arena she had preferred a club to throwing weapons . . .

But where was the rack? Where was Fenella Pruin? It was still too dark for anybody with normal eyesight to find his way around in the theatre and he had now lost all sense of direction.

"Fenella!" he shouted.

"Here!" Then, "Get a bloody move on!" she cried.

He stumbled in the direction from which her voice had come. He found the rack the hard way, crashing into it, falling full length on to her nude body. She snapped irritably, "I want you to cut me loose, not make love to me!"

This time he had dropped the knife. He slid off her, down to the floor. He scrabbled around under the rack, to both sides of it. Then there was a brief flare of actinic light as one of Shirl's missiles hit some piece of electrical equipment, shorting it out. He saw the gleam of metal close by his groping hand. Just in time he was able to stop himself from picking it up by the blade.

As he cut through Fenella's bonds he realised that the theatre was now very quiet. All of the audience must either have escaped or been killed. (He did not think that they could have put up much of a fight.) Fenella pulled herself to her feet by holding on to his shoulders.

She asked, "What now?"

It was a good question, too good.

He said, after hesitation, "I kill you. Then the other two girls. Then myself."

"What!"

"Do you think that *they* will give us an easy death after all this?"

"So you want to die? *I* don't."

And neither did he, thought Grimes. But what chance of survival was there?

Yet the theatre should have been swarming with armed guards by now. It was not. Surely the show in which he, Fenella, Shirl and Darleen were the stars must have been monitored . . . Perhaps the monitoring was only a recording, with nobody watching it live . . . Perhaps the survivors of the massacre were still trying to find their way through the maze of tunnels and had not yet met anybody to whom to report that the actor and actresses had strayed from the script.

"Shirl! Darleen!" he called.

They came to him, their bodies palely luminous in the near-darkness.

"Some escaped," said Shirl. "We didn't get them all . . ."

"We have to escape ourselves. Find women about your build among the corpses. Strip them. Completely. Get dressed. And you, Fenella."

He found the body of a man. A thrown knife had penetrated his brain through his left eye, so there was not much blood. Grimes, hating the feel of the dead flesh, removed the shirt, the kilt, the underwear. At this latter he wrinkled his nose in disgust. He dressed in the shirt and kilt, found that the dead man's shoes fitted his feet.

Not far from him Fenella Pruin had taken the long dress off a tall, slim woman who no longer needed it, had put it on. She looked at him and said, "Let's go."

"Underwear," Grimes told her.

"But I can't wear that. She . . ."

"People usually do when they die. Take those panties off her and hide them under a seat. When the guards get here they'll find, among the other bodies, four completely naked ones. They'll think—for a short while—that they're us. I hope. Ready, all of you?"

"Ready!" said Shirl and Darleen.

"All right. Let's get out of here."

He led the way along an aisle. All the EXIT lights were out, of course, but surely an egress would not be hard to find. They passed through an opaquely panelled revolving door into a corridor that was, by comparison with the darkness of the theatre, brightly lit.

At the far end of this was a large group of men, running towards them.

Twenty-one

So the guards were on the way at last. How much did they know? Would it be possible, Grimes wondered, to bluff his way past them?

"Leave this to me . . ." whispered Fenella Pruin.

She ran towards the advancing party of armed men, staggering a little. (Her requisitioned sandals, Grimes learned later, were a size too small.) She yelled indignantly, "It took you long enough to get here!" Then, hysterically, "They're all dead in there! *Dead!* And what are *you* doing about it? I didn't pay good money to come here to be *murdered!* It's a *disgrace!* Vicious criminals allowed to run amuck with *weapons!* I'll sue!" She was screaming now. *"I'll sue!"*

The officer, a burly brute in grey leather, brass-studded shirt and kilt uniform raised a hand as though to dam the flood of angry words.

"Lady," he expostulated, "we have only just been told. By another lady who escaped . . ."

"Only just been told! What sort of supervision is there in this dump? Where do I find the manager?"

He ignored this question, asked one of his own.

"How many of them are there, and how armed?"

"With knives, iron bars, *anything.* There are four of them, a man and three women. Or there were . . ."

"There *were?"*

"When they got among us and started killing we managed to hide. Under the seats. And then . . . And then I peeped out and saw that they were fighting among themselves. Like wild beasts they were. So we made a break for it and ran . . ."

"I can't waste any more time on you, lady," said the officer brusquely. "I have to get in there to clear up the mess. He turned to Grimes. "Sir, will you accompany us? You might help to identify a few corpses."

"Not bloody likely!" sputtered Grimes indignantly. "It's *your* mess. You clear it up." He turned to the women. "Come, Angelica." (It was the first name that came into his head.) "And you two ladies. We will make our complaints to the manager."

"As you please, sir." He signalled to his men and led them in a brisk trot to the theatre entrance.

Grimes and the women walked, not too fast, along the corridor. They came to a cross passage, paused to take stock. The women had been quick-witted enough to pick up handbags although Grimes had not thought to tell them to do so. His own kilt had come with attached sporran. In this he found an almost empty note-case and another, much fatter, wallet containing credit cards and other documentation. There was also a passport. The late owner of all this had been a Wilburn Callis, M.D., a native of Carinthia. Photograph and other data did not match Grimes' personal specifications. Then, most importantly, there was a card issued by the Colosseum airport; the late Dr Callis, whose medical researches had been so rudely interrupted, had flown here on his own—or rented—wings.

Fenella Pruin, according to the contents of her handbag, was Vera Slovnik, also from Carinthia. Like Dr Callis, Ms Slovnik had preferred credit cards to folding money. Shirl was Lisbeth McDonald from Rob Roy, one of the Waverley planets, and Darleen was Eulalie Jones from Caribbea. As the two New Alicians could almost have passed for twin sisters this would prove awkward if, for any reason, a show of passports were demanded.

Hastily restowing money and papers the party walked on. Fortunately the corridor that they had taken was not a well-frequented one; almost certainly the main thoroughfare to the theatre from which they had escaped must now be extremely busy, with guards, stretcher parties and, thought Grimes with unkind satisfaction, the meat wagons.

They came to a large, illuminated wall map showing the various levels. There was more than one theatre, Grimes saw. The one from which they had escaped was the Grand Guignol. Then there were the Living Barbecue, the Operating Theatre and the Dungeon. But it was the airport that Grimes wanted. It was not very far from where they now found themselves. He memorised the directions and set off at a brisk walk, the women following. A moving way carried them on the last stage of their journey.

And then they were out into the cool night and Grimes, having handed over the card, was paying the charges due from the late Dr Callis' money. Relief at having escaped from the horrors of the Snuff Palace was making him talkative. No, he told the attendant, he hadn't heard about the disturbance in the Grand Guignol. He and the ladies were checking out because, frankly, they found all this old-fashioned sadism rather boring, as a spectator sport. If members of the audience were allowed to participate—no, not as victims, ha, ha—it would be much more fun . . . So perhaps a spot of hunting at Camp Diana would be more entertaining . . . And the camperfly? Fuelled and provisioned? Thank you, thank you . . . (Money—not too much but just enough—changed hands.) And Aisle D, Number 7? Thank you, thank you . . .

They boarded the chubby aircraft and, with Grimes at the controls, lifted. He told Airport Control that the destination was Camp Diana.

Once they were up and clear Fenella Pruin turned on him and asked viciously, "Why did you have to run off at the mouth like that? It's a miracle that you didn't spill the beans!"

"I thought that it was in character . . ." said Grimes lamely.

"Whose character? *Yours?*"

"Leave him alone!" cried Darleen loyally. "He got us out of here, didn't he?"

"It was just his famous luck," snarled the Pruin. "Just hope and pray that it lasts."

Amen, thought Grimes. *A-bloody-men.*

Twenty-two

There was a full set of charts aboard the camperfly, covering all of New Venusberg. There was electronic navigational equipment. There was an autopilot. It was a much bigger and far more luxurious aircraft than the one that Grimes had hired—how long ago?—at Port Aphrodite, one designed for use by tourists utterly lacking in airmanlike or navigational skills and to whom money would be no object.

Normally Grimes would have sneered at such a machine; he preferred to do things for himself rather than to have them done for him by robots. His contempt for push-button navigators was notorious. But now he would be content to leave things to the electronic intelligence while he got some much needed rest. It could be relied upon—he hoped—to steer a safe course over the seas, through the mountain passes, to Port Aphrodite. *Little Sister* must still be there. Once aboard her he and the women would be able to make their escape from this world of commercialised sex and sadism.

If his luck held.

For a while, however, he flew on manual control, on ostensible course for Camp Diana, until the camperfly was screened from sight of the Colosseum airport by the high hills. (On the chart the name Colosseum was not used; there was just an unnamed valley.) Then he switched to automatic and pushed the Port Aphrodite button, waited until he was sure that the aircraft had come around to the correct heading before going aft into the capacious cabin. Somebody, he saw, had been busy. There was a meal set out on the table—a tray of savoury pastries, a big pot of coffee, a bottle of brandy. Grimes looked and sniffed in anticipatory appreciation. Obviously the late Dr Callis had believed in doing himself well.

Darleen got up from her own seat, made a production of getting Grimes settled into a comfortable chair. Shirl poured him a mug of steaming coffee. Fenella Pruin watched sardonically.

"And now," she said, "perhaps the conquering hero will tell us what he intends doing next."

Grimes sipped his coffee, nibbled a pastry. He said. "I've set course for Port Aphrodite . . ."

"Straight back to your beloved *Little Sister,* of course."

"Do you have a sister, John?" asked Shirl. "You never told us."

"It's his ship," said Fenella.

The soft, background music, of which Grimes had hardly been conscious, was interrupted. "This is a news flash. A camperfly, number SCF2O11, has been stolen from a private mountain resort in Caligula Valley. Its charterer, Dr Wilburn Callis, a visitor to New Venusberg, was murdered. Aboard the aircraft are two underpeople, females, and two true humans, a man and a woman. All four are dangerous criminals. Aircraft are requested to keep a sharp lookout for the stolen vehicle and to report any sighting at once.

"It is believed that the criminals will be heading towards Port Aphrodite."

The interrupted music resumed. Grimes gulped what was left of his coffee but his enjoyment of it had been ruined. Obviously the stolen camperfly was no longer an asset but a liability. He did not know what the aerial capability of the planetary police forces was but was certain that it must be considerable.

"Well," asked Fenella Pruin, "what are you going to do about it?"

He reached out for the box of Caribbean cigars, selected one of the slim, brown cylinders. It would not be as good as a pipe but he had long considered the fumes of smouldering tobacco an aid to thought. He ignited it with a flick of his fingernail, put the other end to his mouth. He inhaled. ShirI poured him more coffee.

"Aren't you going to *do* something?" demanded Fenella Pruin.

"I have no intention of flying into a screaming tizzy," he told her. "To begin with, I'm going to land. There may or may not be something flyable at the Colosseum that has the heels of us, but if there is it'll be after us as soon as they get it airborne . . ."

He got up from his chair, went forward to the control cab. He studied the screen which depicted the terrain over which they were flying, looked at the chart. But before he could bring the camperfly down he would have to get off the rhumb line—Or was it a great circle course?—between the Colosseum and Port Aphrodite. There was enough metal in the camperfly's construction to make it a radar target, an anomalous echo that would be picked up by the instruments of pursuing aircraft.

He switched to manual, made a bold alteration of course to starboard. And was that a deep valley showing in the screen, ahead and a little to port? It was a dark rift of some kind, meandering through the general luminescence. He transferred his attention to the all-around lookout radar. The sky—ahead, astern, to both sides—was empty. So far. But he decided that it would be too big a risk to use landing lights.

At reduced speed he drifted down. The worst part of it was that the control cab was not designed for making a visual landing—not that much could be seen in the darkness. He watched the radar altimeter. Yes, that was a valley, or a canyon, and a deep one. He was directly over it now.

He stopped engines. The camperfly had sufficient buoyancy from its gas cells for its descent to be gentle. There was enough breeze, however, for it to be blown off its planned descent. Grimes restarted the engines to maneuver the unwieldy aircraft back into position, making allowance for leeway. But he could not foresee that at ground level there would be an eddy. The camperfly, instead of dropping neatly into the canyon, the walls of which gave ample clearance, drifted to the leeward rim. The port wing of the aircraft fouled something, crumpled. There was a loud hiss of escaping helium, audible even in the cabin. At first there was a violent lurch to starboard and then, as the damaged wing, no longer buoyant, tore free of the obstruction, a heeling over to port. On its side the camperfly dropped into the gulf. Luckily there was sufficient lift remaining in the undamaged gas cells for the descent to be a relatively gentle one.

She struck, with the port wing acting as a fender, cracking up beneath her. She settled, then almost at once was on the move again. Heavy blows shook her structure from beneath, from both sides. A strange, somehow fluid, roaring noise was audible in the control cab.

Grimes extricated himself from the tangle of female arms and legs into which he had been thrown, not as gently as he would have done in a situation of lesser urgency. He ignored the outraged squeals of the women. The dim lighting in the control cab was still on. He saw, through what had been the upper surface of the transparent dome and which was now a wall, this luminescence reflected from a black, swirling surface.

Water.

The camperfly had fallen into a swift running river and was being borne rapidly downstream. Even if she were holed by the rocks into which she was crashing there would be no danger of her sinking as long as the remaining gas cells remained intact. The situation, thought Grimes, could have been worse. This was better than either the Colosseum or the Snuff Palace.

Out of the frying pan, he thought, *and into the washing up water . . .*

Twenty-three

The women sorted themselves out, crawled aft into the main cabin. They reported that the camperfly did not seem to be making water. Shirl returned with cushions so that Grimes could make himself comfortable, Darleen brought him a bottle of brandy. He should, he knew, stay awake—but he had been through too much. If he forced himself to remain fully conscious for what remained of the night he would be in no fit state to cope with any emergencies that might arise. And he wanted Shirl and Darleen, who had already proven themselves, to be fighting fit when needed.

That left one obvious choice for a lookout.

"Fenella!" he called. "Come here, will you?"

"What for? What's wrong *now?* Are you going to make another of your marvelous landings?"

"Just come here!" shouted Grimes.

She came. It was too dark for Grimes to see her face but he knew that she was glaring at him. "Yes?" she demanded.

"I want you to stand the watch. Here. I'll be staying here myself. Wake me at once if anything happens."

"What about *them?* I'm paying for your services. They aren't"

"They're trained fighters. You aren't. I want them to get some sleep."

She capitulated suddenly.

"Oh, all right. I suppose you're right. Snore your bloody heads off, all three of you."

She plumped down beside Grimes, tried at first to avoid physical contact with him but the curvature of the surface on which they had disposed themselves made this impossible. She lit one of the late Dr Callis' cigars. Grimes inhaled her smoke hungrily. Nicotine might keep him awake for a little longer but was a price that he was prepared to pay.

"Did you bring any more of those things with you?" he asked.

"Yes. Want one?"

Grimes said that he did. He lit up.

She asked in a voice far removed from her usual bossiness, "Grimes, what's going to happen to us?"

He said, "I wish I knew. Or, perhaps, I'd rather not know . . ." The camperfly struck and bounced off a rock, throwing them closer together. "But we're still alive. And officially we're dead; that could be to our advantage. When we turn up, in person, singing and dancing, at Port Aphrodite that's going to throw a monkey-wrench into all sorts of machinery . . ."

"You said *when,* not *if* . . . And as for the singing and dancing, I'm going to sing. To high heaven. That's what I'm paid for—but I don't mind admitting that I often enjoy my work. . ." She drew on her cigar, exhaled slowly. "But I do wish that I'd be able to do something about these girls from New Alice . . ." She lowered her voice in case Shirl and Darleen should still be awake in the cabin, and listening. "But they're obviously underpeople. Some crazy Australian genetic engineer had kangaroo ova to play around with and produced his own idea of what humans should be. But they have no rights. As far as interstellar law's concerned they're nonhuman. Oh, I suppose I could try to get GSPCA interested, but . . ."

Grimes was dozing off. His cigar fell from his hand, was extinguished, with a sharp hiss, by the small amount of water that had entered the control cab. His head found a most agreeable nesting place between Fenella's head and shoulder. She made no attempt to dislodge it.

". . . a slave trade's a slave trade whether or not the victims are strictly human . . ."

Dimly Grimes realized that somebody was snoring. It was himself.

". . . the river seems to be getting wider . . ."

"Mphm . . ."

". . . the . . ."

And that was the last that Grimes heard.

He was awakened by bright sunlight striking through the transparency of the control cab bubble. By his side Fenella Pruin was fast asleep, snoring gently. A duet of snores came from the cabin. He should have stayed on watch himself, he thought. Nobody in the party, however, would be any the worse for a good sleep.

From the bubble he could see ahead and astern and to port, but not to starboard. He could see the river bank, densely wooded and with high hills in the background. The scenery was not moving relatively to the camperfly—so, obviously, the camperfly was not moving relatively to the scenery. The bank was at least five hundred metres distant.

He extricated himself from the sleeping Fenella Pruin's embrace, clambered aft into the cabin. Shirl and Darleen were sprawled inelegantly on a pile of cushions and discarded clothing. They seemed to be all legs, all long, naked legs. Reluctantly Grimes looked away from them to what had been the starboard side of the cabin, to what was now the overhead. There was a door there. He could reach it, he thought, by clambering on the table which, bolted to the deck, was now on its side.

The table had only one leg. It was strong enough for normal loads but had not been designed to withstand shearing stresses. It broke. Grimes was thrown heavily on to the sleeping girls.

They snapped at once into full and vicious consciousness. Darleen's hands closed about his throat while Shirl's foot thudded heavily into his belly.

Then—"It's you," said Darleen, releasing him while Shirl checked her foot before it delivered a second blow.

Grimes rubbed the bruised skin of his neck.

"Yes. It's me. Can the pair of you lift me up to the door? There . . ."

They were quick on the uptake. Their strong arms went around him, hoisted him up. He was able to reach the catch of the door, slide it aft. They lifted him still further. He caught the rim of the opening, pulled himself up and through. He was standing just abaft the starboard wing. It must have acted as a sail; with wind was blowing across the river and had driven the camperfly on to a sandy beach. Beyond this there were trees and bushes, with feathery foliage, blue rather than green. There were hills in the not distant background. Darleen—she must have been lifted by Shirl—joined him.

She said, a little wistfully, "We could live here . . . There must be animals, and fruits, and nuts . . . And roots . . ."

"Mphm," grunted Grimes. Many years ago he had been obliged to live the simple life in Edenic circumstances and this was not among his most pleasant memories. "Mphm."

"Help me up!" came a voice from below.

Darleen fell supine to the surface on which she had been standing, lowered an arm through the aperture. Shirl's head appeared through the opening, then her shoulders, then her breasts, then all of her. She stood by Grimes, looking, as Darleen had looked, to what must have been to her a Promised Land.

"This is beaut," she said in a flat voice.

"Too right!" agreed Darleen, who was back on her feet.

"We could start a tribe," said Shirl.

Count me out as a patriarch, thought Grimes.

"Just the three of us," went on Shirl, "to start with . . ."

And did that mean the three women, Grimes wondered, or the two New Alicians only partnered by him, with Fenella Pruin somehow lost in the wash? The way that Shirl and Darleen were looking at him the answer to the question was obvious.

"This is just like the Murray Valley at home," said Darleen.

"Too right," agreed Shirl.

"But we can't stay here," said Grimes.

"Why not?" asked the two girls simultaneously.

"We have to get back to Port Aphrodite," he said.

"Why?" they countered.

Fenella Pruin's voice came from inside the camperfly. "Where is everybody? Grimes, where are you?"

"Here!" he called.

With some reluctance the two New Alicians helped her up to the side of the camperfly. Steadying herself with one hand on the up-pointing wing she looked around.

"All very pretty," she said at last, "but where are we?"

"Home," said Darleen.

"Home," said Shirl. "We will settle here—Darleen, John Grimes and myself. We will start a tribe . . ."

"You can stay if you like," said Darleen generously.

Fenella laughed. "I'm a big city girl," she said. "And, in any case, you'll have to ask the owners' permission before you set up house."

"The owners?" asked Grimes.

"Yes." She pointed. "The owners . . ."

They were coming down from between the trees and bushes, making their way to the beach. They were . . . human? Or humanoid.

Their arms were too short, their haunches too heavy. The women were almost breastless. Their skins were a dark, rich brown. Some of them carried long spears, some cruciform boomerangs, some heavy clubs.

They stared at the stranded camperfly, at Grimes and the three women.

"Good morning!" Grimes shouted.

"Gidday!" came an answering shout.

"Where are we?" he called.

"Kangaroo Valley!" came the reply.

Twenty-four

It had been a long day.

Grimes had supervised the stripping and dismantling of the camperfly, its breaking up into pieces that could be carried into the bush and hidden. Matilda's Children—as this tribe called itself—possessed some metal tools, saws, hammers and axes, and the construction of the aircraft was mainly of plastic. Nonetheless it had not been easy work.

And now it was late evening.

A fire was burning in the centre of the clearing, now little more than glowing coals. Over it, on a crude spit, the carcass of some animal, possibly a small deer, was roasting. The hot coals flared fitfully as melted fat and other juices fell on them. (Grimes remembered, all too vividly, some of the things that he had witnessed during his incarceration in the Snuff Palace. He did not think that he would want any meat when the meal was ready.) There were crude earthenware mugs of some brew that could almost have passed for beer. Grimes had no qualms regarding this.

"You're as safe here, cobber," said the grizzled Mal, who appeared to be the tribe's leader, "as anywhere else on this world. *They* don't bother us. They leave us be. An' we could use a bastard like you, with a bit o' mechanical knowhow. An' Shirl an' Darleen'll be good breedin' stock. They're young . . ." He looked over the rim of his mug at Fenella. "About you, lady, I ain't so certain . . ."

She laughed shortly. "And I ain't so certain about you, Mal. But could I have your story again? Everybody was so busy during the day that they couldn't find time to talk to me . . ."

"We're Matilda's Children," Mal told her. "We come from New Alice. We were brought here by a man called Drongo Kane who said that he was one of us, although he came from another planet. He promised us loads of lolly if we'd work on this world. An' there was loads of lolly, at first. An' then we, the first ones of us, started gettin' old. The fat, rich bitches from all over, an' their husbands, wanted younger meat. Nobody wanted us any more. Not for *anything.*

An' we had no skills apart from rogering. An' there was no way, no way at all, of gettin' back to where we belong . . .

"We were just turned loose . . .

"We found this valley. Over the years others of our people have joined us, some of them too old to work among the red lights any more, some of them escaped from places like the Colosseum. We get by."

"And why do you call this place Kangaroo Valley?" asked Fenella.

"It's a tradition, sort of. Whenever our people have lived together in a strange city, on a strange world, it's called Kangaroo Valley . . ."

And there was a Kangaroo Valley in London, on Old Earth, thought Grimes. In a place called Earls Court. His father had told him about it when he was doing research on a historical novel the period of which was the Twentieth Century, Old Style. But the people living there had not been descended from kangaroos . . .

"But why Kangaroo Valley?" persisted Fenella. "What *is* a kangaroo?"

"An animal from our Dream Time," said Mal. "An animal that lived in Australia, on Earth, where our forefathers came from. On New Alice the kangaroo hunt is one of our traditional dances. It is performed here, for money, on New Venusberg."

"I've seen it," said Fenella.

"I've been it," said Shirl.

A humpy, a rough shelter of leaves and branches, had been allocated to Grimes and Fenella as their sleeping quarters. They retired to this after the feast. Grimes, unable to face the barbecued meat, had dined on rather flavourless but filling roots that had been roasted in the ashes. Fenella, in many ways tougher than he, had enjoyed the venison.

Settee cushions, salvaged from the camperfly, were their beds. They stretched out on these, each with a cigar from the aircraft's now much-depleted stock.

"Poor bastards," whispered Fenella. "Poor bastards, thinking themselves human when they're so obviously not. That reversion to their ancestral characteristics with age . . . In only a few years' time your precious Shirl and Darleen will look just like the older women. All that *they* lack is tails . . ."

"They're still victims of a white slave trade," said Grimes.

"Yes. But legally only animals. How do you think they started?"

"It must have been very similar to what happened on Morrowvia. One of the old guassjammers, driven off course by a magnetic storm, lost in Space and making a landing on the first world capable of supporting our kind of life . . . Probably a crash landing, with very few survivors, among them a genetic engineer . . . Fertilised kangaroo ova—but the Odd Gods of the Galazy alone know why!—in the ship's plasm bank . . ."

"Mankind," she said, "has made a habit of spreading its own favourite animals throughout the galaxy . . ."

"True. There are kangaroos on Botany Bay. Well, anyhow, the era of the gaussjammers was also the era of the underpeople. It got to the stage when the politicians, bowing to the pressure exerted by the trade unions, whose members found their livelihood being taken away by physically specialised underpeople, brought in legislation to make the manufacture of imitation human beings illegal. Of course, it was the imitation human beings themselves who were the main sufferers. And after all these many years the prejudice still persists . . ."

"Tell me," she asked, "have you ever conquered *your* prejudice against underpeople? In bed, I mean . . ."

"I don't think that I have any such prejudice."

"And did you and Shirl . . . Or Darleen . . . ?"

"No," he said.

"The way that they look at you I thought that you and they must have been having it off. But you have this odd hang-up, don't you? You're afraid that when it's open and ready for you it's going to bite you . . ."

Yet her words did not wound, were not intended to do so. It was not what she was saying but the way that she was saying it that robbed them of their sting. The old Fenella Pruin—temporarily at least—was dead. This was a new one, engendered by the perils that they had faced together. The intimacy of this crude humpy was hardly greater than the intimacy of *Little Sister*'s living quarters, and yet . . .

He heard the rustle as she removed the dress that was her only clothing. He was not ready for her when she came to him but was aroused by the first kiss, by the feel of her body against his. She mounted him, rode him, rode him into the ground, reaching her climax as he reached his, as his body purged itself of the months of humiliations and frustrations.

She spoiled things—but only a little—when she murmured, "I got you before those two marsupial bitches did!"

But what would it be like, he wondered as he drifted into sleep, with Darleen? Or Shirl?

Twenty-five

Grimes expected that Fenella Pruin would be all sweetness and light the following morning. She was not. She started complaining almost as soon as she opened her eyes. To begin with it was the toilet facilities—a unisex trench latrine in the bushes, a cold bath in the billabong using a crude, homemade soap that would have been quite a good paint remover. Then it was breakfast—the remains of the previous night's feast, not even heated up, with only water to wash it down.

Then, puffing furiously at the last cigar, she led Grimes on a tour of inspection of the camp. She complained bitterly about the lack of a camera or other recording equipment and was more than a little inclined to blame Grimes for this deficiency. Grimes told her that she'd just have to make a thousand words worth one picture. She did not think that this was funny.

They were joined by Shirl and Darleen, who seemed to be in little better temper than Fenella. Shirl muttered, "They live rough, these people. Too rough . . ." Darleen said to her, "We should have got our paws on to some of those cushions . . ."

"There were plenty of cushions in the camperfly," said Grimes.

"And Mal's got them. Him and his wives," was the reply.

Fenella Pruin said something about male chauvinist pigs.

"Rank has its privileges," said Grimes.

She stalked on, stiff-legged, the others tailing after her. They came to what seemed to be an open air school. There were the children, squatting on the ground around their teachers. One of these, an elderly woman, was fashioning throwing spears, using a piece of broken glass to shape the ends of the straight sticks to a point. Another one, a man, was demonstrating how to make fire by friction, rubbing a pointed piece of hard wood up and down the groove in a softer piece that he held between his horny feet.

This teacher was Mal.

"Good morning," said Fenella, inplying by the tone of her voice that it wasn't.

Mal looked up. "Gidday. I'll find jobs for yer soon as I've finished with this mob."

Fenella ignored this offer. She asked. "These children . . . Were they born here? In Kangaroo Valley?"

"Most of 'em. But all born on this world."

"Were they all conceived here?" She was looking hard at one of the naked boys, who seemed to be in his early teens.

"Conceived?" asked Mal.

"Started. *You* know . . ."

"Oh. That. Some here. Some on the way here, from New Alice . . . Like Kev."

Grimes looked at Kev. There was something vaguely familiar about the youth's appearance. Physically he would not have attracted much attention on a bathing beach.

"And what ships did you come here in?" persisted Fenella Pruin.

"Just . . . ships."

"They must have had names."

"Yair. Lemme see, now. I came in one called Southerly something. *Southerly Buster.* Yair. That's it. Some o' the others in *Willy Willy.* An' *Bombora* . . . But yer wastin' my time an' it's time you did somethin' to earn yer own keep. What do yer do?"

"I'm doing it," she told him. "Now. I want to help you, Mal. You and your people . . ."

"You can help by bringin' in some firewood."

"You can help—yourself as well as us—by telling us how to get back to Port Aphrodite."

"You must be round the bend."

"I'm not. I have friends in Port Aphrodite. John Grimes has a ship there. Get us there and we'll be able to lift the lid off this planet."

"An' what good will it do *us?"*

"Plenty, I assure you. You'll be repatriated to your own world, if you so desire . . ."

"Rather stay here. I'm somebody here. A chief."

"But wouldn't you like to be recognised as such by the New Venusberg government? With rights, definite legal rights, for you and your people? Look at the money you could make from tourists, money that you could spend on little luxuries . . . Decent beer instead of the muck you brew yourselves from the Odd Gods of the Galaxy alone know what . . ."

"Nothin' wrong with *our* beer . . ."

But Mal, Grimes knew, had promptly commandeered the remaining bottles of Venuswasser from the wreck of the camperfly.

"An' there'll be women, Mal. Tourist women . . ."

"You're too skinny," he told her.

"Maybe I am. But before you were too old to perform in the house where you worked you must have enjoyed all the foreign pussy."

"I'm not too old!" he roared. "If you weren't such a bag o' bones I'd soon show yer! I was caught on the nest with the boss's wife—that's why I'm out here!"

"I never really thought that you were too old," said Fenella Pruin placatingly. She had moved so that she was between the morning sun and the chief, so that the strong light revealed the outlines of her body under the single, flimsy garment.

"Too bloody skinny," muttered Mal. "No bloody thanks!"

"Skinny perhaps," she said. "But rich certainly. Help us and I'll pay."

"What with?" he asked sceptically.

"I've money, plenty of money in the safe aboard Captain Grimes' ship."

"But it ain't here."

"I'll make out a promissory note . . ."

"There's only one thing that such a piece of paper would be any use for here."

"My word is good," she said. "And I have a name, a famous name . . ."

"Not to me it ain't."

Grimes was aware that Darleen was tugging at his sleeve. She had something to say to him, in private. He followed her into the bushes. Shirl accompanied them.

As soon as they were concealed from view, out of hearing from Mal and Fenella, she opened the shoulder bag that she was carrying, extracted a purse. It was very well filled, with notes of large denominations. So was the purse produced by Shirl. Evidently the dead women whose personal effects the New Alicians had appropriated had not believed in credit cards.

Grimes counted the money. It came to twelve thousand, three hundred and fifteen. Federation Credits.

"You take it," said Darleen. "On our world women do not handle business."

Grimes stuffed the notes into his sporran, walked back to where Mal and Fenella were still arguing.

"How much do you want to help us?" he asked bluntly.

Mal looked at him. "I was wonderin' why the hell you were lettin' this skinny bitch do all the dickerin'. How much have yer got?"

"How much do you want? A thousand?"

"Fifteen hundred. For you. But the tribe could do with three new women." He laughed nastily. "The ones we've got wear out pretty soon."

"The woman . . ." He corrected himself when he saw the way that Shirl and Darleen were looking at him. "The women come with me."

"That will cost yer, mister."

"Then an extra five hundred for each woman."

Mal spat. "Surely they're worth more to you than that. There's years o' wear in each of them."

"This is degrading!" flared Fenella Pruin.

"Isn't it?" agreed Grimes. "But keep out of this, will you?" Then, to Mal, "They aren't worth more than six hundred apiece."

"She ain't. All she's good for is collectin' firewood. But the other two sheilahs . . . Good breeders, by the looks of 'em. An' they're from my world. They're Matilda's Children, like me. So they'll be hunters. They'll be able to pull their weight."

"Six hundred for *her,* then . . ."

"You bastard!" snarled Fenella.

"Shut up! And a thousand each for the other two."

"Two thousand each."

Until now Grimes had been enjoying the chaffering. Now he was annoyed. "You mean," he demanded, "that they're worth more than me?"

"Too bloody right, mate. I need a spaceman in this camp like I need a hole in the head."

"Fifteen hundred each."

"No go. Two thousand. Cash on the nail and no bits of useless bumfodder."

Oh, well, thought Grimes, it wasn't *his* money. He said, "I have to talk this over, Mal."

"Don't take too long or I'll up the price."

Back in the bushes, with Fenella, Darleen and Shirl watching, he counted out the money. He had not wanted Mal to know how much was in his pouch. Six thousand, one hundred credits exactly; it was just as well that there was no need to ask Mal to make change.

The chief took the notes, made his own count.

"All right," he said. "You've sealed the bargain. You can loaf around all day, an' then ternight, when Cap'n Onslow comes by in his *Triton,* I'll get yer on board. He owes me a coupla favours."

Twenty-six

It had been too easy, thought Grimes. So far. He said as much to the women. Fenella said that it had been easy because he had been throwing money around like a drunken spaceman. Shirl said that Mal would not have been so keen to help had not two of his own people been involved. Fenella said that good money had been paid out but, at the moment there was only the vague promise of assistance. Darleen said that a New Alician's word was his bond. Fenella said, changing the subject slightly, that it was indeed strange that Mal was willing to get rid of his fellow Matilda's Children. Shirl said that the chief had set a far higher value on herself and Darleen than on Fenella.

Before the catfight got out of control Grimes steered the discussion on to what he hoped would be a safe track. He said, "The two of you were still yapping around the fire after Fenella and I turned in last night. What did you find out?"

"Kangaroo Valley ain't entirely cut off from the world," said Darleen. "It's left alone because it's useful. There's a sorta lizard livin' in rocky places. It ain't good eatin'—but there's some demand for parts of its guts. Haveter be dried in the sun, then roasted, then ground into a sorta powder . . . It sells at fancy prices in the cities . . ."

"What's it used for?" asked Grimes stupidly.

"What would anything be used for on this world? Mal doesn't sell it all, o' course. He keeps some for his own use. For all his big talk he's gettin' old, over the hill. He wanted us, last night. Both of us. An' he knew that he could only manage one with the amount of juice that he has in his batteries at his age. So he charged himself up . . ."

"An' the worst of it was," said Shirl, "that after he was quite finished he wouldn't let us sleep on the cushions in his humpy but bundled us off to get what rest we could on a bed o' leaves . . ."

"He's a jealous bastard, that Mal," went on Darleen. "He thought that you'd been havin' it off with us an' didn't want you bustin' in and interferin'. But if the stuff is mixed in drink—like beer—an' if the mug is shared by two people—like you an' Fenella did once last night—it's supposed to work for that couple only . . ."

Grimes looked at Fenella.

She looked at him.

She said coldly, "So that's why you were capable last night."

He thought, *So that's why you weren't your usual bitchy self.*

He said, "That stuff must be pricey."

"Even wholesale it's not all that cheap," she agreed.

"Then why is this camp so primitive?"

"Mal likes it that way. Matilda's Children like it that way."

"What happens to the money?" persisted Grimes.

"It's banked. It builds up. Then, every year, there's a lottery. The winner gets a passage back home, to New Alice."

"And yet," said Fenella Pruin, "Able Enterprises never seem to have any trouble in getting new recruits for the brothels—and worse—of this planet. Surely those lucky winners spread the word about how things really are on New Venusberg . . ."

"I met one," said Shirl, "just before I came out here. The lying bitch! New Venusberg, according to her, was the original get-rich-quick-in-luxury planet. Ha!"

"Do you think that she was in Drongo Kane's pay?" asked Grimes.

"Not necessarily," said Fenella Pruin. "A thorough brain-scrubbing, then artificial memories . . ."

"But that's not legal," said Grimes.

"Some of the things that happened to us weren't legal. But they happened just the same. The only crime here is not having enough money to be able to break interstellar law with impunity. So . . . But what else did you two find out during your night of unbridled passion?"

Shirl and Darleen gave her almost identical dirty looks.

"Mal didn't want us for talking to," said Shirl. "But after he threw us out we slept in a big humpy with two of his wives. They wanted to spend what was left of the night nattering. They told us what a hard life it was catchin' the lizards, an' gutting 'em an' all the rest of it, an' how the only thing to look forward to was Cap'n Onslow comin' in to collect the . . . the . . ."

"Aphrodisiac," supplied Fenella.

"Yair. He always brings some decent beer an' some tins o' food, luxury items, like. He's from some world where the people have a thing about ships—the sort of ships that sail on the sea, I mean . . ."

"Atlantia?" asked Grimes. "Aquarius?"

"Aquarius. I think. He was a shipowner there, an' a captain. He sold out, came here for a holiday. He decided to stay after he found out that a little ship, with no crew to pay, could make a living sniffing around little settlements like this, pickin' up little parcels of cargo . . ."

"Sounds like a good life," said Grimes.

"You should know," said Fenella. "But perhaps he doesn't have the same uncanny genius for getting into trouble that you have."

"From here," Shirl went on, "he sails direct for Troy—that's a seaport just south of New Bali Beach. It's not all that far from Port Aphrodite."

"And then it's only a short tube ride back to my own ship," said Grimes.

"You hope," said Fenella Pruin. "We all hope. But first of all we must hope that this Onslow person will agree to carry us to Troy."

Twenty-seven

Late in the afternoon, just before sunset, *Triton* came up river. She was a smart little ship, gleaming white with a blue ribbon around her sleek hull. Her foredeck, abaft the raised fo'c's'le, was one long hatch served by two cranes, one forward and one aft. Her high poop seemed to be mainly accommodation. Atop the wheel house were antennae and the radar scanner, also a stubby mast from which flew Captain Onslow's houseflag, a golden trident on a sea-green ground. From the ensign staff fluttered the New Venusberg banner—the *crux ansata,* in gold, on crimson.

Grimes expected that she would be anchoring in the stream as Kangaroo Valley was devoid of wharfage. But she did not. With helm hard over she turned smartly through ninety degrees, ran up on to the beach. She moved smoothly over the sand until only the extremity of her stern was in the water. Then she stopped. From the port side of her poop a treaded ramp extended itself, the lower end of this resting on the ground.

There was movement in *Triton*'s wheelhouse as whoever was there left the control position. Shortly afterwards a short, solidly built man appeared at the head of the gangway, walked decisively down it. He was bare-footed and clad, somewhat incongruously, in a garishly patterned sarong and a uniform cap, the peak of which was lavishly gold-encrusted. He was brown-skinned, red-bearded.

He greeted Mal, who was standing there to meet him, "Hello, you old marsupial bastard! How yer goin'?"

"I am not a marsupial, Cap'n Onslow," said Mal stiffly, obviously not for the first time.

"There're marsupials in yer family tree, Mal . . ."

"Kangaroos don't climb, Cap'n."

Then what was an old-established ritual was broken. Onslow stared at Fenella who, with Grimes and Darleen and Shirl, was standing a little apart from the villagers. She was clothed, while all the other women were naked—but even if she had not been her differences from them would have been obvious.

"Hello, hello," said Onslow slowly, "who's *this*?" Then, "Don't I know you, lady?"

"You may have seen my photograph, Captain," Fenella told him.

"M'm. Yes. Could be. But where?"

Another Faithful Reader, thought Grimes.

"Star Scandals," she said.

"And what's a nice girl like you doing in a place like this?" asked Onslow with a leer.

"Getting a story," she said.

"Ah!" exclaimed the seaman. "Got it! Fenella Pruin! I like your stuff. This is an honour, meeting you."

Mal interrupted. "Cap'n, we have business . . ."

"You mean that you want some cold beer, you old bastard. All right, come on board." He turned back to Fenella. "I'll see you later, Miz Pruin."

He led the chief to the gangway, then up into *Triton*'s accommodation block.

"Why did you have to tell him your name?" Grimes demanded.

"I could see that he recognised me. It cost me nothing to be nice to him, to get him on our side from the start."

"Dreeble recognised you—and look where that got us!"

"He recognised *you* first, and that was the start of our troubles."

Onslow had come back to the head of his gangway, was calling out, "Miz Pruin, will you come on board? And bring him with you."

Grimes didn't much like being referred to as "him" and, to judge from their expressions, Darleen and Shirl resented being excluded from the invitation. They looked after him reproachfully as he walked with Fenella across the firm sand, followed her up the ramp.

Onslow—he was still wearing his cap with the ornate badge and the huge helping of scrambled egg—threw the girl a flamboyant salute as she reached the deck. He took her elbow with a meaty hand to guide her through a doorway into the accommodation. He had to relinquish his grip when they came to the companionway; it was too narrow for two to walk abreast. He went up first. Fenella followed. Grimes followed her.

As they climbed to the captain's quarters Grimes looked about curiously. They passed a little galley with an autochef that would not have looked out of place aboard a spaceship. There was a deck which was occupied by what seemed to be passenger cabins. Finally, directly below the wheelhouse-chartroom, was Captain Onslow's suite. There was a large sitting room with bedroom and bathroom opening off it. In the sitting room, sprawling in one of the pneumatic chairs, Mal was drinking beer from a can bedewed with condensation. Three empty cans were on the deck beside him.

Onslow ushered Fenella into another pneumatic chair, took a seat himself.

Grimes sat down in another of the modified bladders; he had not been invited to do so but saw no reason to remain standing. The captain reached out to the low table for a can of beer, opened it and handed it to Fenella. He took one for himself. Mal helped himself to another one.

"May I?" asked Grimes, extending his hand to the table.

"Go ahead. This is Liberty Hall; you can piss out of the window and put my only sister in the family way."

"Don't you have a ship's cat, Captain?" asked Grimes.

"No. But what's it to you?"

"He's just being awkward," said Fenella Pruin. "He's good at that."

"He looks the type," agreed Onslow. "Now, Miz Pruin, Mal tells me that you're in some kind of trouble, that you want to get back to Port Aphrodite without using the more usual means of public transport. As you've noticed, I have passenger accommodation. I understand that you require passage for yourself, for the two New Alice girls who're with you and for Mr . . . Mr . . . ?"

"Grimes," said the owner of that name. "Captain Grimes."

"Captain, eh? Spacer, aren't you? Must be. I know all the seamen on this planet. There aren't all that many of us." His manner towards Grimes was now more affable. "What's your ship?"

"Little Sister," said Grimes.

"Little Sister . . . Captain Grimes . . . There was something about you in the news a while back . . . Now, what was it? Oh, yes. You and some wench called Prunella Fenn went missing on a flight from Vulcan Island to somewhere or other in a hired camperfly . . . *Prunella Fenn* . . ." He looked hard at Fenella and laughed. "I've read your stories in *Scandals,* Miz Pruin. How you've often had to sail under false colours to get them. But I never dreamed that I'd ever meet you while you were doing it—or meet you at all, come to that!

"And what will you be writing about New Venusberg? You don't have to dig very deep to turn up muck here. Will it be about Big Mal and his people? About how they got to Kangaroo Valley? About the lottery rip-off?"

"Possibly," she said. "You'll read it in *Star Scandals.* I doubt very much if that issue will be on sale here. I'll send you a copy."

"And will you autograph it for me?"

"I just might," she said.

"I'll be looking forward to it. But shall we get down to business? The cargo should be down to the beach by now; I want to get it loaded so that we can start the party. Now—passage for four aboard *Triton* . . ." He looked at Fenella. She looked at him. "Make that passages for three. You, Captain, and your two popsies. Three times fifteen hundred comes to four thousand, five hundred credits. Food provided, drinks extra."

"I thought," said Grimes, staring at Mal, "that we'd already paid."

"You paid," said the chief, "just for the . . . arranging . . ."

You money-grubbing bastard, thought Grimes, but without overmuch bitterness. Agents, after all, are entitled to their fees, although a mere 10% is the usual rake-off. He did mental arithmetic. He could afford the fares and have something left over for booze and tobacco. Fenella's drinks and smokes would be, he was quite certain, on the house.

"All right," he said to Onslow.

"Cash on the nail, Captain Grimes."

Grimes fumbled in his sporran, produced the money demanded.

He asked, as he handed it over, "Do we get tickets?"

"You don't. The First Galactic Bank still owns a large hunk of this ship—according to my reckoning it's from the fo'c's'le head to about the middle of the main hatch—and the less they know about what I make on the side the better. Thank you, Captain." He got up, put the money into a drawer in his desk. "Finish your beer, Mal. Let's get up top and see about loading your precious prick stiffener."

Grimes and Fenella accompanied Onslow and Mal up to the wheelhouse. Looking down on to the foredeck Grimes saw that a dozen Matilda's Children were already on board, waiting for the hatch to be opened. They were all women, as were the other stevedores standing around the big heap of bulging plastic bags on the sand just off *Triton*'s port side.

Onslow threw the cover off a console below the port window of the wheelhouse. He touched a button and this opened, the glass panel sliding downwards. He fingered another control and the forward deck crane came to life, the jib lifting and slewing, coming to rest as soon as the captain was satisfied that everything was in working order. A small lever was flicked over and the hatch lids lifted, running almost noiselessly to their stowage just abaft the fo'c's'le, leaving the forward end of the hatchway open. A vertical ladder was revealed just inside the coaming. Down this clambered the Matilda's Children, looking like abnormally heavily rumped naked apes.

The weighted crane hook dropped into the aperture, rose after a short interval with a tray, on a double bridle, hanging from it. This swung outboard, was lowered to the sand. Working fast and efficiently the women on the beach loaded it with a dozen plastic bags. It was lifted, swung inboard and dropped swiftly into the hatch.

Grimes watched, fascinated by this combination of modern automation with methods of cargo handling almost as old as the sea-going ship. It seemed to be working all right. He said as much.

"And why the hell shouldn't it?" demanded Onslow. "Human beings—or, as in this case, their facsimiles—are only machines. Non-specialised machines. On some worlds they cost a damn sight less than the sort o' machines that are built out of metal and plastic. An' who the hell is going to pay for roll-on-roll-off and containerisation facilities in little, used-once-in-a-blue-moon ports like Kangaroo Valley?"

The stack of bags on the beach was fast diminishing as Onslow played his crane with practised ease. The sun was well down but it was not yet properly dark when the last tray was brought on board. The stevedores came up the ladder, their bodies glistening in the glare of the floodlights shining down from the bridge superstructure, from the crane jib. The hatch lids, like a pack of cards toppling, piece by piece, from an on-edge position, ran back into their places, settled with an audible *thunk*.

"That's that," said Onslow smugly. "Loading completed. Now all I have to do is sail when I feel like it—which won't be until not too bright and early tomorrow morning."

"Aren't you going to check the stowage, Captain?" asked Grimes.

"Why should I? All that those bitches had to do was make a single tier of bags over what was already there, cases of canned lemonfish from Port Poseidon . . ."

"Lemonfish is quite a delicacy, isn't it. What about pilferage?"

Onslow laughed. "With the stevedores stark naked? And they're *big* cans . . ." He lowered the jib of the crane into its crutch, switched off everything on the console, replaced the cover. He turned to Mal. "I'm ready for the party whether you are or not. Have some of your people come on board for the beer and all the rest of it. All this cargo handling has given me an appetite. And a thirst."

Twenty-eight

It was a wet party.

It was too wet for Grimes, who was not in the mood for heavy drinking that night. It was too wet, presumably, for Fenella Pruin and Captain Onslow, who absented themselves before the orgy got properly under way. Mal vanished too, and with him both Shirl and Darleen. The fat lady who was plying Grimes with can after can of beer (now lukewarm) and who was trying to spoonfeed him with some sort of salty fishpaste straight from the tin was not at all to his taste.

He broke away from her at last. (It was like disentangling himself from the embraces of a hot-blooded octopus; surely she possessed more than the usual quota of arms and legs.) He walked a little unsteadily down the beach to *Triton,* the high-flaring bonfire behind him casting a shadow before that wavered even more than he himself was doing. Raucous shouts, screams and drunken laughter were unmusical in his ears.

Triton was in darkness save for the light at the head of the gangway and a single flood at the fore end of the bridge superstructure. Grimes climbed the treaded ramp. The door into the accommodation was closed. He had to stand there until the security scanner, which had been programmed by Captain Onslow to recognise his passengers, identified him. It took its time about it while Grimes, in growing discomfort, shifted from foot to foot. He had taken too much beer and, away from the fire, the night air was chilly. Finally a bell chimed softly and the door opened. He hurried up to the passenger deck, went first of all to the common bathroom. Then, feeling much lighter, he looked into the cabin that had been allocated to Fenella Pruin. She was not there, of course. Neither were Shirl and Darleen in their berths. He had not expected them to be. He conceded grudgingly that Mal and Onslow were entitled to their *droit de signeur.* He, himself, was entitled to nothing and would not be until he was back on board his own ship.

He turned in.

* * *

He was awakened by an odd grinding noise that came from somewhere below, sensation as much as sound. He was aware that the ship was moving. She must be sliding stern first down to the river on the rollers set into her flat keel. (That peculiar construction had seemed outrageous to him but it seemed to be working all right.) He slid out of his bunk, pulled on his kilt and shirt. (He should have washed the drip-dry garments before retiring; they were unpleasantly sticky on his skin.) He went into the alleyway. He looked briefly into Shirl's and Darleen's cabins. They were aboard. Shirl had her back to him. Darleen, sprawled on her back and snoring, looked very much the worse for wear.

He went up to the wheelhouse.

Onslow was there, in his inevitable rig of the day, sarong and uniform cap, busy at the manoeuvring console. Fenella, in a borrowed sarong, was standing beside him, sipping noisily from a big mug of coffee.

She turned to look at Grimes.

She said, "Stick around. You might learn something about shiphandling."

Grimes watched with interest. It all looked very simple. *Triton* had backed out into midstream and now was swinging to head down river. Onslow's big hands played over the controls like those of a master pianist. Then, satisfied, he made a last setting and stepped back.

He told his audience, "She'll look after herself now. Radar controlled steering'll keep her in mid-channel . . ."

"Shall we go down for breakfast, Clarrie?" asked Fenella.

"I'll be staying up here until we're over the bar. In narrow waters anything might happen." He turned to Grimes. "Can you handle an autochef, Captain? The one here is the standard spaceship pattern. You'll find eggs in the galley, and sliced bread, and ham . . . What about an omelet? And some more coffee?"

"Given an autochef to play with," said Fenella, "he kids himself that he's in the *cordon bleu* class."

"I'll manage," said Grimes. He would have preferred to stay in the wheelhouse to admire the passing scenery but he wanted breakfast. Obviously that was a meal which he would not enjoy unless he cooked it himself.

He went down to the galley. He found the eggs and the ham, broke a dozen of the former into the labelled funnel—FLUIDS & SEMI-FLUIDS—and fed hunks of ham into another one—SOLIDS. On the keyboard he typed *Omelets—Ham—3. Execute.*

The autochef hummed happily to itself while Grimes poured a mug of hot, black coffee from the dispenser. He was still drinking it when the *Ready* gong sounded. He put the mug down and threw slices of bread into the toasting attachment. Almost immediately the gong sounded again.

Oh, well, thought Grimes, he would just have to finish his coffee on the bridge.

He found a big tray, and plates and eating irons. He took the omelets from the autochef. They looked and smelled good. He loaded the tray. He knew how Fenella liked her coffee; he guessed that Onslow would want his black and sweet.

He managed to get up the companionways to the wheelhouse without dropping or spilling anything. He had expected that he would be welcome, but he was not. Fenella was leaning out of a forward window; Onslow was close, very close, behind her. Grimes coughed tactfully.

Onslow stepped back from Fenella, adjusting his sarong. Hers was on the deck about her ankles. She stooped to pull it up about her slim body before she turned. She glared at Grimes while Onslow looked at him almost apologetically.

She snarled. "You took so bloody long that we . . ."

Onslow pulled up a folding table, said, "Just put the tray down here, will you?"

Grimes did so.

"Thank you," said Onslow. "Yes, we can manage three omelets, I think, between the two of us." Then, "Oh, by the way, Captain Grimes, I don't encourage passengers on my bridge, especially in pilotage waters."

So Fenella wasn't a passenger? thought Grimes. But she was working her passage, of course . . ."

He left the wheelhouse, his prominent ears aflame.

On his way back to the galley he paused on the passenger deck. Shirl and Darleen were still sleeping, both of them snoring. So he would have to eat alone. This time he gave rather more thought to the preparation of the meal, using a tomato-like fruit and a sprinkling of herbs as well as ham for the filling of his omelet. He found a bottle of brandy and added a slug to his coffee.

He ate sitting on a small hatch on the little area of deck abaft the bridge superstructure, watching the scenery slide past, the wooded banks, the shallow bays with their golden beaches. He was joined by Shirl (or Darleen; they had been dressed differently on making their escape from the Snuff Palace but now that they had reverted to nudity he had trouble telling them apart) on the hatch. She was carrying a mug of coffee. She looked enviously at the remains of Grimes' breakfast, helped herself to a slice of toast and cream cheese.

She said plaintively, "I could pour myself a coffee but I couldn't manage that machine . . ."

"I'll do you something, Shirl."

"Darleen. I've a sort of birthmark here . . ." She indicated a mole on her upper thigh. "See."

"What about in the dark?" asked Grimes.

"You can feel it . . ."

She guided his hand to the spot.

"I'm *hungry,*" complained Shirl, coming out to join them. "I thought that passengers were supposed to be fed. I went up to the . . . the control room to ask and they, the captain and that Fenella, threw me out. They were . . ."

"I can guess," said Grimes.

He got up from the hatch and led the two girls into the galley. They both wanted grilled fish for breakfast. (Whoever that long-ago genetic engineer had been he had made considerable modifications to the original stock; kangaroos are herbivores.) They returned to the lazarette hatch, Grimes with more coffee for himself. Sitting there in the warm sunlight with an attractive girl on either side of him he was reminded of a painting he had once seen. What was it called? Picnic On The Grass, or something. But in that there was only one naked woman, surrounded by fully clothed—even to tophats!—men. Here it was a single clothed (more or less) man surrounded by naked women.

And why should he be clothed? The air was warm and the shirt, which should have been washed the previous night, was uncomfortably sticky. He took it off. Darleen, on his right, was sitting very close to him. So, on his left, was Shirl.

Shirl said, "I've a birthmark too, John . . ."

(Grimes wondered just how telepathic these women were.)

"Just under my left breast . . . If it's dark you can feel it . . ."

"It's not dark now," said Grimes, but allowed his hand to be guided to the place. Somehow his fingers finished up on her nipple—and the fingers of the hand that Darleen had taken also strayed.

It was Darleen who fell back supine on to the hatch, pulling Grimes with her. It was Shirl who found the fastening at the waistband of his kilt, who pulled the garment from him. He was the meat in an erotic sandwich, with Darleen's moist, hungry mouth beneath his, with Shirl's breasts, with their erect nipples, pressed into his naked back, with her teeth gently nibbling his right ear.

From above there came laughter and the sound of hand-clapping.

The girls would have ignored this but Grimes could not. He extricated himself, not without difficulty, from the dual embrace. He looked up. The obnoxious Onslow and the even more obnoxious Fenella Pruin were at the rail at the after end of the bridge, grinning down at them.

"Now you know what it's like to be interrupted!" said the Pruin.

Twenty-nine

Grimes was used to odd voyages, to pleasant ones and to unpleasant ones. He was used (of course) to ships, although not at this stage of his career to vessels plying planetary seas rather than the oceans of deep space. But a ship is a ship is a ship, no matter in what medium she swims. Oars, sails, screw propellers, hydraulic jets, inertial drive units or whatever are all no more (and no less) than devices to move tonnage, small or considerable, from Point A to Point B fast or economically or, ideally, both.

Apart from the captain's quarters and the wheelhouse Grimes had the run of *Triton.* Onslow, infatuated with Fenella Pruin, let it be understood that his other passengers could look after themselves, preparing their own meals in the galley, signing for whatever liquor or cigars they took from the bar stores. Grimes did all the cooking for himself and Shirl and Darleen. He was used to getting the best out of an autochef, the two New Alicians were not. Anything they tried more complex than a simple grill was a culinary disaster.

Triton seemed to be navigating herself. Her pilot-computer had been programmed to keep her on a safe track along the coast, to compensate automatically for wind and current, to keep clear of other sea-borne traffic and, Grimes leaned on one of the rare occasions that he met Onslow in the galley and had a brief conversation with him, to sound an alarm if the ship had gotten herself into a close quarters situation or any other potential danger.

Grimes, who spent most of the daylight hours on deck, watched the passing ships with interest. There were bulk carriers. There was an occasional huge cruise liner, white-gleaming with deck upon deck upon deck. There were fishing boats—some, dowdily utilitarian, obviously commercial, others so flashily painted and equipped that they must be catering to wealthy tourists wishing to combine their boozing and wenching with some outdoor sport.

Of these charter boats a few had what looked like a cannon mounted forward. This intrigued Grimes; those little vessels could not possibly be warships. Then, one morning, he was privileged to see a gun in action. He watched, through borrowed binoculars, a harpoon streaking out to hit what, until the moment of impact had been no more than an almost totally submerged, immobile object that he had assumed was a waterlogged tree trunk.

There was more to it than had been visible above the surface, much more. The thing exploded in a frenzy of activity, thrashing the water in its agonies. There was a maned head at the end of a long, slender neck, there was a thick tail with flukes at the extremity, a barrel-shaped body with three pairs of flippers. After the initial flurry it sounded. The harpoon line stretched taut and the bows of the chaser almost went under. Then it was moving fast, under power, relieving the tension on the line as it pursued the stricken sea beast.

"They call them Moby Dicks," volunteered Darleen who, with Shirl, was standing with Grimes on the afterdeck.

"Moby Dicks? Couldn't they have found a name out of Greek mythology?" asked Grimes.

"What's that?" asked Shirl.

"Never mind. But what do they hunt them for? Are they good to eat?"

"No. But the tourists like sport—as *we* know."

"Too right," said Grimes.

"Even the Shaara hunt the Moby Dicks," said Darleen. "But they do it from their own airships. Their. . . blimps."

"They would," said Grimes. Then, reminiscently, "I used to think that the Shaara were a harmless, peace-loving people. I learned differently."

"They're only human," said Shirl.

"Mphm," grunted Grimes.

The chaser was hull down now, only its upperworks showing over the sea horizon. Grimes felt sorry for the Moby Dick. It had been basking on the surface, minding its own business and had been jerked into wakefulness by a harpoon, fired by some moneyed lout, in the guts. And after it had been messily slaughtered it would just be left drifting, to decompose . . .

He looked at his watch. It was almost lunchtime. He was beginning to feel hungry. The previous night, spent in the company of the New Alicians, eager to demonstrate the professional skills they had learned on New Venusberg, tolerant of the inadequacies engendered by past traumatic experiences and that he had yet fully to overcome, had been a wearing one.

Onslow was in the galley, setting the controls on the autochef, wearing the inevitable sarong. He looked pale under his tan. He, too, must have spent a wearing night.

He looked at Grimes, grinned weakly. "Good morning, Captain. Just fixing brunch for her ladyship. Just between ourselves, I shan't be sorry when this voyage is over . . ."

"When do we get there?" asked Grimes.

"Sixteen hundred hours tomorrow. You'll all have to keep out of sight while we're berthing, of course, and not leave the ship until after dark. I've ironed all the details out with Fenella."

"I'm sure you have, Captain."

"And how's *your* ironing going on, Captain? Very nicely, by the looks of you."

"Mphm."

The gong sounded. Onslow unloaded a tray from the autochef. He said, "Be good. Don't do anything that you couldn't do riding a bicycle." He left Grimes to his own devices.

After a good lunch Grimes decided to take the sun on the deck above the wheelhouse while the two girls retired to their cabins for an afternoon nap. Although the wheelhouse itself was, so far as he knew, still out of bounds to passengers Onslow had made no mention of the monkey island. He took with him a box of cigarillos and some reading matter that he had found. Perhaps inevitably this consisted of a few dog-eared copies of *Star Scandals*. Among the other sensational stories there were a few by Fenella Pruin. In spite of the overwriting he found her account of life among the Blossom People on Francisco quite absorbing.

He became vaguely aware of a droning noise different from the subdued hum of *Triton*'s engines. He raised himself on his elbows, looked up and around. He saw it then, out to starboard, flying seaward from over the hazy coastline. It was a Shaara blimp.

He remembered being told that the Shaara hunted the things called Moby Dicks, using their own blimps rather than the charter chasers. And these must be Moby Dick waters; where there had been one there must be others. His sympathies lay with the victims of the chase rather than with the hunters but he did almost hope that the arthropods would sight one of the great beasts; he was curious to see how an airship would be able to cope with the playing of a harpooned prey. And how, he wondered, did the Shaara handle the recoil problem of the harpoon gun?

At first it seemed that the airship was going to pass well astern of *Triton* but it changed course, so as to fly directly over her. That was natural enough. It was going nowhere in particular and its crew might well be wanting a closer look at the smart little surface vessel.

As it approached it lost altitude. That, too, was natural enough. Grimes feeling mellow after his filling lunch with rather too much chilled beer to wash it down, prepared to forgive and to forget all the indignities he had suffered at the hands of the Shaara, got to his feet and waved cheerfully.

He should have had more sense.

The blimp flew directly overhead. He could see Shaara heads, with their antennae and huge, faceted eyes, peering down from over the gunwale of the car. He could see, too, the harpoon gun mounted forward, was interested to note that it was a rocket launcher rather than a cannon proper. Then he realised that nobody had answered his salutation.

Fuck 'em! he thought. *Snooty bee-bastards. Fuck 'em.*

The airship turned, coming around slowly. A Shaara, a princess, thought Grimes, was standing beside the rocket launcher working the laying wheel, depressing the launching rack. The barbed head of the missile was pointing directly at him.

Surely they wouldn't . . . he thought—and knew that they would. He ran for the ladder on the starboard side of the monkey island trying to get down to the bridge, to put the wheelhouse between himself and the harpoon. He tripped on the stack of magazines that he had brought up with him, fell heavily. Half stunned, he was still trying to get to his feet when the rocket was fired. He heard the swoosh of it and thought, *This is it . . .*

Below him there was a screaming roar and a great crashing and clattering. Working it all out later he came to the conclusion that some minor turbulence had caused the blimp's nose to dip at the crucial moment so that the harpoon, missing him, drove right through the wheelhouse, through the port window and out through the starboard one. But at this moment all that mattered was that he was still alive. He wanted to stay that way. He fell rather than clambered down the starboard ladder to the bridge wing, trying to get to cover before the Shaara could reload. He hardly noticed the pain as his bare foot came down on a sharp-edged shard of plastic, part of the wreckage of the wheelhouse windows.

Then, automatically, his Survey Service training taking over, he began to assess damage. Looking into the wheelhouse he saw that the controls seemed to be undamaged. The harpoon must have plunged into the sea to starboard; its line, gleaming, enormously strong but light wire, was trailing aft. Grimes, who knew something about surface craft, wondered if he should stop the engines before the screw (or screws) got fouled. But *Triton,* with her hydraulic jet propulsion, had no external screws. Out to port the line, dipping in a graceful catenary, stretched to the blimp which was now running parallel to the surface ship. At the forward end of the car the figures of Shaara were busy about the rocket launcher, reloading it.

"What the hell's going on?" Onslow was roaring.

He had come up into his devastated wheelhouse, not bothering to dress, in his bewildered fury, his hairy nakedness, looking like the ancestral killer ape in person. He grabbed the taut harpoon line, shaking it viciously. He glared through the broken window at the blimp.

"Get under cover!" shouted Grimes. "They're going to fire again!"

"Two can play at that game!" yelled Onslow. He flung open the door of a locker on the after bulkhead of the wheelhouse, snatched from it a rifle. With the barrel he completed the destruction of the starboard window so that no remaining pieces of plastic obstructed his aim. He brought the butt of the weapon to his shoulder, sighted, fired. Grimes had expected that his target would be the Shaara who were now swinging the rocket launcher around to bear—but it was not. The burst of rapid fire was directed at the after end of the car, to the engine. Grimes saw the tracers strike, saw the coruscation of vividly blue sparks as broken circuits arced and fused. The pusher screw ceased to be a shimmering circle of near invisibility as the blades slowed and stopped. The airship dropped astern, still secured to *Triton* by the harpoon wire, being towed by her like a captive balloon.

"You should have gone for the gunners, Captain," Grimes told him. "They'll have us well within range as long as the wire holds . . ."

"And if I murder one of those murdering swine where will I be? Behind bars—or in the Colosseum arena! They're rich, Grimes, *rich*—and justice, like everything else, is for sale on this world!" He grabbed Fenella—who had come up to the wheelhouse unnoticed until now—by the arm. "Here, now, make yourself useful! I taught you how to steer. Don't bother with a compass course. Just zig-zag . . ."

"Aren't you going to report this to the authorities, Captain?" asked Grimes.

"What with?" Onslow gestured towards the transceiver which was sited just below the sill of the starboard window. The harpoon itself had missed it but the line had sliced the box almost in two. "What with? Keep an eye on things up here while I go down to get tools to cut this blasted wire!"

His bare feet thudded heavily on the treads as he ran down the companionway.

Grimes took stock of the situation. Fenella—she had taken time to put on a sarong before coming up to the wheelhouse—was standing behind the binnacle, her hands on the two buttons used for manual steering. She pressed first one and then the other; the ship's head swung to port and to starboard obedient to the helm. She knew what was required; her alterations of course were sufficiently random to throw off the aim of any gunner not gifted with precognition.

She looked at him and grinned. "Boy! What a story I'll be writing!"

If you survive to write it, he thought but did not feel unduly pessimistic. He picked up the heavy rifle from where Onslow had put it down, went out to the starboard wing of the bridge. Shirl and Darleen, who had come up by an outside ladder, were there. Unlike Fenella they had not bothered to cover themselves. They were staring aft at the tethered blimp, dipping and yawing at the end of its long towline.

"What's doin'?" asked Shirl.

"They're after me," said Grimes. "The Shaara. It's an old grudge."

"After us too, like as not," said Darleen. "We killed four of the bastards in the Snuff Palace . . ."

The blimp's rocket projector fired. The missile fell into the sea at least half a kilometre on *Triton*'s starboard beam. Grimes laughed. Only a very lucky shot could hit the ship and the supply of harpoons must be limited. And once Onslow came up with something to cut the wire the Shaara would fall away rapidly astern, utterly impotent.

But what were they doing now?

First one dark shape dropped from the car, then another, then three more. Even at this distance Grimes could see the irridescent blur of their rapidly beating wings. They were overhauling *Triton* very slowly but they had less than two kilometres to fly and were, Grimes well knew, very strong fliers. Princesses, drones or worker-technicians? He could not tell. Armed or unarmed? The sunlight was reflected by something glitteringly metallic carried by one of them. A knife, possibly, or a handgun . . . But it didn't much matter. He, Grimes, had Onslow's rifle.

He checked the magazine.

It was empty.

He ran into the wheelhouse, to the locker from which the captain had taken the weapon. It was completely bare. But there must be some more ammunition somewhere.

Onslow came up from below, carrying a laser cutting torch.

"Where's your spare ammo?" asked Grimes.

"Haven't got any. This ain't a warship. Now, where do I cut this wire? It's going to lash back if I'm not careful . . . Now if I stand right in the middle of the wheelhouse to cut it I'll be safe, but the rest of you won't be. A spacer like you wouldn't know how a parted wire under a strain whips back . . ." (Grimes did know but this was no time to tell the other man.) "So either get below decks or up on monkey island." He patted Fenella's arse affectionately. "You're safe. You're right on the centreline."

"But the Shaara . . . They're coming after us. They'll be boarding shortly."

"They'll just have to wait till I've finished here. This harpoon wire is a bastard to cut through, even with laser . . ."

He switched on the pistol-like tool and the surface of the wire began to glow where the almost invisible beam impinged upon it.

Grimes ran out on to the bridge wing. He could not understand what the two New Alicians were doing. Stooping, the posture making their big rumps very prominent, they were gathering fragments of sharp-edged, shattered plastic from the deck, discarding some and keeping others.

"Get off the bridge!" he shouted. "This wire's going to go!"

They obeyed him but they did not run below, as he was expecting. They scampered up the ladder to monkey island. He followed them. They would be as safe from the flying ends of wire there as anywhere else and would be able to see what was happening.

Astern the blimp was still bobbing and weaving at the end of its towline. The five Shaara who had left the crippled airship were close now—-two, the larger ones, princesses, the other three drones. If the things that they were carrying had been firearms they would have used them by now. Short spears, Grimes decided. Probably the weapons used in the final stages of the Moby Dick hunt—and such weapons could be, would be used against him. Perhaps he should have run below to find something with which to defend himself—a spanner or hammer from the engineroom workshop, a knife from the galley. But now it was too late. The wire must surely be going to part at any moment and if he were on the bridge when it did so he would be sliced in two.

Behind him and to either side of him Shirl and Darleen shouted. He heard the whirring noise as the fragments of flung plastic whirled past his head on either side, watched their glittering trajectory. One struck the leading princess, shearing off her iridescent wings at the left shoulder joint. The other would have hit the drone flying beside her had he not swerved and dipped. The injured Shaara fell to the sea, legs and the remaining wings thrashing ineffectually.

Again the makeshift boomerangs were thrown. The other princess was hit, but on the heavily furred thorax. She faltered in her flight, falling behind the three drones, but kept on coming. Grimes could see the spears clearly now, nasty looking tridents. He picked up a shard of plastic, flung it viciously. He gashed his hand but did no other damage while Shirl, exhibiting far greater skill, decapitated a drone.

Then the wire parted. The end on the starboard side of the wheelhouse, with the harpoon trailing from it, slid harmlessly overside. The other end whipped up and back towards the towed airship. The princess was in the way of it. The two halves of her body plummeted to the water.

That left two drones.

These abandoned the chase, dropping to the sea to go to the aid of the injured princess. The last that Grimes saw of them they were flying slowly back to the drifting blimp, carrying between them the body, possibly still living, of their superior.

Thirty

Triton came to Troy.

Her entrance into port was delayed; Onslow had not been able to notify the authorities of his impending arrival by radio telephone, the transceiver damaged by the Shaara harpoon being irreparable. So she had to lay off to seaward of the breakwaters while her captain tried to establish communication by daylight signalling lamp. His Morse was rusty, although no rustier than the Morse of the duty officer in the signal station. Finally he was able to find out where he was to berth and to order his linesmen; as *Triton* was crewless a mooring party would have to board as soon as she entered the harbour.

Grimes would have liked to watch the berthing procedure but he, with the three women, had to stay in his cabin until Onslow gave the all clear. So the four of them sat there waiting—Fenella in the single chair, Grimes between the two New Alicians on the bunk. The view from the port was very limited, affording only glimpses of cranes and gantries and, once, a huge bulk carrier.

They felt the bump as the launch with the mooring party came alongside. Then there was the vibration as the hydraulic jets were employed to give lateral thrust and, finally, another bump as *Triton*'s starboard side made contact with the wharf fendering. Not long after there was the sound of footsteps as two people came up the companionway from the poop deck. They passed through the passenger accommodation, carried on up to the captain's quarters.

Port officials? The ship's agent? Police?

The four of them sat there in silence. Fenella was smoking, one cigarillo after another. So was Grimes, although he would sooner have had a pipe. Shirl and Darleen did not smoke.

At last there was the sound of footsteps again. Three people were coming down the companionway. They did not pause on the passenger deck. After a short delay one person came on up, rapped sharply on the locked cabin door.

It had to be Onslow, thought Grimes as he opened up.

It was.

"The harbourmaster and my agent," reported the captain. "They wanted to know what the hell had happened to my wheelhouse. I told them the story that *you* cooked up, Fenella. They believed it." He laughed. "They'd have believed and liked the true story still more. They don't love the Shaara."

"My story is safer," Fenella Pruin said. "For all of us, you included. Don't forget that Grimes and I are officially dead until we elect to bob up again. You've never seen us, any of us. You were just steaming quietly along on your lawful occasions when a Moby Dick surfaced to starboard. Out to port there was this Shaara blimp with a hunting party. The trigger-happy bastards opened fire on their quarry, even though you were between it and them. Something went wrong and the harpoon went right through your wheelhouse, missing you by millimetres. You, looking after your own ship, decided to cut the wire—which had the harpoon, in the water, at one end of it and the blimp at the other. You did so. When you came out on deck you saw Shaara bodies in the water and a couple of drones picking one up. Some of them must have come out of the airship and were flying down to have a few words with you when the wire parted. A couple or three must have been caught by one of the ends when it whipped back . . .

"Is that what you told them?"

"Yes."

"With no improvements of your own manufacture?"

"No."

"Good. If anybody else asks questions, stick to my version. I doubt very much if even the Shaara, arrogant insects that they are, would dare to admit to attacking a New Venusberg ship on the high seas. After all, they're the foreigners and you're the native . . ."

"Native?" asked Grimes.

"Clarry's naturalised," Fenella told him. "He had to be before he was allowed to command a New Venusberg ship." She turned to the shipmaster. "And now, how soon can we get out of here?"

"It'll be sunset in a couple of hours and there's not much twilight in these latitudes." He looked at her as he added, "I'll be rather sorry to see you go."

"I'm sure that you will."

Onslow transferred his attention to Grimes. "And who's going to pay for the repairs to my wheelhouse?"

"Your insurance," Grimes told him. "Or you can sue the Shaara."

"But if *you* hadn't been on board . . ."

"I paid my passage, which is more than somebody else did . . ."

"And I'm still paying *you,* Grimes, so shut up!" snapped Fenella Pruin. She said to the shipmaster, "Let's go up to your cabin, Clarry. It's a bit less crowded than here. We can talk things over there."

Plainly neither Grimes, Darleen nor Shirl was included in the "us." They remained sitting on the bunk while Onslow and Fenella Pruin left the cabin. Grimes hoped that they would make each other very happy.

They helped themselves to a last meal before leaving *Triton;* they did not know where the next one was coming from as, after paying the bar bill, Grimes had only a few credits left. They dressed in the clothing that, supplied by Onslow, was to be part of their disguise. (When captured and when escaping from the Snuff Palace none of them had been wearing sarongs.) Padded brassieres were contrived for Shirl and Darleen—"False upperworks!" laughed Onslow as he, personally, adjusted them on the girls' chests—as well as binding to reduce the size of their prominent rumps. From the neck down, at least, they no longer looked like New Alician women. Syntheskin from *Triton*'s medicine chest was used to gum Grimes' prominent ears flat to his skull. Onslow found a wig—it had been left behind by some past female passenger—for Fenella. It transformed her into a quite pretty redhead, somehow softened her features.

Grimes and the two Matilda's Children were first down the gangway. They waited on the wharf while Fenella and Captain Onslow made a last, passionate farewell on the poop deck. Her wig fell off. Grimes just caught it before it fell into the narrow gap between the ship's side and the wharf stringer.

At last she came down, took the artificial head covering from Grimes without a word of thanks, put it back on. She waved one last time to Onslow. Then, with Grimes in the lead they made their way to the Port Troy subway station. They kept away from the bright lights. This was easy as the only ship working cargo was a big bulk carrier. Apart from the activity about her the port area was very quiet. They met nobody during their short walk.

The entrance to the station was just an entrance, lacking either crude or subtle sexual symbolism. There were no other intending passengers; the only similitude to life was that presented by the animated, pornographic advertisements to either side of the escalator and on the platform.

There was no through car to Port Aphrodite; they would have to change at New Bali Beach. That station was fairly busy. While they waited on the platform for the Port Aphrodite car Grimes felt uneasily that everybody was staring at them. He told himself firmly that this could not be so; their appearance was no more outré than that of the average tourist on this planet.

But there was one fat woman, herself sarong clad, who was subjecting Grimes, and Grimes only, to an intense scrutiny. He had seen her before somewhere, he thought.

But where?

When?

Then he remembered. She was one of the witnesses to his humiliation on Bali Beach when the Shaara had bombed him with garbage. She was the one whom he, rather childishly, had humiliated in her turn on the Platform of the Port Aphrodite subway station.

She approached him tentatively. She asked, "Isn't it Captain Grimes? I never forget a face . . ."

"My name, madam," said Grimes, "is Fenn." (It was the first one that came into his head. He realised that Fenella Pruin was glaring at him—but she did not hold a copyright on the alias.) He laughed. "I must have a double."

"I do beg your pardon, Mr Fenn. But you *are* like Captain Grimes—apart from your ears, that is. And I'm sorry, in a way, that you're not him . . ."

Is there a reward out? he wondered.

"Why?" he asked, trying to make his voice unconcerned.

"Because if you were him he'd still be alive. He was such a charming young man, in spite of his wealth so utterly unspoiled. There aren't many like him in the galaxy . . ."

"What do you mean, madam?" asked Grimes. "My friends and I are new here. We've yet to look at a newspaper or listen to a bulletin . . ."

"Oh, you must be passengers on that big ship that came in yesterday. I can't remember her name but my hubby, who used to be in shipping—on the business side, of course—told me that she's one of the Commission's Beta Class liners under new ownership. But this Captain Grimes is—or was, but they haven't found any bodies yet although they found wreckage—a shipowner as well as being a space captain. Only a little ship but built, so they say, of gold. I can't believe that but she shines like gold. He came here with just one passenger, a girl as rich as himself. They chartered one of those camperflies and flew off for a tour. They never came back. They were last seen taking off from Vulcan Island. Pilot error it must have been, although you'd think that a man who could take a spaceship all around the galaxy would be able to manage a *camperfly.* Even my hubby can, although he's certainly not either a spaceman or an airman. He just sets the controls on automatic and presses the buttons for where he wants to go. Perhaps that was the trouble. Would a *real* captain be happy to let his ship do his thinking for him?

"And then, of course, he had a beautiful young lady with him . . . Perhaps, when he should have been piloting, he was doing something else. I don't want to speak ill of the dead but the girl—what was her name?—was free with her favours. There was that fat Port Captain for one; I did hear that he actually burst into tears when he heard that his lady love was missing . . . Now what was *her* name? It's on the tip of my tongue. Prudence something or other—but she wasn't very prudent, was she?

"No, what am I thinking about? Not Prudence. Prunella. Yes, that was it. Prunella . . . ? Prunella Fenn. You wouldn't be her brother, would you? Or perhaps her husband, come here to find out what happened to her . . . ?"

"No," said Grimes. "No relation."

"But what a coincidence! You looking like Captain Grimes—but much better looking!—and with the same name as the young lady who was with him when he vanished . . ."

Fortunately the Port Aphrodite car came in. Grimes practically shoved his three companions through the open door into the interior. He paused briefly to say, "Thank you for the talk, madam." He laughed. "After what you've told us *we* shan't be hiring a camperfly! A very good night to you."

The door closed before he had taken his seat. The car sped through the tunnel.

"Did you have to use Fenn as a name?" asked Fenella coldly.

"It's as good as any other," said Grimes. "Or is it? Anyhow, we've learned a bit. We—you and I, that is, Fenella—are definitely missing, presumed dead. Your fat friend Jock is heartbroken. He'll be overjoyed to see you again. You—we—had better concoct a story to satisfy him. We'll probably need his help to get back on board *Little Sister*."

"All right, Mr *Fenn.* What are *your* ideas?"

"You're the writer."

"Not a fiction writer."

"No?" He raised his eyebrows, winced as this caused a sting of pain in the skin of his skull under his gummed down ears. "No? Judging from some of your pieces that I read in *Star Scandals* . . ."

"None of them," she told him, "more fantastic than the story of what's happened to us on this world."

Thirty-one

No other passengers boarded the car at the two stops before arrival at Port Aphrodite. Grimes and Fenella were able to work out the details of what they hoped would be a plausible story. It did not tally with the one that Captain Onslow had told the authorities in Troy but, hopefully, *Little Sister* would be well up and away from New Venusberg before there was any thorough checking up.

They would tell Captain McKillick that they had visited Vulcan Island in the rented camperfly. Returning to the mainland they had seen, on the surface, a huge sea beast, a Moby Dick. Fenella Pruin—Prunella Fenn, rather—had wanted a closer look at the monster. They had been flying only a few metres above it when it had lashed up and out with its tail, which had done the aircraft no good at all. It had crashed into the water and broken up.

Grimes and Fenella had gotten away, using one of the camperfly's wings as a raft. (Although the gas cell was holed there was still sufficient buoyancy for it to stay afloat.) They had drifted on to a small island and had stayed there, living on fruit and roots and shellfish, until they had been fortunate enough to attract the attention of the passing *Triton.* Then, during the voyage to Troy, there had been another unfortunate incident. Grimes, sunbathing on the upper deck, had been recognised by one of the crew—probably that princess whom he had first met in Lady Luck's—of a Shaara blimp on a Moby Dick hunting expedition. This spiteful being had taken a shot at him with the blimp's rocket harpoon. She had missed Grimes but scored a hit on *Triton*'s wheelhouse. When the wire had parted an end of it, whipping back, had killed or injured a few hapless Shaara who had left their airship to make an assessment of the situation.

It was decided that Fenella would try to call *Triton,* from a public call box, as soon as they got to Port Aphrodite. Onslow had told her that he intended to have his damaged transceiver replaced that night; in fact the technicians had been due on board only half an hour or so after the fugitives had left the ship. The captain would then be able to amend his story to make it agree with theirs.

The car arrived at the Port Aphrodite station.

There were people on the platform awaiting the transport to carry them to various pleasure establishments. None of these was at all interested in Grimes and his three companions. There were public call boxes at the head of the escalator. There were a few moments of panic when Grimes could not find the much depleted notecase that he had tucked into the waistband of his sarong. While he was fumbling it fell to the floor between his feet. He picked it up, gave it to Fenella.

She went into the box. Grimes and the two New Alicians watched her through the transparent door and walls as she fed one of the plastic bills into the slot. The screen lit up, showing the face—that of a silver woman—of the rob-operator. Fenella said something. The robot replied, the metallic lips moving mechanically. There was a short delay. Then the original picture in the screen faded, was replaced by one of the bearded face of Captain Onslow. He was not alone; there was a brief glimpse of a head of luxuriant blonde hair in the background, of smooth, sun-tanned skin. *A girl in every port,* thought Grimes amusedly, *as well as girls between ports wherever possible . . .*

Onslow did not seem at all pleased to be seeing and hearing his recent lady love so soon after the fond farewell. His initial scowl, however, was replaced by a somewhat spurious smile. He said little, let Fenella do most of the talking. He looked relieved when the conversation was terminated.

Fenella came out of the box. She seemed amused rather than otherwise. She said, "He didn't waste much time, did he? Off with the old love, on with the new . . . Just one of those things . . ."

"Shits that pass in the night," said Grimes.

"Very funny!" she snapped. "Very funny. Well. Anyhow, he's agreed to change his story the next time that anybody asks him how his wheelhouse got busted up. I didn't have much trouble persuading him. He was wanting to get back to that brazen floosie he had with him."

"Mphm."

"And now let's get back to *your* precious ship."

They left the station, walked out into the soft night. The spaceport was almost as it had been when they left it. There were two freighters working cargo with glaring lights all about them. There were the cruise liners. There was *Little Sister,* goldenly agleam in her berth between two big ships. One was the Shaara vessel that had been there when they arrived. The other was one of the Interstellar Transport Commission's Beta Class passenger liners. But was she still owned by the Commission? A flag, softly floodlit, flew from the telescopic mast extruded from her sharp stem, an ensign of imperial purple with, in glowing gold, the CR monogram, the symbol representing the Credit, the galaxy-wide monetary unit.

It was the flag of El Dorado.

And why not? The El Doradans, Grimes well knew, enjoyed kinky sex as much as anybody and could afford to pay for it better than most.

But the name of the ship . . .

He could read it now, in golden (of course) letters on the burnished grey shellplating under the control room.

Southerly Buster III . . .

Southerly Buster . . . Drongo Kane . . .

And Kane, through his Able Enterprises, pulled far heavier Gs on New Venusberg than Grimes or even Fenella Pruin.

He said as much to her as they walked towards *Little Sister.* She agreed with him but said that it was of no consequence; once they got off this cesspit of a planet she would lift the lid off the whole, stinking can of worms.

There were guards around *Little Sister—not* only a Customs officer but two armed men in uniform—modelled on that of the Federation Marines—of the spaceport police.

One of these said sharply, "Halt! I'm sorry, gentlepersons, but nobody is allowed near this ship."

"I am the master," said Grimes, with deliberate pomposity. "I am Captain Grimes."

"If you are," said the guard, "you don't look anything like your photograph. Captain Grimes has *ears.* Yours are quite normal."

"The airlock door is coded to me," said Grimes. "It will let me in."

"I'm sorry, sir. My orders are that nobody, but nobody, is to approach this ship."

"But I am Captain Grimes. I am the master. The owner."

"So *you* say, sir."

"I am Prunella Fenn," said Fenella Pruin.

"Somebody else who doesn't look much like her photograph!" laughed the guard.

"Captain McKillick will soon identify me—but I most certainly do not wish to be kept hanging around until tomorrow morning!"

"You can see the Port Captain now, lady. He is in his office, still. Some business over the El Doradan ship."

"All right," she said. "We'll see him now. And you'll soon find out who we are."

McKillick, as the guard had said, was in his office. Apart from those with whom he was discussing business the administration block was empty; there was nobody to detain Grimes and the three women on their way up to the top floor.

The office door opened silently as they approached it. The Port Captain, studying papers spread over his desk, did not notice. Neither did the two people, a man and a woman, sitting in chairs facing him. The man was wearing a purple uniform with heavy golden epaulettes. The woman was clad in translucent white beneath which her body glowed goldenly. Diamonds glittered in the braided coronet of her glossy auburn hair, in the pendants hanging from her ears.

"As far as I know," the fat McKillick was saying, "Captain Grimes and his passenger, Prunella Fenn, were lost when their hired camperfly crashed in the sea shortly after lifting off from Vulcan Island. I blame myself for the tragedy. I should never have allowed them to leave Port Aphrodite. Grimes I did not trust. The man was no more than an adventurer, battening on wealthy women . . ."

"Captain Grimes," said the woman coldly, "was—or is—an extremely competent shipmaster."

"Be that as it may," went on McKillick, "that camperfly did crash in the sea. A search was made but only the wreckage of the aircraft was found. The cause of the disaster could only have been pilot error."

"Indeed?" the woman said. "The story that *we* heard, in a Carlottigram from Captain Dreeble of *Willy Willy,* was a rather different one. That camperfly may or may not have crashed—but Captain Grimes wasn't in it. At this moment he's probably one of the star attractions at the Colosseum—if he's still alive, that is. He had better be."

"He will be," growled her companion. "His famous luck more than compensates for his many shortcomings."

"Mphm," grunted Grimes indignantly.

McKillick lifted his eyes from the papers on his desk. He stared at Grimes and the three women. The purple-uniformed man and his companion swivelled around in their chairs, also stared.

"Grimes . . ." murmured Drongo Kane at last. "Live, on stage, in person. Singing and dancing. But what's happened to your ears?"

"Grimes . . ." said the Baroness. "Grimes. I was very worried when Commodore Kane got that message about you from Captain Dreeble, especially when he told me about the Colosseum. I'd no idea—believe me, John, I had no idea—what sort of entertainments are available on this planet . . ."

"Grimes!" shouted McKillick. "Grimes! But who are those people with you? What did you do to Prue?" He was on his feet, looking as though he were about to clamber over his desk to shake the truth out of *Little Sister*'s captain. "Where is she? Tell me, damn you, where is she?"

"Here," said Fenella.

"But . . . You?"

She snatched off her disguising wig.

"Prue! You're safe! You're safe!" McKillick did not clamber over his desk but ran clumsily around it. He threw his arms about her, pulled her to him in a bear-like hug. Her face wrinkled in distaste.

"Very touching," remarked Drongo Kane, his carelessly assembled features under the straw-coloured hair creased in a sardonic smile. Then, to the Baroness, "I told you that Grimes would muddle through, as usual, Micky."

Fenella Pruin managed to extricate herself from McKillick's embrace. "Later, Jock," she said. "Later." Then, to Grimes, "This appears to be some sort of re-union as far as you're concerned. Would you mind doing the introductions?"

"Er, yes, Fenella—sorry, Prunella—may I present you to the Baroness Michelle d'Estang of El Dorado?"

"Am I supposed to curtsey?" asked Fenella.

The Baroness looked at her disdainfully. "You may if you wish."

"And to Captain Drongo Kane . . ."

"You've got it wrong, cobber," said that gentleman. "It's Commodore Baron Kane, of the El Doradan Navy."

"Commanding a merchant ship," sneered Grimes. "A cruise liner. A space-borne gin palace."

Kane laughed. "A cruise liner she may be—but she's rated as an auxiliary cruiser. But who are those two sheilahs with you?"

"Shirl," said Shirl.

"Darleen," said Darleen.

"New Alicians, ain't you, with those faces and accents? Matilda's Stepchildren. What are two nice girls like you doing mixed up with Grimes and this muckraking news hen?"

"Muckraking news hen?" asked McKillick bewilderedly.

"Didn't you know, Captain? This is Fenella Pruin, the pride and joy of some local rag on her home planet and the even greater pride and joy of *Star Scandals.* It wouldn't at all surprise me if you were one of her Faithful Readers. She's just been using you, the same as she's used men on hundreds of worlds. She's all set and ready to spill all the unsavoury beans about New Venusberg."

"And what about you, Commodore or Baron or whatever you call yourself?" she shouted. "What about *your* interests here? Your nasty little slave trade from New Alice to the New Venusberg brothels—and worse!"

"Slave trade, my dear? But the New Alicians are under-people, have no more rights than animals. The ships that bring them here are cattle ships, not slave ships."

"Are they? *Are they?* Wasn't it ruled, some many years ago, that underpeople are to be reclassified as human as long as interbreeding between them and true humans is possible?"

"In this case it ain't, Miss Pruin. It's obviously impossible. The ancestors of the New Alicians were marsupials, not placental mammals."

"Their *ancestors,* Mr Kane. And, in any case, I imagine that the crews of your slave ships—sorry, cattle ships—aren't too fussy about having intercourse with them."

"Of course not. I don't recruit my personnel from Sunday schools."

"You can say that again. But I have seen—I'm not telling you where—a New Alician boy who bears a very strong resemblance to his father. To *your* precious Captain Dreeble."

Kane laughed, although he looked uneasy. "I've often entertained doubts about Dreeble's own ancestry," he said.

Grimes laughed. "Morrowvia all over again, isn't it?"

"So the New Alicians are legally human," remarked the Baroness. "So what? All that we have to do is get them to sign proper contracts. What does worry me is that Captain Grimes' current inamorata—I've noticed before that he has the most deplorable taste in women!—is all set and ready to make a big splash in her gutter rag about New Venusberg. Once again—so what?

"El Dorado has big money invested in this world and I, speaking for my fellow El Doradans, shall welcome the free advertising that New Venusberg will be getting. But . . ." she turned to Kane . . . "there will have to be a thorough housecleaning. I did not know of the existence of such establishments as the Colosseum and the Snuff Palace until you told me." Suddenly there was icy contempt in her voice. With pleasure Grimes saw that she was making Kane squirm as, so often during the days aboard *The Far Traveller,* she had made him squirm. "*You* thought that it was a great joke that Grimes would end his days slaughtered in the arena. We are two of a kind, I know—but only up to a point. And beyond that point I refuse to pass. There will be a thorough investigation of the state of affairs on New Venusberg—but without overmuch publicity."

"Yes, Micky," said Kane.

McKillick was at last able to make himself heard. "Prunella!" he bleated to Fenella Pruin. "How could you have done this to *me?* You—a spy!"

"The name is Fenella Pruin," she told him coldly.

"But, Prunella . . ."

The Baroness interrupted. "Port Captain, will you expedite the Outward Clearance of *Little Sister*? Get the necessary officials, Port Health, Customs and the like, out of their beds, or whatever beds they happen to be occupying. Captain Grimes isn't safe on this planet and I want him off it. Rightly or wrongly he will be blamed for the upheaval that will soon take place."

"What about consumable stores?" asked Grimes.

A tolerant smile softened the Baroness's patrician features. "You haven't changed, John. Even though you no longer have Big Sister to pamper you I imagine that you make sure that you never starve."

"Too right," said Grimes.

While they were talking they drifted towards the door, which opened for them, out of the office, into the corridor. He could hear, faintly, the voices from inside the room—Drongo Kane at his hectoring worst, McKillick pitifully bleating, Fenella Pruin emitting an occasional outraged scream. Shirl and Darleen did not seem to be making any contribution to the argument. But he was no longer interested. He was too conscious of the close proximity of that filmily clad body to his. He could smell what once had been, during his tour of duty as captain of her spaceyacht, her familiar scent, cool yet warm, sensual yet unapproachable.

She said, "At times—not all the time, but increasingly so—I'm sorry that Captain Kane turned up when he did. Just when we, alone in the pinnace, were about to do what we'd been putting off for far too long . . ." She put her slender hands on his shoulders, turned him to face her, regarded him with what he realised was affection. "You're an awkward brute at times, for most of the time, but there's something about you. An integrity. I'm fond of Peter, of course . . ." *(Peter?* wondered Grimes. But "Drongo" was probably not Kane's given name.) "I'm fond of Peter—in a way. He's masterful, which I like, but rather too ruthless at times. And he thought that it was a huge joke when he received that message from Aloysius Dreeble—that poisonous little rat!—telling him that you'd been condemned to the Colosseum. (It was only then that I learned that there was such an establishment on this world.) I persuaded him to cancel the ship's visit to New Sparta and to make all possible speed here to try to save you, if it were not too late . . .

"But, of course, you'd already saved yourself."

"With assistance, Michelle."

"Perhaps. But I'm sure that *she,* that muckraker, wasn't much help. It must have been those others, with the horse faces and the ugly names . . . There's a certain strength about them . . ."

"And they throw a wicked boomerang," said Grimes.

"I wish I could have seen it." She laughed softly. "And there's another thing I'd like to see. Again. *The Far Traveller*'s pinnace. I like the name that you gave *her—Little Sister.* And we have unfinished business aboard her, don't we?"

Grimes remembered well that unfinished business—when he, naked, had been holding the naked Michelle in his arms, when the preliminaries to their lovemaking (never to be resumed) had been interrupted by the obnoxious voice of Drongo Kane from the Carlotti transceiver.

He said, "She's under guard. The guards wouldn't let me board her."

"They will," she said, "when I tell them to . . . Come."

They seemed to have stopped arguing in the Port Captain's office. As Grimes and the Baroness turned to make their way to the escalator the door opened. Drongo Kane emerged, scowling. He glared at Grimes.

"Ah, there you are. Well, Micky, orders have gone out that the Colosseum and the Snuff Palace are to be closed down immediately, pending a full enquiry. Of course, you realise that this is going to play hell with our profits. *Your* profits as well as mine."

She said, "There are more things in life than money."

"Name just two!" he snarled. Then, to Grimes, "This is all your doing. As usual. I thought that at long last you'd be out of my hair for keeps—but Her Highness here had to shove her tits in!"

There was a noise like a projectile pistol shot as the flat of her hand struck Kane's face. He stood there, rubbing the reddened skin—and then, surprisingly, he smiled. Even more surprisingly it was not a vicious grin.

He said, admiringly, "I always did like a woman with spirit, Micky."

"There are times," she told him coldly, "when a woman with spirit finds it very hard to like you." She addressed Grimes, "I think that the sooner you're off the planet the better. I can't guarantee your safety. Or that of your companions. Not only will the proprietors of some of the establishments here be gunning for you but there is also my . . . consort, who never has liked you." She allowed a small smile momentarily to soften her features. "But I should imagine that you are already aware of that."

"I shall want stores before I go," said Grimes.

"Then you're out of luck," Drongo Kane said smugly. "McKillick was able to arrange your Outward Clearance but, at this time of night, it was impossible to find a ship chandlery open."

"That presents no problem," the Baroness said. *"Southerly Buster* is well stocked with everything. Peter, will you see to it that what is necessary is transferred from your ship to Captain Grimes' vessel?"

"Am I a philanthropic institution?" bellowed Kane.

"Perhaps not. But *I* am the major shareholder in your Able Enterprises."

"All right," grumbled Kane. "All right. And as for you, Grimes, I suggest that you and your popsies get your arses aboard your little boat while they're still intact."

"Pinnace," corrected Grimes stiffly.

"Or lugger, if you like. Once aboard the lugger and the girls are yours. But not *my* girl." He put a possessive arm about the Baroness's waist.

She disentangled herself, turned to face Grimes. She was as tall as he and did not have to hold her face up to be kissed—and the kiss was not a light one.

"Goodbye, John," she said. "Or *au revoir* . . ."

"Break it up, Micky," snarled Kane. And to Grimes, "It's time that I didn't have to look at you!"

"Goodbye, John," said the Baroness again. "Look after yourself, and those two nice girls. As for the other one—I shall want a few words with her before she joins you aboard *Little Sister.*"

Shirl and Darleen were already in the corridor, watching and listening with interest. Fenella Pruin was still in the office, no doubt saying her farewell to Captain McKillick. The Baroness, followed by Kane, went back into the Port Captain's sanctum. It was not long before he heard, through the closed door, Fenella Pruin's indignant screams. She seemed to be very annoyed about something.

But he could not distinguish what was being said and he wanted to get back aboard his ship to see that all was in order. With the two New Alicians, one on either side of him, he made his way out of the administration block. The guards at his airlock must have been told to allow him through. They saluted him smartly, stood aside.

Back in *Little Sister* he felt much happier. He checked everything. Apart from the legal formalities he could be ready to lift off within minutes. Even the stores were of no great importance provided that one was willing to put up with a monotonous diet.

Fenella Pruin came aboard.

She was crestfallen, sullen. She glowered at Grimes.

"*Your* friends!" she spat. "Her Exalted Highness the Baroness of Bilge! And the Lord High Commodore! Ptah!"

"He's no friend of mine," said Grimes. "Never has been."

"But she is. And that's not all. She's a major shareholder in Star Scandals Publishing. So . . ."

"So what?"

"Do I have to spell it out for you? Are you as dim as you look? She put the pressure on. I shall be graciously permitted to write a story, a good story even but nothing like as good as it should have been. I shall have to keep both feet firmly on the soft pedal. She laid down the guidelines. For example: 'Due to an unfortunate misunderstanding Captain Grimes and I were arrested and sentenced to a term in a punishment and rehabilitation centre for vicious criminals. We were released, with apologies, as soon as our identities were established . . .'" She laughed bitterly. "Ha! Ha bloody ha!"

"But things are going to be cleaned up here," said Grimes. "Such establishments as the Colosseum are going to be closed down. And that's more important than your story."

"Is it? Is it? And how do you know, anyhow?"

"She promised."

"And you believed her?"

"Yes," said Grimes firmly.

Thirty-two

There was somebody at the outer airlock door wanting admittance.

It was a supercilious young El Doradan officer in purple uniform, a single gold band on each of his sleeves. He looked curiously at the women, his expression conveying the impression that he had seen much better. He looked with disapproval at Grimes' informal sarong, asked, "You *are* the captain?"

"I have that honour," said Grimes, blinking at the other's purple and gold resplendence. He looked hard at the young man s face, was both relieved and disappointed when he could find there was no resemblance to himself. His own son, of whom the Princess Marlene was the mother, would be about the age of this youngster.

"Commodore Kane told me to find out what consumable stores you will be requiring. Sir."

"Come through to the galley while I make a check . . ." The officer followed Grimes into the little compartment. "Mphm . . . Would you have any pork tissue culture in your vats? And we shall be needing fresh eggs. And bacon . . . And coffee. And table wines, of course . . ."

The young man took notes. His manner toward Grimes oscillated between almost contemptuous disapproval and respect. After all, he was an El Doradan and therefore to him Money was one of the many Odd Gods of the Galaxy—and *Little Sister,* in her construction and appointments, reeked of Money. If only her captain had the decency to dress the part . . .

A Customs officer, a surly, middle-aged woman obviously rudely awakened from her much-needed beauty sleep, came on board with papers for Grimes to sign. He put his name to them, wondering as he did so who had paid *Little Sister*'s port dues. He had not and had no intention of doing so unless compelled. He asked the woman to unseal the locker in which the small arms and the crystals from the laser cannon had been stowed. She complied with his request reluctantly, telling him sternly that he was not to replace the crystals until he was off New Venusberg. He examined the pistols. They were in order. It was ironical that he had weapons now that the need for them (he hoped) was gone.

The stores were brought aboard from *Southerly Buster.* The young officer handed Grimes a parcel, wrapped in parchment and tied with a golden ribbon, said, "With Her Excellency's compliments, sir."

Grimes opened it. There were two large tins of tobacco and, in its own case, a beautiful brier pipe.

"Thank Her Excellency for me, please," he said.

"Certainly, sir." The young man smiled unpleasantly. "And the commodore asked me to say that he hopes it chokes you."

"You can tell Commodore Kane, from me, to . . . Oh, skip it. He knows what I think about him."

Grimes went into the galley, supervised the two stewards in their stowage of the various items, put the pork into the cooler until such a time as a vat could be readied for its reception. He followed them back into the cabin. They wished him *bon voyage* and went out through the airlock. The officer saluted stiffly, then left *Little Sister.*

Fenella Pruin looked at Grimes, looked at Shirl and Darleen.

"Well?" she asked.

"Well what?" countered Grimes.

"Aren't you going to say your fond farewells?" she demanded.

"To whom?"

"Those two."

"They're coming with us," said Grimes.

"What?"

"Of course. What will their lives be worth if we leave them here? They're wanted for a few murders, you know. And we were accessory to some of those killings."

"Always the space lawyer, aren't you? I know something about the law myself, Grimes. I would remind you that I am chartering this ship."

"Your employers are."

"And *I* decide what passengers may or may not be carried."

"Her Excellency," said Grimes, "is your employer, as you discovered this evening. She charged me to look after Shirl and Darleen. She didn't as much as mention *you,* by the way."

He brushed past her, stamped forward to the control cab, sat down firmly in the pilot's seat. He turned to look aft into the main cabin. He could see Fenella, in profile. She was glaring at Shirl and Darleen. They were staring back at her defiantly. He pushed the button on the control panel that closed the airlock doors, sealed the ship. He said into the microphone of the NST transceiver, "*Little Sister* to Aerospace Control. Request permission to lift ship."

"Permission granted, *Little Sister.*"

The voice was familiar. Yes, that was McKillick's fat face in the screen of the transceiver.

There was no *bon voyage.* There were no pleasantries whatsoever. If looks could have killed Grimes would have died at his controls.

The inertial drive grumbled and *Little Sister* detached herself from the concrete, rose vertically. To one side of her was the towering *Southerly Buster,* to the other the great, metallic skep that was the Shaara ship. There was activity in this latter's control room; Grimes could see huge, faceted eyes peering at him through the viewports. He wondered briefly what their owners were thinking. But for all their wealth and influence they were only tourists on this planet. The real power lay with human capitalists, of whom the Baroness was one. Once he had almost—at least!—hated her but, now, he both respected and trusted her. He had no doubt that the worst abuses on New Venusberg would be put a stop to.

Just in time he turned to look out and down to *Southerly Buster.* There was a white-clad figure in the big ship's control room, one hand raised in a gesture of farewell. He lifted his own arm in reply, hoped that she would see. Then *Little Sister* was high above the spaceport. In the keel viewscreens were the toylike ships and buildings, the dwindling, floodlit form of the wantonly asprawl White Lady. A lot had happened since he first set eyes on that piece of pornographic landscape gardening.

"Goodbye, *Little Sister,"* said McKillick. "Don't come back."

"If 1 do," said Grimes, "it will be fifty years too soon."

He heard the sound of quarrelling female voices behind him.

This would not be, he predicted to himself, one of the more pleasant voyages of his career.

But it would be interesting.

Star Loot

One

For the first time in his life Grimes was rich.

But money, he was coming to realize, does not buy happiness. Furthermore it is, far too often, a very expensive commodity. It has to be paid for and the price can be high. The cost of his newly acquired wealth was *Little Sister,* the beautiful, golden, deep-space pinnace that had been given him by the Baroness Michelle d'Estang. He had hated parting with his tiny ship but financial circumstances had been such that there was almost no option. The fortunes of Far Traveler Couriers were at an extremely low ebb and Grimes, long notorious for his hearty appetite, wanted to go on eating.

At first the courier business had been moderately successful. There seemed to be no shortage of small parcels of special cargo to be carted, at high freight rates, hither and yon across the known galaxy. Then the commercial climate deteriorated and Grimes gained the impression that nobody at all wanted anything taken anywhere in a hurry and at a price. His last employment had been the carriage of a small shipment of memory-and-motivation units from Electra to Austral, the consignee being Yosarian Robotics. There was absolutely no suitable outward cargo for *Little Sister* available on Austral—and the First Galactic Bank was getting restive about Far Traveler Couriers' considerable overdraught.

Grimes went to see Mr. Yosarian. He knew that the fantastically wealthy roboteer often manufactured very special models for very special customers, some of whom must surely wish delivery in a hurry. He was admitted into an outer office on the very top floor of the towering Kapek Komplex, an assemblage of three glittering tetrahedra of steel and plastic with a fourth tetrahedron mounted on this spectacular foundation.

He sat waiting in a deep, comfortable chair, watching the blonde secretary or receptionist or whatever she was doing something at her desk, languidly prodding a keyboard with scarlet-nailed fingers, watching some sort of read-out on a screen that presented a featureless back to the visitor. She was not at all inclined to make conversation. Grimes wondered idly if she was one of Yosarian's special robots, decided that she probably wasn't. She was too plump, too soft looking and there had been nothing metallic in her voice when she condescended to speak to him. He tried to interest himself in the magazines on a low table by his seat but all of them were trade journals. An engineer would have found them fascinating—but Grimes was not an engineer. From his cadet days onward he had displayed little mechanical aptitude and, quite naturally, had entered the spaceman branch of the Survey Service.

He filled and lit his vile pipe, got up from his chair and strolled to one of the wide windows overlooking the city of Port Southern. The tall, elongated pyramid was a feature of local architecture. Between these towers and groupings of towers were green parks, every one of which seemed to have its own fountain, each a wavering plume of iridescent spray. In the distance was the spaceport, looking like a minor city itself. But those gleaming spires were the hulls of ships great and small, passenger liners and freighters.

Grimes could just see the golden spark that was the sunlight reflected from the shell plating of a ship by no means great—*Little Sister.* She had brought him here, to this world. Would she take him away from it? She wouldn't, he thought bitterly, unless there were some cargo to make it worth her while, some paid employment that would enable him to settle his outstanding bills.

The blonde's voice broke into his glum thoughts. "Mr. Yosarian will see you now, sir. Go straight through."

"Thank you," said Grimes.

He looked around for an ashtray, found one, knocked out his pipe into it.

"That," said the girl coldly, "happens to be a flower bowl."

"But there aren't any flowers in it," he said defensively.

"A ship is still a ship even when there's no cargo in her holds," she told him nastily.

That hurt. She must know how things were with him. Probably everybody in Port Southern, on the whole damned planet, knew. With his prominent ears flushing angrily he went through into the inner office.

Like a statue of some corpulent Oriental deity Yosarian sat behind his huge desk, the vast, shining expanse of which was bare save for two read-out screens. He did not rise as Grimes entered, just regarded him through black eyes that were like little lumps of coal representing the visual organs in the white face of a snowman. His too full red lips were curved in a complacent smile.

He said, "Be seated, Captain." His voice was just too pleasant to be classed as oleaginous, but only just.

Grimes started to turn. The nearest chair had been against the wall, near the door by which he had entered. But it was no longer there. Walking rapidly but silently on its four legs, it had positioned itself behind him. The edge of its padded seat nudged Grimes just below the backs of his knees.

He sat rather more heavily than had been his intention.

Yosarian laughed.

Grimes said, "Quite a trick."

"But little more, Captain. You should see—and use—some of the robot furniture that I design and manufacture. Such as the beds. Custom made." He leered. "And what do you think of *these?*"

A drawer in the desk must have opened—by itself, as both Yosarian's fat hands were sprawled on the polished surface. Something was coming out of it. A tiny hand found purchase on the edge of the desk top, then another. It—*she*—pulled herself up. She was only a mechanical doll but she could have been alive, a miniature golden girl, perfect in every detail from her long, yellow hair to the toes of her golden feet. She pirouetted and as she did so she sang wordlessly. High and thin was the music but with an insidious rhythm. She was joined by two more dolls, both female, one white-skinned and black-haired, the other whose body was a lustrous black and whose hair shone like silver. They carried instruments—the white girl a syrinx, the black girl a little drum. They sat cross-legged, piping and drumming, while the golden doll danced and sang.

"These come life-size, too," said Yosarian. "Special orders. Very special orders. . . ."

"Mphm," grunted Grimes thoughtfully and disapprovingly.

"And you wouldn't believe that they're made of metal, would you?" He raised his hands, clapped them sharply, then with his right index finger pointed at Grimes. The musicians stopped playing, the dancer halted in mid-step. Then all three of them ran gracefully to the edge of the desk, jumped down to the thick carpet. Before Grimes realized what was happening they were swarming up his legs, on to his lap. His ears flamed with embarrassment.

"Go on, touch them. They aren't programed to bite, Captain."

Gingerly, with the tip of a forefinger, Grimes stroked the back of the golden dancer. It could almost have been real skin under his touch—almost, but not quite.

Yosarian clapped again. The dolls jumped down from Grimes' lap, ran around to Yosarian's side of the desk, vanished.

"You must often, Mr. Yosarian, get special orders for these . . . toys," said Grimes.

"Toys? You offend me, Captain. But there are special orders. Only a short while ago the Grand Duke Oblimov on El Dorado wanted a pair of dancing boys, life-size. Do you know El Dorado, Captain? I have thought, now and again, of retiring there. I've more than enough money to be accepted as a

citizen, but I'd be expected to buy a title of some kind—and that I would regard as a sinful waste of hard-earned credits! As a matter of fact it was an El Doradan ship that carried the small shipment to the Grand Duke. She was here on a cruise and all the passengers were Lord this and Lady that. The master of her called himself Commodore, not Captain, and *he* was a Baron. The funny part of it all was that I used to know him slightly, years ago, when he was skipper of a scruffy little star tramp running out of Port Southern. . . ."

"Commodore Baron Kane," said Grimes sourly.

"You know him? It's a small universe, isn't it? But what can I do for you, Captain Grimes? I'm sure that you didn't come all the way from the spaceport just to talk to me and watch my pretty mini-robots perform."

"You have mentioned special orders, Mr. Yosarian. I'll be frank; I need employment for my ship and myself very badly. I was wondering if. . . ."

"I am sorry, Captain. The last special order was the one to El Dorado; the next one will be—" he shrugged and spread his hands—"who knows when? But perhaps you have not wasted your time after all. . . ."

"Then you do have something?"

"You have something, Captain Grimes. Something that I want, for which I am prepared to pay. I will tell you a secret. When I was very young I wanted to become a spaceman. As you know, your Antarctic Space Academy on Earth accepts entrants from all the Federated Planets—as long as they can pass the preliminary examinations. I almost passed—but *almost* isn't good enough. So I had to go into my father's business—robotics. He wasn't exactly poor—but I am rich. I have been thinking for some time of purchasing a little ship of my own, a spaceyacht, something so small that I am not required by law to carry a qualified master. I have the know-how—or my people have the know-how—to make a computer pilot capable of navigating and handling life-support systems and all the rest of it. I may have to import a special m-and-m unit from Electra, but that is no problem. They can send it with the next big shipment that I have on order."

"You mean . . ." began Grimes.

"I mean that I want your ship, your *Little Sister.* I know how things are with you. There is word of a forced sale, engineered by the First Galactic Bank. So I'm doing you a favor. I will pay a good price. And you will know that your ship will not be broken up just for the precious metal that went into her building. She will survive as a functioning vessel."

"As a rich man's toy," said Grimes.

Yosarian chuckled. "There are worse fates, much worse fates, for ships, just as there are for women. And a ship such as yours, constructed from an isotope of gold, will keep her looks. I shall cherish her."

"How much?" asked Grimes bluntly.

Yosarian told him.

With an effort Grimes kept his face expressionless. The sum named was far in excess of what he had expected. With such money in his bank account he would be able to retire, a young man, and live anywhere in the galaxy—with the exception of El Dorado—that he wished. But was it enough? Would it ever be enough?

"I think. Captain," said Yosarian gently, "that mine is a fair offer. Very fair."

"Yes," admitted Grimes.

"And yet you are still reluctant. If I wait until your many creditors force a sale I may be able to buy your ship at a mere fraction of this offer."

"Then why aren't you willing to wait, Mr. Yosarian?" asked Grimes.

The fat man looked at him shrewdly, then laughed. "All right, Captain. It's cards on the table. I happen to know that Austral Metals wants your ship. It is quite possible that they would outbid even me—and that, I freely admit, would mean more money in your pocket after all the legal technicalities have been sorted out. But do you know what they would do with her if they got her? They would regard her as no more than scrap metal—precious scrap, but scrap nonetheless. They would break her up, melt her down. Only the Electrans know the secret of producing the isotope of gold of which your *Little Sister* is constructed. Austral Metals use that very isotope in some of their projects—and have to pay very heavily for what they import from Electra. Your ship, her hull and her fittings, would be relatively cheap.

"If I have read you aright, Captain Grimes, you are a sentimentalist. Although your ship is only a machine you feel toward her almost as you would toward a woman—and could you bear to see the body of a woman you loved cut up and the parts deposited in an organ bank?" He shuddered theatrically. "If *I* get *Little Sister* I'll look after her, pamper her, even. If Austral Metals gets her they'll hack her and burn her into pieces."

And I can't afford to keep her, thought Grimes. Always in the past something had turned up to rescue him from utter insolvency—but this time nothing would. Or something had. If he accepted Yosarian's offer it would save *Little Sister* from the breakers as well as putting him back in the black.

"You really want her as a ship?" asked Grimes. "You don't intend to turn out a line of indestructible golden robots?"

"I give you my word, Captain."

Grimes believed him.

"All right," he said. "I'll take your price—on condition that you clear my overdraught and all my other debts."

Had he overplayed his hand? For long moments he feared that he had. Then Yosarian laughed.

"You drive a hard bargain, Captain Grimes. Once I would have haggled. Now

I will not. At least twice—the first time many years ago, the second time recently—I have tried to get the price down on something I really wanted. Each time I failed—and failed, in consequence, to attain my heart's desire."

Grimes wondered what it was that Yosarian had been wanting to buy, decided that it might not be politic to ask. He felt an odd twinge of sympathy.

"My lawyers," said the fat man, "will call on board your ship tomorrow morning to arrange the details. Please have a detailed statement of your liabilities prepared for them."

"I shall do that," said Grimes. "And . . . thank you."

He got up from his chair, turned to leave the office. A slight noise behind him made him stop, turn again to see what was making it. Another mechanical toy had emerged from one of the drawers of Yosarian's big desk. This one was a miniature spaceship, perfect in every detail, a replica of an Alpha Class liner only about fifteen centimeters in length. The roboticist gestured with his fat right hand and, with its inertial drive tinkling rather than clattering, it rose into the air and began to circle the opalescent light globe that hung from the ceiling. It could have been a real space vessel, viewed from a distance, in orbit about some planetoid.

So, thought Grimes, he was letting *Little Sister* go to somebody who would regard her as no more than an ingenious toy.

But in a harshly commercial universe that was all that she was anyhow.

Two

Much to Grimes' surprise the formalities of the sale were concluded late the following morning. (When Yosarian wanted something he wanted it *now.*) It was early afternoon when *Little Sister* was handed over to her new owner. Grimes was both hurt and relieved to discover that Yosarian did not expect him to stay around to show the new owner where everything lived and what everything did; in fact the roboticist made it quite plain that he wished to be left alone to gloat over his new possession.

"If that is all, Mr. Yosarian. . . ." said Grimes.

"Yes, that is all, Captain. I've made a study of ships, as you know. And, in any case, much of the equipment here is of my own design. The autochef, the waste processor. . . . There seems to be nothing here that is a departure from normal practice."

"Look after her," said Grimes.

"You need have no worries on that score, Captain. When something has cost me as much as this vessel I look after it."

He extended a fat hand for Grimes to shake. Grimes shook it, then went out through his—no, *the*—airlock for the last time. Yosarian's ground car was waiting to carry him to his hotel, his baggage already stowed in the rear compartment. There were two large suitcases and a mattress cover that had been pressed into service as a kitbag. (When one is in a ship for any length of time personal possessions tend to accumulate.) Before boarding the vehicle Grimes paused to pat the gleaming surface of the golden hull.

At least, he thought, *you aren't being broken up. . . .*

The chauffeur, a little, wizened monkey of a man in severe, steel-gray livery, watched him dourly. He said, "Old Yosie won't like it if you put greasy pawmarks all over that finish."

"She's had worse on her," said Grimes. "Like blood."

"You don't say, Captain?" The man looked at Grimes with a new respect. Then, "Where to, sir?"

"The Centaurian," said Grimes, taking his seat beside the driver.

The car sped smoothly and silently toward the spaceport gate. It did not reduce speed for challenge and inspection by the duty customs officer; the flag flying from the short mast on the bonnet, black with a golden Y set in a golden cogwheel, was pass enough.

"That *blood,* Captain. . . ." hinted the chauffeur.

"Not human blood," Grimes told him. "Shaara blood. Or ichor. A couple of drones were trying to burn their way in with hand lasers. So I went upstairs in a hurry, out of a dense atmosphere into near vacuum. They . . . burst."

"Messy," muttered the driver.

"Yes," agreed Grimes.

And where was Tamara, who had shared that adventure with him, he wondered. Probably back on Tiralbin, once again the desk-borne Postmistress General, no longer directly involved in getting the mail through come hell or high water. And where were Shirl and Darleen, also one-time passengers aboard *Little Sister?* And the obnoxious Fenella Pruin. . . . And Susie. . . . Susie had never set foot aboard the golden pinnace herself but she belonged to the *Little Sister* period of his life.

He may have lost his ship but he would keep the memories.

The driver was saying something.

"Mphm?" grunted Grimes.

"We're here, Captain. The Centaurian."

The hotel was the usual elongated pyramid. A porter, who could have been a Survey Service High Admiral making an honest living for a change, was lifting Grimes' baggage out of the back of the car, sneering visibly at the bulging mattress cover.

"Thank you," said Grimes to the chauffeur. He supposed that he should have tipped the man but, although he had a fortune in his bank account, he had almost nothing in his pockets. He disembarked, followed the porter into the lobby to the desk. The receptionists, he could not help noticing, were staring at the mattress cover and giggling. But the girl whom he approached was polite enough.

"Captain Grimes? Yes, we have your reservation. Room number 5063. And for how long will you be staying, sir?"

"Probably until *Alpha Sextans* comes in. She's the next direct ship for Earth."

"Have a happy stay with us, sir."

"Thank you," said Grimes.

He accompanied the porter in the lift up to the fiftieth floor, was ushered into a room from the wide windows of which he could enjoy a view of the city and the distant spaceport. *Little Sister* was there among the gray towers that were the big ships, no more than a tiny, aureate mote. He turned away from the window to the resplendently uniformed porter who was waiting expectantly.

He said, "I'm sorry. I'm out of cash until I get to the bank."

"That's all right, sir," said the man, conveying by the tone of his voice that it was not.

He left Grimes to his own devices.

Grimes explored his accommodation.

He treated himself to a cup of coffee from the tap so labeled over the bar. He lowered himself into one of the deep armchairs, filled and lit his pipe. Suddenly he was feeling very lonely in this comfortable but utterly characterless sitting room. He wondered how he would pass the days until he could board that Earthbound passenger liner. He would not, he told himself firmly, go near the spaceport before then. He had made his clean break with *Little Sister;* he would do his best to keep it that way.

The telephone buzzed.

He reached out, touched the acceptance button. The screen came alive, displayed the pretty face of one of the hotel's receptionists.

"Captain Grimes, a lady and a gentleman are here to see you."

"Who are they?" Grimes asked.

"A Ms. Granadu, sir. A Mr. Williams."

The names rang no bells in Grimes' memory and it must have shown in his expression.

"Spacepersons, sir," said the girl.

"Send them up," said Grimes.

He had just finished his coffee when the door chimes tinkled. He had not yet recorded his voice in the opener so had to get up from his chair to let the visitors in. Yes, he thought, the receptionist had been right. These were certainly spacers; the way in which they carried themselves made this obvious. And he, a spacefarer himself, could do better than merely generalize. One spaceman branch officer, he thought, fairly senior but never in actual command. One catering officer.

The spaceman was not very tall but he was big. He had a fleshy nose, a broad, rather thick-lipped mouth, very short hair the color of dirty straw, pale gray eyes. He was plainly dressed in a white shirt and dark gray kilt with matching long socks, black, blunt-toed, highly polished shoes. The woman was flamboyant. She was short, chunky, red-haired, black-eyed and beaky-nosed. Her mouth was a wide, scarlet slash. In contrast to her companion's sober attire she was colorfully, almost garishly clad. Her orange blouse was all ruffles, her full skirt was bright emerald. Below its hem were stiletto-heeled, pointed-toed knee boots, scarlet with gold trimmings. Jewels scintillated at the lobes of her ears and on her fingers. It looked, at first glance, as though she had a ring on every one of them.

"Williams," said the big man in a deep voice.

"Magda Granadu," said the woman in a sultry contralto.

"Grimes," said Grimes unnecessarily.

There was handshaking. There was the arranging of seats around the coffee table. Magda Granadu, without being asked, drew cups of coffee for Williams and herself, replenished Grimes' cup. Grimes had the uneasy feeling that he was being taken charge of.

"And what can I do for you, gentlepersons?" he asked.

"You can help us, Captain," said Williams. *"And* yourself."

"Indeed?" Grimes was intrigued but trying not to show it. These were not the sort of people who, hearing somehow of his sudden acquisition of wealth, would come to ask him for a large, never-to-be-repaid loan. "Indeed?"

"That ship in parking orbit—*Epsilon Scorpii.* You must have seen her when you came in."

"I did."

"She's up for sale. It hasn't been advertised yet but it soon will be."

Grimes laughed. "And so what? The Interstellar Transport Commission is always flogging its obsolescent tonnage."

"Too right, Captain. But why shouldn't you be the next owner of that hunk of still spaceworthy obsolescence?"

"Why should I?" countered Grimes. "I've just sold one ship. I'm in no hurry to buy another."

"You would not be happy away from ships," said the womgn, staring at him intently. "As well you know."

She's right, thought Grimes.

He said, "All right. Just suppose that I'm mad enough to buy this Epsilon Class rustbucket. What is *your* interest?"

"We want to get back into space," said Williams.

"And what makes you think that I'd help you?" Grimes demanded.

"The *I Ching* told us," said the woman.

Grimes regarded her curiously. With her features, her flamboyant clothing, her garish jewelry, she could well have passed for a Romany fortune teller, one of those who plied their trade in tea rooms and other restaurants. But such women usually practiced palmistry or worked with cards, either of the ordinary variety or the Tarot pack. To find one who consulted the *Book of Changes* was . . . weird. And what was a spacewoman doing as a soothsayer anyhow?

She went on, "We're old shipmates, Billy—Mr. Williams—and I. In the Dog Star Line. Billy was second mate, waiting for his promotion to mate. I was catering officer and purser. Billy was married to a girl on this planet who did not like having a husband who was always away on long voyages. So, just to please her, he resigned and found a shore job. A little while later I resigned too.

I had a bachelor uncle on this world whom I used to look up every time that the ship came here. He was an importer in a small way but big enough to have amassed a neat little fortune. He . . . died. When his will was read it was discovered that he'd left everything to me. So, having said my fond farewells to the Dog Star Line, I thought I'd start a restaurant. I'm still running it although I had some very bad patches; now the bank owns most of it. I've come to realize that I was far happier as a spacewoman.

"Billy's of the same way of thinking. He's very much at loose ends since his wife left him."

"You can say that again!" growled Williams.

"It was all for the best," Magda Granadu told him. "Well, Captain, Billy often comes around to my place just about closing time. We have a few drinks and talk about old times. You know. Anyhow, a few nights back we were crying into each other's beer and telling each other how we'd sell our souls to get back into deep space, then Billy suggested that I tell our fortunes, his and mine. No, don't laugh. Quite a few of my customers come to the Tzigane as much for my fortune-telling as the food. I've made some lucky guesses. Up to now I've always used the cards and it's only recently that I've gotten interested in the Oracle of Change. So I got the book out and threw three coins—I don't use yarrow sticks—and constructed a hexagram. *Ta Ch'u,* it was. It told us to place ourselves in the service of the king and that it would benefit us to cross the great water. The great water is, of course, deep space. And the king—*you.*"

"Me, a king?" demanded Grimes incredulously.

"You were a sort of god-king once, weren't you? The story got around. And, in any case, who more kingly than a ship-master who owns his own ship? The local media gave you a good coverage when you brought *Little Sister* in."

"I no longer own her," said Grimes.

"We are well aware of that, Captain, but you were still owner-master when I consulted the oracle. It puzzled us; surely you would not require a crew in such a small ship. Yet yours was the name that came to mind. Too, there was the business of the coins that I used. . . ."

"The coins?" asked Grimes bewilderedly.

"Yes. I used these." She fished in one of the capacious pockets at the front of her skirt, brought out three discs of some silvery alloy. Grimes stared at them. He had seen similar coins in his father's collection. They had been minted on Earth as long ago as the twentieth century, old style. One side bore the head of a woman, Queen Elizabeth, in profile. On the other was a stylized bird with a tail like an ancient lyre, and the number 10. An Australian ten-cent piece, very old yet in good condition.

"Where did you get these?" Grimes asked.

"They're Billy's."

"My father gave them to me years ago," said Williams. "They're out of his collection."

"My father has coins like them in his collection," said Grimes.

"And they're *Australian* coins," said Magda. "And you're Australian. There's a tie-in."

"Mphm," grunted Grimes dubiously.

"So the *I Ching* pointed to you," she insisted. "But we couldn't see how you could help us. And *then,* a day or so later, we heard that you'd sold *Little Sister* to Yosarian at some fantastic price. And we heard, too, that *Epsilon Scorpii* was coming up for sale. My restaurant is a popular place for business lunches and I often overhear conversations at table. Pinnett—he's Planetary Manager for the Interstellar Transport Commission—was entertaining a couple of ITC masters. They were talking about the *Epileptic Scorpion.* Pinnett was saying that he wished that there was somebody on Austral who'd buy her. He'd get a nice commission on the deal."

"Mphm," grunted Grimes again.

"You're the king the *I Ching* told us of, Captain. At the moment you're a king without a kingdom. But you could buy one."

Why not? Grimes asked himself. *Why not?* A sizeable tramp, carrying sizeable cargoes, might make a living. But he would be obliged by law to carry at least a minimal crew in such a vessel.

"What about crew?" he said. "All right, I seem to have two volunteers. One control room officer. I suppose that you hold a Master Astronaut's Certificate, Mr. Williams? One catering officer cum purser. But I shall require two more control room officers. And engineers, both Mannschenn Drive and inertial drive. And a Sparks. Where do I get them from? More important—where would I get cargoes from? *Little Sister* couldn't make one man a living. Could this Epsilon Class rustbucket make a living for a crew of at least a dozen?"

"To answer your first question, Captain," said Williams, "there are quite a few retired spacers on Austral, many of whom would love to make just one more voyage, and one more after that. . . . To answer the second one—a tramp can always make money if her owner isn't too fussy, if he's willing to carry cargoes that the major shipping lines wouldn't touch, to go to places where the big shipping companies wouldn't risk their precious ships. . . ."

"Take a gamble, Captain," cajoled Magda Granadu. "Ride your famous luck."

"My luck?"

She smiled and said, "You're famous for it, aren't you?"

"Let the *I Ching* decide for him," said Williams.

Magda handed him the three antique coins, then from her capacious pocket produced a book bound in black silk. Grimes recalled past encounters with fortune tellers. There had been that drunken Psionic Communications Officer aboard *Discovery* who had read the cards for him with uncanny accuracy, and the old Duchess of Leckhampton on El Dorado who had also read the cards, although she had favored the Tarot pack.

"Shake and throw," ordered the woman. "Shake and throw."

He rattled the coins in his cupped hands, let them fall to the carpet. Two heads and a tail. "Yang," he heard the woman whisper as she drew a line on a piece of scrap paper. "Eight." He picked up the coins, shook them, threw again. Two tails and a head. "Yin," he heard. "Seven." Then there was another yin, another seven. And another. Then three heads—yang, nine. And finally two heads and a tail—yang, eight.

"That will do," she said.

"Well?" he asked. "What's the verdict?"

"Wait," she told him.

She opened the book, studied the chart. She turned the pages.

"Upper trigram Sun," she murmured. "Lower trigram Chen. Increase. There will be advantage in every undertaking. It will be advantageous even to cross the great water. . . ." She looked up at Grimes. "Yes. You are destined to make a voyage."

"That is my intention in any case," he said. "But as a passenger."

"I haven't finished yet," she told him sharply. "It goes on like this. If the ruler strives to dispense benefits to his people and to increase the general level of prosperity he will be given loyalty in return. Thus he will be able to do great things."

Hogwash, Grimes almost said, would have said if he had not felt that in some weird way he was standing at the focus of cosmic lines of force. *Hogwash,* he thought again—but he knew that he was standing at the crossroads.

And he must make his own decision.

He put a hand down to the floor, picked up one coin.

"Heads I buy the ship," he said. "Tails I don't."

He sent the little disc spinning into the air.

It came up heads.

Three

The next morning, bright and early, Magda Granadu and Billy Williams joined Grimes as he was finishing his breakfast in the hotel's coffee shop. The previous evening they had stayed with Grimes to discuss with him the problem of manning; they, as merchant officers, knew far more about such matters than he did. In the Survey Service his crews had been found for him and, except for his tour of duty in the couriers, he had always been used to a superfluity of personnel. As master of *Epsilon Scorpii*—or whatever name he would give her once she was his—he would have no Bureau of Appointments to dip its ladle into the barrel to procure for him his entitlements. (There had been times when he had been obliged to cope with what was at the bottom of the barrel.)

Williams looked at his watch. "As soon as you've finished your coffee, Skipper, we'll ring Pinnett. He should be in his office by now."

So it was "Skipper" now, thought Grimes. If—if!—Williams became one of his officers such familiarity would not be tolerated. It might be all right for the Dog Star Line but not for any ship that Grimes might command.

He drained his cup, taking his time about it. He did not like being rushed. Then, with Williams and Magda on either side of him, he took the elevator up to the fiftieth floor. He found that the cleaning robots were in his suite, noisily dusting, polishing, changing towels and bed linen. One of the spider-like things was making a major production of quite unnecessary housekeeping in the telephone alcove, buffing each button on the selector panel with loving care.

Williams put his big hands about its bulbous body, lifted it down to the floor and gave it a gentle shove toward the center of the room. It staggered no farther than a meter on its spindly legs and then turned around, scampering back to its appointed task. Again Williams tried to shoo it away. Again it came back.

"Get rid of that bloody thing!" growled Grimes.

"Aye, aye, Skipper!"

Williams kicked, hard. The little robot flew through the air, crashed against the wall. Its plastic carapace shattered and there was a coruscation of violet sparks and the acridity of ozone. But it still wasn't dead. It began to crawl back toward the telephone, bleeding tendrils of blue smoke from its broken body.

Williams stamped on it, jumped on it with both feet.

Grimes said coldly, "That will do. I suppose you realize that I shall have to pay for this wanton damage."

"You can afford it, Skipper!" Williams told him cheerfully.

Grimes snarled wordlessly, then touched the D button for Directory. He said, speaking slowly and distinctly, "Interstellar Transport Commission." On some worlds he would have been put through automatically, but not here; he would have to do his own button pushing once he got the number. Luminous words and numerals appeared on the screen: INNIS & MCKELLAR, SOUTHPORT COMPREDORES—0220238.

Grimes snarled again, stabbed X for Cancel, prodded D and repeated his order in the kind of voice that he had used in the past for reprimanding junior officers.

The blanked-out screen returned to life. INTRACITY TRANSIT CORPORATION—02325252.

"You're getting closer, Skipper," said Williams encouragingly. "But the number is 023571164."

"Why the hell didn't you tell me before?"

"You never asked."

Grimes touched the buttons as Williams called out the numerals. After what seemed far too long a delay a sour-faced, gray-haired woman looked out at them from the screen, not liking what she was seeing from her end.

"Interstellar," she snapped. "At the service of the universe."

"Mr. Pinnett, please," said Grimes.

"Whom shall I say is calling?"

"Captain Grimes."

The picture of the woman faded, was replaced by a gaudy representation of a spiral nebula. This faded in its turn when the woman came back.

"Mr. Pinnett," she said, "is in conference."

"Have you any idea when he will be free?"

"I am afraid not."

"Perhaps," said Grimes, "somebody else might be able to help me."

"I can tell you now," she said, "that we have no vacancies for space crew. In any case we always endeavor to avoid recruiting on outworlds."

With an effort Grimes kept a hold on his temper. He said, "I understand that your ship, *Epsilon Scorpii,* is up for sale."

"From whom did you obtain that information?"

"It doesn't matter. I'm interested in buying her if the price is right."

She did not say it but she was obviously thinking, *Spacebums can't buy ships.* Grimes' name had meant nothing to her. She said, "Even an obsolescent Epsilon Class tramp is very expensive. I do not think that any offer that you can make will be of interest to Mr. Pinnett. May I suggest that you waste no more of my time?"

The screen went blank.

"Good-bye, prune-puss," muttered Williams.

"Would you know the number of Yosarian Robotics?" Grimes asked him.

"No, Skipper, but I'll get it for you."

Williams punched the D button, said the words. On his first attempt he got YOUR SAURIAN PET SHOP. Grimes said that he was interested in buying a scorpion, not a lizard. Williams kicked the console. Something tinkled inside it. He tried again and this time got YOSARIAN ROBOTICS and the number. He stabbed the keys with a thick forefinger. The face of the plump blonde appeared on the screen. She looked at Williams without recognition and said cheerfully, "Yosarian to save you labor. Can I assist you?"

Grimes moved so that he was within the scope of the scanner.

"Good morning, Captain Grimes," she said.

"Good morning. Can I talk to Mr. Yosarian, please?"

"He is down at the spaceport, aboard your ship. Sorry, Captain—*his* ship. Perhaps if you called him there. . . ."

Grimes did.

After some delay the roboticist appeared. He looked as though he had been working: there was a smudge of oil on his fat face. He snapped, "What is it? Can't you see that I'm busy?" Then, "Oh, it's you, Captain. If you want your *Little Sister* back it's just too bad."

"I do want a ship," said Grimes, "but not *Little Sister.* I've been trying to get through to Mr. Pinnett, the local boss cocky of the ITC, to find out how much he wants for *Epsilon Scorpii.* Some frosty-faced female gave me the brush-off."

Yosarian laughed. "Pinnett's tame dragon. She's quite notorious. But are you really thinking of buying that decrepit bitch? Still, there's an old saying, isn't there, about the dog returning to his vomit. . . ."

"And also there's 'Once bitten, twice shy,'" said Grimes wryly. "But I'm willing to take the risk of getting bitten again."

"It's your money, Captain. But what do you want *me* to do about it?"

"Perhaps if *you* rang Mr. Pinnett and told him that you know of a potential buyer for his superannuated scorpion. . . . You pull heavier Gs on this world than I do."

"All right, Captain. I'll do that. You're staying at the Centaurian, aren't you? I'll tell him to call you back there. Oh, by the way, I'm having trouble getting your autochef—*my* autochef—working properly. You must have abused it considerably when *you* were using it. . . ."

His face faded from the screen.

Grimes and his companions were halfway through their second cups of coffee when the telephone buzzed. He accepted the call. A craggy-faced black-haired man looked out at Grimes suspiciously. "Captain Grimes? I'm Pinnett, Planetary Manager for the Commission. Mr. Yosarian called me and said that you might be interested in buying *Epsilon Scorpii* and assured me that you possess the necessary funds. I cannot understand why you did not approach me directly."

"I did," said Grimes. "Or tried to."

"Oh." Pinnett looked slightly embarrassed. "But how did you know that the ship is up for sale? Head Office, on Earth, has yet to advertise."

"I just heard it somewhere," said Grimes. "And I also gained the impression that it would be to your advantage if you, personally, handled the sale."

"How did you . . . ? Oh, never mind, there's always gossip." His manner brightened. "Suppose we take lunch together to talk things over. 1300 hours. Do you know the Tzigane, on Moberley Square?"

Magda's place, thought Grimes. "I can find it," he said.

"Good. 1300 hours then."

His face vanished.

"I hope that you aren't allergic to sour cream and paprika, Skipper," said Williams.

The Tzigane was the sort of restaurant that Grimes categorized as being ethnic as all hell. Its interior tried to convey the impression of being that of a huge tent; its human waiters and waitresses were attired as romanticized Romanies. Magda was there, of course, generally supervising, but gave no indication of knowing Grimes, although she greeted Pinnett personally. The food was good, rich and highly spiced, and the portions generous. Pinnett did not allow business to interfere with the more serious business of eating and drinking and it was only when large mugs of coffee, laced with some aromatic spirit, were placed before them that he was willing to discuss the possible sale of *Epsilon Scorpii.*

"Well, Captain," he said around a slim, black cigar, "you'll be getting a good ship."

"If I buy her," said Grimes. Then, bluntly, "How much do you want for her?"

"Nine million," said Pinnett. "A bargain."

"She's not an Alpha Class liner, straight from the builder's yard," said Grimes.

"I know she's not. But she's a good, reliable workhorse, even if she's not built of gold. She's not a toy."

"At her age," said Grimes, "she'll need a lot of maintenance."

"Don't you believe it, Captain. We look after our ships in the Interstellar Transport Commission."

"I'd like to inspect her," said Grimes. "As soon as possible."

"I'm afraid that you'll have to wait a few days," Pinnett told him. "Arranging a shuttle at short notice isn't easy. Our own tender, *Austral Meteor,* is being withdrawn from service for annual survey."

"There are tugs," said Grimes. He strongly suspected that Pinnett did not wish to have the ship inspected until some attempt had been made to have her looking her best for a potential purchaser.

Pinnett smiled—regretfully or with relief? "There are space tugs here, of course. But they aren't here right now. Hadn't you heard that *Punch* and *Percheron* have both gone out to the Dog Star Line's *Samoyed?* A complete engine-room breakdown, all of a light-year from here."

"What about the met. satellite tenders?"

"You know what bureaucrats are. By the time that the Bureau of Meteorology made its mind up about hiring one to us our own tender would be back in service and the two tugs sitting on their backsides in the spaceport, waiting for the next job."

"I think I can arrange something," said Grimes. "I see a telephone there. . . ."

As he got up from the table he saw that Magda Granadu was bearing down upon it, holding a pack of cards in her hand. No doubt she was about to offer to tell Pinnett's fortune—a prognostication, thought Grimes, that would predispose the ITC manager not to hang out for too high a price for the ship.

"You again, Captain Grimes!" complained Yosarian. "Just when I'm in the middle of getting the innie properly tuned. Did you know that it was delivering only ninety percent of its true capacity?"

"But it's working, isn't it? Mr. Yosarian, I'd like to hire *Little Sister* for a day. There's no shuttle available to take me out to *Epsilon Scorpii,* and I want to make an inspection as soon as possible."

"I'm not hiring her out," said Yosarian. Then he grinned. "But I want to see how she handles. We'll regard this as a sort of trial run. I can be ready for space in thirty minutes. That suit you?"

Four

Yosarian, as promised, had *Little Sister* ready for space in half an hour. There were delays, however, before she could lift off. Only two spacesuits were on board; others had to be borrowed from the Interstellar Transport Commission's stores. Luckily the storekeeper was able to find one large enough to accommodate the roboticist's corpulence. Meanwhile Pinnett got in touch, by radio telephone, with *Epsilon Scorpii*'s ship-keeping officer to make arrangements for the reception of the boarding party.

Finally, with everybody and everything aboard *Little Sister,* the pinnace was buttoned up. Yosarian, not without diffidence, took the pilot's seat in the control cab. Grimes sat beside him. Billy Williams and Pinnett disposed themselves in the main cabin. Permission was received from Aerospace Control to lift off. Yosarian looked at Grimes, who nodded.

The fat man's pudgy hands hesitated briefly over the console, then turned on the inertial drive. *Little Sister* shuddered as the thrust built up. The drive hammered more loudly as the little ship lifted from the apron. Yosarian increased the rate of ascent and said to Grimes, "Can't you feel the difference? The innie needed tuning very badly."

It sounded the same to Grimes as it always had—but as long as Yosarian's tinkerings kept him happy that was all right by him. He did not interfere with the roboticist as he pushed *Little Sister* up and up, through wisps of high cirrus, into a sky which rapidly deepened to indigo, into the airless blackness where the unwinking stars were brightly shining. The pinnace's new owner seemed to know what he was doing and was not so arrogant as to attempt himself tasks that were better carried out by the computer. He fed the elements of *Epsilon Scorpii*'s synchronous orbit, which he had obtained from Pinnett, into *Little Sister*'s electronic brain and switched control from manual to automatic. Before long a spark appeared on the radar screen, a point of light, tiny at first, that expanded into a glowing blob that grew steadily.

He turned to Grimes and said, "Well, there she is, Captain." He paused. then asked, "How did I do?"

"Very nicely, Captain," said Grimes.

Yosarian blushed happily and said, "Would you mind taking over now, Captain Grimes? You're more used to this sort of thing than I am."

"But you have to get some practice. Just match orbital velocity; it shouldn't be difficult. Edge her in until we're half a kilometer off target, then put her back on automatic. . . . He transferred his attention to the NST transceiver. *"Little Sister* to *Epsilon Scorpii. . . ."*

"Eppy Scorpy to *Little Sister.* I read you."

A slightly effeminate voice, thought Grimes. Some very junior officer, he decided, not an old retired captain augmenting his pension with a shipkeeper's salary. (But he had been a shipkeeper himself although he had been neither old nor retired. He had needed the money.)

"Is your airlock ready?" he asked. "We will board as soon as we're suited up."

"Opening outer door now," came the reply.

Little Sister was on station, maintaining the correct distance off. In the cabin Pinnett was getting into his spacesuit; it was obviously not the first time that he had been required to wear such a garment. Yosarian, however, required assistance to get into the especially large outfit that had been borrowed for him. When the roboticist was at last suited up Grimes got into his own space armor. He realized, once he had sealed himself in the garment, that it was not the one that he had regarded as his own while he had been *Little Sister*'s owner and master. The last person to have used it must have been Tamara Haverstock; after all this time a trace of her perfume still persisted. He allowed his memories briefly to take over his mind. Who else had worn this suit? Only Tamara, he decided—and she, now, was no more than a recollection of somebody whom he would never see again, any more than he would ever see again those other lost ladies—Jane Pentecost, Fenella Pruin, Shirl, Darleen, Susie, Una Freeman. . . . *1 must be wanting a woman,* he thought, *if it takes no more than a fugitive whiff of scent to start me wandering down memory lane. . . .*

"Are you all right, Skipper?" asked Williams sharply, his voice distorted but still recognizable as it came from the helmet speaker. The big man had seated himself in the chair vacated by Yosarian, was speaking into the NST transceiver microphone.

"Of course, Mr. Williams," said Grimes. He added, lamely, "I was just thinking." He continued, speaking briskly, "All right. You're in charge until we get back. We're locking out now."

The small airlock could accommodate two persons—but not when one of the pair was as bulky as Yosarian. Grimes and Pinnett, therefore, went out first after Grimes had told the roboticist that, according to protocol, he, as captain, should be last out of the ship. Before long the three men were hanging outside *Little*

Sister's golden hull, staring at the great hulk of *Epsilon Scorpii* gleaming against the backdrop of stars. Sunlight was reflected from most of her shell but the open airlock door was in shadow. That was all to the good; it made it much easier to see the bright green light that illuminated the chamber.

"Grimes to Pinnett. Go!" ordered Grimes.

Pinnett went. He handled himself not unskillfully, launching himself into the void with an economically short blast from his suit reaction unit, making only one trajectory adjustment before he braked himself just outside the open air-lock door. Grimes watched him, his figure in black silhouette against the green illumination, as he pulled himself into the chamber.

"You next, Mr. Yosarian," said Grimes.

"I . . . I don't think. . . ." Then, in a burst of embarrassed frankness, "This is the first time that I've done this sort of thing. . . ."

"So we take no risks," said Grimes.

He positioned himself behind the fat man, put both gloved hands on the other's armored shoulders, took a firm grip.

He said, "Whatever you do, don't touch your reaction-unit controls. I don't want a hole blasted in my belly. Just relax. . . ."

Pushing Yosarian before him, he jetted toward *Epsilon Scorpii.* The short flight was a clumsy one. He was grateful that there were not many witnesses. He managed to turn around when halfway to his objective, fired a short braking blast. He missed the open doorway, fetched up with a clang on the ship's side a meter from the rim. Fortunately Pinnett was spaceman enough—like most of the Interstellar Transport Commission's managers he had done his stint as a ship's purser—to extend a helping hand, pulling Grimes and his bulky, ungainly tow into the chamber.

There was ample room for all of them in the airlock and they were able to get themselves sorted out, all standing the same way up, their magnetically soled boots holding them to the deck. The outer door closed and the illumination changed from green to red, indicating that they were in a hard vacuum environ-ment. It acquired a yellowish tinge, became amber, showing that atmosphere was being fed into the chamber. It became green once more.

The inner door opened.

The shipkeeper was waiting to receive them.

She spoke into the little transceiver that she was wearing on her left wrist.

"Come in," she said sourly. "This is Liberty Hall. You can spit on the mat and call the cat a bastard. I hope that one of you is an engineer. The autochef is play-ing up again. I've lost count of the number of times that I've reported it. And isn't it time that I got some new spools for the playmaster? And. . . ."

Grimes stared at her. She was wearing a well-filled T-shirt and very short shorts. The sandals on her rather large feet were secured by string, the original straps being no more than broken ends. Her free-floating hair made a dingy green halo about her head. A pair of vividly green eyes glared at the boarders. Even her skin—and there was plenty of it on view—had a greenish tinge. She would have been a good-looking enough wench, thought Grimes, had she been cleaner (to judge from the state of her shirt and even her face she was a messy feeder), had her expression been less surly. But even after a bath and looking happy she would have been too strong featured to suit his taste in women.

A Donegalan, he decided. (He had visited New Donegal once, during his career in the Survey Service.) Human ancestry, but with a slight genetic drift from the norm. A woman-dominated society. No spaceships of Donegalan registry but, each year, a few promising girls sent to the Antarctic Academy on Earth—where the Commandant and his officers made sure that none of them did well enough to graduate into the Survey Service. Most of them, however, did qualify for entry into the Interstellar Transport Commission and other shipping lines. There was more than male chauvinism involved in the Academy's attitude toward the Donegalans. They were notorious for always carrying chips on their shoulders, and such an attitude on the part of junior officers could seriously impair the efficient running of a warship.

Faceplates were opened.

"Ms. Connellan," said Pinnett, "this is Captain Grimes." Grimes nodded. "And Mr. Yosarian. . . ." The roboticist managed, even in his bulky spacesuit, a quite courtly bow. Pinnett went on, "Ms. Connellan is one of our second officers. . . ."

"Demoted to watchperson," she snarled. "I've a Master's ticket—and this is the best job that the bloody Commission can find for me!"

"Shipkeeping officer," Pinnett corrected her. "With very generous hard-lying money over and above your salary."

"Which I earn, in this rustbucket where damn all works the way that it should!"

"What exactly is not working, Ms. Connellan?" asked Grimes pleasantly.

"The autochef, for a start. And the NST transceiver only works if you know just where to give it a clout. You were lucky that it wasn't on the blink when you came up from Port Southern; the last time that you condescended to call on me, Mr. Pinnett, you had to hammer on the control-room viewports to attract my attention. Then, a couple of days ago, I tried to actuate the Carlotti transceiver, just so that I could find out what ships are around. It just spat sparks at me and died. Oh, and just to pass the time I've been browsing through the logs. It seems that Captain Taine had one helluva job establishing this wreck in orbit. I know that he's not the best ship handler in the universe but the fact that the innies were playing up made him even worse than usual. And. . . ."

"That will do, Ms. Connellan," snarled Pinnett. "That will do!"

"Like hell it will. What about the nutrient pumps for the tissue culture vats? I've had to dump the lamb and the beef and the pork. Would *you* like chicken for every meal?"

"That will do!"

"It will *not* do, Mr. Pinnett. I demand that you find me a deep space appointment."

"I am not the Commission's astronautical superintendent, Ms. Connellan."

"Too right you're not. But you're a planetary manager, aren't you? Somebody in the top office must listen to you sometimes."

"Captain Grimes," said Pinnett, trying hard to ignore the irate shipkeeper, "may I suggest that we start the tour of inspection?"

"It's what we came here for," said Grimes. "Ms. Connellan, will you lead the way? We'll start in the control room and work aft."

"Are you really thinking of buying this . . . *thing?"* asked the girl interestedly. "You must have more money than sense."

Perhaps I have, thought Grimes. *Perhaps it's always been that way, even when I've been flat broke.*

Grimes was glad that Yosarian had come along. Even though the roboticist was not an astronautical engineer he knew machines; too, there was his keen interest in spaceships.

"The people who were here," he complained, "just did not care. All over there is lack of proper attention. . . ."

"I should have been given the time to get the shore gang up here to do some cleaning up," said Pinnett stiffly.

Yosarian ignored him as he continued his inspection of one of the offending pumps on the farm deck.

"Look at this!" he spluttered. "Every lubrication point clogged! Small wonder that it seized up. . . ." He stared reproachfully at the woman. "Surely even you should have seen what was the trouble."

"I'm employed as a shipkeeping officer," she snapped, "not as a mechanic!"

Yosarian shook his head sadly. "But your own comfort. . . . Your own safety, even. . . ."

"I've told you that I'm not an engineer."

"That is glaringly obvious," he said.

"Mr. Pinnett," she demanded, "did you bring this man here to insult me?"

"But this is Mr. Yosarian," said Pinnett.

"And so what? Am I supposed to fire a twenty-one-gun salute? But if there were any guns in this ship they wouldn't be working, any more than the pumps are."

"So the pumps aren't working," snarled Pinnett. "You are at least partly responsible for that."

"The butterfly-brained Terry apes who were the alleged engineers of this scow on her last voyage were responsible, and you know it!"

"Let's get on with the inspection," said Grimes tiredly.

Throughout the ship it was the same story, a glaring example of the "she'll be all right" principle carried to extremes. There were many things, such as those nutrient pumps, that Ms. Connellan could have put right. And, with all the time on her hands, she might have done something about the state of the inertial drive room. Hasty repairs of some kind seemed to have been carried out at the very conclusion of the voyage while the ship was being established in parking orbit—and then the tools employed had not been returned to their clips but had been carelessly dropped, were now, in these free fall conditions, drifting around dangerously in the air eddies set up by the body movements of the inspection party.

Grimes began to round up the wandering spanners and such, returning them to their proper places on the shadow board. Yosarian assisted. Although the roboticist was not used to working in the absence of gravity, he could not bear to see machinery neglected.

Neither Ms. Connellan nor Pinnett made any attempt to lend a hand.

Farther aft it was discovered that one of the propellant tanks for the auxiliary reaction drive had been leaking; that level would have been a suitable habitat for goldfish but not for human beings.

"If I am going to buy this ship," said Grimes, "I shall require new certificates of spaceworthiness."

"But the last annual survey," the manager told him, "was only five standard months ago."

"Then a lot happened in that five months," said Grimes. "And one helluva lot, in the way of maintenance, didn't happen!"

Back at his hotel in Port Southern Grimes conferred with Billy Williams and Magda Granadu.

"Pinnett will come down in price," he said. "But it was just as well that we had Yosarian along as a sort of independent witness. He can bring some pressure to bear."

"I'm sorry that I didn't get to meet that shipkeeping officer," said Williams. "To judge from what I heard of her on the NST radio it's a bloody good thing that she doesn't come with the ship!"

"I've shipped with Donegalans," said Magda. "They're bitter, resentful. On New Donegal they're on top. They're just not used to accepting men as equals, let alone superiors. Too, this Connellan woman knows that the shipkeeping job was just the Commission's way of sweeping her under the carpet."

"Well," Grimes said, "they'll just have to find her another deep-space posting when they sell the ship from around her." He grinned. "And may the Odd Gods of the Galaxy help the unfortunate master who gets saddled with her!"

Five

The details of the sale were ironed out with surprising ease and for a sum quite a bit lower than the original asking price. Yosarian pulled considerable Gs on his home world and even the mighty Interstellar Transport Commission listened when he talked. One of his engineers, an ex-spacer, went out to *Epsilon Scorpii* to make sure that the ship's inertial drive was in proper working order, then acted as engine-room chief while Grimes, assisted by Bill Williams, brought the vessel down to the spaceport. (During this operation Ms. Connellan made it quite clear that she was employed as a shipkeeping officer only and was not required to lend a hand with any maneuvers.)

So Grimes had his "new" ship sitting on the apron, handy to the spaceport workshops whose facilities he was using. The obnoxious Ms. Connellan was no longer on board; she had left, with her baggage, as soon as the ramp was down. It was now up to Pinnett and the Commission to find for her suitable employment.

The next four weeks were busy ones. Grimes and Williams went through the ship from stem to stern with the Lloyd's and Interstellar Federal surveyors, pointing out the things that needed doing while Pinnett, who had reluctantly agreed that the Commission would bear the cost of making the vessel spaceworthy, tried to argue that many of the proposed repairs were only of a cosmetic nature. The trouble was that the Federation surveyor tended to side with him, saying more than once to Grimes, "You aren't in the Survey Service now, Captain. This isn't a warship, you know."

Grimes got his way (he usually did) but it was costing him much more than he had anticipated. For example, he had been obliged to foot the bill for making the auxiliary reaction drive fully operational, such an additional means of propulsion being no longer mandatory for merchant vessels. The charge for the work involved was not a small one.

He had been temporarily rich but he was no longer so; what money had been left after the purchase of *Epsilon Scorpii* was fast being whittled away. If his luck ran out again he would be back where he started—only instead of having a golden white elephant on his hands it would be one constructed of more conventional and far less valuable materials.

Nonetheless he felt an upsurge of pride when she was renamed. To have the new nomenclature fabricated in golden letters was a needless extravagance but one that pleased him. It was a tribute to Big Sister, the almost too human computer-pilot of *The Far Traveler.* It was also a sort of memento of *Little Sister.* As for the second half of the name, it was just there because it went naturally with the first, Grimes told himself—although the lady so commemorated was part of what he was already thinking of as the *Little Sister* period of his life and about the only one from whom he had not broken off in acrimonious circumstances.

SISTER SUE. . . .

He stood on the apron looking up at his ship, at the golden name on the gray hull gleaming brightly in the afternoon sunlight. Williams joined him there.

"Very pretty, Skipper," he commented. Then, "Who was Sue?"

"Just a girl," said Grimes.

"She must have been somebody special to get a ship named after her. . . ." Williams shuffled his big feet, then went on, "I'm afraid I've bad news for you, Skipper."

"What now?" demanded Grimes. "What now?"

This was too much, he thought. He now had, not without a struggle, a spaceworthy ship, a sturdy workhorse, and all that he needed was a little bit of luck to make a go of things.

What had happened to his famous luck?

"It's the manning, Skipper," Williams said. "We're all right for engineers. We've old Crumley lined up; he's a bit senile but he's qualified, a double-headed Chief's ticket, inertial drive and reaction drive. For the Mannschenn Drive there's Professor Malleson. He passed for Mannschenn Chief before he came ashore to go teaching. As I told you before, he's taking his sabbatical leave from the university. Also from the university there'll be a couple of bright young Ph.D.s to act as his juniors. And we've a Sparks, another old-timer, retired years ago but wanting to get back into space. . . ."

"So what's the trouble?"

"In the control room, Skipper. According to the Manning Scale we should have three control-room watchkeeping officers—although we can lift with only two as long as we get a permit. Well, you've got me, as mate. You should have got old Captain Binns—he used to be in the Dog Star Line—as second mate. But he got mashed in a ground-car accident last night. At his age it'll be at least six months before he's grown a new left arm and right leg."

"There are times," said Grimes, "when I strongly suspect that the Odd Gods of the Galaxy don't like me. So Binns is out. Is there nobody on this benighted planet to fill the gap?"

"Well, er, yes. There is."

"So what's all this talk of bad news?"

"The Green Hornet," said Williams, "has let it be known that she's had the Interstellar Transport Commission in a big way."

"The Green Hornet?"

"Kate Connellan. 'Green Hornet' is her company nickname. Anyhow, she had a knock-down-and-drag-'em-out row with Pinnett. She resigned—about a microsecond before Pinnett could fire her. And, as far as we're concerned, she's qualified and she's available."

"Oh," said Grimes. "Oh."

Could he possibly afford to wait until somebody more suitable turned up? He could not, he decided. He had been lucky enough to have a consignment of government cargo offered to him, but if he could not lift it by the specified date somebody else would be found to do the job.

"She has a master's ticket," said Williams.

"But she's still an eleven-trip officer," said Grimes.

"Eleven trips, Skipper? How do you make that out?"

"One out and one home," Grimes told him.

Six

Articles were opened.

Grimes, having done all the autographing required of him in his capacity as captain, stood behind the counter in the shipping office, watching his officers affixing their signatures to the agreement while the shipping master checked their qualifications and last discharges, if any.

Billy Williams was the first to sign. He said cheerfully, "I'll get back on board, Skipper. They should be just about ready to start the loading."

Magda Granadu signed and followed the mate out of the office. Mr. Crumley, a frail, white-bearded, bald-headed old man, produced one of the old-fashioned certificates bound in plastic rather than in flexisteel and a discharge book held together with adhesive tape.

"You'll find that times have changed since you were Chief of the *Far Centaurus,* Mr. Crumley," said the shipping master cheerfully.

"A ship's a ship and engines are engines, aren't they?" grumbled the ancient spaceman.

His three juniors signed. They possessed neither certificates nor discharge books, only diplomas from the Port Southern College of Technology. One of them, Denning, had been employed by Yosarian Robotics, the other two, Singh and Paulus, by the Intracity Transit Corporation. They were squat, swarthy, youngish men who could almost have been triplets—competent mechanics, thought Grimes snobbishly, rather than officers.

Malleson, looking every inch the gray-haired, untidy, stooping, absent-minded professor, signed. His two juniors, tall young men, briskly competent, with fashionably shaven heads and heavily black-rimmed spectacles, signed.

Old Mr. Stewart, the electronic communications officer, signed. His certificate and discharge book were as antique as Mr. Crumley's. *Shave his head,* thought Grimes, *and stick the hair on his chin and he'd be old Crumley's double. . . .*

"You don't have a doctor, Captain?" asked the shipping master.

"I've got three," said Grimes. "Ph.D.s."

"Ha ha. But you have tried to find one, haven't you? A medical doctor, I mean. So I'll issue you a permit to sanction your lifting off undermanned. You realize, of course, that you'll have to pay your crew an extra ten credits each day in lieu of medical services. . . . Cheer up, Captain. You'll be getting it too."

"But *I'll* be paying it," growled Grimes. "Out of one pocket and into the other."

"Ha ha! Of course. It's not very often that I get masters who are also owners in here. In fact the only one before you was a Captain Kane. I don't suppose you've ever run across him." Grimes said nothing and the shipping master, who was checking the entries in the Articles of Agreement, did not see his expression. "H'm. We were talking of permits, weren't we? I take it that you still haven't been able to find a third mate. . . . And where *is* your second mate, by the way?"

"She was told what time she was to be here," said Grimes.

"She?" echoed the shipping master, looking at the preliminary crew list. "Oh. The Green Hornet. But I thought that she was with the Commission."

"She *was."*

"And now you've got her. Do me a favor, will you, Captain. Don't bring her back to Port Southern. I'll never forget the fuss she kicked up when she was paid off from *Delta Crucis,* threatening to sue the Commission, the Department of Interstellar Shipping and the Odd Gods of the Galaxy alone know who else! To begin with she was screaming wrongful dismissal—but, of course, she wasn't being dismissed but transferred. To *Epsilon Scorpii.* Then there was a mistake in her pay sheet—twenty cents, but you'd have thought it was twenty thousand credits. And. . . ."

Grimes looked at his watch.

"I certainly wish that I didn't have to have her," he said. "But I have to. Where *is* the bitch?"

"Do you know where she's staying?"

"Some place called The Rusty Rocket."

"Cheap," sneered the shipping master. "And nasty. You can use my phone, Captain, to check up on her. They might know where she's got to."

He showed Grimes through to his private office, seated him at the desk. He told Grimes the number to punch. The screen came alive and a sour-faced blonde looked out at them.

"The Rusty Rocket?" asked Grimes.

"This certainly ain't The Polished Projectile. Waddya want?"

"Is a Ms. Connellan staying with you?"

"She was. She won't be again. Ever."

"Where is she now?"

"In the right place for her. Jail. I hope they throw away the key."

After a little prodding Grimes got the story. The previous night there had been a nasty brawl in the barroom of The Rusty Rocket, the focus of which had been Kate Connellan. There had been damage, injuries. The police had been called. Arrests had been made.

Grimes thanked the woman and disconnected.

He said to the shipping master, "Now I suppose I'll have to pay her fine or bail or whatever." He sighed. "More expense."

"I'm afraid that's out of the question, Captain. In the old days the police authorities were only too pleased to get rid of drunken spacers as soon as possible—but not anymore. Not since the new Commissioner was appointed. Now any spacer who makes a nuisance of himself—or herself—is given a stiff sentence and has to serve it. Every minute of it."

Grimes sighed again. He owed no loyalty to the troublesome Ms. Connellan, he told himself. Had her name been on his Articles she would have been one of his people—but she had not yet signed.

He said hopefully, "I see no reason why I shouldn't lift off with only the mate and myself as control-room watchkeepers. After all, in *Little Sister* there was only me. I was the cook and the captain bold. . . ."

"Regulations," the shipping master told him. "A vessel of *Little Sister*'s tonnage is classified as a spaceyacht, even though she may be gainfully employed. Your *Epsilon Scorpii*—sorry, *Sister Sue*—is a ship. The manning scale calls for a master and three mates. I can issue a permit to allow you to lift with only two mates. But you may not, repeat not, lift with only one qualified control-room officer in addition to yourself."

"And I must lift on time," muttered Grimes. "If I don't the penalty clauses in the charter party will beggar me." He filled and lit his pipe, puffed furiously. "Do you think that if I made a personal appeal to this Police Commissioner of yours, putting all my cards on the table, it might help?"

"It might," said the shipping master. "It might—but the Commissioner has a down on spacers. Your guild has already lodged complaints—which have been ignored. Still, you can try. As long as you watch your language you should be able to stay out of jail."

Grimes borrowed the telephone again and ordered a cab.

In a short time he was on his way from the spaceport to the city.

Like most of the other buildings in Port Southern, that housing Police Headquarters was a pyramid. But it was not a tall, graceful one, all gleaming metal and glittering glass, but squat and ugly. The material used for its construction looked like dark gray stone although it was probably some plastic.

Grimes walked in through the frowning main entrance, approached a desk behind which a heavily built man, with silver sergeant's stripes on the sleeves of his severe black uniform, was seated.

"Your business, citizen?" asked the police officer.

"I wish to see the Commissioner.

"Your name, citizen?"

"Grimes," said Grimes. "Captain Grimes."

"A spacer, eh? The Commissioner doesn't like spacers." The sergeant laughed briefly. "In fact. . . ."

A bell chimed softly from the telephone set on the desk. A female voice—that of a secretary, Grimes supposed, although it was oddly familiar—said, "Send Captain Grimes up, sergeant."

The policeman raised his heavy eyebrows in surprise. He growled, "So the Commissioner will see you. What have you got that all the other spacers haven't? The elevators are over there, citizen. The Commissioner's office is on the top floor." He laughed again. "The apex of our pyramid."

Grimes thanked the man, walked to the bank of elevators. As he approached the indicator, lights showed that a cage was descending. The door opened as he got to it. There was nobody inside. The door closed again as soon as he had entered and the lift started to rise before he could touch the button of his choice.

Service, he thought. *With a smile?*

The car stopped gently. The door opened. Grimes stepped out. The walls of the apex of the police pyramid were all glass, overhead automatically polarized to reduce the glare of the sun. There were elaborate arrays of screens, some of which displayed ever-changing pictures while in others numerals flickered into and out of being. There was a big desk behind which was sitting a woman, a large woman in black and silver uniform with what looked like commodore's braid on her shoulderboards.

She looked at Grimes. Grimes looked at her. Beneath her glossy brown hair, short cut, the face was too strong for prettiness, the cheekbones pronounced, the pale-lipped mouth wide over rather too much jaw.

"Una . . ." he said softly. "Long time no see."

"Commissioner Freeman," she corrected him harshly. "I knew, of course, that you were on this planet but I was able, quite successfully, to fight down the urge to renew our old . . . acquaintanceship. But now that you have come to see me I let my curiosity get the better of me.

"And what do you want? Make it quick. I'm a busy woman."

"I didn't know that you were the Police Commissioner here, Una. When did you leave the Corps of Sky Marshals? How. . . ."

"This isn't a social call, Grimes. *What do you want?"*

"Your men, Una. . . ." She glared at him. He started again. "Your men, Commissioner Freeman, arrested one of my officers. I'd like her back. I'm willing to pay her fine." He added hastily, "Within reason, of course."

"One of *your* officers, Grimes? The only spacer at present in our cells is a known troublemaker, a Kate Connellan, whose most recent employment was with the Interstellar Transport Commission. She faces charges of assaulting a police officer, occasioning bodily harm. There are three such charges. Also to be considered, and compensated for, is the damage done to the uniforms of those officers. There are five charges of assaulting civilians. There are charges of violent and abusive behavior. There are charges of damage to property—mainly furniture and fittings of The Rusty Rocket. Need I go on?"

"It seems enough to be going on with," admitted Grimes glumly.

"But how is it that you can claim that this person is one of your officers, Captain Grimes?"

"I opened Articles today, Commissioner Freeman. Ms. Connellan was supposed to sign on as second mate. I'll be frank. She wouldn't have been my choice but she was the only qualified officer available."

"Still the male chauvinist pig, Grimes, aren't you?"

"Her sex has nothing to do with my reluctance to employ her. And, in any case, I must have her if I'm to lift off on time."

"You should have kept that *Little Sister* of yours. To judge from my experiences while under your command—ha, ha!—a glorified lifeboat is just about the limit of your capabilities. But you had to have a *big* ship, didn't you? *Epsilon Scorpii*—or *Sister Sue,* as you've renamed her. Who was Sue, by the way?"

"Just a girl," said Grimes.

"Spoken like a true male chauvinist pig. I hope that she has happier memories of you than I have. Even now I can't force myself to eat baked beans. And as for bicycles. . . ."

"You can't blame me for either," said Grimes hotly.

"Can't I? Well, after that most peculiar mess that you got me into I was allergic to space as well as to beans and bicycles. I resigned from the Corps—although I'm still supposed to be on their reserve list. And I've found that useful. Sky Marshals pull heavy Gs with most of the planetary police forces."

"So when you came here you started at the top," said Grimes as nastily as he dared.

"Not at the top, although my having been a Sky Marshal entitled me to inspector's rank. After that my promotion was strictly on merit."

"Local girl makes good," said Grimes.

"Do you want to be arrested too? I can soon think of a few charges. Insulting behavior to a police officer for a start. . . ."

"I can see that I'm wasting my time," said Grimes. He turned to walk back to the transparent tube in the center of the room that housed the elevator.

"Hold it, Grimes!"

Grimes halted in mid-stride, turned to face Una Freeman.

"Yes, Commissioner?"

"I am disposed to be lenient. Not to *you,* Captain, but to Ms. Connellan. I have heard accounts of what actually happened at The Rusty Rocket. She was provoked. You aren't the only male chauvinist pig around, you know. It is unfortunate that she attacked my officers after dealing with those . . . *men* who had been taunting her. Nonetheless she is not a very nice person. I shall be happy if she is removed from this planet.

"Pay her fines to the desk sergeant on your way out and she will be released to your custody. Bear in mind that you will be responsible for her good conduct for the remainder of her stay on this world."

"Thank you," said Grimes.

She laughed harshly and asked, "Will you still thank me after you've been cooped up in a ship with The Green Hornet for a few weeks? Am I doing you a good turn, Grimes? Think that if you want. But I sincerely hope that by the time you get to Earth you'll have changed your tiny mind!"

Grimes stood there silently, looking at her. He remembered how things had been between them before everything had turned sour. He remembered the long weeks in the accommodation dome of that unmanned beacon station, the continual bickerings, the monotonous diet of baked beans, with which delicacy the emergency food stores had been fantastically well stocked.

It was a pity that things had gone so badly wrong. He, for a while at least, had loved her after his fashion. She had reciprocated. But when the beacon tender, making its leisurely rounds, had finally arrived to pick them up they were no longer on speaking terms.

Even so. . . .

"Thank you," he said again.

"For nothing," she growled and then, ignoring him, began to study the papers on her desk.

She ignored his good-bye as he left her.

Seven

The Desk Sergeant must have been given his orders while Grimes was on the way down from the Commissioner's office. There were forms ready for signing. There was a receipt book.

"What have *you* got that other spacers haven't, citizen?" he asked. "But as long as you've got money that's all that really matters. Ha, ha. Now, the fines. . . . Grievous bodily harm to the persons of three police officers at five hundred credits a time. . . . That's fifteen hundred. Replacement of one complete uniform. . . . One hundred and seven credits and fifteen cents. . . . Repairs and dry cleaning to two other uniforms. . . . Twenty-three credits fifty. . . . Medical services to the assaulted officers. . . . One hundred and fifty credits. . . . Riotous behavior, breach of the peace etc. . . . Two hundred and fifty credits. One night's board and lodging in our palatial cells. . . . One hundred and twenty-five credits. Ten percent service charge. . . Two hundred and fifteen credits and fifty-seven cents. Making a total of two thousand, three hundred and seventy-one credits and twenty-two cents."

"Is there no discount for cash?" asked Grimes sarcastically.

The policeman ignored this.

"A check will be acceptable," he said, "or any of the major credit cards."

Grimes pulled out his checkbook and looked at the stubs. He was one of those people who prefer to keep their own accounts rather than put himself at the mercy of the computers. He was still quite a way from being flat broke. He made out a check for the required amount, signed it and handed it over, was given a receipt in exchange.

"And now, citizen, if you'll sign these. . . ."

These were official forms, and by affixing his autograph to them he made himself entirely responsible for Ms. Connellan during the remainder of her stay on Austral. He would be liable for any debts that she had incurred. He would be liable, too, for any further fines, for the costs of any civil actions brought against her and so on and so on and so on.

Una Freeman was striking a very hard bargain. It was a seller's market.

He signed.

When he straightened up from the desk he turned to see that the Green Hornet, escorted by two policewomen who looked even tougher than herself, had been brought up from the cells. She was not a prepossessing sight. One of her eyes had been blackened. Her green hair was in a tangle. Her clothing was soiled and torn.

She scowled at Grimes.

She said sullenly, "I suppose you're expecting me to thank you. But you're only helping yourself, aren't you? We both know that."

"That's the way of it," said Grimes. "And now we'll get you to the Shipping Office to sign on, and then you'll report straightaway to the chief officer, aboard the ship. He'll find you a job to keep you out of mischief."

"What about my gear?" she demanded. "All my things are still at The Rusty Rocket. I can't join a ship without so much as a toothbrush or change of underwear."

"We'll stop off on the way to the Shipping Office," Grimes told her.

There was a public telephone in this ground-floor office. Grimes used it to order a cab. He said a polite good day to the sergeant and the two female constables then went outside to wait, almost pushing Ms. Connellan ahead of him. He realized that he was afraid that Una Freeman might change her mind and was anxious to remove himself from close proximity to her as soon as possible.

The Green Hornet asked him for a cigarette. He told her that he did not use them. He produced and filled his pipe, lit it. She snarled at him, saying, "It's all right for *you*."

He told her, "Just stand to leeward of me and you'll be getting a free smoke." She snarled at him again, wordlessly.

The cab came. Grimes got in beside the driver so that she could sit in solitary state on the back seat. The ride to The Rusty Rocket was made in silence; the driver, unrepresentative of his breed, was not a conversationalist and Ms. Connellan seemed to be sulking. This suited Grimes, who was in no mood to be ear-bashed.

They arrived at the shabby hostelry, a small, pyramidal building with functionless vanes giving it a faint similitude to an archaic spaceship. Grimes asked the driver to wait for them. He and the Green Hornet went inside.

There were unpleasantries.

Ms. Connellan did not have—or said that she did not have—the money to pay her bill. Grimes had been expecting that. What he had not been expecting was to be presented with another bill, a heavy one, to cover repairs to the replacement of various pieces of equipment and furniture. It was obvious, he was obliged to admit, that the playmaster had had its face smashed in, and recently. On the other hand the thing looked as though it had been on the point of dying of old age when it had been put out of its misery. There were two broken bar stools. There was a dent in the stained surface of the bar. There was a bin of broken bottles which, according to the sour-faced manageress, had been swept off the shelves behind the bar by the berserk Green Hornet.

"Did you do this damage?" asked Grimes exasperatedly.

"I did not!" snapped Ms. Connellan.

"She did!" yelped the manageress. "Like a wild beast she was! Screaming and shouting. . . ."

"I had to scream to make myself heard! I had to fight to defend myself!"

"If there was a fight, *you* started it!"

"I did not!" She turned to Grimes. "Pay no heed to her, Captain. She's lying like a flatfish!"

"Lying, you say, you deceptive bitch! Who's lying, I ask. Not me. And I'm holding on to your bags until I'm paid for all the wanton destruction!"

"You'll let me have my baggage," snarled the Green Hornet, advancing threateningly on the landlady, "or . . ."

"Ladies, ladies," admonished Grimes, interposing himself between them.

"Ladies. . . ." sneered Ms. Connellan. "I'll thank you not to tack that archaic label on to me!"

"She admits it!" jeered the other woman. "She's no lady!"

"Who are *you* calling no lady, you vinegar-pussed harridan? I'll. . . ."

"You will not!" almost shouted Grimes, pushing Ms. Connellan to one side before she could strike the manager. "Now, listen to me! Unless you behave yourself I'll put you in the hands of the police again. The Commissioner's an old friend of mine. . . ." (Well, she had been a friend, and rather more tban a friend, once, a long time ago.) "I'll ask her to keep you under lock and key until I'm ready to lift ship. And as for you, madam. . . ."

"Don't talk to me like that, buster. I'm not one of your crew."

"Can I see that bill again, madam?" She thrust the sheet of dirty and crumpled paper at him. "Mphm. I see that you're charging for a *new* playmaster. And that I am not paying. One quarter of the sum you've put down should buy a good second-hand one, one far better than that . . . wreck. The bar stools? I'll let that pass, although I still think that you're overcharging. The dent in the bar? No. That's an old damage, obviously. And now, all these bottles. . . . Were they all *full* bottles? I'll not believe that, madam. I note, too, that you've charged retail price. Don't you buy your liquor at wholesale rates?"

"I'm an honest woman, mister!"

"Tell that to the Police Commissioner," said Grimes. "I've no doubt that she's already well acquainted with your honesty." He began to feed figures into his wrist companion. "One second-hand playmaster. . . . I've seen them going for as low as one hundred credits, quite good ones. . . . Six bottles of Scotch at four credits each wholesale. . . . Twenty-four credits. . . . But as they were almost certainly no more than half full, that makes it twelve credits. . . ." He raised his eyebrows. "Brandy, at twenty-four credits a bottle? Even as a retail price that's steep."

"Either you pay," said the woman stubbornly, "or I call the police."

"Do just that," Grimes told her. "As I've said already, Commissioner Freeman is an old friend of mine."

"Like hell she is. She hates spacers."

"In general, yes. But in particular? Ask yourself why she released Ms. Connellan to my custody, although usually she insists that spacers serve their full sentences, with no fines and no bail."

"All right," said the woman suddenly. "All right. I'll take your word for what you say you owe me. Just don't come back in here again, ever. And tell that green bitch of yours to keep clear of my premises."

"Who are you calling a green bitch, you draggle-tailed slut?" screamed Kate Connellan. "I'll. . . ."

"You will not!" snapped Grimes. "Collect your bags and put them in the cab. And now, madam, if you'll make out a receipt for two hundred and ten credits. . . . That covers the playmaster, the bar stools and a very generous estimate of the cost of liquor lost by breakage."

Check and receipt changed hands.

Grimes went out to the waiting cab in which the Green Hornet, two battered cases on the seat beside her, was sullenly established. He got in beside the driver, told him to carry on to the spaceport.

Eight

The cab brought them into the spaceport, to the foot of *Sister Sue*'s ramp.

Grimes was pleased to see that the loading ramps had been set up around his ship, that already streams of crates and cases were being whisked up from the apron to the yawning cargo ports. This was *real* freight, he thought, not the little parcels of luxury goods that he had been carrying in *Little Sister.* He could read the consignee's title stenciled on each package: SURVEY SERVICE RECORDS, PORT WOOMERA. There had once been a major Survey Service Base on Austral, which had been degraded to a Sub-Base. Finally, only a short while ago, it had been closed down altogether. The transport *Robert A. Heinlein* had lifted off personnel and all the really important stores and equipment. There had been no great hurry for the rest of the stuff, mainly records going back almost to man's first landing on Earth's moon, until the warehouse accommodating the material was required for a factory site.

So perhaps, thought Grimes, this was not real freight after all, except in terms of tonnage. Anybody with any sense would have ordered all that junk destroyed—but the Survey Service, as well he knew, was a breeding ground for planet-based bureaucrats whose dusty files were the temples of whatever odd gods they worshipped.

Nonetheless he had been lucky to get this cargo.

Quite fantastically it had tied in with Magda Granadu's reading of the *I Ching.* She had thrown the coins and constructed a hexagram on the afternoon of the day that Grimes had renamed the ship. *Huan,* it had been. *Dispersion. There will be progress and success. The king visits his ancestral temple. It will be advantageous to cross the great water and to act with firm persistence.* And in the first line there had been the reference to "a strong horse"—and the Epsilon Class tramps had long been known as the sturdy workhorses of the Interstellar Transport Commission.

Yet Grimes had been dubious, at first, about the wisdom of carrying *that* cargo to *those* consignees. He had left the Survey Service under a cloud, had resigned hastily before he could be brought to face a court-martial. But, apart from the obnoxious Delamere's attempt to drag him back to Lindisfarne Base from Botany Bay, there had been no moves made to arrest him, although more than once, as a civilian shipmaster, he had been in contact with Survey Service vessels and personnel.

He had gone to Captain Taberner, Resident Secretary of the Astronauts' Guild on Austral, for advice.

"Not to worry, Captain," that gentleman had told him. "You're one of ours now. We look after our own. You'll get the finest legal defense if—and it's a big 'if'—the Admiralty takes any action against you. We fought an illegal arrest case a few years back—you may have heard about it—when some officious destroyer skipper seized a ship called *Southerly Buster.* Captain Kane's ship. You must have heard about *him.* Anyhow, we won and Drongo Kane was awarded very heavy damages."

So that was that, Grimes thought. If the Guild's legal eagles could save the bacon of an unsavory character like Kane they should be able to do at least as well by him.

He let the Green Hornet board first while he walked around the ship. He told her to report as soon as possible to Mr. Williams.

Finally he climbed the ramp to the after airlock, took the elevator to the No. 3 cargo compartment. Williams was there with a human foreman stevedore who was directing the spidery stowbots. The mate was harassed looking and his slate gray uniform shirt was dark with perspiration. "Tell those bloody tin spiders of yours," he was shouting, "that it's the heavy cases bottom stow and those flimsy crates on top!" He turned to face Grimes. "I had to chase the Green Hornet out of here. Her idea of stowage was big packages under and little packages over, regardless of weight." He switched to a falsetto voice. "'That's the way that we always did it in the Commission. . . .'" He snorted. "It certainly ain't the way we did it in the Dog Star Line!"

"Where is she now?"

"I told her to make a check of the navigational equipment."

Grimes left the mate attending to the stowage, carried on up to Control. There he found Ms. Connellan sulkily tinkering with the mass proximity indicator. She was still dressed as she had been when released from jail.

"Why aren't you in uniform?" he asked.

"What uniform am I supposed to wear?" she countered. "All my trappings are Interstellar Transport Commission."

"Then find out," he told her, "the name of a local uniform tailor. Mr. Williams should know. Get on the telephone and order full sets of uniform trappings for all hands."

"Including you, Captain?"

"Not including me."

Some time in the past Grimes had had his own Far Traveler Couriers insignia made up—the cap badge a stylized rider on a galloping horse, in silver, with two golden comets as the surround; the same horse and rider, but in gold, over the four gold stripes on his epaulets. When he could afford it he would put his people into Far Traveler Couriers uniform but it could wait.

"I suppose you know, sir," said Ms. Connellan, the tone of her voice implying that he didn't, "that the shipowner is responsible for supplying his personnel, at his expense, with uniform trappings."

"I know," said Grimes.

After she left him he began to reassemble the MPI. Luckily she had done no more than to remove the hemispherical cover.

A spacelawyer . . . he thought.

In any astronautical service, naval or mercantile, such are crosses that their commanding officers have to bear.

Nine

Yosarian came to see Grimes shortly before *Sister Sue* was scheduled to lift off. He was carrying a parcel, a gift-wrapped box. Grimes, taking it from him, was surprised at how heavy it was.

"Just a small gift, Captain," said the roboticist. "From myself, and from another . . . friend. I hope that you will like it."

"Thank you, Mr. Yosarian. But the other friend . . . ? Apart from you I don't have any friends on this planet."

The fat man laughed.

"Open the parcel," he said, "and you will see."

Grimes put the package on his desk. The tinsel ribbon around it was tied with a bow that came undone at the first tug. The metallic paper fell away to reveal a box of polished mahogany with brass fittings. The two catches holding down the hinged lid were easy to manipulate. Inside the box was foam plastic packing. Grimes pulled it out carefully, saw the rich gleam of metal, of gold.

He stared at what was revealed. There was a tiny bicycle, perfect in every detail. Seated upon it was one of Yosarian's mechanical dolls, a miniature golden woman, naked and beautiful. He recognized her—or, more correctly, knew whom she represented.

"Una Freeman . . ." he murmured. "Commissioner Freeman."

"As I said, Captain, an old friend of yours. And a friend of mine for quite some years. A charming lady."

"Mphm."

"When I mentioned to her that I was going to give you one of my dolls as a farewell gift she said that she would like it to be from both of us. But I got the impression that the combination of naked lady and bicycle was some sort of private joke."

"At least she didn't ask you to include a golden can of baked beans. That's another private joke."

"But what is the meaning of this?" asked Yosarian. "I was able, easily, to make the lady and her steed to her specifications. But a bicycle . . . ?"

"Miss Freeman and I were working together. It was when she was a member of the Corps of Sky Marshals and while I was in the Survey Service. It's a long story; you must get her to tell it to you some time. But, fantastic as it may sound, the two of us were cast away on an almost desert planet with two bicycles for company. Mphm. Rather *special* bicycles."

"I gathered that."

Carefully Grimes lifted the exquisitely made models from the box, the little woman still sitting on the saddle, her tiny hands grasping the handlebar, her feet on the pedals. He set the toy—or the toys; he did not think that the assemblage was all in one piece—down onto the desk. He let go of it hastily when one foot lifted from the pedal, went down to make contact with the surface on which the bicycle was standing.

"It—she—is attuned to your voice, Captain," said Yosarian. "Tell her to ride around the desk top."

"Ride around the desk top," ordered Grimes dubiously.

The golden foot was back on the golden pedal after giving a backward shove; both feet were on the pedals and the golden legs were working smoothly, up and down, up and down, and the golden filaments that were the wire spokes of the wheels glittered as they turned, slowly at first, and then became a gleaming, transparent blur.

Round the desk she rode, balancing on the very edge of its top, cutting no corners, faster and faster. And then she was actually over the edge with the wheels running on the shallow thickness of the rim, machine and rider no longer vertical to the deck but horizontal.

This was fascinating, but Grimes had to think about getting his ship upstairs in the very near future.

He asked, not taking his eyes from the fascinating golden figurine, "Are there batteries? How is she powered?"

"From any light source, natural or artificial."

"How do I stop her?"

"Just tell her, Captain."

Grimes restrained himself from saying Stop, realizing that if he did so the golden toy might fall to the desk, damaging itself.

"Back onto the desk top," he said. (Sometime, he thought, he must make a slow motion recording of that graceful gymnastic maneuvering.) "Back into the box." (The bicycle ran up the vertical side of the container with ease, hovered briefly in the air before plunging downward.) "Stop."

"You're getting the hang of it, Captain," said Yosarian.

"All I can say," said Grimes, "is thank you. Thank you very much."

"You should also thank Commissioner Freeman. The nature of the gift was her idea—and she was the model for part of it."

"Then thank her for me, please."

"I will do so." Yosarian got up from the chair on which he had been sitting. "And now I must go. There is still work for me to do aboard *my* ship." He extended his hand. Grimes shook it. "Bon voyage, Captain. And good fortune. Oh, I have a message from the Commissioner. She told me to tell you that bicycles aren't always what they seem, and to remember that." Something seemed to be amusing him. "Bon voyage," he said again, and left.

Grimes pottered about his day cabin, making sure that all was secure. He lifted the box containing Yosarian's—and Una's—farewell gift down from the desk, stowed it in his big filing cabinet. (There was room for it; the ship, under her new ownership, had yet to accumulate stacks of incoming correspondence and copies of outgoing communications.) He made sure that the solidograph of Maggie Lazenby was secure on the shelf on which he had placed it while he was settling in. He would have to find a suitable site for Una and her bicycle, he thought; it would be a crime to leave her to languish unseen in the box. He remembered another gift from another woman, the miniature simulacrum of Susie. He remembered, too, the troubles that it had brought him. But the mini-Una, he told himself, for all her motility would be no more dangerous than the image of Maggie.

His telephone buzzed. The fleshy face of Williams appeared on the screen.

"Mate here, Skipper. Mr. Yosarian's ashore now. I'm sealing the ship."

"Thank you, Mr. Williams."

"And Aerospace Control confirms that we're all set for lift-off at 1400 hours."

Grimes looked at the bulkhead clock. The time was 1350. He left his quarters and went up to the control room.

Ten

Sister Sue lifted from Port Southern.

It was not, of course, the first time that Grimes had handled her; he had brought her down from the parking orbit to the spaceport. This, however, was his first lift-off in the ship. He could not help thinking that she appreciated his touch on the controls—and inwardly laughed at his subscription to the pathetic fallacy. But he persisted in his imaginings. *Little Sister* had been little more than a girl, eageriy responsive to his lightest caress. *Sister Sue* was a woman, no longer young, an experienced woman. She required—demanded, even—a heavier hand.

She lifted steadily, accelerating smoothly. Below her the glittering city dwindled and the horizon began to display curvature. Up through filmy upper clouds she drove, up through the last, tenuous shreds of atmosphere, into the blackness and the hard vacuum of space.

Soon it was time to set trajectory for the interstellar voyage. Grimes cut the inertial drive, then used the directional gyroscopes to swing the vessel about her axes. He brought the bright star that was Sol directly ahead, then made the small correction for galactic drift. He started the inertial drive.

The temporal precession field built up.

As always there was disorientation, visually and aurally, while colors sagged down the spectrum and perspective was distorted. As sometimes, although not always, happened there was prevision, a consequence of the warping of the fabric of space and time.

Grimes stared at what, at first glance, had seemed to be his reflection on the inner surface of one of the viewports. With a shock he realized that it was the image of a much older man than himself that was staring back at him. There were the same prominent ears, there was a foul-looking pipe clamped between the teeth. (The here-and-now Grimes' pipe was still in his pocket.) The apparition was gray-haired. He was, like Grimes, in uniform but the gold braid on his shoulderboards was a single broad stripe, not four narrow ones. Above it was a winged wheel device, not the Far Traveler stylized courier. Somehow the name of the ship was in the background but the letters were wavering, squirming as though alive, dissolving, reforming. They stabilized and no longer spelled *Sister Sue* but *Faraway Quest*. . . . And was that Williams there beside this other—this future—Grimes? An older Williams, just as it was an older Grimes in the reflection.

Then, the field established and holding, things snapped back to normal—or as normal as they ever could be in a ship running under interstellar drive. The pseudo reflections vanished. Outside the control room the warped continuum now presented an uncanny, even to a seasoned spaceman, aspect with every star no longer a sharp point of light but a writhing, coruscating spiral nebula, slowly but visibly drifting across the field of vision.

Grimes looked at Williams. Williams looked at him. There was mutual acknowledgment that their futures were somehow interlinked. Then Williams looked at the Green Hornet, slumped and sulky in her chair. He grinned at Grimes as though to say, *Whatever happens, whatever is going to happen, we won't be saddled with* her, *Skipper.*

With slow deliberation Grimes filled and lit his pipe. He said, "Deep space routine, Mr. Williams." He turned to the girl and told her, "You have the first watch, Ms. Connellan."

"I still haven't had time to unpack properly. Sir."

"That will have to wait until you come off duty. The chief officer has been watch on and stay on ever since we opened Articles."

She glowered at him but said nothing. Grimes wondered if, should he log and fine her for the crime of dumb insolence, he could make it stick. He looked back at her coldly, then released himself from his chair and walked to the hatch leading down to the axial shaft. Williams followed him.

"A stiff drink before you get your head down, Number One?" asked Grimes.

"Thanks, Skipper. I could use one."

Grimes led the way into his quarters. He went to the liquor cabinet. Williams asked for beer. Grimes mixed himself a pink gin. Seated, the two men faced each other across the coffee table.

The mate raised his condensation-bedewed can in salutation. "Here's to a long and prosperous association, Skipper."

"I'll drink to that, Mr. Williams. Oh, by the way, when the time-twister was warming up did *you* see anything?"

Williams laughed. "I saw myself as a frosty-faced old bastard—and you even frostier faced! I've had these glimpses of the future before and, just between ourselves, they're more reliable than Magda's *I Ching!"*

"On one occasion," Grimes told him, "I was treated to the prevision of a naked lady riding a bicycle. . . ."

"I doubt if *that* came true, Skipper!" laughed Williams.

"But it did. By the time it was all over I was allergic to both the wench and her velocipede!"

He got up, went to the filing cabinet and brought out the mahogany box. He opened it, lifted out the beautiful . . . toy, set it down on the deck. "Ride around the cabin," he ordered. "Slowly."

Williams stared as the naked cyclist made her leisurely rounds.

"Where did you get that, Skipper? One of Yosarian's specials, isn't it?"

"Yes," said Grimes. "A parting gift. From him, and. . . ."

"And?" Williams bent down in his chair to look more closely at the tiny, golden cyclist as she glided past him. "And? Surely not! Isn't that our beloved Police Commissioner?" He laughed. "But she is a friend of Yosarian's. And I know that she was a Sky Marshal before she settled down on Austral. Don't tell me, Skipper, that she was the lady in your, er, vision!"

Grimes allowed himself a small grin.

"Gentlemen don't tell," he said.

"Come off it, Skipper! We aren't in the wardroom of a Survey Service warship; this is a merchant ship. Religion, politics and sex are quite permissible topics of conversation. In any case it's highly unlikely that any of us will ever be seeing Commissioner Freeman again—and thank the Odd Gods of the Galaxy for that!"

"All right," said Grimes. "I met Sky Marshal Freeman, as she was then, when she was supposed to be taking possession of the pirated, then abandoned *Delta Geminorum.* You may recall the case. The ship was just wandering around, going nowhere in particular, with her Mannschenn Drive in operation. Ms. Freeman called upon the Survey Service for assistance. I was between ships at the time and was put in charge of the prize crew. We—Ms. Freeman, the people in the prize crew and myself—went out in the Lizard Class courier *Skink* to intercept the derelict. We found her and synchronized temporal precession rates. It was arranged that Ms. Freeman and I would be the first to board her; we left *Skink* in a Class A boat, practically a spaceship in miniature, complete with mini-Mannschenn, Carlotti radio, life-support system and all the rest of it. As far as we could work things out afterward there was some sort of interaction between the temporal precession fields of the ship, *Delta Geminorum,* and the boat as we made a close approach. This caused the detonation of the bomb which the pirates had left as a booby trap. It was a thermonuclear device. We were as near as dammit at ground zero—and, as I've said, there was this interaction between temporal precession fields.

"We weren't killed. . . ."

"That's obvious, Skipper!"

"It wasn't at the time. Not to *Skink*'s captain and his crew, and to my prize crew, who were still aboard his ship. They all thought that Sky Marshal Una

Freeman and Lieutenant Commander John Grimes had been well and truly vaporized, together with the boat and the derelict. It was so reported. Of course I was able to report differently some time later, after our return to this universe."

"I've heard all these stories about alternate universes," said Williams, "but I've never quite believed them. Oh, there were a few odd stories about *Delta Geminorum* and Ms. Freeman and yourself—but most people thought that they were some sort of Survey Service smokescreen, covering up something with serious political implications, or. . . . When Ms. Freeman first came to Austral—with her Corps of Sky Marshals background she started in the police force with senior inspector's rank—a few of the local rags and stations tried to interview her. All that she'd say about the *Delta Geminorum* affair was that it was classified. I hope that you won't say the same."

"I'm a civilian shipmaster now," said Grimes. "I don't even hold a reserve commission. But if I tell you, keep it to yourself, will you?

"We were flung, somehow, into a more or less parallel universe. There had been a galaxy-wide war, resulting in the destruction of all organic life. Life, of a sort, had survived—the intelligent machines. The ruling entity, regarded as a god and with godlike powers, wanted to give his late creators, the human race, a fresh start. (Not that they'd been human, as we understand the term. They'd been more like centaurs.) Una—Ms. Freeman—and I were captured. We were set down in an oasis on an otherwise desert planet. There were plants, animals. There was water and a wide variety of edible fruits and nuts. The implication was that we were to become the Adam and Eve of the new race. Una wasn't all that keen on the idea—and neither was I. After her last contraceptive shot wore off we were very, very careful.

"There were guardian angels in this Garden of Eden—although we didn't realize that they were until they tried to force us to do the bidding of the robot god. . . ."

"What form did they take, Skipper?"

"Bicycles," said Grimes.

Williams' eyes followed the little golden Una as she rode around the day cabin on her graceful golden steed. He laughed.

"So she has a sense of humor! The only time that I met her personally I thought that she was humorless. But what happened in the end?"

"I don't like uppity robots," said Grimes. "I never have. After we discovered the true nature of those bicycles I . . . disposed of them. It wasn't all that easy. If you've ever been a cyclist you'll know that even an ordinary bicycle can be quite vicious at times. The robot god made his appearance. He'd decided that we were not fit and proper persons to be the parents of the new race. He banished us from the garden. He slung us back into our own universe. Luckily he had us put back in the boat first.

"We found ourselves in orbit around a world—Tamsin IV, as a matter of fact—with one of those unmanned beacon stations. I tried to convert the beacon into a transmitter so that I could send a call for help. Frankly, I rather buggered it up. So we had to wait until the beacon tender dropped by on its normal rounds. The station had emergency stores, luckily. Unluckily there wasn't much variety. Can you imagine a steady diet of baked beans in tomato sauce for seven weeks?"

"What was wrong with honeymoon salad, Skipper?" asked Williams. "Just lettuce alone, with no dressing."

"The honeymoon was over, Mr. Williams, before we were expelled from the garden. Conditions weren't right for its resumption."

"From what I've seen of Commissioner Freeman," said Williams, "I'm surprised that conditions were ever right." He looked again at the unwearying golden cyclist. "But, to judge by that, she doesn't look too bad out of uniform."

Eleven

The voyage from Austral to Earth was a relatively short one—long enough, however, for Grimes to get the feel of his ship and to make an assessment of his crew. The ship he liked. He knew that during her service under the Commission's flag she had been regarded as a notoriously awkward bitch; he did not find her so. Perhaps the change of ownership had sweetened her nature. Already—at least insofar as Grimes was concerned—she was as comfortable as an old shoe.

Regarding his personnel he was not so happy. Only the mate, Billy Williams, and the Catering Officer, Magda Granadu met with Grimes' almost unqualified approval although he was developing a liking for a few of the others.

One day he amused himself by making out a Voyage Staff Report. Had he been still in the Survey Service this would have been required of him, as it would have been had he been in command of a vessel owned by any of the major shipping lines. As owner/master he could report only to himself.

Williams, William, he wrote. *Chief Officer. A very good second in command. A tendency to be overzealous. Competent spaceman and navigator. Pleasant personality.*

He filled and lit his pipe, cogitated on what he had written. If this were a real report he would have no hesitation in signing it and sending it in.

He resumed writing. *Connellan, Kate. Second Officer. A typical Donegalan female chauvinist bitch. Carries a perpetual chip on her shoulder. Is perpetually complaining about the ship, her shipmates, the meals, etc., etc. and etc. Barely competent as spaceperson and navigator.*

And that, he thought, would be letting her off lightly. If Billy Williams or Magda Granadu were called upon to make a report on her their words would scorch the paper. At every change of watch she would annoy the Chief Officer with her complaints and comparisons. "In the Commission's ships we used to get so-and-so and such-and-such. In the Commission's ships we used to do it *this* way. . . ." The Catering Officer had tried her best to please everybody, but the Green Hornet could not—would not—be pleased. There was no Donegalan whisky in the bar stores. Donegalan national dishes never appeared on the menu. (Among the edible vegetables grown on the farm deck were no potatoes.) She was allergic to paprika. Sour cream made her come out in spots.

But there would be no need to put up with her any longer once *Sister Sue* got to Port Woomera. There should be no trouble in filling any vacancies on Earth.

Stewart, Andrew. Radio Officer. Conscientious and competent. Has no interests outside his profession.

Just an old-time Sparks, thought Grimes, and none the worse for that.

Crumley, Horace. Chief Engineer, Reaction and Inertial Drives. Another old-timer. Extremely conscientious.

And as boring as all hell, thought Grimes. All his conversation is along "when I was in the old so-and-so" lines.

Denning, Fred. Second Engineer. A refugee from a bicycle shop but reliable. Not, unfortunately, officer material.

Snobbish bastard! he admonished himself.

Singh, Govind. Third Engineer. A refugee from the Port Southern Monorail. Would be happier aboard a train than a spaceship—and, possibly, a little more useful.

Mr. Singh had endeared himself to Grimes by fixing the playmaster in the captain's day cabin; after his ministrations the thing would present a picture only in black and white with sound no louder than a whisper. Fortunately old Mr. Stewart had been able to get the thing working properly.

Paulus, Ludwig. Fourth Engineer. Another refugee from the Port Southern Monorail. Has not yet been given the opportunity to demonstrate his incompetence but when the times come will not be found lacking.

Come, come, Grimes, he thought reprovingly. Your innies are working, aren't they, and working well. So are the life-support systems. Just because people haven't been through the Academy and learned which knives and forks to use at table and how to wear a uniform properly it doesn't mean that they're no good as spacemen.

Malleson, Phillip. Chief Engineer, Mannschenn Drive. Very much the academic but he knows his job. Good conversationalist. . . .

But he's being paid to run the time-twister, isn't he, not to be the life and soul of the party. Still, it always helps when an officer is a good shipmate as well as being highly efficient.

Federation Survey Service, then Trans-Galactic Clippers. A typical big ship engineer of the better kind.

Watch that snobbery, Grimes!

Trantor, George. Second Engineer, Mannschenn Drive. And Ph.D., and makes sure that everybody knows it. As snobbish in his way as I am in mine. Must know his job, otherwise Malleson wouldn't tolerate him.

Giddings, Walter. Third Engineer, Mannschenn Drive. Another Ph.D. Like Mr. Trantor tends to hold himself aloof from the low, common spacemen.

Granadu, Magda. Catering Officer/Purser/Acting Bio-Chemist. An extremely capable person and a good shipmate. An inspired touch with the autochef. Farm deck always in perfect order. Works well with members of other departments—as, for example, with the engineers in necessary maintenance of LSS. Very popular with almost every member of the crew. I have no doubt that if this vessel becomes known as a happy ship she will be largely responsible.

Somebody was knocking at his door.

"Come in," he called.

It was the Green Hornet.

"Yes, Ms. Connellan?" asked Grimes, trying to hide his distaste.

"Sir. It is bad enough having to keep watch and watch. But when I am not being fed properly the situation becomes intolerable!"

Grimes looked at her. The sealseam at the front of her uniform shirt was under great strain. So was the waistband of her shorts. And it was obvious that she had not been feeding herself properly; there was a splash of half-dried sauce over her left breast and another on the right leg of her lower garment.

"Lunch," he said, "was very good."

"All right for people who like mucked up food with the real flavor disguised by garlic and pepper!"

'There is always choice, Ms. Connellan."

"What choice, sir? I've raised the point with Ms. Granadu, our so-called Catering Officer, time and time again."

"There was a perfectly good steak, to order, with French fried potatoes."

"French fried potatoes my a . . ." She caught herself just in time, finished the sentence with "foot." "Potatoes reconstituted from some sort of flour, molded into shape and then fried. But not *potatoes.* On New Donegal we know our potatoes. I'll say this for the Commission—in their ships you get real potatoes!"

"Your last ship was *Delta Crucis,* wasn't she?" asked Grimes.

"Yes. What of it?"

"A cargo-passenger liner, Ms. Connellan. You get luxuries aboard passenger ships that you don't get in Epsilon Class tramps. You have a bio-chemist on the Articles who is practically a full-time gardener, who can amuse himself by growing all sorts of things in the hydroponics tanks. Here, Ms. Granadu has plenty to occupy her time without bothering about things that are hard to grow in aboard-ship conditions."

"You could have carried a few kilos of potatoes in the stores."

"Storeroom space is limited, Ms. Connellan."

"Everything in this bloody ship is limited. I should have had my head examined before I signed on here."

"I shall be happy to release you as soon as we get to Port Woomera," said Grimes coldly.

"Oh, will you, sir? Isn't that just typical. You use me, exploit me, and then you cast me aside like a worn-out glove."

"If it hadn't been for me," Grimes told her, "you'd still be in the Port Southern jail."

"And probably feeding a damn sight better than I am here."

"Ms. Connellan, you have made your complaint. I have listened to it. You are the only person aboard this ship who has found fault with the food. You are at liberty to make further complaints—to the Guild, to the Shipping Master, to whoever will listen to you—after we get to Port Woomera.

"That is all."

"But. . . ."

"That is all!" snarled Grimes.

She glared at him, turned sharply about and flounced out of his day cabin. Looking at her fat buttocks straining the material of her shorts almost to bursting Grimes thought that it was exercise she needed rather than more starch in her diet. If *Sister Sue* were a warship he would be able to order people to have a daily workout in the gymnasium. But *Sister Sue* was a merchantman and the powers of her captain, although considerable, were only a civilian shipmaster's powers.

Twelve

Sister Sue came to Port Woomera.

Grimes stared into the stern view screen, looking at what once had been a familiar view, the waters of the Great Australian Bight to the south and to the north the semi-desert, crisscrossed with irrigation canals, with huge squares of oddly glittering gray that were the solar energy collection screens, with here and there the assemblages of gleaming white domes that housed people and machinery and the all-the-year-round-producing orchards. Close inshore, confined in its pen of plastic sheeting, was a much diminished iceberg. Farther out to sea a much larger one, a small fleet of tugs in attendance, was slowly coming in toward what would be its last resting place.

Grimes applied lateral thrust to bring the ship directly above the spaceport. He could see clearly the white buildings, assemblages of bubbles, and the lofty control tower. And there were the smaller towers, metallically gleaming, that were the ships, great and small.

His berth had been allocated. He was to bring *Sister Sue* down to the Naval Station, about five kilometers to the east of the commercial spaceport. He could identify a Constellation Class cruiser, a couple of Star Class destroyers and what he thought was a Serpent Class courier. *Adder?* he wondered. That little ship had been his first command. But he doubted if the long arm of coincidence would be stretched to such an extent. It was extremely unlikely that there would be any ships or any people whom he had known, during his days in the Survey Service, at Port Woomera. He had never been attached to the Port Woomera Base.

The triangle of brightly flashing beacons marking his berth was clearly visible. It showed a tendency to drift away from the center of the screen. Grimes put on lateral thrust again to counteract the effect of the light breeze, decreased vertical thrust. On the screen the figures of the radar-altimeter display steadily diminished.

He allowed his attention to wander briefly, looked to the towers of Woomera City in the middle distance. He watched one of the big dirigibles of Trans-Australia Airlines coming into its mooring mast at the airfield at the city limits. Soon, he thought, he would be aboard one of those airships. His parents, in Alice Springs, would be looking forward to seeing him again after his long absence from Earth.

Looking back to the radar altimeter read-out he stepped up vertical thrust. *Sister Sue* was not a Federation Survey Service courier, or a deep-space pinnace like *Little Sister,* in which a flashy landing would be relatively safe. It wouldn't do for a ship of this tonnage to drop like a stone and then slam on thrust at the very last moment. Nonetheless, he thought, she would be able to take it. She was a sturdy enough brute.

One hundred meters to go. . . .

Ninety-five. . . . Ninety. . . .

Slight drift, thought Grimes. *Lateral thrust again. . . .*

He turned to look at his officers. Williams, he noted, was watching him approvingly. The Green Hornet hastily wiped a sneer from her face. Without his being a telepath Grimes knew what she was thinking, *Anybody would think that the bloody ship was made of glass!*

To hell with you, he thought. *I won't have to put up with you for much longer.*

Deliberately he took his time over the final stages of the descent.

At last *Sister Sue*'s stern vanes made gentle, very gentle contact with the apron. She rocked ever so slightly, then was still. Shock absorbers sighed as they took the weight when the inertial drive was shut down.

"Finished with engines," said Grimes smugly. He pulled his pipe from a pocket, filled it and lit it.

"Finished with engines, Skipper," repeated Williams and passed this final order on to the inertial-drive room. Then, "Shall I go down to the airlock to receive the boarding party? I see them on the way out."

"Do that," said Grimes.

Through a viewport he watched the ground cars scurrying out across the apron. Customs, he supposed, and Port Health and Immigration. One of them, however, was a gray vehicle looking like a minor warship on wheels—probably the Survey Service officer responsible for arranging for the discharge of *Sister Sue*'s cargo. But what was that broad pennant fluttering from a short mast on the bonnet of the car? He got up from his seat, swung the big mounted binoculars to bear.

A black flag, with two golden stars. . . .

Surely, he told himself, a Rear Admiral would not be concerning himself with the offloading of an unimportant consignment of outdated bumf.

Was the Survey Service still after his blood?

But if they were going to arrest him, he thought, they would have sent a squad of Marines, not a flag officer.

Nonetheless there was cause for worry. In his experience Admirals did not personally welcome minor vessels, minor merchant vessels especially.

He went down to his quarters to change hastily into the least shabby of his uniforms and to await developments. As he left the control room he heard Ms. Connellan singing softly to herself—and at him.

"Sheriff and police a-coming after me. . . ."

Bitch! he thought.

Thirteen

"So we meet again, Grimes," said Rear Admiral Damien.

"This is a surprise, sir," Grimes said. Then, "Congratulations on your promotion."

Damien laughed. "Once I no longer had *you* to worry about, once I wasn't always having to justify your actions to my superiors, I got my step up."

Grimes waited until his guest was seated then took a chair himself. He looked at Damien, not without some apprehension. Apart from the extra gold braid on his sleeves his visitor looked just as he had when he was Commodore Damien, Officer Commanding Couriers, on Lindisfarne Base. He was as thin as ever, his face little more than a skull over which yellow skin was tightly stretched. He still had the mannerism of putting his skeletal fingers together, making a steeple of them over which he regarded whomever it was he was addressing. So he was now looking at Grimes, just as he had so often looked at him in the past when Grimes, a lowly lieutenant, had been captain of the Serpent Class courier *Adder*. On such occasions he had either been taking Grimes to task for some misdeed or sending him out on some especially awkward mission.

"Coffee, sir?" asked Grimes.

"Thank you, er, Captain."

Grimes called Magda on the telephone. Almost at once she was bringing in the tray with the fragrantly steaming pot, the cream, the sugar and the mugs. She looked at Damien curiously, then at Grimes.

She asked, "Will that be all, sir?"

"Yes, thank you, Magda."

She made a reluctant departure. Probably everybody aboard *Sister Sue* would be wondering why an Admiral had come to visit Grimes, would be expecting her to have the answers.

Grimes poured. He took both sugar and cream in his mug. Damien wanted his coffee black and unsweetened.

He said, "I suppose you're wondering, just as your Catering Officer was wondering, what I'm doing aboard your ship."

"I am, sir."

"It all ties in with my new job, Grimes. My official title is Coordinator of Merchant Shipping. When I learned that a star tramp called *Sister Sue,* commanded by John Grimes, was due in I was naturally curious. I made inquiries and was pleased to learn that *Sister Sue*'s master was, indeed, *the* John Grimes."

"You flatter me, sir."

"Nonetheless, Grimes, this is not altogether a social call. No, I haven't come to place you under arrest. Or not yet, anyhow. There were, of course, very extensive inquiries into the *Discovery* mutiny and you were more or less cleared of culpability. More or less. There are still, however, those in high places who would like your guts for garters."

"Mphm."

"Cheer up, Grimes. I haven't come to shoot you." He sipped. "Excellent coffee, this, by the way. But you always were notorious for your love of life's little luxuries." He extended his mug for a refill. "I suppose that this ship keeps quite a good table."

"I like it, sir."

"I must invite myself to lunch some day. But this morning we will talk business."

"Business, sir?"

"What else? You're not only a merchant captain, you're a shipowner. You're the one who has to arrange future employment for your ship, yourself and your crew."

"That thought had flickered across my mind, sir. Perhaps you could advise me. It is some many years since I was last on Earth."

"I've found you jobs in the past, Grimes. Whenever there was something too out of the ordinary for the other courier captains you were the one who got it. Now, I'll be frank with you. As Coordinator of Merchant Shipping I work very closely with Intelligence. And Intelligence doesn't consist only of finding out what's happening. Sometimes it's making things happen. Do you get me, Grimes?"

"Dirty Tricks, sir?"

"You can put it that way. Also countering other people's dirty tricks. You know El Dorado, don't you?"

"I was there once, sir, when I was a junior officer in *Aries.* And for a while I was yachtmaster to the Baroness Michelle d'Estang, one of the El Doradan aristocracy."

"And you know her husband, Commodore Baron Kane."

"He's hardly a friend, sir."

"But you know him. Well, I want *you* on El Dorado. There's a shipment of luxury goods to be carried there; wines, caviar, fancy cheeses and such. Normally one of the Commission's ships would be employed—but, as requested by the Admiralty, the Commission will not have a vessel available. So they will have to charter something. And that something will be your *Sister Sue.* Who *was* Sue, by the way?"

"Just a girl. . . ."

"The young lady on the bicycle exchanging glares with our Commander Lazenby?" Damien got up from his chair to look at, first of all, the solidograph of Maggie, then at the golden statuette of Una Freeman. "H'm. I seem to have seen that face before somewhere. . . . On Lindisfarne Base, wasn't it? That Sky Marshal wench you were supposed to be working with. But, unless my memory is playing tricks, her name wasn't Susan. . . ."

"It wasn't," said Grimes. "It still isn't."

"Of course, you've seen her recently. . . ."

(Was that a statement or a question?)

"She's the Port Southern Police Commissioner," said Grimes.

Damien seemed to lose interest in Grimes' art gallery, returned to his chair.

"Now, Grimes, this charter. . . ."

"What's the catch, sir?" asked Grimes. "I somehow can't believe that anybody in the Admiralty loves me enough to throw lucrative employment my way."

"How right you are, Grimes. You'll have to work your passage. To begin with, you will be reenlisted into the Survey Service—on the Reserve List, of course, but with your old rank. Commander."

And when I'm back in the Service, thought Grimes, *they'll have me by the balls.*

He said, "No thank you, sir. I'm a civilian and I like being a civilian. I intend to stay that way."

"Even though you have civilian status, Grimes, you can still be compelled to face a court-martial over the *Discovery* affair."

"I thought you said that it had been swept under the carpet, sir."

"Carpets can be lifted. Quite a number of my colleagues would rather like to lift that one."

"I'm a member of the Astronauts' Guild, sir. They've tangled with the Survey Service more than once in defense of their people—and usually won."

"They probably would in your case, Grimes—but you must know that the legal profession doesn't know the meaning of the word 'hurry.' While the lawyers were arguing your ship would be sitting here, idle, with port dues and the like steadily mounting, with your officers wanting their three square meals a day and their salaries. It'd break you, Grimes, and you know it."

Damien was right, Grimes knew.

He said, "All right. But if I do join the Reserve I'd like a higher rank, with the pay and allowances appertaining while on active duty."

Damien laughed. "Always the opportunist, Grimes! But there's no such animal as a Reserve Admiral and you'll find Reserve Commodores only in the major shipping lines." He laughed again. "Far Traveler Couriers can hardly be classed as such."

"Captain will do," said Grimes magnaminously. "But what exactly do you want me for, sir? How does it tie in with that charter to El Dorado?"

"I can't tell you that until you're officially back in the Service. Damien got slowly to his feet like a carpenter's rule unfolding. "But I'll not rush you. I'll give you until tomorrow morning to make your mind up. Don't bother to come with me, Grimes. I can find my own way down to the airlock."

As soon as he was gone Grimes rang for Magda Granadu. "And bring the coins and the book with you," he said.

Head and two tails . . . Yin. And again, and again, and again, and again, and again . . . *K'un.*

"The superior man," said Magda, "faithfully serves those who can best use his talents. There will be advantage in finding friends in the south and west, and in losing friends in the north and east. In quiet persistence lies good fortune. . . ."

"But I've already found friends in the south," said Grimes. "On Austral, at Port Southern. Yosarian. You and Billy Williams. Even Una Freeman. But where does the west come into it?"

"There are still southerly aspects to consider. Woomera, where we are now, is in Earth's southern hemisphere. And perhaps we should take initial letters into consideration. 'S' for south, 'W' for west. 'S' for Survey Service. 'W' for Woomera."

"Mphm? But finding friends here? Commodore Damien was never a friend of mine."

But wasn't he? Grimes asked himself. *Wasn't he?* Time and time again, during his captaincy of *Adder,* the little Serpent Class courier, Grimes had gotten away with murder, now and again almost literally. Damien, then Officer Commanding Couriers, must have stood up for him against those Admirals who wanted to make an example of the troublesome young officer.

"I think," Magda said, "that the Rear Admiral *is* a friend of yours. He looked into my office for a brief chat on his way ashore. He said, in these very words, 'You've a good captain here. Look after him.'"

"Mphm. Well, he's not such a bad old bastard himself. Bitt we still have that prophecy about losing friends in the north and east. El Dorado is to the galactic north. And its name starts with an 'E'. . . ."

"And do you have friends on El Dorado, Captain?" she asked.

"Well, I did. The old Duchess of Leckhampton. . . . I wonder if she's still alive. And the Princess Marlene. . . . And the Baroness Michelle d'Estang. . . . All friends, I suppose. . . ."

She read again from the book. "The superior man finds a true master and chooses his friends among those whose natures are compatible with his own."

Grimes snorted. "There's one person aboard this ship whose nature is not compatible! The Green Hornet. I'd like you to get her pay made up so that I can get rid of her. There should be no shortage of qualified officers here, on Earth."

"On what grounds will you discharge her, Captain?"

"Just that her face doesn't fit."

She frowned thoughtfully. "I'm afraid that you'll not be able to make it stick. Hasn't Billy told you about the Guild on this world? It's just a junior officers' trade union. When I was late here, in *Borzoi,* the Old Man tried to get rid of the third mate, one of those really obnoxious puppies you get stuck with at times. He paid him off—and then the little bastard ran screaming to the Guild. The Guild not only refused to supply a replacement but brought a suit for wrongful dismissal. And slapped an injunction on us so that we couldn't lift until the case had been heard. Captain Brownlee didn't improve matters by saying, in court, just what he thought about the legal profession. It did not prejudice the judge in his favor. So he lost the case and we had to take the third mate back. The Dog Star Line was far from happy, of course. Their ship had been grounded for weeks. The captain showed me the Carlottigram he got from Top Office. It was a long one, but one sentence sticks in my memory. 'We judge our Masters not by their navigation or spacemanship but by the skill with which they walk the industrial tightrope.'"

"And what happened to Captain Brownlee?" asked Grimes.

"Transferred to a scruffy little ship on one of the Dog Star Line's more unpleasant trades."

"At least," said Grimes, "I don't have any owners to worry about."

"But you have an owner's worries, Captain. You can't afford to be grounded by legal hassles when you should be flitting around the galaxy earning an honest living."

"That's true. But are you sure that Ms. Connellan will scream to the Guild if I try to pay her off?"

"She's already screamed."

"Oh. I'd have thought, to judge from the way that she's been complaining, that she'd be glad to see the last of us."

"She's not altogether a fool," said Magda. "She knows that she's virtually unemployable. She's got a job and she means to hang on to it."

Fourteen

By the time *Sister Sue* was linked up to the Port Woomera telephone system, Grimes' intention had been to ring his parents in Alice Springs as soon as possible but, after his conversation with Magda, decided first of all to have things out with the Guild.

He got through to the local secretary, in Woomera City, without trouble. The face looking out at him from the screen was not a young one and at first Grimes hoped that he would be given a sympathetic hearing.

He said, without preamble, "I'd like to get rid of my second mate, Captain Davis."

"Ms. Connellan has already talked with me, Captain Grimes, and I must say that her complaints of sexual and racial discrimination seem quite valid."

"I'm not practicing discrimination. I just want her out of my ship."

"Then I must warn you, Captain Grimes, that the Guild will give full support to Ms. Connellan."

"I'm a Guild member too. Shouldn't you be looking after *my* interests?"

Davis smiled sadly. "You must realize, Captain, that shipmasters comprise less than twenty-five percent of Guild membership. Junior officers are in the majority. You might say that I am their employee. There is another point. You are a shipowner as well as being a shipmaster. As far as the majority of our members are concerned, shipowners are the natural enemies of all good spacemen. . . ."

"Ms. Connellan is not a good spaceman," growled Grimes. "She is a bad spacewoman."

"Perhaps, perhaps. But I've only your word for that, Captain."

"My chief officer will bear me out. And my catering officer. And my radio officer. And my senior engineers."

"Among whom only the chief officer is a Guild member."

"So you're not prepared to help me, Captain Davis?"

"I have heard Ms. Connellan's story. You were happy enough to engage her in Port Southern when you desperately needed an officer."

"That was then," growled Grimes. "This is now."

"As you say, Captain Grimes, this is *now.* You are no longer in Survey Service with godlike powers over your crew."

Grimes snorted. Any Survey Service captain who tried to come the heavy deity would very soon be smacked down to size by the real gods—not only the admirals but the bureaucrats and the politicians.

He asked, "Were you ever in the Service yourself, Captain Davis?"

"No."

"I thought not," said Grimes. "If you had been you wouldn't be talking such a load of crap."

That ended the call—and, no matter what the *I Ching* had told him, this was one friend that he had not found in the south and west.

He smoked a pipe and then put a call through to Alice Springs. His mother and father were pleased to hear his voice and see his face again—although not as overjoyed as he thought that they should have been. But they had their own interests, he thought, and he had long since ceased to be one of them.

"When are you coming out?" his father asked.

"As soon as I've got various pieces of business tidied up here. Things, quite suddenly, seem to have become a little complicated."

Grimes senior laughed. "I've always thought that you were a sort of catalyst. Things happen around you. But come as soon as you can."

"I will," promised Grimes.

His mother's face replaced that of his father on the screen. She had changed very little; slim, rather horse-faced women keep their looks far more successfully than do their more conventionally pretty sisters. She reminded him, fleetingly, of Shirl and Darleen. . . . (But surely she had no kangaroos in *her* ancestry. . . .)

"We'll be waiting for you, John," she said. "I'll see to it that we have a good stock of gin and a bottle of Angostura bitters."

"And ice," he said.

"And ice. Don't keep us waiting too long—otherwise the ice will melt."

"Or I'll drink all the gin," said his father, back on the screen.

"I'll have to hang up now," Grimes said. "I've things to see to. Look after yourselves."

"Listen to who's talking," his mother said.

Fifteen

The next morning discharge of *Sister Sue*'s cargo commenced under the supervision, from the shore end, of a bored Lieutenant Commander (S) and, aboard the ship, an increasingly exasperated Billy Williams.

"Damn it all, Skipper," he complained to Grimes, "did you ever see such a shower of nongs? Stowbots that Noah must have used to load the fodder for the animals aboard the Ark and brassbound petty officers running them who wouldn't be capable of navigating a wheelbarrow across a cow paddock! I'm not surprised that you resigned from the Survey Service if this is a fair sampling of their personnel!"

"That will do, Mr. Williams," said Grimes coldly.

He looked out from the cargo port and saw the ground car wearing a Rear Admiral's broad pennant approaching the ship. So here, he thought, was Damien coming to ask him if he had made his mind up yet.

He went down to the after airlock to receive his visitor, stood waiting at the head of the ramp. Damien extricated himself from his vehicle, came briskly up the gangway. Grimes saluted him while Kate Connellan, who was just happening by, sneered. The admiral glared at the second mate, then allowed Grimes to usher him into the elevator cage. They were carried swiftly up to the master's quarters.

In the sitting room Damien, as though by right, seated himself behind the desk. Grimes looked at him resentfully, then took a chair facing the man who had once been his immediate boss. *He needs something to rest his elbows on,* thought Grimes, *so that he can make a really good production of steepling his fingers. . . .* Damien did just that and regarded *Sister Sue*'s captain over the digital spire.

He said—and it was as much statement as question—"You have accepted the charter to El Dorado."

"Yes, sir. Conditionally."

"And your conditions?"

"My promotion to captain if I reenter the Survey Service."

"That has been approved. You are now Captain John Grimes, Federation Survey Service Reserve. The necessary documentation should be aboard shortly."

"I haven't finished yet, sir. I have a particularly awkward second officer and I'd like to get shot of her."

"That young lady in the airlock? A Donegalan, isn't she?"

"Yes. She's got the Guild on her side and I'll be involved in wrongful dismissal suit if I empty her out."

"Then you don't empty her out, Grimes. It is essential that you lift on time for El Dorado."

"Mphm. Well, I was hoping to pick up a third mate here. That would improve matters. At the moment the Green Hornet is fifty percent of my control-room staff. But the Guild doesn't seem to be in a mood to help me. . . ."

"I wonder why not," said Damien sardonically. "You know, of course, that all telephone calls made out from the Naval Station are monitored? No? Well, you know now. But not to worry, Grimes. I have already made arrangements for additional personnel for you. A Mr. Venner, who holds the rank of a Reserve Lieutenant Commander, will be applying to you for employment. He is a Guild member, of course, so there should be no difficulties. You will also be carrying a passenger—although actually he will be under your orders. If merchant vessels still carried psionic communications officers he would be on your books—but if you signed him on as PCO it would look suspicious."

"A PCO, sir?"

"Yes. A Mr. Mayhew. Or Lieutenant Commander Mayhew."

"Mphm. And I suppose that your Lieutenant Commander Venner has some skills not usually possessed by the average merchant officer."

"He has, Grimes. His specialty is unarmed combat—and combat using any and all material to hand, however unlikely, as a weapon."

"I remember one instructor, when I did a course," said Grimes, "who demonstrated on a lifelike dummy the amount of damage you can do with a pipe. . . ."

"Iron pipe? Lead pipe?"

"No, sir. This sort of pipe," said Grimes, filling and lighting his.

"By asphyxiation?" asked Damien.

"No." Grimes made a stabbing gesture. "Used as a dagger."

"A poisoned dagger at that. Tell me, what arms do you carry aboard this ship?"

"A Minetti projectile pistol. Two hand lasers. That's all."

"And that's all that there will be. *Sister Sue* is not a warship."

"But, now, commanded by a Survey Service Reserve officer and with two other Survey Service officers on board."

"Agreed. But you must be wondering, Grimes, just what all this is about."

"Too right, sir."

"You've been to El Dorado, haven't you? You know the sort of people who live there. The filthy rich. You may have noticed that no matter how rich such people are they always want to be richer. And, too, there's the lust for power. Your old friend Drongo Kane is in many ways a typical El Doradan, although he was granted citizenship only recently. Before he became an El Doradan he attempted to take over an entire planet, Morrowvia. You were able to shove a spanner into his works. He tried again, on the same world, some years later. Again you were on hand, as master of the Baroness d'Estang's spaceyacht. The Baroness, an El Doradan, was well aware of Kane's criminality. Nonetheless she married him. . . ."

"I think that she rather regrets it now."

"Does she? Oh, she got you out of a nasty mess on New Venusberg rather against her ever-loving husband's wishes, but that doesn't mean that a marriage dissolution is imminent.

"Well, we have learned that he has interested his El Doradan fellow citizens in another scheme of his, an ambitious one although not involving territorial acquisition. As you may know, El Dorado now has a navy. . . ."

"One ship," said Grimes. "An auxiliary cruiser, usually employed as a cruise liner, with Commodore Baron Kane as the captain."

"Correct. But El Dorado, through Kane, has been chartering sundry obsolescent tonnage and not so obsolescent weaponry."

"And upon whom is El Dorado going to declare war?"

"Nobody. But, as you know, there are always brushfire wars going on somewhere in the galaxy. Recently the Duchy of Waldegren put down a breakaway attempt by one of its colonies. The Shaara Galactic Hive has done the same, more than once. In such cases the rebel colonists have been outgunned and easily beaten. But suppose such rebels had been able to employ a mercenary navy?"

"Mercenaries like to be paid," said Grimes. "Mercenaries with warships expect much higher pay than do, say, infantrymen."

"Agreed. Now, just suppose that you're the king or president or whatever of some world that's decided to break away from whichever empire it's supposed to belong. Your imperial masters take action against you. Your trade routes are raided, your merchant ships destroyed or captured. And then somebody presents himself at your palace, cap in hand, offering his services. At a price. It's a price that you can't afford to pay, especially since the salesman makes it quite clear that he's not interested in the paper money that's being churned out by your printing presses. But he makes a proposition. He offers his services free. Free to *you,* that is. All that you have to do is to issue Letters of Marque to his ships, which then become privateers. As such they raid the imperial trade routes, capturing rather than destroying. Your own navy, such as it is, is then free to deal with the imperial navy while the privateers make their fortunes harrying the merchantmen."

"Mphm."

"Now I'm demoting you, Grimes. You're no longer this rebel king or prince or duke. You're just the owner/master of a scruffy star tramp, delivering a cargo to El Dorado and not knowing where the next cargo is coming from. Or going to. You know people on El Dorado. You know Kane. He knows you. It may surprise you to learn that he has quite a high opinion of you. Or a low opinion. He's been heard to say, 'They call *me* a pirate—but that bloody Grimes could give me points and a beating if he really set his mind to it!'" He laughed. "And he could be right!"

"I'm flattered," said Grimes, making it plain that he was not.

"I thought that you would be," said Damien. "And I don't mind telling you that Kane's opinion of yourself coincides with mine."

"Thank you. Sir." Grimes scowled even more heavily. "So the idea is that I join Kane's ragamuffin navy and then, somehow, switch sides."

"More or less, although I don't visualize any overt side switching. Hopefully you will contrive an incident, do something that will give us, the Federation Survey Service, an excuse to clamp down on the privateers. As you are aware, no doubt, the dividing line between privateer and pirate has always been a very thin one. You will, as instructed, break that line. You should be able to do so without any loss of life or injuries on either side, without, even, any serious damage to property—but you will commit an act of piracy. A suitable vessel to become the victim of your depredations has already been selected. She will, of course, carry a PCO who will, of course, be in telepathic touch with your Mr. Mayhew."

"Very ingenious, sir," said Grimes without enthusiasm. "And I suppose that I shall be secretly under Survey Service orders, as will be Mr. Venner and Mr. Mayhew. But what about the rest of my crew? Two refugees from an old men's home. University professors and glorified garage hands for engineers. I can't see any of them taking kindly to a career of piracy."

"Privateering, Grimes, privateering. And you'd be surprised—or would you?—at what people will do when the money is big enough. And they'll think that there's no risk involved, that it will just be a matter of capturing unarmed vessels."

"When a state of war exists, sir, merchant vessels are usually defensively armed."

"You needn't tell your people that."

"The real spacemen will know without my telling them. And Billy Williams, my chief officer, was in the Dog Star Line—and *they* have always made a practice of arming their ships when they're running through trouble zones."

"So much the better. It will mean that you'll have three reasonably competent gunnery officers aboard *Sister Sue*—yourself, Williams and Venner."

"You're forgetting one thing, sir."

"And what's that, Grimes?"

"I have a conscience. I don't mind hiring myself out as a mercenary but I like to be able to approve of my employers."

"Until this mess has been cleaned up, Grimes, *we,* the Federation Survey Service, are your real employers."

"There have been times, Admiral Damien, when I have not approved of the Survey Service."

"You do not surprise me. Many times I strongly suspected that. Nonetheless, you have never approved of Kane. This will be your chance to pay off old scores."

And that, thought Grimes, was one quite good reason for accepting the assignment. Another reason was the prospect of making an honest, or a dishonest, profit. And—although he would never admit this to Damien—the Survey Service had been his life for so long that the prospect of returning to it, even as only a temporary reservist, was almost like coming home.

Sixteen

Although the discharge of *Sister Sue*'s inward cargo had been only two days' work, with no overtime involved, there was a delay of over a week before her loading for El Dorado could be started. Grimes took advantage of this respite to fly to Alice Springs to visit his parents. Williams could be trusted to look after things during the captain's absence and Damien had raised no objections. (Grimes wondered if legally the Rear Admiral could have done so but deemed it polite to ask his permission before leaving Port Woomera.)

The city of Alice Springs had changed little since Grimes' last time there. There were, he thought as the dirigible made its approach from the south and he looked out and down through the promenade deck windows, a few more white domes in the residential districts, an increase of the market garden acreage, vividly green in the desert, crisscrossed by shining irrigation canals. There seemed to have been a proliferation of the gray yet scintillant solar power collection screens.

His father and mother were waiting for him in the lounge at the base of the mooring mast. His maternal parent had changed very little; she was still tall and straight and slim, still with gleaming auburn hair that owed little to artifice. But his father had aged, more so than had been apparent in the small screen of the telephone when Grimes had called from Port Woomera. He, too, was tall but stooped and his abundant hair was white. His face was heavily lined. Yet the old boy, thought Grimes, looked prosperous enough. His historical romances must be paying him well.

They boarded the family electric runabout and drove to the Grimes home on the outskirts of the city, Matilda Grimes at the controls while the two men sat and talked in the back. His parents, Grimes discovered, had moved to a much larger house, one surrounded by a lush, sprinkler-fed garden. When the car stopped, a housebot of the latest model emerged to handle the baggage and contrived somehow to register disapproval of the single, small, battered case brought by the guest. *Another uppity robot,* thought Grimes, but said nothing.

Finally the three humans disposed themselves in the comfortably furnished sitting room, sipping the fragrant tea that Mrs. Grimes had made personally.

"There are some things," she said, "that robots just can't do properly." Her son agreed with her.

Afternoon tea gave way to pre-dinner drinks as the colors of the garden, seen through the wide picture window, dimmed and darkened in the fast gathering twilight. But not every plant faded into near invisibility. Grimes was pleased to see that the Mudooran sparkle bush that, as little more than a seedling, he had brought to his parents as a gift had not only survived but flourished, was now a small tree decorated with starlike blossoms, softly self-luminous, multicolored.

His mother saw what he was looking at.

She said, "We have always loved that bush, John. We've told ourselves that as it survived in what, to it, is an alien environment so you would survive. And, like it, you have not only survived but done well. A captain *and* a shipowner." She frowned slightly. "But I still wish that you could have become a captain in the Survey Service."

Grimes laughed. "So you still think that your illustrious ancestor. . . ."

"And yours!" she snapped.

". . . would not have approved of my career. You'd have liked to have seen me become Admiral Lord Grimes, just as he became Admiral Lord Hornblower. But unless I emigrate to the Empire of Waverley I'll never become a lord. Not that I can imagine King James elevating me to the peerage."

"But John *was* a captain in the Survey Service," said the elder Grimes.

"At times," his wife told him, "you display an appalling ignorance of naval matters, inexcusable in one who is not only an historical novelist but who prides himself on the thoroughness of his research. John was captain of a Serpent Class courier—but his actual rank was only lieutenant. He was captain of bigger ships—first as a lieutenant commander, then as commander. But he never wore the four gold rings on his sleeve."

George Whitley Grimes laughed. "Anybody who is in command is a captain, no matter what he does or does not wear. What do you say, John?"

"I'm a captain," said Grimes. "I'm called that."

"But a *merchant* captain," said his mother. "It's only a courtesy title. And the uniform you wear is only company's livery."

"But *my* company," Grimes told her. "Far Traveler Couriers. And what Survey Service captain owns the ship that he commands or wears uniform trimmings of his own design?"

"But you still aren't a Survey Service captain," said his mother stubbornly.

But I am, my dearest Matilda, he thought. *I'm Captain John Grimes, Federation Survey Service Reserve. It's a pity that I can't tell you.*

* * *

Later during his stay Grimes talked with his father about the old-time privateers, trying to draw upon the old man's fund of historical knowledge.

"Perhaps the most famous, or notorious," said the author, was Captain Kidd, although most people think that he was a pirate. He was tried as such, found guilty and hanged. For murder as well as piracy. During a heated altercation with his gunner, one William Moore, he broke that officer's skull with a wooden bucket."

"I murdered William Moore as I sailed," sang Grimes tunelessly.

"I murdered William Moore as I sailed,
I knocked him on the head
Till he bled the scuppers red
And I heaved him with the lead
As I sailed. . . ."

"So you know something of the story," said Grimes' father.

"Yes. But carry on, George."

"Kidd was commissioned as a privateer. He was authorized both to seize French vessels—at that time England was at war with France, a very common state of affairs—and to hunt down pirates. It was alleged that he joined forces with these same pirates and accumulated a huge treasure, which. to this day, has not been found. . . ."

"If you can't lick 'em, join 'em," said Grimes.

"Not a very moral attitude, young man. But it seems possible, probable even, that Kidd was framed. There were some very dirty politics involved. The Governor of New York, then a British colony, had his reasons for wishing Kidd silenced. Permanently."

"Mphm," grunted Grimes. What dirty politics would he be getting mixed up in, he wondered.

"And then," his father continued, "there was the literary buccaneer, Dampier. He was one of the first Europeans to reach Australia. He made his landings on the west coast and was impressed neither by the country nor its inhabitants. He actually started his seafaring career as a pirate but somehow acquired a veneer of respectability. He was actually appointed by the British Admiralty to command one of their ships on a voyage of exploration. After that he sailed as a privateer, making two voyages. On the second one he hit it rich. . . ."

"So there was money in privateering," said Grimes.

"Of course. Why else should a group of merchants buy a ship and fit her out and man her as what was, in effect, a privately owned man-o'-war? But the days of the privateer, on Earth's seas, were finished by the Second Hague Conference in 1907, Old Reckoning. Then it was ruled that a warship must be a unit of a national navy."

"You've been swotting this up," accused Grimes.

"As a matter of fact, I have. I'm working on an If Of History novel. About the Australian War of Independence, which started with the Massacre at Glenrowan, when the Kelly Gang slaughtered all the police aboard the special train. In actual history, of course, the special train was not derailed—the Glenrowan schoolteacher, Curnow, flagged it down before it got to the torn-up track—and it was the Kelly Gang that was wiped out. . . ."

"I know, I know. And Ned Kelly is supposed to have been a freedom fighter. But he was a bushranger, not a privateer."

"Let me finish, John. Among the characters in my novel is a millionaire American shipowner who's very anti-British. And he has two of his ships fitted out as privateers to harry Pommy merchantmen."

"Cor stone my Aunt Fanny up a gum tree!" exclaimed Grimes. "The things you come up with! I'd just hate to be a character in one of your books!"

"I still think that the Australian War of Independence was a possibility," said the writer. "And, back in 1880, privateering was still legal. Anyhow, I got interested in the subject and carried on with more research. As far as I can gather, the 1907 Hague Conference ruling still holds good—but possibly only insofar as the Federated Worlds are concerned. It could be argued that any planet not in the Interstellar Federation can make its own rules. On the other hand, I have learned that the Federation's Interstellar Navigation Regulations are observed by just about everybody."

"I could have told you that," said Grimes. "They're taken as a model by all spacefaring races. But, getting back to the subject of privateering, there have been astronautical precedents. The notorious Black Bart, for example. He—like Captain Kidd—is widely regarded as having been a pirate. But he always maintained that he was a privateer. His planetary base was within the sphere of influence of the Duchy of Waldegren. The Duchy tolerated him, as long as he paid the taxes. They tolerated and, at times, used him. They weren't very fussy about whom they employed—they still aren't—any more than Black Bart was fussy about who employed him."

"Why all this interest in privateering, John?" asked his father.

"Oh, well, I guess that it's an interesting topic."

"You aren't thinking of going privateering?" asked the old man sharply.

"Who? *Me?"* countered Grimes.

"I wouldn't put it past you. But if you do, don't let your mother know. It's bad enough that you never got to be a four-ring captain in the Survey Service, but if you become a privateer she'd tell you never to darken her door again."

And what if I became both? Grimes asked himself.

But he said nothing.

Seventeen

Grimes returned to Port Woomera; Billy Williams had telephoned to say that Rear Admiral Damien required his presence aboard *Sister Sue.* Grimes' father overheard some of the conversation.

He asked, a little suspiciously, "Why should an admiral be wanting you, John? You're a civilian shipmaster, aren't you?"

Grimes thought hard and fast, then said, "At the moment the ship is berthed in the Survey Service area of the spaceport. I will have to shift her to one of the commercial berths to load my outward cargo." (He probably would have to do just that but it would not be for a few days yet.)

He made his booking. His parents came to the airport to see him off.

"Look after yourself, John," his mother told him. "And try not to make it so long between visits."

"I'll try," he promised.

"And try to stay inside the law," said his father.

How much did the old man suspect? The author, Grimes well knew, at times had telepathic flashes and, more than once, while Grimes was still a schoolboy, had seemed to be able almost to read his mind. And there were others possessing psychic talents. Magda Granadu was one such.

She came to see Grimes as soon as he was back in his quarters aboard *Sister Sue.*

"Captain," she demanded, "what is happening?"

"We shall be carrying a cargo of luxury goods to El Dorado. That's common knowledge."

"But I feel uneasy. It's not the first time that I've had such premonitions."

"It must be the time of the month," said Grimes.

She flushed angrily and snapped, "It is not!"

"Sorry."

"I've brought the book," she said. "And the coins."

"Oh, all right," said Grimes. It would do no harm to humor the woman.

He took from her the three metal discs, shook them in his cupped hands, let them drop to the deck of his day cabin.

Two heads and a tail . . . *Yang.* Then another *yang.* And another. Then two tails and a head . . . *Yin. Yang* again, then a final *yin.*

"Well?" he demanded.

She consulted the book.

"Hsu," she murmured. "Biding one's time. Sincerity will lead to brilliant success. Firmness will bring good fortune. It will be advantageous to cross the great water."

"And what the hell's wrong with that?" asked Grimes.

"I haven't finished yet, Captain. Here's the commentary. Peril lies ahead, but despite the urge toward activity which is shown, he will not allow himself to be involved in a dangerous situation. Firm persistence in a right course of action will ensure great success. But strength and determination are needed to make the most of the progressive trends now operating. It is an auspicious time to commence a major undertaking. The strong man's inclination when faced with danger is to advance on it and combat it without delay; but here one would be wise to wait until success is assured."

Grimes laughed. "And what's wrong with that for a prognostication?" he asked. "It's an excellent weather forecast before the start of a voyage."

"But it counsels caution. It talks of danger."

"If we were afraid of danger, Ms. Granadu, we should not be spacers."

"My own reading," she said, "was much more ominous. It was *Po.* It will not be advantageous for me to make a move in any direction. The forces operating against me will be too great for me to prevail against them. I have to wait for a change for the better."

"And do you want to wait here, on Earth? I can pay you off, you know, although you should have given me more notice. But I don't want to lose you; you're a good catering officer and a very good shipmate."

"And I don't want to leave this ship, Captain. We shall just have to heed the warnings and be very, very careful."

You can say that again, thought Grimes. If all went as planned, he would find himself dealing with Drongo Kane—and he who sups with the devil needs a long spoon.

His door buzzer sounded.

"Come in," he called.

Damien was there, in uniform, and with him were two youngish men in civilian shirts and slacks. One of them was short, stocky, with close-cropped sandy hair over a broad, craggy face, with little, very pale blue eyes under almost nonexistent brows. The other was tall, weedy almost, with fair hair that was more than a little too long, with sensitive features just short of being effeminate and eyes that seemed to vary in color.

"Here is your new third officer, Captain Grimes," said Damien. "Mr. Venner."

The short man bowed slightly and then took the hand that Grimes extended to him. His grip was firm and, Grimes knew, would have been painful had full strength been exerted.

"And this is Mr. Mayhew, an old friend of mine. . . ."

Like hell I am! the words formed themselves in Grimes' mind. He looked at Mayhew suspiciously. "He asked me if I could arrange passage for him to El Dorado and beyond. He's spending his Long Service Leave traveling. . . ."

"And what's your line of business, Mr. Mayhew?" asked Grimes, genuinely curious as to what the cover story would be.

"Senior clerk, Captain, with Pargeter and Crummins, Importers. You may have heard of them."

Grimes hadn't—yet this Mayhew was suddenly looking like a senior clerk, like a man who had spent all his working life at a desk. Nobody would take him for a spaceman—nobody, that is, who was seeing the telepath as he wished to be seen.

"Magda," said Grimes, "will you see to it that the third officer's cabin is ready? And one of the spare rooms for Mr. Mayhew."

"Very good, sir."

She left.

When the door had closed after her, Mayhew's appearance underwent another subtle transformation. Now he looked like what he, in actuality, was—a Survey Service officer in one of that organization's specialist branches, a typical commissioned teacup reader. . . .

"I have often wished," said Mayhew, "that I could meet the man who first called us that."

"Probably an engineer," said Grimes.

"But *you* thought it, Captain. Just now."

"Don't bother to say that you're sorry, Captain Grimes," said Damien. "He'll know that you're lying."

"If he does," Grimes said, he'll be doing so in gross contravention of the Rhine Institute's code of ethics."

Mayhew smiled. It was a likeable smile. He said, "There are some minds, Captain Grimes, into which I would no sooner probe than dive into a cesspit. Yours, sir, is not one of them."

"Thank you," said Grimes. "But I'll be greatly obliged if you don't make a habit of invading my mental privacy."

"Mr. Mayhew will be doing his job, Captain," said Damien. "I have no doubt that you will find his services extremely valuable. And Mr. Venner's. But I'll give you fair warning. Don't ever play cards with him."

This appeared to be some kind of private joke.

Grimes asked, "Does he cheat? Or is he just abnormally lucky?"

Venner grinned while Damien said, "Neither. You're the one who's notorious for having luck." He laughed. "Just stay that way."

"I hope I do," said Grimes. "But some famous privateers, such as Captain Kidd, weren't so lucky."

"Captain Morgan was," said Damien.

"Sir Henry Morgan," Grimes said, "wasn't a privateer. He was a pirate."

"What's the difference?" asked Damien.

Grimes sighed. It was all very well for the Rear Admiral to adopt such a could-hardly-care-less attitude. If things should go badly wrong it would not be he who would be left holding the baby.

Eighteen

Sister Sue lifted from Port Woomera.

She had a full loading of commodities that even on their planet of origin were expensive, some of them hellishly so. Freight charges would make them even more costly. Beluga caviar, champagne, truffles, paté de foie gras. . . . Guiness Stout from Ireland, cheeses from Holland, France, Switzerland and Italy. . . . Whiskies from Scotland, Ireland, North America and Japan. . . . Salami sausages—Italian, Polish and Hungarian. . . . Smoked salmon, vintage sardines, anchovies, olives. . . .

To sit on top of such a cargo for a voyage of weeks' duration, thought Grimes, would be to suffer the tortures of Tantalus. (He had not been nick-named Gutsy Grimes for nothing.) In a ship with an uninspired catering officer and an ailing autochef the temptation to pilfer cargo would have been well nigh irresistible. Luckily *Sister Sue* was not in that class.

The lift-off was uneventful.

Venner, the new third officer, was obviously an experienced spaceman. Kate Connellan was slightly less surly than usual; she must, thought Grimes, have been able to blow off steam in some way during the ship's stay in port. Williams was cheerfully competent. Old Mr. Stewart, manning the control-room NST transceiver, knew the drill. (At his age he should have.)

Mayhew occupied one of the spare seats, a privilege now and again accorded to passengers. He had assumed his senior-clerk-on-vacation persona and was asking stupid questions as part of his cover.

The ship drove up into the clear sky, her inertial drive thudding healthily. The altimeter readings displayed in the sternview screen shifted from meters to kilometers, mounted steadily. The picture of the spaceport diminished, faster and faster, became no more than white and silver specks on the ruddy desert. More desert, but with great green squares of artificial irrigation, came into view to the north while to the south were the dark waters of the Great Australian Bight. The horizon acquired curvature. Grimes looked out through the viewports. He thought that he could distinguish in the distance, the city of Alice

Springs. In the opposite direction he could see the white glimmer of the Antarctic Ice Barrier.

Sister Sue was in space, clear of the atmosphere, plunging through the Van Allens. It was almost time to set trajectory.

The inertial drive was shut down; the ship had built enough velocity for her to continue to fall outward. The big directional gyroscopes turned her about her axes until the target star was lined up directly ahead. There was a small adjustment for galactic drift.

Grimes actuated the Mannschenn Drive.

There were the usual eerie effects as the temporal precession field built up—but, in Grimes' case, with a difference. He did not see anything but he heard a voice. His? It could have been, although it was not tuneless enough. It was singing the old song, The Ballad of Captain Kidd, with which he had afflicted his father's ears during that talk about privateers.

I murdered William Moore as I sailed, as I sailed,
I murdered William Moore as I sailed,
I knocked him on the head
Till he bled the scuppers red
And I heaved him with the lead
As I sailed. . . .

The voice faded to a whisper as inside the control room colors returned to normal and the warped perspective straightened itself out. The only sound was the thin, high whine of the ever-precessing rotors of the interstellar drive. Grimes restarted the inertial drive machinery and again there were *up* and *down* and the sensation of weight engendered by the steady acceleration.

He realized that Mayhew was looking at him. An ironical smile quirked the telepath's lips.

See you on Execution Dock, Captain. . . .

The words formed themselves in Grimes' mind.

He glared at Mayhew and thought, willing himself to transmit, *Very funny. Very bloody funny.*

Mayhew grinned.

After watches had been set Grimes invited Mayhew down to his cabin for a drink.

Before either man could set glass to lip he demanded, "What did *you* see, Mr. Mayhew? What did *you* hear?"

"What you did, Captain. Oh, I wasn't snooping. I wasn't trying to get inside your mind. But you were . . . broadcasting so strongly that I couldn't help picking up the words of that song. If it's any comfort to you I've looked through your crew list and there aren't any William Moores."

"There could be," said Grimes, "at some future date. But I hope not."

Mayhew sipped his gin then said, "I'm assuming, sir, that you wish me to function as a PCO does aboard a Federation Survey Service warship."

"I suppose that that's one of the reasons why Admiral Damien seconded you to me. But snooping is part of a PCO's duties of which I've never approved. Especially when it's against my own crew, my own shipmates."

"If you hadn't been so squeamish, sir, the *Discovery* mutiny might never have happened."

"You could be right, Mr. Mayhew. Mphm. But I still wish you to adhere to the Rhine Institute's Code of Ethics, at least insofar as this ship is concerned."

"If you insist, Captain."

"And as for your real duties, Mr. Mayhew, how is it that you don't have a psionic amplifier with you? I've never liked those naked dogs' brains in their tanks of nutrient fluid but I know that you can't function without them, not over any great range, that is."

Mayhew smiled. "It would hardly do for a mere passenger, a chief clerk blowing his life's savings on an interstellar voyage, to have such a pet. But I do have a psionic amplifier." He tapped his forehead with a long index finger. "Here. You know, of course, that there are such things as telepathic robots. There aren't many of them, mainly because they're so fantastically expensive. And the tiny piece of miniaturized circuitry that I now carry was more expensive still. And it has a limited life."

"Will it last until such time as you have to get in touch with your colleague aboard the . . . incident ship?"

"I hope so." Mayhew held out his empty glass. Grimes refilled it, topped up his own. "I hope so."

"Now, Mr. Mayhew," said Grimes, "I'm going to break one of my own rules. Your mention of the *Discovery* mutiny is why. I'm going to ask you what you, as a professional telepath, think of this ship, of her people."

For what seemed a long time Mayhew said nothing, sipping his drink thoughtfully.

Then he murmured, "You've a good second in command, sir. He's one of those men who must have a leader to whom to be loyal—and now you're it. But he's loyal, too, to his principles. Never forget that.

"Your second officer. The Green Hornet. She's a vicious bitch. Her only loyalty is to herself. Watch her.

"Your third, Venner, I know him personally. He's not really a Reservist, you know. That's just part of his cover. Oh, he ships out as a merchant spaceman, just as he has with you, but he's really employed, full time, by the Intelligence Branch of the Survey Service. As a hit man. His loyalties are to his real employers, not to you. If he were ordered to terminate you with extreme prejudice he would do just that."

"I'd guessed as much," said Grimes.

"And now, your catering officer," went on Mayhew. "In her you have a gem. Like Williams, she's loyal. And—this could be of real value—she has the power."

"What power?"

"Prevision. Some of her kind use cards, either ordinary playing cards or the Tarot pack. Some read teacups. Some look into crystal balls. Oh, as you know, there are all sorts of lenses that can be used to focus attention on the future, on to the most probable of an infinitude of possible futures. She uses the *1 Ching."*

"I know. She threw the coins for herself before this voyage started. She told me about it. Something about it's not being advantageous to make a move in any direction. And small men multiplying and having far too much to say for themselves. And the only course of action being just to ride it out and to hope for better times. . . ."

Mayhew laughed. "And it's true—but in a funny, quite trivial way. She's a good catering officer but the way that she programs the autochef the meals are too fancy for some of the juniors. And every time that she tried to turn out something plain it's . . . uninspired. For example. . . ." He frowned in concentration and said, "I'm snooping, Captain. With your permission, I hope. Two of your junior engineers are wondering what they're going to get for lunch. One of them has just said to the other, 'I suppose that the Romany Queen will be giving us more of her foreign, mucked-up tucker!' And the other replied, 'I must have lost at least ten kilograms since I joined this bloody ship!'"

"If that's who I think it is," growled Grimes, "he's as fat as a pig. And getting fatter."

"It could be glandular," said Mayhew.

"Once you've seen him eating you'll not think that."

"And now he's saying, 'Of course, she's the Old Man's pet. . . .'"

"Enough," said Grimes. "Enough. Carry on with the rundown, please."

"All right, sir. Listeners seldom hear good of themselves, do they? Now, old Mr. Stewart. My electronic rival. As long as he has his toys to play with, he's happy. He'd be radio officer for anybody, in any ship in any service, and ask no questions. If Sir Henry Morgan had been blessed with radio your Mr. Stewart would have been as content in his ship as he is here, just sending and receiving as ordered.

"The other old-timer, Mr. Crumley, your inertial/reaction chief. . . . A rather similar type to Stewart. A ship, any ship on any trade, is no more than a platform on which his precious engines are mounted.

"Now, his juniors. Denning, Singh and Paulus. They're all little men. Not physically little necessarily—but *little.* They resent having to take orders—yours, their chief's, anybody's. They hate having to wear a uniform and mutter about your Survey Service bullshit. But I don't think you'll have any trouble with them on El Dorado when—if?—Drongo Kane recruits you and the ship for his privateer navy. Privateering can be a very lucrative business and, when the victims are unarmed merchantmen, almost without risk.

"Malleson, your Mannschenn Drive king . . . Similar to Crumley and Stewart but—he kids himself—on a far higher plane. He's a master mathematician whereas the other two are mere mechanics. He likes money, so he'll not object to privateering. His loyalty? Essentially only to that weird, time-twisting contraption in the Mannschenn Drive room.

"Trantor and Giddings. . . . Little men again, hating authority, intellectual snobs who look down on rough, half-educated spacemen such as yourself. And Malleson they regard as an old has-been. But for all their intellectual veneer they're out of the same barrel as Denning, Singh and Paulus.

"All in all, Captain, not the best of crews to go privateering with."

Grimes laughed. "Competence at their jobs is all I can ask. As for their characters—well, the average privateersman must have been actuated by greed rather than by patriotism. But Billy Williams and Magda. . . . *They* have principles. . . ."

"As you do. You'll just have to convince them that we shall be fighting on the right side."

"I shall have to convince myself as well."

"No. You, sir, will just be taking orders—as Venner and myself will be. You're an officer of the Reserve recalled to active duty. You should have thought of all the implications when you accepted that commission."

"It seemed a good idea at the time," said Grimes.

Nineteen

The voyage from Austral to Earth had been a short one, barely long enough for *Sister Sue*'s people to get to know the ship and each other. That from Earth to El Dorado occupied all of two standard months. Dislikes that had been engendered on that initial trip now had ample time to develop, to fester. Grimes did not need Mayhew's psionic snooping to make him aware of the lack of harmony. Continually, it seemed, there was somebody at his door to complain about somebody else. The Green Hornet was a frequent visitor. According to her everybody aboard the ship was a male chauvinist pig, with the obvious exception of Magda Granadu. She was even more contemptible; she had sold out to the enemy, was a traitor to her sex. Then there were the inertial/reaction drive juniors with their never-ending whinges about the food, and the Mannschenn Drive juniors to lay complaint about the table manners, in the duty engineers' mess, of those whom they despised as mere mechanics. There were squabbles all the time about what programs should be shown on the playmaster. Even Williams—and it took a lot to ruffle him—said his piece. He practically demanded that Kate Connellan be paid off on El Dorado.

"I'd like to do it, Billy," said Grimes. "By all the Odd Gods of the Galaxy I'd like to do it! But she's a Guild member, just as you and I and Mr. Venner are. Unless she does something justifying instant dismissal we're stuck with her. Even then, I doubt if the El Doradans would allow us to turn her loose on their precious planet. They're very fussy."

"You've been there, Skipper, haven't you?"

"Yes. Once, years ago. When I was a very junior lieutenant in the cruiser *Aries.* The El Doradans were polite enough but they made it quite plain that we, from the Old Man down, were no more than snotty-nosed kids from the wrong side of the tracks. . . ."

That wasn't quite true, thought Grimes, remembering. The old Duchess of Leckhampton had been kind enough to him—and the Princess Marlene von Stolzberg rather more than kind. But they had used him, nonetheless. Still, he had been told that he could return to El Dorado to become a citizen once he had made his first billion credits. . . . The two main requirements for citizenship were noble ancestry and money—and of them money was by far the more important. Titles can be purchased. Grimes wondered how much Drongo Kane, Commodore Baron Kane, had paid for his. . . .

"But you're a shipowner, now, Skipper," said Williams, "not a mere hairy-arsed spaceman."

"But I'm not a *rich* shipowner, Billy. . . ."

And Drongo Kane, of course, was a rich shipowner. And, being Drongo Kane, wanted to be richer still.

"What's El Dorado *like,* Skipper?"

"It's a garden world, Billy. Huge estates, with mansions and even castles. At least one of those castles was shipped, stone by stone, from Earth. Schloss Stolzberg. I was a guest there."

"And who was your host? Some crusty old Prussian baron?"

"No. As a matter of fact it was a very charming princess."

"And yet you say that you were treated like a snotty-nosed kid from the wrong side of the tracks?"

"No. Not *treated* like. After all, aristocrats have very good manners when they care to exercise them. *Regarded as* would be a better way of putting it. And we were welcome only because they wanted something from us. Once they got it, it was on your bicycle, spaceman!"

The telephone on Grimes' desk buzzed sharply.

"Yes?" he demanded.

Keyed to his voice the screen came alive. Looking out from it was Magda Granadu. She was pale, her expression worried.

"Captain, can you come down to the general room? There's trouble. A fight. . . ."

"Who's involved?"

"Mr. Venner and two of the engineers. It's two of them, the engineers, against one. . . ."

"We'll be right down," said Grimes.

Williams followed him out into the circular alleyway around the axial shaft. As usual, when there was any hurry, the lift cage was decks away. It came up at last—but then was reluctant to commence its descent.

The fight was over by the time that they hurried into the general room. Venner was standing there, scowling ferociously. There were the beginnings of a bruise on his right cheek. Also standing were Malleson, the Mannschenn Drive chief, and Giddings, one of his juniors. Not standing were Singh and Paulus. They were sprawled on the deck and making a mess on the carpet. Blood mingled with vomit.

"Captain!" Malleson stepped forward. "That man is dangerous! He should be put under arrest!"

Magda Granadu came back into the general room, overheard what Malleson was saying.

"It was two against one!" she cried. "It was self-defense!"

"But Mr. Venner was fighting to hurt, to kill," stated Malleson.

Venner said, "Why else should one fight?" He turned to Grimes. "I was watching the playmaster, sir. As a matter of fact I had it hooked up to the computer so that I could learn something about El Dorado. Mr. Malleson was watching it too. Mr. Giddings was reading. Then Mr. Singh and Mr. Paulus came in. Mr. Paulus said, 'Who the hell wants this? What about one of those good sex spools we got at Port Woomera?' He switched off the playmaster. I made to switch it back on. Then he struck me."

"Is that true, Mr. Malleson?" asked Grimes.

"Yes, Captain. But it still doesn't justify the savagery of Mr. Venner's counterattack. He used his feet, and the edges of his hands. . . ."

"And why not?" asked Venner. "I do have certain skills. Why should I not use them?"

"A fist fight is a fair fight," insisted Malleson.

"When it's two against one?" asked Venner. "You saw how Singh was taking a swipe at me before I'd finished with Paulus. And what's all this rubbish about fist fighting being somehow manly, even noble? The noble art of self-defense? Why don't you grow up?"

"Mr. Venner!" snapped Grimes.

"Sorry, Captain. But I just don't like being mauled by drunks while I'm quietly minding my own business."

"Were Mr. Singh and Mr. Paulus drunk?" Grimes asked.

"They may have been drinking," admitted Malleson.

Meanwhile Magda, carrying a first-aid box, had come back into the general room, was wiping clean the faces of the two half-conscious engineers, and spraying their cuts and bruises with antiseptic syntheskin.

She said, "I'd like to get these two to the dispensary so that I can look at them properly."

"Will you give me a hand, Mr. Giddings?" asked Williams.

He and the Mannschenn Drive engineer got Paulus to his feet, supported him as he staggered out into the alleyway. After a short while they returned for Singh. Him they had to carry.

"I'll see you in my day cabin," Grimes said to Venner.

"And do you want me, Captain?" asked Malleson. "I was a witness."

"I may want to see you later," Grimes said. Then, to Venner, "Come with me."

* * *

"You realize, Mr. Venner," said Grimes, "that I shall have to make an entry in the Official Log."

"Of course, sir."

"You realize, too, that this could blow up into an inter-union dispute. Mr. Paulus and Mr. Singh are members of the Institute of Interstellar Engineers. They were required to join before they signed Articles at Port Southern. I shan't be at all surprised if they send a Carlottigram to the Institute as soon as they're recovered."

"You seem to be remarkably well versed in industrial matters. Sir."

The man wasn't quite insolent although he was not far from it.

"I've been reading through the industrial files left by my predecessors on this ship," said Grimes. "They had their worries."

"The sort of worries, sir, that need not concern us. We're Survey Service, not civilians."

"As far as this ship is concerned, Mr. Venner, we *are* civilians. We must comport ourselves as such. I am asking you—no, ordering you—to apologize to the engineers. I know that they asked for trouble, and got it, but I don't want to get involved in any legal/industrial hassles after we've set down on El Dorado."

Venner scowled. "All right," he said at last. "I'll apologize. Under protest."

"Just say that you're sorry," advised Grimes, "for having used overmuch force to protect yourself. After all, you did not strike the first blow."

Somebody was hammering on the door. The Green Hornet, thought Grimes. She would be coming off watch now—and she, for some reason, hated to use the buzzer.

"Come in," he called.

She came in. She looked at Grimes coldly, glared at Venner.

"Captain," she almost shouted, "there are times when the Guild must stand by the Institute and this is one of them. I have heard how this man beat up Mr. Singh and Mr. Paulus. I demand that you *do* something about it."

"Mr. Venner is a member of the Guild," pointed out Grimes mildly. "As Mr. Williams is. As I am. Mr. Williams feels, as I feel, that Mr. Venner was merely defending himself from an unprovoked assault."

"There must be a proper inquiry," said Kate Connellan. "There must be punishment, a heavy fine at the very least."

"Yes," Grimes said thoughtfully, "I suppose that I could fine Mr. Paulus for his unprovoked assault on Mr. Venner. . . . Although, possibly, he has been punished enough."

"Are you mad?" she demanded. "It is Venner who should be punished."

"*Mr.* Venner," Grimes corrected her.

"There must be an inquiry," she insisted, "with proper entries in the Official Log."

"There will be log entries," said Grimes at last. He had better make such, he supposed, just to clear his own yardarm, if nobody else's. Neither the Guild nor the Institute would have representation on El Dorado but *Sister Sue,* as a merchant ship, would in the future be visiting worlds on which the Astronautical unions maintained officials. "Get back up to the control room, Ms. Connellan, to relieve Mr. Williams for a few minutes. I shall want him to countersign what I put down."

"But why the mate? I can write, Captain."

"You were not a witness to any of what happened. Mr. Williams was."

"Then I insist that I be allowed to read the entry."

Grimes sighed. "You, Ms. Connellan, as second officer of this vessel, as part of your duties, make all the routine log entries—arrivals, departures, drills, inspections. The log is, therefore, accessible to you at any time. Relieve Mr. Williams, please."

"Aye, aye, Captain, sir!" she replied sardonically and was gone.

Grimes used his telephone to call Malleson, the main witness, and old Crumley, who was the department superior of the two injured junior engineers. He called Magda Granadu, who told him that Mr. Singh had been fit enough to go on watch and that Mr. Paulus was also fit for duty. Grimes asked her to come up with the two senior engineers.

Williams came down from control. He seemed to be amused about something. Malleson, Crumley and Magda arrived shortly afterward. The engineers took seats as far away from the scowling Venner as possible.

Grimes said, "I am making a log entry on these lines. I shall say that in my opinion, Mr. Venner overreacted to the threat against his person. He is prepared to apologize to Mr. Paulus and Mr. Singh for this overreaction. I am stating that Mr. Paulus struck Mr. Venner after a slight argument over the playmaster programing, that Mr. Venner acted in self-defense. Mr. Singh came to the assistance of his friend and was also dealt with by Mr. Venner.

"Is that a fair statement of the facts?"

"Yes, sir," said Venner.

"Two of my engineers were badly injured, Captain," complained Crumley.

"They're fit for duty, aren't they?" demanded Magda.

"Mr. Malleson?" asked Grimes.

"It is, I suppose, a statement of the facts," admitted the Mannschenn Drive chief grudgingly. "But it takes no account of the . . . the. . ."

"Poetic justice of it all," supplied Williams.

"No. The unwarranted savagery exercised by Mr. Venner."

"I have training in the martial arts, Chief," said Venner. "I possess skills—and I use them. My intention was to punish, not to incapacitate."

"That will do, Mr. Venner," said Grimes sharply.

He made the entry in the official log, signed, with a flourish, *John Grimes, Master.* Venner, the engineers and the catering officer left the day cabin. Grimes looked at Williams and asked, "Just why should our female chauvinist bitch be getting her knickers in a twist over the well-deserved misfortunes of mere males, engineers at that?"

Williams grinned.

"Don't you *know,* sir?"

"I'm only the captain," said Grimes. "Nobody tells me anything."

"Our Green Hornet is a woman. Mr. Paulus is a man. Personally, Skipper, I regard an affair between a control-room officer and an engineer as miscegenation. Early in the trip dear Kate tried to indicate to me that she was ready and willing. I wasn't interested. . . ."

"Why not?" asked Grimes interestedly.

Williams flushed, then said, "I'd have thought that that would have been obvious. I've known Magda for a long time. Well, she tried it on with me, then with Mr. Venner. Once again, no dice."

"Oh. One day," said Grimes, "somebody will make a regulation requiring ships with mixed crews to maintain an even balance of the sexes."

"It still wouldn't work," said Williams. "Apart from anything else there're all the in-betweens . . . Like the old joke. The male sex, the female sex, the insex and the Middlesex."

"It's time you got back on watch. But sign the log before you go." Leaving a generous space he printed, in capitals, the word MATE under his own signature. He turned the book around, pushed it toward the chief officer.

Williams signed.

William Moore Williams instead of his more usual *W. M. Williams.*

But he should have known, thought Grimes. He had sighted Williams' Certificate of Competency when Articles had been opened at Port Southern. On it the mate's name was given in full, and had been entered in full in the Articles by the Shipping Master. On the crew list, however, it was *Williams, W. M.* And Mayhew had seen the crew list but not the Articles.

I murdered William Moore as I sailed. . . .

"What's wrong, Skipper?" asked Williams concernedly. "Somebody walking over your grave?"

"No," Grimes said.

Not mine, he thought.

But what about the flash of prevision when he had seen himself, much older, with a much older Williams, the pair of them obvious shipmates?

He went on, "These aboard-ship squabbles always upset me."

"You aren't as upset as those two pig-iron polishers!" Williams laughed.

He went up to the control room to resume his watch.

Twenty

Venner's justifiable beating up of Paulus and Singh was not the only outbreak of physical violence on the ship before her arrival at El Dorado, although it was the most serious one. There was the fight between Paulus and Trantor, no more than an undignified exhibition of inexpert fisticuffs. The reason for it, Grimes discovered, was the transferal of Ms. Connellan's affections from one engineering department to the other. He lectured all those concerned, telling them sternly that even while he did not subscribe to archaic moral codes he was still a strong believer in the old standards of shipboard discipline and good conduct.

Paulus muttered something about Survey Service bullshit.

Grimes said coldly, "I'm inviting you to say that again. Louder, Mr. Paulus—and warning you that if you do I'll throw the book at you. Insolent and contemptuous behavior toward a superior officer will do for a start—and that carries a fine of one hundred credits."

The engineer lapsed into surly silence.

Grimes dismissed the bruised combatants and the glowering Green Hornet. Williams remained with him.

"Billy," asked Grimes, "what am I going to do with that bitch?"

"You could have her fitted with a chastity belt, Skipper," suggested the mate.

"Yes. And a scold's bridle. But would the engineers make them?" He laughed. "Old Mr. Crumley might. I think that he's past it as far as women are concerned."

Williams laughed too. "Could be. But suppose he does make a belt. . . . Who's going to fit it about dear Katie's female form divine? The fat. . . . And that sweaty, greasy, green skin of hers. . . ." He glanced at the bulkhead clock. "But I must ask you to excuse me, Skipper. I promised Magda that I'd lend her a hand thinning out the lettuces on the farm deck."

Grimes felt a stab of envy. The engineers—or some of them—were getting theirs. Williams was getting his. And what did *he* have? A solidograph of a naked woman on one shelf, an animated golden statuette of another naked woman on a ledge on the opposite bulkhead. And both ladies were light-years distant. . . .

He said, "All right, Mr. Williams. Go and do your gardening. The Green Hornet for Second Mate . . . Mr. Greenfingers for Mate. . . ."

And the Captain green with envy?

Williams said, "Magda's promised us that Vietnamese dish for dinner, Skipper. You know. The one where you scoop up the pieces of meat, fish and whatever with lettuce leaves."

"I can hardly wait," said Grimes a little sourly although the meal was one of his favorites. He, in fact, had told the Catering Officer how to prepare, cook and serve it. "Off you go, then."

He buzzed Mayhew, who was in his cabin, asked him to come up for a drink and a talk.

"Well, Mr. Mayhew," asked Grimes after glasses had been filled and sipped, "what do *you* think of this shipload of malcontents? Will they be any good as the crew of a privateer?"

"You told me, sir, that I was not to snoop."

"But even if you aren't snooping you must pick things up, without trying to or wanting to."

"But I am not supposed to pass what I . . . hear on to anybody else." He laughed softly. "All right, all right. I know, and you know, that in the Survey Service the PCO is the captain's ears. It's no secret that we're fast getting to the stage where everybody hates everybody. Well, almost everybody. The honeymoon's not over yet for Mr. Williams and Ms. Granadu—and it's been going on for quite a while. Ms. Connellan? She despises the men she uses, just as they despise her. Oh, I know that she kicked up a song and dance when Mr. Venner made a mess of Mr. Paulus—but that was only because she resented having *her* property damaged by somebody else. . . ."

"Never mind the moral issues, Mr. Mayhew. What I want to know is this. If—*if*—Admiral Damien's plot succeeds, if I'm admitted to Drongo Kane's gang of pirates, what about my crew?"

"No real worries there, Captain. Pirates and privateersmen have usually been malcontents. Of course, there *is* the danger of mutiny—but not even warships of the Federation Survey Service are immune to that."

"No need to remind me, Mr. Mayhew."

Mayhew ignored this. "In the case of the *Discovery* mutiny, Captain, there was an officer quite capable of taking over the command of the ship from you. Here there is not. Your Chief Officer, Mr. Williams, is personally loyal to his Captain. Your Third Officer, Mr. Venner, is loyal to the Survey Service—and to you, as long as you are his legally appointed commander. The Green Hornet? There's no loyalty there—but, assuming that the engineers do think of mutiny they have no confidence in Ms. Connellan's abilities. The feeling is that she couldn't navigate a plastic duck across a bathtub."

"No more could she. I have known many extremely capable women, but she is not one of them."

"They are, though," said Mayhew, looking from the solidograph to the golden figurine.

"Yes," agreed Grimes. He thought, *I could do with either one of them here, although not both at once. . . .*

Mayhew said, "I don't think that a Police Commissioner, an ex-Federation Sky Marshal, would approve of privateering."

Grimes laughed. "Come to that, she didn't approve of me much. Although, if it hadn't been for her, I'd never have lifted from Port Southern on time."

"Perhaps," said Mayhew, "she had her orders."

"You mean that Damien—may the Odd Gods of the Galaxy look sideways at him!—was behind my getting the contract to carry Survey Service records from Austral to Earth?"

"It is hard to keep secrets from a telepath," said Mayhew. "But our beloved Admiral had no hand in your purchase of this ship. He's just an opportunist."

And Damien, thought Grimes, could have had nothing to do with the truly beautiful gift that Yosarian and Una Freeman, jointly, had presented to him. He got up from his chair, carefully lifted the golden cyclist and her steed down from the shelf, set her gently on the carpeted desk.

"Ride," he ordered. "Ride. Round and round. . . ."

Fascinated, he and Mayhew watched as she circumnavigated the day cabin, slowly at first and then with increasing speed. Grimes remembered the real Una in the garden, the Eden from which they had been evicted by the robot deity. He remembered her graceful nudity in delightful contrast to the equally graceful machine that she had ridden.

"There's something *odd* about that bicycle. . . ." murmured Mayhew.

Keep out my memories! thought Grimes. Yes, there had been something odd about the bicycles that both of them had ridden on that faraway world in another universe. He recalled that final showdown when he had been obliged to fight the things. . . .

"Sorry, Captain," apologized Mayhew. "But I couldn't help getting pictures of you as a naked bullfighter, with a bicycle playing the bull!"

Twenty-one

There was the unpleasantness when Kate Connellan, who had taken too much drink before dinner, expressed her disapproval of the menu by hurling the contents of a bowl of goulash at Magda Granadu. It missed its target but liberally bespattered the unfortunate Mr. Stewart. For this assault by her upon a fellow officer Grimes imposed as high a fine as he legally could. There were mutterings from those who had been or were currently recipients of the Green Hornet's favors but even they knew that she had overstepped the mark. Then there was an undignified brawl between Mr. Singh, Mr. Trantor and Mr. Denning, two of whom disapproved of Ms. Connellan's latest change of sleeping partners. This was broken up by Mr. Venner. There was the screaming match when the second mate discovered that the potato plants, installed in one of the hydroponics tanks before departure from Port Woomera, had died. Ms. Connellan alleged that these hapless vegetables had been murdered by Ms. Granadu so as to deprive her of New Donegal's renowned culinary delicacy.

"As long as *you* can have your stinking garlic," she had yelled at Grimes, *"you're* happy!"

There was another entry in the Official Log, another fine.

Grimes was not the only one relieved when, at long last, her interstellar drive shut down, *Sister Sue* was in orbit about El Dorado. His officers were at landing stations, Aerospace Control had granted permission for descent.

"All is ready for you at Bluewater Spaceport, *Sister Sue,"* said the mechanical voice.

"Sounds like a robot, Skipper," commented Williams.

"Probably is," replied Grimes. "A small human population, living in great luxury, pampered by hordes of mechanical servitors. At least, that's the way that it was when I was here last, years ago. . . ."

"Bluewater Spaceport. . . . A pretty name," said Williams. "According to the directory there's another port, on the other side of the planet. Port Kane. . . ."

"That's new," Grimes told him.

"I don't suppose that we shall be seeing it," said Williams.

You've a surprise coming, thought Grimes.

He applied just enough thrust to nudge *Sister Sue* out of her orbit and she began her controlled fall, dropping down through the clear morning sky toward the almost perfect azure ellipse, visible even from this altitude, of Lake Bluewater. The last time that he had made a landing here it had been in an almost uncontrollable, rocket-powered reentry vehicle; in those days such archaic contraptions were still carried by major warships and some captains liked to see them exercised now and again. Grimes and another junior officer had been sent down in this dynosoar, as the thing was called, to be the advance landing party for the cruiser *Aries.* He had splashed down into the lake and had fallen foul of the Princess Marlene von Stolzberg, who had been enjoying an afternoon's water skiing, and her watchbirds.

He found that he was remembering that day very well. Would she remember him? he wondered. He had heard from her only once since that long ago visit to El Dorado. Would she want to be reminded, now, of what had briefly flared between them? Would she have told her son who his father was? His thoughts drifted away from her to another El Doradan lady, Michelle, Baroness d'Estang. Was she on planet? He had last seen her, not so long ago, on New Venusberg and she had strongly hinted that there was unfinished business between them.

He envisaged a cozy little dinner party aboard his ship at which his only two guests would be the princess and the baroness. He chuckled.

"What's the joke, Skipper?" asked Williams.

"Nothing," said Grimes.

"Aerospace Control to *Sister Sue,*" came the voice from the NST transceiver. "Surface wind northeast at three knots. Unlimited visibility. . . ."

"I can see that," grumbled Grimes. Then, to old Mr. Stewart who was seated by the transceiver, "Acknowledge, please. Oh, just ask him—or it—not to foul up my landing with any flocks of tin sparrows. . . ."

"Sir?"

"You heard me."

Williams, Venner and Ms. Connellan looked curiously at Grimes as the radio officer repeated the request.

The reply was not long in coming.

"If your second landing on this world is as eventful as your first, Captain Grimes, the fault will be yours alone."

Williams laughed. "They seem to know all about you, Skipper!"

"The Monitor," said Grimes coldly, "sees all, hears all, knows all and remembers all."

"The Monitor?"

"The electronic intelligence that runs this world—although the human El Doradans are quick to point out that it is only a servant, not a master."

He returned his attention to the controls. *Sister Sue* was dropping fast, the arrhythmic beat of her inertial drive little more than an irritable mutter. Visible in the stern view screen was Lake Bluewater with, on its northern shore, the huddle of white buildings that was the spaceport, the tall control tower. A regular flashing of scarlet light indicated the position of the beacons; soon, now, they would be visible as three individual lights set in a triangle. Through the viewports could be seen the evidence of what great wealth and expensive technology can do to a once barren world. This planet, when first purchased by the El Dorado Corporation, had been absolutely lifeless; now it was all park and garden, cultivated field and orchard. There were lakes and rivers, small seas, ranges of snow-capped mountains, forests. There was only one city, named after the planet, about fifty kilometers north of the spaceport, but there were chateaux, castles and manor houses sparsely scattered throughout the countryside. There were mines and factories—El Dorado was rich in valuable minerals—but all industry was underground.

"What was all that about tin sparrows, Skipper?" asked Williams.

"Watchbirds," replied Grimes. "Every El Doradan has his team of personal guardians. The flying ones have modified and improved avian brains in mechanical bodies."

"So if you made a pass at a local lady," said Williams, "you'd be liable to have your eyes pecked out."

"You've got a one-track mind. . . ." Grimes was going to say, but the Green Hornet got in first with, "No more than you'd deserve!"

Venner laughed and old Mr. Stewart chuckled.

"Quiet, all of you!" snapped Grimes. "Keep your eyes on your instruments. Let me know at once if you pick up any flying objects on the radar, Mr. Venner. Let me have frequent radar altimeter readings Ms. Connellan." (This last was not really necessary as there was a read-out in the stern view screen.) "Maintain an all round visual lookout, Mr. Williams."

"Anybody would think this was a bloody battle cruiser," muttered the second mate.

Grimes glared at her. "I've still plenty of pages in the official log," he said.

Sister Sue continued her controlled fall. The marker beacons showed now as a triangle of three bright, blinking lights. Grimes brought this configuration to the very center of the screen. He stepped up the magnification. There were no other ships in port; the apron was a wide, empty stretch of gray concrete. A long streamer of white smoke was now issuing from a tall pipe at the edge of the landing field. It became particolored—an emission of white, then of red, then black, then white again. It gave an indication of wind velocity as well as of direction.

Compensating for drift was no problem. The inertial drive became louder as

Grimes increased vertical thrust, slowing the rate of descent. He watched the diminishing series of figures to one side of the screen, noted irritably that the Green Hornet, reporting those same readings from the radar altimeter, was lagging badly. But this was not, after all, a battle cruiser.

Yet.

Down crawled the ship, down, at the finish almost hovering rather than falling. The tips of her vanes at last gently kissed the concrete. Grimes cut the drive. *Sister Sue* shuddered and sighed, then relaxed in the tripodal cradle of her landing gear. There were the usual minor creakings and muted rattlings as weight readjusted itself.

"Finished with engines," said Grimes, then refilled and relit his pipe.

Twenty-two

At a normal spaceport, on a normal planet, ground cars would have brought the various officials—Customs, Immigration, Port Health and all the rest of them—out to a newly arrived ship. Here, at Port Bluewater, there was only a solitary figure walking out from one of the white office buildings, pacing slowly over the gray apron. It was wearing a uniform of some kind, black with gold trimmings. It looked human.

Grimes went to the big mounted binoculars, swung and focused them. He looked at the dull-gleaming, pewter-colored face under the gold-embellished peak of the cap. A robot. So none of this world's human inhabitants considered it worth their while to receive him and his ship.

He said to Mr. Venner, "Go down to the after airlock to meet that . . . that tin Port Captain. Take him—no, *it*—up to Ms. Granadu's office. She'll have all the necessary papers ready for our Inward Clearance." He allowed himself a laugh. "At least I shan't be put to the expense of free drinks and smokes for a pack of bludging human officials!"

"He might want to plug into a power point, Skipper, to get a free charge," said Williams.

Venner left the control room. The Green Hornet began, in a desultory manner, to tidy things away.

Williams said, "I suppose I'd better go down to the office myself. There might be some word about discharging arrangements."

"I'll come with you," said Grimes.

Anywhere but here he would have waited in his day cabin for the ship's agent, there to discuss matters over coffee or something stronger. He did not, however, feel like entertaining in his own quarters what he had already categorized as an uppity robot.

The elevator was not immediately available so Grimes and Williams made their descent into the body of the ship by the spiral staircase. Magda was waiting in her office. All necessary documentation was arranged neatly on her desk, as also was a box of cigarillos. On a table to one side was a steaming coffee pot with the necessary crockery and containers of cream and sugar.

"You can put those away," said Grimes, gesturing.

"Not so fast, Skipper," said Williams. "*We* can use some coffee. And I'm never averse to a free smoke."

"All right. Pour me a cup while you're about it."

"Why should the coffee and the smokes not be required, Captain?" asked the catering officer.

"You'll see," said Grimes.

Venner appeared in the doorway.

"The Port Captain, sir," he announced, then withdrew.

The robot entered.

It said, in a quite pleasant, not overly mechanical voice, "Yes. That is my title. I am also Collector of Customs, Port Health Officer and Immigration Officer. If I may be allowed to scan your papers I shall soon be able to inform you whether or not all is in order."

Grimes had seen the thing's like before, both on El Dorado and aboard the Baroness d'Estang's spaceyacht. It could have been a handsome, well-made human being with a metallic skin. Williams and Magda, however, were familiar only with the common or garden varieties of robot, only crudely humanoid at the best. (They had seen, of course, the exquisite, golden figurine that had been given to Grimes before lift-off from Port Southern—but she was only a beautiful miniature, not life-size.)

The automaton moved to the desk, went through the papers like a professional gambler dealing playing cards. It seemed to have no trouble reading things upside down. After only seconds the documents were back in their original order.

The subtly metallic voice said, "You are cleared inwards."

"Don't I get certification?" asked Grimes.

"That, Captain, is not required. The Monitor has cleared you. You will, however, be issued the usual Outward Clearance documents prior to your departure."

"When will discharge be started?" asked Grimes.

"Your cargo is not urgently required, Captain. Perhaps tomorrow the shipment of caviar will be off-loaded. The other items? At the moment there is no warehouse space available."

"So I have to sit here," exploded Grimes, "with my ship not earning money, paying wages to my crew and feeding them. . . . And you, I suppose, will be charging port dues."

"Of course, Captain."

"Demurrage . . . ?" wondered Grimes aloud. "Compensation for delay?"

"That is not applicable in your circumstances."

Perhaps, perhaps not, Grimes thought. He would have to make a careful study of *The Shipmaster's Business Companion.*

"Another point," he said. "I was last here as an officer of one of the Survey Service's cruisers."

"We are aware of that, Captain Grimes."

". . . so I had no cause to find out what facilities are available to merchant vessels. Is there a Shipping Office here? I may have to pay off one of my officers."

"There is no Shipping Office here. In any case, as you should know, outworlders may not be dumped on this planet. And that seems to have concluded all immediate business. Should you require stores, repairs or other services you may call the Port Master's office on your NST. I wish you good day."

"Is my NST hooked up to the planetary telephone service?" asked Grimes.

"It is not, Captain. You may, however, use the telephonic facilities in the reception area in the main office. Such calls will be charged against you. Again I wish you a good day."

The Port Captain turned, strode out of the office. They could hear his (its) footsteps, too heavy to be those of a human being, in the alleyway outside—and, for quite a while, on the treads of the spiral staircase leading down to the after airlock.

Grimes, Billy Williams and Magda Granadu looked at each other with raised eyebrows.

Williams said, "I don't think that I shall like this world, Skipper, where even robots treat us like dirt."

"The last time I came here," said Grimes, "there was a human Port Captain. The Comte Henri de Messigny. He wasn't must better than his tin successor."

"What happened to the . . . Comte?"

"He . . . died."

"Were you involved, Skipper?"

"Yes," said Grimes shortly. "And now, Mr. Williams, you'd better see to it that the caviar is ready for discharge when somebody condescends to send a team of stowbots out to us. And you, Ms. Granadu, can let the Port Captain's office know what stores you require. Try to confine yourself to inexpensive items, will you? That is, if anything here *is* inexpensive . . . Mphm." He poured himself another mug of coffee, sipped it thoughtfully. "I think I'll take a stroll ashore," he went on. "I might make one or two phone calls. . . ."

"Looking up the old girl friends, Skipper?" asked Williams cheerfully.

"Surely you don't think, Mr. Williams," said Grimes coldly, "that any El Doradan lady would have anything to do with a mere spaceman?"

"There are precedents," said the mate. "Drongo Kane, for a start. . . ."

And me before him, thought Grimes—but maintained his sour expression.

Twenty-three

The spaceport was almost as he remembered it, with only a few minor additions and alterations. And regarding these, he thought, his memory could be playing him tricks. He walked slowly across the apron to the Port Control building, a gleaming, white truncated pyramid topped by the graceful latticework pylon of the control tower. The main door was composed of two huge panels of opalescent glass which swung inward, to admit him, as he approached. He walked over the highly polished floor with its swirling inlaid designs toward the spiral staircase that rose from the center of the huge, high-ceilinged room. He stepped on to the bottom tread. Nothing happened. The last time that he had performed this action—how many years ago?—he had been borne smoothly upward to what were to be his temporary quarters and to much appreciated refreshment. This time, obviously, there were to be no free meals and drinks.

He turned away from the spiral staircase, walked to an open booth against one of the walls. There was no panel with dials or buttons but he could recall the procedure. Inside the booth, facing the rear wall, he said, "Get me the Princess Marlene von Stolzberg."

The rear wall became a screen, three dimensional. From it stared a robot servitor, pewter-faced, clad in archaic livery, black, with silver braid and buttons and white lace ruffles.

"Who is calling?" asked the metallic voice.

"John Grimes. Captain John Grimes."

The servant moved away from the screen. Grimes was looking into a room, dark paneled, with antique suits of armor ranged against the walls. *So she's still living in the same place,* he thought. *That gloomy Schloss of hers. . . .*

The picture flickered, faded, was replaced by that of one of the other rooms in the castle, a boudoir, frumpishly feminine in its furnishings.

And she . . . she was not quite a frump, Grimes decided, although she was no longer the golden girl whom he had known. She was not quite fat, although the fine lines of her face were partially obscured by the overlay of fatty tissues.

The padded robe that she was wearing concealed her body but, Grimes thought, it must have thickened. (When he had known her she had been a hearty eater.) Her hair was still golden but somehow dulled.

She looked out at him through blue eyes that were clear but cold, cold.

"Grimes," she said without enthusiasm. "John Grimes. Captain John Grimes. Should I congratulate you on your having achieved command? But I see from your uniform that you are no longer in the Survey Service. You are a commercial shipmaster?"

There was a note of disdain in her voice as she asked the question—or made the statement.

"Yes, Marlene. But I'm also a shipowner. I own my ship."

"The correct form of address, Captain Grimes, is Your Highness. As you should remember."

"Your Highness," repeated Grimes, his prominent ears flushing angrily.

"And why have you called me, Captain Grimes?"

"I . . . Well . . . Surely you remember, M . . . Sorry. Your Highness. You sent me a solidograph of yourself and . . . And a baby."

"Yes. I remember. *My* son. The Graf Ferdinand von Stolzberg."

"I . . . I wonder if I could see him. . . ."

"To satisfy your idle curiosity? The Graf and yourself would have nothing in common. Are you trying to tell me that you have paternal instincts, Captain Grimes? Ferdinand has never felt the need for a father—and even if he did would not wish to acknowledge a common spaceman as such."

"I apologize for wasting your time, Your Highness," said Grimes at last.

"The pleasure, if any, was all yours," she said.

The screen went blank.

Grimes filled, lit and smoked a soothing pipe. Then he said, slowly and deliberately, "Get me the Baroness Michelle d'Estang."

The screen came alive. This time the robot servitor had the appearance of a human female, a pretty, golden girl in severe black and white lady's maid uniform.

"Who is calling, please?"

"Captain John Grimes, late of *The Far Traveler* and *Little Sister,* now master/owner of *Sister Sue.*"

The face and upper body in the screen were replaced by those of a man.

"Micky's out, Grimesy," said Drongo Kane. "Will I do?"

Grimes stared at his old enemy, at the face that looked as though it had been shattered at some time and then reassembled by a careless plastic surgeon, topped by an untidy shock of straw-colored hair.

"Please tell the Baroness that I called, Commodore Kane," said Grimes.

"I'll do that. You're looking quite prosperous, Grimesy. And I hear that you've got yourself a real ship at last. But I warn you—you'll not find it so easy to find cargoes to fill her. I should know."

"I've managed so far," said Grimes.

"And how many voyages have you made in that rusthucket of yours? Two, to date. Well, if you get stuck here you can always give me a call. I might, I just might, have something for you."

"That'll be the sunny Friday," said Grimes.

(For him to have replied otherwise would have been out of character.)

"Don't go looking gift horses in the mouth, Grimes. I'm prepared to let bygones be bygones. But I can always change my mind. And remember—sunny Fridays have a habit of coming around."

The screen went blank.

There was one last call that Grimes thought that he would make.

"Get me," he ordered, "Her Grace the Duchess of Leckhampton."

The robot servant looking out from the screen was, save for his gray metal face, a traditional English butler.

"Good morning, sir. Who shall I say is calling?"

"Captain John Grimes."

"Very good, sir. I shall ascertain if Her Grace wishes to speak with you."

After a very short wait the butler was replaced in the screen by the Duchess. She looked no older. (But she had never looked young.) Her thin white hair was carelessly arranged. Her cheeks were painted. She was wearing a gaudy emerald and scarlet shirt. There was a necklace of glittering stones that looked far too large to be genuine diamonds—but which almost certainly were genuine—about her wrinkled throat. Her black eyes sparkled from among the too liberally applied eye shadow.

"Young Grimes," she cackled, "but not so young any longer. And a captain. This is a pleasure."

"It is a pleasure," said Grimes, not untruthfully, "seeing you again."

"And when are you coming out to see me, John Grimes? What about this evening? Can you get away from your ship? But of course you can. You're the captain now. It is short notice, but I should be able to arrange a little party. I'll ask Marlene. . . ."

"I've already talked to her," said Grimes. "She didn't seem all that pleased to see me."

"Too bad. She's a silly girl, and dotes on that useless son of hers. But I shouldn't have said *that,* should I? After all, he's yours too. But whom else can I ask? Michelle? You know her, of course. And that husband of hers. And Baron Takada. And Chief Lobenga and the Lady Eulalia. . . . Just leave it to me. And perhaps you could bring one or two of your senior officers. . . ."

"But where do you live, Your Grace?"

"In El Dorado City, of course. I'll send a car for you. Can you be ready to leave your ship at 1800 hours?"

"I can, Your Grace."

"Good. I am looking forward to meeting you again, Captain Grimes."

He left the Port Control Office, walked back to the ship. He saw that a conveyor belt had been set up to connect with one of the upper cargo ports and that at its base a medium-sized air truck and a couple of spidery stowbots were waiting. As he watched, the first of the cartons slid out of the aperture in the hull, was followed by others in a steady stream. With a smooth economy of motion the robot stevedores loaded them into the body of the truck.

He walked up the ramp into *Sister Sue*'s after airlock, took the elevator to the cargo compartment in which the shipment of caviar was stowed. He found Williams there and also the Port Captain, the agent or extension of the Monitor, who, wordlessly, was supervising the activity of the pair of stowbots which were loading cartons onto the top of the belt.

"Mr. Williams," said Grimes, "I think that our friend here can be trusted to function as a master stevedore. Come up to see me, please, and collect Ms. Granadu on the way."

"Aye, aye, Skipper. I'll just see the next tier broken—It's rather tightly stowed—then I'll be with you."

Grimes carried on up to his quarters, sat down in his day cabin to wait. Before long the mate and the catering officer had joined him.

"Sit down," he said. Then he asked, "Are you free this evening?"

"Free, Skipper? You have to be joking. We're confined to the vicinity of this blasted spaceport. There's no public transport. I asked the so-called Port Captain if we could use one of the ship's boats to take a run into the city and I was told that intrusion into El Doradan air space by outworlders is prohibited."

"I've been asked to a dinner party, Mr. Williams, by the Duchess of Leckhampton. She suggested that I bring two of my senior officers with me. Does the Dog Star Line run to mess dress?"

"Only in their passenger ships, Skipper, and I was never in them. But I've a civilian dinner suit."

"That will do nicely. I won't be wearing uniform myself. And you, Magda?"

"I've an evening dress, Captain."

"Good. The Duchess's air car will be calling for us at 1800 hours."

Magda Granadu appeared to be thinking deeply. She said at last, "I feel that this will be an *important* meeting. . . ."

"Too right it is," said Williams. "It'll be the first time in my life that I've had dinner with a Duchess!"

"More important than that, Billy," the woman told him. "Important for all of us. I think that we should consult the *I Ching,* Captain."

"We can wait until we get to Her Grace's mansion," said Grimes, "and she can read the Tarot pack."

"Does this Duchess have the gift?" asked Magda.

"I . . . I think so. When I was here before she came up with a rather uncanny prediction."

"And was she working for you—or for herself?"

"For El Dorado, I suppose," said Grimes.

"And my *Book of Changes* will be working for you, Captain. For us. Would you mind if I went down for the book and the coins?"

"Go ahead," said Grimes.

"She really believes it," said Williams when she was gone. "Do you, Skipper?"

"Do you, Mr. Williams?"

Magda came back, holding the black silk-covered book. She handed the three silvery coins to Grimes. He shook them in his cupped hands, let them fall to the deck. Two heads and a tail. The second throw produced the same result, as did the third. Two tails and a head, then two heads and a tail again. The last throw was a head and two tails.

"Upper trigram, *K'an,*" said the woman. "Lower trigram, *Ch'ien.* The hexagram is *Hsu. . . .*" She read from the book. "Biding one's time. . . . Sincerity will lead to brilliant success. Firmness will bring good fortune. It will be advantageous to cross the great water. . . ."

"That's our job, isn't it?" asked Grimes.

"I suppose so," she said. "But the Image is . . . interesting and possibly apposite. 'Clouds drift across the sky as if biding their time. The superior man, in accordance with this, eats and drinks, feasts and enjoys himself.'"

"There's no reason," said Grimes, "why we should not enjoy a free meal."

After they had left his cabin he called Ken Mayhew.

"Mr. Mayhew," he said, "I suppose you know that I've been invited to dinner with the Duchess of Leckhampton. I'm taking Mr. Williams and Ms. Granadu with me. I'd have liked to have taken you—for obvious reasons—but the old bat said that I could bring two of my officers with me. And unless we break your cover you're not one of my officers. You're a passenger, and only a senior clerk on holiday. They're a snobbish bunch here."

"I have already gained that impression, Captain. I have been . . . eavesdropping, receiving unguarded thoughts from all over, trying to pick up something concerning *you.* There was a woman who came through quite strongly. She was vocalizing her thinking. *Should I see him again? But if I invite him here he will be almost certain to meet Ferdinand—and Ferdinand could notice the facial resemblance, even though I had his ears fixed while he was still only a baby. He believes that Henri was his father and I want him to go on believing that. Better a dead aristocrat than an impossibly bourgeois spaceman. . . .*"

"Mphm," grunted Grimes indignantly. "Am I impossibly bourgeois, Mr. Mayhew?"

"I don't think so, sir," said the telepath diplomatically. "Then there was a man, a spaceman I would say, like yourself. Would it have been this Drongo Kane? *So Grimes, of all people, is here. In a real ship. I could use him. After all, he held command in the Survey Service. He's been in a few naval actions. The only laws for which he has any respect are those he makes himself. But he's a prickly bastard. I'll have to handle him carefully. But, first of all, I'll have to see to it that there's a shortage of cargoes for his* Sister *Sue—what a name for a ship!—in this sector of the galaxy. I'll have to get old Takada on to it. He's our financial wizard. . . .*"

"The Baron Takada," said Grimes, "is El Dorado's financial wizard. And am I a prickly bastard?"

"You are at times, sir. But to continue. . . . There was a woman, elderly. *Just imagine that young Grimes turning up here after all this time . . . I wish that I were a few years younger. Marlene's a fool; she should have kept him once she'd got her claws into him. She's enough money for two and she could afford genealogical research to turn up some sort of patent of nobility for a commoner husband. Michelle wasn't so absurdly fussy—although you could hardly say that Kane married her for her money. He's plenty of his own. And he'll have plenty more—as we all shall!—if that private navy of mercenaries does as well as he says it will. . . .*"

"I always rather liked the Duchess," said Grimes, "although she's a ruthless old bat. So she's an investor in Kane's Honorable Company of Interstellar Mercenaries. Probably everybody is on this world. I've noticed that the very rich never miss any opportunity to become even richer. And Baron Takada will be pulling his strings and exporters and importers will be dancing to his tune, and I'll be sitting here on the bones of my arse, flat broke and getting broker. . . . And then Drongo Kane will bob up like a pantomime Good Fairy and offer me, and the ship, a job. . . ."

"You have some peculiar friends, sir," said Mayhew dryly.

"Don't I just. Can you sort of tune in to the dinner party tonight? Let me know, when I get back, if you heard anything interesting."

"I think I can manage that, sir."

"Good." He looked at the bulkhead clock. "It's time I was getting changed."

Twenty-four

Grimes and Williams, dressed in what the mate referred to as their penguin suits, stood at the foot of the ramp watching the Duchess's air car coming in. With them was Magda Granadu, also wearing a black outfit, high-necked, long-sleeved and with an ankle-length skirt. Its severity was offset by a necklace of opals, by a blazing, fire opal brooch over her left breast and by what was almost a coronet of opals in her piled-high auburn hair.

You can put an inertial drive unit into any sort of body, of any shape at all, and it will fly. If you want speed through the atmosphere streamlining is desirable. If speed is not the main consideration the streamlining may be dispensed with.

The Duchess's car was not streamlined. It was an airborne replica of one of the more prestigious road vehicles developed during the twentieth century, Old Reckoning, on Earth, even to the silver nymph decorating the square bonnet. It drifted down through the evening air, touched, then rolled the last few meters on its fat-tired wheels. The chauffeur—a gray-faced robot clad in black, high-collared, silver-buttoned livery—got down from the forward compartment, marched stiffly to the three humans and saluted smartly.

"Your transport, gentlemen and lady," he announced in a metallic voice.

He turned, walked back to the car and opened the rear door. Grimes held back to let Magda enter first but she said, "After you, Captain."

She followed him in, so as to sit between him and Williams. Williams entered. The robot chauffeur shut the door, returned to his own seat. There was a sheet of glass or some other transparency between him and his passengers. His voice came to him through a concealed speaker. "Gentlepersons, you will find a small bar in the panel before you. There is a single button in the padding, which you may press."

The car lifted. Grimes, whose mind was a repository of all manner of useless facts, recalled the proud boast of Rolls Royce on one of whose later cars this vehicle had been modeled. *The only mechanical sound you can hear is the ticking of the clock on the dashboard.* So it was here. The inertial drive is inevitably noisy, yet Grimes and his companions had heard only the faintest mutter as the car came in for its landing. Inside the passenger compartment there was not so much as a whisper to indicate that machinery was in operation.

"A drink, Skipper?" asked Williams.

"Just one," said Grimes. "We don't want to arrive doing an impersonation of drunken and dissolute spacemen."

When the button was pushed a section of panel fell back to form a shelf and to expose a compartment containing a rack of bottles, another one of glasses and a tiny refrigerator with an ice cube tray. There was a box of cigarettes and one of cigarillos. There was even a jar of pipe tobacco. (Grimes had smoked the local weed when on El Dorado, years ago, and enjoyed it.)

Magda dispensed drinks—whisky, genuine Scotch, for herself and Williams, gin and bitters for Grimes. She and Williams lit up cigarillos. Grimes scraped out his pipe and refilled it with the fragrant mixture. The three of them sipped and smoked, watching, through the wide windows, the landscape over which they were flying.

Here, between the spaceport and the city, it was well tamed, given over to agriculture. There were orchards, with orderly rows of fruit trees. There were green fields, and other fields that were seas of golden grain. In these the harvesters were working great machines whose bodies of polished metal reflected the rays of the setting sun.

Ahead was the city, a small one, a very small one compared to the sprawling warrens found on the majority of the worlds of man. There were towers, only one of which was really tall, and great houses, oddly old-fashioned in appearance, few of which were higher than four stories. Every building stood in what was, in effect, its own private park. Lights were coming on as the sun went down, in windows and along the wide, straight avenues.

The air car was losing altitude. It dropped to the road about a kilometer from the city limits, continued its journey as a wheeled vehicle. The landing was so smooth that had the passengers been sitting with their eyes shut they would never have noticed it. The vehicle sped on with neither noise nor vibration, a great orchard with golden-fruit-laden trees on either side of it. Then it was running along one of the avenues. There was other road traffic, ground cars which, like their own transport, were probably capable of functioning as flying machines.

Williams was enthusiastic. "Look, Skipper! A Mercedes! And isn't that a Sunbeam?"

That was an open car, with wire wheels and a profusion of highly polished brass. (Or gold, thought Grimes. On this world it could well be the precious metal.) A man in an archaic costume—belted jacket, high, stiff collar with cravat, peaked cap—was at the wheel. By his side sat a woman with a dust coat over her dress, with her hat secured to her head by a filmy scarf tied over it and beneath her chin. Both these persons wore heavy goggles.

The pseudo Rolls Royce slowed, turned off the avenue on to a graveled drive, made its way to a brilliantly illuminated portico beyond which loomed Leckhampton House, gray and solid, a façade in which windows glowed softly like the ranked ports of a great surface ship, a cruise liner perhaps, sliding by in the dusk. The car stopped. The robot chauffeur got out to open the door for his passengers, saluting smartly as they dismounted. In the doorway of the house stood a very proper English butler, pewter-faced, who bowed as he ushered them in. Another robot servitor, slimmer and younger looking than the first, led them to the drawing room, a large apartment illumined by the soft light from gasoliers, that was all gilt and red plush, the walls of which were covered with crimson silk upon which floral designs had been worked in gold.

It was all rather oppressive.

Following the servant Grimes and his companions walked slowly toward the elderly lady seated on a high-backed chair that was almost a throne.

"Your Grace," said the robot, "may I present Captain John Grimes, of the spaceship *Sister Sue,* and. . . ."

"Cut the cackle, Jenkins," said the Duchess. "I've known Captain Grimes for years. Shove off, will you?"

"Very good, Your Grace."

The servitor bowed and left.

"And now, John Grimes, let me have a look at you. You've changed hardly at all. . . ."

"And neither have you, Your Grace," said Grimes truthfully. He looked at her with admiration. She was dressed formally—and what she was wearing would not have looked out of place at the court of the first Queen Elizabeth, richly brocaded silk over a farthingale (Grimes wondered how she could manage to sit down while wearing such a contraption), ruff and rebato. A diamond choker was about her neck. There were more diamonds, a not so small coronet, decorating the obvious auburn wig that she was wearing over her own hair.

"Introduce me to the young lady and the young gentleman, John."

"Your Grace," said Grimes formally, remembering the style used by the rudely dismissed under butler or whatever he was, "may I present Miss Magda Granadu, my Catering Officer and Purser? And Mr. William Williams, my Chief Officer?"

"So you're the commissioned cook, Magda," cackled the old lady. "By the looks of John you ain't starving him. And you're his mate, Billy, somebody to hold his hand when he gets into a scrape. Do you still get into scrapes, John-boy?"

"Now and again," admitted Grimes.

Then there were the others to meet—in Grimes' case to meet again. There was the Baron Takada, his obesity covered with antique evening finery, white tie and tails, the scarlet ribbon of some order diagonally across his snowy shirt-front with its black pearl studs. There was the Hereditary Chief Lobenga, tall and muscular, darkly handsome, in a high-collared, gold-braided, white uniform. There was his wife, the Lady Eulalia, her glistening black hair elaborately coiled above her face with its creamy skin, the nose too aquiline for mere prettiness, the mouth a wide, scarlet slash. Through the pale translucence of her simple gown her body gleamed rosily.

An under butler circulated with a tray of drinks. Grimes did not have to state his preference for pink gin; it was served to him automatically.

"You remember my tastes, Your Grace," he said.

"Indeed I do, John-boy. For drinks and for. . . ."

The butler made a stately entrance into the room.

"The Princess Marlene von Stolzberg," he announced. "Commodore the Baron Kane, El Doradan Navy. The Baroness Michelle d'Estang. . . ."

So she had come to see him after all, thought Grimes. It was a pity that Mayhew had not been able to warn him. She had put on weight, he thought, and remembered regretfully the slim, golden girl whom he had seen, skimming over Lake Bluewater, on the occasion of his first landing on this world. And yet she was more beautiful than she had seemed when he had talked to her by telephone. Like Eulalia she was simply but expensively attired in a robe of smoky spider silk—but her dress was definitely opaque.

She recognized his presence with a distant nod. He bowed to her with deliberate stiffness.

But Drongo Kane was cordial enough. Like Grimes and Williams he was in civilian evening wear; unlike them he gave no impression of being dressed up for the occasion. His suit looked as though it had been slept in. His black bow tie, obviously of the clip-on variety, was askew.

He seized Grimes' hand in a meaty paw, almost shouted, "Grimes, me old cobber! Welcome aboard!"

"This happens to be *my* party, Baron, in *my* house," said the Duchess coldly.

"But *I* am the naval authority on this planet, Duchess," Kane told her cheerfully. Then, to Grimes, "Let by-gones be by-gones is my motto. I've even brought Micky along to see you again."

"I brought myself," snapped the Baroness. She looked at Grimes and he at her. Her dress was modeled on the Greek chiton—but of the style worn by artisans, warriors and slaves. It was short, very short, secured at the left shoulder by a brooch that was a huge diamond surrounded by smaller stones. Her arms and her right shoulder were bare. Her gleaming, auburn hair was braided into a coronet in which precious stones reflected, almost dazzlingly, the gaslight. Her fine features were illumined by a sudden smile.

"John, it's good to see you!"

"And it's good to see you. . . ." How should one address a Baroness? he wondered. "Your Excellency. . . ."

"Not here," she told him. "That was for when I was off planet, in my own ship, with ambassadorial status. Call me Michelle." She glared at her husband as she added, "But don't call me Micky!"

Grimes would have liked to have talked longer with her but Drongo Kane was an inhibiting influence. So he circulated. He tried to make conversation with the Princess Marlene but it was heavy going. And then he was unable to escape from Baron Takada who evinced a keen interest, too keen an interest, in the financial aspects of shipowning.

Then the robot butler announced in sonorous tones, "Your Grace, dinner is served."

Grimes realized that he was supposed to escort the Duchess in to the dining room. She put her hand lightly into the crook of his left elbow, indicated that they should follow the stately mechanical servitor. They marched slowly into the dining room, a huge apartment the walls of which were covered with broad-striped paper in black and white. At the head of the table, covered with a snowy-white cloth on which the array of golden cutlery and crystal glassware glittered, was the tall-backed chair, of ebony, which was obviously Her Grace's. The illumination, from massed candles in golden holders, was soft but adequate.

The Duchess seated, Grimes stood behind his chair, at her right, waiting for the other ladies to take their places. Opposite him was Marlene. Below her was Baron Takada, then the Lady Eulalia, then Hereditary Chief Lobenga. Williams was at the foot of the table. On Grimes' right was Michelle, with Drongo Kane below her, then Magda.

There was no scarcity of robot footmen. In a very short time all the guests were seated, a pale, dry sherry was being poured into the first of the glasses, and plates, of fine gold-trimmed porcelain, were set down at each place. Grimes looked at his curiously. Surely this could not be a rose, a pink rose? But it was not, of course. It was smoked salmon, sliced very thinly and arranged in convincing simulation of petals.

He raised his glass to the Duchess and said, "Your very good health, Your Grace."

"Down the hatch, Skipper!" she cackled in reply.

Across the table the Princess looked disapprovingly both at her hostess and at that lady's guest.

Course followed course, each one beautifully cooked and served. English cookery is often sneered at but at its best it is superb. There was a clear oxtail soup, followed by grilled trout, followed by game pie. There was a huge roast of beef, wheeled around on a trolley and carved to each diner's requirements. (By this time Grimes was beginning to wonder if he would be able to find any room for some of that noble Stilton cheese he had noticed on the ebony sideboard.) There was tipsy cake, with thick cream. And there were the wines—the sherry, obviously imported, a hock that was a product of the Count Vitelli's vineyards and none the worse for that. With the game pie came a delightfully smooth claret, and with the beef a heavier but equally smooth Burgundy. Vitelli Spumante accompanied the sweet.

After all that Grimes could manage only a token sliver of the delicious Stilton. He looked down the table a little enviously at Williams, who was piling the creamy, marbled delicacy high on to crackers and conveying them enthusiastically to his mouth.

During the meal the conversation had been pleasant and interesting—and at times, insofar as Grimes was concerned, a little embarrassing. The Baroness told a few stories of their voyagings together in *The Far Traveler*. "If I had let her," she said, "Big Sister—that was the name that we had for the yacht's pilot-computer—would have spoiled John as much as you've been spoiling him tonight. She even made pipe tobacco for him; I think she used dried lettuce leaves for the main ingredient. . . ."

"It was still a good smoke," said Grimes.

"Talking of smoking," said the Duchess, "shall we leave the gentlemen to their port wine and cigars?"

All rose when she did. She was escorted from the dining room by her major-domo, the other ladies by robot footmen.

The gentlemen resumed their seats.

Twenty-five

A servitor brought in a large decanter of port wine, another a box of cigars, a third golden ashtrays and lighters. When these had been set down on the table the robots retired. Drongo Kane got up from his chair, took, as though by right, the Duchess's seat at the head of the table. Baron Tanaka was now sitting opposite Grimes, with the Hereditary Chief next to him. Williams moved up to sit next to his captain.

The decanter circulated. Kane filled his glass to the very brim. So did Williams. Cigars were ignited.

"Perhaps we should have a toast," said Kane. He raised his glass. "Here's to crime!"

And it was a crime, thought Grimes, how that uncouth bastard gulped that beautiful wine as though it were lager beer on a hot day.

"But it is not crime," said Baron Takada, "if it is legal."

"As a banker, *you* should know, Hiroshi," Kane said. "What do you think, Grimes?"

"I always try to keep on the right side of the Law," said Grimes.

"Don't you find it rather a strain at times? A man like you. I've always thought that you'd make a good pirate. I haven't forgotten what you did to my ship that first time on Morrowvia."

"I thought that you were letting by-gones be by-gones."

"I am, Grimesy-boy, I am. I might even put some business your way. Some *honest* crime. Or legal crime."

"You're contradicting yourself, Kane."

"Have you ever known me to do that?" He refilled his glass, to the brim again, looked over it at Grimes. "Tell me, have you never regretted having left the Survey Service? Have you never felt naked swanning around in an unarmed ship when, for all your spacefaring life prior to the *Discovery* mutiny, you've had guns and missiles and the gods know what else to play with?"

"Are you offering me a commission in the El Doradan navy?" asked Grimes.

Kane laughed. "To be an officer in our navy you have to be of noble birth and I don't think that you qualify."

"If you're a fair sample of nobility, Baron Kane, I'm glad that I don't."

"Temper, temper, Grimes!" Kane wagged his cigar reprovingly. "Anyhow, you're a trained fighting spaceman." He turned to Williams. "And so are you, Mister Mate. You're out of the Dog Star Line—and they've always made a practice of defensively arming their ships when necessary."

"I have been in action, sir," admitted Williams.

"And there's your Third Officer, Grimes," Kane went on. "Your Mr. Venner. A Survey Service Reserve officer."

"How do you know all this?" asked Grimes.

"From your ship's papers, of course. The data was fed into the Monitor when you were cleared inward."

"And what are you driving at?" Grimes demanded.

Kane did not reply but Baron Takada murmured, "In times of economic stress the armed and armored man survives."

It sounded profound, probably more so than it actually was.

"Economic stress?" echoed Grimes.

"Yes, Captain. A state of affairs to which you are no stranger. My reading of your character is that you are a man who would take up arms to defend what is his. And has it not been said that attack is the best defense?"

So, thought Grimes, the first feelers were being put out. It would be out of character for him to be too eager to take the bait.

He said, "This is all very interesting, gentlemen, but I don't see how it concerns me. I own and command a ship, fully paid for. I show a profit on my voyage from Earth to El Dorado. Presumably there will be some cargo from here to elsewhere in the galaxy."

"I am afraid that there will not be," said Baron Takada. "The Interstellar Transport Commission has the contract for the shipment of our metal products off El Dorado. Too, I can tell you that there are no cargoes for ships such as yours, independently operated star tramps, in this sector of the galaxy." He smiled apologetically. "It is my business to know such things. The Duchess asked me if I could be of help to you in finding you employment, or in advising you where to find employment. I command a fine commercial and financial intelligence service and I have set it to work on your behalf. All inquiries have been fruitless."

"Something will turn up," said Grimes.

"Still riding your famous luck, Grimesy-boy?" laughed Kane. "I sort of gained the impression that it had been running out lately. If I hadn't pulled you out of the soup on New Venusberg. . . ."

"I gained the impression," Grimes said, "that it was the Baroness who was largely responsible for my rescue."

"I was there too." Again he filled his glass, then sent the decanter on its rounds. Baron Takada waved it on. Hereditary Chief Lobenga helped himself generously. So did Williams. So did Grimes. He knew that he should be keeping a clear head but this wine was of a quality that he rarely encountered.

Kane continued, "Just suppose your luck does run out, Grimes. Just suppose that you're stuck here, waiting for news of employment somewhere, anywhere, with port dues mounting and your bank balance getting lower and lower. And just suppose that I, your old cobber, offer you and your ship a job. . . ."

"A charter?" asked Grimes.

"Sort of," said Kane.

"What cargo, or cargoes?" Grimes persisted.

"What you can pick up," Kane told him.

For some reason he found this amusing. So did Lobenga, who laughed loudly. Even Baron Takada smiled.

"Cards on the table, Grimesy-boy," said Kane. "I'll spill the beans and see if you're ready to lick them up. If you aren't now, you may be in a few days' time, when you're still stuck here, with bills piling up and nobody in any hurry at all to discharge your cargo. You may have heard that I'm assembling a fleet at Port Kane. Owner-masters, not too scrupulous, down on their luck. . . ."

"Like you," said Grimes.

"Not like me. I'm not down on my luck. But you are. There's *Pride of Erin,* Captain O'Leary. And *Agatha's Ark,* Captain Agatha Prinn. *Spaceways Princess,* Captain MacWhirter. . . . All of 'em, like your *Sister Sue,* one-time Epsilon Class tramps in various stages of decrepitude. All of them armed. Oh, nothing heavy. A laser cannon, a quick-firing projectile cannon, a missile launcher. All of them with temporal precession synchronization controls fitted to their Mannschenn Drive units. Small arms, of course, for the boarding parties. . . ."

It was Grimes' turn to laugh.

"Just who do you think you can fight with an armed rabble like that?"

"Unarmed merchantmen, of course."

"Piracy?"

"No. Not piracy. Privateering," stated Kane.

He went on to tell Grimes what he already knew, what Damien had told him back at Port Woomera. He made it all sound as though it would work, and work well. Williams, to whom all this was new, listened entranced. Grimes did his best to look both disapproving and doubtful.

"And meanwhile," he said, "your gallant, money-hungry captains are sitting snug in Port Kane, eating their heads off and being paid for doing nothing."

"There is a retaining fee, of course," admitted Kane. "And no port dues are charged. And the ships will soon be lifting." He nodded toward the Baron. "Over to you, Hiroshi."

"You will appreciate, Captain Grimes," said Takada, "that a successful interstellar financier must maintain an intelligence service. Do you know, or know of, the Hallichek Hegemony? Of course you do. A not very pleasant avian matriarchy. On one of the worlds under their control, one of their colonies, the males have succeeded in becoming dominant. Soon, very soon, the Prime Nest will be endeavoring to restore the status quo. A punitive expedition will be dispatched to Kalla, the rebel planet. The Kallans have a space navy of their own, a small one and a good one. The Kallan government is prepared to issue Letters of Marque to outsiders, such as ourselves, so that the Hegemony's merchant shipping may be raided and seized, leaving their own fighting ships to defend the planet."

"As an idea," said Grimes, "it's strictly for the birds!"

"But it could be fun, Skipper," said Williams.

It could be, Grimes thought. He was a human chauvinist at times and had never liked the Hallicheki, those cruel, dowdy, yet strutting and arrogant old hens. The males of their species were, by human standards, much more likeable.

"Think about it," said Kane. "Sleep on it. Remember that this is a golden opportunity to get in on the ground floor of what could be, what will be a very profitable business. Big profit, small risks. The arms that you carry will remain the property of the El Doradan Corporation so you will not have to buy them. The Corporation will make the necessary modifications to your ship, free of charge. We can also provide gunnery training facilities—although in your case it should not be necessary. You, and your mate and your third mate, already have experience with weaponry. . . ."

"Give it a go, Skipper!" urged Williams who, obviously, had overindulged in the excellent port wine.

"Mr. Williams," said Grimes, "seems to be enthusiastic. But what about my other officers?"

"Any merchant spaceman left by his ship on El Dorado," said Kane, "is regarded and treated as a criminal, jailed until such time as somebody can be persuaded to take him off planet. Such few unfortunates as have experienced the hospitality of our prison system have not been pampered. We do not believe in needless expense."

"No?" asked Grimes sardonically, looking around at the rich appointments of the dining room.

"Unless," went on Kane, "it is for ourselves." He got to his feet. "Shall we join the ladies?"

Twenty-six

The ladies were playing bridge, with the exception of the Princess Marlene. She was sitting by herself, idly leafing through a magazine. Kane looked at the dedicated quartet about the card table, turned to the other men and asked, "What about making up another four, Grimes?"

"I'm not a millionaire," Grimes said. "I can't afford to play with El Doradans."

"Your tabby's doing all right," said Kane.

And so she should be, thought Grimes. Magda was partnered with the Duchess, which lady was on the point of pulling off a Misere in no trumps. Was it fair, he wondered, that two women with psychic gifts should be allied? But Michelle and the Lady Eulalia could afford to lose money. Magda could not. Neither could he nor Williams. Too, he did not much care for the variety of bridge, with its Misere bids, that was being played. No matter what his cards were he played—not always successfully—to win. (And now, he thought wryly, he was being paid by Rear Admiral Damien to lose. . . .)

"All right," said Kane. "If you're chicken we'll adjourn to the music room." He called to the Duchess, "Is it okay to use your playmaster, Lecky? Could we watch those spools you've just got in from New Venusberg?"

The Duchess looked around and up to him, stared at him coldly. "You may use the playmaster, Baron Kane. It will exhibit whichever programs you order."

"New Venusberg . . ." murmured Williams. "Hot stuff. . . ."

Too hot for me, thought Grimes. He had been an unwilling performer in New Venusberg entertainments and his memories of that period of his life were not among his happiest.

The Princess had closed her magazine and put it down on her lap. She was looking at Grimes. Was that invitation in her expression? Could her attitude toward him have changed so suddenly? And if so, why? The El Doradans, as he well knew, did not believe in giving something for nothing.

He sauntered over to her, bowed stiffly. Her nod in reply was not stiff. She dropped the magazine on to the low table by her chair, extended a plump hand to him. He took it, helped her to her feet.

She said softly, "I thought, John, that we might take a stroll in the conservatory . . ."

He said, "That will be a great pleasure, Your Highness."

She was very close to him as they walked slowly out of the drawing room, her rounded—too well padded?—right hip brushing against his left one. They passed the music room. Looking in through the open door Grimes could see the wide, deep screen of the playmaster, alive with a vivid depiction of the Colosseum arena where naked gladiators, men and women, were battling to the death. He was fortunate, he thought, that on his one appearance there he and the others on his team had been pitted only against wild beasts.

Marlene guided him through a labyrinth of corridors, gaslit tunnels, stone-floored, walled with panels of some dark wood, gleaming with satin polish. They came to a door which opened before them. Beyond it was a dimly illumined cavern—it seemed at first—a green gloom that was alive with the rustle of lush vegetation, the tinkling of falling water. The air was warm, moist, redolent with the scent of growing things. Gradually the intensity of the light increased, was reflected from fleshy, scarlet flowers, from the glowing, golden globes that were exotic fruit of some kind.

"The one part of Leckhampton House," remarked Marlene, "that's not a slavish imitation of Old England. Although, I believe, the conservatories of some of the ancient establishments maintained by the nobility were hothouses in which all sorts of foreign plants flourished. . . ." She waved an arm in the direction of a luminous display of great, polychromatic blossoms. "I'm sure that if Her Grace's ancestors could have gotten a specimen of Tandoro Spectrum Flowers they would have done so."

They paused by the fountain, looked into the big basin in which the Locomotive Lilies—an ugly name for a quite beautiful plant—were cruising slowly around and around, each an almost circular pad of green leaves supporting a creamy blossom, with trailing root-tendrils that, as well as providing motility, snared the tiny, almost invisible water insects that were the lilies' food.

She didn't drag me in here to give me a lecture on botany, thought Grimes.

She had turned to face him, still standing very close. The scent that she was wearing competed with the natural perfumes of flowers and foliage. It was not a losing battle.

She said, "At first, when I heard that you were coming back to this world, I was far from happy. Now I am not so sure. We had something once. I wonder if we still have it. . . ."

Her upraised face was an invitation for a kiss. He kissed her, on her open mouth. Her lips were warm, moist. He could feel her breasts against him, more full than they had been—how many years ago?—but still firm. His own body was showing signs of interest.

His right hand slid down her back, moving easily over the smooth, silky material of her dress, to the cleft of her buttocks. His fingers closed over a fleshy mound, squeezed gently.

She pulled away from him, quite violently. He thought that she was going to strike him but she did not. Then her face relaxed, the lines of emotion—but what emotion?—smoothing out. Her eyes, thought Grimes, were hard, cold, calculating.

Yet her voice was soft.

She said, "Not here, John. Not now. The Duchess knows everything that happens in this house of hers."

"She knew what happened before," said Grimes. "When. . . ."

"That was then," said the Princess. "This is now."

But she was close to him again, very close. There was another kiss. He restrained, with something of an effort, his hands from wandering.

She said, "You must stay with me again. At the Schloss."

He said, "As master I have considerably more freedom than I did when I was here before, as a junior officer."

"I wish that you could come out with me tonight," she told him, "but the castle is not in a fit state for the reception of a guest."

With hordes of robot servants on the job for twenty-four hours a day and seven days a week? he thought.

She sat down on the rim of the fountain basin, let her hand dangle in the warm water. The lilies clustered about her wrist, attracted by her body heat, by her perfume? Grimes submerged his own right hand. The drifting, motile plants avoided it.

She turned to face him again, looked at him with apparent frankness.

She said, "It is not in my nature to ask favors—but there is one that I must ask you. You know that the Graf von Stolzberg is your son. He does not know that you are his father. He believes, as do many people on El Dorado, that he was sired by the Comte Henri de Messigny. I have made no demands on you until now. . . ." She paused. "No, I am not demanding. I am asking. This. If you enter Baron Kane's service will you, as it were, take Ferdinand under your wing?"

I wish that I'd had some say in naming the boy, thought Grimes.

He said, "But how can I?"

She said, "Then Baron Kane has not told you everything? But you will have to know sooner or later. Perhaps you have wondered what is to stop one of the privateers from deciding not to return to El Dorado with his spoils, from proceeding with all speed to, say, the Duchy of Waldegren or some other worlds or world where loot could be sold at a profit without too many questions being asked. This is what has been arranged. Each of the ships will carry an El Doradan supernumerary officer, seconded from our navy. These officers will make their reports, by Carlotti radio, at regular intervals, to our admiralty. Coded reports, of course."

"And if one of them fails to report, so what?" asked Grimes.

"I haven't finished yet. You know of our watchbirds. . . ."

"I do. But I just can't imagine such a contraption flapping around inside a spaceship."

"I should not need to tell you that our guardians are not necessarily in avian form. But guardians there will be, in the guise of some animal that might be carried aboard a spaceship as a pet. They will be programed to kill in defense of their masters. They will also be programed to self-destruct, catastrophically, should their masters be dead."

"And you think that young . . . Ferdinand will be appointed to my ship, to *Sister Sue?"*

"Of that I cannot be sure. It might be better if he is not. It could prove embarrassing. But this I do know. Baron Kane has said that his fleet of privateers must have a commodore and that you are the obvious man for the choice. As commodore you will have overall responsibility. You will be able to protect my son—*our* son—from danger."

"But he's a naval officer," said Grimes. "A spaceman. . . ."

And what was the El Doradan Navy? A rich men's yacht club, its flagship a luxury cruising liner rated as an auxiliary cruiser. . . .

"He has never been in any sort of action," said the Princess. "But he's young and foolish. He hopes that there will be fighting."

"If I have my way," said Grimes, *"if* I join Drongo Kane's private gang, *if* I'm put in command of his ragtag fleet, there won't be. We shall keep well clear of real warships and confine our attentions to unarmed merchantmen."

"But you will enter Baron Kane's service," she pressed.

She was pressing in more ways than verbally. She was sitting very close to him on the basin rim, almost melting against him.

Damn you, he thought, *do you want it or don't you?* His arms were about her, hers about him. This time she made no objection to his straying hands. Her mouth was hot on his, open, her darting tongue busy. No matter what her motivations—anxious mother? Drongo Kane's recruiting sergeant?—she was as ready for him as he was for her. What if the conservatory were bugged? (It almost certainly was; on this world the Monitor saw all, heard all, knew all.)

He had worked her dress down over her shoulders, exposing her breasts. Her nipples were erect under his insistent fingeys. She moaned, kissing him ever more hotly. One of her hands was at his crotch.

She. . . .

He. . . .

They overbalanced, fell with a loud splash into the fountain basin.

The water was neither deep nor cold but the sudden shock killed desire.

He scrambled out, then assisted her out of the pool. She glared at him as she hastily adjusted her clothing. Then she laughed. It was genuine amusement with nothing vicious about it. She was still laughing when two of the Duchess's robot lady's maids appeared, solicitously wrapped her in a huge white towel and led her away. Grimes, chuckling ruefully, followed.

"There *is* a swimming pool, John," said the Duchess when he made his dripping appearance in the drawing room, "but it is not in the conservatory. I hope that none of my lilies are damaged."

The footman's livery that had been found for him fitted well enough and, in fact, was of far better quality than any of his own uniforms. Nonetheless he thought that it was time that he was getting back to his ship.

"What *did* happen, Skipper?" asked Williams as the air car bore them swiftly back to the spaceport.

"Nothing," grunted Grimes.

"But something must have happened, Captain," said Magda.

"All right," Grimes said. "I didn't cross the great water. I fell into it."

Twenty-seven

Back aboard the ship, in his quarters, Grimes buzzed Mayhew and asked him to come up to see him.

The telepath looked sardonically at Grimes' borrowed livery and asked innocently, "Did you have a nice swim, Captain?"

Grimes glared at him and growled, "You know, of course, what happened in the conservatory. What else do you know?"

"I know, Captain, that *they* want you to play a major part in their venture. Your Survey Service background and training. Your reputation. You'll be an ideal figurehead, in more ways than one. . . ."

"How so?" asked Grimes.

"If things come badly unstuck, Kane thinks, you'll be left holding the baby. He looks forward to seeing that almost as much as he does to making another fortune or two."

"The bastard!" swore Grimes.

"Of course," went on Mayhew, "the Baroness is at least partly to blame for his attitude toward you. She's inclined to nag. 'John Grimes would never have done this. John Grimes would never have done that. . . .' She has a soft spot for you and she lets it show."

"I'm glad that somebody loves me," said Grimes.

And what about Marlene? he thought. Then—*No*, he decided. *I'll not ask. She's entitled to her privacy.*

"The old Duchess quite likes you," said Mayhew, "although she's quite prepared to use you. The Hereditary Chief Lobenga despises you—but he despises all honkies, as he thinks of white men. He is amused that the honkies, Baron Kane, you and the others, will be going to all this trouble to put money into his bank account. The Lady Eulalia? She has no racial prejudices. Her blood line is so mixed that she can hardly afford them. She doesn't care where the money comes from, or how it is made, as long as it comes in. Baron Takada? A money man pure and simple—or not so simple. The Princess von Stolzberg? She is genuinely concerned about her son and wishes that he had not volunteered to become one of the El Doradan liaison officers with the privateer fleet. And there is something more. . . ."

"What?" demanded Grimes.

Mayhew smiled and said softly, "You were thinking very strongly on the subject of the Princess's privacy, sir. I respect that privacy, since it is your wish. But. . . . No matter. Just don't go looking gift horses in the mouth."

"And what about Trojan horses?" asked Grimes. "What about the El Doradan puppies, with their lethal pets, who'll be infesting our ships?"

"Those who have invested in the project," said Mayhew, "not unnaturally wish their investment to be protected. The Trojan horses, as you refer to them, are one means of doing this. There are other methods, less immediate but effective nonetheless. Baron Takada's net is flung wide, very wide. Should a liaison officer defect or be rendered ineffective, should his deadly pet be somehow destroyed without the subsequent destruction of all around it, then the lucky ship would find itself to be an extremely unlucky one, unable to find a market for its stolen goods, harried by officialdom throughout the galaxy."

"Perhaps," said Grimes. "Oh, you didn't include the Baroness in your rundown. . . ."

Mayhew laughed. "You have a friend there, John. A very good one. But like all the other El Doradans she loves money. Too, she is a jealous woman. For whose benefit did she dress the way she did for Her Grace's dinner party? And then—with whom did you go for a swim—sorry, walk—in the conservatory?"

"She was playing cards," said Grimes. *"And* she had her husband in tow."

"And as I said, she is a jealous woman. And now, sir, there are matters of immediate concern. The natives are becoming restless."

"What natives?"

"Your own crew, Captain. Oh, I didn't have to do any snooping. I just flapped my ears in what you would describe as the normal, human manner. The Green Hornet's the most outspoken. At dinner tonight she went off at the deep end. 'What about shore leave? It's all right for His Survey Service High and Mightiness, and his two pets, to go wining and dining with the snobocracy, but what about *us?* Stuck aboard this stinking ship and told that the entire bloody planet's off limits to us. I've a good mind to take one of the boats to fly to that city of theirs!' The junior engineers, both departments, were with her. Venner told her to shut up. She tried to pull rank on him. Then Malleson and Crumley ordered their people to have nothing to do with getting a boat ready. But even they are resentful at being confined to the ship. So is old Mr. Stewart."

"I'll see what I can do about it in the morning," said Grimes.

"You'd better, Captain. One of the things that the Green Hornet shouted was, 'If he's not bloody careful he'll have another bloody mutiny on his hands!'"

"Mutinies," said Grimes coldly, "are usually a result of too much shore leave. It happened to Bligh. It happened to me, in *Discovery.* But I admit that I should have raised the point with Kane. It'd be useless talking to that tin Port Captain about it."

Twenty-eight

The next morning, after a leisurely breakfast in his quarters, Grimes went ashore to the Port Office to make his telephone calls. First he got through to the Duchess, thanking her for a very enjoyable evening and apologizing for any inconvenience that he may have caused. She thanked him for the pleasure of his company and assured him that no great damage had been done to the lilies and told him that his evening clothes, cleaned and pressed, would very shortly be sent out to him. She hoped that she would be seeing him again shortly and asked him to present her best wishes to Mr. Williams and Ms. Granadu.

Then he called Kane.

"Yes, Grimesy-boy? Are you dried out yet?"

Grimes ignored this. He said, "You're the naval authority on this world, Commodore. I'm asking you if it would be possible for my crew to have any shore leave."

"It's a pity that you aren't at Port Kane, Grimesy. I've set up some quite good entertainment facilities there for the privateers. A bar, a cabaret . . . manned—or womanned—by volunteers. It's surprising how many of the local ladies don't mind a night's slumming among the drunken and licentious spacemen. But Port Kane's a long way from Port Bluewater, isn't it? Oh, how's your discharge going, by the way?"

"It isn't," said Grimes.

"Too bad. Haven't you made your mind up yet? If you did, *the right way, that is,* you and your boys would soon be wallowing in the fleshpots of Port Kane. *And* you'd be a commodore, like me. Doesn't that tempt you?"

"Not especially," Grimes said.

"Stubborn bastard, aren't you?" remarked Kane. "Face the facts, Grimes. As an owner/master you're finished—unless you charter your ship and hire your services to me. You don't like the Hallicheki. (Who does?) Why not turn your dislike into money?"

"I'll think about it," said Grimes. "Meanwhile, what about shore leave for my personnel?"

"I'll fix it," said Kane. "I'm a spaceman myself and I know what it's like being stuck aboard the ship when you're in port."

Grimes called the Schloss Stolzberg.

The face of a pewter-visaged servitor appeared on the screen. Then the Princess put in her appearance. Grimes wondered how it had been that he had thought her dowdy. She had matured—but why should she not have done so? Her blue eyes were far from cold. (Whatever had given him the idea that they were?) She smiled at him from inside the screen.

"John! It was fun last night, wasn't it?"

"I trust that you suffered no ill effects, Your Highness."

She laughed. "Shall we forget the titles? I'll call you John, not Captain. You may call me Marlene. When can you come out to stay with me again?"

"My time is my own," said Grimes. "I'm owner as well as master."

Her expression clouded briefly. She said, "At the moment I'm rather tied up. Perhaps after you've shifted your ship from Port Bluewater to Port Kane. . . ."

He said, "I have to finish discharge first. In any case I still haven't said that I'm willing to join Drongo Kane's private navy."

"But you've no option," she said. "Have you? There is nobody else whom I can trust to look after Ferdinand."

Grimes winced. "Tell me," he asked, "why *that* name?"

"Don't you like it, John?"

"Frankly, no."

"It is one that has been in my family, on my mother's side, for a very long time. Even you will admit that the Graf Ferdinand von Zeppelin was illustrious. My Ferdinand—*your* Ferdinand—is descended from an aeronaut. He is an astronaut.

"Is it not, somehow, fitting?"

"Mphm," grunted Grimes.

Twenty-nine

Shore leave was arranged for that evening.

"You'd better go with the boys, Captain," said Mayhew. "If it's going to be as grim as I think that it will be you'll have to be seen sharing the vicissitudes of your gallant crew. I'll come along too. I'm not officially on your Articles but I don't think that anybody will notice."

"Very noble of you," grunted Grimes.

"I shall find it interesting," said the telepath.

Williams—lucky man, although he did not know it yet—was shipkeeping. Magda Granadu had elected to keep him company. Mr. Singh, sulking hard, was remaining on board to look after the essential services. There was small likelihood that anything would fail, but Grimes had modeled his own, Far Traveler Couriers, regulations on those of the Federation Survey Service.

The liberty party, attired in a variety of civilian clothing, was waiting at the foot of the ramp when the Wilberforce air car came to pick them up. *Not the sort of company I'd choose for a night ashore,* thought Grimes snobbishly. The Green Hornet, in an outfit of slightly soiled scarlet flounces, was talking with Denning and Paulus, the first in a suit of garish plaid, the other in a shirt of poisonous green with a bright orange kilt and sagging socks of the same color. A not very high-class tart, Grimes thought, trying to entice two honest mechanics enjoying a night out in the big city into her brothel. . . . And Venner, in rusty black, could have been a bouncer from the same establishment. Trantor and Giddings, Malleson's juniors, were holding themselves aloof from the others, already trying to put the message across, *We don't really belong with this mob.* They were neatly, too neatly attired in conservative dark gray with gleaming white shirts and black cravats. Malleson was every inch the tweedy, absentminded professor. Old Mr. Crumley and old Mr. Stewart, both coincidentally rigged out in dusty brown, looked as though they should be occupying rocking chairs on the porch of a senior citizens' home. Mayhew, gray-clad, was also wearing his senior clerk persona. Grimes himself was looking smart enough in sharply creased white trousers over which was a high-collared black tunic with, on its left breast, his own badge, the horse and rider worked in gold.

The big air car, almost an air bus, came bumbling in from the north. This was no fantastically silent, superbly styled, pseudo Rolls Royce. It was, essentially, only an oblong box on wheels. It dropped down for a clumping, graceless landing. The robot chauffeur remained in his seat although he did condescend to press the button that opened the doors. The officers boarded the vehicle, Grimes last of all. He sat with Malleson and Mayhew on the rear transverse seat. Before he was properly settled the air car lifted. The sonic insulation was of very poor quality and the cacophony of the inertial drive unit inhibited conversation. Nonetheless Malleson tried to talk.

"This Countess of Wilberforce, Captain. . . . Do you know her?"

"No," Grimes almost shouted. "But I know of her."

"What's she like?"

"Filthy rich, like everybody else here."

"Why has she invited us to her bunstruggle?"

"Charity."

"Charity?"

"She's a notorious do-gooder."

"What have you got us into, Captain?"

"You all wanted shore leave, Chief. This was the only way that I could arrange it."

Conversation lapsed.

Grimes looked glumly out of the window, at the twilit landscape below, sliding rapidly astern. He could not see ahead but he could tell that the car was now descending. Jarring contact was made with the road surface and the vehicle rolled along the broad avenue with the mansions, each in its own extensive grounds, on either side. It turned into a driveway, shuddered to a halt.

Wilberforce Hall was a red brick building of three stories, graceless but without enough character to be actually ugly. Inside the open main doorway stood one of the inevitable robot butlers and with him a tall, thin woman, black-gowned but with touches of white at throat and wrists. Her dark hair was scraped back from a high, pale forehead. Her bulging, pale gray eyes were set too close together over a beaky nose. Her mouth was small, the lips wrinkled. Her chin was almost nonexistent.

"Come in, boys and girls!" she cried in a high, sickeningly playful voice. She tittered. "Sorry. Boys and *girl* I should have said!"

Grimes made the introductions. He and the others were led into a chilly hall where there were hard chairs and little tables, where a few girls, mercifully prettier than their hostess, brought them weak tea and plates of uninteresting sandwiches and hard little cakes.

Grimes, with Malleson, Crumley and Stewart, sat at a table with the Countess.

"It is so good to have you here, Captain," she gushed. "I have been blessed with wealth and I feel that it is my responsibility to bring joy to others."

"Mphm." Grimes pulled out his pipe and tobacco pouch from a pocket, began to fill the former.

"Please don't think me stuffy," said the Countess, "but I would be so pleased if you wouldn't smoke, Captain. You are doing your lungs no good, you know, and there is even the possibility of brain damage. . . ."

Grimes put his pipe away.

"And we have such a treat for you this evening. As you may know I am the patroness of a number of missionary societies. Bishop Davis has very kindly sent me records of the work of his people among the Carolines. . . ."

The Carolines? Yes, Grimes recalled having read about them. They were a lost colony, descended from the survivors of a long-ago wreck, that of the gaussjammer *Lode Caroline.* They had been fortunate enough to make their landing on an almost paradisal world, one on which nature was kind, too kind perhaps. They had lived there happily, latter day lotus-eaters, until the Survey Service's exploration ship *Starfinder* had stumbled upon their planet. Their "lotus," a fleshy leaved plant which was their staple diet, had been investigated by *Starfinder*'s scientists. Its organic chemistry was such that synthesis of the complex amino acids would be almost impossible. Daily ingestion of the leaves—raw, or cooked in various ways, or mashed and fermented to make a sort of sweet beer—ensured longevity, freedom from all minor and some major ills and, as a not unpleasant side effect, a state of continuous mild euphoria.

New Caroline was now a commercially important world.

And, thought Grimes, almost certainly the El Dorado Corporation had a dirty finger in that financial pie.

Two robot servants pulled aside the heavy drapes that covered one of the walls of the hall, revealing a huge playmaster screen. As this came to glowing life, depicting a green, blue and gold sphere slowly spinning in space, the lights in the room dimmed.

A sonorous voice announced, "New Caroline—where every prospect pleases but only man is vile. Where only man *was* vile until our coming, until we, of the New Reformed Missionary Alliance were able to bring to the unhappy people the Way, the Truth and the Light. . . .

"The Federation Survey Service has made available to us records taken by the personnel of *Starfinder.* These we show you so that you may judge for yourselves the depravity of the Lost Colonists, the degradation from which we have rescued them."

The planetary globe faded from the screen, was replaced by a village by a wide river, huts of adobe, grass roofed. The time seemed to be late afternoon. A woman emerged from one of the huts, raised her arms and yawned widely. Her teeth were very white against the red of her mouth, the dark, golden tan of her face. She was naked, firmly plump rather than fat. (The Countess looked reprovingly at Grimes as, at one of the other tables, Denning whistled loudly and Paulus remarked, in a carrying whisper, "A lovely dollop of trollop. . . .") She sauntered to a clump of purplish vegetation, aimost like a huge artichoke, growing between her hut and its neighbor. She broke off the tip of a succulent leaf, brought it to her mouth, chewed slowly. She spat out a wad of fibrous pulp.

"Observe," intoned the commentator, "the shamelessness of these people, living in filth and squalor. . . ."

(Grimes did not approve of people spitting chewed cuds all over the place but that village looked neither filthy nor squalid—and certainly that sun-tanned body looked clean enough.)

Other people were emerging from their huts—men, women, children of various ages, all innocent of clothing. There was an absence of anybody very old—but that, thought Grimes, could be attributable to the beneficial effects of their staple diet. All the men were heavily bearded. Each of them? had a nibble of lotus leaf and then all of them strolled down to the slow flowing river, waded through the shallows and then swam lazily up and down. Grimes ignored the rantings of the commentator and did his best to enjoy the idyllic scene.

"That was *then,*" came the annoying voice. "This is *now.* During the few years that we have been on New Caroline we have made great strides. The naked have been clothed. The people have been aroused from their sinful indolence and now experience the benefits deriving from honest toil. . . ."

There were shots of long, neat parallel rows of the artichoke-like plant between which overall-clad Lost Colonists, their clothing dark-stained with perspiration, were working—weeding, spraying fertilizer from backpack tanks, plucking tender young leaves and putting them into baskets. Strolling foremen—Grimes could not be sure, but these men had the appearance of Waldegrensians—supervised, at times seemed to speak harshly to the workers. (Apart from the commentary there was no sound track.)

"And after the day's gainful employment there is the joy that only true religion can bring. . . ."

There was an exterior shot of an ugly chapel constructed of sheet plastic. There was an interior shot of the same building—the pews with the worshippers, dowdily clad in what looked like cast-off clothing from a score of worlds in as many styles—although every woman's dress was long, high-necked and with sleeves to the wrist. There was the pulpit where the black-robed priest was holding forth. There was a small organ at which a woman sat, hands on the keyboard, feet pedaling vigorously. Although an agnostic, Grimes had a weakness for certain hymns, especially those of the Moody and Sankey variety. But what this dispirited congregation was singing failed to turn him on. Not only were the words uninspired but the wheezy apology for a tune was not one to set the feet tapping or the hands clapping.

For many a year we lived in sin
And never knew the Lord;
But now we have been taken in
And glorify His Word . . .

Oh for a good, honest, Salvation Army band, he thought, *with blaring brass and thumping drums and the lassies with their tambourines. . . .*

Grimes awoke with a start and realized that the film was over.

". . . noble work, Captain," the Countess was saying. "And the contrast! Those poor sinners wallowing in squalor, and then the happy, industrious people at the finish. . . ."

"Mphm," grunted Grimes, who did not feel like telling any lies.

"And now you must excuse me, Captain. I have my humble part to play."

She got up from her chair, walked to the portable organ, the harmonium that had been wheeled in to below the now dark and empty screen. The pretty girls who had been helping to entertain the spacemen distributed hymn sheets. The Countess played. The girls waved *Sister Sue*'s people to their feet and started to sing. Reluctantly, hesitantly, the spacemen joined in. It was hard to say which was more dismal, the words or the music.

Sinners all, we beg for grace
And grovel at Thy feet,
And pray that even in this place
We find Thy Mercy Seat!

Holding that thick sheaf of printed matter in his hands Grimes feared that the ordeal would go on for hours. But the fourth sheet was not part of a hymnal; it was the beginning of a brochure.

THE HAPPY KANGAROO, Grimes read with some amazement.

MUSIC, DANCING AND GIRLS, GIRLS, GIRLS!

Meanwhile the portable organ had fallen silent and the Countess had risen to her feet.

"Thank you all for coming!" she cried. "I am glad that I was able to bring some happiness into your drab lives. The air car is waiting for you outside, but before you leave there will be a collection for the Mission. I am sure that you will all welcome this opportunity to contribute . . ."

One of the girls was circulating with a collecting bag. She grinned at Grimes and the others at his table.

"The party's over, spaceman," she whispered, "but if you come to Port Kane the entertainment will be more to your taste!"

Grimes made to put the hymn sheets and the other literature down on the table.

"Keep all the paper, Captain," she said. "You may be needing it." She laughed softly. "It'll please old Florry no end if she thinks you're holding revival meetings aboard your ship. And now. . . ."

She shook the bag suggestively.

The smallest money that Grimes had on him was a fifty-credit bill. He sighed as he made his contribution to the good cause. He wondered who else had contributed, managed to peak inside the bag and saw that, apart from his note, it was empty.

The Countess stood at the door bidding her guests good night.

"Please come again. . . ."

"Not bloody likely," was a too audible whisper from the Green Hornet.

"It was so nice having you."

"That's what you think," muttered somebody. Denning, Grimes thought.

"And you have seen, now, what good work we do among the disadvantaged, how we have raised a backward people to full civilization. . . ."

"I'm crying for the Carolines," Grimes could not resist saying.

"But there is no need for you to cry for them now, Captain. They have been saved, *saved.* Good night, good night, and bless you all!"

Grimes, at last tearing himself away to board the air car, was met by the hostile stares of his officers.

Back aboard the ship he told an amused and sympathetic Billy Williams what the evening had been like, enjoyed coffee and *real* sandwiches with him and Magda before going up to his quarters. Mayhew joined him there.

"Well," growled Grimes, "what did *you* make of it?"

The telepath grinned. "The Countess is genuine enough, in her way. She's not the first example of a too wealthy woman who's tried to buy her way into heaven. Too, the missionaries have opened up New Caroline to exploitation—which has been a good thing for the El Dorado Corporation."

"Those girls," demanded Grimes. "And this bumf. . . ."

He pulled the hymn sheets and the brochure from his pocket, threw the papers down on the coffee table.

"The girls," said Mayhew, "were both spies and recruiting agents. They were circulating among the juniors, subtly sounding them out, not so subtly promising them a good time if the ship should come to Port Kane." He picked up the brochure, leafed through it to the picture of a dancer. "Recognize her?"

"Mphm. She was the one carrying the collection bag around, wasn't she? Who'd ever have thought that she was like that under the frumpish black dress?"

"Never judge a parcel by its wrapping," said Mayhew philosophically.

"Clothes make the woman what she really isn't," countered Grimes. "That cuts both ways."

"Too true. Anyhow, Captain, before long the boys will be asking why you can't shift ship to Port Kane where there's some real action. Too, I have the feeling that your old friend Commodore Kane will be calling around shortly, promising to expedite discharge if you agree to join his private navy. I suggest that you convey the impression that (a) you could use some money, preferably in great, coarse hunks. . . ."

"You can say that again, Mr. Mayhew!"

". . . and (b) that you're craving a spot of excitement."

"Which I'm not."

"Aren't you, sir? And, in any case, I should not need to remind you that you are acting under Survey Service orders as much as Mr. Venner and myself are. Your job, for which you are being paid a four-ring captain's salary and allowance. . . ."

"I haven't seen the money yet."

"You—or your estate—will receive it as a lump sum when the mission has been brought to its conclusion. You are being paid, as I say, to infiltrate, and then to contrive an incident."

"All right, all right. I have to take the plunge some time. I just don't want to appear too eager."

"Perhaps," said Mayhew, "you should allow the Princess von Stolzberg to talk you around. That would be in character."

"Would it?" demanded Grimes. "Would it? I think that you had better go now, Mr. Mayhew."

Thirty

Grimes was finishing a late breakfast—almost always he took this meal in his own quarters—when the telephone buzzed. He thought that it would be one of his officers wishing to tell him something.

"Captain here," he said, facing the instrument.

The little screen came alive. To his surprise it was the face of Drongo Kane looking out at him. He thought, at first, that the piratical commodore was aboard the ship, was calling from the mate's or the purser's office. That tin Port Captain had told him that it would not be possible for the ship's telephones to be hooked up with the El Doradan planetary communications system. But the background scenery was wrong. None of the bulkheads in *Sister Sue*'s accommodation was covered with blue wallpaper on which, embossed in gold, was a floral design.

He said, "How did you get through to me? I was told that I could use the ship's telephones only to talk to the port office."

"We can make calls to you," said Kane smugly. Then, "I hope that you and your merry crew enjoyed last night's outing."

"Ha!" growled Grimes. "Ha, bloody ha!"

"Your people," Kane went on, "would be far happier at the spaceport that the corporation, in recognition of my services, named after me. And you'd be much happier too, knowing that your ship was earning money again. Once she's on charter she gets paid, even when she's sitting on her big, fat arse, at my spaceport, waiting for the balloon to go up."

"I'm thinking about it," said Grimes grudgingly.

"Just don't be too long making your mind up, Grimesyboy. Until you do there'll be no cargo worked—and then only if you make your mind up the right way. I'll be waiting to hear from you."

The screen went blank.

Grimes poured a last cup of coffee, filled and lit his pipe. It was very fortunate, he thought, that Kane did not, as he did, have the services of a tame telepath. He had raised this point already with Mayhew, had been told that the

El Doradans would not tolerate the presence on their world of anybody capable of prying into their precious minds.

The telephone buzzed again.

"Captain here," he told it.

It was another outside call. It was the Princess Marlene.

"Good morning, John." She laughed prettily. "I hear that you had a very boring time last night. I feel that I should offer some small compensation. Are you free today?"

"I am, M . . . Sorry. Your Highness."

She smiled out at him. "Marlene would have been better. So you are free. Then I shall call for you at . . . 1100 hours? Will that be suitable? Good. Can you stay overnight at the Schloss? Excellent. Until eleven, then."

She faded from the screen.

"Mphm?" grunted Grimes, recalling Mayhew's advice. "Mphm."

He called for Williams.

The chief officer, as soon as he set foot in Grimes' cabin, started complaining.

"I've been on the blower to that so-called Port Captain," he said. "He—or it—just couldn't tell me when any more cargo would be worked. You've your contacts here, sir. Can't you do anything?"

"Just be patient, Mr. Williams," Grimes told him.

"Patient, sir? You should have heard the growls over the breakfast table. And the engineers were waving those pamphlets about—*you* know, the advertising for all the fancy facilities at Port Kane. I told them what it would mean if we did shift ship there, the privateering and all the rest of it. They got interested and wanted to know if there was any money in it. And *your* pet, the Green Hornet, said, 'Forget it! Our saintly captain would never dirty his hands with piracy! All that he's fit for is dragging us to prayer meetings, like last night!'"

"There have been pious pirates," said Grimes. "One of my ancestors was one such. But tell me, what would your reaction be if I accepted Commodore Kane's offer of employment?"

"I'd be with you, sir," said the mate at last. "After all, privateering is not piracy. It's legal. And there should be money in it. The way I understand it is that the people financing the venture—in this case the El Dorado Corporation—would be entitled to a large percentage of the take, the balance being divvied up among the crew, according to rank. Something like a salvage award. . . ."

"Sound people out, will you?" Grimes looked at the bulkhead clock. "And now, you'll have to excuse me. I have to get packed."

"You're leaving us, sir?"

"Only for a day. The Princess von Stolzberg will be picking me up at eleven. I shall be staying at the Schloss Stolzberg overnight. You'll know where to find me if anything horrid happens."

"Will do, Skipper. And so Her Highness has forgiven you for the swimming party. . . . If you can't be good, be careful."

"I'll try," said Grimes.

He was waiting at the foot of the ramp when the Princess's air car came in. It was not the gaily colored mechanical dragonfly in which he had ridden with her before, years ago. It was a far more sober vehicle, although conforming to the current El Doradan fad or fashion. "A Daimler . . ." whispered Williams reverently to his captain as the elegant black vehicle, its silver fittings gleaming in the late mormng sun, came in to an almost noiseless landing.

"A bloody hearse," muttered Ms. Connellan. "It's even got vultures following it!"

But they were not, of course, vultures. The pair of watchbirds, circling alertly overhead, were more like ravens.

Two doors of the car opened, one forward, one aft. The Princess, Grimes saw, was sitting in the front seat. She turned her head to smile at him invitingly. She looked softly maternal in a frilly pink dress—and yet there was more than a hint of the slim, golden girl whom Grimes had once known.

He threw his overnight bag into the rear of the vehicle, wondering if he was doing the right thing as he made to board at the front end. Apparently he was; the inviting smile did not fade as he took his seat by his hostess.

The doors closed.

Marlene's hands remained demurely folded on her lap, were not lifted to take the controls.

"Home," she ordered.

The car lifted. Inside it was as silent as the pseudo-Rolls had been.

She broke the silence, asking, "Do you remember the last time, John?"

"Yes, Marlene."

"You will find little changed," she told him. "The Croesus Mines are still in operation. . . ."

Yes, there was the low, spotlessly white building in the shallow, green valley. Below it, Grimes knew, were the fully automated subterranean workings. He wondered over how great an area these now extended.

"And the Laredo Ranch. . . . Senator Crocker is still playing at cowboys, rounding up his herds and all the rest of it. He's conquered his prejudice against robot ranch hands now. . . ."

Looking down, Grimes saw that a round-up was in progress, a milling herd of red-brown cattle with horsemen keeping the beasts grouped together. Which one of them was Crocker and which were the robots? They all looked the same from up here.

"Count Vitelli's vineyards. His wines are improving all the time."

"The Baroness d'Estang," said Grimes, "kept a good stock of them aboard her yacht, *The Far Traveler. . . .*"

"I still find it hard to understand," she said, "how and why you—of all people!—became a yachtmaster. And to *that* woman, of all possible employers!"

"Mphm."

"Some people," she went on cattily, "think that she married beneath her. If anything, the reverse is the case. The Baron is descended from an English lord. He had no trouble at all establishing his claim to the title. . . ."

I wonder how much it cost him? thought Grimes.

"And she, of course, is descended from a French pirate. . . ."

"A privateer," said Grimes. He would have liked to have said, *And you, my dear, are descended from German robber barons. . . .* He thought better of it. He would not bite the hand that, hopefully, was going to feed him.

"A privateer," she repeated. "What's the difference? Oh, there is a difference now, of course. The Baron's fleet will do nothing illegal. If I thought otherwise I would not have allowed Ferdinand to volunteer to serve as a liaison officer.

"Will Ferdinand be at the castle?" asked Grimes, half hoping and half fearing that the answer would be in the affirmative.

"No. He is at Port Kane with the other El Doradan officers. Perhaps it is as well. It could be embarrassing if you met him in my company." Her hands went up to the wheel, grasped it firmly. It was an indication, thought Grimes, that she was determined to control the course of events. "And it will be as well, John, if he never knows that you are his father."

"Will he be seconded to my ship?" asked Grimes. "Assuming, that is," he added hastily, "that I join the enterprise."

"No. If he were it is possible that the relationship would become public knowledge. He will be attached to *Agatha's Ark,* under Captain Agatha Prinn. A strange woman, John, but, I believe, a highly competent spaceperson. Meanwhile, I understand that Baron Kane intends to appoint you commodore of the privateers. As you will be in overall charge you will be able to keep a watchful eye on my son. Our son."

"I haven't decided yet," said Grimes, "if I'm going to take Kane's offer."

"But you will," she said.

She relinquished her hold on the wheel so that she could point ahead. There, on a hilltop, was the grim, gray pile, a castle that was straight out of a book of Teutonic mythology. Schloss Stolzberg. As before, Grimes wondered how much it had cost to transport it, stone by numbered stone, from Earth. *I wish that somebody would give* me a *job like that,* he thought. He tried to arrive at a rough estimate of what the freight charges would have been.

Thirty-one

Slowly, smoothly, the car drifted down to a landing in the central courtyard, dropping past flagpoles from which snapped and fluttered heavy standards, golden heraldic beasts rampant on fields of purple, past turrets and battlemented walls, down to the gray, rough flagstones. From somewhere came the baying of hounds. Then as the doors of the vehicle opened, there was a high, clear trumpet call, a flourish of drums.

"Welcome, again, to Schloss Stolzberg," said the Princess.

"It hasn't changed," said Grimes.

"Why should it have done so, John?" she asked.

To this there was no reply.

He got out of his seat, stepped to the ground, then helped the Princess down. Her hand was pleasantly warm and smooth in his. She thanked him, then turned to address the car.

"We shall not be needing you again," she told it. "You can put yourself to bed."

A melodious toot from the vehicle's horn was the reply. The thing lifted, its inertial drive unit purring almost inaudibly. It flew toward a doorway that suddenly and silently opened in the rough stone wall, then quietly closed behind it.

She put her hand in the crook of his left arm, guided him to a tall, arched portal. The valves were of some dark timber, heavily iron studded, and as they moved on their ponderous hinges they creaked loudly. Grimes did not think, as he had his first time here, that this was an indication of inefficiency on the part of the castle's robot staff. Those hinges, he had been told, were meant to creak. It was all part of the atmosphere.

They were in the main hall now, a huge barn of a place but, unlike a real barn, cheerless. Only a little daylight stabbed through the high, narrow windows and the flaring torches and the fire that blazed in the enormous hearth did little more than cast a multiplicity of confused, flickering shadows. Ranged along the walls were what, at first glance, looked like space-suited men standing at rigid attention. But it was not space armor; these empty suits had been worn by men of Earth's Middle Ages. By men? By knights and barons and princes, rather; in those days the commonality had gone into battle with only thick leather (if that) as a partial protection. Marlene's ancestors had fought their petty wars ironclad. Grimes wondered what they would think if they could watch their daughter being squired by a man who, in their day, would have been only a humble tiller of the fields or, in battle, a fumbling pikeman fit only to be ridden down by a charge of metal-accoutered so-called chivalry.

Grimes, you're an inverted snob! he chided himself.

She led him across the hall, past a long, heavy banqueting table with rows of high-backed chairs on either side. She took the seat at the head of it, occupied it as though it were the throne it looked like. In her overly feminine ruffled pink dress she should have struck a note of utter incongruity, but she did not. She was part of the castle and the castle was part of her.

She motioned Grimes to the chair at her right hand. It was far more comfortable than it looked. He saw that a decanter of heavy glass had been set out on the table and with it two glittering, cut-crystal goblets. Marlene poured the dark ruby wine with an oddly ceremonial gesture.

She raised her glass to him, sipped.

Grimes followed suit. He remembered that on that past occasion she had given him Angel's Blood from Wilsonia, one of the worlds of the Denebian system. She was giving him Angel's Blood again. It was a superb wine, although a little too sweet for his taste. It was also far too expensive for his pocket. Even duty free and with no freight charges it was forty credits a bottle.

She said softly, "I'd like to think that we're drinking to us. Do you remember how, years ago, I told you that you could come back here to live, to become a citizen, when you had your first billion credits?"

"I remember," said Grimes. (That was not among his happier memories.)

"You're a shipowner now, not a penniless Survey Service lieutenant. . . ."

"And I'm still not worth a billion C."

"But you could be, John. If the privateering venture is successful."

"Mphm."

"*Must* you grunt?"

"Sorry."

"I'm telling you, trying to tell you, that now you have the opportunity to become a citizen of El Dorado. A title? Proof of noble ancestry? That's no problem." She laughed. "It has been said, and probably quite correctly, that everybody in England has royal blood in his veins. Some monarchs did their best to spread it among their people. . . ."

"Such as Charles the Second," said Grimes. "But I'm Australian."

"Don't quibble."

"I like me the way I am," said Grimes. "A shipmaster. A shipowner."

"And a father."

"Ferdinand," he said, "is *your* son."

"And yours, John. You were there too. Or have you forgotten?"

He had not. He accepted the fresh glass of wine that she poured for him. (The decanter, not a small one, was now almost empty.)

"You have a responsibility," she went on.

Why didn't you engineer my discharge from the Survey Service, as, with your wealth, you could so easily have done? he thought. *But, of course, 1 didn't have that billion credits and then it didn't look as though I ever would. . . .*

A robutler in black and silver livery removed the now empty decanter and goblets from the table. Another one set down mats on the polished wood. More wine was brought, a chilled Riesling. And there were fat, succulent oysters on the half shell and a plate of brown bread and butter. Despite his nickname, Gutsy Grimes, the spaceman rarely, these days, enjoyed a large lunch, preferring to start the day with a good breakfast and to finish it with a good dinner, with possibly a substantial supper if he were up late.

"From the beds in the Green River," said Marlene. "I think that you will find them to your taste, John. Their ancestral stock is the Sydney Rock Oyster."

Grimes enjoyed them. So did Marlene. He thought, patting his lips with a napkin of fine linen, *If that was lunch, I've had it. And liked it.* But there was more to come—steak tartare, with raw egg, raw onion sliced paper-thin, gherkins, capers and anchovies, with a Vitelli Burgundy to accompany it. There was cheese, locally made but at least as good as any Brie that Grimes had sampled on Earth. There was, finally, aromatic coffee laced with some potent spirit that Grimes could not identify.

He looked at Marlene through eyes that he knew were slightly glazed. She looked at him through eyes that, as his were, were indicative of the effects of a surfeit of good food and good wine.

She said, "You look rather tired, John."

He said, "I'm all right, Marlene. It's just that I usually have a very light meal in the middle of the day."

"But you *are* tired. Don't you have a saying, This is Liberty Hall, you can spit on the mat and call the cat a bastard? This is Liberty Hall. If a guest of mine wants an afternoon siesta, then he shall have one."

She pushed her chair back from the table. Grimes rose from his own, moved to assist her to her feet. For a second or so she hung heavily in his arms.

She said, "I'll show you to your room."

She guided him through corridors, then up one of the spiral staircase escalators that were a feature of El Doradan architecture. They came to a suite that consisted of sitting room, bedroom and bathroom, plainly but very comfortably furnished. The wide bed, seen through the open door of the sitting room, looked very inviting.

"Mix us drinks, please, John," said Marlene, indicating the bar to one side of the sitting room. "I would like something long and refreshing. Use your own discretion."

She went through into the bedroom, then to the bathroom.

Grimes went to the bar, studied the array of bottles. The labels of some of these were familiar, others were not. Those that were not looked very, very expensive.

He thought, *I'd better play it safe.*

He found gin. In the refrigerator there were bottles of tonic water, the real stuff, imported from Earth. There were ice cubes, and lemons. He busied himself quite happily and, before long had prepared two tall, inviting glasses, each with its exterior misted with condensation.

And now, where was his hostess?

She was in the bed, her plump, naked shoulders creamily luminescent against the dark blue bed linen, her golden hair fanned out on the pillow. Her smile was both sleepy and inviting.

Oddly, for him, Grimes was feeling guilty.

The censor who lived in his mind and who, now and again, made himself heard was telling him that he should not be enjoying himself.

Grimes, she's fat. *She's not your sort of woman at all. . . .*

But she was a most comfortable ride.

Grimes, she's just using you. . . .

And didn't women always use men?

Grimes, you're using her. You're letting her persuade you to do just what you've come to this world to do. . . .

But why shouldn't he, he thought rebelliously, enjoy whatever fringe benefits came with the job into which he had been press-ganged by Rear Admiral Damien?

The feeling of guilt diminished but did not quite go away.

All right, all right, the Princess was a mercenary bitch, a founding member of the money-hungry El Dorado Corporation. Grimes, as a privateer commodore, would be a valuable employee of the Corporation. But. . . . But she was also a mother, concerned about the safety of the son whom he, Grimes, had yet to meet.

They shared a shuddering climax after which she continued to hold him tightly, her body soft and warm against his. Now he really wanted to go to sleep.

But she said, "John. Darling. What we had so many years ago has not been lost after all. . . ."

"No . . ." he lied.

(Or was it the truth? After that heavy lunch and the strenuous bedroom gymnastics he did not feel inclined to analyze his feelings.)

"You will make me very happy if you agree to become commodore of the privateer squadron. I shall know then that Ferdinand will be safe."

"I've always wanted to be a commodore," said Grimes.

"Then you will become one? For us?"

"Yes," said Grimes.

He wondered if his consent had been registered by the monitor. It almost certainly had been. There was no backing out now.

"John, darling, you've made us very happy. . . ."

Her soft lips brushed his ear as she whispered the words.

"And I'm happy to be of service to you," he replied.

They drifted into sleep then, limbs intertwined. It was a pity, he thought, that she snored—but the almost musical noise did not prevent him from following her into sweet unconsciousness.

Thirty-two

When he awoke it was late evening. He was alone in the big bed.

Well, he thought philosophically, *it was nice while it lasted.*

Somebody had come into the sitting room of his suite. *Marlene?* he wondered. (Hoped?) But by the gradually increasing illumination he could see that it was one of the robot servitors, carrying a large tray which was set down on a low table visible through the bedroom door.

Tea? wondered Grimes. He hoped that it was. Then the robot moved away and he could see that it was a silver ice bucket from which protruded the slender neck of a tall bottle. There was a tulip glass—no, glasses. There was what looked like a dish of canapés.

Marlene appeared in the doorway. The subdued lighting was kind to her. She was wearing a diaphanous robe through which her full—too full?—body was clearly visible. (But she was no plumper, thought Grimes, than fat Susie had been before her remodeling.)

"You are awake, darling," she murmured. "I had hoped to wake you in the time-honored way. . . ."

Nonetheless she billowed into the bedroom, planted a warm, moist kiss on his not unwilling lips. She seemed to be inclined to carry on from there—but Grimes had more urgent matters on his mind.

He said, as he tried to break away from her embrace, but not too abruptly, "You'll have to excuse me for a few moments, Marlene. I have to go to the bathroom. . . ."

"Then go."

She released him but remained seated on the bed.

Grimes got from under the covers, feeling absurdly embarrassed. (Had it not been for the knowledge that each of them was using the other his nudity would not have worried him.) He went into the bathroom, closed the door behind him, did what he had to do. He was relieved to find a dressing gown of dark blue silk—it seemed to be a new garment—hanging there. He put it on. When he emerged he found that the Princess was in the sitting room, sprawled rather inelegantly in one of the chairs by the low table.

"Open the bottle, John darling," she said.

Grimes untwisted the wire and eased the old-fashioned cork free, hastily poured before too much of the foaming wine was lost.

"To success," toasted the Princess.

"To success," repeated Grimes.

They clinked glasses. She regarded him over the rim of hers. He wished that he had missed the coldly calculating gleam in her blue eyes. He wished that she were loving him for himself, not for what he could do for her.

The telephone—an instrument that Grimes, until now, had not known was part of the sitting room's appointments—chimed. The Princess, facing the corner just beyond the bar, said, "Marlene here."

The air shimmered and then a holographic projection of the pewter-faced majordomo appeared.

"Your Highess, an officer from the ship, *Sister Sue,* is calling. He wishes to speak with his captain."

"Very well, Karl. You may put him through."

The image of the robutler faded, was replaced by that of Williams. He seemed to be looking directly into the room—as, in fact, he was. Grimes wished that he were wearing something more formal than a dressing gown, that Marlene's negligee were not so transparent. The mate—blast him!—was trying hard not to leer.

"Sorry if I interrupted anything, Skipper," he said cheerfully.

"What is it, Mr. Williams?"

"The Baron, sir. Commodore Kane. He's just been on board. He asked me to call a meeting of all hands—which, of course, I did. He treated us to a fine sales talk on the pleasures and profits of privateering. Yes, it was a sales talk all right. He could sell a pair of hairbrushes to a bald man. . . ."

"Get on with it, Mr. Williams. Are the people willing to join Kane's enterprise?"

"Too right, Skipper. Even Magda. She insisted on going through her ritual with the coins and the book and came up with the *Chieh* hexagram." He looked at a scrap of paper that he was holding. "Regulation. There will be progress and success. But if the regulation is too severe and difficult, its good effect will not last long. . . ."

"So? Is that a good forecast?"

"It is, Skipper. You'll just have to ride with a loose rein, that's all."

"Mphm. You all seem to be sure that I shall agree to charter my ship to the El Dorado Corporation."

"The commodore gave us to understand, Skipper, that you'd agreed."

Grimes looked at Marlene. She looked back at him rather too innocently. Grimes turned his attention back to the solid-seeming image of Williams.

"All right, all right. Then why call me to tell me about it?"

"There's more, Skipper. We're to complete discharge at Port Kane. The commodore wants you back so that you can shift ship so as to be at Port Kane tomorrow morning, their time. There's a twelve-hour differential."

Grimes looked again at Marlene. She looked back at him, shook her head ever so slightly. Did that mean what he thought it did?

He said, "Mr. Williams, must I make it clear to you that Drongo Kane is neither the owner nor the master of *my* ship? Furthermore, the charter party has not yet been signed. Until it is, I am a free agent."

"But the officers," Williams said, "are looking forward to getting away from this cheerless dump to Port Kane. . . ."

"My nose fair bleeds for them, Mr. Williams. I shall return to the ship tomorrow morning. . . ." The Princess nodded almost imperceptibly. "I shall return to the ship tomorrow morning to make all the necessary arrangements. A very good night to you."

Williams flickered and vanished.

"I'm glad that you were firm, John," said Marlene.

"Now I suppose we'll have Kane on the blower," grumbled Grimes.

"We shall not." She spoke firmly toward the corner of the room, "Karl, you are to accept no more incoming calls."

"Very good, Your Highness," came a disembodied, mechanical voice in reply.

"What if he calls around in person?" asked Grimes.

She laughed. "My watchbirds never sleep. And they are vicious."

She drained her glass, held it out for the refill. She helped herself to a savory pastry, then to another. Grimes decided that he had better start nibbling too, otherwise he would not be getting his share. It would have been a shame to have missed out; the creamy filling in the flaky cases, some sort of fish, he thought, was delicious.

Then the dish was empty save for a few crumbs. The tall bottle, now standing to attention in the ice bucket, was a dead marine. The Princess sighed, inelegantly wiped her mouth on the back of her hand.

"I could order up more," she said, "but it might spoil dinner. I thought that we would have it served here. It would be such a waste of time getting dressed and then getting undressed again. . . ."

Grimes thought wryly of the evening dress that he had packed, the resplendent mess uniform that he had worn while he had been master of the Baroness d'Estang's space yacht. It had been altered only inasmuch as the gold buttons now bore the crest of his own company, Far Traveler Couriers. He had affected to despise what, privately, he had called his organ grinder's monkey suit but had been looking forward to giving it an airing in the proper surroundings.

She said, "I think that we shall be more comfortable on the settee."

He got up from his chair, helped her to her feet. He thought, *If I married her I'd rupture myself carrying her across the threshold* . . . He deposited her at one end of the sofa, sat himself down at the other. She pouted at him but before she could move toward him the robot servants came in, cleared the low table of the debris of the pre-prandial snack and then set it down between them, laying out on its surface napery and cutlery, a selection of glasses. Then there was caviar, glistening black pearls piled high in a crystal bowl nestling in a larger vessel in which was crushed ice, with paper-thin toast and butter. With this there was vodka, poured by the attentive robot waiter from a bottle that was encased with an ice block.

Grimes made a pig of himself. So did Marlene.

There was paté, rich and flavorsome, in which a profusion of truffles was embedded. There was lobster, served in its split carapace and drenched with garlic-flavored butter. There was duck—or some bird like it—with a crisp, honeyed skin and a cherry sauce, with tiny new potatoes and green peas. (By this time Grimes' appetite was beginning to flag although Marlene, whose face had become quite greasy, was leaving nothing on her plate.) There was steak, tender and rare, smothered with mushrooms. There was a fruit tart, topped by a minor mountain of whipped cream. There were the wines—white and rosé and red with, at the finish, an imported champagne with the sweet.

There was coffee.

Grimes took his black, Marlene with cream, lots of it.

Grimes repressed a belch.

Marlene did not.

Grimes said, speaking with some difficulty, "Thank you for a marvelous dinner."

Marlene giggled and said, "The laborer is worthy of his hire. Besides, it is very rarely, on this world, that I can enjoy a meal in the company of somebody who appreciates good food as much as I do."

Grimes took a cigar from the box proffered by the majordomo—genuine Cuban, he noticed. Marlene selected a slimmer smoke, a panatella. The robutler presented, first to Grimes then to his mistress, a metal index finger from which white flame jetted.

Grimes inhaled, wondering dimly that there should be room for anything else, even something so insubstantial as smoke, in his overfed body. He sat back, watching the silent, efficient robots removing the final plates and glasses, the coffeepot and cups. The table was shifted back to its original position between the two chairs and a large ashtray was placed on the richly carpeted floor.

Marlene, grunting a little with the effort, slowly shifted herself along the settee toward him. She covered the distance and then fell on to him. Her still-burning panatella dropped between their two bodies. Frantically he fished it out before it could do any damage, put it into the ashtray. Regretfully he placed his own cigar beside it. He was drowsy, so very drowsy. Marlene was sleeping, imprisoning him beneath the soft weight of her body. He tried to extricate himself, then gave up the struggle.

It may have been a dream but almost certainly it was not.

Awakening in the morning, alone in bed, as a robot servitor set down the morning tea tray, he had a confused memory of warm, pale flesh in the semi-darkness, of plump, naked limbs that imprisoned him, of hot, moist lips on his face and body, of an explosive release. . . .

"And what do you wish for breakfast, lord?" asked the liveried servant.

"Some more tea will do nicely," Grimes said. "After I've had my shower and all the rest of it. . . ."

Surprisingly he did not feel at all bad. He just did not feel hungry.

"Very well, lord. Her Highness wishes me to tell you that the car will be ready, to return you to Port Bluewater, as soon as you desire."

The old brush-off, thought Grimes. *On your bicycle, spaceman. She's got what she wants, had what she wanted, and that's it.*

He finished his second cup of tea, then got out of bed and went through to the bathroom.

Thirty-three

He emerged from the bathroom refreshed and rather less torpid. He saw that his bed had been made and that on the coverlet fresh clothing—slacks, jacket and underwear—had been laid out. Presumably his case was already in the car.

He dressed and was not surprised to find that the waistband of his trousers was tight. He filled and lit his pipe; he would have a quiet smoke while waiting for the second pot of tea.

The majordomo entered the sitting room carrying a big tray. He (it) was followed by Marlene. Clothed—this morning in pale blue—she looked no more than pleasantly plump. She sat down in one of the chairs by the coffee table, motioned to Grimes to take the other. The robutler put down the tray and left.

She said, "I thought, perhaps, that we might partake of only a light breakfast. . . ."

On the tray were both teapots and coffeepots, with milk and cream and sugar. There was a large pitcher of some chilled fruit juice. There were croissants, with butter and a syrupy conserve with whole strawberries.

"Nothing for me, thanks, Marlene," said Grimes. "Or, perhaps, some fruit juice." She poured, handed him the glass. "And I think I've changed my mind. I told the servant tea, but that coffee smells delicious. . . . Yes, two sugars." She filled his cup. "And I wonder if I might have just a nibble of croissant. . . ."

She laughed. "What I liked about you when I first knew you was your hearty appetite. I've heard that your Survey Service nickname was Gutsy Grimes. . . . And what of it? Good food is meant to be enjoyed."

She managed four croissants to Grimes' three and was more generous with butter and conserve than he was. Satisfied, she lit a cigarillo. Grimes resumed his pipe.

"And now, my dear," she said practically, "we have to get you back to your ship."

She was friendly enough, thought Grimes, but little more than that. The events of the previous night might never have happened.

She got to her feet unassisted, walked toward the door. Grimes followed.

She led him through corridors and down spiral staircases to the courtyard. The gleaming Daimler was awaiting them and, standing by it at stiff attention, were the majordomo and four liveried footmen. Grimes wondered wildly if he was supposed to tip them. (What sort of gratuity would a robot expect?) But they bowed stiffly as their mistress and her guest approached and the robutler assisted her through the open door of the car. Grimes sat down beside her. The doors closed. The car lifted and, escorted by the watchbirds, flew silently northward.

Its passengers, too, were silent. Grimes, at first, attempted to make conversation but the Princess made it plain that she did not wish to talk. There was not, after all, much to say. On a mental plane, he realized, they had little in common—yet he admitted to himself that he did feel some affection for her. The silence was not an uncomfortable one.

Lake Bluewater showed up ahead, and the white buildings of the spaceport on its farther shore. And there was *Sister Sue,* gleaming silver in the strong light of the late morning sun. And that was where he belonged, thought Grimes, not in the castle owned by a member of this planet's aristocracy.

She spoke at last.

"I've brought you back, John, to where you really want to be."

He said, "I wanted to be with you." Then, bending the truth only slightly if at all, "I want to be with you again."

She laughed—regretfully?

"Do you? I'm no Michelle, and I know it. If you were to settle on El Dorado—and if Commodore Kane's enterprise is successful you might well be financially qualified—you would range farther afield than Schloss Stolzberg. I should not be able to hold you. There's too much of the tomcat in you. You're capable of feeling cupboard love—but, until you meet the right woman (if ever you do) little more. . . .

"But it was good having you. . . ."

Grimes tried to believe that she really meant what she said.

She was facing him now, holding her face up to his. He put his arms about her, kissed her. Her lips tasted of strawberries.

They broke apart as the car began its descent. Probably Williams and several of the others would be watching. He did not wish to be the subject of ribald comment.

The vehicle grounded gently on the apron, ran silently to the foot of the ramp. (Yes, Williams was there, and the Green Hornet.) The door on Grimes' side opened. He inclined his head to the hand that she extended to him, kissed it lightly. He dismounted, then reached through the other open door to retrieve his bag. He heard her order, "Home," as the doors shut. The car rose swiftly, dwindled fast to a mere speck in the southern sky.

"Sorry to have called you back, Skipper," said the mate cheerfully while Ms. Connellan scowled at Grimes. "But the Commodore is very insistent. He wants us at Port Kane as soon as possible, if not before."

"Are the engines ready?"

"Yes. I told Mr. Crumley to be ready for the shift. Oh, and the Commodore told me to ask you to call him as soon as you got back. You'll have to use the phone in the office." He scowled. *"They* can call us aboard the ship but we can't call them from the ship. . . ."

"All right," said Grimes. "Would you mind taking my bag aboard for me, Ms. Connellan?" The Second Mate scowled at him but wordlessly took his luggage. "And come with me, Mr. Williams."

Together they walked into the port office. In the doorless booth Grimes said, "Get me Commodore Baron Kane." The holographic image of a golden lady's maid appeared and told him, "The Commodore will speak with you shortly." She faded. Kane appeared.

"Ah, Grimes, back at last after your wallow in the von Stolzberg flesh pots. Anybody would think that you were not eager for gainful employment."

"I had a duty to my hostess," said Grimes stiffly.

"I'm sure you did. Now, listen. Port Kane is twelve hours ahead of Port Bluewater. The hop should take you four hours, at the outside; I imagine that your innies are capable of delivering enough lateral thrust. If you lift off at, say, 1400 your time you should be at Port Kane at 0600 my time, just before sunrise. There'll be the usual beacons to mark your berth. Keep in touch with Aerospace Control to confirm your ETA and all the rest of it. The Port Captain will bring you a gnomonic chart and a plan of Port Kane."

"And also the bill for my port charges here?" asked Grimes.

"They'll be just a matter of bookkeeping, Grimes, to be deducted from whatever profit you make as a privateer. After your arrival—not immediately after, of course; like you I enjoy my sleep—I shall call aboard you with the charter party for your signature. Also I shall be introducing you to the other captains. Is everything clear, Grimes?"

"Yes, Kane."

Drongo Kane scowled, then grinned sourly. "All right, all right. I should have called you Captain Grimes. Soon it will be Commodore Grimes. Does that make you happy?"

"I'm rolling on the deck, Commodore, convulsed with paroxysms of pure ecstasy."

"That will do, you sarcastic bastard. I'll see you tomorrow morning."

Kane's image faded.

* * *

Later, in *Sister Sue*'s control room, Grimes and Williams studied the gnomonic chart. It would be a simple enough operation to shift ship—although something of a nuisance. Luckily the ship possessed a rarely used gyro compass, which had now been started, with a repeater on the bridge. Williams had painted a mark on the inside of one of the big viewports to coincide with the lubber's line. That would be, for the purposes of this short voyage, "forward." The Green Hornet, grumbling that this was a spaceship, not an airship, had not been capable of working out the great circle distance and courses so Grimes had done it himself.

Grimes looked at his watch.

"All right, Mr. Williams, make it lift off stations. I shall want Control fully manned until we're underway, then just one officer besides myself until we're ready to set down."

He took his usual seat, controls at his fingertips, displays before his eyes. He waited until the others—Williams, Connellan, Venner and Stewart—were at their stations before putting the inertial drive on standby. Mr. Venner obtained permission from Aerospace Control to lift ship.

Sister Sue shuddered then rose slowly from the apron. Grimes set course by turning her about her vertical axis, watching the repeater card until the lubber's line was on the correct reading. Then there was the application of lateral thrust and, at an altitude of only two kilometers, the ship was underway on the first leg of the great circle course.

The officers watched interestedly. Save as passengers, during spells of planetary leave, atmospheric flights were outside their experience. Grimes, of course, during his Survey Service career had often handled pinnaces proceeding from point to point inside a world's air envelope. He had done so often enough, too, in *Little Sister.*

Sister Sue swept majestically—and noisily; would there be any complaints from the pampered people in the mansions and chateaux and castles over which she was clattering?—in an east northeasterly direction, the fast westering sun throwing her long shadow over fields and forests. Grimes increased vertical thrust to give her safe clearance over the Golden Alps, a range of snow-capped crags bare of vegetation for most of their towering height, whose sheer yellow rock faces reflected the sunlight as though they were indeed formed from the precious metal.

Beyond the mountains the ship dropped again, into shadow, into deepening dusk, into darkness. There were no cities on the land below her, no towns, no villages even. There were only sparsely scattered points of light, marking the dwelling places of the very rich. It was like, Grimes thought, the night sky of the Rim Worlds, out toward the edge of the galaxy, an almost empty blackness.

He flew on toward the dawn, toward Port Kane.

Thirty-four

Port Kane was a cluster of white domes, dominated by a graceful, lattice-work control tower, on the western bank of the broad, slow-flowing Rio del Oro. There was something familiar about that tower, thought Grimes. Then he laughed. It was obvious that Michelle must have had some say in its design. It was almost a replica of a far more famous erection in the city of Paris, on far-away Earth. It dwarfed the relatively squat, far more solid in appearance, towers that were the spaceships. All three of them, like *Sister Sue,* had started their working lives as Epsilon Class tramps of the Commission's fleet. They had been altered, however, the one-time symmetry of their hulls broken by added sponsons. A laser cannon turret, another turret for the quick-firing projectile cannon, a third one for the missile launcher. . . . Two of the ships gleamed dull silver in the light of the rising sun. The third one had been painted a green that once had been vivid, that now was dull and flaking. A hundred or so meters clear of this vessel—*Pride of Erin,* she had to be—the triangle of scarlet flashing beacons had been set out.

"Port Kane Control to *Sister Sue,"* came the mechanical voice from the NST speaker. "Control to *Sister Sue.* Set down between the beacons."

Mr. Stewart acknowledged. Grimes applied lateral thrust until he had the triangle of beacons centered in the stern view screen. He cut vertical thrust, just enough so that the ship was almost weightless. She fell gently, touched, shuddered and then was still.

"Finished with engines," ordered Grimes.

He looked out through a viewport, saw a group of figures standing on the pale gray concrete of the apron and staring up at him. He took a pair of binoculars from the box, looked down at them. There were two men and a woman. One of the men was short, with a ruddy face and a neat, pointed, white beard. He was wearing a green uniform with four gold bands on each sleeve. The other one, also a captain to judge from his sleeve braid, was tall. His face was almost obscured by a luxuriant, red-gold hirsute growth. His uniform was black with a black-and-gold kilt in lieu of trousers, with a gold trim on his long socks. The woman, too, was tall. What she was wearing could have been a short-skirted business suit in sober gray had it not been for the rather ornate golden epaulets. The lines of her face were harsh, her mouth wide but with thin lips, her nose a prominent beak.

Grimes said to Williams, "Looks like the bold masters of *Pride of Erin, Spaceways Princess* and *Agatha's Ark* down there. I may as well meet them now. You can come with me."

The ramp was just being extended from the after airlock door as they stepped out of the elevator cage. They marched down the gangway, Williams in the lead. Once they were on the ground the mate fell back to let Grimes precede him.

"Captain Grimes?" asked the little man in the green uniform.

"Yes. And you're Captain O'Leary, aren't you? And Captain MacWhirter, and Captain Prinn. A very good morning to you all."

"And the top o' the morn to you, Captain. Or should I be sayin' Commodore? We didn't think that we should like havin' the Survey Service—no disrespect intended to yourself—bossin' us around, but the way things are, you could be the lesser of two evils. We thought we'd be after seein' you, bright an' early, before Drongo tells you his side of it. . . ."

"I'm only ex-Survey Service," said Grimes, not realizing that he had lied until the words were out. "And I'm not your commodore yet. But what seems to be the trouble, Captain?"

"Oh, 'tis these El Doradan Navy liaison officers, or gunnery officers, or observers, or whatever they're supposed to be when they're up an' dressed. Space puppies, all of 'em, but puttin' on the airs an' graces of admirals. I've a still wet behind the ears junior grade lieutenant callin' himself the Honorable Claude Ponsonby. His daddy is Lord Ponsonby—whoever *he* might be. Captain MacWhirter has a Count—not that he counts for much! An' Captain Prinn has a Count too—although he calls himself a Graf. . . ."

"The Graf von Stolzbert," said Grimes.

"Yes. How did you know?"

"His. . . ." He corrected himself. "Commodore Kane told me. And it's Commodore Kane who makes the rules. What can I do about it?"

"You're Survey Service, Captain Grimes. Or ex-Survey Service. You've been a senior officer in a *real* navy, not a glorified yacht club. Drongo Kane says that you're to be in charge of things. We're relyin' on you to call the puppies to heel."

"Do any of you have any naval experience?" asked Grimes.

"No, Captain," O'Leary said. "I was with a small outfit called the Shamrock Line, out of New Erin. You may have heard of the New Erin Sweepstake? I won it. At about the same time the Shamrock Line went broke. Thinkin' that I was well on the way to winnin' an even larger fortune I bought one o' their ships. . . ."

"An owner/master, like myself," said Grimes. "And you, Captain MacWhirter?"

"I was in the Waverley Royal Mail," said the Scot. "My old uncle Hamish died and left me the lot. In whisky, he was. In those days I was a religious man an' a total abstainer. So I sold the distillery an' all the rest of it an' bought me a bonny wee ship." He laughed mirthlessly. "It's driven me to drink, she has."

"I know what it's like," said Grimes sympathetically. He turned to the tall woman, who was regarding him through cold gray eyes that matched the short hair swept severely back from her high, pale forehead. "Captain Prinn?"

"Captain Agatha Prinn," she corrected him, "to distinguish me from Captain Joel Prinn, my late husband. I was a rich woman, an heiress, on Carinthia. You have heard, perhaps, of the Davitz Circus and Menagerie? I was a Davitz, the last Davitz. But circuses bore me and I have no great love for animals. I sold my interests in the family business and went for a cruise in a Cluster Lines ship, where I met my future husband, at that time a Chief Officer. He paid off on our return to Carinthia and we were married. He persuaded me to buy for him the Commission's *Epsilon Puppis,* which was up for sale. He renamed her *Agatha's Ark*. . . ." She smiled frostily. "I can see that you're wondering how I came to be a shipmaster myself. I accompanied my husband on his voyages, signed on as purser. I became interested in navigation and spacemanship and studied. Finally I passed for Master on Libertad." She smiled again. "Libertad qualifications are recognized throughout the galaxy."

But only just, thought Grimes. He wondered just how much that Certificate of Competency had cost. He wondered, too, what had happened to Captain Prinn I. Obviously Captain Prinn II wasn't going to tell him.

"So," he said. "So." He looked at *Pride of Erin* and at the other two vessels in line beyond her. "I see that you've all been armed."

"Aye," said MacWhirter. "An' every day we've been pittin' our skills against electronic enemies in yon gunnery simulator—" he waved a hand toward one of the white domes—"while the El Doradan Navy puppies have been standin' around an' sneerin'. . . ." He went on enviously, "I don't suppose that ye'll be needin' gunnery instruction, Captain Grimes. . . ."

"A session in the simulator never did anybody any harm," said Grimes. "I'll be using it, and so will Mr. Williams here, my chief officer—although both of us have seen action. And my third officer holds a Survey Service Reserve commission but I'll make sure that he brushes up his gunnery."

"It looks, Captain," said O'Leary enviously, "as though *you'll* have no trouble with whatever puppy they foist on you!"

A uniformed port official, a humanoid robot, approached the party. He saluted Grimes smartly.

"Sir, Commodore Kane instructs that you be ready to commence discharge at 0800 hours. The Commodore will call upon you at 0930."

"Our master's voice," said Agatha Prinn sourly.

And then they all drifted back to their ships.

"Sign here, Grimes," said Drongo Kane. "All four copies."

Grimes signed.

He had read the document carefully and found that its provisions were as good as could be expected. He did not think that he had missed anything in the small print. For a quite substantial consideration he agreed to put his ship, his officers and himself at the service of El Dorado Corporation until such time as the contract would be terminated by mutual consent or, with an option for renewal, after the passage of three Standard Years. He, as master of *Sister Sue,* had been given the rank of Company Commodore with authority not only over the other shipmasters but to deal, on behalf of the corporation, with planetary governments. Items of equipment on loan from the El Dorado Corporation were to be returned, in good order and condition, on expiration of the contract; there was a penalty clause covering failure, for any reason, to do so.

Any and all profits accruing from ventures engaged upon were to be divided between the corporation and the chartered vessel—sixty percent to the charterer and forty percent to the ship. The cost of stores, services and the salary of the El Doradan representative aboard would, however, be deducted from the charteree's percentage. The monies remaining were to be divided among the crew according to the provisions of Lloyd's Salvage Agreement, the higher the rank, the bigger the share. All parties agreed to accept the rulings of the Prize Court which would be set up on El Dorado.

And so on, and so on.

"And now, Commodore," said Kane, "I shall take you ashore, to my office, to introduce you to your captains. You've already met them, I know, but you have not done so yet officially."

"As you please, Commodore," said Grimes.

He put one copy of the Charter Party into his safe while Kane picked up the others from the desk. He took his cap from the hook on which it was hanging, looked at it, at the badge, before putting it on. At least, he thought, there was nothing in the charter party that required him to wear El Doradan uniform.

"Oh, one small thing, Grimes," said Kane.

"Yes?"

"That passenger of yours. You can't leave an outworlder here, you know. And if you have a civilian aboard what will be, essentially, a warship you're liable to run into all sorts of complications. Legally speaking he could be classed as a pirate, you know."

"I'll put him on my Articles," said Grimes. "Assistant Purser or something."

"Do that."

Kane led the way out of Grimes' day cabin.

Thirty-five

They were gathered in a lounge in the main dome of the spaceport administration complex, standing in two groups. There were the three tramp captains; there were four young people, three men and a woman, in the purple and gold uniform of the El Doradan Navy. Grimes looked at these latter curiously and, he was obliged to admit, apprehensively. Which of them was the Graf von Stolzberg, his . . . son? He had half expected to see a mirror image of himself, but. . . . There had been more genes than his involved.

The young man was blond haired, like his mother, and blue eyed. He was much taller than Grimes and with more than the mere suggestion of a paunch. With less fat to smooth them over his features might have been craggy. Yes, the likeness was there. Grimes hated himself for remembering the old saying: Our relations are chosen for us, but thank God we can choose our friends.

"Good morning, gentlebeings," said Kane jovially. "I'd like to introduce you to your leader, Commodore Grimes, master of the good ship *Saucy Sue.*"

"Sister Sue," growled Grimes.

"Sorry, Commodore. So *Sister Sue* isn't saucy."

"Get on with it, man," muttered Captain MacWhirter.

Kane shot a nasty look in the Scot's direction, then continued. "You've already met your captains, Commodore Grimes. But here, with them, are our own liaison officers. The Honorable Claude Ponsonby, attached to *Pride of Erin. . . .*"

"Glad to have you aboard, Commodore," said the tall, weedy, young man, extending his right hand. Grimes, thinking sourly that he, as the senior officer, should have made the first move, shook it. It was limp, almost boneless, in his.

"Count Vishinsky, of *Spaceways Princess. . . .*"

The stocky El Doradan lieutenant, as heavily bearded as MacWhirter, although his whiskers were glossily black, committed the same solecism as Ponsonby although his grip was much firmer. Obviously, thought Grimes, in the opinion of these space puppies an El Doradan aristocrat outranked an outworld commodore.

"The Graf Ferdinand von Stolzberg, of *Agatha's Ark*. . . ."

The Graf looked down disdainfully on the man whom he did not know was his father, clicked his heels and bowed stiffly. Grimes bowed back, repressing the urge to murmur, "Ah, so. . . ."

"And now, Commodore, your own pet. The Countess of Walshingham."

The Countess was a tall, slim blonde with, as revealed by the miniskirt of her uniform, excellent legs. Her jacket bulged in the right places. Her face was strong, with high cheekbones, a square, dimpled chin, a wide, full-lipped mouth, a short, straight nose. Her gray eyes looked at Grimes, who had extended his hand, disdainfully.

"Go on, Wally," urged Kane. "Shake paws with the commodore!"

"Don't call me Wally!" she snapped. "The correct title, *Baron,* is Countess."

Nonetheless she touched hands briefly with Grimes.

"And now," said Kane, motioning the others toward the round table.

They seated themselves—Grimes on Kane's right, the three tramp captains on the right of him, then the El Doradan officers. A robot steward brought in a tray with a huge coffeepot, mugs, a bowl of brown sugar crystals, a jug of cream. There was a pause in conversation while the drinking vessels were filled.

"And now," said Kane again. "You have all heard of your commodore. He was quite famous while he was an officer in the Federation Survey Service. Or should I have said 'notorious'? As an owner-master—although only recently of a *real* ship—he has maintained his Survey Service reputation. For a short while he was captain of the spaceyacht owned by my wife, the Baroness Michelle. She speaks highly of him. You may rest assured, ladies and gentlemen, that I would have never trusted command of our enterprise to anybody less capable than Commodore Grimes. . . ."

"When do I get my medal?" Grimes asked sardonically.

"You're in this for money," Kane told him. "Not for honor and glory. But, before we go any further, does anybody not approve of the commodore's appointment?"

MacWhirter muttered, "I'm no historian, Commodore Kane, but didnae the old time pirates, on Earth's seas, elect their commanders?"

"You are not pirates, Captain MacWhirter. At the moment you're not anything. You're just shipmasters whose vessels have been fitted with defensive armament. Once the Letters of Marque have been issued you will be privateers."

"You never used to be so fussy about legalities, Commodore," Grimes could not resist saying.

"In the old days, Commodore," said Kane, "I was not a naval officer. I am now. But didn't you, when you were in the Survey Service, bend the law now and again? But enough of this. Kalla had been blockaded, although so far no large force has been dispatched to deal with the rebels. Our agents on the planet have informed us that the Kallan government will be happy to issue Letters of Marque so as to leave their own navy free for planetary defense. Work will begin on mounting your armament tomorrow, Commodore Grimes. I suggest that you and your officers avail themselves of the battle simulators, and that your Mannschenn Drive chief acquaint himself with the temporal precession synchronizer. . . ."

"I have already raised that point with Mr. Malleson," Grimes said. "He tells me that he was among those involved in the development of the device."

"Good. Well, ladies and gentlemen, I shall want you off planet, on your way to Kalla, as soon as your commodore is ready. Meanwhile—as most of you know already—all the facilities of Port Kane are open to you and your crews." He smiled expansively. "Enjoy, enjoy!"

The meeting was over.

Grimes walked back to his ship in the company of the other tramp captains. He was pleased to see that discharge was well under way, was going fast and smoothly with busy stowbots stacking crates and cases and cartons into trucks that carried them into one of the domes.

"Yon's The Happy Kangaroo," said MacWhirter, pointing. "The liquor was runnin' a mite low. Would there be Scotch in your cargo, Commodore?"

"Yes," said Grimes.

"An' haggis, maybe?"

"I'm afraid not."

"Ah, weel. A man canna have everything. . . ."

"As long as there're willing popsies, Mack," said Captain O'Leary, "why worry?" He turned to Grimes. "But that'll not be worryin' you, Commodore, will it now? I saw your Catering Officer—a bit of all right as long as you like red hair. An' a green-skinned wench—a New Donegalan, would she be? An' now you're gettin' the Countess. . . . Whoever said that rank has its privileges wasn't far off the mark!"

"I consider this conversation quite disgusting, Captain O'Leary," said Captain Prinn. "I am sure that Commodore Grimes would never consider a liaison with one of his female officers."

"One of them might consider a liaison with him, Aggie," said O'Leary.

"I do not think that Commodore Grimes is that sort of man," said Captain Prinn.

Evidently, Grimes thought, she had taken a shine to him. He wondered if she would take a shine to the Graf von Stolzberg.

The others left him at the foot of his ramp. He looked up at the gantry that was being erected to one side of the ship, presumably for the installation of the armament. He was joined there by Williams.

"How did it go, Skipper?" asked the mate. "Everybody happy in the Service?" He did not wait for an answer. "The boys are happier now. Most of the engineers are already across at The Happy Kangaroo. Their chiefs let them go. Mr. Malleson and old Mr. Stewart are playing with some newfangled gadgetry in the Mannschenn Drive room—a synchronizer or some such. The Green Hornet's sulking hard because I wouldn't let her go ashore with her boyfriends. I let Vic off, though. He's gone to brush up his gunnery in the battle simulator they have here. I shouldn't mind a bit of a refresher course myself. . . ."

"Off you go, then, Mr. Williams. I shall be staying on board. Ms. Connellan can look after the discharge."

"That's what she's doing now. The stowbots here are so good that she'll not be able to do any damage."

Grimes went up to his quarters, where he was joined by Mayhew.

"I suppose, Captain—or should I say Commodore—that you'll be wanting a rundown on this morning's meeting," said the telepath.

"Yes."

"All right. First, Captain O'Leary. He rather resents having you placed in authority over him; he thought that he'd be able to roar through space on his ownsome, seeking whom he might devour. But he realizes that an experienced naval officer in charge will be to everybody's benefit. He will do what he's told—but more often than not will argue about it first.

"Captain MacWhirter. His general attitude is very similar to O'Leary's, although he's less of a romantic and far more of a real mercenary. And, unlike O'Leary, he has a great respect for titles of nobility. That comes of his being a citizen of the Empire of Waverley. If only *you* had a title, preferably a Scottish one, he'd follow you into a black hole.

"Captain Prinn. For all her appearance and manner another romantic. And she, too, has that absurd respect for titles. She's thrilled to be having a real Graf, the son of a real Princess, as a junior officer aboard her ship. He will be pampered. I wonder what she would think if she knew who the Graf's father is. . . ."

"That will do, Mr. Mayhew."

"Sorry, Commodore. And would you like my analysis of the El Doradans?"

"Please."

"First, the Honorable Claude Ponsonby. Don't be fooled by his appearance and manner. He's tough, and could he vicious. His god is money and he's determined that the operation will be a success, no matter who suffers. He, like the other liaison officers, will receive a substantial percentage of the profits.

"Now, Vishinsky. For all the dissimilarity in appearance and manner a man cast in the same mold as Ponsonby. He'll see to it that Captain MacWhirter toes the line.

"The Graf von Stolzberg? He's an El Doradan, of course, despite his ancestry. . . ." Grimes winced. "But, because of his ancestry, he's also something of a romantic. He hides that side of his character beneath his stiff manner. I think that he will get along *very* well with Captain Prinn—she, too, is a repressed romantic. . . ."

"The prince and the pirate queen," sneered Grimes. "I hope that they will be very happy."

"Come, come, sir," chided Mayhew. "You may be commodore—but that doesn't give you *droit du seigneur* over your subordinates, especially those who're captains of their own ships. Do you wish me to continue?"

"Yes. Go on."

"There is little more that I can say about the Graf von Stolzberg. He's young and romantic and an affair with an older woman, such as Captain Agatha Prinn, will do him far more good than harm. Out of uniform and with hardly more than a hint of cosmetics she will be a very attractive woman."

"Stop harping on it, Mr. Mayhew."

"Very good, sir. Now, the Countess of Walshingham. . . . I'll describe her this way. If she and our own Green Hornet could swap bodies and accents you'd never know that there had been an exchange. The other three El Doradans are, in their ways, loyal to their planet. She is loyal only to herself. Furthermore she is a man-hater."

"Another female-chauvinist bitch," said Grimes.

"It was Commodore Kane's idea of a joke to appoint her to your ship," Mayhew said.

"That bastard!"

"Just so, sir. Just so. I, like yourself, am firmly of the opinion that he must have ridden to his parents' wedding ceremony on a bicycle. Anything more, Commodore?"

"That's enough to be going on with, I think. Oh, you might see if Ms. Granadu has any shipboard uniforms, shorts and shirts, in the slop chest your size. She's a fairish needlewoman and should be able to knock up a pair of assistant purser's shoulderboards for you."

"Some get promoted," said Mayhew with a grin, "and others demoted. But as one of your officers I shall be entitled to my share of the spoils."

"If any," said Grimes.

"If any. Aren't you just a little sorry that you accepted that commission in the Reserve?"

"Just a little," admitted Grimes. (It is useless trying to lie to a telepath.) "Oh, and when you see Miss Granadu ask her to come up and see me."

"And I'll tell her to bring the coins and the book," Mayhew said.

Grimes shook the three antique coins in his cupped hands, let them fall to the deck. Two tails and a head. Seven. Two heads and a tail. Eight. Three heads. Nine. Another three heads, another nine. Then eight, and again eight for the final throw.

Kou. Sudden encounters. A bold, strong woman appears on the scene. One should not contract a marriage with such a woman. . . .

Nine in the third place. He proceeds with difficulty, like one who has been flayed. His position is fraught with danger, but despite this he will commit no great error. . . .

"Well," said Grimes, "that, at least, is comforting."

"There's more—and worse—to come, Captain," said Magda.

She continued reading.

Nine is the fourth place. The inferior men have escaped from restraint, like fish from a bag. This will give rise to evil. . . .

"Didn't we have this once before?" asked Grimes.

"Yes. But that time the lines were not so ominous."

"And that time," said Grimes thoughtfully, "there was only one strong woman to worry about. Now there are two."

Thirty-six

The few days at Port Kane were busy ones for Grimes. Personally he oversaw the installation of *Sister Sue*'s armament—the laser cannon, the quick-firing projectile gun and the missile projector. There was the fire-control console to be fitted in the control room; instrumentation required for normal, peacetime purposes had to be relocated to make room for it. Malleson, too, was busy. The operation of the precession synchronizer would be his concern. He assured Grimes that he had been one of those involved in the original development of this device and that he was looking forward to seeing it in operation.

When he could spare the time Grimes played around with the battle simulator, pitting his wits and skills against the computer representing an enemy commander unless, as sometimes happened, one of the other captains was on hand to play that part. When he was matched against O'Leary or MacWhirter, maneuvering the blob of light that represented his ship in the tank, every simulated battle was for him a walkover. With his one vessel against both of theirs he invariably won; the tramp masters seemed to be quite incapable of deploying all their armament simultaneously. There was always the time lag when they switched from laser to quick-firer to guided missile. But whoever came up against Captain Agatha Prinn, he conceded, would have to be *good.* She took to naval gunnery like a duck to water.

Now and again his captains would be accompanied by their El Doradan officers who, having affixed their signatures to the privateers' Articles, signing on as fourth mates, were now wearing the uniforms of their putative employers. The Honorable Claude looked faintly absurd in the *Pride of Erin*'s green, although his outfit was far better cut and of greatly superior quality to Captain O'Leary's. The *Spaceways Princess* rig of tunic and kilt suited Vishinsky, especially since his robot tailor had succeeded in imparting a cossack quality to the upper garment. In *Agatha's Ark*'s severe gray business suit with the touch of gold on the shoulders the Graf von Stolzbert looked more like a diplomat than a spaceman. Perhaps, thought Grimes, watching the young man as he played the attentive squire to his captain, a diplomat was what he should have been. He was rather ruefully amused. He wished that he were able to advise his son. But then, what would he, could he say? Beware of older women? Beware of *all* women? And who was he, Grimes, to dish out such advice? Don't do as I do, my boy, do as I say. . . .

Williams and Venner were frequent visitors to the dome housing the battle simulator, as were the control-room officers from the other ships. Now and again the Green Hornet condescended to try her hand, usually in the company of the Countess of Walshingham. The Countess was still wearing her El Doradan uniform and had yet to sign *Sister Sue*'s Articles.

It was not all work and no play for the privateers, however. There was The Happy Kangaroo, the pleasure dome which Grimes and his people had first learned about at the Countess of Wilberforce's prayer meeting. There were refreshments, solid and liquid, all of high quality. There was a gaming room. (Kane, in a jovial mood, told Grimes that the returns from this were almost sufficient to pay for the other entertainments.) Grimes was no gambler but he looked in one evening to watch O'Leary, Vishinsky and other officers, including his own Mr. Venner, playing *vingt et un.* The dealer and banker was the girl who had carried around the collection bag at the finish of that dreary evening in El Dorado City. She seemed to be doing far better for Drongo Kane than she had been doing for the missionaries. She was dressed differently, too, wearing a bunny uniform that showed her long, sleek legs to best advantage.

But Grimes was watching Venner more than he was watching her. Rear Admiral Damien had warned him not to play cards with the man—yet he was losing heavily, as was everybody except the house.

There was music, and there was dancing, and there was a cabaret whose underclad performers made up in enthusiasm for what they lacked in terpsichorean skill. And there was enthusiasm, Grimes knew, off stage. Slumming these girls might be but they were enjoying it. *Sister Sue*'s junior engineers were no longer fighting among themselves for Ms. Connellan's favors; they had far better and tastier fish to fry.

Grimes knew what was going on and felt the occasional stab of jealousy. He could have had his share of what was going—but he did not like sharing. He was a snob, and he knew it, but the thought of sampling delights that Denning, Singh or Paulus (his pet dislikes!) had already sampled repelled him. He wanted a captain's lady, not an officers' mess.

Now and again he would call the Schloss Stolzberg to talk with Marlene. She was polite enough but that was all. He suggested that he come to the castle for a brief visit before departure; she told him that as a commodore he had far too many responsibilities. He asked her if she would come to Port Kane; after all, he told her, she would wish to see her son again before the privateers set off on their venture. She smiled rather sadly and said that she knew that Ferdinand was being very well looked after and that the young man might be embarrassed if his mother, a woman some years younger than Captain Prinn, made her appearance. Of course, Ferdinand would be spending his last night on El Dorado in his mother's home and it certainly would not do for Grimes to be there to.

He hoped that the El Dorado Corporation or Drongo Kane or whoever would soon decide that it was high time that the privateer fleet was underway.

Thirty-seven

He sat at a table in The Happy Kangaroo, by himself, nursing his drink. He did not, unlike most of the other spacers, consider that free liquor was a valid excuse for getting drunk. Malleson and Mayhew had been with him but the Mannschenn Drive chief had wanted to try out a new system in the gaming room, where a roulette table was in operation. Mayhew had gone with the engineer. Was he a telekineticist as well as a telepath, Grimes had wondered idly. A few tables away the Green Hornet and the Countess of Walshingham were sitting. They were not actually hand in hand but conveyed the impression that they were. Elsewhere in the room were three kilted officers from *Spaceways Princess,* another trio from *Pride of Erin* in their green and gold finery and a quartet from *Agatha's Ark,* their noisy behavior in contrast to the gray sobriety of their uniforms. A dozen of the volunteer bunnies were looking after them. He wondered briefly where most of his own people were. Williams, he knew, was staying on board, with Magda Granadu to keep him company. Neither Mr. Crumley nor Mr. Stewart was much of a shore-goer. And he had heard talk of a picnic and bathing party at a nearby ocean beach—a beer and bunnies orgy, he thought sourly. That would account for the absence of his junior officers.

He watched the stage more with censorious interest than with enthusiasm. Once he would have enjoyed a turn of this nature; now it rather repelled him. He thought that he knew why. Years ago, when he had been a watchkeeping officer aboard the Zodiac Class cruiser *Aries,* one of his shipmates had been a reservist, a lieutenant who, in civil life, was a second mate in Trans-Galactic Clippers. This young man had a fund of good stories about life in big passenger ships. There was one captain, he told his listeners, who was a notorious womanizer. "We even used to pimp for the old bastard," said the storyteller. "If he got fixed up at the beginning of the voyage the ship was Liberty Hall. . . . But if, for some reason, he failed to score it was *hell.* . . . We all had to observe both letter and spirit of company regulations *and* a few extra ones that he thought up himself just to make our lives miserable!"

Grimes had no real desire to emulate the TG captain, but. . . .

He looked morosely at the stage, at the naked girl who was dancing, an old-fashioned waltz, with a gleaming, humanoid robot. Great art it was not. It was not even good pornography. The girl was gawky and her movements were stiffer than those of the automaton. Her feet were too big.

Somebody dropped into the chair that had been vacated by Malleson. He was dimly conscious of a white collar with a black bow tie, of smooth shoulders, of long, gleaming legs. *A bunny,* he thought. *Another rich bitch putting on the Lady Bountiful act. . . .*

She said, "You look as though you'd rather be in The Red Kangaroo, on Botany, John."

He turned his head to look at her properly.

"Michelle," he said.

It was by no means the first time that he had seen her scantily clothed but this bunny rig imparted to her a tartness. It suited her, he decided.

She raised a slim hand commandingly and a robar glided up to their table on silent wheels. She said, "I can see what you're drinking. I'll have the same." She addressed the frontal panel of the machine, gay with little winking lights, and ordered, "Two pink gins."

"Coming up," the thing replied in a mechanical voice. A section of panel dropped down to form a shelf and on to it slid two misted goblets. Grimes reached out for them, put them on the table.

He said, "And some little eats."

A dish of nuts of various kinds appeared on the shelf.

"Still Gutsy Grimes," murmured the Baroness.

"Just blotting paper," said Grimes, between nibbles.

She raised her glass to him and said, "Here's looking at you. . . ."

"And at you," he replied.

She sipped—not as daintily as had been her wont when he first knew her, thought Grimes—and then gestured toward the amateur performer on the stage.

"Ashley," she said scornfully, "thinks that she's the best since Isadora Duncan, but. . . ."

"Who's she?"

"Lady Ashley Mortimer."

"No, not her. Isadora Duncan."

"Really, John, you are a peasant. She was a famous dancer who lived in the twentieth century, old style. But don't you find the entertainment here boring?"

"I do, frankly."

She said, "I'd rather like to see your ship."

He looked at her intently and asked, "Won't Drongo mind?"

"The Baron," she said, with a subtle emphasis on the title, "is in El Dorado City, in conference with Baron Takada and others. It is my understanding that very soon now you will be given orders to lift for Kalla." She tossed the remains of her drink down her throat. "Come on." She rose to her feet.

Grimes finished his drink, snatched up a last handful of the nuts and then extricated himself from his chair. Together they walked to the door, out into the warm night.

The four ships stood there, floodlit towers of metal, three silvery in the glare, one a dull green. On the side of one of the silver ships a flag had been painted, a purple burgee with a gold ball in the upper canton, a commodore's broad pennant.

"That's her," said Grimes. *"Sister Sue."*

She said, "I wish that somebody would name a ship after me."

"You could always ask Drongo to do that little thing."

"Him!" she snorted with such vehemence that Grimes was not only embarrassed but felt an upsurge of loyalty to his own sex.

They strolled slowly over the apron to the foot of *Sister Sue*'s ramp. There was a sentry on duty there, one of the omnipresent robots, attired in approximation of the uniform of the Federation Survey Service Marines. The thing saluted with mechanical smartness. Grimes acknowledged with deliberate sloppiness.

He and Michelle walked up the gangway to the open airlock door, into the vestibule. The elevator cage, already at this lower level, carried them swiftly and smoothly up to the captain's flat. Grimes ushered his guest into his sitting room. She sprawled with elegant inelegance in one of the armchairs by the coffee table, her long, slender legs stretched out before her. Grimes took the seat facing her. He saw that Magda had laid out his usual supper—a thermopot of coffee, a large dish of napkin-covered sandwiches. Michelle, too, noted this offering. She bent forward and lifted the napkin. The sandwiches were of new bread, with the crust left on, cut thick—as was the pink ham that was the filling.

She smiled. "You have a female catering officer, don't you? It looks as though she spoils you as thoroughly as Big Sister used to. . . ." Her expression clouded slightly. "I hope that I am not . . . trespassing. Or poaching."

"No, Michelle. She's already spoken for."

"Oh. Do you think I could have some coffee?"

"Of course."

There was only one mug on the tray but there were others in a locker. Grimes got one out. He filled both vessels with the steaming, aromatic brew, remembered that she preferred hers unsweetened. He added sugar liberally to his own drink.

She nibbled a sandwich.

She said, "Marriage—or marriage to Baron Kane—seems to have coarsened me. Once I would sneer at this sort of food. Now I enjoy it."

"Mphm," grunted Grimes through a mouthful.

"This cabin," she said, "is more *you* than your quarters aboard *The Far Traveler*. . . . And even if you don't have a golden stewardess you do have a golden girl. . . ." She waved a half-eaten sandwich toward the miniature Una, astride her gleaming bicycle, on the shelf. "Rather pretty. Or even beautiful."

Grimes got up and lifted the figurine and her wheeled steed down to the deck. "Ride," he ordered. "Ride. Round and round and round. . . ."

She clapped her hands gleefully. "One of Yosarian's toys, isn't she? But aren't they rather expensive?"

"I didn't buy her," said Grimes stiffly. "She was a gift. From Mr. Yosarian and. . . ."

"And from the lady who was the model?" She laughed. "No doubt one of your ex—or not so ex—girl friends. You know, I've always been sorry that you were so overawed by me when you were my yachtmaster. But now that you're an owner-master, *and* a commodore. . . ."

"But not a baron," said Grimes.

"But still a privateer," she told him, "as the first Baron d'Estang was. . . ."

There was something more than a little sluttish about her posture. Her bodice had become unbuttoned. The pink nipple of one firm breast seemed to be winking at him. The invitation was unmistakable.

Yet when he got up from his chair and moved toward her she put up a hand to fend him away.

"Wait," she said. "I have to use your bathroom first. Through there, isn't it?"

"Yes."

She rose sinuously from her seat, walked, with swaying buttocks, to the bedroom, through which were the toilet facilities. Grimes poured himself the last of the coffee from the thermopot. He was still sipping it when she came back, standing in the doorway between day and sleeping cabins.

The glossy white Eton collar and the black bow accentuated her nakedness. A highborn lady she might be—and, at this moment, a tart she most certainly was.

But a high-class tart, thought Grimes, as he got up and went to join her in the bedroom.

In the day cabin the miniature Una Freeman continued her tireless rounds while the solidograph of Maggie Lazenby looked down disapprovingly.

"And now," he whispered, "what was all this about, darling?"

She murmured, "The laborer is worthy of his hire."

He said, "But this was a bonus."

"And for me, John. And for me. Besides. . . ."

"Yes?"

"I don't pretend to possess the faculty of prevision. . . . But. . . . But I don't think that you'll be coming back here, ever. I just had to take this chance to do with you what we should have done a long time ago."

"Thank you," he said.

She kissed him a last time, her lips moist and warm on his, then gently disengaged herself from his embrace. She swung her long, long legs down to the deck, swayed gracefully into the bathroom. When she came out she was dressed again in her bunny costume.

"Don't get up," she told him. "I can see myself ashore."

"But. . . ."

"Don't get up, John." She blew him a kiss. "Good night. Good-bye, and the very best of luck."

She vanished through the doorway.

She screamed briefly. Grimes flung himself off the bed and ran to the door. She straightened up from rubbing her right foot and glared at him.

"That bloody golden popsy of yours," she snarled. "It was *intentional!*"

"She's only a toy," said Grimes.

"And a dangerous one." She grinned. "I'd better go before I kick her off her bicycle and then jump on her!"

She waved and then was gone.

Grimes told the tiny cyclist to stop, picked her up and put her back on her shelf. The integument of the metal body in his hands seemed almost as real as the human skin that, only minutes ago, he had been caressing.

Thirty-eight

Sister Sue's control room was fully manned.

Grimes was in the command chair, and Williams seated at the stand-by controls. Old Mr. Stewart was looking after the NST transceiver and Ms. Connellan and the new fourth officer, the Countess of Walshingham, were at their stations by the radar equipment. Venner was attending the recently installed battle organ. It was SOP in the Survey Service to have all armament ready for instant use during lift-off and, thought Grimes, what was good enough for a regular warship was good enough for a privateer.

He looked around him at his officers. Williams was his usual cheerful self and old Mr. Stewart looked like an elderly priest performing a ritual of worship to some electronic deity. Venner, with violent death at his fingertips, was grinning mirthlessly. He would welcome the excuse, Grimes knew, to push a few buttons. The Green Hornet seemed to have a smaller chip on her shoulder than usual. The Countess was conveying the impression that she was holding herself icily aloof from everybody except the second mate.

Grimes didn't like her. He did not think that anybody, save Ms. Connellan, would or could like her. She had made a scene—only a minor one, but still a scene—when, at long last, she had deigned to affix her signature to *Sister Sue*'s Articles of Agreement. She had scrawled, in a large, rather childish hand, *Walshingham.* "What are your given names?" Grimes had asked her. "That's no concern of yours, Captain," she had replied. "How do we address you?" he had persisted. "As Your Ladyship, of course." "You are a junior officer aboard this vessel," he had told her. "Here you are not a Ladyship." "I am a Ladyship anywhere in the galaxy. But you may address me as Countess."

(The Green Hornet, Grimes knew, called her new friend Wally. He said, "You will be addressed as Miss Walshingham. Or, if you prefer it, Ms.")

"Port Kane Control to flagship," came a voice, Kane's voice, from the NST radio speaker. "Lift when you are ready. *Pride of Erin, Spaceways Princess* and *Agatha's Ark* are under your orders."

Grimes turned to face the transceiver with its sensitive microphone. "Commodore Grimes to Commodore Kane and to masters of *Pride of Erin, Spaceways Princess* and *Agatha's Ark.* The squadron will proceed in echelon—first *Sister Sue,* then the *Pride,* then the *Princess,* then the *Ark,* as rear commodore. . . ."

The Green Hornet muttered something about Survey Service bullshit.

"Ships will lift at twenty-second intervals and will maintain station. Acknowledge in order named."

The acknowledgments came in.

"Stand by!" At Grimes' touch on his controls the mutter of his hitherto idling inertial drive deepened to a rumble. "Execute!"

Sister Sue shook herself, then clambered slowly into the calm morning air toward the blue sky with its gleaming, feathery streaks of high-altitude cloud. Grimes looked out and down through a viewport, saw that there was a small crowd of women outside the dome that housed The Happy Kangaroo. The volunteer hostesses, he thought. Most of them were still in their bunny costumes. Several of them were waving. Michelle was not among them and he felt a little stab of disappointment. Probably she would be with Kane, watching the privateer fleet's departure from the control room at the top of the lattice-work tower. He transferred his attention to the glassed-in cage but could see nobody; the sunlight reflected from the windows was too dazzling. And was Kane, he asked himself wryly, playing King David to his Uriah the Hittite? But it was a far-fetched analogy. Apart from anything else it was the ill-fated Uriah who had been the cuckolded husband.

He wished, too, that the Princess had come to the spaceport to watch the ships, carrying both her son and the man who was his father, set out.

Grimes, he admonished himself, *you're a sentimental slob.*

The Countess announced in a high, clear voice, "*Pride of Erin* is lifting, Commodore."

"Thank you, Miss Walshingham."

He stepped up the thrust of his inertial drive.

"*Spaceways Princess* is lifting. . . ."

"Thank you."

In the stern vision screen the spaceport buildings were dwindling fast.

"*Agatha's Ark* is lifting."

"Good."

Up drove the four ships, and up. The flickering altimeter numerals in the screen told their story of ever and rapidly increasing distance from the ground. Soon, thought Grimes, it would be time for the first test of his captains—and of himself. Never before had he been called upon to assume responsibility for the movements of more than a single ship. He had discussed the maneuver that he was about to attempt with the three other tramp masters, had told them that it was one frequently carried out by Survey Service squadrons shortly after lift-off. He had instructed them in signals procedure. It was a quite spectacular evolution, especially during the hours of darkness, but as long as everything was working properly there was no risk.

"Stand by inertial and reaction drive controls," he ordered. "Acknowledge."

In the screen he saw paired brilliant lights, one red and one blue, blossom into life on the gun turrets of the other ships, so sited as to be visible to all concerned. *Sister Sue* was now displaying similar illuminations.

His hand poised over his inertial drive controls, he looked to Williams, whose fingers were on the light switches. The mate nodded.

"Execute!"

The clangor of the inertial drive ceased suddenly. In the screen Grimes saw the blue lights on the other ships wink out as one. He felt the inevitable weightlessness as *Sister Sue* began to drop.

"Execute!"

As the red lights were switched off blue incandescence and white vapor burst from the sterns of the ships. Acceleration slammed Grimes down into his chair.

Not bad, he thought, *not bad at all. . . .*

"*Pride of Erin* is out of station," said the Countess coldly. "She is lifting relative to us."

"She's not going to come sniffing up our arse, is she?" asked Grimes coarsely.

"No, sir.

He had seen worse, he remembered. There had been one quite spectacular balls-up many years ago when he had been a junior officer aboard *Aries.* The cruiser, with four escorting destroyers, had lifted from Atlantia. One of the destroyers had not only accelerated violently but had deviated from trajectory, missing the flagship of the squadron by the thickness of the proverbial coat of paint, searing her plating with the fiery backblast.

Anyhow, there was no point in wasting reaction mass. He ordered the required signals to be flashed, cut the reaction drive and restarted inertial drive simultaneously.

The fleet lifted steadily.

Once clear of the Van Allens, trajectory was set for the Kalla sun. Grimes wondered what prevision, if any, he would experience during the moments while the temporal precession field of the Mannschenn Drive built up. What visions of battle and carnage would he see?

But there was only a voice—his voice—singing, not very tunefully.

I murdered William Moore as I sailed, as I sailed,
I murdered William Moore as I sailed,
I knocked him on the head till he bled the scuppers red
And I heaved him with the lead
As I sailed. . . .

Then inside the control room the warped perspective snapped back to normality and colors resumed their proper places in the spectrum. Outside, the stars were no longer points of brilliance but resembled writhing nebulae.

Grimes looked at Williams.

The mate, obviously, was unaware that his captain was destined to kill him. *But,* thought Grimes, *there is an infinitude of possible futures. There are probabilities and improbabilities—but there are no impossibilities.*

He unbuckled himself from his chair, went to look into the screen of the mass proximity indicator. All the ships were there, as they should have been. Soon, thought Grimes, he would carry out trials of the synchonizers with which the privateers were fitted, and then there would be a few practice shots. There was no urgency, however. Until those Letters of Marque were issued *Sister Sue* and the others were just innocent merchantmen proceeding on their lawful occasions.

"Deep Space routine, Mr. Williams," he ordered. "You know where to find me if you want me."

He went down to his day cabin, where he was joined after a few minutes by Mayhew.

Thirty-nine

"I have that damned prevision again," he told the telepath. "The Ballad of Captain Kidd. I murdered William Moore, and all the rest of it."

"I know," said Mayhew.

"You would. But I don't like it. There're a few people aboard this ship who tempt me to commit murder—but Williams isn't one of them."

"But it's not a certainty, Commodore. It's no more than one of the many possibilities."

"A probability, Mr. Mayhew."

"But still not a certainty."

"Then I'll just have to hope for the best. Now, you've got your fingers on the pulse of the ship. Is everybody happy in the service?"

"At the moment, sir, yes. Even Her Highness the Countess of Walshingham."

"She's not a 'highness.' She's only a Countess."

Mayhew grinned. "Of course, sir, you are more familiar with aristocratic ranks and ratings than we low, common spacemen are. Oh, have you seen dear Wally's pet yet?"

"No."

"I have. The thing gives me the creeps. Outwardly it's no more than a cat—a big one, black, with a white bib and socks. But the fur's synthetic and the claws are razor-sharp steel and the skeleton is steel too. And the battery that powers its motors will deliver at maximum capacity for all of twelve standard months. The brain's organic, though. A feline brain, modified, with absolute loyalty to the Countess. And it's programed to kill—anybody or anything—to protect her or if she so orders it. And it's programed to self-destruct if its mistress dies."

"So there's a bomb of some kind inside it," said Grimes.

"That I don't know, sir. I don't possess X-ray vision."

"Presumably dear Wally knows."

"But unless she's actually thinking about it there's no way that I can tell."

"What is she thinking about now?"

Mayhew looked pained.

"First you tell me that you do not approve of . . . snooping. Now you tell me to snoop." He creased his brow in concentration. Suddenly and surprisingly he blushed. "Oh, no," he muttered. "No. . . ."

"What is it, Mr. Mayhew?"

"It's embarrassing, that's what. Ms. Connellan and the Countess are both off watch. How would *you* like to experience the sensation of that green, greasy skin against yours? Those fat, floppy breasts. . . ."

"That will do, Mr. Mayhew."

The telepath grinned. "Well, you asked for it, sir, and you got it. The trouble is that I did too."

Forty

Sister Sue and her consorts fell steadily through the warped continuum toward the Kalla sun. Now and again the Mannschenn Drive would be shut down aboard all vessels so that a practice shoot could be held; this was necessary as the targets used would be outside the temporal precession fields and therefore visually invisible. At fairly close range, of course, they would show up in the screens of the mass proximity indicators—but MPIs are essentially indicators only and do not fix the position of an object, large or small, with the accuracy of radar. This latter, naturally enough, can be employed only in Normal Space Time. Too, as Grimes never ceased to impress upon his own officers and the other shipmasters, to change a vessel's mass while the interstellar drive is in operation is to court disaster.

"You'll warp the field," he would say. "You'll finish up lost in time as well as in space. You won't know if it's last Christmas or next Thursday. Of course, when there are two ships in close proximity, with temporal precession fields synchronized and overlapping, it will be possible to use missiles or projectile weapons *as long as what you throw does not leave the effective limits of the combined field.* But laser, of course, you can use in any circumstances."

For the first practice shoot Grimes had released from his ship a large balloon with a skin of metallic foil. He ordered his fleet into line astern formation and drove out and away from the target until it was no more than a tiny spark on the screens. He then steered a circular trajectory about the target. Much to the annoyance of Williams and Venner, who wanted to demonstrate their skill, he let *Pride of Erin* be the first to engage the make-believe enemy, using the quick-firing cannon. The target was unscathed. Then it was the turn of *Spaceways Princess.* The flashes of the bursting shells could just be seen through the control-room binoculars but the speck of light in the radar screen still shone, indicating that the balloon was still intact. Finally *Agatha's Ark* had her turn. The spark vanished as the balloon was torn to shreds.

"Well done, *Agatha's Ark,*" said Grimes into the microphone of the NST transceiver.

"She must have been using the gunnery computer," came O'Leary's aggrieved voice.

"I was *not,* Captain O'Leary," said Agatha Prinn tartly.

"An' why should we not use the computer?" demanded O'Leary. "It's supposed to be used, isn't it, Commodore? In an actual battle we'd all be usin' our computers. . . ."

"In an actual battle," said Grimes, "you could have suffered one or more direct hits, playing merry hell with your electronics. But as long as your seat-of-the-pants gunnery is up to scratch you stand a chance of surviving."

Another balloon was launched and this time laser was used against it. *Agatha's Ark* opened the action but without success. *Spaceway Princess* did no better; neither did *Pride of Erin.* Then Venner sulked while Williams took over the fire control. The Green Hornet and the Countess looked on disdainfully, as did the big black cat with its white markings that had accompanied its mistress to the control room.

The mate stared into the repeater screen. "Range . . ." he muttered. "Acceleration. . . . With laser there's no deflection to worry about. . . ." He manipulated the controls with sure fingers. Then with his left forefinger he stabbed down—once, again and again, loosing off one-second pulses.

"Got it, Billy!" said Venner, who was watching the main display.

From the transceiver came Agatha Prinn's voice. "Nice shooting, *Sister Sue."*

And then there was O'Leary complaining again. "I'd have got that damn' balloon if ye'd let me use my laser like a sword. Just one good slash, an'. . . ."

Again Grimes had to explain. He said patiently, "As I told you before, you've suffered direct hits. Your jennies have packed up. All you have to give you juice is your power cells. When they're dead, you're dead. You *must* conserve energy."

"Ye're a mon after me own heart, Commodore," broke in Captain MacWhirter.

So it went on. It became obvious that somebody aboard *Agatha's Ark,* probably Captain Prinn herself, was a very good gunner. The *Princess* would never be better than fair and those aboard *Pride of Erin* would not be able, as Williams put it, to shoot their way out of a paper bag. Grimes had three good gunnery officers aboard his own ship—himself and Williams and Venner.

The privateers graduated from balloons to moving targets—practice missiles fired from *Sister Sue* and programed to steer a random trajectory. Reluctantly Grimes conceded that against these it was necessary to make use of the battle computers.

There were other drills—these in the use of the field synchronizers and, just as important, the techniques to be employed in breaking free from synchronization. It was extremely unlikely that any merchantmen would be fitted with the synchronizing device but all too probable that Hallicheki warships would be so equipped. As with the gunnery, *Agatha's Ark* put up the best show, with *Spaceways Princess* a runner-up. *Pride of Erin*'s performance left much to be desired.

"They couldn't *wriggle* out of a paper bag," said Williams disgustedly. "I hope that Captain O'Leary never tangles with a real warship."

"I hope that none of us do," said Grimes. "Come to that, I hope that the Hallicheki haven't gotten around yet to defensively arming their merchantmen. We're in this business, Mr. Williams, to make money, not to take lives."

"Rather strange words to be coming from you, Skipper," said the mate. "If only half the stories one hears about you are true you've done more than your fair share of killing."

"When I was pushed into it," Grimes told him. "Only when I was pushed into it."

And would this William Moore Williams push him into it? he asked himself. He hoped that he would not. Yet, twice, there had been the warning, the prevision.

I murdered William Moore as I sailed. . . .

The voyage continued.

Daily there was Carlotti radio communication with Port Kane, coded messages back and forth. These messages were not only to and from Grimes; the Countess of Walshingham was also keeping old Mr. Stewart busy. The radio officer should not, legally, have informed his captain of this traffic but he did so. Her signals, out and in, were coded. Grimes ran them through the coding machine with which he had been supplied by Kane—and it was at once obvious that the El Doradan was using a code of her own.

So Grimes called in Mayhew.

"More snooping, Captain?" asked the telepath. "This privateering is having a bad effect on your ethical standards."

"We haven't started privateering yet," said Grimes. "Well, as you almost certainly know, dear Wally is in daily communication with her happy home world. All messages out and in are in a code to which I don't have the key. I'd like to know what's cooking."

"At this moment," said Mayhew, "dear Wally, as you call her, is engaged in romantic dalliance with our other non-favorite lady. I have no desire again to intrude upon their sweaty privacy. But this is what I can do. The purser's office is on the same deck as the radio office. When I see Wally making a call on Stewart I'll snoop. She's bound to be thinking about the message that she's getting off."

Grimes did not have long to wait.

"What she is sending," Mayhew told him, "is daily reports on the conduct of the voyage, and her estimation of the capabilities of yourself, your officers and of the other captains. *You* are 'a typical Survey Service officer, a slave to routine and lacking in imagination. . . .'"

"I don't think that her boss, Commodore Kane, shares that opinion," said Grimes.

"He does not, Captain. I took the liberty of eavesdropping now and again during your conferences back on El Dorado. His evaluation of your good self was, 'cunning as a shit-house rat.'"

"Now you tell me. But, more important, what is Kane telling Wally?"

"Mainly routine acknowledgments of her signals. But he is impressing upon her that she must accompany you when you call on the High Cock of Kalla."

"What a title!" laughed Grimes.

"It gains absurdity in the translation," said Mayhew.

"And suppose that I don't wish to have my fourth mate with me when I do my dickerings with His Avian Majesty?"

"Probably you'll be getting orders on that subject from the El Dorado Corporation, through Kane. Even commodores, service or company, have to do as they're told by their superiors."

"And well I know it, Mr. Mayhew. What makes it complicated in my case is that there are two parties giving me orders."

"And you were never very good at taking orders, were you?" said Mayhew.

Forty-one

The privateer fleet came to Kalla.

Grimes was relieved to discover that the Hegemony had not yet established a blockade of the rebel planet. Without doubt they would be attempting to do so eventually—but the Hallicheki, he knew from past experience of the avian race, were apt to run around in circles squawking like wet hens before they actually got around to Doing Something. When they did take action, however, it would be with a cold-blooded viciousness.

Kalla is an Earth-type world, although with a somewhat denser atmosphere. It has the usual seas, continents, islands, rivers, mountain ranges, deserts, fertile plains, forests, polar ice caps and all the rest of it. There is agriculture and there are industries, although there is little automation. The main means of freight transport is by towed balloon, the more or less streamlined gas bags being dragged through the atmosphere by teams of winged workers. Before the revolution these were caponized males. After the revolution it was the hens who had to do the heavy work.

Sister Sue established first contact with Kalla Aerospace Control, by Carlotti radio, while still seven standard days out. Four days out she was challenged by a vessel of the Insurrectionary Navy. This warship made a close approach and attempted to synchronize precession rates with the privateers' flagship. Had she attempted to do so with *Pride of Erin* she would almost certainly have been successful. Grimes' Mannschenn Drive engineer, Malleson, knew all about the synchronizer, its uses and abuses. Although the blob of light representing the guard ship was bright enough in the screen of the mass proximity indicator not so much as the faintest ghost of her was ever seen through the viewports.

Then she did what she should have done at first, calling *Sister Sue* on the Carlotti radio.

A squawking voice issued from the speaker. "*Karkoran* to leader of squadron. *Karkoran* to leader of squadron. Come in. Come in.

The screen came alive and from it looked out the face of a great, gaudy bird—hooked beak, fierce yellow eyes, a golden crest over green and scarlet plumage.

"*Sister Sue* here," said Grimes. "Company Commodore Grimes commanding. Identify yourself, please."

"Flight Leader Kaskonta, Commander of the Inner Starways. I am to escort you and your squadron to Kalla."

"I am obliged to you, Flight Leader."

"I shall be obliged to you, Commodore, if you will allow me to synchronize."

Grimes hesitated briefly. He told Williams and Venner, both of whom were in the control room, to stand by the ship's fire control. He did not expect any trouble—there were never any male avians aboard the warships of the Hegemony—but it would cost nothing to be prepared. He called Malleson, who was in the Mannschenn Drive room.

"All right, Chief. She's one of ours. I hope. Let her synchronize. But stay handy."

There was a brief, very brief period of disorientation. Outside the viewports the stars were still pulsating nebulosities—but against their backdrop, big and solid, was the Kalla ship. It was strange, Grimes thought not for the first time, how spaceship design varied from race to race. The insectoid Shaara, for example, with their vessels that could have been modeled on old-fashioned beehives. . . . The Hallicheki, whose ships looked like metal eggs sitting in lattice-work eggcups. . . .

This was one such.

Probably she had started life as a merchantman but she was far more heavily armed than any of the privateers, a real cruiser rather than an auxiliary cruiser. Her fighting capabilities, however, would depend as much upon the quality of her crew as upon that of her armament. Grimes, who tended at times to be a male chauvinist, thought that she would be able to take on a comparable warship of the Hegemony with a fair chance of success. He did wonder, though, how and where these fighting cocks had received the necessary training. Probably this had been financed, for some promised consideration, by the El Dorado Corporation.

All officers were now in the control room.

"Put out a call to *Pride of Erin, Spaceways Princess* and *Agatha's Ark,* Mr. Stewart," ordered Grimes. "Tell them that we are proceeding to Kalla under escort. Tell them, too, that the authority still rests with myself."

The squadron, with *Karkoran* still in watchful attendance, established itself in synchronous orbit about Kalla. Grimes had been told that none of the ships would be allowed to land but that he could make the descent in one of his boats for an audience with the Lord of the Roost. He talked with Captain Prinn by NST radio, told her that until his return she would be in charge of the little fleet. This did not go down at all well with Captain O'Leary. And Williams, left in command of *Sister Sue* during Grimes' absense, was not pleased either. "You mean that she's the commodore now, Skipper?"

"I appointed her vice-commodore at the beginning of the trip, Mr. Williams."

"I thought that it was rear commodore, sir. And rear is junior to vice. Of course, I'm only a Dog Star Line man, not used to all these naval titles. . . ."

"Don't try to be a space lawyer too, Billy. Captain Prinn, in my opinion, is the person most suitable to be my deputy. I called her the rear commodore because hers is the sternmost ship of the squadron."

"But I thought, sir, that during the commodore's absence his second-in-command would be in charge."

"You're in temporary command of *Sister Sue,* and that's all. And that's plenty. Should you want to get in touch with me, my wrist transceiver will be within effective range of the ship."

He went down to his cabin to pick up his best uniform cap, the one with the scrambled egg on the peak still untarnished, with the especially large horse-and-rider badge. Apart from that he was making no attempt at ceremonial dress. He was not in the Survey Service any longer—apart from that Reserve Commission which was a secret to all save Mayhew and Venner—and did not have in his wardrobe such finery as an epauleted frock coat, with sword belt and sword, or a gold-trimmed fore-and-aft hat. His shipboard shorts and shirt would have to do. He had made inquiries and learned that Port Kwakaar, near which the Lord of the Roost had his palace, was well within Kalla's tropics.

Williams accompanied him to the boat bay. Mayhew, wearing a uniform that looked as though he had slept in it, was awaiting him there. So was the Countess of Walshingham. Her shirt and shorts could have been tailored by one of the big Paris houses. Her cat—that evil beast!—was with her.

Grimes said, "We are not taking *that* down with us, Ms. Walshingham."

"Why not, Commodore?"

"Because I say so. In case you don't know, the Hallicheki are an avian people. There's a strong possibility that they may not like your pet, and an equally strong one that your pet will not like them. It is vitally important that we do not annoy the planetary ruler. I have to get the Letters of Marque from him for a start. And I want to get permission for the ships to land to take aboard such stores as are necessary."

"Birdseed?" she sneered. "Or nice, fat worms?"

He said, "If Commodore Kane had not requested that I take you with me you would be staying aboard. Commodore Kane said nothing about the cat."

"Go to my cabin," she told the . . . animal? "Go to my cabin and wait for me."

It made a noise that was more growl than mew, stalked out of the boat bay. Sulkily the Countess clambered into the fat torpedo hull of the boat. Mayhew followed her. Grimes, after saying, "She's all yours, Mr. Williams. Don't start any wars in my absence!" went in last. He found that the fourth officer was already seated forward, at the controls. He resisted the urge to tell her to get aft, with the telepath. After all, she was a qualified spaceperson. And he was a captain—no, a commodore—and as such should not be doing his own chauffeuring.

The Countess seemed to be capable enough.

She sealed the little spacecraft and made the necessary checks. She reported readiness to depart to the control room.

"Shove off when ready," came Venner's voice from the transceiver. The little inertial drive unit grumbled, then snarled. Ahead of the boat the door in the shell plating opened, exposing the chamber, from which the air had already been evacuated, to space, to a view of black, starry sky and the curved, luminous limb of the planet, glowing greenly.

The inertial drive almost screamed as the Countess made a needlessly abrupt departure from *Sister Sue,* the sudden acceleration forcing Grimes and Mayhew back in their seats.

"We are not a guided missile, Ms. Walshingham," said Grimes sternly when he had recovered his breath.

"Time, Commodore, is money," she said. "As soon as we get those Letters of Marque we shall be able to start making a profit."

Probably, thought Grimes, she was a shareholder in the El Dorado Corporation—and as money hungry as the rest of them.

Forty-two

Port Kwakaar was, in some ways, just another spaceport. In other ways it was exotic. The administration buildings, for example, were domes that looked as though they had been woven from straw, and the control tower was a huge tree on top of which another such nest was perched. There were ships on the apron—not only Hallicheki vessels but a couple of the Commission's Epsilon Class star tramps. There were mooring masts to which were tethered sausage-shaped balloons below which were slung flimsy-looking baskets. There were Kallans in the air, male birds to judge from their gaudy plumage. These gave the descending boat a wide berth.

"*Sister Sue*'s small craft," squawked a voice from the transceiver speaker, "land by the beacon. Land by the beacon."

The Countess acknowledged, then slammed the boat down alongside the tripod atop which a bright, scarlet light was flashing. Grimes winced. On the return trip to the mother ship, he decided, he would take the controls himself—and if dear Wally didn't like it she could go and cry on the Green Hornet's shoulder.

"Open up, Ms. Walshingham," he ordered.

He was first out of the boat and saw two figures walking toward him, one human, one Hallicheki, both male. The man was dressed in an expensive looking gray coverall suit, the bird only in his brilliant plumage. Grimes recalled a dictum of his academy days: *If it moves, salute it; if it doesn't move, polish it.*

So he saluted.

The man inclined his head in reply. The bird lifted his right wing, on the end of which was a claw-like hand.

"Commodore Grimes?" asked the human, the faint disdain in his voice and on his fine-featured face conveying the impression that, as far as he was concerned, commodores were six a penny.

"Yes," said Grimes.

"I am Lord Francis Delamere, Ambassador for El Dorado on Kalla."

"Delamere?" asked Grimes. "I know two Delameres. Cousins. One is a

Commander—probably a Captain by now—in the Federation Survey Service. The other is a Dog Star Line Company Commodore."

"Indeed? Younger sons of younger sons of younger sons, possibly. But let us not waste time talking about obscure members of my family—if, indeed, they are members."

"There is a strong facial resemblance, Lord Francis."

"Indeed? You will leave your boat here, Commodore Grimes, and you and your officers will be taken to the palace of the Lord of the Roost by airship. . . ."

"In one of *those* things, Franky?" demanded the Countess, who had just disembarked. "You must be out of your tiny mind!"

"In one of those things, Wally," said Lord Delamere coldly. "When in Rome, do as Rome does."

"And when in Baghdad," added Grimes, "do as the Baghdaddies do."

Not only did Delamere and the Countess and the Kallan look at him coldly; so did Mayhew.

"Come!" ordered the avian and set off toward the mooring masts with an odd scuttling motion, the tips of his claws/hands just brushing the ground. The humans followed him toward the mooring masts, to a flimsy-looking ladder that was propped against the basket of one of the balloons. Delamere was first up this and as soon as his weight was in the car the aerostat started to fall. He threw out a bag of some sort of ballast—sand or earth to judge by the sound that it made when it hit the concrete—and restored buoyancy. Grimes was next, and did his own ballast dumping. Mayhew followed him, then the Countess. It was obvious that she had no intention of doing any manual work so Grimes had to oblige.

Five dejected-looking hens, their drab plumage dusty, appeared. The cock bird picked up lines that were made fast to the car at one end, trailing on the ground at the other, and attached them with cliphooks to collars about the scrawny necks of four of the females. The fifth one climbed clumsily up the lattice-work mooring mast and, using her beak, cast loose the line securing the nose of the balloon to the skeletal tower. Delamere threw out another bag of ballast, a small one. The male took to the air, his wings beating strongly, squawking orders in his own language. The females flapped their pinions and lifted, straining against the towlines. The untethered bird lifted too, flying abeam of and a few meters distant from the basket. She turned her head to glare at the occupants. If looks could kill they would all have died at once.

It was not a comfortable ride. There was no seating inside the car and its last use, to judge by a lingering, acrid odor, must have been for the carriage of organic fertilizer. There was a swaying motion and, now and again, jouncing as minor turbulence was encountered. The treetops beneath them, viciously spiked coronals with leaves like bayonets, looked far too close. The air through which they passed was heavy, hot and humid.

And then, ahead of them, on the summit of a low hill was the palace of the Lord of the Roost, a towering structure that could have been made of wickerwork but which gleamed metallically, pierced at intervals with circular ports. The hapless hens fought to gain altitude. Grimes suggested to Delamere that more ballast might be dumped. Delamere told Grimes that he was a spaceman, not an airman, and that, in any case, any attempt to make the work of the towing team easier would be frowned upon by the male Kallans.

"You have to remember," he said, "that these hens are being punished for the crimes that they committed when they were the rulers."

The male bird, well in the lead by now, flew into a port at the very summit of the tower. The free female followed him but did not enter the building and perched on a protruding spar. The balloon labored ahead and upward. When it was close enough the hen dropped from her perch, swooped down and caught the dangling mooring line in her beak, flew with it to the pole on which she had been sitting, made it fast. Grimes watched proceedings with great interest mingled with apprehension. He could foresee what he categorized as one helluva tangle. But he need not have worried. Delamere, who knew the drill, unsnapped the towlines from the forward end of the car as they slackened, threw them out and clear. The hens flapped wearily groundward. The breeze, such as it was, was just enough to push the balloon in toward the building, although there was no actual contact.

"Do they expect us to *jump?"* demanded the Countess.

Grimes had been just about to ask the same question.

He could see movement inside the circular opening. From it a gangway was pushed out, an affair of woven slats that did not look as though it would support a healthy cat. But it was rigid enough and did not sag sufficiently to make contact with the basket rim.

"You first, Commodore," said Delamere. "I have to stay to valve gas."

Carefully Grimes clambered out of the car until he was kneeling on the flimsy gangway. He was tempted to make the short passage to the safety of the tower on his hands and knees. There was no handrail of any kind. But to crawl to an audience with the Lord of the Roost would not, he knew, enhance his image. He pushed up and did a little jump forward. He was standing. He did not look down. He knew that as long as he walked toward a light that gleamed in the very center of the port he would be safe. (He knew it—but he did not quite believe it.) He walked, fighting down the temptation to break into a near run, to get it over with as quickly as possible. He proceeded with befitting dignity until a sidewise glance told him that he was in safety.

Then he turned to watch the others cross the perilous bridge.

He hoped that he had not looked so unhappy as the Countess and Mayhew were looking. Lord Delamere, after valving a last dribble of gas, sauntered across exuding insouciance.

Forty-three

Grimes supposed that the dimly lit apartment into which they were led could be called a throne room. There was no throne, however. There was a horizontal bar at human eye level on which the Kallan leader was roosting, gripping the perch with his huge, clawed feet. There were other bars at lower levels on which lesser dignitaries stood (sat?). All the avians were males, brightly plumaged. Among the feathers of some of them precious metals and jewels reflected what little light there was, seemed to concentrate it before throwing it back. In one corner of the big room sophisticated recording equipment was humming almost inaudibly, panel lights gleaming. There was a rather unpleasant acridity in the air. Grimes managed to restrain himself from sneezing. The Countess did not even make an effort.

"Your Winged Mightiness," said Lord Delamere, "I present to you the privateer commodore and his officers."

The Lord of the Roost squawked derisively, "He is a cock, and he has a hen officer!"

"She is only a very junior officer, Mightiness."

"She may remain, but she will keep silent." The glaring, yellow eyes turned to Grimes. "I am told that you have an offer to make to me, Commodore. Speak."

"Your Winged Mightiness," Grimes began. He tried to think of what to say next. He had assumed that Lord Delamere would be doing the haggling, would already have done the haggling. "I have come," he went on, "to offer my services, the services of myself and my ships. I have learned that Kalla is threatened by the Hegemony. Your own fleet, gallant though it is, will be fully employed protecting your world." He paused for thought. "Warfare is more than actions between opposing fleets of warships. There is economic warfare. . . ."

"Are you a spaceman or a banker?" demanded the great bird.

"I am a spaceman, Mightiness. Perhaps my words were ill chosen. By economic warfare I mean the destruction of the enemy's commerce. . . ."

"Which you will do for your profit." The Lord of the Roost emitted a discordant sound that could have been a laugh. "But do not bother me any more with your talk, Commodore. You are a spaceman, not a salesman. I have seen you now, as well as having heard many reports about you. The Lord Delamere has already made the deal on your behalf. You will harry Hallicheki shipping, for the benefit of the El Dorado Corporation and, of course, for your own benefit. The Letters of Marque have been drawn up. You will be fighting for money, whereas our ships will be fighting for Kalla's freedom from the harsh rule of the Hegemony. Korndah will give you your precious papers, then you may go."

One of the lesser birds hopped down from his perch, scuttled to a very prosaic looking filing cabinet that was standing beside the recording apparatus, opened a drawer, used his beak to withdraw a bundle of documents. He hopped/shuffled to Grimes, dropped the papers into the commodore's hands. Grimes removed the elastic band securing them. He tried to read what was on the top one but in the dim light it was impossible.

"Do not worry, Commodore," squawked the Lord of the Roost. "All is in order. You can read the authority that I have given you at your leisure. Now you may go, back to your ships, and commence operations as soon as possible."

"Your Mightiness," said Grimes, "there is one favor that I wish to ask of you."

"Speak."

"I request permission for the fleet to land and to replenish certain items of consumable stores."

"The permission is not granted. You can replenish your storerooms from those of your victims."

"But I also want to top up the water tanks. On leaving El Dorado I ordered an exercise in the use of reaction drive. As a result of that our stocks of reaction mass have been reduced."

"I am not a spacebeing, Commodore." The Lord of the Roost gabbled briefly in his own language to one of his aides, received a raucous reply. Then, "Very well. I am told that in warfare the rocket drive, the reaction drive, might be employed. Your fleet may come in to the spaceport at first light tomorrow morning, and will depart as soon as the tanks have been topped up."

"Thank you, Mightiness," said Grimes.

"Oh, one more thing, Commodore. Do not trust hens."

The audience was over.

At the end of the corridor they found that the towing team had again been harnessed to the balloon car, were hanging on to projections on the tower, the lines slack. Delamere was first into the basket and began to dump ballast. During the time that they had spent with the Lord of the Roost, Grimes realized, more bags of sand had been loaded and gas replenished. The Countess was next aboard. She and her compatriot obviously did not love each other and were avoiding physical contact. Mayhew was next, and then Grimes, the precious Letters of Marque tucked into his shirt, made the short but perilous passage.

The balloon was cast off from the mooring spar and the towing team beat their wings clatteringly, then pulled the clumsy aircraft out and away from the tower. The flying escort took up their stations. On the return trip Grimes did not admire the scenery but looked through the documents. There was one set of papers for each ship. That issued to *Sister Sue* authorized her to make war upon all enemies of the Independent Nest of Kalla, wherever found. It stated, too, that one Commodore Grimes, while master of this vessel, was fully responsible for the conduct of *Pride of Erin, Spaceways Princess* and *Agatha's Ark.* The signature was a jagged scrawl written with some brownish medium. *Blood?* wondered Grimes. There was an ornate gold seal, bearing the likeness of a rapacious bird with outstretched wings, its taloned feet gripping a planetary orb. The other Letters of Marque were in duplicate—one copy for each captain, the other for the commodore. In each of them it was stated that overall responsibility for the operation rested with Grimes.

So, he thought wryly, *whoever carries the can back it's going to be me. He who sups with Drongo Kane needs a long spoon. So does he who sups with Commodore—correction!—Rear Admiral Damien. . . .*

The balloon sagged down toward the spaceport mooring masts. Lord Delamere valved gas. He miscalculated and had to compensate by dumping a small bag of ballast.

Grimes was amused and thought, *He's no more perfect than his cousins umpteen times removed. . . .*

Mooring procedure was carried out quite efficiently. The humans clambered down the light ladder to the ground.

Delamere said, dismissively, "I'll see you tomorrow morning, Commodore."

Grimes led the way to the waiting boat. Inboard, he took the pilot's seat. The Countess glared at him but went aft to sit with Mayhew. Grimes, starting the inertial drive, lifted with deliberately exaggerated caution. He heard the girl mutter something about Survey Service throw-outs with only two speeds, Dead Slow and Stop. His prominent ears reddened but he maintained his sedate ascent.

Forty-four

"Well, Mr. Mayhew?" asked Grimes.

"To begin with, sir, the Lord of the Roost is not human. . . ."

"A blinding glimpse of the obvious. I'm not a telepath but even I could see that."

Mayhew flushed. "Let me finish, sir. I meant that his thought processes are not human. He would be incapable of being devious. He despises you for fighting for profit but realizes that you will be useful to him in the struggle for Kallan freedom."

"The free rooster in the free barnyard," said Grimes. "I don't think that our two liberated ladies would approve of such freedom."

"With the Hallicheki," said Mayhew, "it's a clear choice. Either the cocks or the hens must rule and roost. The cocks are the more intelligent, the more honest. The hens have mean, petty minds. And didn't the ones who were towing us *hate* us! All the time they were thinking of tearing the flesh from our bones with their sharp beaks. Oh, we're on the right side, sir. No doubt of that."

"And Delamere?"

"I think that what you were thinking about him was quite correct."

"Talking of Delamere, I suppose that his distant relative is still in the Survey Service."

"Very much so. He's a four-ring captain now, and loved by everybody."

The telephone buzzed.

"Commodore here," said Grimes.

Williams' face formed in the little screen and he said, "The boat's back and inboard, sir. Wally's finished her mail run. The way she's carrying on it must be beneath her dignity to act as postwoman."

"My nose fair bleeds for her. Tell Mr. Stewart to arrange NST hook-up between all ships. I'll give the captains time to read their Letters of Marque, then I'll be up to control to give them a pep talk."

Forty-five

One by one, at thirty-minute intervals, the four ships dropped down to the spaceport. By the time that *Agatha's Ark* was landed the hoses connected to *Sister Sue*'s intake valves were already throbbing as tons of reaction mass—water—were being pumped into her tanks and teams of dingy, sullen hens, bullied into activity by strutting male birds, were connecting the pipes to *Pride of Erin* and *Spaceways Princess*.

There was, of course, no planet leave for the privateer crews. Those officers who had come ashore to supervise the work about their ships would not stray from the spaceport. They were all too conscious of the smoldering hate with which the work-hens regarded them, of the haughty disdain for mere mammals evinced by the arrogant cocks.

Grimes stood at the foot of *Sister Sue*'s ramp to await Lord Delamere. Mayhew was with him. They were approached by a stocky, dark-featured man wearing master's uniform with the badge of the Interstellar Transport Commission on his cap.

This person made a sketchy salute. Grimes replied.

"Good morning, Captain," said the ITC master.

"Good morning, Captain," replied Grimes.

"Jones is the name, Captain. Of *Cross Eppie.*" He waved his hand toward one of the two Epsilon Class tramps. "Or *Epsilon Crucis,* if you want to be formal."

"Grimes," said Grimes, introducing himself.

"Of *Sister Sue,*" said Jones unnecessarily. Then, "What is this? An invasion? Four ex-Epsilon Class tramps, all armed to the teeth. . . . We've been half expecting a couple or three Hegemony cruisers to come roaring in, but. . . . And you must be on *their* side. . . . The Kallan rebels, I mean."

"Mphm," grunted Grimes, filling his pipe.

"Why all the lethal ironmongery, Captain?" persisted Jones.

"Defensive armament," muttered Grimes through a cloud of acrid smoke.

"Are you blockade runners, then? And have you any idea of the sort of punch packed by one of the Hegemony's cruisers? Those vicious hens'd chew you up and shit you out in five seconds flat."

"Thank you for the information," said Grimes coldly.

"I'm just trying to be helpful, Captain. I *know* these people. I've been running to the various Hallicheki planets for the last twenty years. I think that the commission's very foolish to be maintaining trading relations with Kalla."

"So you're a blockade runner too, Captain Jones. And, like me, you just go where you're sent."

Jones would have made a reply, a heated one possibly, but there was a clattering noise from overhead. The men looked up. Dropping down from the murky sky was a helicopter, a small one, little more than a basket dangling beneath rotors. It landed. Delamere stepped out of the flimsy-looking cab. Grimes saluted him—not the sort of salute that he would have given to an admiral or to a pretty girl but a curt greeting to an equal. The El Doradan nodded in reply.

"Excuse me, Captain Jones," said Grimes. "I have matters to discuss with my agent."

Followed by Mayhew he walked toward the little aircraft.

"I have arranged for you to see the ex-Minister of Star Shipping," said Delamere. "She will be able to give you information about the Hallicheki trade routes."

"That will be useful," said Grimes. "Do you have transport laid on?"

"Not necessary, Commodore. The . . . prison is only a short walk from here."

The prison—or that part of it in which the ex-Minister was confined—was no more than a hovel, a dingy *kraal.* In it a filthy, more-dead-than-alive hen was chained by one leg to the central pole, was squatting in her own filth. Her skin was scabbed where feathers had been plucked out and the dun plumage around these patches was darkly matted. Where one eye had been was a still oozing wound.

There were two cockbirds in the malodorous hut. Guards? Interrogators? Delamere—who must have been an accomplished linguist—addressed one of the gaudy beings in the Hallicheki language. It sounded like a comedian imitating a parrot. There was a squawking reply from one of the avians.

"She will not talk," said Delamere to Grimes. "But do not worry. There are . . . methods."

There was a cacophony of squawks from the larger and gaudier Kallan, answered only by the female's sullen silence. There was a tearing out of a beakful of feathers from the hen's breast—which elicited an agonized screech. There was a vicious beak poised menacingly over the remaining eye—and a low, gobbling sound from the prisoner which Grimes did not need to be told was supplication.

The ex-Minister talked. When she faltered she lost yet more plumage. That of newly shed blood was added to the other stinks in the hut. But she talked and Delamere translated. Mayhew recorded the interrogation.

At last, to Grimes' great relief, it was over. He, with Delamere and Mayhew, left the hut. The air outside was warm, humid, heavy and, compared to the atmosphere inside a well managed starship, almost unbearably stuffy. Compared to that inside the hut it was like champagne after pond water.

"Happy now, Commodore Grimes?" asked Delamere.

"I'm not, My Lord. I thought that I should be fighting on the right side; now I'm not so sure. Was that cruelty necessary? There are other ways—drugs and the like—to get beings to talk."

"The Hallicheki, male or female, are a cruel race, Grimes."

"I still don't have to like them."

"As long as you do what your Letters of Marque entitle you to do, likes and dislikes don't come into it."

"I suppose not."

As they approached *Sister Sue* Grimes saw that the water hoses had been withdrawn and were being reeled in. They were still connected to the other three ships. He saw, too, that officers from the two ITC tramps were talking with people from the privateers, looking up at the armament as they did so. It didn't matter. Only one person knew what trajectory the fleet would follow once it was clear of the Kallan atmosphere—and that one person was Grimes. (And, he realized, Mayhew—but he and the telepath were working for the same boss.)

"Good luck, Commodore, and good hunting," said Delamere.

The two shook hands briefly, without much enthusiasm on either side. The El Doradan clambered into his helicopter and clattered skyward.

"Well, Mr. Mayhew?" asked Grimes when they were back on board and sitting in the commodore's day cabin.

"She spoke the truth, sir," said Mayhew. "And Lord Delamere's translation was a faithful one. The trade route between Kookadahl and New Maine seems the most promising. Much of the freight is carried in the ships of the Hegemony. From Kookadahl to New Maine there are tree pearls, mainly for transshipment to other human worlds. Quite precious, as you know. Attempts have been made to grow the pearl tree, from smuggled seeds, on other planets but they have never been successful."

"Spare me the botany lesson, Mr. Mayhew."

"Sorry, sir. Tree pearls, and *ferancha* skins and ingots of gold and platinum.

. . . The other way the pickings wouldn't be so good. A horrid sort of fish meal that they make on New Maine for the Hallicheki market. Things like eels, pickled in brine. Too—and this is what suits *our* purpose—one of the Terran ships, the Commission's *Epsilon Draconis,* selected to be a possible victim of piracy, is on that trade. Her assistant purser is really, like myself, a PCO from the Survey Service."

"But will the Hallicheki institute a convoy system?" wondered Grimes aloud. "Will they arm their merchantmen?"

"I don't think so," Mayhew told him. "Or, at least, not at first. Even if there are spies for the Hegemony among the crews of the ITC tramps—which is extremely unlikely—it will take some time to organize convoys, to fit defensive armament and all the rest of it. The Hallicheki Admiralty will be at least as slow as ours when it comes to dedigitating."

"You could be right," conceded Grimes. "You probably are right."

He dismissed Mayhew and sent for Magda Granadu.

She brought the coins and the book.

Grimes shook the ancient discs of silvery alloy in his cupped hands, feeling—as he had before—that he was standing at the focus of supernatural lines of force. *It's no more than superstition,* he told himself. *But. . . .*

The coins clinked between the concavities of his palms. He let them drop to the deck.

Two tails and a head. . . . Yin. . . .

Two heads and a tail. . . . Yang. . . .

Three tails. . . . Yin. . . .

Three heads. . . . Yang. . . .

Two tails and a head. . . . Yin. . . .

Three tails. . . . Yin. . . .

The trigrams: Chén, thunder, arousing. K'an, water, dangerous. . . .

The hexagram: Hsieh. Escape. . . .

"It all looks rather ominous," said Grimes to the woman.

"It is," she murmured as she consulted the book.

Escape. Advantage will be found to the south and west. If no further expeditions are called for, good fortune will come from returning home. . . .

"That doesn't sound too bad," he said. "But the south and west? Austral and Port Woomera?"

"There's more," she told him. "There's the commentary, and the lines. . . ."

Here the trigram depicting danger is confronted by that depicting powerful arousal. By movement there is an escape from peril. . . .

"A blinding glimpse of the obvious," he said.

The lines. . . .

Sixth in the third place. He travels in a carriage, with a porter to handle his baggage. Such behavior will tempt robbers to attack him. However firm and correct he may try to be, there will be cause for regret. . . .

"But *I'm* supposed to be the robber," he said.

Nine in the fourth place. Remove your toes. Friends in whom you can trust will then approach.

"Remove my *toes,* Magda?"

"The interpretation, Commodore," she told him, "is that you remove hangers-on from your immediate circle, thus allowing true friends to approach."

"Hangers-on?"

"I could name a few. Her Highness Wally, for one. And for all the use the Green Hornet is, she's another. And. . . ."

"That'll do."

Six in the sixth place. The prince looses an arrow from his bow and hits a falcon sitting on top of a high wall. The effect of this action will be in every way advantageous. . . .

"A falcon," said Grimes. "So I shall be taking some Hallicheki ships."

"You should not take it literally, Commodore. According to the interpretation—he removes the most powerful of his enemies and escapes from their domination."

"It could be worse," he said. "Much worse."

"But there's still danger," she told him.

Forty-six

Through the warped continuum fell the four ships, their temporal precession rates unsynchronized, using their mass proximity indicators to maintain a rather ragged line astern formation.

Grimes ordered frequent drills. He had been able to stock up on missiles and ammunition for the quick-firing cannon on Kalla. (He had, too, been appalled at the price charged for these martial necessities by the Kallans.) He decided to let Captain O'Leary make the first capture. The sooner that *Pride of Erin* was on her way to El Dorado with her prize and out of the commodore's hair the better. Captain MacWhirter would be the next to go. *Spaceways Princess* came in the barely competent category. *Agatha's Ark* he would keep with him as long as possible. Then, when *Sister Sue* was a ship alone, it would be time to instigate the incident that would give the Survey Service the excuse to crack down on the privateers. He would be rather sorry, he admitted to himself, when the time came. He was enjoying being a commodore, with a small fleet under his command. He was looking forward to deploying his squadron, even though it would be against only unarmed merchantmen.

The ships maintained a Carlotti listening watch but broke radio silence rarely, and then transmitted only on very low power. Aboard the flagship was a plotting tank and in it Grimes was able to record the positions of merchant shipping traversing a sphere light-years in diameter. It was a fascinating exercise, requiring considerable navigational skill. Vessels outbound from New Maine to Kookadahl would not be worth bothering with. What value would a cargo of stinking fish paste be? But, at last, there was a ship, one of the Hegemony's freighters, bound from Kookadahl to the Terran colony.

The squadron steered an intercepting trajectory.

Presumably the Hallicheki captain would have a mass proximity indicator in her control room. Possibly she would become perturbed to see an obvious formation heading toward her. She might assume that it was a squadron of Kallan warships, commerce raiders, and squawk for help.

In *Sister Sue*'s Main Carlotti Room old Mr. Stewart was standing by, watching his rotating Mobius Strip antennae, his dials and oscilloscopes. He had his orders. As soon as *Krorkor*—that was the name of the Hallicheki ship, learned from her transmissions in English to the Carlotti station at New Maine—began to send, a characteristic squiggle would appear in one of the screens. Immediately Stewart's especially designed computer would match crests with troughs, troughs with crests. In the oscilloscope the wavy line of green luminosity would be replaced by one almost straight. From the speakers of any transceivers tuned to the Hallicheki ship would issue . . . nothing.

Grimes, now, rarely strayed from the control room, taking catnaps in his command chair, nibbling snacks and drinking coffee brought up to him by Magda, fouling the atmosphere with the acrid fumes from his vile pipe. He was reasonably happy when Williams or Venner had the watch, distinctly uneasy when Ms. Connellan was in charge. As fourth officer the Countess of Walshingham should have been sharing the chief officer's watchkeeping duties but Grimes had told his mate, "Find some sort of job for that snooty bitch, Billy, that doesn't bring her anywhere near Control!"

Mr. Stewart was undergoing a far less wearing time than his captain. The responsibility for jamming the victim's transmissions, should she attempt to make any, was divided between *Sister Sue, Spaceways Princess* and *Agatha's Ark.* Captain O'Leary had been ordered to instruct his radio officer to monitor all Carlotti signals originating from anywhere at all. *Pride of Erin* was the squadron clown, one of those ships incapable of doing anything right, inevitably slow off the mark. It would be good to be rid of her.

Slowly, steadily, the range closed, could be measured in light-minutes and, at last, in kilometers. The Hallicheki captain finally squawked—or tried to squawk. Stewart, who had the Carlotti watch, jammed her before she could do more than clear her scrawny throat prior to speaking. Grimes, no longer in his chair, stood over the main MPI screen, staring into the sphere of velvety blackness in which were the four bright sparks—the potential victim, the other three privateers and, in the exact center, *Sister Sue*'s reference marker. He saw that relative bearings were no longer changing as they had been. He realized what had happened, was happening. The Hallicheki had shut down her drives—Mannschenn and inertial—as the preliminary to a major alteration of trajectory. This, inevitably, was a time-consuming process. And when the gyroscopes had swung the ship, turning her hull about its axes, which way would she be heading? Grimes guessed—and, as it turned out, correctly—that the panic-stricken hen would put the raiders right astern and then increase not only the thrust of the inertial drive but the intensity of the temporal precession field.

"Stop Mannschenn!" he ordered Williams, who was in the 2 I/C seat. "Stop inertial drive. Pass the order to all ships. Make it Action Stations!"

"I've only one pair of hands, Skipper," the mate grumbled—but it was a good-humored whinge. The subdued clangor of the inertial drive slowed and ceased while Grimes was still making his way back to his own chair. He managed to pull himself into the seat despite the cessation of acceleration and the consequent free fall. The thin, high note of the Mannschenn Drive deepened to a hum, then died away. As the temporal precession field faded the stridulation of the alarms shrilled to near inaudibility. Colors sagged down the spectrum and perspective was a meaningless concept.

And there was that song again.

I murdered William Moore as I sailed, as I sailed. . . .

Then everything snapped back to normal—colors, sounds, perspective. Grimes stared into the two miniature repeater screens before him—mass proximity indicator and radar. The Hallicheki ship was a radar target now, just inside the extreme range of two thousand kilometers. So she had not yet restarted her interstellar drive, was still in normal space-time. Obedient to the touch of the captain's fingers the powerful directional gyroscopes deep in *Sister Sue*'s bowels rumbled and Grimes felt himself pressed into the padding—under his buttocks, along his spine and his right side—of his chair by centrifugal forces. He brought the tiny spark that was the merchantman directly ahead, held it there and then reactivated the inertial drive, on maximum thrust.

"General chase!" he ordered and heard Venner repeat the words, heard acknowledgments from the other ships. He hoped that all that he had ever heard about Hallicheki spacemanship—not held in very high regard by the Survey Service's officer instructors—was true. By the time that the fumbling hens had gotten their vessel onto the new trajectory, with inertial and interstellar drives restarted, the privateers would be almost within range. (Of course, if the avian captain had any sense she would steer toward the pursuit, not away from it. Grimes remembered a ride that he had taken in a ground car, years ago, through the Australian countryside, and a witless hen that had run ahead of the vehicle, swerving neither to left nor right. He *knew,* somehow, that his quarry would be equally witless.)

He glanced up and out through the viewports. The stars were hard, bright—and there were those other, unnatural constellations, the recognition lights of the vessels of the fleet, ahead of *Sister Sue* now after the alteration of trajectory. Closest was the vividly green display of *Pride of Erin.* Grimes did not need to look into his radar screen to see that the range was closing, that *Sister Sue* would soon sweep past her. O'Leary's spacemanship must almost be down to Hallicheki standards. And there was *Spaceways Princess,* scarlet, and *Agatha's Ark,* blue. Grimes thought of perpetrating a pun about arclamps but thought better of it.

In the radar screen the tiny, distant spark that was the merchantman vanished but still showed in the MPL So she was underway again.

"Stop her!" ordered Grimes, suiting the action to the words as far as his own ship was concerned. "Pass the order."

"To all ships. Stop inertial drive," he heard the Countess's voice.

So Venner must now be at his battle console, thought Grimes.

"Mr. Williams," he said, "set up the graticules and graduations in the main MPI. Let me know how much, if at all, I must come around to keep the target ahead. . . ."

"Aye, aye, Skipper!"

"Ms. Connellan, stand by the NST transceiver. . . ."

"But we'll not be needing it for a long while yet. Sir."

"Stand by the NST!"

That would keep her from getting underfoot.

"We're lucky, Skipper!" he heard Williams say. "Just bring her right ahead, and keep her there, and we've got her!"

"Good. To all ships, Ms. Walshingham. Put target ahead. Restart all drives. General chase!"

There was again the brief period of complete disorientation as the temporal precession field built up, as the tumbling, precessing gyroscopes of the drive dragged the ship with them into her own warped continuum.

And again Grimes heard the ballad of Captain Kidd.

And what can I do about it? he asked himself. *What can I do about it? Captains, even privateer captains, don't go around murdering their senior officers. . . .*

But Captain Kidd had done so.

Forty-seven

It is axiomatic that a stern chase is a long chase.

The chase would have been a very long one, and quite possibly unsuccessful, had not Survey Service pattern governors—obtained from whom, and at what expense?—been fitted to the Mannschenn Drive units of the four ships when, at Port Kane, the other modifications had been made. With this hyperdrive in operation things were uncomfortable. There was always the feeling of walking a thin, swaying wire over an abyss that was the Past, maintaining balance with extreme difficulty. There was the frightening knowledge—in Grimes' mind at least—that he and all aboard *Sister Sue,* as was the ship herself, were at the mercy of a swirling field of force and of the man controlling—trying to control!—it. But Malleson was better than highly competent. He was designer as well as engineer. He knew—Grimes hoped—what he was doing. He would allow not the slightest fluctuation of field strength.

Obviously Captain O'Leary's Mannschenn Drive chief was neither so confident nor so competent. *Pride of Erin* straggled badly. She was well astern when the flagship and *Spaceways Princess* and *Agatha's Ark* finally overhauled their fleeing quarry and stationed themselves about her, the three points of an equilateral triangle.

"Make to *Princess* and *Ark,"* ordered Grimes, "synchronize at will!"

He heard the Countess repeat the order into the Carlotti transceiver microphone as he pressed the button that had been installed among the other controls of the wide arms of his chair.

The thin, high keening of the Mannschenn Drive wavered, took on an odd, warbling quality. Inside the control room things . . . flickered. It was like watching one of the very earliest movies in some museum of the cinematic arts. It was like being inside such a movie.

Abruptly the flickering ceased and the whine of the drive resumed its normal quality. Looking through his viewports Grimes could see the hard, bright, colored sparks that were the recognition lights of the *Ark* and the *Princess* against the backdrop of blackness and stars that still had the semblance of vague nebulae. Of the Hallicheki ship there was, as yet, no visual sign although she was showing up on the radar screen as well as in the MPI. To all practical intents and purposes the four wheels were sharing their own tiny universe; relative to them the rest of the continuum was warped.

"Let us see the target, please, Mr. Venner," said Grimes.

The laser cannon could be used as a searchlight. It came on now. Yes, there she was—a distant, silver egg sitting in a silver skeleton eggcup. She could not escape by throwing herself out of synchronization. She could not even stop her Mannschenn Drive so as to emerge into normal space-time. To all intents and purposes her interstellar drive was a mere slave to the more powerful units aboard the privateers and would be so for as long as the synchronizers were in operation. But the Hallicheki captain still exercised full control over her inertial drive. Suddenly she reduced thrust and began to fall astern, out of the trap. Almost immediately, almost as one, the three raiders fell back with her, regained their stations. She applied a lateral component—but before she was dangerously close to *Agatha's Ark* Captain Prinn was doing likewise and Grimes and MacWhirter were maintaining their distances off with contemptuous ease.

"Ms. Connellan, Ms. Walshingham," ordered Grimes, "try to raise her on NST and Carlotti."

The two women obeyed. It was the Green Hornet who got through on the normal space-time radio. In the screen appeared a bird's face—yellow beak, dun plumage, mad yellow eyes.

"Who are you? Who are you? What are you doing?"

Ms. Connellan passed a microphone to Grimes.

He said, "You are under arrest. You will complete your voyage to such port as we shall decide under escort. Do not attempt to escape."

"But you are . . . human." (She made it sound like a dirty word; in her language it most probably was.) "The Hegemony is not at war with Earth!"

"At the moment, no," admitted Grimes smugly.

"You are pirates!"

"We are not," Grimes told her. "We hold Letters of Marque issued by the Lord of the Roost on Kalla."

"Rebel worm! We will pluck the feathers from his skin, the skin from his flesh and the flesh from his bones! We. . . ."

"You'll have to catch him first, Captain. Meanwhile, are you coming quietly?"

"No!" came the screeched reply. "No! No!"

And somebody must be playing with the Hellicheki ship's inertial drive controls like a demented pianist; ahead and astern she darted, to one side and the other. It was all quite useless.

"This," said Grimes, "is getting to be rather boring. Mr. Venner, tickle the lady, will you. Use the quickfirer. Reduced charges, of course, and solid shot. And for the love of all the Odd Gods of the Galaxy, don't miss!"

This admonition was necessary. To diminish the mass of a ship running under interstellar drive is to ask for trouble and, almost certainly, to get it. But *Sister Sue* was now part of a four-ship system enclosed by a common precession field. As long as those projectiles hit and adhered to their target the overall mass of the system would not be changed.

The merchantman's last application of lateral thrust had brought her almost dangerously close to *Sister Sue.* This suited Grimes. At this range not the most incompetent gunnery officer could miss his target—and Venner was highly competent. From the muzzle of the quickfirer issued a stream of bright tracer that, with apparent laziness, drifted across the black gulf between the two ships like a swarm of luminous bees, striking her in a ragged line from stem to stern.

The noise inside that ovoid hull, thought Grimes, must be deafening—but, at the very worst, there would be no more than a very minor puncture or two that would be automatically sealed.

"Piracy!" the Hallicheki captain was screeching, her words almost drowned by the drumbeat of the striking shot.

"That was just a sample," Grimes told her.

"Terry pirate! I demand. . . ."

"You are in no position to do any demanding, Captain. You are a prize of war. Do you want another taste of gunfire? After all, it is your cargo that I want, not you and your crew. Your bodies, alive or dead, are of no importance."

"Pirate! Filthy pirate! All right. I . . . surrender. But as soon as I can I will scream to the Hegemony!"

"And much good may it do you, Captain."

Meanwhile, where the hell was *Pride of Erin*? Captain O'Leary had been told that he would be taking the first prize in. Captain O'Leary, Grimes saw, was no more than a dim spark right astern, just within range of the mass proximity indicator.

"Ms. Walshingham," he said, "call *Pride of Erin.* Tell her to shake the lead out of her pants. Gods! She'd be late for her own fucking funeral!"

The Countess spoke into the microphone of the control-room Carlotti transceiver. Her voice was cold and arrogant. It was that of the lady of the manor tearing a strip off a delinquent under gamekeeper, using what she would consider to be lower-class vocabulary for effect but retaining her upper-class diction.

"Sister Sue to *Pride of Erin. . . ."*

"Pride of Erin. I've been after havin' me troubles. . . ."

"Sister Sue to *Pride of Erin.* Shake the lead out of your pants. Gods! You'd be late for your own fucking funeral!"

"What did you say?" shouted Grimes to the fourth officer. "That was no way to make a signal to another ship!"

"I said what *you* said, sir."

Insolent bitch! he thought. *I'll deal with you later.*

Captain O'Leary's voice came from the speaker of the Carlotti set. It was obvious that the man was holding himself in with an effort. He, he was implying, could be correct even when his alleged superior could not.

"I'm doin' me best, Commodore, but I'm not a miracle worker. I'll be with you as soon as me time-twister can get me there. I'll. . . ."

There was a confused gabbling. There were yells.

There was nothing.

Grimes stared into the repeater screen. The Hallicheki ship and the *Ark* and the *Princess* were still there. *Pride of Erin* was not.

"Mr. Williams," he said, "check the main MPI. See if you can find *Pride of Erin*."

But he knew that O'Leary, his ship and his people were gone, tumbling down the temporal gulfs like a dead leaf whirled to oblivion by an autumnal gale.

If the Walshingham bitch had not spoken as she had, the thin-skinned master of *Pride of Erin* would have taken no risks with his malfunctioning interstellar drive.

But why blame her?

I'm a fine commodore, he thought. *My first action, with nothing fired but a few practice shells, and one of my ships lost. . . .*

He hoped that in the remote past or the distant future O'Leary and his crew would find a world to their liking.

If they survived.

Forty-eight

So it was *Spaceways Princess* that took in the first prize while *Sister Sue* and *Agatha's Ark* continued their cruise.

Shortly after Captain MacWhirter's ship had been detached from the squadron Captain Prinn made a personal call to Grimes. He was glad that it was during Williams' watch. It was bad enough that he should overhear what was said; it would have been far worse had it been any of the other officers.

She looked out at him from the screen of the control-room Carlotti transceiver, her normally harsh face even harsher than usual. Behind her Grimes could see others of the *Ark*'s crew, among them the young Graf von Stolzberg. All of them were regarding him with condemnation.

"Commodore Grimes," she said, "I am serving notice that after this cruise I shall refuse to put out again under your command. It is my opinion, and that of my officers, that you deliberately goaded Captain O'Leary into taking unjustifiable risks. Why could you not have done as you did eventually, ordering Captain MacWhirter to take charge of the prize? That would have given Captain O'Leary time to make the necessary adjustments or repairs to his Mannschenn Drive. But you were foolishly inflexible and insisted that he close the main body of the fleet without delay. Furthermore you couched your message in words of a kind that should never be used by a commanding officer to those serving under him. That brutal message was contributory to the disaster."

She moved to one side. Marlene's son (Grimes' son) came forward.

"Commodore Grimes, speaking as the El Doradan representative aboard this vessel, I put myself as being in complete agreement with what has been said by Captain Prinn. I shall report to Commodore Kane and to the El Dorado Corporation upon your unfitness to command any further privateering expeditions."

And what about your fellow El Doradan? Grimes thought but did not say. *What about the El Doradan representative aboard* my *vessel? She's one of* your *lot, Ferdinand my boy.* She *made O'Leary blow his top. . . .*

He asked coldly, ignoring the young officer, "Is that all, Captain Prinn?"

"That is all, Commodore Grimes. Over and out."

"She's got it in for you, Skipper," said Williams sympathetically.

"And rightly so, Billy. Rightly so."

"It was that bloody Wally's fault!"

"Everything that happens aboard a ship," said Grimes tiredly, "is the captain's fault. And everything that happens in a squadron is the commodore's fault." He laughed without much humor. "It's a pity that O'Leary's given names were Patrick Joseph, not William Moore. That would have taken one weight off my mind . . ."

"But *I'm* William Moore, Skipper," said the mate. "William Moore Williams."

"I know," said Grimes.

He went down to his day cabin, sent for the Countess of Walshingham.

When she came her cat was with her. The animal(?) sat down on the deck and stared, in an oddly hungry manner, at the golden figurine of Una mounted on her golden bicycle. It ignored Grimes—which was just as well. Did it, he wondered, recognize a fellow robot? Did the mini-Una possess some sort of organic brain, just as the evil black and white beast did?

"Must you bring that creature with you?" Grimes demanded irritably.

The tall girl stood there, superb in her tailored uniform, looking down at him disdainfully as he sat behind his desk.

"I thought you knew, sir," she said, "that all El Doradans have their guardians, their watch animals. Felix is my protector. Should anybody attempt to do me harm he will attack."

"And you think that I might attempt to do you harm?"

"You would like to, sir, wouldn't you? You wish that you possessed the punitive powers of the old-time captains on Earth's seas."

"Frankly, Ms. Walshingham, I do wish just that. What you did merits a flogging, if nothing worse. How are you people trained—if at all!—in the El Doradan Navy? Don't you know that an officer passing on a message from his captain to another captain is supposed, if necessary, to . . . to *edit* the message, to put it into the proper Service terminology?"

"Since when, sir, was this armed rabble a Service?"

Grimes kept his temper. He said slowly, "It may interest you to know, Ms. Walshingham, that Captain Prinn, blaming me for what happened to Captain O'Leary. . . ."

"That bog-Irish slob!"

"Quiet, damn you! Captain Prinn put through a personal call to me. She holds me responsible for what happened to *Pride of Erin* and condemns me for it. So do all her officers—including *your* compatriot the Graf von Stolzberg."

"That mother's boy!"

"I have not yet written my report on your conduct and capabilities. When I do so I shall see that you read it. I do not think that Commodore Kane will continue to think highly of you when *he* has done so."

"I could hardly care less, sir. The Commodore is not a true El Doradan."

"He is your commanding officer. So, come to that, am I as long as you are on my books."

She flushed. "As the representative, aboard this ship, of both the El Doradan Navy and the El Dorado Corporation. . . ."

"You are still my fourth mate. That will do, Ms. Walshingham. Get out, and take that animal with you!"

"With pleasure, sir."

When they were gone Grimes sent for Mayhew.

"That *bitch,*" he said. "That arrogant *bitch!* Did she realize what she was doing, what the results were likely to be, when she passed that message?"

"I don't think so, sir. She is, as you say, arrogant. Captain O'Leary was a member of the lower orders. She feels no more sorry for him and his crew than she would for a dog or a cat belonging to somebody else and not to her."

"But there was an El Doradan officer aboard *Pride Of Erin.*"

"A *man,* Captain. She despises all men, aristocratic or otherwise. Even so, she has her needs."

"I thought that the other bitch, the green-skinned one, was satisfying them."

"So did I. I have been refraining from prying into their sweaty amours. I'm not a prude, sir, but I am fastidious. And, I suppose, something of a snob. I could not bring myself to make love to a woman who was not, like me, a telepath. And, very unfortunately, such women are usually either very plain or very unintelligent. Or both."

Grimes poured more gin for both of them.

He said, "It's dear Wally's love life that I'm concerned about, not yours. As long as she's getting her odd form of satisfaction she's a little less of a bitch than she would be normally. That goes for the Green Hornet, too."

"That's the odd thing, Captain. The pair of them are passing through a heterosexual phase. Not all the time, but for a lot of the time. Bestowing their favors upon the junior engineers. I don't suppose you want to know the details. . . ."

"I don't."

"That's just as well, Captain. I'd hate to have to find them out for you."

"Ours is a nice ship, ours is," said Grimes glumly.

Forty-nine

The next capture was effected without incident and Captain Prinn was ordered to escort the merchantman to port. Her farewell was a cold one. She did not even wish Grimes the usual good luck and good hunting when she and the prize were detached. Alone in the warped immensities *Sister Sue* cruised the space lanes, maintaining her listening watch, waiting for the Terran ship that was to be the next victim, that was to be the excuse the Survey Service needed to put a stop to the El Doradan privateering operations.

Grimes' officers sensed that something was wrong.

Vessels, within easy range, were picked up by the mass proximity indicator. Some of those ships, identifiable by their routine Carlotti radio transmissions, were of Hallicheki registry, bound for New Maine with their rich cargoes. Yet Grimes ignored them. There were mutterings. Soon, everybody knew, *Spaceways Princess* and *Agatha's Ark* would be allocated their shares of prize money—and *Sister Sue* had yet to earn a more or less honest cent.

There was one ship, passing quite close, that, like *Sister Sue* herself, was maintaining radio silence. Grimes knew who she was—after Mayhew had told him. She was the FSS destroyer *Denebola.* She had among her people a Psionic Communications Officer. Through the telepaths her captain sent a message to Grimes. It was: "Continue cruising until you fall in with *Epsilon Draconis,* New Maine to Carinthia with valuable transshipment cargo. Her master has been instructed to surrender without a real struggle. Her PCO, on articles as assistant purser, is a Survey Service officer. All other officers hold Reserve Commissions and know what is expected of them."

"Long-winded bastard," commented Grimes. "Commander Cummings, isn't it? Never uses one word when three will do."

"It shouldn't be much longer now," said Mayhew. "That's just as well, sir. The natives are getting restless. I quote, 'When is the old bastard going to take his finger out and find us a prize?' According to Sparks he's missed at least four good chances since Aggie left us . . . And, 'He's scared, that's why. He needs at least one other ship to hold his hand when he makes like a bold, bad pirate. . . .'"

"Mphm!" grunted Grimes indignantly around the stem of his pipe.

At last a spark of light that could only be the Epsilon Class tramp appeared on the MPI screen. Mr. Stewart monitored her routine transmissions. Mayhew established telepathic contact with her PCO. Trajectories converged.

"But, sir," expostulated Williams, "she's a Terran ship!"

"Carrying the Hegemony's cargo," said Grimes. "That makes her a legal prize, a blockade runner."

"Are you *sure,* Skipper?"

"Of course I'm sure. Our Letters of Marque empower us to seize Hallicheki cargoes, no matter by whom carried."

"Even transshipment cargoes?" asked Williams.

"Yes," said Grimes firmly.

(He would have to check that point later, he thought. Probably what he was about to do was piracy—and that was what Damien wanted, anyhow.)

The interception and the capture went as planned.

Epsilon Draconis went through the motions of attempting to escape from the precession synchronization field. Captain Mulligan, his fat, florid face filling the screen of the NST transceiver, raved and ranted convincingly, shouting, "You'll swing for this, you bloody pirate!" Mr. Venner went into his act with the quickfirer, raking the struggling prey from stem to stern. "Accidentally," there was one round in the drum that did not have a reduced charge and that did carry a high explosive warhead. This blew a large hole in one of the stern vanes.

"Was that necessary?" roared Mulligan.

This time he was not play-acting.

"Are you coming quietly?" asked Grimes.

"Yes, damn you. But somebody is going to get the bill for repairs—and I hope it's you!"

"He's very annoyed with you, sir," said Mayhew when, after the setting of a new trajectory for privateer and prize, he and Grimes were discussing matters in the commodore's day cabin.

"That's his privilege," said Grimes. "I just wanted my act of piracy to look realistic."

"You did just that. Well, sir, I've been in touch with *Denebola.* She's making all speed to intercept. She has one of the new Mark XX Mannschenns so she'll be showing up in the MPI screen at any time now. And now, if you'll excuse me, I'll go down to the wardroom to mingle with the peasantry. Venner, Malleson and Magda want me to make up a four at bridge."

"Do you play for money?" asked Grimes.

"Of course, sir. It discourages wild bidding."

"Isn't it cheating, as far as you're concerned?"

"It would be, if I used my talent. But I don't. When I sit down at the card table I . . . switch off. If—*if!*—I win it's just due to luck and skill, nothing more."

"Mphm." Grimes grunted, then laughed. "I remember that Rear Admiral Damien warned me against playing cards with Venner, but he didn't mention you."

"In ships where I am known for what I am," said Mayhew, "I don't play cards. For obvious reasons. And I do enjoy a game now and again. . . ."

He got to his feet and drifted out of the cabin.

Fifty

From: Kenneth Mayhew, Lieutenant Commander (PC) FSS
To: Rear Admiral Damien FSS, OIC Operation Jolly Roger

Sir,

I have to report as follows on the circumstances of the death, in the line of duty, of Lieutenant Commander Victor Venner FSS.

As planned by yourself and others the Interstellar Transport Commission's ship *Epsilon Draconis,* Captain Mulligan FSSR, was intercepted and seized by *Sister Sue,* Captain Grimes FSSR. After the capture normal deep-space routine—or deep-space routine as normal as possible in the circumstances—was resumed. After discussing various matters with Captain Grimes I went down to the wardroom for a game of bridge with Mr. Malleson, the Mannschenn Drive chief engineer, Ms. Magda Granadu, the ship's purser and Lieutenant Commander Venner. Rather unusually no other off-duty personnel were in the compartment.

I freely admit that I should have used my telepathic powers to make a check. I did not do so for two reasons. Firstly, when I play cards with non-telepaths I deliberately "close down" the portion of my brain that acts as psionic transceiver. Secondly, I had become increasingly disgusted by the glimpses I had caught of the off-duty activities of various officers, these being Ms. Kath Connellan, second mate, Ms. Walshingham (the Countess of Walshingham), fourth mate and El Doradan liaison officer, Messrs. Denning, Paulus and Singh, junior inertial drive engineers, and Messrs. Trantor and Giddings, Mannschenn Drive juniors.

I did not foresee that my prudishness would have such disastrous consequences and accept, without reservation, whatever punishment you may consider called for.

We were, as I have said, playing bridge. I was partnered with Ms. Granadu; Lieutenant Commander Venner with Mr. Malleson. I had opened the bidding with one no trump. Mr. Malleson bid two hearts. Ms. Granadu bid two no trumps. We were waiting, it seemed a long time, for Lieutenant Commander Venner to make his bid. I realized that he was staring at the door into the alleyway. I turned to look at what had attracted his attention. It was Ms. Connellan. She was holding a heavy pistol—later identified as a Bendon-Smith scattergun, El Doradan Navy issue—and pointing it straight at us. Behind her were Denning and Paulus, both of them armed with wrenches, and Trantor, with a big screwdriver.

She said, "Freeze, all of you! We're taking the ship. Grimesy isn't the only bastard around here who can play at pirates!"

I "switched on" then. What I received was garbled, the outpourings of minds that were vicious, greedy and—insofar as the men were concerned—not a little scared. The women—the Green Hornet (as she was nicknamed) and the Countess—were the ringleaders. Later I was to learn that the intention had been to seize *Sister Sue* and to take her and the prize to one of the planets of the Duchy of Waldegren. The immediate attention, however, was to capture and restrain the captain and all loyal officers.

"Get away from the table," ordered Ms. Connellan. "Get down onto the deck, on your faces, with your hands behind you!" She made a jerking motion with her gun as she said this. For a second, for less than a second, we were no longer in the field of its fire.

The first card that Lieutenant Commander Venner flipped from his hand caught Ms. Connellan in the throat. The sharp plastic sliced through skin and flesh, severed a major blood vessel. I remember being surprised to see that her blood was red and not green. She fired her pistol before she dropped it to put her hand up to the spurting wound. The pellets tore a wide, ragged gash in the carpet but did no other damage.

Before she had fallen, before she had even started to fall, Lieutenant Commander Venner's second card caught Mr. Denning just above the eyes. He screamed and threw his arms out violently, letting go of the heavy wrench that he had been holding. I think that if Lieutenant Commander Venner had not been concentrating on his third shot, the one that sliced off Mr. Trantor's right ear, he would have seen the clumsy missile coming and dodged it. As it was, it struck him on the left forehead, killing him instantly.

Ms. Granadu picked up the pistol and covered Mr. Trantor and Mr. Denning, both of whom were bleeding profusely, and Mr. Paulus. They were cowed and allowed themselves to be driven into one of her storerooms, which she locked. Mr. Malleson and I tried to do something for Lieutenant Commander Venner but he was beyond aid. As a telepath I knew that the spark of life had been extinguished. Ms. Connellan expired while we were kneeling by our dead shipmate. . . .

Scrawled comment, signed Damien.

Vivid writing. The man's wasted in the Survey Service; he should be a novelist. If we weren't so short of trained telepaths I would encourage him to forsake space to enter the literary profession.

Fifty-one

The Countess entered Grimes' day cabin without knocking. The big, evil cat stalked behind her.

He looked up from the papers on his desk.

"Yes?" he demanded sharply. Then he saw that she was holding a pistol, a stungun, and that it was pointing at him. She pressed the trigger. Grimes was paralyzed but not unconscious. Perhaps she had used the weapon on lower power only or, possibly, the metal desk had acted as a partial shield.

He heard, from somewhere on a lower deck, the sound of an explosion.

She smiled viciously and remarked, "I let Katy have the heavy artillery. It sounds as though she's used it."

He said nothing. He could not. But he thought, *Billy will have heard the shot. He'll investigate.*

She said, "Don't expect the mate to come to hold your hand. I've already dealt with him. I hope that Katy soon finishes what she's doing. There should be somebody more or less conscious in the control room. . . ."

She strolled around the day cabin, the cat at her heels.

"Not bad, not bad. . . . This accommodation will do for me as soon as I've had you . . . removed. I might even keep your . . . ornaments. Old girl friends, are they? As you may have guessed, my tastes run more to the female form divine than to the hairy-arsed male version. . . . That one on the bicycle . . . she's rather butch, isn't she?"

With an effort Grimes was able to turn his head. (The paralysis was wearing off.) He saw the Countess lift the tiny golden woman on her little gleaming steed down from the shelf, set the models down on the deck.

"How do you make this thing work?" she asked. "I'd like to see it in action."

As though in obedience to her words the slim, golden legs, with feet on the pedals, began to move. The bicycle and rider made one circuit of the cabin and then, as though demonstrating her skill as a cyclist, the miniature Una released her grip of the handlebars—which turned so that the handles were pointing forward. From each of them projected a blade. Grimes remembered having seen this sort of thing once before. That time he had been the subject of attack by a murderous bicycle.

The Countess aimed her pistol and fired, again and again. Against the tiny robot it was quite useless. The cat pounced, but it was too slow. One of the blades caught the girl on her vulnerable right heel. It came away red. She screamed and fell to the deck. The bicycle dashed in for the kill. The blades drove into her right temple, piercing the skull, penetrating the brain.

And now, thought Grimes dully, *for the Big Bang.* Its mistress dead, the cat would self-destruct. How powerful was the bomb hidden in its body? Powerful enough to devastate the day cabin and all its occupants, living and dead. Powerful enough, probably, to blow the nose off the ship.

But the Countess was still living—after a fashion. Her long legs were twitching. The fingers of her outstretched hands were opening and closing, scrabbling at the deck. She was moaning softly and wordlessly.

The cat was chasing the deadly, glittering toy which, twisting and turning, was trying to get itself into a position to deliver an attack. A heavy paw went out, batted the tiny rider off her saddle, knocking the bicycle off balance. It fell to its side and lay there briefly, its wheels still spinning. The front one turned at right angles to the frame as it tried to right itself. But the animal was too fast for it. Jaws opened wide and closed, metal on metal, and . . . crunched. There was a brief sputter of blue sparks, the acridity of ozone.

The rider, the tiny golden woman, was running now. The cat dropped the twisted remains of the bicycle, started after her. The beast was fast, agile, but its prey was even—although barely—more so. How long could the chase go on? How long would the Countess go on living? How long would it be before the watch beast realized that its mistress was dead and detonated the explosive device built into it?

"Captain!" somebody was saying. "Captain!"

Grimes withdrew his horrified attention from the macabre chase, saw that Mayhew had come into the cabin. There was blood on the telepath's hands and clothing (not his own, Grimes was to learn later).

"We must get it out of the ship," Mayhew said urgently. "We must get it out before it detonates!"

Grimes found that he could speak.

"We . . . can't. Not while the drive is running. We must not . . . discharge mass."

"You were firing off guns."

"That was . . . different. All the mass stayed within the combined fields."

"Then shut down the drive. Come up to control. I can handle both Una and the cat."

Handle Una? wondered Grimes. Surely that figurine did not run to a brain, either electronic or organic.

He felt strength seeping into him. From Mayhew? He managed to get up from the chair in which he had been slumped. The cat, still chasing the little golden woman, brushed against his leg but ignored him. The Countess was beyond noticing anything. Mayhew went to him, supported him, led him to the door. As soon as they were through, the figurine scampered out into the alleyway, followed by the animal.

He ignored them. Painfully, he pulled himself up the ladder and through the hatch into Control. Williams was there, slumped in his seat, unconscious. He staggered to the command chair, sank into it. His fingers went to the controls set in the armrests.

"The overall monitor," urged Mayhew.

He activated the rarely used Big Brother Is Watching system. In the stern vision screen he could see, at will, into every compartment of the ship. He was able to follow the sternward progress of the little golden girl, the vicious black-and-white predator, the flight and pursuit down the spiral staircase surrounding the axial shaft.

"Mr. Malleson is in the Mannschenn Drive room," said Mayhew.

Don't nag me, he thought.

He said, "Tell *Epsilon Draconis* that I'm shutting off the synchronizer and shutting down the drive. . . ."

He heard, from the NST transceiver, "What am I supposed to do? Make a break for it, or what?"

Tell him to get stuffed, he thought.

He said, "Ask him to stand by, please. We have problems."

He looked out through the port. *Epsilon Draconis* was there, hard and distinct against the background of vaguely swirling darkness, the nebulosities that were the stars. As the whine of *Sister Sue*'s drive deepened to a rumble and then died she faded, vanished, and abruptly the stars became hard points of light.

And. . . .

And, *I murdered William Moore as I sailed, as I sailed. . . .*

But William Moore Williams was there, sprawled in his seat and snoring.

Grimes returned his attention to the screen.

Deck after deck after deck, the tiny golden woman, the big black-and-white cat, hunted and hunter, while in the commodore's day cabin the ham-strung Countess breathed her last. Deck after deck after deck. . . .

He took a sideways look. *Epsilon Draconis* was still with him. She, too, had shut down her Mannschenn Drive, was standing by to render assistance should it be required.

Deck after deck after deck. . . .

"Open inner airlock door," he said to Mayhew.

"Door opening, Captain."

The miniature Una was in the chamber, the cat hard upon her heels.

"Close inner door. Open outer."

He switched to an exterior view of the hull. He saw the door open, saw the sudden flurry of ice crystals. The cat now had the golden figurine in its mouth, was tumbling over and over as it fell into the nothingness.

There was an eye-searing flash and then the screen was dead.

"What *are* you doing?" came Captain Mulligan's petulant voice from the NST transceiver.

"Tell him," said Grimes to Mayhew, "just dumping garbage."

He regretted the words as soon as he had uttered them. The Countess's cat had been no more than garbage, dangerous garbage at that, but the figurine of Una had been not only a gift, a thoughtful gift evocative of old memories, but it had saved his life and the lives of all those aboard *Sister Sue,* all of those, that is, who still had lives to save.

Fifty-two

"I suppose," said Grimes, "that we shall have to return her effects and papers to her next of kin on El Dorado. . . ."

As Billy Williams and Magda Granadu watched, he looked through the listing of personal possessions and then, finally, picked up the dead woman's passport.

A waste, he thought, as he stared at the three-dimensional photograph. *A waste. But she was a vicious bitch, after all. A female-chauvinist bitch. . . .*

And then he started to laugh.

"What's the joke, Skipper?" asked the mate.

"Her name, Billy. Wilhelmina Moore, Countess of Walshingham. . . ."

"But what's so funny about that?" asked Williams.

Fifty-three

The three ships hung there, in the warped continuum, the destroyer's synchronizer making slaves of the Mannschenn Drive units of the other two vessels.

From the NST transceiver came the voice of the destroyer's captain.

"Denebola to *Sister Sue.* You are under arrest."

"Acknowledge," said Grimes to Williams.

"Sister Sue, stand by to receive boarders."

"Acknowledge, Mr. Williams. Then carry on down to the after airlock to do the courtesies."

The mate was all concern.

"Sir, can't we fight? What will they do to you?"

"Not as much as they'd like to," said Grimes. "Don't worry, Mr. Williams. It will all come right in the end."

"I said, sir, that we should never have taken a Terran ship. . . ."

"But we did. Never mind, it was by *my* orders. You're in the clear. Off with you, now. Be polite, but not servile. I shall be in my cabin."

He got up from the command chair, turned to Mayhew.

"You're in charge, Ken, until Billy comes back. You know where to find me if you want me."

He went down to his day cabin, lowered himself into his armchair. *Let the Survey Service take over now,* he thought. *I've done their dirty work for them. It was rather dirtier than I thought that it would be—but isn't it always that way?*

He filled and lit his pipe, looked up through the blue smoke that it emitted at the empty shelf upon which the figurine of Una Freeman had stood. He found that he regretted the loss of that gift very deeply. If—*if!*—he ever saw Una again he would tell her of the circumstances. Meanwhile he could expect a quiet voyage back to Earth, under escort and with a prize crew on board, an official rapping of the knuckles, an unofficial pecuniary reward and then a resumption of his tramping life. He hoped that Williams would stay with him, and Magda Granadu. Old Mr. Stewart probably would. Malleson and Crumley probably would not. As for the others—he would not wish to be in their shoes. But their defense, almost certainly, would be that they had mutinied against a captain who had turned pirate.

There was a knock at his door.

"Yes?" he called.

"Sir," said Williams, "the officer in charge of the boarding party to see you."

"Send him in."

"You are under arrest," she said.

Grimes stared up at her. On the shoulders of her silvery spacesuit were the scarlet tabs that showed that she was a member of the Corps of Sky Marshals. She had removed her helmet and was holding it under her left arm. Her face, given a coat of gold paint, would have been the face of the figurine destroyed by the killer cat.

"Aren't you pleased to see me?" she asked.

"Yes. Of course. But aren't you . . . ? Shouldn't you, I mean, be on Austral?"

"I was recalled to the Corps for a refresher course. And piracy, as you know, is the concern of the Sky Marshals as well as of the Survey Service."

"Mphm. Well. Glad to have you aboard, Una."

"I'm glad to be aboard, John. This is far more capacious than that bloody lifeboat."

"Yes. I'll tell my purser to organize a cabin for you."

She said, "Don't bother. This will do very nicely." She grinned. "I have to have some place to interrogate my prisoner. Somewhere well away from the other accommodation so that the screams won't be heard."

"Oh."

"Don't just sit there grinning. Put that vile pipe out for a start—and then you can help me out of my spacesuit. And the rest . . ."

"But I have to get up to Control, Una. To give some orders."

"Don't worry," she told him. "I'll be giving the orders from now on."

More than once during the voyage back to Earth Grimes would think, *Where is that bloody cat now that I need him?*

The Anarch Lords

One

"You got off lightly, Grimes," said Rear Admiral Damien.

Grimes's prominent ears flushed angrily as he scowled at the older man across the vast, gleaming surface of the desk, uncluttered save for telephone, read-out screen and the thick folder that must contain, among other documents relating to himself, a transcript of the proceedings of the recent Court of Inquiry.

"You got off lightly, Grimes," Damien repeated.

His elbows on the desk, the tips of his steepled, skeletal fingers propping his great beak of a nose, he stared severely at the owner and erstwhile master of the star tramp (the privateer, the pirate) *Sister Sue.* Grimes thought irreverently, *If it weren't for that schnozzle his face would look just like a skull . . . Come to that, his uniform tailor must use a skeleton for his dummy . . ."*

Briefly he entertained the ludicrous vision of a spidery tailorbot, fussily measuring and recording, scuttling around and over an assemblage of dry, articulated bones.

He grinned.

"What are you thinking, Grimes?" demanded Damien sharply.

"Nothing, sir."

"Ha. Of course. Nothing that you'd dare to tell me, you mean. May I remind you that the crime of Dumb Insolence, with its penalties, is still listed in Survey Service Regulations despite all the efforts of the Human Rights League to have it removed? And even though your Master Astronaut's Certificate of Competency was suspended by the court you still hold your Survey Service Reserve commission. And you have not yet been released from Active Duty."

"I was under the impression, sir," said Grimes stiffly, "that my Reserve Officer's commission was a secret."

"Was—and is. But *I* know your status. I can still throw the book at you if I feel like it." Then Damien allowed himself a grin and, briefly, looked almost genial. "But I didn't send for you so that I could haul you over the coals, although it has been like old times, hasn't it?" (That grin, Grimes decided, had become wolfish.) "Officially I'm supposed to be conducting a little inquiry of my own. The safe passage of merchant shipping is among my responsibilities—so, quite naturally, I'm interested in such activities as privateering. And piracy. But I already have your confidential report. And Mayhew's. I know what really happened—which is more than can be said for Lord Justice Kirby and his assessors, or for the boarding party that brought your ship in under arrest. That ex-girlfriend of yours—or not so 'ex'—did a good job of brainwashing your officers. My people thought that the apparatus she brought aboard *Sister Sue* was just an aid to interrogation, not for the implantation of false memories."

Damien laughed. "And it was a good story that the witnesses told the court, wasn't it? The wicked Kate Connellan and the even wickeder Countess of Walshingham seizing the ship at gunpoint and forcing you to embark upon a career of piracy . . . But somebody had to carry the can back. They didn't survive—and you did."

He opened the thick folder, found the right page. "And what did that old fogey Kirby say? Ah, here we are. 'Nonetheless I am of the strong opinion that the master, John Grimes. was not entirely blameless. He deliberately set his feet onto the downward path into violent crime when he placed his ship, his people and himself at the service of the notorious Commodore Baron Kane, as he is now known. John Grimes should have pondered the truth of the old adage, *He who sups with the devil needs a long spoon.* But John Grimes was like too many in this decadent day and age, money hungry. Had his avarice put only himself at risk I should not think so hardly of him—but all of his crew, merchant spacemen and women, ignorant of the arts—if they may so be called—of war, were compelled, willy nilly, to share the perils to which their captain had deliberatly exposed himself, persuaded by him that privateering is no risk and all profit . . .' Sanctimonious old swine, isn't he? 'And some of his crew whom he deluded were not even experienced spacemen. His engineering officers, for example, young men recruited from industry and the Halls of Academe on the world of Austral, true innocents abroad. . . .'"

"Those bastards!" exploded Grimes. *"They* were with the Green Hornet and Wally!"

"I know, I know. But they don't, not now. They have that fine set of false memories. They're little, woolly, innocent lambs, all of them, in their own minds, and in old Kirby's mind." He switched to his imitation of the judge's voice.

"'It is obvious to me that John Grimes is unfit to hold command. I have considered the cancellation of his qualifications but have decided to temper justice with mercy, hoping that in the fullness of time he may come to see the error of his ways. Therefore I order that his Certificate of Competency be suspended for a period of ten Standard Years.'"

"And what am I supposed to be doing with myself for all that time?" asked Grimes.

"You still have your ship. We released her to you. We'll see that she finds employment. I've no doubt that your mate—your ex-mate, rather—will make quite a good master . . ."

"While I sit and sulk in the owner's suite when I'm not getting into his hair. No, sir. That wouldn't be fair to Billy Williams. Come to that, it wouldn't be fair to me. It'd be worse than just being an ordinary passenger." He got to his feet, began to pace up and down. He pulled his pipe from a pocket of his civilian slacks, filled and lit it. He said, speaking through an eruption of acrid fumes, "I think that the Service should do something for me in the way of employment."

"I didn't give you permission to smoke, Grimes. Oh, all right, all right. Carry on asphyxiating yourself. As far as the universe knows you're a civilian shipmaster—ex-shipmaster, rather—and I have no jurisdiction over you. *But* you're still on pay, captain's salary. We'll not let you starve even if *Sister Sue*'s running at a loss."

"Thank you, sir. I'll not hurt your feelings by refusing my pay. I've earned it. ButI want to be *doing* something."

"Why don't you write a book, Grimes? Your autobiography should make fascinating reading."

"And would the Survey Service provide legal defense if I were sued for libel? And if such a case were heard by Lord Justice Kirby the best lawyers in the universe couldn't save me."

Damien laughed. "All right, all right. If you wrote the book I'd probably be among those screaming libel. Now, Grimes, sit down and listen. I sent for you so that I could sound you out. I've an offer to make that I'd not be making if you'd indicated that you'd be quite happy bumbling around in that rustbucket of yours even if not in command of her.

"Have you ever heard of Liberia?"

"In Africa?"

"No. Not the province. The planet. The colony."

"Oh. *That* Liberia. Founded by a bunch of freedom-loving anarchists during the days of the gaussjammers. I've heard about it but I've never been there."

"How would you like to go?"

"Doing what? Or as what?"

"As Governor."

Two

“You have to be joking,” said Grimes at last.

“I’m serious,” Damien told him.

“Then this is another piece of dirty work for you.”

“On the contrary, Grimes. If you take the job it will be in the nature of a clean-up operation.”

“That sounds even worse. Sir.”

“Grimes, Grimes, you have a suspicious mind.”

“With very good reason.”

“Do you want the job, or don’t you?”

“Tell me about it first,” Grimes said.

“Very well. Liberia is a Federated Planet but not now fully autonomous. I’ll not bore you with a detailed history; you’ll be able to read it up before you are installed in the Governor’s Lodge. Suffice it to say that the original colonists, the idealistic Anarchists, after a bad start during which their settlement almost perished, became devotees of the goddess Laura Norder . . .” *(I’d better laugh,* thought Grimes, *to keep the old bastard in a good mood.)* “Their numbers increased and eventually they were able to exercise control over their environment. There was a resurgence of Anarchism and armed revolt against the authorities. The president—he was more of a dictator, actually—appealed for help to the Federation. After the mess had been more or less cleaned up it was decided that the Liberians would be far happier if governed by an outsider, somebody whom everybody, right, left and center, could hate. So now there’s an elected president who, in effect, just does what the Earth-appointed governor tells him.

“Liberia is an agricultural planet. When it was first settled it was little more than a mudball crawling with primitive yet motile plant life. Now it is all, or almost all, wheatfields and beanfields and orchards. It has been called the granary of the Shaula Sector. There is only light, very light industry. In the past all heavy agricultural machinery has had to be imported. Now, as such equipment wears out it is not replaced.”

"So they have their own factories?" asked Grimes.

"No. They're getting away from the use of machinery. They're using manpower."

"They must be gluttons for hard work."

"They're not. They import their labor."

"But who would ever emigrate to such a world, to sweat in the fields?"

"Quite a few, Grimes. Quite a few—although I doubt if they were expecting what they got. Have you ever wondered what happens to all the refugees? There was the so-called Holy War on Iranda, sect against sect. The losers—those of them who had not been slaughtered—were evicted. They were evacuated by Survey Service transports. Liberia, very nobly, offered to give a new home to those hapless people. And do you remember when the New Canton sun went nova?"

"Before my time," said Grimes. "But I've read about it."

"A large number of the New Cantonese finished up on Liberia," Damien said. "Wars, revolutions, natural disasters—all have contributed to the build-up of Liberia's vast pool of slave labor."

"Slave labor?"

"It's not called that, of course. It's indentured labor. It's got to the stage where the Liberians need no longer import expensive machines. It's got to the stage where they're pampered aristocrats, waited on hand and foot. (I wonder what their anarchistic ancestors would have thought!) The real ruler of the planet is not the governor, or the president, but the commanding officer of the peacekeeping force, Colonel Bardon, Terran Army. He's got the president eating out of his hand."

"And the governor?"

"The last governor—your predecessor?—met with an accident. It seems that he tried to put a stop to many of the abuses. The military didn't like it. His aircraft crashed when he was on the way to investigate conditions at one of the orchards. The Board of Inquiry decided that the disaster—killing the governor, his wife and his personal pilot—was attributable to pilot error."

"A not uncommon cause of such disasters, sir."

"The Board of Inquiry, Grimes, consisted of Major Timms, Captain Vinor and Lieutenant Delaney, all of them Bardon's officers. And there were witnesses who saw the aircraft—a helium-filled blimp with electric motors—explode and come down in flaming fragments."

"Oh. I'm surprised that they, too, didn't meet with accidents."

"Most of them did. The one who didn't managed to stow away aboard a bulk carrier and make it to New Maine. He told his story to our Sub-Base Commander there, who passed it on to Survey Service Intelligence."

"Then why isn't this Colonel Bardon relieved of his command?"

"Politics, Grimes. Politics. For quite some time now the Army has been the Lord Protector's pet. For some reason he despises the Survey Service. And Field Marshal von Tempsky refuses to believe anything bad about any of his people, especially when the complaint is laid by us. Nonetheless, it's a known fact that the Army sweeps all its misfits and bad bastards under the mat by shipping them off to outworld garrison duties."

"And the Survey Service is doing the same, sir?"

Damien chuckled. "You're a misfit, Grimes, but even I wouldn't call you a bad bastard. Your forte has always been giving bad bastards what they deserve. People like Colonel Bardon, for example. . . ."

"So you want me to become governor of Liberia so that I can put a spoke in Bardon's wheel?"

"You could put it that way."

"But since when, sir, has the Survey Service been appointing colonial governors?"

"A good question, Grimes. We never have done so. But the Protector of the Colonies—Bendeen—is a friend of mine. We were midshipmen together. He got as high as lieutenant commander, then married into a political family. Not long after he resigned his commission and went into politics himself. His wife's family found a safe seat for him and he was elected to the Assembly. Surprisingly, despite his idealism and an honesty more typical of spacemen than politicians, he attained ministerial rank. He has his sights set on the Lord Protectorship but I don't think he'll make it. He tramples on too many corns."

"And he wants to trample on Field Marshal von Tempsky's corns?"

"Yes. And those of the Cereal Consortium. He hasn't forgiven them for the engineered famine on Damboon, which resulted in the downfall of the Free Democrat regime."

"Mphm." Grimes knocked out his pipe in Damien's wastepaper disposer, refilled and lit it. "Mphm. So I'm supposed to be Protector Bendeen's cat's paw. If I take the job, that is. . . ."

"You could put it that way, Grimes."

"Mphm. But won't it look fishy? A Survey Service dropout, a master astronaut who's lost his ticket after a widely publicized inquiry, appointed to a governorship. . . . Won't there be questions asked, in the World Assembly, by the media, on every streetcorner?"

"Our rumor factory will be working overtime, Grimes. The El Dorado Corporation has its tentacles everywhere. It will be hinted that El Dorado is behind the appointment, that highly placed people on that world are pulling strings to find a soft, highly paid job for a man who was one of their officers, a Company Commodore, and who served them to the best of his ability. Bendeen will try to convey the impression that your appointment is not one that he would have made of his own free will."

"You should have become a politician yourself, sir."

"Whatever makes you think that I didn't?" asked the Rear Admiral.

Three

Grimes watched *Sister Sue* lift off from Port Woomera.

He stood there, on the stained and scarred concrete of the commercial spaceport apron, staring up at the dull-gleaming spindle that was the ship—*his* ship—climbing steadily until it was no more than a speck in the cloudless blue sky, listening to the cacaphony of the inertial drive until it was no more than a faint, irritable mutter. And then the sky was empty and the only noises were those normal to a working spaceport at ground level—the whining of motors, the occasional clank and rattle from conveyor belts and gantries, now and again a shouted order.

Williams would do all right, he thought, despite his initial diffidence, even though the ex-Mate had made it plain that he had hoped that Grimes would be along in an advisory capacity.

("The old ship won't be the same without you, skipper," he had said. Then, "I'll look after her for you. You'll be back. I know you will." And Grimes had thought, *But ten years is a long time*.)

And now *Sister Sue* was up and away, outbound for Caribbea with a cargo of manufactured goods, everything from robotutors to robutterflies, the beautiful little devices that had been developed to deal, lethally and expeditiously, with flying insect pests. (They would sell well enough, Grimes thought, while the craze lasted.) Her discharge completed she would go on Time Charter to the Interstellar Transport Commission, carrying anything and everything anywhere and everywhere.

At least, thought Grimes, Williams had a good crew. Magda Granadu was still Catering Officer/Purser and the two old-timers, Crumley and Stewart, were still Reaction Drive Chief and Radio Officer respectively. The other engineers, Reaction Drive and Mannschenn Drive, were *real* space engineers, not refugees from universities and bicycle shops. (Their predecessors, together with their false memories, had been given passage back to Austral.) The Chief, Second and Third Officers were all young, properly qualified and actually employees of the Commission which, by the terms of the charter party, was required to supply necessary personnel.

So that was that.

Ex-Captain Grimes, ex-Company Commodore Grimes, soon-to-be-Governor Grimes climbed into the ground car that had been waiting to take him to the airport from where he would fly to Alice Springs to spend a few days with his parents before leaving for Liberia.

They met him in the waiting room at the base of the mooring mast.

Grimes senior, a tall, white-haired old man, greeted his son with enthusiasm. "I envy you, John," he said. "I really do. I just write about adventures; you have them!"

Matilda Grimes—also tall, red-haired and pleasantly horsefaced—frowned disapprovingly. "Don't encourage him, George. Ever since he left the Survey Service he's been doing nothing but getting into trouble. I hoped to see him become an admiral one day. I never dreamed that he'd become a pirate." She turned on her son. "And what do you intend to do now, John? You've had your Certificate taken from you . . ."

"Only suspended," said her husband.

She ignored this. "You'll never command a ship again, not even a merchant vessel. And after that trial. . . ."

"Court of Inquiry, my dear."

". . . nobody will ever employ you."

"As a matter of fact, Matilda," Grimes said, "I shall shortly be going out to take up a new appointment."

"What!"

"What as?" asked Grimes's father.

"Governor, as a matter of fact. Of Liberia."

"I've always thought," said his mother, "that the standard of intelligence in the World Assembly is appallingly low. Now I am sure of it. And I've never trusted Bendeen. Any man who would give up a career in the Survey Service for one in politics must have something wrong with him. Appointing a pirate as governor. . . ."

"There are precedents," said George Whitley Grimes. "Sir Henry Morgan, for example." He realized that the other people in the lounge were looking curiously at the small family party and said, "I suggest that we continue this discussion at home."

* * *

The robutler brought in drinks. *The Old Man must be doing well,* thought Grimes. The machine was one of the very latest models, a beautifully proportioned and softly gleaming cylinder moving on silent treads rather than something unconvincingly humanoid. From a circular port midway up the thing's body a sinuous tentacle produced the drinks ordered—dry sherry, chilled, for Matilda Grimes, a pink gin for Grimes and beer for his father. A dish of assorted nuts, placed on the coffee table, followed.

"Here's to crime," toasted George Whitley Grimes, raising his glass.

"I'll not drink to that!" snapped his wife. Nonetheless she gulped rather than sipped from hers.

Grimes sampled his pink gin. He could not have mixed a better one himself.

He said, "You seem very prosperous, George."

"Yes. It was that *If Of History* novel."

"The Ned Kelly idea that you were telling me about the last time that I was here?"

"No. The one after that, based on the Australian Constitutional Crisis. *If* Gough Whitlam, the Prime Minister, had refused to relinquish office after the Governor General fired him. . . ."

"Don't go putting ideas into his head," admonished Matilda. "The last time that he was here the pair of you talked about privateering and piracy—and look what happened! The next thing we hear will be that he's fired the President of Liberia!"

"Perhaps I shall," murmured Grimes. "Perhaps I shall. . . ."

His father looked at him intently over the rim of his condensation-beaded glass. He said softly, "Tell me, John, did you really leave the Survey Service?"

"I did."

"Did they call you back?"

"Did they?" pressed his mother, suddenly alert.

It was useless, he knew, to try to lie to her.

He said, "No comment."

"And isn't it true," his father went on, "that after your piratical antics a bill was pushed through the Assembly making privateering illegal anywhere in the Federation of Worlds?"

"You read, watch and listen to the media, George."

"I do. And there have been some nasty rumors recently about Liberia. But you can't tell us anything, can you?"

"I can't. And I think that you'd both be wise to keep your suspicions to yourself."

"We shall," promised his father. "But I shall be tempted, mind you, to give them an airing in a novel."

“Please don’t. The El Dorado Corporation might add two and two to make five and then be after my blood.”

“All right.” The older man finished his beer and, ignoring his wife’s frown, demanded a refill from the robutler. “And now, young John, I am going to put an idea into your head—one that even Matilda will approve of. You’re really a spaceman, aren’t you? That’s all you want to be, ever will want to be. And you don’t want to wait ten years to get your Certificate back—especially when you’ve a ship of your own of which you should be the captain. You’ll be governor, of a world called Liberia. When in Liberia do as the original Liberians did. . . .”

He talked, drawing upon his historical knowledge.

Grimes listened intently, as did his mother.

When his father was finished Grimes grinned happily. “It could work,” he said. “By all the Odd Gods, I’ll make it work!”

“But you will have to finish the job that you’re being sent out to do,” said his mother, frowning worriedly. “You’ll have to finish that job first.”

“Of course,” Grimes assured her. “Of course.”

Four

Grimes took one of the regular airships to Sydney and then a ramjet to New York. The World Assembly was housed in the old UN Building which, miraculously, had survived all the troubles that had plagued the city since the United Nations had taken up residence there. Staring down at Manhattan as the jet descended to the airport Grimes wondered what it had looked like during the days of its glory. He had seen photographs, of course, but would have liked to have been able to recognize, in actuality, such fabled towers as the Empire State and World Trade Buildings; the ornamental lakes that occupied their sites were all very well but, from the air, were no more than irregular puddles of blue water. But there was Brooklyn Bridge, rebuilt only recently to the old design. And that must be the Chrysler Building. . . . It was too bad that this was to be a brief business visit only.

An official World Assembly car was waiting for him and whisked him swiftly to the Assembly's headquarters. He was expected there; a young officer in a smart, sky-blue uniform escorted him along moving ways and up escalators, delivered him to the office of the Protector of the Colonies.

Bendeen—a slim man, not overly tall, gray-haired and with a heavily lined face—came from behind his littered desk to greet Grimes. The WA lieutenant withdrew and the door automatically closed behind him.

"So you're the famous—or notorious—Grimes," said Bendeen. "All right. You can admit it. This office is bugproof—or so the experts loaned to me by Rear Admiral Damien assure me. We can talk. Officially, as you may have learned, I was pressured into finding you a job. In actuality you were strongly recommended to me by the Rear Admiral. Drink?" What Grimes had taken for just another filing cabinet detached itself from the wall, rolled up to them on silent casters. A tray was extruded from it; on it were two glasses of what looked like pink gin. "As you see, Governor, I share your taste in tipples. Your very good health."

"And yours, Protector," Grimes replied.

(His father's robutler, Grimes thought, was much better at mixing drinks than this thing of Bendeen's.)

"You're booked out, Grimes, on *Sobraon.* The VIP suite, of course. She lifts from Port Woomera tomorrow so that means another ramjet flight for you. Can't say that I envy you. I hate those things. If God had meant us to fly He'd have given us an ample supply of non-flammable, lighter-than-air gas. Which, of course, he did. But where was I? Oh, yes. Your commission as Governor. It's on the desk somewhere. Ah, here it is. A splendid example of the engraver's art with eagles and dragons and hammers and sickles and lions and unicorns and hammers and sickles and rising suns and . . . oh, yes, emus and kangaroos all over it. And the Grand Seal of the Assembly. No not a *seal,* but a seal. Red wax, you know. And your name, in Gothic script. It'll look fine when you have it framed on the wall of your gubernatorial office. . . ."

"Isn't there any sort of swearing in ceremony?" asked Grimes, at last getting a word in edgewise.

"You'll have to wait until Libertad—that's the capital of Liberia—for that. I'm told that the president likes to put on shows to impress the oppressed masses. And they are oppressed, you know. Not only is there the hard, manual work for precious little pay but there're all the lucrative rackets indulged in by Bardon's boys. I don't know what Bardon's got on von Tempsky but, as far as VT is concerned, the colonel can do no wrong. I've tried to have him replaced but the Field Marshal piles on more Gs with the Lord Protector than I do. So I'm relying on you to catch Bardon with his hand in the till—or in the pocket of one of the indentured laborers. From what Damien has told me about you you're used to playing by ear. And you're a sort of catalyst. Things sort of happen all around you and, more often than not, you turn them to your advantage.

"There's a case waiting for you at the airport with plenty of light reading for your voyage—spools and spools of it. The VIP suite, of course, has a playmaster. You'll get a good idea of the world you're going to—history from the first settlement to the present. And now, finish your drink. The car's waiting to take us out to Kennedy. Don't forget the commission—there's a case for it somewhere. Ah, here . . ."

They emerged from the Protector's office into the corridor. Bendeen's manner changed, became stiff, hostile even. He said, as they passed through the door, ". . . this appointment was none of my choosing. But you are now the Governor—until such time as you are relieved."

Which will not be soon enough, implied the Protector's expression.

Grimes took the hint. This corridor must be well covered by audio-visual bugs. He kept his distance from the Protector, set his face into sullen lines. The two men maintained their charade until they shook hands, with a marked lack of enthusiasm, at the airport and Grimes boarded the ramjet for Woomera.

Five

The master of the Trans-Galactic Clipper *Sobraon* was well-accustomed to the carriage of Very Important Passengers and to playing the urbane and courteous host. VIPs who were also ex-pirates were, however, outside his normal experience. He had heard of Grimes—who among the spacefaring community had not?—and had never been among his admirers. Even as a small boy he had not considered pirates and privateers glamorous; as a shipmaster he regarded them as vicious and dangerous criminals. When he had been shown his passenger list for the forthcoming voyage, with the names of those worthy of special attention marked with a star, he had stared at it incredulously.

"Not *the* Grimes?" he had demanded of his purser.

"I'm afraid so, sir," she had replied.

"But . . . A *governor* . . . Can't you be mistaken, Liz? Surely there must be more than one John Grimes in this universe."

"Not with jug-handle ears. His photograph was among all the others in the Security parcel."

"But he was on trial for piracy."

"A Court of Inquiry, sir, not a trial."

"Even so, he had his Certificate dealt with. The judge and the assessors must have thought that he was guilty of something. And with good reason. And am I supposed to have him at my table?"

"With all the other VIPs." She grinned. "At least he'll be less boring than the others."

He scowled at her. "The man's a pirate, with blood on his hands. Get this straight, Liz, I don't want you and your tabbies fawning on him as though he were the latest tridi heart-throb. All that concerns us is that we're to deliver him from Port Woomera to Port Libertad with celerity and enjoying a far greater standard of luxury than he deserves. If I had *my* way I'd put him in one of the J Deck dogboxes!"

"You still could, sir. You're the master."

"Ha! And how long should I stay in one of the Line's senior ships if I did that? He must be treated correctly, Liz—with *icy* correctness. Convey subtly that any respect accorded to him is to his rank, not to himself. But subtly, Liz, subtly. Perfect service—but without the personal touch. The liquid hydrogen hand in the velvet glove . . ."

"Is velvet a good insulator, sir?"

"How the hell should I know? That will do, Liz; you've plenty to look after."

When the girl was gone he rang for his chief officer and then issued to that gentleman instructions as to how the VIP was to be treated.

Sobraon lifted from Port Woomera, slowly at first and then with increasing velocity as the thrust of her inertial drive built up. Grimes was a guest in the liner's control room, such courtesy often being extended to senior astronauts traveling as passengers and to civilian VIPs. He strongly suspected that the invitation had been extended to him in the second capacity. He looked out through the viewports at the fast receding scenery—to one side the semi-desert with its green rectangles of irrigated land, crisscrossed with silvery canals, to the other the dark sea with, far to the southward, the white glimmer of the Antarctic ice barrier. Twice recently he had been on Earth, he thought, and on neither occasion had he paid a visit to the Space Academy in Antarctica. The first time he might have done so, as a graduate who, despite the circumstances of his resignation from the Survey Service, was now a successful shipowner. On the second occasion it might not have been politic. A privateer-turned-pirate would hardly have been regarded by the Commandant as an Old Boy whose career should be emulated by the cadets.

He heard one of the officers whispering to another, "I wonder what he's thinking about? Is he working out how he could skyjack the ship?"

He looked around to see who it was.

It must have been Kelner, the liner's chief officer, who flushed and turned away hastily as Grimes's eye caught his. The ponderously portly Captain Harringby must, too, have heard that whisper—but the expression on his heavy face was approving rather than otherwise. Then the shipmaster looked at Grimes who, although no telepath, could tell what he was thinking. *I invited you up here only because Company Regulations require that I give you the VIP treatment. But I don't have to like you.*

Grimes shrugged. So he was *persona non grata.* So what? It was not for the first time in his life, almost certainly would not be for the last. He would stick it out, seated stolidly in the spare chair. He would, after trajectory had been set, graciously accept the invitation, no matter how grudgingly offered, to partake of the ritual drink with the captain and his senior officers. Throughout the voyage to Liberia he would be the very model of a modern Governor General. *(All right, all right,* he told himself irritably, I *know that it should be Major General and, in any case, I'm only a Governor.* He looked at Harringby, smugly omnipotent in his command chair, and thought, *And I'd sooner be a shipmaster again.)*

Trajectory was set (competently enough, Grimes admitted) and *Sobraon* was falling down the warped continuum on the first leg of her passage, Earth to Liberia. (This was, actually, no more than a deviation; Trans-Galactic Clippers specialized in carrying rich passengers around the truly glamorous worlds of the Galaxy—to Caribbea, with its warm seas and lush, tropical islands, to Atlantia for the big game fishing and the ocean yacht races, to Morrowvia, with its exotic cat people, to New Venusberg, with its entertainments to suit all warped tastes, to Waverley, with its reconstruction of a Scottish culture that owed more to myth than to actual history, to Electra, where those of a scientific bent could feast their eyes on the latest marvels.)

Trajectory was set, the powerful gyroscopes pulling the ship around her axes until the target star was ahead, then making the necessary adjustment for galactic drift. (Grimes flexed his idle hands on the arm rests of his chair; for so long he had been doing what Captain Harringby was doing now; it seemed—it was!—all wrong that he was no longer doing it.) The Mannschenn Drive was actuated. Deep in the bowels of the great ship the rotors began to turn, to spin, to precess, to tumble down and through the warped dimensions as the temporal precession field built up.

There was the usual brief disorientation, the transient nausea and, for Grimes at least, a flash of prevision.

He saw, as plainly as if she had been standing there in person, one of his fellow privateers, Captain Agatha Prinn of the star tramp *Agatha's Ark.* She was dressed—how else?—in her uniform of severely cut, short-skirted business suit, gray, with minimal trimmings of gold braid. She was holding a paper bag. She dropped it. It burst when it hit the ground, releasing a cloud of fine, white powder . . .

Colors, perspective and sounds snapped back to normal.

Grimes blinked, found that he was staring out of a viewport to an interstellar night in which the stars were no longer bright points of unwinking light but were amorphous nebulae.

Agatha Prinn and a flour bomb? he wondered. *What the hell was all* that *about?*

He realized that Captain Harringby was addressing him.

"Your Excellency," (but that's *me*! thought Grimes) "we are now on trajectory. Would you care to join me for liquid refreshment before lunch?"

It would make the old bastard's day if I said no, Grimes told himself.

"Thank you, Captain," he said as he unbuckled himself from his seat.

Six

It was a peculiar voyage, not altogether unpleasant, with its mixture of ostracism and adulation and downright pampering. Governor Grimes took his meals at the captain's table—and Captain Harringby, presiding over this lavish board, accorded the governor the respect due to him while making it plain that he did not approve of Commodore Grimes, the pirate chief. Now and again he permitted himself a flash of unkind humor, such as when the wine stewardess was dispensing a vintage Burgundy to accompany the roast beef. "I suppose, Your Excellency, that you must, now and again, have acquired some very fine wines among your other . . . er . . . loot?"

"The Hallichecki," Grimes had replied stiffly, "do not use alcohol." He added, after sipping from his glass, "My privateering operations were against the shipping of the Hegemony."

"But didn't you seize a Terran ship? One of the Commission's liners?"

"That happened after a mutiny, Captain. It all came out at the Court of Inquiry." He added, "And, in any case, the attempted piracy was unsuccessful."

The others at the table were looking at him, some with disapproval and contempt, others with what was almost admiration. There was the fat Joachim Levy, one of the Dog Star Line's managers taking his Long Service Leave and bound for New Venusberg. He pursed his thick lips, then said, *"Our* ships are used to coping with piracy. When necessary they are armed—and their crews know how to use their weapons."

"I know," Grimes told him. "My Mate was ex-Dog Star Line. He was a very good gunnery officer."

Levy scowled and the plump, artificially blonde Mrs. Levy laughed. "So all the drills that the Dog Star Line officers have to go through are some use after all!" She smiled quite prettily at Grimes. "But wasn't it *fun,* Your Excellency? Sailing the seas of space with the Jolly Roger at the masthead and a cutlass clenched between your teeth?"

"Mphm," grunted Grimes.

"In the *good* old days," said Ivor Sandorsen, who was a Lloyd's underwriter, "you would have been hanged from your own yardarm. Your Excellency."

"As a matter of fact," said Grimes, "one of my ancestors was."

"Thus establishing a precedent."

"Another, better known, pirate," said Grimes, "established another precedent. Sir Henry Morgan. He became a governor."

"Had Lloyd's been in existence in those days, sir, he would have paid the just penalty for his crimes."

"In any case," said Harringby with a superior smile, "I think that His Excellency will admit that the governorship of Liberia is hardly a plum as such appointments go. More of a rotten apple, perhaps."

"Have you been there, Captain?" asked Mrs. Levy, who seemed to have appointed herself Grimes's champion.

"No, madam. Nor do I want to. I shall place my ship in orbit about that world and a tender will rendezvous to pick up His Excellency. Then I shall be on my way."

"Rejoicing?" asked Grimes.

"I shall most certainly not be weeping."

"And you, Your Excellency," asked Dorothea Taine, tall, dark, intense, author of a best seller which Grimes's father had scornfully dismissed as *Womens' Weekly* rubbish, "will you be weeping or rejoicing?"

"That remains to be seen," Grimes told her.

"Sir—Your Excellency, I mean—what's it really like being a pirate? Sorry. A privateer. . . ."

The young Fifth Officer made his diffident approach to Grimes as he was just dismounting from one of the exercise bicycles in the liner's gymnasium.

"There are better and safer ways of earning a living," Grimes said.

"Safer, perhaps, sir. But . . . Would you know if Commodore Kane is still trying to find volunteers for his privateer fleet?"

"Drongo Kane is better stayed away from. In any case, as you must have heard, the Survey Service is smacking down on all privateering operations."

"Mr. Barray!" The Chief Officer had just come into the gymnasium for his own exercise session. "Here you are. I thought that you were supposed to be checking the equipment in your lifeboat."

"I . . . I've finished that, sir. It's all in order."

"Then find Mr. McGurr and lend him a hand in hydroponics. This is his tank cleaning day."

Crestfallen, the young man left the gym. Shedding his robe and, clad only in trunks, the Chief Officer mounted the bicycle that Grimes had vacated. As he started to pedal he said, "Even you, Your Excellency, must know that young men often evince enthusiasm for the most unworthy people and causes."

"Are you implying that I'm unworthy, Mr. Kelner?"

"I never said so, Your Excellency."

"I can *use* you, Your Excellency. Or may I call you John? After all, I know your father; I've met him at Australian Society of Authors meetings . . ."

Grimes looked at Dorothea Taine over his coffee cup. He was taking this midmorning refreshment in the lounge; he did not see why he should be confined to his quarters, luxurious though they were, even though he was something of a social leper.

"Use me?" he asked.

The writer smiled. Her teeth were too large for her small mouth. The heavy-rimmed spectacles that she affected made her big, black eyes look even bigger in her sallow face.

"I want to use you . . . John."

"How, Ms. Taine?" asked Grimes dubiously.

"Dorothea, please. Or you may call me Dot. I'm starting a new novel. One of those If stories. *If* Dampier, the buccaneer and privateer, had established a settlement on the West Coast of Australia, long before the one was established at Botany Bay. After all, he was there. . . ."

"And he didn't think much of it."

"But something could, just could, have made him change his mind. He could have fallen madly in love with a beautiful Aboriginal girl. Perhaps she could have saved his life, just as the Princess Pocahontas saved the life of Captain John Smith in Virginia . . ."

Grimes entertained a fleeting vision of a naked black girl getting in the way of a boomerang flung at the piratical Captain Dampier by her irate father.

"Mphm," he grunted around the stem of his pipe.

"You see, John, I want to make Dampier a *real* character. I can't go back in time to meet him. But there's one real life character, aboard this very ship, who could serve as a model. You. Dampier wasn't only a pirate and privateer, he was also an officer, a captain, in the Royal Navy. You've been a privateer and a pirate—and also an officer, commanding ships, in the Survey Service . . . If I could only get *inside* you . . ."

I don't want to get inside you, thought Grimes unkindly. *You're too skinny, for a start. And you gush.*

"Perhaps some evening, or evenings, after dinner . . . We could get away by ourselves somewhere and you could tell me all about yourself . . ."

"It would be very boring for you," said Grimes.

"It would not. John. It couldn't possibly be."

"I'm sorry," he told her, "but all my evenings are fully taken up. I've all the spools on Liberia to study. After all, I'm being paid to be governor of the damn place so I'd better know something about it before I get there. . . ."

"Do you mind if I join you, Your Excellency? Joe's gotten himself involved in a non-stop poker game and I'm just a bit lonesome."

"Please do, Mrs. Levy. What are you drinking? A Black Angel?" Then, to the bar stewardess, "Another pink gin, please, and a B.A."

"I *like* this little bar. . . . Your very good health, Excellency."

"And yours, Mrs. Levy."

"That sounds dreadfully formal."

"Vee, then."

"Only Joe calls me that. I prefer Vera."

"Your very good health, Vera."

"I only found this little bar a couple of days ago, John. (Do you mind?) It's so . . . private. Not like the main bars, always crowded and always that so-called music so that you can't hear yourself think. I guess that there're still parts of this big ship that I haven't seen. We—the Dog Star Line, that is—don't have anything in this class."

"But you are getting into the passenger trades."

"Glorified cattle boats," she sneered. "Nothing like *this.* But I don't suppose that Joe will ever be important enough to qualify for the VIP suite. I would so like to see how the VIPs live. . . ."

"I must throw an official cocktail party before we get to Liberia," said Grimes. "You're invited, of course. . . ."

After all, he thought, *I might want a job in the Dog Star Line some day. Mr. Levy, for all his apparent inattention to his wife, looked as though he might prove to be a very jealous husband. . . .*

"Never mind," she said with sudden coldness. "I'll just take my place in the queue. Goodnight, Your Excellency."

She finished her drink and left—and Grimes knew that he would never be employed by the Dog Star Line as long as she was the wife of one of that company's managers.

"Satisfied?" he asked sleepily.

"Yes . . . and no, darling. But we've several hours before Jane brings in your morning tea."

"You'd better be out of here before then, Liz."

"It's not important really. We tabbies stick together, even though some of us have gold braid on our shoulders and some haven't. Jane would never run screaming to old Herring."

"Herring?"

"Captain Harringby. Haven't you ever noticed the fishlike look he has sometimes?"

"What if he did find out? What would he do?"

"Nothing, darling. Nothing. He's all show and no blow. Like practically every other passenger ship master he's scared shitless of the Space Catering Officers and Stewardesses' Guild. We have the power to make any voyage a hell for all concerned."

"Mphm."

No matter how successful I am, he thought, *I shall never be fool enough to buy a big passenger ship.*

He persisted, "But you didn't answer my question properly . . ."

"About being satisfied? Well, you aren't exactly bad in bed, although you could be better. But I'll educate you, darling. What satisfies me is that I've won the sweep."

"The sweep?"

"Yes. We all put in twenty credits and the prize goes to the first member of *Sobraon*'s female staff to go to bed with the notorious pirate. You. And I get the prize."

"So that's why the purser brought up my supper tray in person tonight instead of entrusting the task to one of her underlings! All right, Liz. You've won. But it's been touch and go." He laughed. "I wondered why my personal needs were being attended to by different stewardesses every day and night. A fair go for all, I suppose. I almost succumbed this morning when that little carroty cat . . ."

"Sue . . ."

". . . intimated that she'd just love to wash my back while I was taking my shower."

"And now I'll rub your front and hope that you'll rise to the occasion."

Seven

Sobraon was in orbit about Liberia.

Alongside her was one of that planet's meteorological satellite tenders, airlock to airlock and with the short gangway tube sealed in place, a means of transfer of personnel from spaceship to spaceship with which Grimes was unfamiliar. In the Survey Service spacesuits and lifelines were good enough for anybody, from admirals down. But now he was no longer a spaceman. He was a first class passenger. And he was a governor.

He was dressed as such, in the archaic finery that must always have seemed absurd to any intelligent human being, a rig neither functional nor aesthetically pleasing. Starched white shirt, stiff collar and gray silk cravat . . . Black tail coat over a gray waistcoat . . . Gray, sharply creased trousers . . . Highly polished black boots . . . And—horror of horrors!—a gray silk top hat.

He stood in the vestibule of the liner's airlock; at least Harringby had put the inertial drive back into operation so that Grimes was spared the indignity of floundering about clumsily in his hampering clothing. Nonetheless he was sweating, his shirt damp on his chest, sides and back. He derived some small pleasure from the observation that Captain Harringby was far from comfortable in his own dress uniform; obviously it had been tailored for him before he started to put on weight. The Chief Officer's black and gold finery fitted him well enough but his expression made it plain that he hated having to wear it. Liz, the Purser, carried her full dress far better than did the Captain and the Mate. She looked cool and elegant in her long, black skirt, her white blouse with the floppy black tie, her short, gold-trimmed jacket.

Also present were the Third Officer, who would be looking after the airlock, and two Cadets. The young men were comfortable in normal shirt-and-shorts rig. Grimes envied them.

Harringby saluted stiffly. Grimes raised his top hat. Harringby extended his hand. Grimes took it with deliberate and (he hoped) infuriating graciousness.

"Good-bye, Your Excellency," said the shipmaster. "It's been both an honor and a pleasure to have you aboard."

Bloody liar, thought Grimes. He said, "Thank you, Captain."

The Chief Officer saluted, waited until Grimes extended his hand before offering his own.

"The best of luck, Your Excellency."

Do you mean it? wondered Grimes.

Liz brought her slim hand up to the brim of her tricorne hat, then held it out to Grimes who, gallantly, raised it to his lips while bowing slightly. Harringby scowled and the Chief Officer smirked dirtily. Grimes straightened up, still holding the girl's hand, looking into her eyes. He would have liked to have kissed those full lips—and to hell with Harringby!—but he and Liz had said their proper (improper?) good-byes during the night and early morning ship's time.

"Good-bye, Your Excellency," she murmured. "And—look after yourself."

"I'll try to," he promised.

Harringby coughed loudly to attract attention, then said, "Your Excellency, I shall be vastly obliged if you will board the tender. It is time that I was getting back to my control room."

"Very well, Captain."

Grimes gave one last squeeze to Liz's hand, relinquished it reluctantly and turned to walk into the airlock chamber and then through the short connecting tube. The tender's airlock door was smaller than that of the liner and had not been designed to admit anybody wearing a top hat. That ceremonial headgear was knocked off its insecure perch. As Grimes stooped to retrieve it he heard the Chief Officer laugh and an even louder guffaw from one of the tender's crew. He carried his hat before him as he completed his journey to the small spacecraft's cabin. His prominent ears were burning furiously.

The crew of the tender—Liberia possessed only orbital spacecraft—were young, reasonably efficient and (to Grimes's great envy) sensibly uniformed in shorts and T-shirts and badges of rank pinned to the left breast. The Captain asked Grimes to join him in the control cab. He did so, after removing his tail coat and waistcoat, sat down in the co-pilot's chair. He looked out from the viewport at the great bulk of the liner, already fast diminishing against the backdrop of abysmal night and stars, saw it flicker and fade and vanish as the Mannschenn Drive was actuated. He transferred his attention to the mottled sphere toward which the tender was dropping—pearly cloud systems and blue seas, brown and green continents and islands.

"It's a good world, Your Excellency," said the young pilot. He grinned wrily. "It *was* a good world. It could be one again."

Grimes looked at him with some curiosity. The accent had been Standard English, overlaid with an oddly musical quality. The face was olive-skinned, hawklike. Native-born, he thought. The original colonists—those romantic Anarchists—had been largely of Latin-American stock.

"Could be?" he asked.

"That is the opinion of some of us, Your Excellency. And we've heard of you, of course. You're something of an Anarchist yourself . . ."

"Mphm?"

"I mean. . . . You're not the usual Survey Service stuffed shirt."

"A stuffed shirt is just what I feel like at the moment."

"But you've a reputation, sir, for doing things your own way.

"And where has it got me?" asked Grimes, addressing the question to himself rather than to the tender's pilot.

"You've commanded ships, sir. Real ships, deep space ships, not . . . *tenders.*"

"Don't speak ill of your own command," Grimes admonished.

The young man grinned whitely. "Oh, I like her. She'll do almost anything I ask of her—but if I asked her to make a deep space voyage I know what her answer would be!"

"Fit her out with Mannschenn Drive and a life support system," said Grimes, "and you could take her anywhere."

"If I were qualified—which I am not. Master Astronaut, Orbital Only—that's me."

"But you're still a spaceman, Captain. I'd like to have a talk, spaceman to spaceman. But . . ."

"Don't worry about Pedro and Miguel, sir. They're like me, members of the OAP, the Original Anarchist Party. We're allowed by our gracious President to blow off steam as long as we don't *do* anything. . . ."

"What could we do, Raoul?" came a voice from behind Grimes.

He turned to see that the other two crew members had taken seats at the rear of the control cab.

He said softly, "What could you do? I don't know. Yet. I spent the voyage from Earth running through all the official spools on Liberia . . ." (He remembered guiltily that there had been times when instead of watching and listening to the playmaster in his suite he had been doing other things.) "Before I left I was given a briefing of sorts. I still don't know nearly as much as I should. You have the first-hand knowledge. I don't."

"All right, sir," said Raoul. "I'll start at the top. There's our revered President, Estrelita O'Higgins. . . ."

"Mphm," grunted Grimes. He remembered how she had looked in the screen of the playmaster. Tall, splendidly bosomed, black-haired and with rather too much jaw to be pretty. But she was undeniably handsome. In the right circumstances she might be beautiful.

"Then there's your boy, Colonel Bardon. . . ."

"Not *my* boy," said Grimes.

"He's Earth-appointed, isn't he? Just as you are, sir. Most people say that he's got Estrelita eating out of his hand—but it could well be the other way around."

"Or mutual," said Grimes.

They made a good pair, Estrelita and the Colonel, he had thought when he saw them in one of the sequences presented by the data spools. The tall, handsome woman in a superbly tailored blue denim suit, the tall, handsome man in his glittering full dress. Like her, he had too much jaw. In his case it was framed by black, mutton chop whiskers.

"Whoever is eating out of whose hand," Raoul went on, "it's the Terran Garrison that really runs Liberia. They get first pick of everything. Then the Secret Police get their pickings. Then the ordinary police. The real Liberians don't get picked on much. There's some grumbling, of course, but we aren't badly off. It's the slaves who suffer. . . ."

"The indentured labor," corrected Grimes.

"You're hair-splitting, sir. When an indenture runs out the only way that a laborer can obtain further employment is to sign up again. All his wages, such as they are, have gone to the purchase of the little luxuries that make life bearable. And not only luxuries. There are habit-forming drugs, like Dassan dreamsticks. . . ."

"They're illegal," said Grimes, "on all federated worlds."

The pilot laughed harshly. "Of course they are. But that doesn't worry Bardon's Bullies." He returned his attention to his instruments and made minor adjustments; the beat of the tender's inertial drive changed tempo. "I've time to tell you a story, sir, before we come in to Port Libertad. There was a girl, a refugee, from New Dallas. You must have heard about what happened there. An independent colony that thought that it could thumb its nose at the Federation and at everybody else. Then the Duchy of Waldegren wanted the planet—and took it. We took a few thousand refugees. A lot of the prettier girls finished up in the houses owned—not all that secretly—by Bardon. Mary Lou was one of them. That's where I met her, in a dive called the Pink Pussy Cat. And—don't laugh, please!—we . . . fell in love. I was going to buy her out of that place. But some bastard got her hooked on dreamsticks and. . . ."

"She withered away to nothing," said Miguel.

Grimes said nothing. What could he say?

Raoul broke the silence, speaking in a deliberately brisk voice. "There's Port Libertad, sir. That statue you can see, just to the north of the spaceport, is Lady Liberty. She was copied from the old Statue of Liberty in New York harbor, on Earth. Those two big ships are bulkies, here to load grain. Some worlds, though, prefer to import the flour that's been milled here, on Liberia. Don't ask me why; I'm a spaceman, not an economist. Do you see that smaller ship? She's a fairly regular visitor. *Willy Willy,* owned by Able Enterprises. The master's Captain Aloysius Dreeble. A nasty little bastard on a nasty trade. He comes here to recruit entertainers—so called—for the brothels on quite a few of the frontier worlds."

"And New Venusberg," said Grimes. "That's where I last met him."

"You know him, sir?"

"All right, all right. I don't like him. And he doesn't like me."

Looking out and down Grimes could see the triangle of winking, bright, scarlet lights that marked the tender's berth. He picked up a pair of binoculars and stared through them. He could make out a body of men drawn up in military formation, flags streaming from portable standards, the burnished metal of musical instruments from which the afternoon sun was brightly reflected. A guard of honor and a band. . . .

From the speaker of the transceiver, through which the tender had been in communication from Aerospace Control, came a sudden blast of music, the drums almost drowning out the trumpets.

"They're warming up," said Raoul sardonically. "Be prepared to be deafened by our glorious planetary anthem as soon as you set foot on Liberian soil."

"And a twenty-gun salute?" Grimes asked, half seriously.

"No. I did hear some of the Terran Army officers discussing it before I boarded to lift off for the rendezvous with *Sobraon.* It seems that if you'd been landing in a Terran warship the Captain would have been able to accord the courtesy of a salute, in reply, to Madam President. But as you've no guns to fire you get none fired in your honor."

"This protocol," said Grimes, "is a complicated business."

"Isn't it, sir? We should never have strayed from the simple ways of our ancestors. They'd have given a gun salute to an Earth-appointed governor—and not with blanks, either!"

Looking at Raoul's face Grimes saw that the words had been spoken only in jest—but Miguel, when he spoke, was serious enough.

"If all that we've heard of Governor Grimes is true. Raoul, Bardon's Bullies would love to give him his twenty guns, each one loaded with H.E.!"

"There are more subtle ways of getting rid of unpopular governors than that," Raoul Sanchez said with sudden bitterness. Then, to Grimes, "My brother was the late Governor Wibberley's personal pilot."

A man with motive, thought Grimes. A double motive. His girlfriend and his brother, both . . . murdered.

He asked, "Are you qualified for atmosphere flight, Captain?"

"Yes, sir. Both LTA and HTA." He grinned. "Are you offering me a job, Your Excellency? I already have one, you know."

"I'm offering you a job. I warn you that it mightn't be good for your health."

"It wasn't good for my brother's health, either. All right, I receive your signal, loud and clear. You think that I might be interested in . . . revenge?"

"That thought had flickered across my mind."

"I am so interested. And now, sir, if you'll excuse me, I'll try to get this crate down in one piece."

And had he fallen into a trap? Grimes wondered. Wasn't it too much of a coincidence that these young men in the shuttle should all be OAP members, opposed to the present regime on Liberia? Were Raoul's stories, about his girl and his brother, true? (That could be checked.)

But he would have to employ some personal staff and he would prefer, whenever possible, to make his own choices. Any made for him by Colonel Bardon would be suspect from the start. And, thought Grimes, if Captain Sanchez were Bardon's man air travel, at least, would be safer for him than it had been for Governor Wibberley. Raoul didn't look the type to commit suicide just to help somebody else commit murder.

Eight

A blast of sound assailed Grimes's ears as he stepped out of the tender's air-lock, onto the top platform of the bunting-bedecked set of steps that had been wheeled into position. With an effort he identified it as music—the brass too strident and the drums too insistent—and with a further effort as the Terran Planetary Anthem, one of those forgettable songs with words and music composed to order by an untalented committee of lyricists and musicians. He stood to attention, his right hand holding his gray silk topper over his breast, his left hand grasping the cylindrical, gold-trimmed leather case in which was his Commission. It must look, he thought wryly, like a Field Marshal's baton. But would Bardon give him the respect that he would accord to a Field Marshal?

Sons of Terra, strong and free came to its blaring conclusion. Thankfully Grimes relaxed, put his hat back on to his head. Then there was a roll of drums, followed by more *music—Liberia's sons, let us rejoice* . . . He whipped off his hat, came again to attention. That anthem was over at last and he took a step towards the edge of the platform—and again froze. This time it was *Waltzing Matilda.*

The familiar words ran through his mind as he listened to the band.

Up came the squatter, riding on his thoroughbred,

Down came the troopers, one, two, three . . .

And there were the troopers, and there were more than three of them. There were Bardon's Bullies, drawn up for his inspection, resplendent in their dress uniforms of blue and gold and scarlet.

Up jumped the swagman, sprang into the billabong . . .

Grimes thought, *And this is one helluva billabong that I've sprung into this time* . . .

After *Matilda* there were no more anthems but Grimes was in no hurry to descend the steps to the ground but made a slow survey of his immediate surroundings. That must be Bardon down there, waiting to receive him, even more splendidly attired than his soldiers, his finery topped by a plumed helmet. And the tall woman with him, in a superbly tailored suit of faded blue denim, had to be Madam President.

There was a crowd, but only a small one. There was a group of men and women, attired as was their President. There were the inevitable school children waving their little flags—the Federation star cluster on a black field, the Terran opalescent sphere on dark blue, the Australian national ensign with the British union flag in the upper canton and the Southern Cross constellation in the fly. There were spaceport workers in shabby, dirty, white overalls, small statured men and women, dark skinned and with Mongoloid features. There were officers from the ships in port. Grimes recognized one of these men—the weedy, ferret-faced Aloysius Dreeble, master of *Willy Willy.* Dreeble recognized him, grinned and raised two fingers in a gesture that would have been, had his palm been outward, V for Victory.

Grimes looked coldly at his old enemy and then turned away. He descended the steps with dignity. At the foot of them stood Bardon. The Colonel saluted smartly. Grimes raised his hat. The Colonel said, "Glad to have you aboard, Your Excellency." Grimes said, swapping lie for lie, "I'm happy to be here, Colonel Bardon."

"Your Excellency, may I introduce you to Madam President?"

Grimes removed his hat, put it to his chest and bowed. She inclined her head graciously. When they had both resumed normal posture they stood facing each other. Her eyes, gleaming black under heavy black brows, were level with his and looking at him appraisingly. The skin of her face was smooth and pale, her lips wide, full and very red. Her jaw was too heavy for a woman. But her smile, revealing strong white teeth, was quite pleasant.

She said, "I never dreamed that I should one day welcome a famous pirate as Governor of Liberia."

"Not a pirate, Madam President. A privateer."

"Pirate or privateer, Captain Grimes, you are bound to be an improvement over your predecessor."

"Indeed?"

"Yes. He was a psalm-singing do-gooder. You must know the type."

"I have met such people."

"Your Excellency," interrupted Bardon, "may I suggest that we inspect the Guard of Honor?"

The President shrugged and, with that well-fitting jacket of soft denim, the effect was spectacular.

She said with a smile that was not altogether malicious, "The Colonel wants us to help him play with his toy soldiers, Captain Grimes."

Bardon scowled, but not fiercely, and said, "My men are not toys, Madam."

It was, thought Grimes, very like an essentially light-hearted exchange of insults between husband and wife. But sometimes such apparently friendly gibes are symptomatic of well-hidden hostilities.

He walked with the President and the Colonel along the ranks of the Honor Guard, preceded by a Lieutenant with a drawn sword, with other officers bringing up the rear. At close quarters the men were not so impressive as they had seemed from a distance. Even so, Grimes could not fault the uniforms, well-tailored from spotlessly clean and sharply pressed cloth, with gleaming natural leather and brightly burnished metal. The archaic rifles, weapons brought out only for ceremonial occasions, held now at Present Arms, were beautifully maintained. On the features of each man the facial hair, a down-sweeping moustache, was brushed and trimmed into exact uniformity with the whiskers to right and to left. But even those tailored scarlet jackets could not hide the paunches or the wide, gleaming, cross-straps and belts hold them in. And there were the sagging jowls and the shifty eyes, some of them bloodshot.

Bardon's Bullies, thought Grimes. *They look it.*

He said, "Thank you, Colonel. A fine body of men."

"I am pleased that you found them so, Your Excellency. You can rely upon them for loyal service."

"Thank you, Colonel."

"I prefer soldiers in undress uniform," said the President, turning her sultry gaze on to Bardon. And then, to his rather embarrassed surprise, Grimes was treated to a similar, lingering glance. "And I am sure, Your Excellency, that you would feel far happier in something less formal."

"Too right," said Grimes.

She said, "You may dismiss your troops. Colonel Bardon."

Bardon turned to Grimes and asked, "Permission to dismiss the Guard, Your Excellency?"

Who gives orders to whom on this bloody planet? Grimes asked himself.

He said, "Dismiss the Guard, Colonel."

Orders were barked, Colonel to Lieutenant, Lieutenant to Sergeant, Sergeant to the enlisted men. Smartly, with a jingle of accoutrements, the detachment formed fours and, behind the band, stepping in time to the thud and rattle of the drums, marched toward the spaceport's boundary fence. Chattering shrilly, the schoolchildren followed their teachers in the wake of the departing military. The ground staff drifted back to their jobs. The spacemen strolled toward their ships.

Vehicles drove up—a huge, scarlet-enameled limousine for the President with the symbol of a clenched fist, holding a torch, in black, on each of its doors, an olive-drab-painted armored car for the Colonel and one of the Lieutenants, a superb RR Whispering Ghost, gleaming black and shining silver with the forward-leaning nymph on its bonnet holding a staff from which flew a Terran ensign, for Grimes. There was a civilian chauffeur, a young man with a full beard, denim-clad and with a scarlet neckerchief. Beside him, on the front seat, were two soldiers in drab battle dress.

Bardon said to Grimes, "Your ADC will look after you, Your Excellency, and will . . . er . . . show you the ropes at the Governor's Residence. Lieutenant Smith, please see that His Excellency is at the President's Reception, at 2000 hours this evening."

Smith saluted. He was old for his rank, his face both pudgy and sulky. The decorations on the left breast of his tunic were of the variety that Grimes referred to as Good Attendance Medals. If he had ever been in a war, even a police action, he had failed to distinguish himself.

"Until this evening, Your Excellency," said Estrelita O'Higgins.

"Until this evening, Madam President," said Grimes.

"Until this evening, Your Excellency," said Bardon, saluting.

"Until this evening, Colonel," said Grimes, raising his hat.

He had to take it off again when he climbed into the car, through the door which the ADC had opened for him. Smith followed him into the vehicle.

Nine

Rather to Grimes's disappointment the drive out to the Residence did not take him through the city of Libertad but through countryside that, in a natural state, could have been beautiful but, with its too orderly orchards, was rather boring. He remembered that although cereals were Liberia's main exports here was also a considerable trade in various processed fruit products. Working in the aisles between the trees were the laborers, small, dark-skinned people, clad only in loincloths, picking the golden fruit and filling baskets with the gleaming globes. lt was not the first orange plantation that Grimes had seen—but it was the first one in which machines had not been doing the harvesting.

Then there were terraced rice paddies, and more orchards and, eventually, a low hill on which stood the Governor's Residence. It was a low, rambling building, white-walled, its shallowly pitched roofs red-tiled. The main entrance was an imposing portico, with white pillars and a proliferation of intricately patterned iron lace. There was a wide, velvety lawn fringed with flowering bushes—plants indigenous to Liberia, thought Grimes, who was no botanist. There was a tall flagstaff at the peak of which the starry banner of the Federation stirred lazily in the light, uncertain breeze.

A small detachment of Terran Army troops—a Sergeant and six men—was drawn up before the portico. Unlike the Honor Guard at the spaceport they were wearing khaki, not full dress uniform, and were armed not with archaic but aesthetically pleasing rifles but with modern, ugly and viciously effective sprayguns. Like the Honor Guard, however, they looked far better from a distance.

Behind the soldiers were the livened civilians, men and women in long, white trousers or skirts under high-necked, royal blue jackets. Some of these jackets were absolutely plain, others were decorated with silver buttons and varying quantities of silver braid. One man was wearing a chef's high, white hat. There was a civilian who was not in uniform, a short man, stocky, bald-headed, wearing a plain gray suit.

Grimes stared.

These, obviously, were the servants—but a mob like this to look after one man, even though he was a governor!

He voiced his disapproving surprise.

It was the chauffeur who made reply. He said smugly, "The Residence is a large building, Your Excellency. Even though there is only one level above ground there are three sub-surface ones.There is all the cleaning to do, and the cooking, and. . . ."

"And machines to do such work," said Grimes.

"Not here," said the chauffeur. "Not on Liberia. Not now. In order to create employment for the refugees whom we have accepted from all over the galaxy we have reverted to the use of human labor wherever possible."

"I thought," Grimes said, "that this principle applied only to large-scale enterprises, such as agriculture. Not to menial work."

"Are you calling *me* a menial?" demanded the man.

"Of course not," said Grimes hastily. The driver already seemed more interested in the conversation than the handling of the car; if he got involved in a real argument he might forget to stop and plough into and through the reception committee.

He did stop; only just in time, it seemed to Grimes. The doors opened. The ADC was first out. Grimes followed, putting on his top hat. He raised it in response to the Sergeant's smart salute. The short, stocky civilian came forward and bowed, presenting his shiny, bald pate to the Governor's inspection. He straightened up and said, "Jaconelli, Your Excellency. David Jaconelli. Your secretary."

Grimes took his clammy hand, pressed it briefly.

He said, "I am pleased to meet you, Mr. Jaconelli."

One of the servants, the one with the most lavish display of braid and buttons on his tunic, presented himself and bowed far more deeply than had the secretary. His sparse gray hair, Grimes noted, was scraped back and plaited into a neat queue, a pigtail. He came erect and regarded Grimes from black, slanted eyes. His face was thin, the skin tightly stretched over the bone structure, his complexion ivory yellow. A wispy beard decorated his far from prominent chin.

He said, in a high-pitched voice that was not quite a twitter, "Welcome, Your Excellency, from myself and from all of your servants."

"Thank you," replied Grimes. Then, "You are . . . ?"

"My name is Wong Lee, Your Excellency. I have the honor to be Your Excellency's majordomo."

"I am pleased to meet you, Mr. Lee." (Or should that have been Mr. Wong?) "You may tell the other servants to return to their duties." Orders were given in a high-pitched voice in a language that Grimes thought was Chinese. "And now, if you will be so good as to escort me to my quarters. . . ."

Led by Wong Lee, accompanied by Lieutenant Smith and Mr. Jaconelli, Grimes walked into what would be his happy home until such time as his gubernatorial employment was terminated. Would he be able to resign before he got fired? he wondered.

The four men marched through what seemed, to Grimes, like miles of corridors, over long reaches of gleaming parquetry, past a never-ending display, on either side, of works of art, copies—but excellent ones—of paintings of all periods, representative of every school since some inspired Cromagnard daubed his crude but enduring pigments onto a cave wall. There was a Turner—*Spaceship out of sight in a gas nebula,* thought Grimes irreverently—and a Picasso—*Portrait of a lady after a Mannschenn Drive malfunction.* And a Rubens . . . Grimes had no objection to naked blondes but preferred them less fat. A Norman Lindsay. . . . None of his undressed ladies could be classed as skinny but they were far more to Grimes's taste than the models of the old Dutch master. Inevitably there was that famous woman who daren't smile properly—thought Grimes, cultural barbarian that he was—for fear of exposing her carious teeth. Then there were more Australian artists. There was Nolan, with his weirdly compelling perpetuation of a myth, the giant in his fantastic armor astride a horse that could have been borrowed (or stolen!) from Don Quixote. A myth? But there had been a Ned Kelly, whose name and fame had survived while those of countless far worthier citizens were long forgotten. And if the cards had fallen only a little differently at Glenrowan what might have happened? The course of Australian history, of Terran history, even, could have been changed.

Wong Lee noticed Grimes's interest in the Nolan paintings.

"A folk hero, Your Excellency?" he asked.

"Mphm. Yes, I suppose."

"Perhaps an honorable ancestor . . ."

"Not as far as I know."

They came to the Governor's suite.

There was a large, comfortable sitting room with, off it, an office—big enough, thought Grimes, for a full meeting of the entire Board of Admiralty. While the others watched respectfully he took his seat behind the vast, gleaming desk, enjoying the feeling of power. He had commanded ships and, recently, a flotilla—but this was different. Now he was boss cocky of an entire planet—on paper, at least. *De jure.* But *de facto*? That remained to be seen. He looked down to his reflection in the highly polished surface of the desk, saw behind his face the crossed flags, the banners of Terra and of the Interstellar Federation. He saw too, with something of a shock, that he was still wearing the absurd top hat. But he was the Governor, wasn't he? This was his Residence, wasn't it? If he couldn't make his own rules of etiquette, who could? Nonetheless he removed the head covering, skimmed it across the desk top to Wong Lee.

He got up then and, followed by the others, made a tour of his living quarters. There was a luxurious bedroom. He saw that his baggage had already been deposited there; it must have been offloaded and transported while he was inspecting the Guard of Honor at the spaceport. Somebody had begun to unpack and had laid out his civilian full evening dress on the bed. That somebody was a girl—tall, with glossy black hair swinging in a pageboy bob about her face, wearing a royal blue tunic and a long, white skirt that was slit to hip level, revealing a delectable length of smooth, ivory-skinned leg. She straightened up from what she was doing, turned to Grimes and bowed. Like the other servants she was of Mongoloid stock—a descendant, Grimes supposed, of those New Cantonese refugees. But there was some mixed blood—that wide mouth, the almost—but no more than almost—harsh angularity of the facial bone structure.

"This is Su Lin, Your Excellency," said Wong Lee. "She is to be your . . . handmaiden. I decided that you, as a space gentleman, accustomed to the ministrations of stewardesses aboard your ships, would prefer a personal attendant of the female sex."

"I like to make my own decisions," said Grimes.

"Then, Your Excellency, I will see to it that Peng Yuan, who was valet to your late, revered predecessor, performs the same duties for your honored self."

"I've already told you, Mr. Wong," said Grimes stiffly, "that I like to make my own decisions. I am sure that Miss Su will be quite satisfactory."

"It is not customary, Your Excellency, to use an honorific when addressing or referring to under servants."

Jaconelli and Smith exchanged glances, each permitting himself as much of a sneer as he dared.

Grimes restrained himself from saying that he was the Governor and that he made the rules. It would not do at all to cut the old man down to size in the presence of a subordinate and of the ADC and the secretary. As he knew from experience a wise captain does not unnecessarily antagonize his chief steward.

He looked at his wrist companion, the chronological function of which had been set to local time.

He said, "I think, now, that I'd like to get cleaned up and all the rest of it. What time should I leave the Residence for the Palace, Lieutenant?"

"1900 hours, sir."

"Thank you. And Mr. Jaconelli. . . ."

"Sir?"

"I take it that all of the late Governor Wibberley's papers will be accessible to me? In the office, perhaps. . . ."

"No, sir."

"No? Why not?"

"After the accident all documents were taken by Colonel Bardon. He said he was shipping them back to Earth."

"But there must have been copies."

"Yes, Your Excellency. But. . . ."

"But what?"

"He took them too."

"Why didn't you . . . ?"

"Sir, I am only the Governor's secretary. Until your arrival the Colonel was the senior Terran officer on this planet."

"Mphm." Grimes glared at Smith, who had been listening to the exchange with interest and enjoyment. "You may go, Lieutenant. Be waiting for me in the car at 1900 hours."

"Very good, Your Excellency."

"And Mr. Jaconelli. . . . Please arrange with the Bureau of Meteorology for the release of Captain Raoul Sanchez, the shuttle pilot who brought me down from *Sobraon,* to serve as my atmosphere pilot."

"It was my understanding, Your Excellency, that Colonel Bardon was to second one of his officers to your service."

"Then tell the Colonel that I am making my own arrangements. Oh, and I'd like a crew list."

"A *crew list*?"

"A list of all the Residence staff. Age, sex, birthplace, national and/or planetary origin, qualifications, if any, etc. etc. and etc."

"Very good, Your Excellency. Will that be all?"

"Yes, thank you."

When the ADC and the secretary were gone the majordomo asked, "Will you require my services any further, Your Excellency?"

"No, thank you, Mr. Wong. You may leave. And you, Su Lin."

She objected. "But, Your Excellency, I am your body servant. I am to serve you in all ways."

"It is customary among our people, sir," said Wong Lee. "There is the help to be given to a great man in the removal of his formal attire and the donning of other ceremonial clothing. There is the bringing of refreshment when he so desires it. There is. . . ."

Meanwhile Grimes had succeeded in getting his pipe out of a pocket in his too-tight-fitting trousers and, after another little struggle, his tobacco pouch. He filled the vile brier and was patting his coat pockets in a vain search for a box of the old-fashioned matches that he preferred to other means of ignition.

And then Su Lin was holding a golden lighter, a miniature flame thrower from which issued a jet of incandescence. Grimes hated having his pipe lit for him but submitted to her ministrations. If he refused to submit to other, more intimate ones he would be likely to hurt her feelings. He would just have to see to it that the ministrations were not too intimate. During his Survey Service career he had always despised commanding officers who had engaged in liaisons with their personal stewardesses. (He was, in some ways, a snob; he had never shied away from the occasional affair with female shipmates who held commissioned rank.)

Wong Lee bowed deeply and glided away.

Grimes said to the girl, "Lin—or should it be Su?"

"Whichever pleases Your Excellency."

"All right. Su. Please wait in the sitting room while I get undressed and showered."

"But I am your body servant, Your Excellency."

Already she was helping him out of his tail coat and was loosening the cravat about his neck. He let her go ahead with it. After all, he thought, this was the girl's job, one for which she had been trained. And, he admitted, he liked being pampered, especially by attractive women. Her nimble fingers coped expeditiously with studs and buttons. (Why could not the items of formal dress be secured by sealseams?)

Surprisingly soon he was naked, unembarrassed but determined that things would go no further. He walked to the open door of the bathroom, into the shower cubicle. Before he could put a hand to the controls a slim, bare arm slid past his shoulder and a long, scarlet-nailed finger pushed the WARM button. He felt smooth, soft nudity against his back. He turned to face the girl and said, "I am quite capable of washing myself, Su Lin. Please wait for me in the bedroom." Then, lest the order be misconstrued, he added, "And get dressed."

She stepped away from him and bowed, saying, her voice expressionless, "As Your Excellency pleases."

She turned gracefully and glided away from him; her smoothly working buttocks were like peaches poised on the long, slender (but not too slender) stems of her legs.

Feeling excessively virtuous Grimes continued with his shower. The water temperature was just right. He pushed the DETERGENT button, then the one labeled SCRUBBERS. The soft brushes worked up a scented lather all over his body. He thought that her hands would have made an even better job of it. Although the feeling of virtue persisted he was beginning to feel something of a bloody fool. But one of his own rules, which he was determined not to break, was NEVER PLAY AROUND WITH THE HIRED HELP.

"You stinking snob!" he muttered.

And, talking of stinks, he would have to get the detergent dispenser charged with something less redolent of a whore's garret.

The blowers soon dried him and he returned to the bedroom. The girl was waiting for him, once again respectably attired. Her face, utterly devoid of expression, could have been carved from old ivory. Expertly she helped him into his full evening dress, the archaic white tie and tails, with decorations. When he was fully clad he surveyed himself in the full length mirror of the wardrobe. The effect would have been better, he thought, had he been taller and slimmer, less stocky, but . . . *Not bad,* he thought. *Not bad.* He allowed Su Lin to make the final adjustments to the snowy white butterfly nestling on his Adam's apple.

"Thank you," he told her and walked through to the sitting room.

Lieutenant Smith, in his uniform mess full dress, was waiting for him.

He said, "The car is waiting for us, Your Excellency."

"Thank you," said Grimes.

He followed the ADC to the doorway. Before he could pass through it Su Lin came out of the bedroom carrying his hat, another topper, black this time. Grimes had deliberately forgotten the thing; he took it from her with a brief word of thanks that he hoped she sensed was insincere.

He let Smith pilot him through the labyrinth of corridors.

He thought, *I must tell Jaconelli to get me a chart of this bloody warren.*

Ten

The gubernatorial car was waiting in the portico, the civilian chauffeur, in his livery of faded, frayed denim and red neckerchief, in the front seat and, beside him, two soldiers in khaki uniform. The rear doors of the vehicle opened. Grimes took off his top hat, climbed in. The ADC followed him. Wong Lee and Su Lin bowed deferentially as the Whispering Ghost purred away from the portico.

Grimes tried to make conversation.

"I'm not used to having an ADC," he remarked pleasantly to the Lieutenant.

"ADC, Officer Commanding the Governor's Guard, liaison with the Officer Commanding the Garrison. . . ." The officer's voice was surly. "I hope that you don't think up any other jobs for me, Your Excellency. If ever there was a penny-pinching operation, this is it. I'm surprised that they don't have me doing the cooking. . . ."

"Talking of cooking," said Grimes, hoping to switch the conversation to a topic dear to his heart, "what's the chef like?"

"Oh, all right, I suppose, if you don't mind mucked-up food. He's New Cantonese, of course. Like all the rest of the Residence mob, with the exception of my men and Jaconelli and myself." He laughed. "I'm surprised that they didn't appoint a New Cantonese as Governor. They'd be paying him much less than they're paying you, Your Excellency."

"Mphm." Grimes managed to make it sound like a reprimand. He didn't like and never had liked moaners. "Some people would think that being appointed ADC to a Governor was an honor."

"I . . . I suppose so, Your Excellency."

They sat in silence while the car sped down the winding road toward the city, taking a different route, Grimes noted, from that which had been taken during the journey from the spaceport. The dusk was falling fast but still work was continuing in the fields to either side of the highway. The last of the daylight was caught and reflected by metal implements, by sickles (sickles! in this day and age!) and the blades of hand-wielded hoes. A few of the laborers paused and straightened up to stare at the passing vehicle but most of them took no respite from their back-breaking toil.

Then there were no more fields but, to either side of the wide avenue, there were houses, each in its own garden. All of these buildings were low and rambling, the architectural style vaguely Spanish. Some—but only a few—of the gardens were well-kept; most of them were miniature jungles. The street lights were coming on but not all of them were working.

There was some traffic in the avenue. There was the very occasional solar-electric car. There was a sudden swarm of cyclists, skimming silently through the dusk. Motorized machines, thought Grimes at first, then saw that all the riders' legs were pumping vigorously. Workers, he decided, domestic servants possibly, returning to their compounds outside the city. And there were trishaws, tricycles with the passengers seated forward, flanked by the pair of leading wheels, with the operator on his saddle astern of them, pedaling hard. Most of the passengers were of Caucasian stock—and all the drivers Mongoloid. Grimes grunted disapprovingly. The use of such transport was justified only during periods of energy crisis—and such days were long past on all of man's worlds.

Ahead, now, was the President's Palace, a blaze of illumination, with its profusion of white pillars more Grecian than Spanish. The vast expanse of lawn surrounding the building was like dark green velvet, the drive along which the car made its approach was surfaced with well-raked yellow gravel. A flock of sheep drifted slowly across the headlight beams; the vehicle slowed to a crawl until the animals were past and clear. The driver turned his head to address Grimes.

"What do you think of our lawn mowers, Your Excellency? They're sort of cobbers of yours, Australian Merinos. Their ancestors came out with the First Fleet."

The ADC snapped, "Do not address His Excellency without permission, Garcia."

"Mr. Garcia to you, Mister. And, anyhow, this is *my* world, not yours."

Grimes shoved his oar in, hoping thereby to avert an acrimonious argument. He asked, "And do you have any other Australian animals here, Mr. Garcia?"

"Only yourself, Your Excellency."

Grimes laughed and the ADC growled wordlessly.

"Our beef cattle are Argentine stock," went on the driver, "and our dairy herds are from some little island back on Earth, Jersey. The pigs and the hens? From anywhere and everywhere, I guess."

The sheep were finally past and the car increased speed, passing a huge statue, a bronze giantess whose heroic proportions were revealed rather than hidden by her flowing draperies. She was holding aloft, in her right hand, a flaming torch. Clouds of flying insects—or insectlike creatures—attracted by the fatal lure of the flaring gas were immolating themselves by the thousand.

"I have often wondered," said the driver philosophically, "why the bastards, since they like the light so much, don't come out during the day. . . ."

An interesting problem, thought Grimes.

The vehicle pulled up in the wide portico. Waiting to receive Grimes was Colonel Bardon, in all the splendor of his mess full dress. With him was a group of local dignitaries—heavily bearded men in black velvet suits, in white, floppy-collared shirts with flowing, scarlet neckties, women in low-cut, black velvet dresses with scarlet scarves about their throats.

The ADC got out of the car first and stood to rigid attention. Grimes got out, putting on his hat. He raised it as Bardon saluted with a flourish, raised it again as the male Liberians swept off their own headgear—black, broad-brimmed and with scarlet bands—and as the ladies curtseyed. Then the party, Bardon and Grimes in the lead, passed through the huge double doors, held open by white-liveried servitors (more New Cantonese, thought Grimes) into an anteroom large enough to serve as a hangar for a fair-sized dirigible. The vast expanse of floor was local marble, highly polished, in which the multicolored veins were brightly scintillant. The high walls were covered with crimson, gold-embroidered silk. Overhead the huge electroliers glittered prismatically.

Attentive servants took hats, carried them away somewhere. Others swung open the enormous doors affording admission to the Reception Hall. This had a floor area that would have been ample for the apron of a minor spaceport. The decor was similar to that of the vestibule but on a much greater scale. Awaiting Grimes was the cream of Liberian society, the black-and-scarlet-clad Anarchist grandees and their ladies. At the far end of the vast hall were two platforms, red draped. On the lower but wider dais was a band, drums and gleaming brass. On the higher one Madam President was sitting in state; her chair was not quite a throne and the tiara adorning her glossy, black hair was not quite a crown. Behind her was a huge, gold-framed portrait of a heavily bearded worthy.

"Who's that?" whispered Grimes to Bardon. "Karl Marx?"

"Better not let anybody hear you say that, Your Excellency. That's Bakunin."

"Oh."

The music started. Grimes stiffened to attention, as did Bardon and the ADC. The Liberians also stood, but without rigidity. Nonetheless it was a mark of respect. Many of them sang. Grimes was both surprised and pleased that so many knew the words.

Once a jolly swagman camped by a billabong
Under the shade of a coolibah tree,
And he sang as he watched and waited till his billy boiled,
'Who'll come a-waltzing Matilda with me?'

Grimes wondered if those jumbuks, grazing on the wide lawns outside the Palace, could hear the national song of their long ago and far away homeland. And did they have an ancestral memory of the sheep-stealing swagman, a man who had been far more of an anarchist than these Liberians who attached that label to themselves.

Then it was the turn of the Terran anthem. Hardly anybody knew the words and the tune was not one to stick in the memory.

Sons of Terra, strong and free,
Faring forth through Time and Space,
As far as human eye can see
We run our sacred, fateful race . . .

Grimes wondered which was worse, the words or the music.

Finally Liberia had its innings. Almost everybody sang.

Liberia's sons let us rejoice
For we are strong and free . . .

"Mphm," grunted Grimes. Who was free these days?

We sing our song with heart and voice
In praise of Liberty!
And praise we, too, our homeworld, so free from want and care,
Stronghold of all the freedoms—
Advance, Liberia fair!

There was a final flourish of drums, then relative silence.

Bardon said, "And now, Your Excellency, I have to present you to Madam President."

"Lead on, MacDuff," said Grimes. He knew that he had misquoted but did not think that the Colonel would be aware of this.

"The name is Bardon, Your Excellency. Colonel Bardon."

The black and scarlet crowd parted like the Red Sea before the Israelites, opening clear passage toward the presidential dais along which Grimes, Bardon and the ADC marched, their heels ringing on the marble floor, keeping time to the rhythmic mutter of a single drum. The new Governor was acutely conscious that he was being observed, that he was being curiously regarded by all these bearded men and handsome women. (There may have been some ladies who could not be so categorized but he did not notice any.) He saw that Estrelita O'Higgins had risen from her thronelike chair, was making a stately descent of the short flight of red-carpeted stairs. If only she were holding a torch, thought Grimes, she would look just like one of those statues of Miss Liberty.

She stood there, at the foot of the stairs, waiting for him.

And who bowed to whom? Grimes wondered. Why had he not made a proper study of the protocol for such occasions? She was the (allegedly) elected ruler of a planet—but he was the appointed viceroy of Imperial Earth. Would she extend a gracious hand for him to kiss? At the spaceport they had bowed to each other, practically simultaneously, but this was the official reception, the state occasion.

She knew the drill (surely for this planet only!) even if he did not. She extended her long, smooth, pale arms and flung them around him, engulfing him in a powerful embrace. She must have been eating something with garlic in it, thought Grimes. But he returned her hearty kiss.

She released him, turning him around so that they were both facing the people.

"Comrades!" she cried in her deep contralto. "Comrades! I present to you our new Governor, John Grimes. The Federation, this time, has made a wise choice. John Grimes is a man of action. John Grimes is a man of the world, of many worlds, who knows that each and every planet has its own character. He knows that we, here on Liberia, have our own character. He knows that we have opened our world and our hearts to the poor, the distressed and the oppressed of many planets. There are people here, our guests, who, were it not for us, would be living lives of deepest misery—or who would not be living at all.

"Governor John Grimes, I am sure, will appreciate what we have done, what we are doing.

"I ask you, comrades, to welcome John Grimes and to take him to your hearts, just as you have taken so very many less fortunate outworlders."

A New Cantonese servant was bowing before them, extending a golden tray upon which were three tall goblets, each filled with a red wine. The President and the Colonel waited until Grimes had taken his before picking up theirs. Other servants had circulated through the hall. Soon everybody was holding a charged glass.

"Viva Grimes!" cried Estrelita O'Higgins, raising her goblet. (She was more than ever like those statues.)

"Viva Grimes!" sounded loudly from the body of the hall. "Viva Grimes!"

And everybody has had a drink but me, thought Grimes wryly.

He waited until the toast had been drunk, then made his own.

"Long live Liberty!"

He was probably more sincere, he hoped, than those who, so noisily, had drunk to his health.

The wine wasn't bad, although a mite too sweet.

Eleven

Guided by Estrelita O'Higgins, accompanied by Colonel Bardon, Grimes made the rounds of the great reception hall. The ADC trailed behind for a while, then lost himself in the crowd. The new Governor was introduced to the people who—in theory—were now his subjects. He made and listened to small talk. Now and again he was able to initiate a discussion on more serious matters. He sampled snacks from the buffet tables and enjoyed the savory, highly-spiced morsels. An attentive servant continually replenished his glass, even after only a couple of sips. On any other world but this, Grimes thought, a Governor would remain in one place and the people would be brought to meet him. Possibly this Liberian way of doing things was better. At least the newly installed dignitary did not go hungry or thirsty.

He met ministers of state and media personalities. He fended off searching questions about his recent experiences as a commodore of privateers. He asked questions himself, some of which were answered frankly while others were not. Politicians, he thought, were much of a muchness no matter what labels they had attached to themselves.

His conversation with Eduardo Lopez, Minister of Immigration, was interesting.

"You must realize, Your Excellency, that I have little choice regarding the ethnicity of our immigrants. To deny any distressed person or persons sanctuary on racial grounds would be altogether contrary to our . . . constitution? Yes. Constitution. . . ."

"I thought," said Grimes, "that a society founded on the principles of Anarchism wasn't supposed to have such a thing."

"Contrary to our principles," said the President firmly.

"You are right as always, Estrelita," said the fat politician gallantly. "Principles. Of course, if I received a request for permission to enter from, say, an El Doradan, a representative of a society notorious for its devotion to capitalism, I should be obliged to refuse. But the poor, distressed and homeless, of whatever race or color, I must welcome with open arms."

"*We* must welcome," said the President.

"As I was saying—we must welcome."

"And can these immigrants become full citizens?" asked Grimes, although he already knew the answer to that question.

"Of course, provided that they show proof that they are fit and proper persons to become Liberians."

Grimes looked around him. Apart from the servants all those present seemed to be of Terran Anglo-Saxon or Latin stock. There were no Orientals, no Negroes.

"Have any outworlders yet achieved citizenship?" he asked.

"Er . . . no. You see, Your Excellency, the major qualification is freedom. As long as a person is in debt to the State he is not free. Once he has earned enough money to repay the debt he is free . . ."

"Debt?" asked Grimes.

"Resettlement is a costly business, Your Excellency, as you as a shipowner must know. Transportation between worlds . . ."

"The responsibility, I understand, of the Federation."

"Even so, there are costs, heavy costs. People come here. They must be fed, housed, found employment. . . ."

"Employment," echoed Grimes. "Menial work. Manual labor, for not very high wages. . . ."

"And would you pay a field hand, Your Excellency, the salary that you, highly trained and qualified, would expect as a shipmaster?"

"The laborer, in any field, is worthy of his hire," said the President.

Her hand firmly on Grimes's elbow she steered him away from Lopez, toward the flamboyantly red-haired Kitty O'Halloran, Director of TriVi Liberia. She was a large woman, fat rather than plump, and she gushed.

"Your Excellency. Commodore. I'm dying to get you on to one of our programs. Just an interview, but in *depth.* Just the story, told by yourself, of some of your *outrageous* adventures. . . ."

"Outrageous?" parried Grimes. "I'm a respectable Governor."

"But you weren't always. You've been a pirate. . . ."

"A privateer," he corrected her.

"Who knows the difference?" She tittered. "From what I've heard, you didn't know yourself. . . ."

Again there was the guiding pressure on his elbow. This time he was to meet Luigi Venito, Minister of Interstellar Trade, a tall, distinguished man with steely gray hair and—unusual in this company—a neatly trimmed beard.

"I thought, Your Excellency," said Venito, "that I might one day deal with you in your capacity as a shipowner. To meet you as a Governor is an unexpected pleasure."

"Bad pennies," said Grimes, "turn up in the most unexpected places."

"Ha ha. But I refuse to believe that the Terran World Assembly would appoint a bad penny to a highly responsible position."

"You'd be surprised," said Grimes. "And, in any case, governments are rarely as moral as those whom they govern." *(There are times,* he thought, *when I feel that I should have a Boswell, recorder in hand, tagging after me . . .)* "I hope that your government is an exception to the rule."

Venito chuckled. "Some say that we shouldn't have a government at all, not on this world. But after the first few years our founding fathers—and mothers, of course, Madam President—were obliged to admit that pure Anarchism doesn't work. A state of anarchy is not Anarchism. But we *are* free, unregimented, doing the things that we want to do as long as we do not infringe upon the rights of our fellow citizens. From each according to his ability, to each according to his needs. My own ability is trade, buying in the cheapest markets, selling in the dearest. All for the greatest good, naturally, of Liberia . . ."

He had been drinking, of course, not too much, perhaps, but enough to loosen his tongue. Grimes ignored the President's attempt to push him along to another group. There was one point that he wanted to clear up, a matter that had not been fully dealt with in the data that he had been given to study on the voyage out from Earth.

He said, "You must have made some interesting deals in your time. . . . Agricultural machinery, for example. . . ."

Venito laughed. "Yes. That *was* a good deal! The new colony on Halvan—and the ship carrying all their robot harvesters and the like months overdue! She's listed as missing, presumed lost, at Lloyd's. I think that the presumption still holds—but that's not important. . . ."

Only to the crew, thought Grimes, *and their relatives.*

"And we had still more refugees coming in and so I said to Lopez, 'Put these people to work in the fields—and I'll flog all our agricultural machinery at better-than-new prices!' And I did just that."

"Clever," said Grimes. "Ill winds, and all that. But it wouldn't have been so good for Liberia if you didn't have the indentured labor system, if your field workers were being paid decent wages."

"What is a decent wage, Your Excellency? Enough to buy the necessities of life—food, shelter, clothing—with a little left over for the occasional luxury. That's a decent wage. On this world nobody goes cold or hungry. What more do you want?"

"The freedom to change your job when you feel like it, for a start."

"But all our citizens enjoy that freedom."

"Yes. All your *citizens,* Minister."

"Citizenship has to be earned, Your Excellency."

The President not only had her hand firmly on his elbow; she pinched him quite painfully. He took the hint and allowed her to conduct him to a meeting with the Minister for Culture and the lady with him, the Chief Librarian of Liberia.

They knew his background, of course, and, talking down from their intellectual eminence, made it plain that they held spacemen in low esteem.

Twelve

The reception was over.

The President and Colonel Bardon, very much like husband and wife getting rid of the guests after a party and looking forward to holding a post mortem on the night's doings as soon as they were in bed, escorted Grimes out to the waiting car, which was at the head of the queue of vehicles. Most of these were trishaws.

The ADC was there, with the two soldiers. All three of them made a creditable attempt at standing to attention. Grimes wondered briefly how the two enlisted men had spent their evening; obviously they had found congenial company somewhere. He knew how the ADC had passed the time; that officer had been mainly in the company of two not unattractive girls who seemed to have monopolized the services of one of the wine waiters. Surely ADCs, Grimes had thought disapprovingly, should always be at the beck and call of their lords and masters. But this was Liberia where all animals—unless they had the misfortune to be refugees—were equal. (But surely a Governor was more equal than the others.)

"Good night, Your Excellency."

"Good night, Madam President." Grimes clasped her extended hand. "Thank you for the party."

"It was a pleasure having you."

"Good night, Your Excellency."

"Good night, Colonel."

Grimes removed his tall hat before climbing into the passenger compartment of the car. The driver turned his head to regard him sardonically.

"Feeling no pain, Gov?" he asked. (He, too, must have spent a convivial evening.)

When in Rome . . . thought Grimes resignedly. He said, "I'll survive."

"More than your predecessor did . . ." muttered the chauffeur.

The ADC and the soldiers embarked. The doors slid shut. The car drove away.

* * *

Grimes drowsed most of the way back to the Residence.

Wong Lee was waiting there to receive him and so, in his suite, was Su Lin. As though by magic the girl produced a pot of fragrant tea, brought it to him on a lacquer tray as he went into his office and sat down at the desk. He sipped from the cup that she poured for him; the steaming liquid cleared his head. The old man and the girl watched impassively as he opened the first of the folders that Jaconelli had laid out for him.

This contained the information on the Terran staff of the Residence.

Jaconelli, Grimes read, had been born in Chicago. His solitary qualification was Bachelor of Commerce, the minimal requirement for any secretarial post. Surely a Governor, thought Grimes, should be entitled to at least a Master to handle his correspondence and affairs.

Harrison Smith, the ADC, was another Bachelor—of Military Arts. He was a graduate of West Point. His birthplace was Denver. His Terran Army career had been undistinguished; he had not played a part, however minor, in even a police action or a brush-fire war.

The Sergeant of the Governor's Guard, Martello, was another American. Although seven years older than his officer he, too, had been lucky enough to avoid action during his Army service.

The privates were a mixed bunch—one New Zealander, three Poms, a Swede and an Israeli. That all of them had reached early middle age without attaining noncommissioned rank did not say much for them.

The New Cantonese file was a thicker one—but only because there were more names in it. Wong Lee had the biggest entry.

The majordomo was old, even older than his appearance and manner had led Grimes to believe. He had actually been born on New Canton, where his parents had been the owners of the Heavenly Peace Hotel and the Jade Dragon Restaurant. As had been the custom of his people he had commenced his training in hotel and restaurant management at a very early age. In spite of his refugee status he had easily obtained such employment on Liberia although he was never allowed to become the owner of his own establishment. He had applied for the post of majordomo to the Governor when the first of such appointments was made by Earth. He had got the job and for many years had kept it.

All the others had been born on Liberia, some of mixed parentage. Among these was Su Lin, with a New Cantonese father and an Irandan mother. And young enough, thought Grimes, to be his own daughter. He looked up at her from the typed pages. She looked back at him and smiled. He frowned back at her.

Finally he got to the transcript of the telephone conversation that Jaconelli had had with the Bureau of Meteorology. The Secretary, pulling rank as the Governor's personal representative, had received an assurance from one of the Deputy Directors (*the* Director had been among those at the reception) that Captain Raoul Sanchez would be released at once from his normal duties and instructed to report at the Residence at 0900 hours tomorrow morning. *Tomorrow* morning? Grimes looked up at the wall clock. *This* morning.

He said, "Thank you, Mr. Wong. Thank you, Su Lin. I shall not be needing you any more tonight. Please see that I am called promptly at 0700 hours."

The old man bowed deeply and then glided out of the office. The girl remained.

Grimes said again, "Thank you, Su Lin. Please call me at 0700 hours."

She said, "But you have yet to retire, Your Excellency. And my duties are to attend you at all times."

"I am capable of putting myself to bed," Grimes told her.

"But, Your Excellency, I have been trained . . ."

"And so have I, from earliest childhood—to undress myself and even to fold and hang my clothes properly."

She laughed at this and it made her even more attractive. If Grimes had not been so well looked after on the voyage out from Earth he might well have yielded to temptation.

"Good night," he said firmly.

"Good night, Your Excellency," she said softly.

A little later, wrestling with the fastenings of his archaic finery, he regretted not having retained her services if only to help him undress.

Thirteen

She called him at seven, placing the tea tray down on the bedside table with a musical clatter and then whispering softly into his ear, "It is morning, Your Excellency. It is morning."

Grimes ungummed his eyes and looked up at her. There must be, he admitted, far worse sights with which to start the day. She smiled at him and poured tea from the pot with its willow pattern decoration into a handleless cup on which was the same design. As soon as he had struggled into a sitting posture, propped by the plump pillows that she had arranged for him, she handed him the cup. He handed it back to her. When he first awoke it was not a drink that he needed but the reverse. With some embarrassment—normally he slept naked—he got out of the bed on the side away from her and padded through to the bathroom. The pressure on his bladder relieved, he returned to his bed and slid the lower portion of his body under the covers. This time he accepted the cup and sipped from it gratefully. He saw that she had brought his pipe from where he had left it in the office and had filled it. She put one end of the stem into her mouth, applied flame to the bowl from a small, golden lighter that she brought from the side pocket of her tunic. When it was drawing properly she handed it to him.

Even an Admiral, thought Grimes smugly, *wouldn't be getting service like this . . .* He wondered if he, as a Planetary Governor, outranked an Admiral. *De jure,* possibly, if not *de facto.*

He sipped and smoked, smoked and sipped.

She asked, "What does Your Excellency desire for breakfast?"

"What's on the menu?" Grimes asked.

"Whatever Your Excellency wishes," she said.

A roll in bed with honey, he thought. Then, *Down, boy, down!*

He said, after consideration, "Grapefruit, please. Then two eggs, sunny side up, with bacon and country fried potatoes. Hot rolls. Butter. Lemon marmalade. Coffee. . . ."

"At once, Your Excellency?"

"No, thank you. I always like to shower and depilate and all the rest of it first. And dress. . . ."

"What will Your Excellency wear this morning?"

And just what was a Governor's undress uniform?

"I leave it to you. Something informal, or relatively so. . . ."

He put the almost empty cup down on to the tray with a decisive clatter, declined the offer of a refill. When she removed the tea things, carrying the tray through to the sitting room, he got out of bed. There was an old-fashioned bolt on the door to the toilet facilities, he shot it. He completed his morning ablutions, depilation and all the rest of it without interruption. On returning to the bedroom he found that the bed had been made and that clothing had been laid out on it—underwear, a ruffled shirt of orange silk, dark gray, sharply creased slacks. Highly polished, gold-buckled shoes stood by the couch.

He dressed and went through to where a low table had been set with crockery and cutlery, a covered dish of hot rolls, a butter dish and another with the marmalade. There was a pot of coffee, a bowl of sugar crystals and a jug of cream. A prepared half grapefruit awaited his attention, as did that morning's issue of *The Liberty Star.* He sat down, propped the newspaper against the coffee pot and made a start on the grapefruit. He read the account of Madam President's reception for the new Governor the previous evening. He was amused to see himself referred to as "an officer who achieved great distinction whilst in the Federation Survey Service" and as "a successful shipowner who has put his great administrative and business talents at the disposal of both his home planet and of Liberia." The piece on Grimes concluded with the pious hope that he, as an experienced captain both of spaceships and of industry, would not feel the urge, as had his predecessor, to meddle officiously in the smooth running of the world that he had been called upon to govern.

The attentive Su Lin—he had not noticed her return—removed the plate with the now empty grapefruit shell, replaced it with that occupied by his eggs and bacon. She asked him how he preferred his coffee. He told her that he liked it black. He held the paper in both hands as she poured.

The eggs, bacon and fried potatoes were just as he liked them. The rolls were crisp. The marmalade, when finally he got to it, was deliciously tangy. By this time he had turned to the INTERSTELLAR SHIPPING—ARRIVALS AND DEPARTURES columns. *Sobraon*'s arrival and departure were listed as *Orbital Only. Willy Willy,* with the obnoxious Dreeble commanding, had lifted off, with passengers for Isa—a world rich in metals, Grimes knew, with mining and smelting as the major industries—while the Governor had been enjoying himself at the reception. One did not need to be clairvoyant, he thought, to know what sex those passengers belonged to or for what employment they had been recruited. *Bulkalgol* and *Bulkvega* were due out very shortly, with grain, one for Waverley and the other for Caribbea. After that it looked like being a slack time, for some weeks, at Port Libertad. One name among the *Future Arrivals* caught Grimes's attention—*Agatha's Ark*. He remembered that old flash of prevision he had experienced while *Sobraon*'s temporal precession field had been building up.

He filled his pipe, brought the stem to his mouth. Before he could strike a match Su Lin was holding the flame from a golden lighter over the charred bowl. Grimes hated having his pipe lit for him but submitted to the attention. He did not mind, however, having another cup of the excellent coffee poured for him.

The Liberty Star, he discovered ran to a daily crossword puzzle. He got up from the breakfast table and sat down in one of the easy chairs. Without being asked the girl brought him a slim, golden stylus from the office. But the puzzle was not to his taste; it was not of the cryptic variety. Furthermore it required of the would-be solver an encyclopedic knowledge of Terran political history—names, dates and all. And that, thought Grimes, was not a subject in which he would ever be awarded full Marx. He savored the pun, knocked out his pipe in a convenient ashtray (it had been burning unevenly), refilled it and, Su Lin being temporarily absent, clearing away the breakfast things, lit it properly himself.

He got up and, trailing an acrid rather than an aromatic cloud of blue smoke, wandered out into the corridor and, to his pleased surprise, found his way to the main doorway of the Residence without too much trouble. Servants bowed to him as he passed, the guard on duty at the entrance to the building saluted smartly.

It was pleasant outside, the morning sun warm but not too much so, the light breeze carrying the scent of the gaudy flowers from the big, ornamental beds. The closely cropped grass of the lawn was springy under the soles of his shoes. Su Lin joined him, walking respectfully to his left and half a pace to the rear. He was conscious of her presence and found himself wishing that their relationship was not one of master and servant.

She broke the silence.

"Your Excellency," she said, "someone approaches from the air."

"Thank you," said Grimes. He had already heard a distant clatter, looked up and seen a dark speck in the sky. He stopped walking and stared at it. Su Lin produced from a pocket a thin, round case, about twenty millimeters in diameter. She did something to it and it opened out into a tapered tube. She removed the covers from each end, handed it to Grimes. He realized that it was a telescope, a sophisticated instrument with a universal focus. He raised it to his right eye, managed to bring the approaching aircraft into the field of it. It was a minicopter, little more than a bubble-enclosed chair with two long skids under it as landing gear and over it the almost invisible rotating vanes.

Grimes recognized the pilot. It was Raoul Sanchez. He raised his free hand to wave. The young pilot returned the salutation, altered course slightly so as to come into a landing close to where Grimes and the girl were standing. Almost immediately the little aircraft was surrounded by a small crowd of indignant gardeners, gesticulating and shouting in high-pitched voices, pointing at the barely visible scars that the landing gear of the minicopter had made on the surface of the lawn. Sanchez grinned and shrugged apologetically. A door slid open in the surface of the transparent bubble.

"Better keep off the grass, Captain," said Grimes. "You'd better shift to the drive before we have a riot on our hands."

"Willco, Your Excellency."

The gardeners scrambled back as the vanes started to spin again. The machine lifted, drifted slowly over to the broad drive, settled down again, the skids crunching audibly on the gravel. By the time that Grimes had walked to it Sanchez had unstrapped himself from the chair and disembarked. He was wearing a suit of faded, deliberately frayed denim and a red neckerchief. He bowed formally to Grimes.

He said, "Your aerial chauffeur, Your Excellency, reporting for duty."

Lieutenant Smith who, accompanied by two soldiers, had come on to the scene achieved an expression that was both sneer and scowl.

Fourteen

Sanchez led the way around the sprawling Residence to what was almost a minor airport. He had been there before, of course, while his brother had been atmosphere pilot to the late Governor Wibberley. There were hangars—two of them occupied and the third, the very big one, empty. Outside this, at a suitable distance, was a tripedal mooring mast.

Smith said, with a gesture toward this construction, "Your airship will be delivered this afternoon, Your Excellency. One of the Army's Lutz-Parsivals. Colonel Bardon has appointed Lieutenant Duggin to be your pilot."

Before Sanchez could protest Grimes said, "I have made my own appointment, Lieutenant. Captain Sanchez will be flying me."

"But the Colonel . . ."

"Is not the Governor. *I* am."

"But Captain Sanchez is a spaceman . . ."

"And a qualified airshipman. Is that not so, Captain?"

"It is, Your Excellency," replied Sanchez as Smith said nastily, "So was his brother."

"That will do, Lieutenant Smith!" snapped Grimes while making a *Pipe down!* gesture aimed at the other man. "That will do. Captain Sanchez is my pilot. And now, Captain, shall we look at what toys we shall have to play with?"

He walked to one of the occupied hangars, into it. The craft housed therein was a small pinnace of a type carried by the larger warships of the Survey Service, a spaceship in miniature. That, thought Grimes, he could fly himself—although legally he couldn't, his Master Astronaut's Certificate having been suspended. (Of course there was his Reserve Commission but that was supposed to be kept a secret.) Sanchez opened a door in the pinnace's side, into the litle airlock. Grimes clambered on board, followed by Sanchez and Smith. He went forward first, to the control cab. With two exceptions the instrumentation on the console seemed to be in order. Certain switches, dials and screens had been removed and replaced by blank cover plates.

"No Mini-Mannschenn?" asked Grimes. "No Carlotti deep space radio?"

"They were removed, Your Excellency," said Smith, "when Colonel Bardon had this pinnace modified for the Governor's use."

"Modified *how*?" demanded Grimes.

"The space occupied by that equipment was required for the bar and for . . . for . . ."

"Mphm," grunted Grimes. He asked suddenly, "Does the Residence run to its own Carlotti transceiver?" (That was one of the many things, he thought, that he should have found out long before he arrived on Liberia.)

"No, Your Excellency," said Smith. "Surely you must have noticed that there are no Carlotti antennae on the roof."

"They could be in the cellar," said Grimes, "and work just as well."

Smith made a show of ignoring this and continued, "The only Carlotti equipment is at the spaceport. It is manned and maintained, of course, by Terran personnel."

And so the Governor, thought Grimes, *can communicate directly with Earth only by courtesy of the Garrison Commander.*

He completed his inspection of the pinnace. He was not overly impressed. He could not refrain from using his memories of *Little Sister* as a yardstick. When he made his way out through the airlock Su Lin was there to help him down to the ground. He waved her aside irritably and then, when he saw her hurt expression, rather hated himself.

He said, "It's all right, Su. I'm a spaceman. I'm used to getting into and out of these things."

With the others he made his way into the other hangar in use. The aircraft there was a helicopter, a rather beat-up Drachenflieger, no doubt one of Bardon's cast-offs. Sanchez looked at the machine disparagingly.

"Governor Wibberley," he said, "never used this. My brother reckoned that it wasn't safe."

"And he, of course," said Smith, "was an expert on aeronautical safety."

"You . . ." the pilot growled, his fist raised threateningly.

"Lieutenant Smith," snapped Grimes, putting a control room crackle into his voice, "you will refrain from making provocative remarks." Then, his voice a little milder, "Captain Sanchez, I will not tolerate brawling among the members of my . . . family. And now, will you take luncheon with me?"

"Thank you, Your Excellency."

"And will you, Lieutenant Smith, please inform us when the airship is approaching?"

"Very good, Your Excellency."

The party walked back to the main entrance to the building, Sanchez beside Grimes, Su Lin the usual half pace to the rear and Smith, sulking hard, well astern.

* * *

It was a leisurely and pleasant meal, with drinks before, served by the attentive Su Lin. The honeyed sand crawlers were especially good, reminding Grimes of the honeyed prawns that he had enjoyed in Chinese restaurants on Earth. With the meal there was rice wine, served warm in tiny cups. When it was over Grimes lit his pipe—waiting until the girl was out of the room—and Sanchez a slim, black cigar.

The pilot said, "I must apologize for having lost my temper with your ADC, Excellency."

"He asked for it," said Grimes. "I've been considering asking Colonel Bardon for a replacement, but . . ."

"Better the devil you know, sir."

"Precisely. You must have seen him, now and again, when you visited your brother here."

"Yes. I never did like him. He didn't like me. And my brother hated him. It was mutual."

"He's Bardon's man, of course."

"Of course," agreed Sanchez.

Su Lin returned with coffee.

"Is it switched on, Su?" asked the pilot.

"Yes, Raoul," she replied.

Grimes stared at them.

"Is *what* switched on?" he demanded.

"A device that I carry," she replied. "A—how shall I call it? A conversation modifier. It takes our voices and—scrambles? shuffles? To any listener you are telling Raoul about some of your deep space adventures and he is asking questions about them."

"And what are you saying?"

"I am urging Your Excellency to take at least one of these *chinrin* cakes with your coffee. *Chinrin* cakes, of course, were a great delicacy on New Canton. The refugees brought *chinrin* seeds with them when they came here and now we have our own little plantations of the shrubs."

"This modifier," asked Grimes curiously. "Does it have to be programmed?"

"Only in the most general of terms. It could almost be said to be intelligent. Perhaps it functions psionically. It could be a form of pseudolife but that I cannot say. I am not a scientist."

"Could I see it?" asked Grimes curiously.

To his surprise she blushed embarrassedly.

"When Su Lin said that she carried the modifier," explained Sanchez, "she didn't mean that she carried it *on* her . . ."

"An implant?" asked Grimes.

"Yes, sir. But not a *surgical* implant. If you know what I mean."

"Oh. So am I to understand that as long as she's around, and along as she has *it* switched on, the bugs with which the Residence must be crawling will be sending absolutely fictitious reports to Bardon's monitors. I suppose that the bugs *are* Bardon's?"

"Of course, sir," said Sanchez.

"Mphm." He turned to Su Lin. "So you're rather more than my faithful handmaiden, it seems—just as Wong Lee is rather more than my faithful majordomo. But this . . . this *thing* of yours . . . where did you get it?"

It was Sanchez who answered.

"Shortly after the late Governor Wibberley's so-called accident there was a salesman here from Electra—not that he called himself a salesman. Trade Representative was his title. He was wined and dined by Estrelita but didn't make any sales. He was allowed to wander around without supervision—after all, what harm could a woolly-witted scientist-engineer do? He enjoyed a liaison with one of our girls, an OAP member." He grinned. "She put the hard sell onto him and made a convert. Probably only a temporary one but still a convert. She told him about our problems and of the way in which the Governor, who had been taking too much interest in the state of affairs here, had been eliminated. . . ."

"Tanya Mendoza is a friend of mine," said Su Lin. "She came to visit me here. It was quite natural that she should bring her Electran friend with her and quite natural that I should show him around the Residence. He had a detector with him—although as far as Smith and Jaconelli were concerned he had nothing on him but the usual camera and recorder carried by tourists. He confirmed our suspicions that—as you have said—the Residence is crawling with bugs. He promised Tanya that he would do something about it, something that would not be obvious to the . . . the . . . buggers. Is there such a word?"

"There is," said Grimes, "although its real meaning is not the one that you have given it."

Looking at her face he saw that she was making some sort of physical effort. He was about to ask what was wrong when Sanchez said. "Very interesting, Your Excellency. Very interesting. . . ."

Then, from behind him, Smith said, "Your Excellency, the airship is approaching now."

So the device had been switched off, Grimes realized. So all conversation from now on was being faithfully and truthfully recorded.

He turned to face his ADC.

"We'll be right out," he said.

Fifteen

The Lutz-Parsival came in slowly and cautiously.

She was a graceful ship despite her chubbiness, her metal skin gleaming brightly in the sunlight. On her tail fins was painted the insignia of Bardon's regiment, a rampant golden lion. He would have to get that changed, thought Grimes. To a kangaroo? Why not?

"He's handling her like a cow handling a musket," muttered Sanchez disgustedly.

Grimes was inclined to agree. The approach was overly careful and then, in the final stages, clumsy. The ship dropped too fast as the helium in the gas cells was compressed and then lifted steeply as water ballast was dumped to compensate, drenching the gubernatorial party.

"If this," said Grimes furiously to Smith, "is a fair sample of the Army's airmanship it's just as well that I've appointed my own pilot!"

"Your Excellency," replied the ADC, "Lieutenant Duggin is a little rusty. . . ."

"If we were made of metal," said Grimes, "we'd be getting rusty!"

With his hand he wiped the water from his face. He would have liked to take his shirt off to wring it out.

"Your Excellency," said Su Lin, "you must go back inside to change into dry clothing."

"It doesn't matter, Su. I'll soon dry out. I want to see what other comic turns that clown up there is going to put on for us.

The airship circled slowly, once again losing altitude. This time her descent could be measured in millimeter/seconds. It was a long and painful process. By the time that the dangling lines had been picked up by the ground party—soldiers of the Governor's Guard supplemented by New Cantonese gardeners—Grimes's clothing was merely damp. And then the pilot did not use his engines for the final approach to the mast but was towed into position by the mooring crew. At last the nose cone was secure in the socket. A ladder was lowered from the control gondola and down it scrambled the plump figure of the pilot, handling himself as clumsily as he had handled the ship. He shambled rather than marched to where Grimes was standing and threw a casual salute in his direction.

"Lieutenant Duggin, Your Excellency. Reporting for duty."

"Lieutenant Duggin, you are relieved from duty," Grimes told him. "Lieutenant Smith will make arrangements for your transport back to barracks."

"But I'm your pilot, sir."

"You are not. But if ever I require a bath attendant I'll send for you."

"But, sir. . . ."

"That is all, Lieutenant. Captain Sanchez, do you wish Lieutenant Duggin to make a formal hand over?"

"It would be advisable, Your Excellency."

"Very well, Captain. See to it, will you?"

He stood with Su Lin and Smith watching as the two pilots walked to the dangling ladder and mounted it. As it took their weight the airship sagged down from the mast and then resumed her horizontal attitude. No further ballast was dumped; no doubt there was an automatic release of pressure from the atmospheric trimming cell or cells.

"Wait here, Mr. Smith, to look after Mr. Duggin after he's handed over," Grimes told the ADC.

He walked with Su Lin back to his quarters in the Residence.

She brought him tea. He sent her away to get another cup so that she could join him in the taking of refreshment.

He asked, "Are you switched on?"

She said, "Yes, Your Excellency."

"And what are we talking about?"

"I am telling you about the New Cantonese festivals that we still observe on this world."

"Fireworks, processions of lanterns and dragons and all that?"

"Yes, Your Excellency."

"I hope to see at least one of your festivals."

"You will be an honored guest."

"Thank you, Su." He sipped from his cup. "Now you can tell me about the underground. What do you do, what do you hope to accomplish?"

"As far as we, and the other refugees, are concerned we want full citizenship. As far as Captain Sanchez and the OAP are concerned they want a return to the egalitarian principles of the original colonists of the planet. All of us are against the regime of Estrelita O'Higgins and Colonel Bardon and the vicious trades that they foster."

"Such as?"

"The shipping of girls—yes, and boys—to the brothels of various worlds where there is a demand for them, such as Isa and Venusberg. The pleasure houses—so-called—on this planet. The drug trade. And the profiteering in all the stores at which the refugees must purchase the essentials of life to ensure that nobody can possibly save enough money to become financially independent."

"So you want a revolution."

"Yes. Not necessarily an armed revolt, although it might have to come that." (And was this, wondered Grimes, his solicitous handmaiden with her limited but courtly English? She was reminding him more and more of a girl he had once known who had been President of the University of Kandral's Young Socialist Club and who had finished up as Vice President of the planet.) "We realize that once we take up arms against O'Higgins we shall also be taking up arms against Earth, against the Federation, as represented here by Bardon. If it is at all possible the change must be made by constitutional methods. The Governor is more than a mere figurehead. He has . . . How shall I put it? He has the power to hire and fire."

"Mphm?" Grimes knocked out and refilled his pipe. Su Lin reverted to her serving maid persona and lit it for him. He thought, I *shall have to try to break her of* that *habit.* "Mphm?"

"Governor Wibberley was conducting his own investigation of the state of affairs here. He had amassed considerable evidence of malpractices. He was almost ready to act. And then. . . ."

"So you want me, as Governor, to sack Colonel Bardon *and* President O'Higgins *and* all her ministers. . . ."

She said, "There have been precedents. There was one, in *your* country, on Earth, many years ago."

He said, "There's more than one Australian precedent. The Governor General, Sir John Kerr, sacked Prime Minister Gough Whitlam. Some years previously the Governor of New South Wales, Sir Philip Game, sacked Premier Jack Lang. . . ."

"You see."

He went on. "And many years before that the garrison in New South Wales deposed the Governor, Captain—as he was then—William Bligh."

"And wasn't Bligh," she asked, "the man who was always having mutinies? You've had a few yourself, haven't you?"

"Which doesn't mean that I like having them, Su."

She laughed. "I suppose not. But there must be ways of doing things constitutionally. And to do them without calling Earth first for approval—always supposing that Bardon let you get a message through."

"Messages did get through, after Wibberley's death," said Grimes. "That's why I'm here."

"As trouble shooter?" she asked. "Or as shit stirrer? In any case, Bardon's made sure that no more messages get through without his knowledge."

"Just who—or what—are you, Su Lin?" he asked.

"You have seen my dossier, Your Excellency."

"For what it's worth."

"There *is* a Su Lin," she told him. "But she is not on Liberia any longer. She was carefully selected out of all the New Cantonese as being almost my double. I required only minor body sculpture to make me her replica."

"Then what is your real name?"

"It doesn't matter. I rather like Su Lin, anyhow."

"Where are you from? You aren't from FIA, are you? Or are you? If you are I should have been told."

"I am not."

"The Sinkiang People's Republic?"

"No. The New Cantonese here are no worse off than they would be on New Sinkiang."

"Then where?"

There was a knock on the door. Grimes saw Su Lin's face go briefly tense as her vaginal muscles switched off the device that she carried.

Sanchez entered.

"I have taken delivery of the Lutz-Parsival, Your Excellency," he reported formally. "She seems to be airworthy in all respects, although I shall have to make a more detailed inspection later." (*To look for hidden bombs,* thought Grimes.) "I have left her at the mast, in the sunlight, to recharge the power cells."

"I think that I'd like to have a sniff round aboard her myself," said Grimes, "if you will be so good as to accompany me."

"Of course, Your Excellency," said Sanchez.

Sixteen

"We shall have to give her a name," said Grimes to Sanchez as he and the pilot made their way along the catwalk running from stem to stern inside the airship. "LPI7 is too . . . impersonal. Ships are more than just . . . *things.*"

"What do you have in mind, Your Excellency?"

Grimes thought hard. There had been quite a few ships for which he had felt a real affection. most recently *Little Sister* and *Sister Sue.* He grinned.

"Fat Susie," he said. "She is rather plump, isn't she? I'll tell Mr. Jaconelli to organize painters for you to put the new name on the envelope. And at the same time they can change the insignia on the tail fins. I want a kangaroo instead of that tomcat of Bardon's."

"People might think," said Sanchez, "that you're naming the ship after Su Lin."

"She's not fat," Grimes told him. "But there was a fat Susie, not so very long ago."

(He wondered where she was now, how she was faring.)

He inspected the comfortable lounge with its wide out-and-down looking windows on either side, the not-too-Spartan sleeping accommodation, the little galley with a standard autochef. This, if he was going to make much use of *Fat Susie,* would have to be modified to his requirements. He spent some time in the control cab, familiarizing himself with the instrumentation. It would not take him long, he thought, to learn how to fly this thing.

"She'll do," he said at last.

He was first down the ladder with Sanchez not far behind him. As he dropped to the ground he heard the air pump start up to pressurize the helium in one of the cells to compensate for the loss of weight.

Sanchez, who would now be living in the Residence, dined with him that evening, the two men taking their meal in Grimes's sitting room. (He had decided to use the dining room only for state occasions.) They were waited upon by Su Lin. The meal was a good one, traditional New Cantonese cookery. The pilot wielded his ivory chopsticks with as much assurance as did Grimes.

There was no need for Su Lin to activate what Grimes thought of as the anti-bug: conversation consisted mainly of generalities and of astronautical shop talk. Finally Sanchez said good night and left. Su Lin brought more tea, for herself and Grimes.

She said, "I am switched on."

"Indeed? And what are we talking about, Su Lin? I have to call you that as I don't know your real name."

She laughed. "As far as the bugs are concerned you're living up to your reputation. Casanova Grimes, the terror of the spaceways."

"Do people really think of me like that?"

"Some of them do. Pirate, libertine. . . . Oh, you've a reputation all right."

"Mphm."

"If Bardon thinks that you're spending all your time womanizing he'll not be expecting you to start putting your foot down with a firm hand."

"Mphm."

He looked at her. It was obvious that she was enjoying being herself and not playing the part of a faithful handmaiden.

He said, "You were just going to tell me who you're really working for when Raoul came in."

"Yes, I was. Do you really want to know, Your Excellency?"

"As long as we're in private you can call me John."

"I am honored, John. I'm with Pat."

With Pat? Did she mean that she had an Irish boyfriend, Grimes wondered, and therefore out of bounds as far as he was concerned? But PAT was an acronym, he remembered. PAT. People Against Tyranny. He recalled the first time that he had heard of this organization; it was during a spell ashore between ships at Lindisfarne Base. A dictatorial planetary president had been assassinated and PAT had claimed the credit for this act of justice. There had been some discussion of the affair in the junior officers' mess.

"Aren't you running rather a risk telling me, Su?"

"I don't think so, Captain Grimes, Survey Service Reserve."

"My Reserve Commission is supposed to be a secret."

"It is—and PAT CC, Pat Central Committee, are among those keeping that secret."

"Do you mean to tell me that Admiral Damien is one of your members? If ever there was a tyrant, he's one!"

"So you say. But we have members everywhere. On Electra, for example. Silverman, the scientist/salesman, really came here just to check the bugs in the Residence and to supply me with the counter measure. But getting back to Damien—didn't it ever occur to you that, when he was O.C. Couriers and you a courier captain, he was always sending you on missions in the hope, usually realized, that you'd throw a monkey wrench into somebody's machinery at the right time?"

"You could look at it that way."

"And when it was necessary to put a stop to the privateering operations of Drongo Kane and the Eldorado Corporation—just who did Admiral Damien pressgang back into the Survey Service?"

"Me. All right, then. Since PAT seems to have been using me for the Odd Gods of the Galaxy alone know how many years, why have I never been asked to become a member?"

"Because you're an awkward bastard. You'd be as liable to throw a monkey wrench into our machinery as into anybody else's."

"Then why are you spilling all these beans?"

"Because I was told to do so. It was decided that you should know that there is a galaxy-wide organization behind you—as long as you're doing the right things. And that if you do the wrong things—there's a nasty, mercenary streak in your nature—you'd better try to make a get-away to the Magellanic Clouds."

Grimes got up from his chair and began to pace back and forth. He managed to light his pipe—on the run, as it were—before Su Lin could do it for him.

He said, "I don't like being manipulated."

"You haven't been manipulated all the time," she told him.

"And this nasty, mercenary streak you accuse me of having. . . ."

"What shipowner doesn't have one?"

"Some more than others. More than me."

"So you say." Her smile robbed the words of offense.

It did more than that, making her look very attractive. And, he knew now, there was no longer that master-servant relationship to deter him from entering into a relationship with her. But would she now renew the offer that she had made when, so far as he then knew, she was no more than a serving girl?

She was still smiling at him, on her feet and facing him. She did not break away when he took her in his arms—but she did not put her own arms about him. She did not turn her lips away from his—but she did not open them.

When the kiss—such as it was—was over she said, "As well as being mercenary, you're snobbish. You had the offer, your first day here, and you turned it down. And now that you know that there's no great social gulf yawning between us you think that we'll fall happily into bed together."

Now Grimes was really wanting her. He kissed her again, brutally, and, holding her to him, walked her backwards into the bedroom. He threw her on to the couch. She sprawled there, looking up at him. And was that contempt in her expression—or pity?

She said, "When I first met you, you were making the rules. Now I'm making them. You can have me when I'm ready—and not before. Once you've proven yourself to be as good a man as Governor Wibberley was. . . ."

"You mean that he and you. . . ."

"Try to get your mind off sex, John. He was a *good* man, a religious man. A Bible-basher you'd call him—but, unlike so many Christians, he really tried to live according to his faith, to comfort and succor the helpless. Even agnostics such as myself could appreciate him, to say nothing of the mess of Anarchists, Confucianists, Buddhists and the Odd Gods alone know what on this planet. We—the various undergrounds and PAT—hope that you will carry on his work, the restoration of hope and dignity to the refugee peoples, the suppression of Bardon's rackets. . . ."

"Get off your soap box, Su," said Grimes tiredly. "I'm here to do a job and I'll do it to the best of my ability. I'll expect some pay for my work—after all, I have that nasty, mercenary streak in me—but, if all goes well, I'll arrange it myself. It won't cost PAT anything. It won't cost *you* anything. And now, if you'll excuse me, I'd like to go to bed. By myself."

"I certainly do not intend otherwise."

She got up from the bed and walked slowly out of the room.

"Call me at the usual time," Grimes called after her.

Seventeen

The next day Grimes had been looking forward to taking a test flight in *Fat Susie* but, while he was having his breakfast, Jaconelli brought him a list of the day's appointments. He was to be host at a luncheon, he learned, for Madam President and her ministers. After this he was to accompany her to the official opening of the new Handicrafts Center just outside Libertad. After that he was free—for what little remained of the day.

He spent the forenoon familiarizing himself with the Residence, guided by Wong Lee and with Su Lin and Lieutenant Smith in attendance. It was one of those buildings that seemed to have just happened, additional rooms and facilities being tacked on to an originally quite small house as required. The servants' quarters were underground, as was the kitchen. Grimes lingered here, using a pair of long chopsticks handed to him by the chef to sample tidbits from various cooking utensils. He did some more nibbling during his tour of the storerooms.

There were the vaults in which the records were stored—or had been stored. Filing cabinets were empty and the only information available from the readout screens was purely domestic—food, light, heating and wages bills for the past decade and the like. Grimes found details of the last official luncheon given by his predecessor. Wibberley had been English and had fed his guests on pea soup, Dover sole (were there sole in Liberia's seas?), steak and kidney pie, trifle and a cheese board featuring Stilton, Wensleydale and cheddar. He wondered how the New Cantonese kitchen staff had coped with this feast. To judge by the two breakfasts that he had already enjoyed they had probably made a very good job of it—just as they would almost certainly do with the menu that he had ordered.

He returned to his quarters to change from shirt and slacks into an informally formal lightweight suit. Su Lin, the dutiful handmaiden, assisted him unnecessarily to dress. She walked with him out to the portico where, with Jaconelli and the ADC, he waited to receive the guests.

Bardon, wearing a dark blue civilian suit that was almost a uniform, rode in with Estrelita O'Higgins in the presidential limousine. The President was in superbly cut blue denim with scarlet touches. The ministers and their companions were similarly clad. Before luncheon there were drinks in one of the big reception rooms.

The Colonel cornered Grimes while the Governor was graciously circulating among the guests.

He said abruptly, "I hear that my Lieutenant Duggin isn't good enough for you, Your Excellency."

"Frankly, Colonel, he isn't," said Grimes. "In any case I'd already made my own appointment of an atmosphere pilot."

"I was hoping, Your Excellency," said Bardon, "that you, with a military rather than an academic background, would be more cooperative with the Garrison than the late Governor Wibberley was."

"A military background, Colonel? Piracy, you mean?"

"I was referring to your Survey Service career, Your Excellency."

"In the Survey Service, Colonel, we expected a reasonably high standard of ship-handling competence."

"Ship-handling, sir? An airship is not a spaceship."

"One did not need to be an airshipman to know that Duggin was not very competent."

"You are entitled to your opinion, Your Excellency."

Grimes wandered on, chatting with the other guests. Most of them, inevitably, asked him what he thought of Liberia and then, before he could make reply, told him what he should think.

And then the sonorous booming of a gong announced that luncheon was about to be served.

Grimes enjoyed the meal in spite of the company; he did not like fat cats and most of the guests could be categorized as such. The Residence chef and his assistants had done very well. Local crustacea, served simply with a melted butter dressing, could almost have been the yabbies that Grimes remembered from his younger days in Australia. The Colonial Goose—leg of hogget, well spiced—could not have been better. The tropical fruit salad, its components marinated in wine, was a suitable conclusion to the meal. There should have been kangaroo tail soup for the first course but the necessary ingredients had not been available on this planet.

It was Estrelita O'Higgins, sitting at Grimes's right, who brought the luncheon party to a close.

"Your Excellency, they will be waiting for us at the Handicrafts Center. Oh, there is no *real* hurry." She smiled. "Everybody of any importance is here. Nonetheless, we have our obligations. Our duties."

She asked for more coffee.

Finally the party made its collective way to the waiting cars. Grimes rode in his own official vehicle, accompanied by his ADC and with two soldiers sitting forward, with the chauffeur. Estrelita O'Higgins led the motorcade.

The new Handicrafts Center was a big, single-storied hall, one of those buildings that manage to show signs of dilapidation even before their completion. It looked like an unprosperous factory. Outside its main entrance, which was bedecked with wilted flowers, was a small crowd. There was a band which, at the approach of the official cars, struck up with a selection of Australian folk songs which, at first, Grimes found it hard to recognize; every one of them sounded like a military march. There were the schoolchildren with their little flags. Most of them, Grimes noted, were New Cantonese. There were older people—teachers?—and they, too, were mainly representative of the refugee population.

The cars stopped.

Estrelita O'Higgins, squired by Colonel Bardon, got out of hers. There was some not very enthusiastic flag waving and a ragged cheer. Grimes, accompanied by his ADC, disembarked. Was it his imagination or was the cheering a little louder?

The President, accompanied by Grimes, Bardon and the Minister of Industry, mounted a temporary, bunting-covered dais. She spoke into a microphone and her amplified voice came from the speakers mounted on the streetlamp standards. She told her listeners how Liberia—that generous host!—had supplied facilities for the fitting education of the children of those to whom refuge had been given.

God bless the Squire and his relations, thought Grimes, *and keep us in our proper stations.*

Manual Silvero, the Minister of Industry, said *his* piece. He extolled the virtues of labor. A fat, short, greasy man he looked, thought Grimes, as though he had never done an honest day's work in his life.

He concluded, "And now it is my honor to request His Excellency, Commodore John Grimes, to open this well-appointed, palatial, even, training establishment."

The President led the way down from the dais. Bardon indicated that Grimes should follow her. The others came after them. They walked to the entrance, which had a scarlet, silken ribbon strung across it. A young man—a native Liberian—approached them, bearing a plump, purple cushion. On it was a pair of golden scissors. Bowing, he presented the implement to the Governor.

Grimes took the scissors, worked them experimentally. They seemed to be in order. He walked the few steps to where the ribbon barred his way to the drab looking interior of the Handicrafts Center.

And was it accidental or did somebody possess both a sense of humor and an acquaintance with Australian folk music?

Click go the shears . . .

Click went the shears and the ribbon parted.

The children cheered (because they had to) and there was a patter of polite handclapping.

Eighteen

Grimes returned to the Residence.

Sanchez was waiting for him in the portico.

He said, as soon as Grimes was out of the car, "I've taken her out, Your Excellency . . ."

Grimes wondered who *she* was.

"She handles quite well . . ."

"Oh. *Fat Susie.*"

"Of course. What did you think I meant, sir?"

"Come with me to my office and tell me about it." Then, to the ADC, "I'll not be requiring you any more today, Lieutenant Smith."

"Very good, Your Excellency."

As soon as Grimes and the pilot were seated Su Lin materialized with a tea tray.

"Are you switched on?" Grimes asked the girl. He realized, too late, that this would be rather a foolish question, one that would cause the snoopers to wonder, to add two and two to make at least five, if she were not.

But she was.

Grimes said, "I want to wander around the city incognito. To see for myself without having to peer through a thick screen of officials, politicians and hangers on."

"Like that Caliph of Baghdad," said Raoul. "Haroun al Raschid or whatever his name was."

"Yes."

"Governor Wibberley used to do it," said Su Lin. "I would help him with his disguise. A denim suit, false whiskers. A voice modulator. . . ."

"But how did he—how do *I*—get out of this place unobserved?"

"Wong Lee has a car," she said. "It's a van, rather, with the back enclosed. He runs into the city now and again, in the evening. He goes to the Golden Lotus Club. This is one of his recreational nights."

"And mine," said Grimes, suddenly making up his mind. "Su, could you disguise me? Is there a denim suit that would fit? Can you still lay your hands on the other things?"

"Of course."

"And would you come with me, Raoul?"

"It will be my pleasure, sir."

"Then what are we waiting for?"

He went through to his bedroom and got out of his informal suit. When he was down to his underwear Su Lin came back with a bundle of clothing and other things. She unnecessarily helped him on with the floppy-collared white shirt and the scarlet neckerchief, the blue denim suit, the black, calf-length boots. There was a full-length mirror in the wardrobe door and Grimes admired himself in it. He rather liked this rig—but he was still him.

The girl told him to sit in a chair, went behind him to carry on the work of disguise. He felt the sticky coldness as some adhesive was dabbed on to his skull behind his ears and then her hands as she firmly pressed the prominent appendages to the fast-setting gum. She came around to stand in front of him and looked down at him.

She said, "That's better. Now, open your mouth, please . . ."

He obeyed.

Her deft fingers inserted a pad, a tiny cushion covered in slick plastic, into each side of his mouth, under each cheek. He was, of course, aware of their presence although they were not uncomfortable.

"Now look at yourself," she told him.

He got up from the chair and did so. He stared at the chubby-faced stranger who stared back at him from the mirror.

He asked, "Don't I get a moustache?"

His voice was as strange as his appearance, high, squeaky almost. He could see his expression of surprise.

She told him, "The voice modulator is incorporated in one of the cheek pads. The way you look and the way you sound nobody will recognize you."

"Perhaps. But just about everybody on this world has face fungus of some kind."

"All right." She went back to the things that she had laid out on the bed and selected something that looked, at first glance, like a large, hairy insect. "This is self-adhesive," she told him. "You'll need a special spray, of course, to get it off."

Grimes looked at himself again.

That heavy moustache suited him, he thought. It was a great pity that his modulated voice did not go with his macho appearance. He supposed, ruefully, that he couldn't have everything.

He took the broad-brimmed black hat, with its scarlet ribbon, that the girl handed him, went through to the sitting room. Sanchez got up from the chair in which he had been sitting when Grimes entered. At first Grimes did not recognize him; the tuft of false beard on his chin was an effective disguise.

Sanchez asked, "Ready, Joachim?"

"Joachim?"

"You have to have a name."

"Joachim, then," agreed Grimes. "I rather like it." He patted his empty pockets. "What do I use for money?"

Su Lin handed him a well-worn notecase and a small handful of silver and copper coins.

She said, "At first you'd better let Raoul do the paying, until you get the feel of the local currency."

"That shouldn't be long," Grimes told her. "As a spaceman I'm used to paying for things, on all sorts of worlds, in all sorts of odd coins and pieces of paper or whatever. And now, as soon as I've found my pipe and tobacco, I'll be ready to go."

"You will *not* smoke a pipe, Joachim," said Su Lin severely.

"I've seen people smoking pipes in Libertad."

"And everybody knows that *you* smoke one. There were cartoons in the newspapers when your appointment was first announced; in every one of them you had a pipe stuck in your face. Pipe and ears—those are your trademarks."

"Mphm."

"Here's a packet of cigars, and a lighter. And now, if both of you will follow me, I'll take you to the truck."

Grimes thought that he had already acquired a fair knowledge of the geography of the Residence; he soon discovered that he had not. There was a door that he had thought was just part of the paneling in the corridor; beyond this was a corridor of the kind that, aboard a ship, would be called a working alleyway. There was a tradesman's entrance. Beyond this was the rather shabby van, in the driver's seat of which the old majordomo was sitting. Wong Lee was not wearing his livery but was looking very dignified in a high-collared suit of black silk, a round black hat of the same material on his head. He ignored Grimes and Sanchez as they clambered into the rear of the vehicle. The door shut automatically as soon as they were aboard. There was a roll of cloth of some kind on which they made themselves comfortable. The only light came from ventilation slits and that—it was all of half an hour after sunset—was fading fast.

The van started, so smoothly that the passengers were hardly aware of the motion. Raoul offered Grimes a long, thin cigar from his pack, took one himself. The two men smoked in companionable silence, broken eventually by the pilot.

He said, "Wong Lee's letting us off on the corner of May Day Street and Tolstoy Avenue. On the outskirts of the city. From there it'll be easy to get a trishaw. He'll pick us up on the same corner at 0100 tomorrow."

"And how do we fill in the time until then?" asked Grimes.

"Easily, Joachim. I'll try to give you an idea of the way in which the refugees are exploited here. We'll do a tour of the pleasure district."

"Combining business with pleasure, as it were," said Grimes.

"You can put it that way," said Raoul coldly, very coldly. Grimes remembered, then, what he had been told when the pilot's shuttle craft brought him down from the orbiting *Sobraon* to Port Libertad, about the New Dallas girl called Mary Lou who had been one of the entertainers in the Pink Pussy Cat.

He said, inadequately, "I'm sorry, Raoul."

"There's no need to be, Joachim. I know that you're not the sort of man who'll get much pleasure from what we're going to see. You're no Holy Joe—as Wibberley was—but you have your principles."

"You hope," said Grimes, adding softly, "and *I* hope."

The van stopped.

The rear door opened on to a warm darkness that was enhanced rather than dispelled by the sparsely spaced, yellow streetlamps.

Grimes and Sanchez got out.

Without a word to them Wong Lee drove away.

Nineteen

It did not seem to Grimes to be a place at which to wait for a cab—or its local equivalent—but, after a wait of no longer than five minutes, an empty trishaw, its operator pedaling lazily, drifted along, halting alongside them when hailed. Yet another New Cantonese, Grimes decided, a little man, scrawny in his sleeveless singlet and baggy shorts yet with muscles evident in his thighs and calves.

Grimes clambered into the basketlike passenger compartment, which was forward of the driver, followed by Sanchez who, before mounting, ordered, "Garden of Delights."

The trishaw operator grunted acknowledgment and, as soon as his passengers were seated, began pumping his pedals. The journey was mainly through quiet side streets and, Grimes decided, more or less toward the locality of Port Libertad, the glare of lights from which was now and again to the right and now and again to the left but always forward of the beam.

They came to a street that, by local standards, was fantastically bright and bustling. There were street stalls, selling foodstuffs, from which eddied all manner of savory aromas. There were brightly lit façades, establishments whose names were picked out in multi-colored lights. *The Pink Pussy Cat . . . The Dallas Whorehouse . . . The Old Shanghai . . . The Ginza . . . The Garden of Delights . . .*

The trishaw stopped.

Grimes got out and began to fumble for money. Sanchez forestalled him, tossing coins to the operator, who deftly caught them. The two men walked into the vestibule of the Garden of Delights where, sitting in a booth that was like a miniature pagoda, an elderly Oriental gentleman who could have been Wong Lee's slightly younger brother was sitting in receipt of custom.

Again Sanchez paid and led Grimes through a doorway, through an entanglement of beaded curtains, into a large, dimly lit room, the air of which was redolent with the fumes of the incense burners standing on tripods along the walls and between the tables. The decor, thought Grimes, was either phonily Terran Oriental or fair dinkum New Cantonese—but he had never been to New Canton and never would go there. (Neither would anybody else; the planet was now no more than a globe of incandescent slag.) There were rich silken hangings. There were bronze animals that could have been either lions or Pekingese dogs. There were overhead lanterns, glowing parchment globes encircled by painted dragons. There was music—the tinkling of harplike instruments, the high squealing of pipes, the muted thud of little drums.

There was a stage at one end of the hall. On it was a girl, gyrating languidly and gracefully to the beat of the music. She was attired in filmy veils and was discarding them one by one. *(And what the hell,* wondered Grimes, *did Salome have to do with China, or New Canton?)* Nonetheless he watched appreciatively. The girl was tall, high-breasted, slender-limbed. Her dance *was* a dance, did not convey the impression that she was disrobing hastily prior to jumping into the shower or into bed.

Grimes's attention was distracted momentarily by a waitress who came to their table. She was wearing a high-necked tunic that did not quite come down as far as possible, golden sandals and nothing else. She had brought two bowls of some savory mess, one of rice, what looked like a tall, silver teapot, two small silver goblets, two pairs of chopsticks. She poured from the pot into the cups, bowed and retreated.

"Your very good health, Joachim," said Sanchez, raising his cup.

"And yours, Raoul."

Grimes sipped. He had been expecting tea, was surprised—not unpleasantly—to discover that the liquid was wine, a hot, rather sweet liquor. He put the cup down, picked up his chopsticks and with them transferred a portion of rice to the sweet-and-sour whatever it was in his bowl. He sampled a mouthful of the mixture. It wasn't bad.

On the stage the dancer was down to her last veil. She swirled it around her—partially revealing, concealing, affording more glimpses, concealing again, finally dropping the length of filmy fabric. She stood there briefly, flaunting her splendid nudity. She bowed, then turned and glided sinuously from the stage. The orchestra (if one could call it that) fell silent. There was a pattering of applause.

Grimes looked around. There were not, he saw, many customers. There were men, dressed as he and Sanchez were. At two of the tables there were obvious spacers. At one of these the waitress was being mauled. Obviously the girl was not enjoying having those prying hands all over her body but she was not resisting.

"You'll not get shows like this out in the country, Joachim," said Sanchez.

(And that, thought Grimes, was the pilot's way of telling him that there could be bugs here. It was very hard, these days, to find a place that was not bug-infested.)

He said, "That was a lovely dollop of trollop. On the stage, I mean."

"She'll not be that way long, Joachim. The signs were there. Her eyes—didn't you notice?"

Grimes admitted that he hadn't paid much attention to her face.

"That faraway look. Dreamsticks. Soon she'll start to wither. The waitresses, too. But there are plenty more where they came from. Don't tell me that you haven't had the recruiters around your plantation yet."

"I thought that they were selling encyclopedias," said Grimes.

"Ha, ha!"

The music had started again, a livelier tune. The dancer who came on the stage might have been beautiful once, still possessed the remains of beauty. But her movements were clumsy; her strip act was just that and nothing more. When she was completely naked she stood there, swaying, beckoning to various members of the audience. Grimes felt acutely ashamed when he, briefly, was the target of her allure. He was ashamed for his cloth when, finally, one of the spacers got to his feet and shambled to the stage.

"They aren't going to do it *here*?" he whispered to Sanchez.

"There are rooms at the back, Joachim. She'll want to go through his pockets in privacy. Her habit's expensive. But let's get out of here. It's not very often that you have a night on the town and there are more places to sample."

"Wait till I've finished my sweet-and-sour," said Grimes.

The Dallas Whorehouse was their next port of call. The girls there were all tall and blonde, the music a piano on which a tall, thin and very black man hammered out old-time melodies. He was far better than the instrument upon which he was performing. Grimes recognized "The Yellow Rose Of Texas" and, in spite of himself, was amused by the very well-endowed young lady who borrowed two twenty-cent pieces from a spacer sitting just under the stage and placed one over each nipple, after which she counter-rotated her breasts without dislodging the coins. When she was finished she deftly flipped them into the cupped hands of the spaceman.

"In a few weeks' time," said Sanchez sourly, "she'll have to use paper money—and stick it on with spit."

"A pity," said Grimes sincerely.

The pilot looked at his wrist companion. “Finish your beer, Joachim. I have to show you that the big city’s not all boozing and wenching, otherwise you’ll be going back home with a false impression.”

“Give me time to finish the tacos and this chili dip,” grumbled Grimes.

Twenty

The next place that they went to was a very dowdy house, one of a terrace, in a poorly lit side street. As they approached it Grimes wondered what sort of entertainment would be offered in such a venue; something unspeakably sordid, he thought.

There was a doorkeeper, a burly man wearing the inevitable frayed denims and the almost as inevitable heavy beard.

"Your contributions, comrades," he growled, gesturing toward a battered metal bowl on the table before him. There was a clink and rattle of coinage as Sanchez paid for himself and Grimes.

The two men passed through a curtained door into a hall, took seats toward the back. Grimes looked around curiously. The room, he saw, was less than half full. There were both women and men there, some of them obviously Liberians, some New Cantonese, some Negroid, some blondly Nordic. As yet there was nobody on the platform, behind which were draperies of black and scarlet bunting, at the end of the room.

Grimes was about to ask what was going on when a tall, heavily bearded man mounted the platform. He was followed by a fat woman, by two other men of average height and, finally, by a girl who was more skinny than slim, whose protuberant front teeth gleamed whitely in her dusky face. She took her seat at a battered upright piano; the others sat behind a long table on which were water bottles, glasses and what looked like (and were) old fashioned microphones.

The thin girl assailed the keyboard of her instrument. The people behind the table stood up. With a shuffling of feet and a subdued scraping of shifted chairs those in the body of the hall stood up. Everybody—excepting Grimes—started to sing.

The faith of our fathers lives on in our hearts,
The flame of their courage burns on,
Their banners still fly, let us lift them on high,
In the light of Liberia's sun . . .

There was more, much more. Grimes hummed along with the rather trite music while he listened to the words. This was a political meeting to which Sanchez had brought him, he decided, a gathering of the Original Anarchists. At last the song was over. Everybody sat down but the big, bearded man on the platform.

"Comrades," said this person. "Comrades, and honorary comrades . . ." (The New Cantonese? wondered Grimes. The refugees from New Dallas and other devastated worlds? So even the OAP was capable of discrimination . . .)

"Comrades. Honorary comrades. Again there is hope. Again Earth has sent us a Governor, one who may take our part, as Governor Wibberley did, against the tyranny of O'Higgins and Bardon. But I must warn you, all of you, not to place too much faith in him. After all, the man is no more than a common pirate. . . ." (Piracy, thought Grimes, wasn't exactly a common trade.) "We will support him if and when he confronts O'Higgins and Bardon. We will stand against him when he attempts to re-impose the rule of Imperial Earth.

"But what manner of man is this new Governor, this pirate Commodore Grimes? With whom shall we have to deal when the time comes? What say you, Chiang Sung?"

One of the New Cantonese got to his feet.

"I am only an under-chef at the Residence, Comrade. I have little contact with him. I have seen him, of course. He has inspected the kitchens. He was very affable. He appreciates good food. It will be a pleasure to work for such a gentleman. But Su Lin, his maidservant, can tell you more than I."

"And where *is* Su Lin?" demanded the fat woman. "Where is the Pekingese Princess? The airs and graces that she puts on when she's no more than a governor's trollop . . . Come to that—where is the Lord High Mandarin Wong Lee? With all due respect to Comrade Chiang Sung, we should exercise far greater discrimination."

"And where," demanded one of the smaller men on the platform, "is *Captain* Raoul Sanchez?" He went on, sneering heavily, "Oh, he came crying to us after that wench of his died and after his brother was murdered—or so he says. But I suppose that now he's found himself a new girl and, as we know, he's inherited his brother's soft job he'll scrub us."

Grimes heard Sanchez growl softly and gave him a sharp nudge with his elbow.

He sat through a long and boring speech by the Comrade Chairman. The more he heard the less he was puzzled by the fact that the Liberian authorities tolerated the OAP. Probably many of the men and women at this meeting were government agents. Possibly these same agents, as dues-paying members, made quite heavy contributions to the OAP working expenses. He listened to horror stories from various refugees, men and women in domestic service whose masters and mistresses, according to them, were unduly harsh. Most of such tales left him unmoved. Those servants would not have lasted long in like capacities aboard any spaceship, naval or mercantile. Those who make a practice of insolence, dumb or otherwise, should not be surprised when their employers take counter measures.

The meeting came to a close just as Sanchez was beginning to fidget and snatch ever more frequent glances at his wrist companion. The pianist again battered the long-suffering keyboard. Everybody stood up.

Arise, ye prisoners of starvation,
Arise, ye wretched of the world,
For Justice thunders condemnation
And the flag of Hope's unfurled!
Then comrades come rally
And the last fight let us face,
Fraternity and Liberty
Unite the human race!

"Time we got going, Joachim," said Sanchez.

They made their way toward the door, accepting handfuls of leaflets as they did so. They were almost out and clear when they were accosted by a large, heavily moustached man.

"New here, comrades?"

"Yes, comrade," said Sanchez. "We're up from our plantation. Somebody told us that there was an OAP meeting so we thought we'd look in."

"Interested, comrades?"

"Yes. We have drifted away from the old ideals."

"I'd like to send you some more literature, comrades. Put you on our mailing list."

"We'd be pleased with that," Sanchez said. He pulled out his notecase, took out a card and gave it to the man. "And now, if you'll excuse us. We have a date. With two of the girls from the Whorehouse."

"But you're contributing to their degradation, comrades."

"Come off it, comrade. They like their work. Or they will with us—eh, Joachim? Come on, man. We mustn't keep the ladies waiting."

As they waited for a trishaw Grimes said, "Raoul, surely you could see that the man was some sort of under cover agent."

"Of course I did."

"But you gave him a card . . ."

"I didn't say that it was mine, did I?" He hailed an approaching trishaw. "Come on, Joachim. We mustn't keep Wong Lee waiting."

Twenty-one

Sitting in the back of Wong Lee's truck they talked.

"What did you think of the OAP meeting, sir?" asked Sanchez.

"Not much," said Grimes frankly. "Just an occasion to blow off harmless steam under the watchful eye of the authorities."

"You're right, sir. And the other places?"

"I've seen worse on other worlds."

"Including the encouragement to drug addiction?"

"Even that."

"But not in the same way, sir. On other planets there are pushers—but surely they are not employed by the government. The policy here, on Liberia, is that the refugees shall become so dependent on dreamsticks and other drugs that they lack the drive to achieve full citizenship."

"Are there any emancipists?" asked Grimes.

"Emancipists?"

"It's a term from Australian history, Raoul. During the days when New South Wales was a penal colony the emancipists were convicts who had been granted their freedom. More than a few of them became wealthy and influential men."

"We do have the equivalent here, sir, but there aren't many of them. There's Calvin McReady, who's one of our minor grain kings and all set to become a major one. There's Sin Fat, who owns the New Shanghai. But they regard themselves as Liberians, not as refugees, or ex-refugees. They are as money- and power-hungry as any of the native-born Establishment."

"So it was, all too often, in New South Wales," said Grimes. "But tell me, Raoul, why are you in the OAP? Is it only for personal reasons?"

Sanchez fell silent for a while, quietly smoking one of his long cigars.

Then, "There are more than personal reasons, sir. When I was a child I was taught the history of Liberia. After I left school—before, even—I could not help but see the disparity between the ideals of our founding fathers and what we have—despite all the lip service—now. . . ."

"Mphm. You went into an odd trade, didn't you, for one of your political beliefs. A spaceman has to accept discipline, take orders. Once he becomes captain he has to give orders."

"But I wanted to become a spaceman," Sanchez said. "I want to become a *real* spaceman, not a ferry master. Oh, I could never stand Survey Service discipline and spit and polish, such as you were once used to—but merchant ships are run on fairly democratic lines."

"Mphm," grunted Grimes dubiously.

"Of course, sir, what would be ideal would be a *little* ship, with no crew, of which I was owner-master. Something on the lines of that *Little Sister* of yours. . . ."

"Either accumulate at least a million credits or hire yourself out as yacht-master to a billionairess who'll give you such a ship as a parting gift." Grimes laughed. "I did it the second way. I certainly couldn't have done it the first."

"But you must *know* people, sir."

"I do, Raoul, I do. Hinting, are you? Well, if all goes well I just might—only might, mind you—be able to get you a berth as a very junior officer in a deep space ship. After that it'd be up to you—getting in your deep space time, passing examinations and all the rest of it. There are no instant captains in deep space. But forget that we're spacemen. I'm a planetary governor who's been traveling incognito among his people. You're my guide. Tell me about the dives we were in tonight."

"First, sir, the Garden of Delights. It's owned by Colonel Bardon and Estrelita O'Higgins. The manager is one Chiang Sooey. Chiang is not yet a citizen but hopes to become one. The turnover rate of entertainers is high—Chiang likes them to take their pay in dreamsticks and the like rather than in money. . . ."

"And the dreamsticks. . . . Where do they come from?"

"One of the main sources of supply used to be the ships owned by Able Enterprises but recently a dreamweed plantation was started by Eduardo Lopez. . . ."

"The Minister for Immigration?"

"The same. There was an influx of refugees from Bangla—there was some sort of Holy War there. Dreamweed comes from Bangla. The people there use it but they're immune to its worst effects. They were recruited to work on the Lopez plantation. The occasional leaves they smoke or chew will not reduce their capacity for hard work."

"And the other people, the customers, who get hooked have to work like bastards to feed their habit."

"Yes. And burn themselves out. And now, the Texas Whorehouse. Owned by a syndicate of Bardon's officers. Managed by Lyman Cartwell, of New Dallas origin. Like Chiang Sooey, not yet a citizen but hopeful of becoming one. It's not at all likely; he's become a dreamstick addict himself."

"I take it that the clipjoints—how much do I owe you, by the way?—that we didn't patronize are all very much the same insofar as ownership is concerned."

"With the exception of the New Shanghai, of course. And I'll let you have a detailed accounting as soon as possible, sir."

"Do that, Raoul."

"To date, sir, you've just seen the glamorous—*glamorous,* ha, ha!—side of the exploitation of the refugees. You've yet to see the conditions on the farms and plantations—the living quarters, the company stores . . ."

"It's time," said Grimes, "that you and I took *Fat Susie* out for an airing. A leisurely tour of my domain. . . ."

"I'd like that, sir."

Obviously the van was slowing.

It stopped and the rear door slid open.

Grimes and Sanchez jumped down to the ground, found themselves standing by the tradesmen's entrance of the Residence. Su Lin was waiting for them there. After a brief word of greeting she led them inside the building and through a maze of passageways to the Governor's quarters. She produced the inevitable tea. After this had been sipped she brought out a bottle of solvent and, applying it with gentle hands, removed Grimes's false facial hair. Sanchez attended himself to the stripping of his own disguise.

The pilot said good night and departed for his accommodation. The girl stayed with Grimes and insisted on preparing him for bed.

She did not offer to share his couch with him.

Twenty-two

After a not too early breakfast Grimes sent for Sanchez.

Su Lin was present while the two men studied charts spread on the desk in the Governor's office. Whatever the bugs picked up and reported would not be what was actually being said.

"I suggest, sir," said the pilot, "that we start by flying to the McReady estate. There are mooring facilities there."

"A surprise visit, Raoul?"

"More or less. We'll give him a call about an hour before we're due. That'll give him time to muster a few hands and to get his own blimp away from the mast and into the hangar."

"It sounds rather high-handed."

"You're the Governor, sir."

"But not an absolute monarch. Mphm."

"If we cast off at noon," said Sanchez, "we should arrive at about 0900 hours. McReady's time, tomorrow morning. The actual flying time will be seventeen hours, weather permitting. At this time of the year there shouldn't be much wind, either with us or against us. Would you mind standing a watch or two, sir? There's an automatic pilot, of course, but I'm old fashioned. I feel that the control room should be manned at all times."

"So do I," said Grimes.

"I can stand a watch too," put in Su Lin. "I may not hold any licenses or certificates but I can handle lighter than air craft."

"Did you fly with Governor Wibberley?" Grimes asked.

"No. I learned . . . elsewhere."

"But what gave you the idea that you were coming with us?"

"The Lord High Governor must have his personal maidservant in attendance, mustn't he? Who's going to make your tea and cook your meals?"

"I can handle an autochef," Grimes told her huffily. "When I was by myself in *Little Sister* I fed quite well. I don't need a huge kitchen, such as here, with hordes of chefs and scullions."

"Three watches will be better than watch and watch, sir," said Sanchez.

"I suppose so. But you're the expert, Raoul. Shall we need any crew apart from the three of us?"

"What for?"

"As long as you're happy," said Grimes, "I am. I don't want any of Smith's nongs in my hair. Come to that—I don't want Smith himself, even though he is alleged to be my ADC."

"He hates flying," said Su Lin. "Whenever possible he found some excuse to avoid accompanying Governor Wibberley on his flights."

"He knew what was going to happen," said Sanchez bitterly.

"Could it happen to me?" asked Grimes interestedly. "To us?"

"*Fat Susie* is clean." the pilot told him. "So far. And I've set up an intrusion recorder that will let me know if anybody has been sniffing around her during my absence."

"One of *your* electronic toys, Su Lin?" asked Grimes.

"Yes."

"Then all right, Raoul. Get *Fat Susie* ready for flight. I'll see Smith and Jaconelli and tell them that I shall be away from the Residence for a while."

"Perhaps you'd better tell Madam President and Colonel Bardon as well," suggested Su Lin.

Sanchez left.

Grimes picked up the telephone on his desk, was able to get in touch with the ADC and the secretary without any trouble. After a very short while they came into the office.

"Good morning, gentlemen," said Grimes.

"Good morning. Your Excellency," they chorused.

"Captain Sanchez and I are going to take *Fat Susie* out for a trial flight. I can't be sure when I shall be back."

"Will you require me, Your Excellency?" asked Smith.

"No, thank you. Somebody has to mind the shop during my absence, to maintain my liaison with the military. . . ." Smith looked relieved. "And you, of course, Mr. Jaconelli, will maintain liaison with the civil government. I'd like you both to pass out the necessary information regarding my temporary absence from the Residence."

"Will you be filing a flight plan, Your Excellency?" asked Smith.

"No. Captain Sanchez and I will just be swanning around, admiring the scenery, letting the wind blow us where it lists. . . ."

"It is a calm day, Your Excellency," said Smith.

"Just a figure of speech, Lieutenant."

"And should we wish to get in touch with you, Your Excellency?"

"*Fat Susie*'s radio telephone system will be operative throughout."

Smith, Grimes noticed, was sneaking glances at the charts laid out on the desk. He wouldn't learn much. The one with the courses plotted on it was under all the others, the one on display was of the Lake Country, west of Libertad.

"I think that's all, gentlemen," said Grimes.

"Thank you, Your Excellency."

"And will you pack an overnight bag for me, Su Lin?"

"Very good, Your Excellency."

After having made sure that his tobacco pouch was full Grimes strolled out of the Residence and made his way to the mini-airport.

Fat Susie was swinging lazily at the low mast. The end of the ladder hanging from her control cab was just clear of the ground. Grimes caught hold of the side rails, got his feet onto the bottom step. He heard, above him, the air pump whine briefly as pressure in the atmospheric trimming cells was reduced to compensate. He climbed up to the cab, through the open door, went forward.

"Permission to board, Captain?" he asked Sanchez, who was feeding information into the auto-pilot.

"Glad to have you aboard, Commodore," replied the young man.

"What courses do you propose to steer?"

"With your permission, sir, north at first to make a circuit of Mount Bakunin. When it's erupting it's very spectacular—but it's been quiet for some years now. Of course, if it were erupting we shouldn't be going near it. After that we follow a great circle to the McReady place. That takes us over Rumpel's Canyon and, a bit farther on, the townships of Vanzetti and Princeps. . . ."

"Should be a scenic trip."

"Yes, sir."

Through an open window came the sound of a female voice.

"Ahoy, *Fat Susie! Fat Susie,* ahoy!"

Grimes looked out and down. Su Lin was standing there, two large suitcases on the ground beside her.

"Your Excellency," she called, "could you send a line down for the baggage?"

"I'll fix it, sir," said Sanchez.

Grimes watched with interest as the pilot opened a hatch in the deck of the cab, lowering through it a wire from a winch secured to the overhead. Su Lin hooked on both bags. By the time that they were inboard she was half-way up the ladder. She did not stay long in the control cab but went up into the body of the ship. Sanchez and Grimes were again discussing the navigational details of the flight when she came back.

"I've checked the autochef," she said. "It's very short on spices. No mace, no cummin, no tumeric. No . . ."

"You've time to get some from the kitchen, Su," said Sanchez. "But make it snappy." He turned to Grimes. *"Women . . ."* he said.

"Don't spoil the ship for a ha'porth of tar," Grimes told him. "Don't spoil the stew for a pinch of salt. Don't spoil the roast for a sliver of garlic. Don't . . ."

"Wasn't your Survey Service nickname Gutsy Grimes, sir?" asked Sanchez respectfully.

"It was. For some obscure reason people still find occasion to remind me of it. What time did you order the ground crew for?"

"They should be along now," said Sanchez.

And there they were, following in the wake of Su Lin, who was carrying a quite large bag. Again the winch was put to use and then, as soon as the girl was aboard, the ladder was retracted. Two soldiers clambered up the other ladder, that inside the metal tripod, to the head of the mast. Sanchez stuck his head out through a forward window of the cab, a portable loud speaker to his mouth.

"Let go!" he shouted.

There was a faint clang as the quick release shackle at the end of the airship's mooring wire was given a sharp blow.

"Lift!" called Sanchez.

Grimes, who had been given instructions on the drill by the pilot, used the airpump to reduce pressure in the midships trimming cell. *Fat Susie* drifted lazily astern, drifted and lifted, going up like an unpowered balloon. She cleared the Residence roof with ease. Grimes, looking out and down, saw that an almost horizontal part of it was being used as a sunbathing area by female members of his domestic staff. Apparently unembarrassed, one of the naked girls got to her feet to wave to the slowly ascending dirigible.

"Back inside, sir," ordered Sanchez. "I'm going to close the windows."

The transparent panels slid silently into place. Almost as silently the motors started. Sanchez put the wheel over, watching the gyro-compass repeater. When he was satisfied he switched to automatic.

Fat Susie, maintaining course and above-ground altitude, would find her own way to Mount Bakunin.

Su Lin came back into the control cab carrying an insulated container.

"I thought," she said, "that you would both like lunch here."

"The Governor," said Sanchez, "would like lunch anywhere."

"I resent that," said Grimes, but jocularly. From the steam that issued from the box when its lid was removed he thought that the girl had conjured up a meal of chili beef. He sat down on the settee, gratefully took the bowl and chopsticks that she handed to him.

Twenty-three

Grimes enjoyed the flight.

He had always loved dirigibles, maintaining that they were the only atmospheric flying machines that were real ships. And now he had one of his very own to play with—although it was a great pity that he was not master as well as being *de facto* owner. When he had time and opportunity, he thought, he would qualify as a pilot of lighter-than-air craft. Meanwhile Sanchez was instructing him in the elements of airship handling, allowing him to take the controls during the circuit of Mount Bakunin.

The snow-covered upper slopes of the great, truncated cone were dazzlingly white on the sunlit side, a chill, pale blue in the shadow. The frozen-over crater lake was like cold, green stone. The lower slopes were thickly forested and even the old scars of lava flows were partially overgrown with scrub. As was to be expected in the vicinity of a high mountain there were eddies and updraughts and downdraughts. Sanchez watched alertly while Grimes steered and Su Lin, acting as altitude coxswain, turned her own wheel this way and that. He said little, just an occasional "Easily, sir, *easily*. . . ." or "Not so fast, Su, or you'll put us in orbit. . . ." *Fat Susie* made her own creaking protests at the over-application of elevators or rudder but these diminished as Grimes and the girl got the hang of their controls.

And then course was set and its maintenance left to the automatic pilot. *Fat Susie* flew quietly and steadily into the darkening east, the flaming sunset astern. Dusk deepened into night and the stars, the unfamiliar (to Grimes) constellations appeared in the sky. Those directly overhead were, of course, obscured by the airship's upper structure but Su Lin was able to point out and identify those not far above the horizon.

"That's the Torch of Liberty," she said. "The bright red star at the tip of it is the Pole Star . . ."

"Mphm." (That constellation, thought Grimes, looked as much like a torch as that other grouping of stars, with Earth's Pole Star at the tip of its tail, looks like a Little Bear.)

"The Hammer and Sickle. . . ."

"I was under the impression," said Grimes, "that the founders of this colony were Anarchists, not Communists."

"They had to call their constellations something," put in Sanchez. "And that one does look like what it's called."

Su Lin went up and aft to the galley, returned after not too long with dinner for them all, a simple but excellent meal of lamb chops and some spicy green vegetable with a fruit salad to follow. Shortly after this Grimes retired to his cabin; he was taking the middle watch at the suggestion of Sanchez. "You'll want to see Rumpel's Canyon," the pilot had told him. "In the *dark*?" queried Grimes. "You'll see it all right, sir," Sanchez assured him.

Stretched out on the comfortable couch he had little trouble in getting to sleep, lulled by the slight swaying motion of the ship and by her rhythmic whispering. He awoke instantly, feeling greatly refreshed, as Su Lin, calling him for his watch, switched on the cabin light. She had brought him a pot of tea.

"Rise and shine!" she cried brightly. "Rise and shine, Your Excellency!"

She put the tray down on the bunkside table and returned to the control cab.

Grimes poured and sipped tea, then got up and went into the tiny toilet facility. He finished his tea while he was dressing. He filled and lit his pipe, then went out into the narrow alleyway toward the control cab. Looking up at the gas cells, their not overly taut fabric rippling from forward to aft, he wondered how it had been in the early days of airships when the only buoyant gas available was hydrogen. It must have been hell on smokers, he thought.

He clambered down the short companionway into the cab. Su Lin turned away from the forward windows, through which she had been peering, binoculars to her eyes.

"The canyon's coming up now," she said.

She handed him the glasses. He adjusted the focus and looked. There was the hard, serrated line of the land horizon, black against the faintly luminous darkness of the sky.

"More to your left," she told him.

A spark of light . . . A town or village? But there was an odd quality about it. It was pulsing as though it were alive. The ship flew on and now there was more than just a spark to be seen. A stream of iridiscence came slowly into view, a winding, rainbow river and then, most spectacular of all, a great cataract of liquid jewels.

At last the show was over, fading astern.

"Luminous organisms," said Su Lin matter of factly. "Found only in the Rumpel River. And now, sir, will you take the watch?"

"I relieve you, madam," said Grimes formally.

"She's on course and making good time. If any of the automatic controls play up the alarm will sound. Call Captain Sanchez—although that shouldn't be necessary. There's a bell in his cabin. Call him, in any case, at 0345. The clock's adjusted to McReady's time."

"So I see." Grimes lifted his hand and spoke into his wrist companion. "Advance to 0045 exactly on the word *Now.*" He watched the changing seconds on the clock. "Now."

"I'm an old-fashioned girl," said Su Lin. "I prefer old-fashioned watches—not contraptions that can do just about anything but fry eggs. Good night, sir. Or good morning, rather."

"Good morning, Su," said Grimes.

His watch passed pleasantly enough. He looked out at the dark landscape streaming past below with the very occasional clusters of light that told of human habitation. He studied the instruments—gyro compass, radar altimeter, ground, air speed and drift indicators and all the rest of them. He looked into the radar screen and saw a distant target, airborne, and finally was able to pick it up visually, a great airliner ablaze with lights along the length of her, sweeping by on course, he decided, for Libertad.

Then, satisfied that all was in order and would remain so, he went briefly aft to the galley to make for himself a mid-watch snack—a pot of tea and a huge pile of thick ham sandwiches. He went to the galley again to make more tea, this time for Sanchez when he called him.

"You shouldn't have done that, sir," protested the pilot. "You . . . You're the Governor."

"Where are your Anarchist principles, Raoul? In any case—you're the captain and I'm only a watchkeeper."

Shortly afterward Sanchez relieved him in the control cab.

He said, "At least you and Su managed to keep your paws off the controls. I was half expecting that you'd go down for a closer look at the canyon."

"I'd have liked to, Raoul, but I was brought up to believe that the captain's word is law."

"And so, surely, is the Governor's."

"That," said Grimes, "I have yet to convince myself of."

All of *Fat Susie*'s people were well-breakfasted, showered (and in the cases of Grimes and Sanchez depilated) when the airship made the approach to the McReady Estate. The morning was fine, almost windless, and below the dirigible the grainfields were like a golden sea. Reaping had been commenced and, like hordes of disciplined ants, the laborers, scythes flashing in the sunlight, were cutting a broad swathe through the wheat, the cut stalks being loaded onto hand-drawn carts. This sort of harvesting, thought Grimes, would be relatively inexpensive only if there were an abundant supply of slave labor—flesh and blood robots. And flesh and blood robots are superior to the metal and plastic ones in at least one respect; they are self-reproducing.

Ahead was what was practically a small town—the threshing sheds, the barracks, mess halls and the like. On a low hill was a sprawling building that seemed to be larger than the Governor's Residence, tall by Liberian standards, all of four stories. In the center of its flat roof was a mooring mast from which a dirigible, smaller than *Fat Susie*, a clumsy looking non-rigid, was just casting off.

"McReady to *Fat Susie,*" came a nasal voice from the speaker of the transceiver. "The mast will be ready for you. The mooring crew is waiting."

"Thank you, Mr. McReady," said Grimes into the microphone.

He had little to do but watch as Sanchez brought the airship in. He thought that the pilot was maintaining full speed for too long—and restrained himself from back-seat driving. But a dirigible, he realized, would lose way very quickly once power was cut. Such was the case. It was Su Lin who started, by remote control, the small winches that let down the weighted lines for the mooring crew to grab hold of and the other winch that paid out the stouter mooring, flexible wire rope, from *Fat Susie*'s blunt nose.

The men on the roof worked efficiently.

A dozen of them held *Fat Susie* in position while two more of them clipped the end of her bow wire to the other wire from the tower. Winches whined, then there was a muffled clang as the airship's stem came into contact with the swivel cone.

"We're here," said Sanchez.

The door on the port side of the cab slid open, the ladder extended downward until it was just clear of the roof surface. Grimes looked out and down to the people awaiting him, to the tall, blue-denim-clad man with the broad-brimmed hat decorated with a silver band, to the almost as tall blonde woman in her denim shirt and full skirt. Both of them, he saw, were wearing riding boots, with silver spurs.

He thought ironically, *Deep in the heart of Texas.*

Twenty-four

Grimes clambered down the ladder to the pebbled roof.

McReady removed his hat in a sweeping salute. The woman curtseyed. Grimes, bareheaded, acknowledged with a stiff bow.

"This is an unexpected honor, Your Excellency," drawled the man.

"I was passing," said Grimes, "and thought that I'd drop in."

The man chuckled and extended his hand. Grimes took it. The grip was firm but unexpectedly cold. And there was coldness, too, behind the pale blue eyes set in the darkly tanned, bluffly handsome features. And McReady's wife, thought Grimes as he shook hands with her, was cast from the same mold as her husband—handsome enough but a cast-iron bitch.

Su Lin came down, followed by Sanchez.

Grimes made introductions.

"This is Su Lin, my personal attendant . . ." The McReady couple nodded coldly to the girl. "And Captain Sanchez, my pilot . . ." There was more handshaking.

"And now, sir, how can we entertain you?" asked McReady.

"With your permission, sir, I'd like to look around your estate," said Grimes. "I want to get the feel of this world—just as a captain likes to get the feel of a ship to which he has been newly appointed."

"But why pick on *me,* Governor?"

"I want to see how outsiders, comparative newcomers, make good on Liberia. After all, this entire planet is a social experiment—and how things are turning out is of great interest to my lords and masters on Earth."

"You've a fancy way with words, sir. And you've caught me at a busy time; unless I get dug into my paperwork I'm goin' to be suffocated under a pile o' bumfodder. But I can spare you Laura. Laura, honey, will you give the Governor the five credit tour?"

"Surely, honey." Then, to Grimes, "Do you wish to start right now, or would you like refreshment first?"

"Now, if you wouldn't mind," said Grimes.

* * *

The "five credit tour" did not include a look over and through the McReady mansion. Grimes and his party were carried by an elevator down to the ground floor and then out to where two trishaws were already waiting. Laura McReady gestured and the driver of the first one dismounted, went through the motions of helping Grimes into the passenger carriage (he did not require such assistance but did not wish to hurt the man's feelings) and then assisted the woman to take her seat beside him. Su Lin and Sanchez boarded the other vehicle unaided.

"Do you wish to see the village, sir?" asked Laura McReady.

"The village?"

"It's what we call where the laborers live."

"That will do for a start, Ms. McReady," said Grimes.

She turned her head and barked an order. The driver began pedaling. The trishaws made their way along a rather narrow but well-surfaced road along the sides of which tall bushes, blue-foliaged and with huge scarlet flowers, were in luxuriant growth. Gaudy insects, gold and crimson and metallic green, hovered in clouds around each blossom. From somewhere came the monotonous song of something that might have been a bird but that probably was not.

The road wound through outcroppings of bare rock, rounded, weatherworn, that gleamed whitely in the sunlight, then through an orchard grown from seeds of Terran origin. The citrus scent was heavy in the warm, still air.

They came to the village—a long street with buildings on either side, with cross streets that were little more than lanes. Bright banners—red, yellow and blue, decorated with ideographs—depended from poles protruding horizontally from the ornate eaves of the single-storied structures.

"Shops," said Laura McReady. "Eating houses. And so forth."

Grimes sniffed the savory aromas that eddied from some of the establishments. "Eating houses? Do you think that we could look inside one?"

"If you wish, sir." Her voice was cold, disapproving. "I'm afraid that I can't recommend any of these places. Mr. McReady and I have always preferred to eat the kind of food to which we are accustomed."

The trishaws stopped. The driver of the leading one dismounted, opened the door of the passenger compartment on Grimes's side. Grimes jumped out before the man could extend a helping hand. Mrs. McReady, however, made a major production of dismounting from the vehicle like a great lady born to the purple. Even the Baroness Michelle d'Estang would not have put on such airs and graces. By the time that she had set her well-shod, silver-ornamented feet on the ground Grimes had been joined by Sanchez and Su Lin.

He led the way into the eating shop. There were a few customers there, seated around small tables. These, seeing who had come in, got hastily to their feet and bowed deeply. (To him. Grimes wondered, or to their mistress?) A middle-aged woman came out from the kitchen at the rear of the premises. She, too, bowed and murmured, "You have honored my humble establishment, Missy Laura. . . ."

"*Your* establishment? Surely it is owned by the McReady Estate, is it not?"

"I am the humble cook and manager, Missy Laura."

"And this gentleman here is the new Governor, Commodore Grimes. He wishes to sample your cooking."

"Please to take a seat, Missy Laura. This way, please . . ."

She led the party to a table, pulled out four chairs. Su Lin pushed back the one intended for her. Here she was no more than a servant. She accompanied the manageress into the kitchen. Before he took his seat Grimes looked around. The customers were still standing respectfully.

"Sit down, please," said Grimes to them.

They ignored him.

"Tell them to sit down, Ms. McReady," said Grimes to her.

"Yes, Your Excellency," she said sweetly—but her expression was not sweet.

She made a gesture and the customers resumed their seats.

She said to Grimes, "You must remember, Your Excellency, that these are only laborers."

"But human beings, nonetheless."

"You are entitled to your opinion, sir."

Su Lin and the plump manageress returned, bearing dishes of tiny spring rolls, bowls of rice and others of interesting looking pickles, chopsticks, a teapot and cups. Laura McReady condescended to take tea and, without speaking, implied that it was not to her taste. Grimes sampled a spring roll; it was delicious. He tried the pickles and liked them. Sanchez, too, was eating with a good appetite. Between them the two men cleared all the edibles on the table.

More tea was brought and with it a dish of small cookies. Grimes took the one nearest to him. It was still warm, hot almost. It must have been freshly baked. He broke the crust and was surprised to see a small square of folded paper inside. So, he thought, they had fortune cookies even on Liberia.

He unfolded the paper. The writing on it was in minuscule characters but very clear.

Pay heed to the manner in which people nourish others, and watch what they seek out for their own nourishment.

Wasn't that from the *I Ching*? He should have Magda with him here, he thought, to throw the coins and consult the Oracle of Change.

He tore the paper into tiny shreds, dropped them into the ashtray.

"What did it say, sir?" asked Raoul. "Mine says that there will be advantage in crossing the great water. I suppose that 'great water' is another way of saying 'deep space'."

Laura McReady sneered silently.

Their meal finished, the party walked out into the street, escorted to the door by the deeply bowing manageress. The question of payment wasn't mentioned; presumably the McReady Estate would be footing the bill. (They could well afford it.) Raoul Sanchez and Su Lin lagged behind, talking in low voices. Then the pilot overtook Grimes and Laura McReady, who were walking slowly along the footpath.

"Your Excellency. . . ."

"Yes, Captain Sanchez?"

"Perhaps we should inspect one of the other eating houses."

"His Excellency has already enjoyed a good lunch," said the McReady woman.

"We can inspect without eating," said Grimes. He suspected that there was some good reason for Raoul's suggestion.

"But when you have seen one you've seen them all," insisted Ms. McReady.

"Not necessarily," said Grimes.

She glared at him. Did he, he wondered, wield, as Governor, the punitive powers that he had possessed as a Survey Service commanding officer? Could he put this woman in the brig on a charge of Dumb Insolence?

Su Lin turned into one of the narrow cross streets. Sanchez followed her. Grimes and the McReady woman brought up the rear. She was almost literally seething with hostility. The girl paused outside the door of a place that was little more than a shack, waited until the others caught up with her. She lifted the bead curtain to allow Grimes, Sanchez and Laura McReady to enter before her.

The lighting inside was dim, the air musty. There were long tables and benches, most of them occupied. One of the diners saw who had come in, got to his feet, still holding his bowl in one hand, his chopsticks in the other, and bowed. There was a scraping and shuffling as other men and women followed suit. And it was not toward himself, Grimes noticed, that this obeisance was directed.

"Tell them to sit down, please," he said to Laura McReady.

She did so.

Su Lin went through to the kitchen. She returned carrying a steaming bowl and a pair of cheap, plastic chopsticks. These, with a bow, she handed to Grimes. He looked suspiciously at the mess in the bowl—like gray, slimy noodles it was, specked with green and yellow—and sniffed the sour vapor. It reminded him of the sort of mess on which he had been obliged to live, for far too long a time, during a voyage in a ship's boat, nutriment that was actually reprocessed sewage.

He lifted one strand with his chopsticks, brought it to his mouth and sucked it in. It was even worse than he had been expecting. He swallowed it, then handed the bowl and the eating implements back to the girl.

He said, "So this is how the poor live."

"Your Excellency," said Laura McReady, "the food served in this establishment satisfies the highest nutritional standards. If this were not so there would never be a good day's work done in the fields."

"Mphm." Grimes filled and lit his pipe, hoping that the fumes of burning tobacco would clear the taste of that . . . sludge from his mouth. "Once I had to eat stuff like this myself. I functioned quite well on it. But I didn't have to like it."

"These people, Your Excellency, are not like you and me. They don't know anything better."

"What about the ones in the first place?"

"Foremen and forewomen. Clerks and the like."

"More highly paid than the laborers in here?"

"Of course. You're more highly paid than . . . than a common spacehand, aren't you? But may I suggest, Your Excellency, that we continue this conversation outside?"

"Not in front of the children, eh?"

"You could put it that way," she said coldly.

They walked through the village, looking into shops in which both luxuries—sweetmeats, spices and pickles to lend savor to the staple diet, cheap jewelry to brighten drab clothing—and necessities were sold. They saw purchases being made and paid for by thumbprints on a screen-pad, recorded by some master computer. They visited a school, in which children, ranging in age from about four to fourteen, were being taught how to be good little field hands. They made the rounds of the barracks, the dormitories for males and females, the married quarters, the hospital. Somehow Su Lin had taken charge—and if Laura McReady's looks could have killed the girl would not have lived beyond that laborers' eating house.

Everything was well-maintained, spotlessly clean.

And everything was drab, drab.

For most of the people on the McReady Estate life was just a matter of going to work to earn the credited pay to buy the food to give them the strength to go to work to earn the pay etc.

Grimes found no evidence to indicate that drugs such as dreamsticks were available to the workers—but there were shops selling a limited variety of alcoholic beverages, most of which seemed to be industrial alcohol with the addition of crude flavorings.

He sampled the so-called rum and even he didn't like it.

Twenty-five

At Grimes's insistence the party then went to the fields to watch the progress of the harvest. Laura McReady did her best to dissuade him but at last, sullenly, gave the necessary orders to the trishaw drivers. On the ride out they passed, bound in the opposite direction, a steady stream of large, steam-driven trucks bound for the threshing floors in the village.

Having observed the nature of the cargoes of these vehicles Grimes asked, "Why don't you thresh on the spot and just bring the grain in?"

"Why should we, Your Excellency?" asked Mrs. McReady. Then she condescended to explain. "The straw and the husks are . . . processed. They, too, have nutritional value. You, yourself, have just sampled some of the food made from such materials."

"Oh," said Grimes. "So that was origin of the sludge we tasted. I thought that it came from something worse."

"Why should we waste good organic manure?" countered the woman.

Grimes pursued the subject.

"So your slaves get the husks and you get the grain. For export."

"Not slaves, Your Excellency. Indentured labor."

"Mphm."

They came to one of the fields, to where a line of steam trucks was awaiting cargo. They dismounted and watched for a short while the huge-wheeled handcarts being pushed in from the slowly receding line of reapers, each piled high with golden, heavy-headed stalks. Men and women, sweating in the afternoon sun, naked save for brief loincloths, tipped the loads out onto the road and then, gathering up huge armfuls of grain-bearing straw, staggered up ramps to the truck beds to restow the harvest. Human beings, thought Grimes, reduced to the status of worker ants. . . . But worker ants do not toil under the watchful eyes of overseers. And these overseers, men and women bigger and tougher-looking than the common laborers, were armed with whips, short-handled but with at least two meters of lash. Usually they just cracked these threateningly while shouting in high-pitched voices—and then Grimes shouted in protest when one of the overseers drew a line of blood on the sweating back of a frail girl.

"The lazy little bitch," said Laura McReady, "deserved it. Look at the load she's carrying!"

"Even so . . ." protested Grimes.

"Your Excellency, you are the Governor. Before you became Governor you were a spaceman. With all due respect to you, what do you know of the management of a large agricultural enterprise?"

"Very little," admitted Grimes. "But I'm learning. And I don't like what I'm learning, Mrs. McReady."

"We all have to learn unpleasant lessons, Your Excellency."

And I shall be teaching some, I hope, thought Grimes.

He led the way onto the field itself, walking between the furrows, his feet sinking into the soft soil. The incoming handcarts swerved to avoid him—or to avoid Laura McReady, who was walking close behind him. Her they knew but they would not know the new Governor. He came up to the line of reapers, stooped and sweating as they wielded their flashing sickles. He heard the cracking of the overseers' whips and their shouted orders. He saw a woman, not young, one of the gatherers, straighten up briefly from her labors and stand there, her face turned up to the uncaring sky. For some reason (and who could blame her? thought Grimes) she was weeping quietly.

She stood in tears amid the alien corn . . . Where did that come from? Not that it mattered. What did matter was that a woman was standing there, in tears, the helpless victim of a harsh economic system and of political hypocrisy.

"Su Lin," he said, "will you ask her what is wrong?"

"What does it matter, Your Excellency?" asked Laura McReady.

"It does to her, madam," said Grimes.

Su Lin went up to the woman and, in a soft voice, spoke to her in her own language. The answer came in a rather unpleasant whining voice, punctuated by sobs.

"She says, Your Excellency," Su Lin told him, "that her husband was promoted to threshing floor foreman. Now he has no time for her. He has taken up with one of the girls working under him."

"You can't blame *me* for that," said Laura McReady smugly.

Grimes ignored this.

"Tell her," he said to Su Lin, "that I am sorry. Very sorry."

And what the hell good will that do? he asked himself.

And what the hell good will that do? Mrs. McReady, to judge from the expression on her face, was obviously thinking.

She asked, "And now have you seen enough, Your Excellency?"

"For the time being," said Grimes.

"Then may I suggest that we return to the manor house?" She added, without enthusiasm, "You and Captain Sanchez will be dining with us, of course."

"Thank you," said Grimes. "And Su Lin?"

"Your servant, Your Excellency, will be able to take a meal with our own domestic staff."

And make sure that you keep your pretty ears flapping, Su, thought Grimes.

Following the line of furrows they made their way back to the waiting trishaws.

Twenty-six

After their return to the manor house Grimes, Sanchez and Su Lin went back briefly into the airship. There the two men showered and changed—not that they had much to change into, just fresh suits of blue denim enlivened by scarlet neckerchiefs. They held a brief conference in the control cab before making their way down to the roof.

"The setup here," said Grimes, "reminds me of what I have read of the plantations in the American deep South before the War Between The States. Instead of Negro slaves there are New Cantonese indentured labor—but the only essential difference is that of skin pigmentation. . . ."

"And nobody is strumming a banjo and singing Negro spirituals," commented Sanchez drily.

"But Commodore Grimes is right," said Su Lin. "The situation is analogous."

"Not exactly," Sanchez insisted. "Far from exactly. Where are the Yankee generals at the head of the Union armies, marching south to free the slaves?"

"It wasn't quite like that, Raoul," said Grimes. "In fact, according to some historians, the question of slavery was only a side issue. The major one was that of secession. And I don't think that Liberia has any desire to secede from the Federation." He got up from the settee, looked out and down from one of the control cab windows. "There's some sort of functionary down there. He seems to be waiting for us. We'd better go and join our gracious hosts at the tucker table."

The McReady butler, a tall, thin, pigtailed man in black-and-white brass-buttoned livery, bowed deeply to Grimes as he stepped from the foot of the ladder to the roof surface.

He said, "The Lord and the Lady are awaiting you, Your Excellency. Please to follow."

He led Grimes and the others into the elevator cage, scowled at Su Lin when she was standing too close to her master, scowled at her again when she moved to stand by him. The downward journey did not commence until the grouping of the passengers was to the butler's satisfaction—he standing in solitary state by the control panel, Grimes and Sanchez in one corner, Su Lin in another.

The downward journey was swift and smooth. The door opened. The butler was first out, bowing deeply to Grimes as he disembarked, saying, "Please to follow, Your Excellency. Then, to Su Lin, "Wait here, woman. You will be sent for."

She smiled submissively and bowed to the upper servant. She winked at Grimes.

The butler, with a slow and stately walk, led the way along a corridor the walls of which were paneled with some dark, gleaming wood, floored with the same material. There were no pictures or other decorations. They came at last to a hinged door which the butler opened with a flourish. Beyond this was a large room, paneled as was the corridor but with wall ornaments. There were the mounted heads of horned beasts and others ferociously fanged. There were highly polished firearms—antique projectile weapons, modern lasers and stun-guns. There were, even, crossed cavalry sabers.

McReady and his wife got up from the deep, black-leather-upholstered arm-chairs in which they had been sitting. They were dressed for the occasion—the man in a silver-braided and -buttoned black jacket over a ruffled white shirt, a kilt in a tartan that Grimes could not identify (he was no expert in such matters), long socks in the same tartan, highly polished black, silver-buckled shoes. Laura McReady was in high-necked, long-skirted, long-sleeved black with a sash in the same tartan as that worn by her husband.

Both of them looked at the formally informal attire of their guests and allowed themselves the merest suggestion of a sneer.

"Your Excellency," said the woman, "we must apologize. We assumed that you, as the Governor, would be dressing for dinner."

"The rank is but the guinea stamp," quoted Grimes. "A man's a man for a' that."

"Indubitably," said McReady. He repeated the word, making it sound anything but indubitable. "But be seated, please. A drink or two before dinner, Your Excellency?"

"That will be a pleasure," said Grimes.

He and Sanchez lowered themselves into deep armchairs, facing the others across the black, gleaming surface of the low round table. There was a decanter already there, a bowl of ice cubes and, standing on ceramic coasters, four glasses, two of which had already been used.

"Whisky, Your Excellency? Captain Sanchez? On the rocks?"

"That will be fine," said Grimes.

"Thank you," said Sanchez.

The whisky, rather to Grimes's surprise, was not Scotch. It was bourbon. He didn't mind. It would have been improved by light conversation during its intake. Words were exchanged, of course, but it was obvious that the McReady couple were trying, without enthusiasm, to be on their best behavior and were annoyed that their guests, sartorially, had themselves made no great effort. After the second drinks—insofar as Grimes and Sanchez were concerned—had been disposed of a gong sounded somewhere outside.

The butler appeared and bowed.

"Lord McReady, dinner is served."

"Your Excellency," said McReady, "shall we proceed to the dining room?"

The dining room was a huge barn of a place, gloomy, the only lighting being from the candles set in ornate silver holders on the long, polished table. The McReady family, thought Grimes, must have a thing about black wood. McReady stood by his high-backed chair at the head of the not very festive board; Laura McReady indicated that Grimes should take one halfway down the table on McReady's right. She moved to her own chair at the foot of the table, leaving Sanchez to find his way to a position facing Grimes.

Everybody sat down.

Grimes, his eyes now accustomed to the near darkness, looked around curiously. There were paintings on the walls, ancient-looking oils, uniformly gloomy, horned beasts standing around drearily in a drizzle, another horned beast—a Terran stag?—understandably perturbed by the harassment of hounds. He had been expecting that the McReady estate would be Little Texas; it was turning out to be, inside the manor house at least, Little Scotland. And what would be for dinner? Haggis? He hoped not.

But there was no kilted piper to play in "the chief of all the pudding tribe." There was only the liveried butler supervising the activities of the New Cantonese maids, pretty little girls in short-skirted uniforms. Somebody, somewhere, had switched on music—and that had no Scottish flavor. Grimes recognized one of the tunes—"The Yellow Rose Of Texas." He wished that the local representatives of the Clan McReady would be consistent.

The first course was a soup that Grimes categorized as lukewarm varnish. The second course was some sort of flavorless fish, steamed, with a bland, uninteresting sauce. This was followed by boiled mutton accompanied by vegetables with all the goodness stewed out of them. Finally there was an overly sweet fruit tart smothered with custard. The wines, Grimes had to admit, were not too bad. Without them the meal would have been quite impossible.

Throughout there was desultory conversation.

"And what do you think of Liberia, Your Excellency?"

"I have hardly been here long enough, Mrs. McReady, to form an opinion."

"Have some more of this mutton, Your Excellency. It's from our own flocks."

"I don't think that I have room, Mr. McReady."

"Oh, but you must. Haven't I heard somewhere, Your Excellency, that your nickname in the Survey Service used to be Gutsy Grimes?"

"Just a slice, then."

"Governor Wibberley used to enjoy his visits here. It was on his way back to the Residence from our estate that he was so tragically killed."

"Oh."

Grimes looked across the table at Sanchez. Sanchez looked at him.

"That is an unusual name that you have given your airship, Your Excellency."

"How so, Mrs. McReady?"

"Fat Susie . . ."

"She's named after a girl I once knew," said Grimes.

"And did you *call* her Fat Susie? To her face?"

"No."

"And was she fat?"

"Well, she was . . . plumpish."

"And where is she now?"

Damn the woman, thought Grimes. *She sits there like a statue all through the meal and now, once the subject of my murky past crops up, she's putting me through the third degree . . . And what was the* official *story of Susie's disappearance?*

"I don't know," he said truthfully.

At last the meal was over.

The party retired to what McReady called the gun room for coffee and brandy and cigars. (Grimes refused the latter and stuck to his pipe.) Mrs. McReady made deliberately halfhearted attempts to stifle her yawns. Grimes said that it was time that he was getting on his way. He thanked his hosts for a very enjoyable day and evening. There was a brief session of not very warm handshaking. The butler escorted the Governor and his atmosphere pilot up to the roof where, black against the darkly luminous sky, *Fat Susie* swung at the mooring mast like an oversized windsock.

Su Lin was waiting for them aboard the airship.

She said, "Look what I found!"

She showed Grimes and Sanchez a small sphere of black metal.

"Where was it, Su?"

"Tucked in between the main gas cells."

"What is it?"

"Just a ball, an empty ball, not hidden very cleverly and bound to show up on the metal detector I used. Just a warning."

"I wish it were a bomb," said Grimes viciously, "so that I could drop it on those bastards!"

"Not selective enough," she told him. "There are quite a few nice people in the servants' quarters."

"And I suppose that you had a nice meal," said Grimes.

"Very nice, as a matter of fact. Satay, and . . ."

"Don't tell me. But if this . . . *thing* is just a warning how did they know that *you* were going to go through the ship with a fine tooth comb and find it?"

"Not me," she said, "but *you.* You are the ex-Survey Service Commander, the pirate Commodore. They're hoping that you will make a better job of cleaning up the mess here than your predecessor did." She laughed. "You know, I think that the dummy bomb was planted not by the baddies but by the goodies."

"A warning nonetheless," said Grimes.

"Too right," she said.

Twenty-seven

As a matter of courtesy Grimes kept in radio contact with both President O'Higgins and Colonel Bardon. There seemed to be no great need for him in the capital—no schools or bridges to be opened, no official dinners or luncheons to attend. During his conversations he was deliberately vague about *Fat Susie*'s flight plan. "Just swanning around," he would say. "Just letting the wind blow me wherever it listeth. . . ."

And that, for much of the time, he was actually doing. During his younger days on Earth he had acquired some expertise as a hot air balloonist and he found his old skills returning. Now he was the instructor and Raoul his pupil. With main engines shut down and only the air pumps in operation he would decrease or increase altitude in the search, usually successful, for a fair wind. The dirigible drifted over the countryside, going a long way in a long time and quite often in the right direction.

Her descents to ground were unscheduled, dropping down with very little prior warning onto the manor houses of the vast estates, her people receiving grudging hospitality ("What the hell is *he* doing here?" Grimes overheard on one occasion) from those whom Grimes, remembering his Australian history, categorized as squatters. In long ago Australia, however, there had been three classes of colonist—the wealthy squatters, the small farmers and the laborers who, in the very earliest days, had been convicts, More than one governor had sided with the little men against the big landowners. Some of them had been socially ostracized by the self-made aristocracy. One of them, the immensely capable but occasionally tactless Bligh, had been deposed by his own garrison, the New South Wales Corps, the officers of which were already squatters or in the process of becoming such.

On Liberia things were only a little different, although there were no small farmers. The status of the refugees was almost that of those hapless men and women who had been shipped out to Botany Bay in the First Fleet and its successors. Bardon's Bullies were not at all unlike the personnel of the New South

Wales Corps. They were up to the eyebrows in every unsavory and lucrative racket.

There was the Lopez dreamweed plantation in the foothills of the Rousseau Ranges, an expanse of low, rounded hills covered with a purple growth that, from the air, looked more like the fur of some great animal than vegetation. The swarming, brown-skinned laborers, gathering the ripened leaves, could have been lice. There was the sprawling, red-roofed manor house with, at its highest point, a latticework mooring mast. There was a ship at this mooring, a large dirigible with military markings, crossed swords below the Terran opalescent sphere on its dark blue ground. It seemed to be taking on cargo of some kind, bales piled on the small area of flat roof space being hoisted, one by one, into its interior.

"And now, sir," said Sanchez, grinning widely, "we shall embarrass them by making our presence known. Give them a call, Su."

"Fat Susie to Lopez Control," said the girl into the transceiver microphone, *"Fat Susie* to Lopez Control. Do you read me?"

"Lopez Control here," came the answer at last in a very bored voice. "What do you want?"

"Request mooring facilities."

"You'll just have to wait, *Fat* . . ." There was a long pause, then, "What did you say your name was?"

"Fat Susie. And, in case you're wondering, the Governor, Commodore Grimes, is on board."

Loading operations had ceased, Grimes saw, looking out and down through his binoculars. Loading operations had ceased but work had not. The remaining bales on the rooftop were being rolled into a large penthouse—from which, no doubt, they would hastily be taken down and stowed somewhere out of sight.

A fresh voice issued from the speaker of the transceiver.

"R273, Major Flattery commanding, to *Fat Susie.* My compliments to His Excellency. I am casting off now so that you may approach the mast. May I ask how long you will be staying here?"

"Tell him," said Grimes, "that I don't know."

Su Lin passed on the message.

"Fat Susie," said Flattery, "please inform His Excellency that I am on urgent military business and have a schedule to keep. I would like to know how long I shall be delayed."

"Tell him," said Grimes, "that I am on governmental business."

"Fat Susie," said the major (he must have overheard Grimes's instructions to Su Lin), "please inform His Excellency that I shall be obliged to inform Colonel Bardon that my schedule has been disrupted. Over and out."

R273 cast off, drifted lazily astern from the mast. Flattery was in no hurry to start his engines. Sanchez, coming in against the wind, passed closely to the larger ship. Grimes could look into the control cab, saw a ferociously moustached face scowling at him through one of the windows. Major Flattery, he assumed. He waved cheerfully. Flattery did not acknowledge the salutation.

The mooring party—dark-skinned men in startlingly white loincloths and turbans—was waiting for *Fat Susie.* She was brought to the mast smartly enough, hooked on. A tall, thin man, in white tunic with a scarlet sash, white-trousered but barefoot, stood at the foot of the ladder, extended a hand to assist Grimes as he stepped down from the platform. Then he put his hands to his turbaned forehead and bowed deeply.

"Sahib. The Burra Sahib and the Burra Memsahib await you."

Amn't I *a Burra Sahib?* wondered Grimes.

He followed the man into the penthouse with Su Lin a couple of steps behind him. Sanchez was staying with the ship; it had been decided not to ignore the warning, dummy bomb that had been planted at the McReady estate. The rooftop shelter was a big one, being intended for the handling of freight as well as passengers. Grimes sniffed suspiciously. The air still carried a sickly sweet aroma. Dreamweed. It would not be wise, he thought, to inhale too deeply.

There was a large car for cargo, a much smaller one for passengers. Inside this cage the air was free of taint. The downward journey was smooth and swift. The vestibule into which they emerged had a tiled floor, black and white in a geometrical pattern which was repeated on the tiled walls. From somewhere came the tinkling music of a fountain accompanied by bird song. This could have been a recording but Grimes didn't think that it was.

The butler led Grimes and Su Lin through a succession of arches, bringing them at last to a large, airy room, the floor of which was covered with beautiful carpets. There were others, even more beautiful, on the walls, tapestries almost, with strutting peacocks, prowling tigers and brightly clad horsemen doing unkind things to fierce looking boars with their long lances.

At a low table Eduardo Lopez and Marita Lopez were sitting on piles of cushions, sharing a narghil. The fat little man, in white silk shirt and trousers, with crimson cummerbund and slippers, could have been an old-time Oriental potentate. His wife, in gauzy white trousers and bodice, could have been an overblown harem beauty.

"Lopez Sahib," announced the butler, "the Governor Sahib and . . ." He paused to look doubtfully at Su Lin. "The Governor Sahib and his servant."

Lopez put down the mouthpiece of the pipe onto the inlaid surface of the table. He got slowly to his feet. His wife remained seated.

"A good day to you, Your Excellency. Had we been expecting you we would have arranged a proper reception."

"I like to keep things informal," said Grimes.

Meanwhile Su Lin had collected more brightly covered cushions, had put them down by the table.

"Please be seated, Your Excellency," she said to Grimes.

Grimes sat, cross-legged. Lopez resumed his own seat. He, his wife and Grimes were the points of an equilateral triangle about the round table. Grimes sniffed the fumes that were drifting from the bowl of the water pipe. Mainly tobacco, he decided, but with some addition.

"You will smoke, Your Excellency?" asked Lopez. He clapped his hands. "Ram Das! A pipe for the Governor Sahib!"

"I'll use my own, thanks," said Grimes hastily. "And my own tobacco."

Su Lin made a major production of filling and lighting the vile thing for him. Mrs. Lopez went into a paroxysm of coughing.

When she was quite finished Lopez inquired, "And how may we serve you, Commodore Grimes? And may I presume to ask why you are honoring us with your presence?"

"A sort of captain's inspection," said Grimes. "A tour of spaceship *Liberia.* Just finding out what lives where and what does what. After all, this world is my new command."

"It could be argued," said Lopez mildly, "that Madam Estrelita O'Higgins is the captain of spaceship *Liberia.*"

"A sort of staff captain, perhaps," Grimes said. "And, carrying on with the astronautical analogy, Colonel Bardon is the master at arms. But I am the master. My name is on the register."

"I am not a spaceman," said Lopez, "but I think I see what you mean. I do necessarily agree with you."

For what seemed a long time the Lopez couple and Grimes smoked in silence, Su Lin and Ram Das watching them impassively. Then Grimes asked a question.

"What was that army dirigible doing here, Mr. Lopez?"

"Major Flattery is a personal friend, Your Excellency. He was paying a social call."

"Indeed? His ship seemed to be loading some sort of cargo."

"It is our custom," said Lopez, "to make small gifts to our departing guests."

"Indeed? And I suppose that these same guests make gifts to you in exchange. Like folding money."

"A plantation owner," said Lopez coldly, "expects to make some small profit."

"Talking of plantations," said Grimes, "I would like to inspect yours."

"I have nothing to hide, Your Excellency," stated Lopez. "Ram Das, ask Mendoza Sahib to attend me here. At the same time arrange for two trishaws to be waiting in the portico."

"To hear is to obey, Sahib."

The butler silently left the room.

Twenty-eight

Grimes looked curiously at Mendoza when that gentleman eventually made his appearance. He could have been a survivor from the long defunct British Raj in India. He was tall and thin, deeply tanned, black-haired and with a pencil-thin moustache. His eyes were startlingly blue against the dark skin of his face. He was clad in spotless white—shoes, trousers with a knife-edge crease, a high-necked, gold-buttoned tunic. Under his left arm was a white sun helmet.

He stiffened to attention as he faced his employer.

"Sir?"

He could have been a subaltern of some crack Indian regiment of the old days called before his colonel to be given his orders.

"Ah, Mr. Mendoza. This gentleman is the new Governor, Commodore Grimes . . ."

Mendoza bowed stiffly in Grimes's direction. Grimes disentangled his legs and, with Su Lin's assistance, got to his feet. He extended his hand. After what seemed to be a long hesitation Mendoza took it. It was like, thought Grimes, getting a fistful of cold, wet, dead fish.

"The Commodore," said Lopez, "would like a tour of the plantation. I assume that his . . . er . . . servant will accompany him."

"Yes," said Grimes, "Su Lin will be coming with me."

"You spacemen!" chuckled Lopez. It was a dirty chuckle. He flinched under Grimes's hostile glare then went on hastily, "I beg your pardon, Your Excellency, but members of your profession do have a reputation, you know."

"If a world such as New Venusberg," said Grimes coldly, "were obliged to depend upon spacemen for its prosperity it would very soon go bankrupt."

"Yes, yes. Of course. I was merely jesting. And now, if you will accompany Mr. Mendoza, he will show you everything that you wish to see. Dinner will be awaiting you on your return. Do you appreciate Oriental cuisine, such as Indian curries?"

Grimes said that he did. Then he and Su Lin followed Mendoza from the room, leaving Lopez and his consort to the enjoyment of their shared pipe.

* * *

The trishaws were waiting in the portico, each powered and piloted by a scrawny man, each of whom had an almost black, dusty skin. Two pairs of yellow eyes regarded Grimes and the girl incuriously, looked to Mendoza with a mixture of respect and fear. Fear was predominant.

"Will you ride with me, Your Excellency?" asked the plantation manager. "Your servant can bring up the rear."

Grimes would far sooner have ridden with Su Lin but the arrangement proposed by Mendoza made sense. He would be able, when sitting alongside the visitor, to point things out and to explain. (He would be able, too, to distract Grimes's attention from things that he should not be seeing.)

He climbed into the passenger basket of the leading trishaw while the driver sat impassively, his gnarled feet on the pedals. Mendoza joined him. The man was redolent of some male perfumery. Grimes sniffed disgustedly. He would much sooner have been smelling Su Lin's clean scent.

Mendoza gave orders in a language strange to Grimes. Then, "Jao!" he snapped. "Juldi jao!"

"Atcha, Sahib!"

The trishaw took off like a rocket, its spinning wheels spattering the loose gravel of the driveway to port and to starboard. Grimes turned his head to look astern. The vehicle with Su Lin was following.

"We shall pass, first, through the laborers' compound," said Mendoza. "As you will see, Your Excellency, our workers are well and adequately housed."

Well and adequately housed they may have been, although Grimes had his doubts. The trishaws sped between rows of barrack-like buildings, drab gray, of poured concrete construction. The windows were tiny, unglazed, some screened by dirty rags fluttering lethargically in the light breeze. There seemed to be children everywhere—black, skinny, naked brats of both sexes. But they were not running and shouting and screaming as children should. They were squatting silently in the dust, staring at nothing. There were a few adults abroad—withered, ancient crones shuffling on their various errands, old men sitting in doorways conversing among themselves in low voices.

These adults, despite their apparent age, seemed to be showing far more life than did the children. They stood up as the two trishaws passed, salaaming deeply. And Grimes thought that he read hate in their yellow eyes.

"Mr. Mendoza," he said, "shouldn't these kids be at school?"

"School, Your Excellency? What for? Whatever skills they will need when they join our work force they will learn from their parents."

"Shouldn't they be . . . playing?"

"Playing, Your Excellency?"

"Yes, I've seen children on more worlds than you've had hot dinners and, more than once, I've cursed the noisy little bastards. But these. . . . Anybody would think that they were doped."

"They are, Your Excellency."

"What!"

"It is their way of life. Their parents start them on the dreamweed almost as soon as they are weaned. By adolescence they have built up at least a partial immunity and are able to function as members of the work force."

"What a life!" exclaimed Grimes.

"They have never known any better, Your Excellency. And who can say that they are not happy, sitting there and dreaming their dreams?"

"Would you want *your* children to grow up like that, Mr. Mendoza?"

"I have no children, Commodore Grimes. It is extremely unlikely that I shall ever be a father. To me the necessary preliminaries, undertaken with a woman, would be extremely distasteful."

His voice must have carried. From the following trishaw came Su Lin's scornful laugh.

The manager lapsed into sullen, haughty silence. The vehicles sped on, hardly slackening speed when, once they were clear of the compound, there were hills to negotiate. The road was now a winding one, threading its way between hillocks on each of which the fleshy stems and leaves of the dreamweed flourished. In this locality the crop was not yet ready for harvesting; the predominant colour of the vegetation was a greenish blue. As they progressed, however, Grimes saw an increasing number of purple leaves.

And then they came to an area in which the harvest was in full swing. On either side of the winding roadway rose the glowing purple mounds, over which crawled the small, dark-skinned people, their white loincloths in vivid contrast to the almost-black of their thin bodies. They were working in pairs—usually it was the man who wielded the knife, hacking the fleshy leaves from the thick, convoluted stems while a woman filled a basket with the yield. Filled baskets stood by the roadside, awaiting collection. Overseers moved among the workers. These wore white jackets and turbans as well as loincloths. Their skin was lighter than those of the laborers, their build heavier. They carried short whips.

The air was heavy with a sweet yet acrid aroma. Grimes wondered if it were safe to breathe. He asked Mendoza as much.

"Perfectly safe, Your Excellency," the manager told him scornfully. "The dreamweed has to be taken orally—chewed and swallowed. If you care to look you will see the field hands doing just that. Doesn't it say in the Bible, 'Thou shalt not muzzle the ox that treads the corn'?" He barked an order to the trishaw driver and the vehicle slowed to a crawl, as did the one carrying Su Lin. "On the other hand, it is not desirable that the ox make a pig of himself. As that man there is doing."

The person indicated was working far more slowly than the others. The leaves that he was hacking from the stems he was stuffing into his busily chewing mouth while his woman, holding her almost empty basket, watched.

An overseer was making his way around and over the tangle of stems, shouting angrily. The man paid no heed, although his woman put out a hand to try to catch his wrist as he was raising another bundle of leaves to his mouth. He shook her off, went on chewing. The overseer was now within striking range. He raised his whip and used it, slashing the addict across the face. The laborer screamed shrilly. He brought up his long, heavy knife to ward off the whip that was descending for a second blow. And then there was a flurry of fast action, after which the whip-wielder was staring stupidly at his right wrist from which the bright red, arterial blood was spurting, then at his hand, still clutching the whip, on the ground at his feet. The woman was wailing loudly; it seemed odd to Grimes that so loud a noise could come from so small a body. But she was soon quieted. The knife silenced her, slashing down onto the juncture of scrawny neck with thin shoulder.

There was blood everywhere.

On the hillock both workers and overseers were scrambling desperately away from the scene of the maiming and the killing. Down in the road the trishaw drivers were attempting to turn their vehicles so that they could return to the safety of the compound. The madman, purple froth spattering from his working mouth, his yellow eyes glaring, was jumping down the hillside toward them, miraculously avoiding being tripped by the tangled roots and stems.

Su Lin's trishaw was around, making off downhill. Grimes's trishaw was turning. As it did so it heeled over. Mendoza fell heavily against Grimes—and Grimes fell out on to the roadway. He scrambled to his feet. He would have run but, in his fall, he had twisted his right leg. He was weaponless. He looked around frantically. A stone to throw at the fast advancing homicidal maniac . . .

But there weren't any stones, and it was a very long time since, as a very junior officer in the Survey Service, he had taken a course in unarmed combat.

He decided that if he were to die all his wounds would be in front. He would not turn his back on his murderer. And perhaps—perhaps!—he might be able to cow the man into submission with his best quarterdeck glare . . .

The killer was down on the road now, loping toward Grimes. Grimes stood there, facing him.

"Stop!" he barked.

And the man did stop and momentarily—but only momentarily—the light of sanity gleamed in his yellow eyes. Then he came on again, the bloody knife upraised.

"Stop! Drop that knife!"

The man came on.

Grimes heard running feet behind him. So Mendoza, he thought, had returned to sort things out. Presumably he was used to such emergencies and, probably, armed.

But it was not Mendoza. It was Su Lin. She ran past Grimes as he shouted at her, "Get back, you stupid bitch! Get back!"

She had something in her right hand, something small that gleamed golden in the sunlight. Grimes recognized it. It was the lighter that she had used to ignite the tobacco in his pipe.

He staggered after her. He had to save her from the madman, even though it cost his own life.

The maniac screamed, dreadfully. Before he threw up his hands, his knife dropped and forgotten, to cover his face Grimes saw the two-meter-long flame, a thin pencil of intense radiance, that slashed across the mad, staring eyes, searing and blackening them. There was a sickening stench of burned flesh in the air. Then the man, hunched and moaning, turned and shambled blindly away. Sightless, he could not keep to the road. He crashed into the dreamweed plants, tripped and fell heavily. His thin, high whining was a dreadful thing to hear.

Su Lin, the lethal lighter back in a pocket, stopped to pick up the knife.

"What . . . What are you going to do?" asked Grimes.

"Finish him off quickly," she said. "It will be the kindest way."

She was right, of course.

Grimes made no attempt to stop her but did not watch.

Twenty-nine

The two trishaws returned.

Mendoza got out of the leading one, walked past Grimes and Su Lin to where the huddled form of the dead maniac was sprawled face down, the hilt of his knife protruding from his back. Two of the overseers were squatting by the corpse, talking in low voices. The manager went to them, was obviously questioning the men. He returned to the governor and the girl. His expression, decided Grimes, was an odd combination of condemnation and disappointment.

He said, "This is a serious matter."

"Too right it is," said Grimes. Then, "And where were *you* when the shit hit the fan?"

"A man is dead, Your Excellency."

"For all the help that you were, I could be dead too. As for your dead man—he is responsible for one death himself. Possibly two."

"But this is a serious matter, Your Excellency. This woman may be your servant but she is a native of this world—and not a citizen. Only citizens may carry weapons."

"Only citizens, Mr. Mendoza?" Grimes gestured toward the dead man. "Was *he* a citizen? What about his knife?"

"A working tool, Commodore."

"And a murder weapon."

Mendoza ignored this.

He said to Su Lin, "Give me your flame-thrower, girl. It will have to be produced as evidence when you are brought to trial."

Grimes thought hard and fast.

He said, "It is not hers to give to you, Mr. Mendoza."

"What do you mean?"

"It is *my* lighter. During my career as commodore of a privateer flotilla I found it convenient to carry on my person gadgets such as that lighter—seemingly innocent but capable of being used in self defense . . ." While he was speaking he was filling his pipe. "I had to use it once," he went on untruthfully, "to quell a mutiny . . ."

"Then what is *she* doing with it?"

By this time the bit of Grimes's pipe was between his teeth. Su Lin lit it for him, using a flame of normal dimensions and intensity.

"You see what she's doing with it," Grimes said through a cloud of acrid smoke. "She regards this as part of her duties."

"Like stabbing a blinded man in the back, Your Excellency."

"He would not have lived," said Su Lin. "Not only was he blinded but his brains were fried."

"This is a matter for Mr. Lopez," said Mendoza stiffly.

"Naturally," agreed Grimes. "After all, it was one of his employees—or slaves—who would have murdered me had it not been for Su Lin."

"It was one of his employees who was murdered by your servant, Your Excellency. At the very least there will be a heavy claim for compensation."

"Quite possibly," said Grimes. "I shall have to look into the legal aspects. I am not as young as I was and being attacked by homicidal maniacs puts a severe strain upon my nervous system. It is likely that I shall require the services of an expensive psychiatrist to undo the mental damage that I sustained." He drew deeply from his pipe and then exhaled the smoke. "But no doubt Mr. Lopez is rich enough to pay both the doctor's bill *and* the damages that I shall demand."

"Your Excellency," almost sneered Mendoza, "is quite a space lawyer."

"As far as this planet is concerned," growled Grimes, "I am the law—and the prophets. The members of my personal staff answer only to me, and don't go forgetting it. Come, Su Lin, we will share a trishaw back to Mr. Lopez's not so humble abode. Mr. Mendoza can do as he pleases."

The two of them clambered aboard one of the waiting vehicles.

"Home, James," ordered Grimes, "and don't spare the horses."

To his surprise the man understood. It was a pity as it meant that he and the girl were not able to compare notes during the ride back to the Lopez establishment.

Understandably Mr. Lopez was not pleased when he heard Grimes's story. He would have been far happier, Grimes could not help thinking, if Mendoza had returned alone with the news of the murder of yet another troublesome planetary governor. And yet, Grimes knew, the messy affair had not been planned. How could it have been? But Mendoza had been quite prepared to let nature take its course and would have been commended rather than otherwise if Grimes had been hacked to pieces.

"A sorry business, Your Excellency," sighed Lopez.

"It could have been sorrier still as far as I'm concerned," said Grimes coldly. And then—he might as well put the boot in while he had the chance—"I was far from impressed by the conduct of your Mr. Mendoza. Any officer of the Survey Service behaving as he did would face a court martial on the charge of cowardice in the face of the enemy."

"My trishaw driver bolted," Mendoza said.

"So did Su Lin's. But she managed to jump out and run back to help me."

"Ah, yes," murmured Lopez, "there is the matter of the weapon that she was carrying, quite illegally."

"Not a weapon," Grimes told him. "A lighter. *My* lighter."

"A very special sort of lighter," insisted Lopez.

"*Anything* can be used as a weapon," said Grimes. "You should see what the average petty officer instructor in the Survey Service, a specialist in unarmed combat, can do with a rolled-up newspaper. And when I was privateering one of my officers could do quite dreadful damage with a pack of playing cards."

"You realize, Your Excellency," persisted Lopez, "that I shall be obliged to make a full report to President O'Higgins's chief of police and to Colonel Bardon."

"Report away, Mr. Lopez. I am Colonel Bardon's superior officer. And, legally speaking, I rank above the president. As far as I am concerned *my* servant took steps, effective steps, to save my life while yours, Mr. Mendoza, was rattling down the road as fast as his trishaw could carry him."

"The driver panicked!" almost shouted Mendoza.

"That's *your* story. Stick to it, if you feel like it. I could hardly care less."

There was what seemed to be a long silence, broken at last by Lopez.

"Well, Your Excellency, what has been done has been done. I suppose that now you will wish to return aboard your airship to freshen up before joining Madam Lopez and myself for dinner. . . ."

"I shall return aboard my airship," said Grimes, "and then I shall order my pilot to cast off."

"But I have instructed my chef to prepare a meal, a very special meal, for the occasion of your visit."

"You'll just have to eat it yourself. Come, Su Lin."

The butler escorted them from the oriental opulence of Lopez's reception room up to the roof. Grimes regretted having missed what probably would have been a superb curry. But, he consoled himself, there might have been some subtle poison in the portions served to him, or, possibly, a stiff infusion of dreamweed essence.

He was relieved when he emerged into the late afternoon sunlight, looking up to the gleaming bulk of *Fat Susie* swinging at the mast. Sanchez looked out from an open control cab window and waved cheerfully. Grimes raised a hand to return the salutation.

Now there would be that blasted ladder to negotiate. The wrenched muscles of his right leg were still painful and he could move the limb only by making a conscious effort.

"Your Excellency," said Su Lin, "I will ask Captain Sanchez to send down a cradle for you."

"You will not."

Slowly, painfully, he went up the ladder, taking as much weight as possible on his arms, Su Lin close behind him. He clambered at last into the control cab.

"What's wrong, Commodore?" asked Sanchez anxiously.

"Just a twisted leg, Raoul. It could have been worse."

"Very much worse," said the girl.

"But what happened?"

"I'll tell you later. Meanwhile, get us the hell out of here."

"The mooring mast is not manned, sir."

"You can actuate your release gear from the cab, can't you? As long as nothing fouls it's quite safe."

Sanchez did as ordered and *Fat Susie* drifted slowly astern, away from the roof of the Sanchez mansion, a winch whining as the short length of wire cable was reeled in. Only Ram Das, the butler, was there to see them go.

"You must rest now, Your Excellency," said Su Lin.

"All right."

"Where do we go, Commodore?" asked Sanchez.

"I'll leave it to you, Raoul. Surprise me."

Walking slowly and painfully he made his way aft to his quarters.

Thirty

Stripped, prone on his bunk, Grimes submitted to the ministrations of Su Lin.

He murmured, "What did I ever do to deserve you? Devoted handmaiden . . . Highly efficient bodyguard . . . And now masseuse . . ."

Under her kneading fingers the soreness and stiffness were dissipating. But there was another stiffness, of which he was becoming embarrassedly conscious. *As long as she doesn't ask me to turn over* . . . he thought.

But she did not.

She slapped his naked buttocks and said cheerfully, "You'll survive, Commodore. But you usually do, don't you?"

"If I didn't," he told her, "I shouldn't be here." He flexed his legs experimentally. "Thanks to you, I shall be able to stand my watch."

"All part of the PAT service," she told him. "And, talking of watches, it's almost time that I was relieving Raoul. You'll be fit to take over at midnight, will you? Good. Then you had better get some sleep."

"I'll do just that," he said.

Sleep was a long time coming—and when it did he was plagued by nightmares—or, rather, by a recurring nightmare. In it he would be standing there, helpless, on the hot road, under a blazing sun, while the madman came at him with bloody machete upraised. Each time he woke up just as the sharp, gleaming blade was descending on his unprotected head.

And then Su Lin was there, switching on the light, putting the tea tray down on his bunkside table.

"Are you all right, Commodore?" she asked. "Do you feel fit enough to take over? If not, Raoul and I can manage between us."

"I'm feeling fine, Su Lin."

"You don't look it."

"I'm a little tired, that's all. The tea will perk me up. Get back to control like a good girl. I'll be with you shortly."

"As you say, Commodore," she said doubtfully.

The tea did refresh him.

He dressed, then made his way forward and then down into the cab. *Fat Susie* was ambling along at cruising speed, almost silently, only the occasional click and whine of servo-mechanisms telling that the auto-pilot was functioning, maintaining course and adjusting attitude and altitude as requisite.

He looked at the chart and at the dotted line of the extrapolated track ahead of the airship's actual position, a trace that, astern of her, was unbroken.

"We're flying over the Unclaimed Territory, as they call it, now," said Su Lin. "No doubt, eventually, it will be tamed—with wheatfields and vineyards and . . . dreamweed plantations. It all depends, I suppose, on what sort of influx of refugee labor—slave labor—there is over the next few years . . ."

"Assuming, of course," Grimes said, "that things continue going on as they have been going on. But aren't we supposed to be throwing a spanner into that machinery?"

She grinned. "We are, Commodore."

"Just what is down there, anyhow?" asked Grimes.

"In places, a jumble of rocks. Deep canyons. Savage animals. Even more savage plants."

"Savage plants? You have to be kidding, Su Lin."

"I'm not. I thought that you had been given a thorough briefing on this planet before you were sent here, *Governor.*"

"I was given a fine collection of spools to study on the way out. I studied them. But they were all concerned with history, politics, economics and sociology."

"I'll see to it that you get a briefing on Liberia's natural ecology when we get back to the Residence. Who knows? It might come in useful some day. It will be interesting, at least."

"As you say." Grimes was still looking at the chart. "I suppose that these names given to the various natural features should tell me something. Mount Horrible . . . Bloodsuckers Canyon . . . Shocking Valley . . . But that sounds more comic than sinister . . ."

He was interrupted by an insistent beeping from the radar. He went to the console, looked into the PPI. Yes, there was a target, an airborne target, just abaft the starboard beam, all of forty kilometers distant. He pushed the extrapolation button. The airship, as he assumed that it must be, was flying on an almost parallel course in the same direction.

Su Lin had gone to the radio telephone transceiver.

"Fat Susie to unidentified aircraft to my starboard. Do you read me?"

The reply came with no delay.

"Citizen Marat to *Fat Susie.* I read you loud and clear. Where bound, *Fat Susie*?"

"Cruising, *Citizen Marat.* Where are you bound? Over."

"Libertad to Rousseauville with mail and passengers. Over."

Grimes, now, was staring out through the starboard window of the cab, binoculars to his eyes. He realized that he could not see the line of the land horizon against the dark luminosity of the sky. And, at this range, he should be able to see the other airship's running lights—but there was nothing there. And something seemed to have blotted out those stars at lower altitudes. He looked ahead. There the stars were dimming, were being obscured.

So *Fat Susie* had driven into a belt of cloud. So what? Radar and radar altimeter were working perfectly. The only traffic was bound in the same direction at the same speed. The extrapolated course was well clear of any mountains.

He heard Su Lin say, "A very good night to you, *Citizen Marat*. And *bon voyage.*"

"Bon voyage to you, *Fat Susie,"* And then the male voice of the other watchkeeper chuckled. "Are *you Fat Susie*?"

"Just Su," she replied. "And not fat."

"I'd like to meet you some time."

"Good night," she said firmly. "Over and out."

"Wolves of the air," commented Grimes. "Off with you now, Su Lin. Get your head down. I have the watch."

Grimes, although he had done his share of atmosphere flying, was a spaceman, not an airman. He did not like this pushing ahead through thick fog. (Cloud, he told himself, cloud, not fog. The air would be clear enough at ground level, clear enough if he pushed *Fat Susie* up and through this vaporous ceiling.) He considered reducing altitude, then decided against it. Airships are not designed for hedge-hopping. Should he lift? But that would mean the dumping of ballast. And Sanchez had set the course, had set it in three dimensions, and might be annoyed, when called to take over the watch, to find that Grimes had been playing silly buggers all over the sky while he slept. All right, all right, Grimes was the pilot's employer. But he, Grimes, was not the master. Sanchez was.

Should he call Sanchez?

And then, Grimes told himself, *he'd have valid grounds for thinking of me as an old woman. Damn it all, I'm a shipmaster, I've commanded far bigger vessels than this little gasbag. As commodore, I've commanded a flotilla. (And,* he thought wryly, *made a jesusless balls of it.)*

Apart from the visually invisible *Citizen Marat* there was no other traffic. There would not be, Grimes knew, over this region of the planet. Grimes consulted the radar. The other airship was on a slightly converging course but she was drawing ahead. Furthermore, she was maintaining an altitude at least a thousand meters in excess of *Fat Susie*'s. She would cross ahead of *Fat Susie* safely enough and without incident.

The watch wore on. The air in the control cab, from the fumes of Grimes's pipe, was almost as thick as the air outside. The airship maintained course and altitude without a human hand at the controls. In the PPI the glowing blip that was *Citizen Marat* was now ahead, was still edging over to port. Grimes stared into the screen, drowsy, hypnotized by the steady rotation of the sweep.

But there was something wrong!

The range was no longer opening; it was closing fast. A glance at the auxiliary screen showed that the other ship was losing altitude rapidly. What the hell was she playing at?

It was one of those occasions when Grimes wished that he had three pairs of hands. Somehow he managed to push the General Alarm button and, a split second later, to initiate the process of switching from automatic pilot to manual control. *Fat Susie*—the stupid bitch!—seemed reluctant to yield the dominance of her functions to a mere human. It seemed ages before the illuminated sign, AUTO, over the wheel and the gyro compass repeater flickered out to be replaced by MANUAL. And all the time there was the urgent stridency of the alarm bells to engender panic.

Sanchez and Su Lin were in the control cab. Neither had taken time to dress. Sanchez stared out through the windows at nothingness, then went to the radar.

"Holy Bakunin!" he muttered. "How the hell did you . . . ?" Then, "Turn away, man! Hard-a-starboard!"

Grimes, at the wheel, spun it rapidly to the right. He felt *Fat Susie* heel over, heard her creaking protests. From above and abaft the control cab there was a peculiarly muffled crash—and, almost immediately afterwards, a noise that could only be that of the discharge of at least one medium caliber automatic cannon. *Fat Susie* lurched, shuddered. Grimes, clinging to the now useless wheel, managed to keep his feet. He stared out through the port window, saw that the colliding airships had, fortuitiously, found a pocket of clear air in the cloud blanket. By the crimson glare of his own vessel's port navigation light he could see a great hulk backing away, under reversed thrust, from its victim.

He could read the name . . .

No, not the name. The single letter and the three numerals.

Wherever the real *Citizen Marat* was, this was not her.

This was the army's *R273,* the rigid dirigible that had cast off from the Lopez mooring mast to make room for *Fat Susie.*

The clouds enveloped her once more and she vanished from sight.

Fat Susie, her main gas cells ruptured, fell almost like a stone.

Thirty-one

"Up into the ship!" shouted Sanchez.

"Why?" asked Grimes stupidly.

"Because the control car is going to hit first, you fool!"

Su Lin was already mounting the short ladder. Grimes followed her. Sanchez followed him. They reached the catwalk that ran fore and aft between the gas cells, these containers wrinkled now, collapsing upon themselves. There was no place else to run. The vertical ladder that gave access to the outside of the envelope was blocked by fold upon fold of limp fabric.

The lights were still burning, running from the emergency power cells. They gave some small comfort. The three members of *Fat Susie*'s crew huddled together in their cave of wrinkled cloth, blocked now at either end, waiting for the crash.

"It can't be long now," said Sanchez at last.

His voice was oddly high, almost a soprano.

He's scared, thought Grimes. *I didn't think that he'd be the type to show such fear . . .*

He said philosophically, "What goes up has to come down, I suppose."

His own voice was high and squeaky, even in his own ears.

The helium, he thought. *There's a lot of it in the atmosphere we're breathing. It's making us sound like refugees from the papal choir . . .*

"She was a good little ship," said Sanchez regretfully. "I'd like to get the bastards who did this to her."

"I'd like to get the bastards," said Grimes, "who did this to us. Did you see the markings on the other dirigible before she backed away?"

"I did," announced Su Lin, her voice faint, almost as inaudible as a bat's sonar squeak. "I did. It was the Army ship that we saw at the Lopez plantation. It was no more *Citizen Marat* than I am."

"You're the wrong sex in any case," quipped Sanchez,

There was no doubt about that, thought Grimes. He was acutely aware of the girl's nudity pressed against him.

He said, changing the subject, "I wonder what premiums Lloyd's would charge to insure the life of a Liberian governor?" He was about to add, "Especially one who travels by airship . . ." when *Fat Susie* struck.

It was an amazingly gentle contact. The catwalk lifted beneath their feet, throwing them together but not violently. From somewhere beneath them there came the sound of a muffled crash. And then there was silence, broken only by the sound of their breathing and the hiss of escaping helium.

The lights did not go out but their illumination was dimmed by the layers of fabric through which it had to shine.

They were huddled together, the three of them, in a sort of cave, the walls and ceiling of which were formed by the fabric of collapsed gas cells. Luckily air was getting in from somewhere. At the same time the helium was getting out. Their voices were reverting to normal timbre.

"Where's that fancy lighter of yours, Su Lin?" asked Grimes. "We can use it to burn our way out."

"Unluckily," she told him tartly, "I don't have any pockets in my birthday suit. The lighter's where I left it when I turned in. On my bunkside table."

"And the door to your cabin," said Sanchez thoughtfully, "should be right behind where you are standing now . . ."

Wriggling, squirming, they managed to turn around. Su Lin's body, Grimes realized, was slippery with perspiration. So was Sanchez's, on the other side of him. They were facing a featureless wall of limp fabric. They tried to lift it up and clear, but it was anchored somehow at its lower edge. They tried to pull it down, then to pull it sideways. Grimes was almost envying the nudity of his companions. His own clothing was becoming soaked. He could feel the sweat puddling in his shoes.

During their struggles with that impenetrable curtain Su Lin's hip was pressing heavily against his right side. There was something hard in his pocket of which he became painfully conscious. His pipe, of course. His pipe—and the old-fashioned matches that he preferred to other means of ignition.

"Raoul," he asked. "This fabric . . . Is it flammable?"

"Of course not."

"Will it melt, if heat's applied?"

"I don't know. I just fly airships. I don't build them."

"Then there's only one way to find out. Su Lin, can you shift a bit to your right? A bit more . . ."

"Normally I should appreciate this," grumbled Sanchez, against whom the girl was now pushing.

Grimes got the box of matches, after a struggle, out of his pocket. It felt damp to his touch. Had his perspiration made them useless? He got one of them out of the box, struck it. It fizzled sadly and went out. He dropped it, extracted a second one. He was careful not to touch either its head or the striking surface with his fingers. This one did burn, but unenthusiastically. The oxygen content of the air in their little cave must, thought Grimes, be getting low, depleted by their consumption of it during their exertions.

Carefully, carefully he brought the feeble flame into light contact with the fabric. It began to smoke and bubble. A vile, acrid stench assailed their nostrils. The match went out. Grimes let it fall, got a third one from the box. By the time that it had burned away there was a small hole with fused edge, just large enough for Su Lin to get her index finger into. She tried to tug downwards but achieved nothing.

Grimes used seven more matches to enlarge the hole in an upward direction. (There were now only three left; he should have put a full box in his pocket before going on watch.) He could, now, get his right hand into the vertical slit. He pulled, sideways, with all the strength that he was able to exert in this confined space. The fabric was stubborn—but there was room, now, for Sanchez to get his left hand into the bole to join the struggle.

Suddenly there was a ripping noise. Slowly, slowly the rent was enlarging while the two men panted from their combined effort. Luckily fresh air, in appreciable quantities, was getting in now.

They paused, to breathe deeply.

Between them the girl said, "Give me a hand, you two. I think I can squirm through . . ."

She did that. With her gone there was room for Grimes and Sanchez to move with much greater ease. They could hear her seuffling progress on the other side of the curtain. They heard her grunt with effort. Was something jamming the door to her cabin? They heard, faintly, what they hoped was a sigh of relief.

At last she was back.

"Stand clear!" she called. "Stand clear!"

The jet of flame—not as long as when the lighter had been used as a weapon but still as glaringly incandescent—swept downwards, and then up. It went out.

She said. "Come in. This is Liberty Hall. You can spit on the mat and call the cat a bastard."

The ship—what was left of her—was theirs again.

They gained access to their cabins.

Sanchez and Su Lin got dressed, then they and Grimes sat in the little wardroom with stiff drinks. They felt that they deserved them but were careful not to overindulge. Grimes wanted to take a torch to go outside to assess the damage but the others vetoed the suggestion.

"We're still alive," Su Lin told him. "If we go outside the ship, at night, we very soon shan't be. This is the Unclaimed Territory. Remember?"

"And as for viewing the wreck," said Sanchez, "that can wait until daylight. One thing *is* certain—*Fat Susie* will never fly again."

"Mphm," grunted Grimes, filling and lighting his pipe. Then, "What time is sunup, Raoul?"

The pilot looked at his watch, just a timekeeper without any fancy functions.

"About an hour," he said. Then, with a wry grin, "Where *has* the night gone to?"

"I'll make some tea," said Su Lin briskly.

She got up from the settee, went from the wardroom into the adjoining galley. After a brief absence she returned.

"Raoul," she said, "there's no fresh water . . ."

Sanchez got up and went back with her into the airship's kitchen. They returned, eventually, to the wardroom. Their faces were grave.

"Commodore," said the pilot, "there's good news and bad news. The good news is that this was a crash that we shall be able to walk away from. The bad news is that we owe our soft landing to the fact that we lost considerable mass during our descent. Our fresh water tanks must have been holed."

"If our luck holds," said Su Lin, "we might find that we're not too far from a stream . . ."

"And that the stream doesn't harbor any life forms big enough to be a serious menace to us," Sanchez said.

"Meanwhile," the girl went on, "we have beer, and table wines, and lolly water. Even if there's no water handy it'll be at least a week before we die of thirst."

"You're a pair of cheerful bastards," grumbled Grimes.

"Don't complain," the girl told him severely. "We're alive. There's no reason at all why we shouldn't stay that way."

"I'm surprised," said Grimes, "that Major Flattery didn't stick around to make sure that we were all very dead."

"I was myself—but, thinking it over, I can see why he just made us crash, *here,* and then flew off," said the girl. "I can see what the official story will be. Steering gear failure and a midair collision, contributed to by the bad airmanship of the vessel sustaining major damage. Flattery's own ship was damaged too, so much so that he could not make an immediate search for survivors—if any . . . In the fullness of time a proper search will be organized—but everybody will be quite sure either that we were all killed at once by the crash or, shortly afterwards, by the local flora and fauna. . . ."

"Why should Flattery make a report at all?" asked Grimes, "except to his boss, Colonel Bardon . . . As far as the rest of Liberia is concerned Governor Grimes will be enjoying himself flying hither and yon about his domain. Eventually there will be a public urinal or something to be ceremoniously opened and people will start to ask, 'Where *is* the Governor?' And Lopez Sahib will have been the last person to have seen me, and he will say that *Fat Susie* was last sighted proceeding east—whereas we were proceeding north. . . ."

"And years from now," said the girl, "when the Unclaimed Territory is opened up for exploitation, somebody will find what's left of *Fat Susie* and what's left of us. If anything."

"And I shall be blamed, posthumously," Sanchez said. "Pilot error. That's what they'll say."

"And what they'll say about me," contributed Grimes, "is that my famous luck finally ran out . . ."

They all laughed, enjoying, briefly, their indulgence in gallows humor.

Then Grimes asked, "Could we make our way back to civilization by foot?"

"Not if we're where I think we are—where I'm reasonably sure that we are—we couldn't. Not even if we had weapons. Did *you* bring any private pocket artillery with you, Commodore?"

"No."

"Su Lin?"

"Only my all-purpose lighter. And there are some quite useful knives in the galley—not that they'd be much use against the local predators. And you, Raoul?"

"There's a laser torch in the workshop. Normally it runs off the mains, although it has a power cell. But the power cell has a limited life."

"We could recharge—or could we?—from the power cells that are supplying juice for the emergency lights," said Grimes.

"And *they,* too, aren't exactly everlasting," Sanchez told him.

"Even so, once the sun is up they should be recharging themselves."

"Yes. Of course. Assuming that things weren't too badly damaged by the collision and the crash. As soon as it's light we'll go outside and see just how well off—or badly off—we are."

Thirty-two

Dawn came, the light of the rising sun striking through but diffused by the tattered fabric that obscured the outside of the wardroom windows. Su Lin led the way into the galley where each of them selected a knife. Grimes did not like knives; he made no secret of his preference for doing his killing from a distance, lobbing missiles and directing assorted lethal rays at some enemy whom he would never meet face to face while, of course, this same enemy would be reciprocating in kind.

These sharp blades, however, were better than nothing—not as good as Su Lin's versatile lighter but the charge in that would not last forever.

The three of them made their way aft, frequently having to hack their way through the tough fabric of the collapsed helium cells. They cut their way into the workshop. They found not only the laser gun—it looked like a weapon, a pistol, but its range would be pitifully short—but also two long-handled spanners, a big screwdriver that might be used as a stiletto, and a hammer.

Egress would not be possible through the control car; comparatively gentle as their fall had been at the finish, that compartment had taken the brunt of the impact. The thin metal skin forming the envelope must, Grimes knew, have been pierced by the sharp prow of Flattery's airship and by the fire of the major's automatic cannon—but none of them could do more than hazard a guess as to where the bigger rents would be. So, even though they were conscious that they were using power which might be badly needed for defense, Sanchez cut through the metallic integument, burning what was, in effect, a large inverted U, a panel that was easily bent out and down.

Fat Susie had found her last home on top of a low, rounded hillock. No, not a hillock. It was an island in the middle of a river. It would be an easy swim to either bank. Furthermore, that stream would be a valuable source of fresh water.

Grimes was the first out through the improvised doorway although the others tried to restrain him. He stood there in the warmth of the morning sun, savoring the fresh air, the light breeze that carried the not unpleasant tang of some vegetable growth. He straightened up from his knife-fighter's crouch, an attitude which he felt must look more than a little foolish. He wished that he had a sheath into which to stick the long, sharp blade.

Su Lin joined him, her golden lighter, ready for action, gleaming in her right hand. Sanchez—the captain, last to leave his ship—jumped down. Unlike the others he did not stand admiring the scenery. He stared up at *Fat Susie,* a great, gleaming beached whale that had been run down and almost cut in two by some passing vessel.

"The bastards!" he muttered with great feeling. "The *bastards!"*

"But not very efficient ones," commented Grimes. "They should have made sure of us."

"But they have, Commodore. They have. This is the Unclaimed Territory."

"All that I see," Grimes told him, "is a quite pleasant little island in the middle of a river, with the eastern and western banks within easy reach of even such a poor swimmer as myself. The banks are well wooded—and that looks like fruit on some of the trees. Is it edible, I wonder?"

Su Lin muttered something about Gutsy Grimes.

"We have to eat, don't we?" Grimes said. *"Fat Susie* wasn't stocked for a long voyage. We have to live off the land." He grinned. "Unless we resort to long pig," he finished.

"The Governor's talking sense, Su Lin," Sanchez admitted. "What do you know, really know, about the Unclaimed Territory? Apart from hearsay, that is. . . ."

"What do *you* know, Raoul?" she countered.

"Not much. Not one quarter as much as I should. It's a reserve of native lifeforms, some of them nasty. . . ."

"Like that?" asked Grimes.

He indicated with his knife something that, moving silently, was almost upon them. It didn't look like much to worry about. It could have been an almost deflated air-mattress, garishly striped in blue, green and orange, flung carelessly down upon the mossy ground. But it was motile, flowing over the irregularities of the surface.

"Just a glorified amoeba . . ." he said.

Foolishly—as he was very soon to realize—he squatted, prodding the wetly glistening surface with the point of the blade. He wondered dazedly what had hit him as he was hurled violently backwards. He sprawled there, paralyzed. He was dimly aware that Su Lin had her lighter out, was directing its shaft of intense flame at the . . . *thing.* There was a strong smell of burning. Grimes was expecting it to be of seared meat but he was surprised. The smoke that irritated his nostrils, that made him sneeze, that made them all sneeze, was one that he would have associated with a grass fire.

He heard rather than saw the flurry of activity as the creature, flapping madly in its death throes, died.

Then Su Lin was beside him, kneeling by him, her strong, capable hands stroking him gently.

"Commodore! Are you all right?"

"What. . . . What hit me?"

"It was an electric shock. I should have remembered what these things look like. . . ."

"What . . . things?"

"Shockers, they call them . . ."

He managed to sit up.

"Then this must be the Shocking River that I saw on the chart. And the shockers themselves . . . Like electric eels and rays back on Earth, and similar animals elsewhere. . . ."

"Yes. But these aren't animals. They're plants. They use their chlorophyl to convert sunlight into electricity. . . ."

Grimes was recovering now, his interest diverting his attention from the pain that persisted in his cramped muscles.

"Plants, you say? Motile plants . . . But why motile?"

"So that they can move from shadow into sunlight to recharge their batteries, crawl back into the shade to avoid an overcharge." She laughed. "I gave this one an overcharge, all right! Too, very often, their victims are thrown away from them by the shock. Then they have to ooze toward them and over them to envelop and ingest them."

Grimes shuddered. He did not fancy being enveloped and ingested.

"By why," he persisted, "are their victims such mugs as to touch them in the first place?"

"Why were you such a mug, Commodore?"

"Mphm. And, come to that, why did I get a shock? The knife has a wooden handle. It should have been a fairly effective insulator . . ."

He was still holding the weapon. He dropped it to the ground, saw the metal studs that secured the hilt to the blade.

"Yes, Su Lin, I was a mug. But *why* are the local animals mugs too?"

"They are attracted by the gaudy coloration—which duplicates, almost exactly, the coloration of other plants, non-motile and without built-in solar power plants, which are very good eating. I hope that we find them so—as we might be here for a very long time."

"If you will excuse me from the natural history lesson," said Raoul, "I'll carry on with my survey of the ship."

"Do that," said Grimes. "Su Lin and I will explore the island, what there is of it, and see what it has to offer in the way of a balanced menu."

"We will keep together," said the girl firmly. "As far as I can recall, from what I have read, the shockers are the least dangerous of the life forms that we are liable to encounter. So, while one is poking around the wreckage, the other two will be keeping a lookout. I shall have my lighter and the Commodore will have the laser pistol."

"I wish it were a *real* pistol," said Grimes.

"We have to make do," she said, "with what we've got."

Thirty-three

There were flying things that sailed through the air with lazy, undulant grace—until they swooped. They were all great, flexible wing, long, sharp beak and huge, bulbous eyes. These creatures, the humans soon discovered, were attracted both by movement and by color. They saw one of them dive from the air onto a shocker, saw it stunned into immobility and, slowly, slowly enveloped by the crawling plant. They were attacked themselves, three times. On the first two occasions pairs of the creatures were easily driven off by the slashing jet of fire from Su Lin's lighter, set to maximum intensity. The third attack was by a solitary flyer, hungrier or more aggressive than the others. It came boring in, vicious beak extended, like some nightmare airborne lancer, until Su Lin, standing her ground, succeeded in blinding it. (*Her favorite technique,* thought Grimes with a shudder. *I'd sooner have her on my side than against me. . . .*) Whining shrilly the thing veered away, flapping clumsily, and fell into the river. Almost immediately its struggling body was attacked by the denizens of the stream—and very shortly thereafter a covey of aerial predators swooped down, not (of course) to rescue their mate but to prey upon the aquatic carnivores that were ripping his (?) body to shreds. Long, writhing, segmented, many-legged bodies were impaled on the sharp beaks, carried into the sky and then dropped from a great height to fall with armor-shattering impact onto a rocky outcrop on the far side of the water.

"That could have happened to us," muttered Sanchez, at last tearing his eyes away from the distant, grisly feast.

"But it didn't," said Grimes, "Thanks to Su Lin. But I suggest that, from now on, we move *very* slowly. It might help."

It did—but working in slow motion was tiring. And although the flying things now seemed to be ignoring them (perhaps they were intelligent and had come to the conclusion that the strange, two-legged beings on the island were better left alone), there were other . . . nuisances. There was a sort of huge worm that, unexpectedly, would extrude its blind head from the mossy ground and attempt to fasten its sucker mouth upon their booted feet and ankles. There was a small army of crab-like things, each with a carapace all of a meter across, each armed with a pair of vicious looking pincers, that marched out of the stream and up the hill in military formation, that milled about in confusion on finding the way blocked by the wreckage of *Fat Susie,* that finally made its way around the stranded airship and then down the hill and into the water.

There was a straggler.

This Grimes killed with the laser pistol. The smell of roast crab made his mouth water.

"That was very foolish, Commodore," chided the girl. "The rest of them might have come back to attack you."

"But they didn't, did they? And I'm very fond of crab."

"These things only look like crabs. Their flesh might be poisonous to us."

"There's only one way to find out. Standard Survey Service survival technique. You take only a very small taste of whatever it is you're testing. If, at the end of an hour, you're suffering no ill effects then it's safe and you can tuck in."

While he spoke he was using his knife to lever up the top of the carapace, like a lid. The smell was stronger, more tantalizing. He scooped out a pea-sized portion of the pale pink, still steaming, flesh with the point of the blade. He was raising it to his mouth when she put out a hand to stop him.

"No, Commodore. Not you. You're the Governor. I'm the guinea pig." Her long fingers plucked the morsel of meat from the knife, brought it to her mouth. "H'm. Not bad, not bad at all. Now, I'll put this thing in the shade. If I'm still healthy at the end of an hour it will be our lunch . . ."

Slowly, painstakingly they continued to make their way about the wreck. They found that a relatively large area of the solar energy collecting screens on top of the envelope was undamaged. Power would be no problem. Hopefully neither food nor water would be—as long as they could fill buckets from the river without being dragged into it and eaten. (None of them had any desire to see the things that had attacked the downed flier at close quarters.) They might even, constructing a raft or canoe from the dirigible's metal skin, be able to get away from the island by crossing the stream or by drifting down-river. But what then? Could they hope to make their way overland or by water to human settlement? So far they had seen only a small sample of the Unclaimed Territory's flora and fauna, and only those creatures that operated by day.

What came out at night?

Yet, thought Grimes, there just could be a way. It all depended on what was in the workshop, what materials there were for making emergency repairs. Too, they would have to gain access to the wrecked control car so that they could study the charts.

"I'm still alive," said Su Lin. breaking into his thoughts. "It's lunch time. I can whip up some mayonnaise, and . . ."

But when they went to pick up the crab-thing they found that the worms had gotten to it first, sucking the shell dry and empty.

Thirty-four

Back in the wardroom they took lunch, eating rather uninteresting sandwiches (Grimes bitterly regretted not having had the crab put in a safe place) and washing them down with mineral water. After the meal and a brief smoke Grimes suggested that they get in a supply of fresh water. There were buckets available; there were some large empty plastic bins that could be filled. Sanchez volunteered to do the actual bucket filling and insisted that it was his duty. While he stooped on the river bank, bending out and down and over, Su Lin and Grimes kept watch—she of the sky and he of the water. Her weapon had a far greater range than his, the laser tool.

The winged creatures did not bother them. The many-legged swimmers did, once they became aware of the humans' existence. Grimes drove off the first attack, by a single predator, without any difficulty. He discovered that if he kept the water boiling or almost so it was a good deterrent. The ugly, vicious things did not venture from the merely warm into the very hot. He was beginning to congratulate himself when, very fortunately, he took a glance upstream. The water centipedes—as he had decided to call them—were coming ashore, were advancing toward them, their two-meter-long bodies wriggling sinuously along the bank. Hastily he and the others retreated up the hill, temporarily abandoning the buckets. Luckily the aquatic predators could not stay long out of their native element. They returned to the river.

But they waited there, their writhing bodies gleaming just under the surface, stalked eyes upheld like periscopes.

Grimes had seen in the workshop some pairs of rubberized work gauntlets. Accompanied by Su Lin and Sanchez he went to get three pairs of these.

"A good idea, sir, now that it's too late," complained Sanchez. "I could have done with these when I was having to dip my hands into that near-as-dammit boiling water . . ."

"They're to insulate against more than heat," Grimes told him.

Su Lin laughed appreciatively; she was quicker on the uptake than the pilot.

They went in search, then, of shockers. It was quite easy to distinguish them from those other gaudy plants that they imitated. If a thing wriggled sluggishly when it was lifted, it was a shocker. If it didn't wriggle and was securely rooted to the ground it wasn't. They were able to build a barricade of the electric plants up-river from where the buckets had been left. Then Grimes, with the laser, heated the water to near-boiling point again, simmering a centipede that was evincing hostile attentions toward him. The other creatures, as before, came ashore upstream. They tried to cross the living, garish carpet to get at their prey. They twitched and died.

Grimes wondered if they were edible—but the motile plants had already made that decision. Very soon the long, twisted bodies were enveloped and the process of ingestion had commenced. Grimes shrugged. Those centipedes hadn't looked very appetizing. Hopefully, perhaps tomorrow, at the same time as today, there would be another procession of crabs. . . .

Anyhow, something had been accomplished. The wreck of *Fat Susie* was now well stocked with water.

"What now, Commodore?" asked Sanchez wearily.

"We get down into the control car to fetch out the charts, Raoul."

"Come off it, sir. Can't it wait until tomorrow? We've put in a very busy day, and it will be advisable for us to keep watches all through the night. We've seen only the daytime beasties—Bakunin alone knows what the nocturnal ones are like!"

"Was Bakunin a xenobiologist?" asked Grimes interestedly.

"Just somebody to swear by, sir—the same as your Odd Gods of the Galaxy."

"We'll continue this theological discussion later," said Grimes. "Right now I want those charts. I want to see what chance we have of getting out of here."

"But we can't even get ashore from this blasted island!"

"Can't we?" asked Grimes gently. "Can't we?"

"Of course we can," said Su Lin, "as long as the Commodore's famous luck hasn't run out."

"I don't think that it has," said Grimes softly. "I don't think that it has. . . ."

They had to cut their way into the control car, using the laser tool. Fortuitously—a case of Grimes's luck!—the aperture that they burned in the deck was directly over the chart table. Fantastically none of the charts sustained fire damage. They took these to the wardroom, spread them out on the carpet, studied them.

"We're here," said Sanchez definitely, drawing a circle around the representation of an island in a wide river with a soft pencil.

"Are you sure, Raoul?"

"Yes, sir. It's not far from where Flattery attacked us. We made very little headway after that—for obvious reasons."

"Mphm. Now find me a small scale chart, one with the Shocking River and this island on it but showing the terrain beyond the Unclaimed Territory."

"This one should do, Commodore."

"Good. Now, how was the wind today?"

"I . . . I didn't notice. . . ."

"Did you, Su Lin?"

"No."

"Well, I did. It's been northerly all the time—no more than light airs during the forenoon but, by now, quite a stiff breeze. Presumably—and hopefully—this weather pattern will persist. From where we are now the shortest distance to what is laughingly referred to as civilization is due south."

"But we still have to get off the island, sir!" protested Sanchez. "And then, when we do, we have to cross at least a thousand kilometers of broken terrain *crawling* with all manner of *things*. . . ."

"I know that, Raoul. Now, am I correct in stating that I saw, in the workshop some tubes of a very special adhesive?"

"Yes, sir."

"Used when you're slapping patches on to ruptured helium cells."

"That's what it's for, sir."

"And did I see some cylinders of compressed helium?"

"You did." Sanchez laughed. "I see what you're driving at, Commodore. A balloon with the envelope made from pieces of our burst gas cells glued together. And suppose we get winds with an average velocity of, say, twenty kilometers an hour . . . A fifty-hour flight—and we're out of this mess!"

"And probably into a worse one," grumbled Su Lin, but smiling as she spoke.

But the supply of adhesive, they discovered, was sufficient only for making the odd repairs. There was not nearly enough to gum together pieces of fabric to make a balloon large enough to support three persons. The helium situation was better—but what would they have to put the lighter-than-air gas in?

Grimes said, "With luck we might be able to make a reasonably airworthy one-man balloon. With luck that one man might make it, then come back to rescue the others. . . ."

"A one-woman balloon," said Su Lin.

"After we've made the thing," said Grimes, "we'll decide who's to go."

Thirty-five

Sanchez stood the evening watch, Su Lin the middle and the morning watch was kept by Grimes. Before they broke up—two to go to their beds and the other to commence his tour of duty—they discussed procedure. Would it be better for the watchkeeper to stay inside the ship or should he go outside? They agreed that an open-air vigil could well be tantamount to suicide. Then there was another question. Should lights be rigged to illuminate *Fat Susie* from the outside, or not? None of them knew much about the flora and fauna of the Unclaimed Territory. Would night prowlers be scared away by lavish illumination or would they be attracted to it?

"We didn't have any unfriendly visitors last night," argued the pilot. "The only lights were those inside the ship—and most of the ports were well screened by wreckage."

"Any nocturnal animals," said Grimes, "could well have been scared away by the descent of a huge monster from the sky. It might not be long before they accept *Fat Susie* as part of the scenery. If we rig lights outside it will make her look unnatural and delay acceptance. Too, if we do have to go outside to fight something we shan't be fighting in the dark."

"That makes sense," said Su Lin. "But the watchkeeper should stay inside the ship, on the catwalk handy for the cabins, and, on no account, go outside by himself. And the watchkeeper will have with him what seems to be our most effective weapon—my lighter." She grinned at Grimes. "And I hope that you, Commodore, will use matches to light your pipe. I don't want the lighter's charge reduced unnecessarily."

They found suitable and powerful lights and ran them, on wandering leads, outside the ship. They stood there, while the darkness deepened, waiting to see if anything would be attracted. They soon came to the conclusion that the gearing lamps would be useful in an unexpected way. Up the hill, from all sides, oozed the shockers, coming to recharge their solar batteries. They soon formed a tight cordon about the wreck, seemingly content to remain there, quiescent, soaking up the radiation. They were far more effective a barricade against intruders than anything that might have been constructed from the available materials could be.

After a not very satisfactory supper Grimes and Su Lin retired to their cabins, leaving Sanchez in charge.

The girl called Grimes at 0345 hours, bringing him the usual tea tray. After a sketchy toilet he dressed, then joined her on the catwalk.

She said, "It's been a quiet night. Either the lights have been scaring things off—or they've been electrocuted. If you don't mind, Commodore, I'll get my head down. We shall have a busy day."

"Off you go," Grimes told her.

He made his way through the ship to the hole that had been cut in her metallic skin, looked out. The external lights were burning brightly, the garish carpet of shockers was still in place. Here and there were sluggish stirrings, lazy undulations. A few of the carnivorous, mobile plants were bulging. They had fed, obviously. On what? On something quite big, that much was obvious. Something that, quite possibly, might have gotten inside the wreck and fed on its human occupants.

Would it be possible, wondered Grimes, to . . . to harvest? Why not? They were plants after all, not animals . . . to harvest the shockers, keep them in captivity and export them at a nice profit? The Survey Service would be a potential customer. Grimes recalled occasions in his own career when he had been involved in the exploration of newly discovered plants. Efficient sentries such as these creatures would have been very, very useful.

Get-rich-quick Grimes, he thought. *That's me.*

At the moment there was only one snag. As Governor of this world he could not, legally, engage in any profit-making enterprise. As Governor? He laughed aloud. If things didn't go as he was hoping he would soon be the late Governor Grimes.

He went back inside, smoked his foul pipe. He went into the galley and constructed a multi-tiered sandwich, made tea. He thought, as he was munching his snack, *We shall have to institute a system of rationing until we find out just what around here is edible.*

The watch wore on.

At 0600 hours he called Sanchez.

Shortly thereafter the two of them went to the hole in the envelope. They could not watch the sun rise as that was on the other side of the ship. They saw the shockers slowly oozing away from the shadow cast by the twisted hull.

Artificial light they liked when there was nothing else—but they preferred the real thing.

"So we can get out," said Grimes, "without having to wear rubber boots . . ."

Until it was time to call Su Lin the two men busied themselves in the workshop, carrying the tools and some of the materials that they would need out of the ship. They did not think that any of the local life-forms would be interested in gas cylinders, shears or tubes of adhesive. They kept a watch for fliers, some of which were already sailing through the sky like, Grimes thought, the manta rays that he had seen in the tropical seas of Earth. Only once did one swoop down upon them but it sheared off at once as soon as Grimes directed a jet of flame, from Su Lin's lighter, in its direction.

Then the girl was called and they had breakfast. She, officiating as cook, looked at Grimes suspiciously.

"I could have sworn," she said, "that there was more bread than this when we finished supper last night. And there were those hard-boiled eggs that I had plans for. And what's this in the gashbin? An empty sardine can . . ."

"I'll get you another crab this morning," promised Grimes.

"You'd better, Commodore. You'd just better . . ."

After the meal—fried eggs (there would be no more after this) and bacon (in short supply but not finished)—they got down to work. Working mainly inside the ship they cut large sections from the fabric of the collapsed helium cells, trying to keep these as big as possible. Sweating with the exertion they—Grimes and Sanchez—lugged these out of the ship, spreading them on the mossy slope while the girl, her weapon once again in her possession, kept watch. They were troubled only by the great worms. Su Lin managed to kill one of these before it could withdraw its ugly, sucker-equipped head back into its burrow. They dragged it out of the hole, carried the still-twitching body—it was like a huge, greatly elongated sausage—into the wreck. There was a chance that its flesh might be edible.

Grimes, using his versatile wrist companion, utilizing its computer functions, had made his calculations the previous evening, had drawn plans and diagrams on the backs of the charts salvaged from the control car. The workshop yielded rulers and tapes and sticks of crayon. Finally, making ample allowance for overlap, it was possible for Grimes and Sanchez to begin cutting out elliptical sections from the gas cell fabric. They worked slowly and clumsily. At last Su Lin could stand it no longer.

"Here, Commodore," she told him, "take this." She handed him the golden lighter. "*You* keep watch. Dressmaking, with the preliminary cutting, is one of my skills. Obviously it's not one of yours."

"I never said that it was," Grimes told her.

So, while the others, on their hands and knees, worked he acted as sentry, scanning the sky and the ground and the river. Right on time the procession of crabs emerged from the water, led by the crustacean whom Grimes was now referring to as The Grand Old Duke Of York.

"Why do you call it that?" asked Sanchez curiously. (He and the girl had stopped work to make way from the procession.)

Su Lin laughed. She recited, in a sing-song voice,

"The Grand Old Duke Of York
He had ten thousand men,
He marched them up to the top of the hill
And he marched them down again . . ."

Meanwhile Grimes had opened fire on the stragglers. This time he got two of them. Work on the balloon envelope was suspended while these were carried into the ship and stowed in the galley for future reference.

Eventually, leaving Sanchez to work by himself, Su Lin went to prepare the midday meal, calling the two men when it was ready. She had boiled one of the crabs, serving it with a sort of sweet-and-sour sauce. It was delicious. The only fly in the ointment was that with her method of cookery she had seriously depleted the fresh water supply. So more had to be brought up from the river, using the same technique as on the previous day.

Nonetheless the work progressed steadily. A wrinkled, empty sausage skin was taking shape. (Grimes found it hard to believe that it, when fully inflated, would be spherical—but each segment of the envelope had been cut according to the formulae presented by the computer function of his wrist companion.) The supply of adhesive was holding out better than he had expected. When sunset came upon them the job was almost finished. All that remained was to gum into place two more panels and to fit a valve cannibalized from one of *Fat Susie*'s gas cells.

Sanchez wanted to go on working under artificial light. Grimes would not permit this. It would be far too easy, he said, for something to swoop down upon them from the gathering darkness overhead, unseen until it was too late to take defensive measures. Su Lin was in complete agreement with him. So the empty, almost-finished baloon was rolled up and placed just outside the doorway cut in the airship's metal skin. It was too bulky for them to lift it inside. It had been bad enough having to lug it from its original position.

The sun was well down when they were finished and dusk was fast deepening into night. The lights were switched on. From inside the wreck they watched the shockers, attracted by the harsh illumination, making their slow and undulant way up the slope. Did the things have a memory? Grimes wondered. Did they recall that they had fed well the previous night? But he just somehow could not accept the idea of a sentient plant.

Before long the castaways were partaking of their evening meal. Su Lin had found time during the day to test the flesh of the huge worm that Grimes had killed earlier. It was non-poisonous but, even with the exotic sauce that she had concocted, not very palatable. Presumably it was nutritious and a strictly rationed one glass of red wine apiece took the curse off it.

As before, they kept watches. But this time, by arrangement, Grimes called the others earlier. They wanted to make an early start on the balloon construction. After a very sketchy breakfast they went outside, emerging from the ship a few minutes before sunrise.

Sanchez was first out and yelled loudly in horror and anger.

"What's wrong?" demanded Grimes.

The pilot pointed.

On top of the rolled up envelope were two of the shockers. Obviously they had eaten only very recently; their bodies bulged in the center like that of a boa constrictor immediately after a very heavy meal. And what juices would have been oozing from them, what corrosive digestive fluids and excretory matter?

Su Lin hurried back inside for the work gloves. The three of them put these on and, with rather more haste than caution, removed the carnivorous plants from the top of the roll of balloon fabric, throwing them to the ground. They were all expecting to find a ragged hole eaten through the material—but it seemed to be undamaged. They felt the surface of the tough plastic with their fingers, prodded it and pinched it. The real test, Grimes knew, would not be until the balloon was inflated. And if all was well insofar as gas-tightness was concerned there was a way in which the aerostat could be furnished with protection from aerial attack during its flight.

But he would not, he decided, say anything to the others until the process of inflation was initiated. A lot would depend on how much of the fast-setting, stick-anything-to-anything adhesive was left.

There was an assault by the fliers while the last panel was being glued into place. Grimes beat this off—but when the last attacker had been disabled (those bulging eyes were very vulnerable) he noticed that the lance of flame from the lighter was neither as bright nor as long as it had been.

He said as much to Su Lin.

She replied, "I warned you that the charge wouldn't last forever. When it's exhausted all we shall have is that almost useless laser and the knives." She added, "This balloon of yours had better work, Commodore."

Then the envelope was finished and the equatorial band, made from strips of gas cell fabric, carefully positioned, held in place by sparing dabs, little more than specks, of the adhesive. Above it was a criss-crossing of webbing. Other strips of material would depend from the band when the balloon was ready for flight. These were attached to one of the light, wickerwork chairs from the wardroom. The aeronaut would travel in something approaching comfort.

The two ends of the filling pipe were connected to their respective valves.

"All systems Go!" said Sanchez, squatting by the gas cylinder.

"Not yet," said Grimes.

"But we have to fill this thing, sir," said the pilot.

"All in good time. But, first of all, *Little Susie* must be fitted with her defensive armament."

"Little Susie?" asked Sanchez.

"She has to have a name, hasn't she?"

"Defensive armament?" asked Su Lin.

"Yes. Shockers. We've found out that they can't harm the fabric. We've seen a flier killed by one of them."

"But with their bright coloring they'll attract the fliers, sir," the pilot said.

"The fliers, Captain Sanchez, are going to be attracted to anybody or anything invading their airspace. I don't fancy trying to fight them off with a galley knife. Come to that—even if I had a decent pistol I couldn't deal with anything up on top of the envelope. Not without shooting holes through my own means of support."

"Get your gloves on again, Raoul," said the girl. "We'll do as the man says and collect a few shockers." She asked Grimes, "Will the adhesive hold them in place?"

"I don't know," he said. "There's only one way to find out. If the glue won't work we'll just have to lash them on to the envelope somehow."

Thirty-six

The inflation of *Little Susie* was still further delayed.

Grimes didn't like the way that the fliers were hovering not overly far overhead, circling watchfully, gliding and soaring against the rising wind, maintaining their position relative to the island. It seemed to him that the airborne predators were far too interested in what was going on.

He said, "It will take three of us to handle this operation. It should be more—but three bodies is all we have. Somebody will have to stand by the valve on the helium cylinder, ready to shut off immediately. The other two of us will be kept busy handling the lines. Nobody will be able to keep a proper lookout."

"We'll just have to carry on and take a chance, Commodore," said Sanchez.

Grimes looked at the young man severely.

"As a spaceman, Raoul, you should know that chances aren't taken, except when the circumstances are such that there's absolutely no option."

"As now, sir."

"No. I admit that we have not had time to explore this island thoroughly—but you must have noticed, as I did, that at the northern end there is quite a miniature jungle of low bushes. In spite of their proximity to the water they are *dry* looking bushes. But not *too* dry. . ."

Get on with it! said the young man's expression although he remained silent.

"All animals," went on Grimes pedantically, "fear fire. That holds good on every world that I have visited. I am sure that this one is no exception. My proposal is this—that we start a fire among those bushes, hopefully not too fast-burning but one with plenty of smoke. The wind will blow the smoke right over us. As we work we shall require goggles and handkerchiefs, well wetted, to tie over our noses and mouths. The fliers—unless they are related to the legendary phoenix—will not be at all inclined to dive into the heart of an apparent conflagration. . ."

"Not so apparent, Commodore," said Sanchez. "But it's a good idea. As long as *we* don't get barbecued."

"We'll try just a small sample of shrubbery first," Grimes told him. "And, at the same time, we'll make sure that this mosslike growth is not flammable. We don't want to have to work with flames licking around our ankles."

"Especially," said Su Lin, "since our getaway craft will carry only one person . . ."

Grimes's plan worked.

The undergrowth at the northern end of the island was flammable but not explosively so; in fact. even with the laser in use, it was not all that easy to start the brush fire. Once Grimes got it going, however, it kept on going. A column of black, almost intoxicatingly aromatic smoke arose, drifting up the slope to cover the activities of the balloon crew, rising into the cloudless sky at an acute angle. Overhead, the fliers departed down wind. Were they really frightened? wondered Grimes, or were they hopeful that land animals fleeing the conflagration could be swooped upon as they ran in panic? The other local predators were doing well for themselves. The shockers, incapable themselves of swift motion, trapped the little, many-legged things that ran over them. In the river the water centipedes were feeding well.

Luckily there were very few sparks. Even though helium, unlike hydrogen, is an inert gas, any large burning fragment could have melted a hole in the envelope fabric. But the slowly swelling balloon was unscathed.

Grimes and Su Lin tended the guy lines, straightened out folds in the slowly distending fabric. They had to work, he said later, like one-armed paperhangers. *Little Susie* slowly took shape, lifting from the ground as she acquired buoyancy. And, although dwarfed by the bulk of the wrecked airship, she was not so little. She was not beautiful either. Despite the careful calculations and the painstaking implementation of these during the cutting and gluing of the segments she was a sadly lopsided bitch. But she was, thought (and hoped!) Grimes, airworthy. She strained at her mooring lines, anchored to the ground by grapnels from *Fat Susie*'s stores. She was eager to be off.

"Shut off and disconnect," ordered Grimes, his voice muffled by the wet handkerchief covering his mouth. "After all this trouble we don't want to burst her. And now, Su Lin, if you'll be so good as to pack me a tucker box I'll be off. Expect me back when you see me. I'll be as quick as I can mustering help."

"But you're not going, Commodore," said Sanchez.

"I'm not going?" (All the time Grimes had assumed that he would be piloting the balloon.) *"I'm* not going? Damn it all, it's my job."

"It is not, Governor Grimes," Su Lin told him. "Raoul and I have talked this over. *You* are the Governor. You are the best hope we have, such as it is, of cleaning up the mess on this planet. You're too precious to risk."

"Me, *precious!"* Grimes exploded. "Come off it, girl!" He turned to

Sanchez. *"You* know, Raoul, that I'm a quite fair balloonist. Didn't I teach you quite a bit about the art of free ballooning?"

"Yes, Commodore, and I learned from you. And I am, after all, a qualified airshipman."

"Even so . . ."

"There's another point," said the girl. "We don't know, we have no way of knowing, where the balloon is going to come down. With a little bit of luck it might be somewhere that's just lousy with OAP members and supporters. On the other hand, it might be somewhere crawling with police, police informers and staunch supporters of Bardon and O'Higgins. Even if the descent is made unobserved, by night, the balloon pilot will still have to feel his way around cautiously, to find people whom he can trust. What chance would you have of doing that, Commodore? For a start, you're an obvious outworlder with an Orstrylian accent that you could cut with a knife. Raoul's a native. He knows people. He knows his way around . . ."

It made sense, Grimes had to admit.

But he didn't like it.

He and Sanchez stood in the billowing, eddying smoke through which the afternoon sun gleamed fitfully. They looked up at the misshapen *Little Susie,* bobbing fretfully at her moorings.

"A poor thing, but mine own," murmured Grimes. "Look after her, Raoul."

"I hope she looks after me," said the pilot.

"You know," went on Grimes, "this is the first time in my life that I've actually designed a ship. I really should be risking my own neck on her maiden flight, not yours . . ."

"You and Su Lin," consoled Sanchez, "will be running plenty of risks staying here."

"Mphm. Why remind me?"

"Sorry, Commodore. What will you do if I'm not back with help within, say, ten days?"

"Then we make a raft or a canoe and try to make our escape down river. In fact, I think we'll make a start on the project tomorrow."

"And that will be a ship, designed and built by yourself, that you will have the pleasure of commanding. But I hope, sir, that it never comes to that." The pilot laughed. "You seem to have a *thing* about the name Susan. Your spaceship, the one in which you went privateering, is *Sister Sue.* The airship is *Fat Susie.* The balloon—*Little Susie.* What will you call the canoe or raft?"

"Wet Sue," said Grimes after a moment's thought.

"That sounds Chinese. It should please Su Lin . . ."

"Were you talking about me?" asked the girl, coming out of the ship with a plastic bag of foodstuffs and a flagon of water.

"Not exactly," said Grimes.

"Oh. Well, here're your provisions for the voyage, Raoul. As long as this wind holds they should last you as far as the nearest cantina."

If you get there, thought Grimes.

"Bon voyage, Raoul," said Su Lin. She put the food and drink into the chair suspended below the balloon (the added weight didn't seem to worry it) and then threw her arms about the pilot and kissed him soundly. Grimes felt a stab of jealousy. *"Bon voyage,* and look after yourself."

Grimes made a show of checking everything before lift off.

"Food . . . Water . . . Ballast . . . Now all we need is the crew. . . ."

"All present and correct, sir!" reported Sanchez briskly, saluting.

"Good. You know the drill, Raoul. That bag of assorted stones is your ballast. Don't throw it all away in one grand gesture. You'll probably have to jettison some weight after sunset when the helium cools and loses buoyancy. But don't be a spendthrift. Once weight has been dumped you'll not be able to get it back. Conversely, gas valved is lost forever . . ."

"Understood, Commodore."

"Then, good luck, Raoul." He extended his hand. Sanchez took it. "Good luck. You'll need it."

"We all need it, sir."

Sanchez hung the flagon of water from one arm of the chair, the bag of food—bread, cold meats and fruit—from the other. He took his seat, buckled on and adjusted the safety belt.

"Ready?" asked Grimes.

"Ready."

"Trip for'ard grapnel."

Sanchez yanked sharply on one of the three mooring lines. The grapnel flukes swiveled, came free of the soil.

"Trip port and starboard grapnels!"

This time it was Grimes and Su Lin who jerked upwards on the lines. The grapnels lost their grip. The balloon lifted. Su Lin did not jump back and clear smartly enough and a fluke fouled her clothing, catching in the loosely buttoned front of her tunic. She was lifted from the ground. Grimes caught her dangling legs, held her. Cloth ripped. *Little Susie* continued her ascent, taking with her Su Lin's upper garment.

Grimes actually ignored the half-naked girl whom he was holding tightly in his arms, stared up and after the rising balloon. She was rising steadily, carried along in the stream of smoke that was still coming from the brush fire. The fliers, well down wind, were staying clear of the reek of the burning. But would they continue to do so?

The diminishing balloon was drifting into clear air.

Su Lin disengaged herself from Grimes's arms—he was hardly aware that she had done so—and was absent from his immediate presence very briefly. Then she was pressing something into his hands. It was a pair of binoculars that she had brought from the ship.

Grimes thanked her briefly, then put the powerful glasses to his eyes. The hemisphere of the balloon that he could see was holding its shape. There were (as yet, anyhow) no leaks, no ripped seams. Sanchez was sitting stolidly in his chair. But, Grimes saw as he adjusted the binoculars to obtain a wider field at the expense of magnification, the fliers, the circling, soaring and swooping carnivores, were closing in. The only weapon that Sanchez had with him was a long knife—and that was supposed to be used in lieu of a ripcord rather than to ward off attack. Too, his view obscured by the bulging gasbag, the pilot quite possibly was not even aware of his danger.

And what use would the shockers be as defensive weaponry? Grimes could see them plainly enough, gaudy patches on the silvery grey envelope. He had applauded his own cleverness in having them attached to *Little Susie*'s skin but now was having his doubts. Contact with them might well be lethal but their bodies would never be tough enough to stop a direct, stabbing assault by one of those long, murderous beaks.

So far there was no direct assault.

The fliers were making rings around the balloon with contemptuous ease, flying in ever diminishing circles. (Surely Sanchez must have seen them by now—but what could he do about them? Did Anarchists pray to Bakunin?) Closer they were coming to the helpless aerostat, closer and closer. And then a leathery wing brushed *Little Susie*'s taut skin—no, not her skin but the garishly colored plant attached to it.

Grimes watched the airborne predator falter in its flight and then fall, its great wings still outspread but unmoving. Dead or merely stunned, it was parachuting down. It did not reach the ground. The others were upon it, tearing it to shreds as it dropped. Grimes was reminded of maddened sharks feasting upon the injured but not yet dead body of a member of their own species.

Little Susie drifted on, steadily diminishing in the field of Grimes's binoculars. Smoke was coming from her. *Smoke?* Yes. Grimes could just see that there was something dangling below the pilot's chair, a bundle from which the thick fumes were issuing. Clothing? Possibly. Perhaps Sanchez' jacket, probably Su Lin's shirt.

The pilot's ingenuity was to be commended, but . . . Weight was being sacrificed. As a result, gas might have to be valved. And then, with sunset (not far off), ballast would have to be dumped.

Was Sanchez sufficiently proficient a balloonist to juggle his buoyancy and ballast and still stay aloft for long enough to complete his voyage?

Grimes, he admonished himself, *don't be a back seat driver.*

Then *Little Susie* was no more than a speck in the sky, and then she was gone. She had not fallen, Grimes told himself. She was still aloft, still flying steadily south. She was just out of sight, that was all.

"This wind is chilly," said Su Lin.

He turned to look at her. She had her arms crossed over her naked breasts. She was shivering. Her creamy skin was speckled with smuts, some of them large, from the dying fire upwind. Her handkerchief mask and her goggles were still in place.

The effect was oddly but strongly erotic.

"There is nothing more that we can do today," she said. "I am going inside. Are you coming?"

Why not? Grimes asked himself. *Why not?*

He followed her into the ship.

Thirty-seven

She did not make her way to her own cabin but into that occupied by Grimes. She sat down on the bunk, stripped off her goggles and the improvised mask, dropped them carelessly to the deck. This was out of character; she was usually fanatically tidy. She . . . slumped. But her breasts were proudly firm, the prominent nipples erect.

She said, "Well, Grimes, this is it. The girl from PAT and the Survey Service's prize trouble shooter alone at last. And for how long? Until Raoul returns at the head of the United States Cavalry to rescue us from this howling wilderness. *If* he does return, that is . . ."

"He'll be back," said Grimes with a conviction that was not altogether assumed.

"But when, Grimes, *when?* And how do we pass the time until we're rescued?"

"We have to keep ourselves supplied with food . . ."

"You would say that."

"We can't live on fresh air and sunshine. And then we have to make a start on building some sort of raft or canoe to get us out of here, down river, if Raoul doesn't come back."

"As far as I'm concerned," she told him, "mucking about in boats has never been one of my favorite pastimes. Especially in homemade boats on rivers *crawling* with large, vicious carnivores . . . Did it escape your notice that this stream runs through Bloodsuckers Canyon on its way to the sea?"

As she spoke she was easing her heavy boots off her feet—her slim, graceful feet with their crimson-lacquered toenails.

"We have to do something to pass the time," said Grimes.

"For a Governor, for a pirate Commodore, for a Captain in the Survey Service Reserve you're remarkably dim. Or are you putting me on?"

"The thought of that had flickered across my tiny mind," said Grimes.

She laughed. "So the man is capable of double entendres. There's hope for him yet. . . ."

Slowly Grimes was removing his sweaty shirt. It was not quite at the stage when it could be stood in the corner but it was not far from it. And, on the bunk, the girl was sliding her trousers down her long, shapely legs. Above the waist her body was besmirched with smoke and smuts; below her navel her skin gleamed with a creamy translucence. The lush blackness of her pubic hair was in vivid contrast to the rest of her and was the focus of Grimes's mounting desire.

But, even though now naked himself, he hesitated before joining her on the not-too-narrow couch.

"Are you still . . . bugged?" he asked. "Or should I say anti-bugged?"

"I've room for only one thing at a time," she told him. "And, right now, that one thing is *you.*"

It was good, very good, but Grimes could not shake off a feeling of guilt. Here was he—and here was Su Lin—reveling in the release of tensions, the all-over skin to skin contact, the intimate moist warmth, the murmured endearments and finally—from the girl—the screamed obscenities. (This rather surprised him; he had expected that one of her race would be a *quiet* lover.) He could not help thinking of Raoul Sanchez, dangling from that crudely cobbled gasbag in the perilous sky, with no one to comfort him through the coming night.

Tenderly and skillfully Su Lin aroused him again.

This time he thought only fleetingly of the young pilot. After all, he was *there* (wherever *there* was) and Grimes was here. Worrying about Sanchez would not make his voyage any safer.

And then, looking up, they saw through the port that darkness had fallen. They did not bother to dress at once. More important was to switch on the outside lights and then to make sure that there were enough shockers, attracted by the illumination, to form a protective cordon about the ship. (To judge from their numbers few, if any of the motile plants had been destroyed by the brush fire, which now seemed to be completely out.) Satisfied that they were about as safe as ever they would be they heated water, refraining from extravagance, and shared a sponge-down. Attired in clean clothing they had a not-too-bad dinner of what Grimes described as tarted-up bits and pieces, washed down with a quite decent local variety of claret. They drew up a watch-and-watch roster.

Grimes—who should have been drowsy but was not, who was feeling exceptionally fit and alert—took the first tour of duty while Su Lin slept in his bed.

Thirty-eight

The night passed.

Grimes, who (thanks to his father's influence) was already something of a maritime historian, began to feel considerable sympathy for those long-ago Terran seamen to whom watch and watch had been routine. He recalled having read somewhere that Bligh—the much and unjustly maligned Bligh!—had been, by the standards of his time, an exceptionally humane captain. He had put his crews on three watches, four hours on and eight hours off. And now Grimes, following in Bligh's footsteps for the second time in his career, was having to revert to the bad old ways and, thereby, was missing out on his beauty sleep.

He didn't like it.

Neither did Su Lin.

"Midnight already?" she complained.

"No," he told her. "It's one bell. 2345. You've fifteen minutes before you're on watch."

"At least you've made tea. Thank you." She sipped from the steaming cup and grimaced. "What did you do? If I weren't a lady I'd refer to this as gnat's piss."

"One for each person and one for the pot," he said.

"What! I'll not believe that you used three spoonfuls of tea to make this feeble brew!"

"Who mentioned spoonfuls? One tea leaf for each person, one for the pot. There's precious little dry tea left in the cannister."

"I think I'll be able to find another packet or two. But you're right. We shall have to be economical. . . ."

Grimes would have liked to have stayed with her, to have watched her as she slid her elegant nudity from under the bed coverings. But he feared that if he did so there would be no middle watch kept. Regretfully he went back out into the alleyway. Before long, dressed in shirt, slacks and calf-length boots, she joined him there.

"All quiet," he told her. "All lights burning brightly. The shockers have been capturing occasional nocturnal beasties but I didn't see what they were. If you're happy, I'll get my head down."

"I have been happier," she told him. "On the other hand—I've been unhappier. . . ."

She kissed him briefly, then broke away before things could develop. He went into his cabin, stripped rapidly and slid between the sheets that were still warm from her body.

It seemed that only seconds had passed when she called him at 0345.

The pot of tea she brought was better—but only a little better—than the one that he had made. There was only one packet of tea remaining in the stores and they would have to make it last.

They shared breakfast—fried rice with the protein component being what was left of the worm. They knew that they must soon make a serious attempt at living entirely off the country but were inhibited from foraging by the activities of the fliers which, almost immediately after dawn, maintained a patrol over the island. And they were now almost weaponless. The charge of Su Lin's lighter was so depleted that it was now useful only for the ignition of the tobacco in Grimes's pipe. (And how long could he make his tobacco last?) The laser tool was effective only at very short range. Knives would not be of much use against something that could dive, without warning, from the sky with at least two meters of sharp, horny beak extended before it.

Water was not, yet, an immediate problem. There were still bottles of various mineral waters in the stores—but once these were gone they would have to go down to the river again. While there had been three of them, one could watch the sky, another keep an eye on the stream and the third one fill the buckets.

"Sometimes," said Su Lin, "I wish I were a mutant. One with eyes at the back of my head."

They spent the day mainly inside the wreck. Grimes, once again using the backs of the charts on which to make calculations and draw plans, tried to work out ways and means of using what wreckage was available to make some sort of boat or raft. A coracle would have been easy—had there been any of the adhesive left. But this had all been used in the manufacture of *Little Susie.* The sheet metal of the skin was very thin and could be bent into shape by hand. The laser pistol was actually a welding tool. Yet a canoe made this way would be almost as flimsy as a coracle and would offer hardly more protection against the aquatic predators.

At sunset Grimes had a sudden rush of brains to the head. Using the laser he killed—at least, he hoped that had killed it—one of the shockers when the creatures, attracted by the lights, took up their stations about the ship. Handling it with heavily gloved hands, careful not to let the still twitching mass touch any other portions of their bodies, they got the thing into the galley, put it onto one of the work surfaces. It overlapped considerably, the edges of it hung down almost to the deck.

Su Lin carved off a slice, then cut from this a very small portion. She chewed thoughtfully. When she spoke, Grimes saw that her teeth were stained green.

She said, "There's moisture here. And possibly—hopefully—some food value. Of course, there must be. The thing eats meat itself. . . ."

After an hour had elapsed she was suffering no ill effects. She and Grimes dined on shocker salad, washed down with shocker juice. (The thing's "battery" yielded a quite refreshing, only slightly acid fluid.) They were well-fed enough but they still felt hungry. Too, probably their diet, although rich in vitamins, would be deficient in many other essentials.

There was another night of watch and watch.

Just before sunrise, before the fliers resumed their diurnal patrol, Grimes was lucky enough to kill a shocker just after it had killed a thing that, he said later, looked like a cross between a spider and an Airedale terrier. He was able, at some risk, to get the animal's body into the wreck before any of the other carnivorous plants could reach it.

This provided them with meat for the day's meals.

The flesh was tough but Su Lin found that marinating it in juice squeezed from a dead shocker tenderized it. The meat was almost flavorless—but it was meat.

It would be possible for Grimes and Su Lin to hold on until Raoul Sanchez returned with help.

If he returned. . . .

If not they would either have to live out their lives as castaways or risk their lives on a hazardous voyage down-river in some cranky, homemade canoe.

Thirty-nine

"Don't . . . stop . . ." she murmured.

But Grimes's body, clasped to hers by her strong arms and thighs, had become motionless. He tried to raise his head from where it had been beside hers on the pillow.

He demanded. "Do . . . you . . . hear . . . it?"

"Hear what? I can hear your heart thumping away like a runaway steam engine . . ."

"Not . . . my heart. Or yours . . . Listen!"

She heard it then. It was very faint, coming from far away. It was the irritable mutter of an inertial drive unit. A small one, thought Grimes, such as are fitted to ships' boats and pinnaces. And there had been a pinnace in one of the hangars at the Residence.

The mutter was now more of an interrupted snarl.

The thing was getting closer.

So Raoul had made it after all.

Grimes tried to disengage himself.

She asked, rather tartly, "Aren't you going to finish what you started?"

He said, "My name is Grimes, not Sir Francis Drake."

She said, "I wasn't aware that we were playing bowls."

They laughed together.

And then doubt assailed Grimes. What if this approaching pinnace or whatever were not piloted by Raoul Sanchez? What if this were Bardon or some of his minions coming to make sure that the troublesome Governor was well and truly dead?

Then this might be the last time.

She said, "I thought you were in a hurry to rush out to repel boarders."

He said, "A man can change his mind, can't he?"

* * *

He completed the act—but it was not as good as it should have been. All the time he was aware of that rapidly approaching pinnace. He rolled off her, hastily pulled on a pair of trousers, picked up the almost-useless laser pistol from the table on which he had left it, went out to the catwalk and then made his way to the hole that had been cut in the metal envelope. He was just in time to see the ship's boat coming in to land.

A ship's boat?

And what was the name on the bows?

No, not a name. Just letters and a number.

AA #1.

The boat touched ground, crushing at least half a dozen of the shockers. A scent like that of new-mown grass filled the air. The cacaphony of the inertial drive unit abruptly ceased. Slowly the outer airlock door opened. From it stepped a woman, not young but far from old, with short, iron-gray hair and matching eyes, dressed in a uniform that was, essentially, a short-skirted business suit, well-tailored from some gray fabric that looked (and probably was) very expensive, with touches of gold braid at the collar and on the sleeves.

She looked at Grimes and at the scantily clad girl standing behind him.

She asked pleasantly. "Have I interrupted something, Commodore?"

And then she, herself, was interrupted as four of the fliers, briefly scared off by the racket of the boat's inertial drive unit but now, with that engine shut down and silent, returning in search of prey, swooped. She would have been skewered had not Raoul Sanchez, jumping out of the airlock, knocked her to one side and then delivered a dazzling exhibition of laser play.

Before the remainder of the circling predators could launch a fresh attack he yanked the woman to her feet, hustled her through the opening cut in *Fat Susie*'s skin and then literally fell in after her.

"Who is your friend, Raoul?" asked Su Lin.

The pilot scrambled to his feet, then said courteously, "Allow me to introduce Captain Agatha Prinn, of *Agatha's Ark.* Captain Prinn already knows Commodore Grimes, of course."

"Of course," she agreed. "We're old flotilla mates. And now the Commodore is a Governor and I'm still a star tramp skipper. But didn't somebody say once, 'Uneasy lies the head that wears a crown'?"

"You're more of an absolute monarch aboard your ship, Agatha," Grimes told her, "than I am on this planet. But tell me, do you still have that young El Doradan officer, the Count von Stolzberg, with you?"

"You mean Ferdinand, your son. . . ."

"How did you know . . . ?"

"Everybody knew. But no, he's no longer with me. A pity. He was a good spaceman. But after the Inquiry into the privateering racket we were told that any El Doradan officers must be repatriated. . . ."

"Excuse me, sir and madam," put in Sanchez, "I really think that this old pirates' reunion can be deferred for a while. What's of pressing urgency is what's happening now on Liberia, not what happened when you were scouring the interstellar spacelanes under the Jolly Roger!"

Grimes glared at the young man, then laughed.

"All right, Raoul. Come into the wardroom and tell us your story. And is there any beer left, Su Lin? Good. This calls for a celebration. Raoul back in one piece, and Agatha with him . . ."

"It's thanks only to Captain Prinn that I am back," said Sanchez.

The flight of *Little Susie*, said Sanchez, had not been too bad an experience. The worst of it had been the way in which he had almost been kippered, sitting in his chair with the smoldering rags—Su Lin's shirt and then his own clothing—directly beneath him. But the smoke had scared off the fliers.

During the first night he had been obliged to drop most of his ballast. The next day, to prevent the balloon from rising to a dangerous altitude, it had been necessary to valve helium. But the wind had been stronger than anticipated and he had made good time. By late afternoon he was out of the Unclaimed Territory. He didn't know quite where he was but, sighting a village on the horizon, decided to make his descent before he was over the settlement. He came down in a wheatfield, one some weeks away from its future harvesting. There was nobody to see his landing.

He extricated himself, with some difficulty, from the smothering folds of the deflating gasbag. He was, he realized, armed only with a galley knife and practically naked; he had stripped himself to his underpants to keep his deterrent fire going. As long as he was airborne he had not felt the cold as he had been traveling at the same speed as the wind. Now that breeze on his bare skin was very chilly.

He made his way toward the lights of the village, finding the going difficult in the fast-gathering darkness. At last he stumbled onto a road. Then he made better progress.

There was nobody abroad. He walked past the slave barracks—the *refugee* barracks, he corrected himself—and heard the sound of voices and of Oriental music and smelled the enticing aromas of exotic cookery. Now he was hungry as well as cold.

He kept on until he was in the village itself. There was the inn. He saw the sign—THE TORCH OF LIBERTY. It was then that he thought that some of Grimes's famous luck had rubbed off on himself. The parents of Miguel, one of his crew aboard the Met. Service tender, were innkeepers. The name of their cantina was The Torch of Liberty. Like their son, they were members of the OAP, the Original Anarchist Party. Raoul knew that there must be many Torches Of Liberty throughout Liberia—but somehow he was sure that this was the right one.

He went round to the back door.

He knocked cautiously.

He went on knocking.

At last the door opened and Miguel was standing there, demanding, "Who is it? What do you want?"

"I still can't get over the fantastic coincidence," said Raoul.

"No fiction writer," Grimes told him, "would dare to use the coincidences that are always happening in real life. But go on."

Miguel was on leave.

Miguel saw to it that Sanchez was fed and clothed and plied with restorative drinks. He listened to the pilot's story. He was of the opinion that the planetary authorities should be ignored and that Grimes should be rescued from the island as secretly as possible. The best way of achieving this, he said, would be to "borrow" one of the Met. Service tenders from Port Libertad and fly directly to the site of the wreck.

Meanwhile, Sanchez learned, already the news had been put about that Governor Grimes and his small entourage had perished in an airship crash. Searches had been mounted—but not one of them had covered the Unclaimed Territory. The Met. Satellites were making continual photographic surveys of Liberia—but the processing of the films was being carried out by Bardon's people. Almost certainly the fire on the island had been seen from orbit but it was being ignored.

Miguel and Raoul flew to Port Libertad in Miguel's 'copter. Both of them in Met. Service uniform, they attempted to take over one of the tenders. But the spaceport guards—Bardon's people—were suspicious. One of them had recognized Sanchez. There had been shooting, a chase. The two men had split up. Perhaps Miguel had escaped; Sanchez hoped that he had. Raoul, by this time little more than a mindless, hunted animal, had run up the ramp into the after airlock of one of the deep space ships in port. . . .

Agatha Prinn took up the tale.

"I was just strolling ashore," she said. "I'd just gotten as far as the airlock, in fact, when I heard shooting. I wondered what the hell was going on. And then this young man came bolting up the ramp, brushing past me. I was curious, naturally. And, having been to this world before, I was inclined to think that anybody in trouble with the authorities couldn't be all that bad. So I told my second mate—he was shipkeeping officer—to keep an airlock watch and to swear to any police or guards or whatever that no strangers had come aboard while, in my own quarters, I heard young Raoul's story.

"And what a story it was!

"As you know, Commodore, we tramp masters neither know nor care who heads the governments of the various worlds that we visit. We deal only with Customs, Immigration and Port Health officials. We never meet Prime Ministers or Presidents or Governors. At first I couldn't believe that *you* were the Governor Grimes of Liberia. But it all tied in. Jughandle ears, ex-Survey Service officer, ex-owner-master, ex-commodore of privateers.

"I've already told you that I've been to this world before, more than once. On any planet, this one included, I like to take one of my boats for a sightseeing cruise around. I log it as Boat Drill, of course. So the Port Authorities didn't feel it worth their while to make close inquiries when, this morning, I told them that I was about to go on my usual sightseeing tour." She laughed. "As a matter of fact one puppy, laughing himself sick over his alleged humor, did ask me to keep my eyes skinned for Governor Grimes and *Fat Susie*."

"And now you've found him," said Grimes.

"And now I take you and your people back to *Agatha's Ark.* I've plenty of spare accommodation. I'll keep you out of sight until we lift—and then you can use my Carlotti equipment to bleat to your bosses back on Earth about what's been happening."

"Why can't I bleat now?" asked Grimes.

"Because it's not legal for any ship to use deep space radio while in port. You should know that. You're Governor, aren't you?"

"Mphm. Well, if you don't mind, Agatha, I'd like you to take us back to the Residence. I'm still Governor—and I want to play hell with a big stick as long as I'm in office. There's Major Flattery for a start. I shall demand that he be arrested and put on trial. There's the dreamweed trade. There's . . . Oh, I could go on and on . . ."

"You can go on and on, Commodore, once you're up and clear from Liberia."

"But that wouldn't be the same, Agatha. Look at what happened in New South Wales. Governor Bligh was deposed—and then what could he do? He got no support from his Lieutenant Governor in Tasmania. He returned to England and was, to all intents and purposes, swept under the mat. Oh, Major Johnston was, eventually, brought to trial but received little more than a rap over the knuckles—and that after leading an armed mutiny!

"I have to stay here.

"I have to exert my authority. I have to show Estrelita and her boyfriend Bardon who's boss."

"As you please, Commodore," said Agatha Prinn. "I wish that I could be of some real help—but *Agatha's Ark* is no longer a privateer. The only arms aboard her are a few privately owned laser and projectile pistols."

"Just take me back to the Residence," said Grimes, "and I'll play it by ear from then on."

Forty

They managed to scamper the short distance between the wreck and the ship's boat without being attacked by anything. Once inside the small craft they made a careful search and were relieved to find that no hostile life form had taken up residence while the boat had been left unattended. Then, with Agatha Prinn at the controls, they lifted from the island and set course for the Residence.

Captain Prinn wanted to deliver Grimes at his own front door but he talked her out of it. It would be better, he said, if he and the others were dropped within easy walk of the gubernatorial palace; that way they could make entry without their being expected by Jaconelli and Smith. Too, Agatha would not be liable to reprisal by the authorities if there were nothing to associate her with the Governor.

"But they must know," she protested. "They must know that I was one of your captains on the privateering expedition."

"They *should* know," he told her, "but they almost certainly don't. If they had associated you with me they would not have allowed you to go flapping off by yourself all over Liberia. Thanks to my father I'm something of a student of history—and I know that very often Military Intelligence has been a contradiction in terms."

They timed their arrival for the beginning of evening twilight. Raoul took the controls and dropped the boat to a field just off the road running up the hill to the Residence. They disembarked—Sanchez first, then Su Lin, finally Grimes. All of them were armed with weapons supplied by Captain Prinn—laser pistols for the pilot and the girl, a Minetti automatic for Grimes. Only Sanchez was wearing anything approximating a disguise, a uniform (which fitted quite well) borrowed from one of *Agatha's Ark*'s junior officers.

"Let me know if I can do anything more, Commodore," said the tramp captain.

"You've done plenty already, Agatha. But if things go too badly wrong you can put in a full report, to Rear Admiral Damien, once you get clear of this world."

"I'll do that."

Surprisingly she took him in her arms and kissed him. He found himself wishing that he could carry on from there but there was no time. Besides, Su Lin was looking in through the open airlock doors, an amused expression on her face.

He broke away.

"Thank you for everything, Agatha."

"It was nothing. And, good luck, John. The very best of luck."

Grimes jumped down to the damp grass.

He stood with the others and watched the boat lift, watched her running lights dim and diminish as she continued her interrupted voyage to the spaceport.

They walked up the road.

They met nobody.

They did not use the front entrance to the Residence but went round to a back door, to what Grimes thought of as the tradesmen's entrance. Surprisingly, there they were met. Wong Lee, the old butler, seemed to have been expecting them. He bowed and said, "It is good that you are back, Excellency."

"I'm pleased to be back," said Grimes. "Too right I am."

He followed the old man through the maze of corridors. They came at last to the Governor's quarters. The sitting room was empty but there were voices coming from the adjoining office. One belonged to Smith, the A.D.C., the other to Jaconelli, the secretary. They seemed to be having a party. There was a clinking of glasses and the speech of each man was slurred.

"Flattery's got his step up to half colonel," Smith was complaining, "but there's no hint that I shall get my captaincy."

"But *you* didn't actually *do* anything," said Jaconelli. "Flattery did do something. He got that bastard Grimes out of our hair for keeps. And that poisonous tart Sue-Ellen or whatever her name was . . ."

"What've you got against *her?*"

"She wouldn't play, that's what. Anyhow, they're all out of our hair. Grimes, the uppity tart and that upstart of a ferry skipper . . ."

"No, they're not," said Grimes, stepping into his office with his Minetti out and ready.

That was just the start.

There were the soldiers of the guard to be disarmed and locked up. They were not so easy to deal with as Smith and Jaconelli had been. There was actually gunfire while Sergeant Martello, holed up in Smith's office, got through on the telephone to Colonel Bardon, quite bravely ignoring Grimes's finally successful attempt to shoot out the lock. (Sanchez's prior attempt, using his hand laser, had succeeded only in fusing this into a mass of metal that held the door as firmly as in its original state.)

Martello got up from his seat at the desk to face the intruders. He was a big, paunchy man, almost bald and with little porcine eyes in his fat face. His hand went to his holstered weapon, then he thought better of it. He raised his hands reluctantly above his head.

"All right," he growled. "You've won—for the time being. But the Colonel will soon fix your wagon . . ."

"That will do, Sergeant!" snapped a voice from the telephone screen. "You have my permission to surrender to the pirate. You will be released very shortly."

Martello moved to one side, away from the scanner.

Grimes looked into Bardon's angry face.

"Colonel Bardon," he said, "you are to place yourself under arrest. Before you do so, however, please see to it that Major—or should I say Lieutenant Colonel?—Flattery is clapped in irons."

"It's you who's under arrest, Grimes. Do you want to hear the charges? Whilst under the influence of drugs or alcohol you, in charge of a dirigible airship, deliberately collided with another such vessel owned by the Terran military establishment on Liberia, causing considerable structural damage. Returning to the Residence, you have threatened officers, noncommissioned officers and enlisted men of the Terran Army with firearms and illegally incarcerated them. A man in your employ, one Raoul Sanchez, attempted to steal a shuttle-craft from the Port Libertad spaceyard. A woman in your employ, one Su Lin, murdered a laborer under the protection of Senor Eduardo Lopez.

"A pirate, sir, is obviously no fit person to be appointed as governor of a civilized planet."

Grimes laughed.

"You must have suspected, Bardon, that I just might get out of the mess that your precious Flattery left me in—otherwise you wouldn't have been so ready with all those charges! But I must correct you on two points. One—I was a privateer, not a pirate. Two—I rather doubt that this is a civilized planet."

"Are you giving yourself up, Grimes?"

"Are you putting yourself under arrest, Bardon?"

"Don't argue with him!" There were two faces in the screen now; the other one was that of the President. "Send your soldiers to take the Residence. *Now*—or as soon as you can get them out of the whorehouses and grogshops!"

"I'll send Flattery to bomb the bloody place!" growled Bardon.

"You will not. The building—and it cost plenty!—is Liberian property. And what about your own men imprisoned there?"

"They wouldn't be much loss," Bardon said.

"I heard that, Colonel, *sir,*" put in Sergeant Martello. "Now, let me tell you that I've never liked working for you and your officers. If the Commodore will have me, I'll fight for him!"

Bardon cursed, then the telephone screen went blank.

Grimes stared at the big sergeant, who was still standing with hands upraised, still covered by the weapons held by Su Lin, Sanchez and Wong Lee.

Was the man sincere?

What was his motivation?

Grimes had . . . glimmerings. A lifetime in the Army, a failure to attain commissioned rank, a growing, festering resentment at having to take orders from officers no better soldiers than himself, quite possibly not even as good. Perhaps harsh treatment by Bardon or officers like him, unjust treatment . . .

Perhaps—it was possible although not probable—the uneasy stirrings of a conscience.

"All right, Sergeant," he said, "I'll believe you—with reservations. I'm not a soldier—so you shall be my advisor. But I'll be obliged if you'll hand your pistol—butt first—to Captain Sanchez. No, cancel that. Keep *very* still while Captain Sanchez takes the gun from its holster . . . Good. Now you can drop your hands. . . ."

They watched him, more than half expecting an explosion of hostile energy. But the sergeant just stood there, grinning.

He said, "You'll not believe this, Commodore, but as a boy I used to read space stories, pirate stories especially, I wanted to be a pirate when I grew up. Now, whatever happens, I'll be able to say that I served under one of the famous pirate captains."

Grimes started to explain, for the thousandth time, the difference between a privateer and a pirate, then decided that he would be merely wasting his breath.

Out of earshot of the sergeant he had a few words with Wong Lee.

"Get word to the spaceport," he said, "to Captain Agatha Prinn of the ship *Agatha's Ark.* I can't use the telephone; Bardon will be monitoring any calls made from here. See that Captain Prinn is told just what's been happening since I got back. Then, as soon as she's off this world, she can make a full report to Earth."

"Very good, Your Excellency."

"How many of your people can use firearms?"

"Most of them, Your Excellency."

"How . . . ? But no matter. Round up all the weapons you can and have men on the roof. That parapet is more than merely ornamental."

Forty-one

Grimes stood with Su Lin on the small, railed platform that was at the highest point of the low-pitched roof. They had binoculars with them, powerful night glasses that converted infrared radiation into visible wavelengths. They swept the terrain on all sides of the residence. Of one thing they could be certain—nothing big was out and moving, although there were small, glowing sparks representing tiny nocturnal animals.

"How is it," asked Grimes, "that so many of the domestic staff—if Wong Lee is to be believed—are expert in the use of weapons?"

She said, "You must have guessed by now that the Underground—or one of the many Undergrounds—has seen to it that the Governor's personal entourage are capable of defending him should the need arise."

"Mphm. But I thought that only full citizens of this world were allowed to own firearms."

"Ever since firearms were invented they've been falling into the wrong hands. Or—in this case—the right hands. Criminals or freedom fighters have always been able to get arms. When you went a-pirating it wasn't in an unarmed ship, was it?"

"For about the four thousandth time," growled Grimes, "I was a privateer, not a pirate."

"Sorry." The laugh following the word indicated that she wasn't.

Grimes broke the short silence.

"Isn't it time," he asked, "that I was put into the picture? After all, should things come entirely unstuck who'll have to carry the can back? Me, that's who."

"Too right," she said, in an imitation of an Australian accent. "But I agree. You have been kept in the dark—by everybody, from Admiral Damien on down. Liberia is on the point of blowing up. Not only is there the OAP but there are the secret organizations of the various refugees. The aim of PAT is that it shall be a *controlled* explosion. We may be People Against Tyranny—but we are also against Anarchy, using the word in its very worst sense, against mob rule and mindless violence. One of our requirements was a Governor who could stand as a figurehead for the rebels and who would recognize whatever sort of government is formed after the revolution.

"We had our doubts about your predecessor. He was a good man, but rather lacking in glamour. But you are a glamorous figure."

"Who? *Me?"*

"Yes. The people will rally behind a famous pirate, a man who was a pirate for the very best of motives. . . ."

"Mphm. Well, Su Lin, where do we go from here? What happens next?"

"Bardon sends a detachment here to arrest you. That will be the signal for rioting to break out in the city, for risings on many of the big estates and plantations. . . ."

"And if the detachment Bardon sends," said Grimes, "is a really powerful one, with hover-tanks and aircraft, we stand a very good chance of winding up very dead."

"Bardon and O'Higgins want you alive, so that you can stand trial for your crimes. And then they'll crucify you. No, not literally. But you'll be crucified, all right. Deported to Earth in disgrace together with a curt note from the President. 'Please do not send us any more criminals as Governors. But, of course, they will have to arrest you first. . . ."

Sanchez came up to the lookout point. Grimes handed him his night glasses and then, with Su Lin, went down to his quarters. He sent for Sergeant Martello. The big man soon made his appearance, escorted by two machine-pistol-toting chefs. He drew himself to stiff attention.

"Commodore, sir!"

"Sit down, Sergeant. And that'll do the rest of you. Oh, Su Lin, will you organize tea for us? Good. . . ."

"You sent for me, sir?" said Martello.

"Obviously. I want your expert advice. I know, of course, what forces the good colonel has at his disposal *on paper*. What's the situation in actual practice?"

"If any hostile power from outside tried to invade this world, sir, they could take it with an armed space tug and a platoon of Boy Scouts. One of the things that sickened me was the way in which equipment has been allowed to deteriorate. I was in charge of the maintenance of armored vehicles at the barracks—and I made such a nuisance of myself trying to get people to do their jobs properly that I was shifted to the Residence Guard, just to get me out of the way. It'd take all of a week to get the hover-tanks in order for any sort of real action. The wheeled vehicles, the armored cars, are in slightly better nick, but they're only lightly armed."

"Aircraft?" asked Grimes.

"Flattery's ship was damaged after that collision with yours. I don't think that anybody has gotten around to starting repairs yet. There's another dirigible but, the last I heard, all the helium cells were leaking badly. Three ex-Survey Service pinnaces, I suppose you'd call them. Inertial drive jobs. Light armament. Half a dozen little helicopters. . . ."

And I've a pinnace of my own, thought Grimes. *And a near-wreck of a helicopter. And, of course, Raoul's little flitterbug. . . .*

He asked, "If you were Colonel Bardon, Sergeant, what would you do?"

"Bardon," said Martello, "has always liked making arrests in the middle of the night or in the small hours of the morning. The same applies to the civil—if you can call those bastards civil!—police. But they've been arresting people who weren't expecting it. And they haven't had to be rounded up from the nightspots to go on duty.

"Believe me or don't believe me as you please, Commodore, but I think that the attempted arrest will be in the morning—and not too early in the morning, either. The approach, I think, will be made by road. Bardon was involved in a minor crash once and he's scared of flying. He'll not be expecting any armed resistance except that from you, your pilot and, possibly, Miss Su Lin. . . ." He looked admiringly at the girl, who had just come in with a tea tray. "However did you organize all the Residence Chinks, miss, right under our noses? I can see by the way they're handling their guns that they know how to use them."

She smiled coldly. "I suppose that I should thank you for the implied compliment, Sergeant. But in China, many, many years ago, there used to be a saying. Horseshoes are made from inferior iron—and soldiers from inferior men."

Amazingly Martello did not take offense. He laughed. "That certainly applies to Bardon and most of his officers!"

But not to the enlisted men? wondered Grimes, but said nothing.

He sipped his tea. So did the sergeant and Su Lin.

He said, "Since it doesn't seem that anything is going to happen tonight—what's left of it—I'll get my head down. You know where to find me if you want me."

He got from his chair, walked through to his bedroom.

He heard Martello whisper to the girl, "He's a cool customer, the Commodore. We could do with a few like him in the Army. . . ."

Nonetheless he was a long time getting to sleep. He was hoping that Su Lin would join him. But she, he reproached himself, would be doing all the work while he caught up on his rest.

Forty-two

Grimes should have given orders that the prisoners be thoroughly searched before they were locked in a storeroom. He was awakened, shortly before sunrise, by the unmistakable clatter of an inertial drive unit. His first thought was that Bardon had mounted an attack by air after all, especially as there was also the rattle of automatic fire. Snatching the borrowed Minetti from his bedside table, pausing briefly to throw a light robe about himself, he ran into his sitting room, stared out through the wide window. He could see people on the lawn, could see the muzzle flashes of the guns that they were firing upwards. The noise of the inertial drive diminished. So the pinnace—as he assumed that it was—had been driven away.

He decided that it would be better if he stayed in one place rather than go running around, making inquiries. He collected his pipe and tobacco from the bedroom, went into his office and sat down behind the big desk. He had succeeded in establishing his personal smokescreen when Su Lin and Sanchez came in.

He grinned at them.

"So you repelled boarders," he said.

They did not grin back.

"We failed," said the girl, "to prevent the prisoners from escaping."

"They were only a liability," said Grimes.

"But they escaped in the pinnace," Sanchez told him. *"Our* pinnace. Worse—before they left they made sure that the two helicopters will never fly again."

"Who let them out?" demanded Grimes. "Martello? I was a fool to have trusted him."

"Come in, Sergeant!" called Su Lin, turning to face the open door into the living room.

Martello entered.

"It was my fault, sir," he admitted.

"So you released your cobbers."

"No cobbers of mine, Commodore. But I should have remembered that Levine was a professional thief before he joined the Army. Yes—and after. Burglar Levine they call him. He used to boast that he could pick any lock ever made. . . ."

"And now you tell me." He turned to Su Lin. "Any of our people hurt?"

"None badly. Two sentries knocked out, but they're recovering."

"So it could have been worse."

"But our aircraft, sir! We don't have any aircraft now!"

"And so what, Raoul?" asked Grimes. "What could we do with them if they were still operational?"

"They'd give us a chance to escape from here."

"All of us, Raoul? All the Residence staff? Cooks and gardeners and maids and scullions and . . . and . . . I'm surprised at you. What about the tradition that the captain should be the last to leave the sinking ship?"

Sanchez flushed ashamedly.

"It's just that, even now, I can't think of the refugees as being part of the revolution."

"But they are," said Su Lin. "And they've far more to rebel about than you romantic Original Anarchists."

Grimes got to his feet.

"Since I'm up," he said, "I might as well stay up. I'd like breakfast, Su Lin, in half an hour's time. But let me know if there's any sign of an attack."

After the others left his quarters he went through to his bathroom.

Forty-three

There was a uniform that he had brought with him in his luggage—his own uniform, that of a Far Traveler Couriers captain. If there was any fighting to be done he would prefer to do it properly attired. So he dressed himself in the slate-gray shorts, shirt and long socks, flicked a few specks of dust off his gold-braided shoulderboards. He contrived a belt from a dressing gown sash, thrust the borrowed automatic pistol into it. He walked into his sitting room just as Su Lin entered with a laden tray.

"No morning paper?" he asked severely.

She looked him up and down with amused approval. She said, "Something seems to have gone wrong with the delivery, Commodore."

"I wonder what?"

He sat down to enjoy his meal. (The condemned man ate a hearty breakfast?) Su Lin sat down to talk to him, sipping coffee from her own cup.

"All quiet," she said. "Too quiet. The telephone's dead. On the credit side, there's no sign of any air activity. Back to the debit side—I'd have been expecting that there'd have been rioting in the city by now."

"How would we know if there was any rioting?"

"There would be fires, explosions. All I can think of is that the various rebel factions are waiting to see which way the cat will jump. And there are so many rebel factions. The OAP and all the planetary organizations. The Texans, for example, would be quite happy to see the New Cantonese pulling the hot chestnuts out of the fire from them."

"And everybody would like to use me as a cat's paw."

"We're here with you, Grimes. Raoul, and all the New Cantonese, and even Sergeant Martello."

"I still can't make him out."

"It's simple. He just hates Bardon, is all. He had his rackets, as do all the Terran troops on Liberia. He was poaching on Bardon's preserves. Bardon became the heavy colonel and put a stop to the sergeant's little games. And then, when

Bardon, during that telephone conversation, made it plain that he didn't give a damn about the safety of his own people in the Residence, that was it."

"So all his other talk, about playing at pirates and the rest of it, was just so much bullshit."

"Mm. Maybe. Maybe not. . . ."

Sanchez came in.

He, too, was in his own version of uniform—the faded blue denims, the scarlet neckerchief.

"Armored cars, Commodore," he announced. "Approaching from the city."

"ETA?" asked Grimes.

"Thirty minutes from now, sir."

"Good." Grimes broke another crisp roll, buttered it and then thickly spread the exposed surfaces with marmalade. "Then I've time to finish my breakfast in comfort."

"But we could ambush the armored cars, sir. There're low walls along the road as they approach the Residence."

"Captain Sanchez," Grimes told him severely, "*we* cannot afford to break the law, such as it is. *They* must be seen to fire the first shot. Besides," he went on, "our firearms won't make much impression on their armor."

"We could get the officers," said Raoul, "before they button up. And the kitchen staff has been making Molotov cocktails."

"Their intentions may be peaceful," said Grimes. "Mind you, I shall be surprised if they are. But, until we know for certain. . . ." He bit into his roll. He did not, now, feel much like eating but he had to consider his reputation—Gutsy Grimes, the man who would not miss a meal even though the Universe were crumbling about his ears.

"I'll get back on top, sir," said Sanchez at last. "I'll let you know what develops."

"Do that, Raoul," said Grimes through a mouthful of roll and marmalade.

Eventually he got up, patted his lips with his table napkin, filled and lit his pipe. Accompanied by Su Lin he took the elevator up to the roof. They joined Sanchez on the lookout platform. Grimes took the proffered binoculars, looked at the advancing armored column. There were a half-dozen of the drab-painted six-wheeled vehicles. Their hatches were open; in each one stood the begoggled car commander. It was all very pretty and, thought Grimes, remarkably archaic. From a staff mounted on the leading car flew a large, white flag.

So there was to be a parley first.

Oh, well, thought Grimes, *I might as well hear what the man wants to say.*

He went down to the portico, stopping off in his quarters to collect his cap. He glanced at himself briefly in the wardrobe mirror. In his rather shabby uniform, with his cap at a rakish angle, with that scarlet dressing gown sash into which the pistol was thrust, he looked like the pirate that many supposed him to be. Then, outside the main entrance, he was standing there, Su Lin and Sanchez beside him and behind him the Residence staff, all armed, their colorful liveries making them look like a smartly uniformed army.

The leading car came to a halt about twenty meters from the portico. The officer climbed down from the turret. He was a man whom Grimes did not recognize. He was carrying, on a stick, another white flag, a small one.

He came to attention before Grimes and then, it seemed, thought better of it. He fell into what could be described only as an insolent slouch.

"You are John Grimes?" he asked.

"I have that honor," Grimes replied.

"You are under arrest. I have to inform you that any resistance will make things all the worse for you and your people."

"You've come to the wrong shop this time, Major Johnston," said Grimes.

"My name is not Johnston," said the major, obviously baffled by the historical allusion.

"Maybe not. And this isn't Sydney, New South Wales. And now, sir, I'm ordering you off my premises. And take your mechanized tin cans with you."

"Very well, sir. You have been warned."

The officer turned, marched back to his armored car. Grimes and the others retreated inside the Residence. The big, solid doors slammed shut but they could not keep out the sound of the highly amplified voice that was shouting, over and over again, "Come out! Come quietly! Come out, or I open fire!"

This ceased when a marksman on the roof scored a hit on the sonic projector. Almost immediately there came the rattle of heavy machine gun fire. The doors shuddered but held. Nothing came through them—but it could not be long before they were literally chewed away. The doors held—but windows shattered. "Down!" Martello was bawling in his sergeant's voice. "Down!"

People were dropping to the floor but none of them was a casualty.

Yet.

Grimes went up to the roof, found his way to the parapet that was little more than a low gutter rim. He crouched behind it, beside one of the chefs who was pouring automatic fire down on the cars. He tapped the man on the shoulder. "Hold your fire until it can do some good," he admonished. "Ammunition doesn't grow on trees. . . ." The man grinned at him cheerfully, inserted a fresh clip into his weapon and blazed away again. But if the defenders were the rankest amateurs the attackers were not much better. Had they continued to concentrate their fire on the main entrance they would have been through it in minutes. But they seemed to be playing at Red Indians attacking a wagon train, circling the Residence. And they were not using their laser cannon. That made sense, Grimes supposed. Lasers could start a disastrous fire and Estrelita O'Higgins had made it clear that she did not want the building too badly damaged. Meanwhile, these circling tactics ensured that nobody escaped. Perhaps the intention was to starve the defenders out.

Then Bardon would have a long wait, thought Grimes wryly. The Residence's larders were very well-stocked. There was a deep freeze that could almost have accommodated a herd of mastodons.

It was a situation approaching stalemate—until one of the armored cars broke down. Martello's tale of slovenly maintenance had been a true one. The defenders on the roof concentrated their fire on the stalled vehicle. There was a chance, just a chance, that a lucky bullet might find a chink in the armor. Eventually the major decided that he had better do something about it. Three cars moved into position to shield the disabled one from the fire from the roof while a fourth one moved into position just in front of it. A tow . . . thought Grimes. A tow. . . . That meant that hatches would have to be opened so that somebody could climb out to fix the towing wires. Where were those Molotov cocktails that he had heard about?

And somehow they were there, ready to hand, ten bottles with rag wicks, not yet ignited. filled with some clear fluid. An aroma more intoxicating than unpleasant was making itself known despite the reek of cordite. And Su Lin was there, her golden lighter in her hand. Grimes got recklessly to his feet, holding one of the bottles. "Light it!" he ordered the girl. She obeyed. The flame blowing back from the flaring wick scorched his arm as he threw.

The missile fell well short, bursting spectacularly but harmlessly.

"I should have played cricket when I was a boy," remarked Grimes glumly. He raised his voice. "Are there any cricketers here? Any fast bowlers?"

(If only the Residence staff were Indian and not Chinese . . .)

"Cricket?" Martello's rough voice was contemptuous. "Baseball was my game. Commodore. Still is. An' I'm a pitcher, not a bowler . . . Gimme!"

He snatched the bottle from Grimes's hand, waited until Su Lin had ignited the wick, then threw. Neither range nor direction could have been bettered. He threw again, and again. From the armored cars there was screaming. At least one of the Molotov cocktails must have found an open hatch.

He let fly with two more bottles.

He was a good target standing there, too good a target. A burst of machinegunfire caught him, threw him back onto the gentle slope of the roof. Crabwise, Grimes scrambled to him but there was nothing he could do. The entire front of the big man's body was . . . shredded. Shredded and pulped. Even his face was gone.

I shall never know what really made him tick, thought Grimes, gulping back his nausea.

Then he heard the explosions.

Crouching, he made his way back to the parapet. Two of the armored cars were burst open, literally. Their ammunition must have gone up. A third was on its side, its wheels spinning uselessly. A fourth, its rear wheels gone, looked ludicrously like a circus elephant trying to sit down.

The two survivors had turned and were retreating, fast. The turret hatch of the down-by-the-stern car opened. From it was poked a rifle barrel to which a white rag of some kind had been tied.

"Hold your fire!" ordered Grimes.

Su Lin repeated the command in a language that the New Cantonese could understand.

Slowly a man clambered out through the hatch, slid down to the ground, stood there with hands upraised. He was joined, after a long interval, by two others.

"We surrender!" shouted the first man, a sergeant.

"We don't want you!" called Grimes. "Just get the hell out of here!" Then, "No! Stop! Look after your mates first!"

They managed, at last, to persuade those in the overturned car to open up. Only two men crawled out.

"Where's the other?" shouted Grimes.

"Dead, sir. His neck's broken."

"I want to see him!"

"Why?" whispered Su Lin.

"Haven't you heard of the Trojan Horse?" he countered.

The corpse was dragged out. The man was obviously dead, his head almost twisted off his body. And, thought Grimes, nothing could possibly be living in the two still-smoking wrecks.

The five men shambled down the road.

"You're too soft-hearted, Grimes," said Su Lin. "You should have made them bury their own dead before you let them go."

"I never thought of it," admitted Grimes.

He was conscious of the smell of burnt meat drifting up from the destroyed cars. He thought ruefully that disposing of the mess left over after a space battle is so much easier than disposing of similar mess on a planetary surface.

Forty-four

The gardeners formed the burial detail and seemed more annoyed at having to mar the beauty of the Residence lawn than by the true, gruesome nature of their work. Martello was laid to rest a little apart from the others. Some day, thought Grimes, the sergeant would have his monument, a statue depicting him in the uniform of a baseball player, not of a soldier, frozen in stone or metal in the act of pitching.

Grimes, as Governor, conducted a brief service, one that he modeled on that used by the Federation Survey Service, whose personnel observed a wide variety of religions or none at all, that was used for enemies as well as friends.

"These men," he said, "did their duty as they saw it. They will be missed by their friends and relations. Let us not dishonor their remains. May they rest in peace."

Then Sanchez, with a work party, set about salvaging weaponry from the wrecked cars. He hoped to be able to dismount both the heavy machine guns and the laser cannon from the two not too badly damaged vehicles. Su Lin and Grimes went to his sitting room to see what news programs, if any, they could find on the playmaster.

They were lucky.

Almost immediately they found a channel on which a grave-faced newscaster was keeping his listeners up to date on what had been happening.

". . . the criminal John Grimes. According to reports that we have received, Colonel Bardon, as instructed by President O'Higgins, sent a force of six armored cars, under Major Jackson, to arrest the ex-Governor. It seems that Grimes and his criminal associates have barricaded themselves in the Residence and are refusing to give themselves up to justice. Two of the military vehicles have returned to the city, to the barracks, where Major Jackson is making his report to Colonel Bardon. The remaining four are maintaining the siege, ensuring that the notorious ex-pirate and his gang do not escape to terrorize the countryside.

"A statement issued by Colonel Bardon assures us that the situation is well in hand."

There followed a report on a game of soccer. Su Lin switched channels. The commentator whom she found could have been an archbishop in mufti.

"... must be made to realize that we, as a proud and independent planet, cannot, will not and must not accept as gubernatorial figureheads men of dubious character. . . ."

Su Lin switched channels again.

"... minor rioting in the Vanzetti Plaza district . . ."

There were shots of police charging demonstrators, of demonstrators pelting police with rocks, bottles and other missiles. There was an explosion, after which the façade of a building crumbled in almost slow motion. A mist of tear gas hung over everything.

And there was the shouting: Grimes! Grimes! Grimes!

"Somebody is acting at last," said Su Lin happily. "I wish I could see who they are. Oh, hell! Here come the water cannon!"

And so that riot, thought Grimes, soon became a washout.

"We shan't get the real blowup," said Su Lin earnestly, "until there's a direct confrontation between you and Bardon, and you win. You've seen how O'Higgins and Bardon have handled the first engagement. Almost certainly there was TV coverage of the action; I shan't be at all surprised if Raoul finds cameras in the armored cars. But those shots will never be shown. Not unless—*until*—we win."

"And I can't see us winning until there's something better than that abortive riot we saw. And I can't see any sort of uprising until we show the people that we can beat Bardon." He thoughtfully filled and lit his pipe. "But why doesn't he use his ground-to-ground missiles? He must have some in his armory. . . ."

"Because he wants you alive. He's not fussy about the rest of us—but he wants *you.* There must be a show trial. And *he* will be on trial as well as you. He must be seen to have acted with moderation despite great provocation. He must present the image of statesman as well as soldier. And then, after you've been found guilty and deported, who will be Governor *de facto,* soon to become Governor *de jure?*

"Bardon, of course."

"I'd never have given him credit for that many brains," said Grimes.

"It's dear Estrelita that has the brains, not him."

"Estrelita may be the statesman, but not the soldier. What Bardon does next is our immediate worry. Mphm. My guess is another attack, by land, tomorrow morning. With full TV coverage—not be released unless things go well. If I were him I'd use a squadron of hover-tanks. . . ."

"Sergeant Martello cast doubts upon their serviceability."

"I hope he was right. I hope most sincerely that he was right. Meanwhile, we'll maintain full watches during the night and have all hands on deck at sunrise."

Forty-five

Grimes—just in case Bardon did mount a bombing attack, either from aircraft or by rockets—ordered that bedding be shifted down from the ground floor into the basements of the Residence. He decided, however, that he would remain in his palatial quarters. Su Lin had almost convinced him that he would be more use to O'Higgins and Bardon alive than dead. He was willing to take chances with his own life—but not with the lives of others.

The armored cars had yielded two useful heavy machine guns and a good supply of ammunition. Their crews, however, had removed the crystals from the laser cannon before abandoning the vehicles, must have taken these with them. This was annoying, but Grimes felt a grudging respect for the men. They were not altogether devoid of the soldierly virtues.

The night was quiet.

The sentries, with their powerful night glasses, maintained their vigil on the roof. The only thing that they reported was a fire of some kind in the city. Grimes went up to look. It did not seem to be a very big conflagration. He and Su Lin caught a late night TV news session on the playmaster and there was no mention of it. There was no further mention of the riot that they had seen earlier. And, they learned to their amusement, Colonel Bardon's armored cars still had the Residence under siege. It would not be long, said the smug announcer, before the notorious pirate commodore was brought to justice.

Grimes turned in.

Su Lin turned in with him.

They knew, both of them, that no matter what the outcome would be they would not be enjoying much more time together. They had been thrown together by circumstances beyond their control—and other circumstances, inevitably, must soon send them on their separate ways.

They would enjoy what they had while they had it.

* * *

When Grimes awoke, in the early morning, Su Lin was no longer with him although her place in the bed was still warm. Had there been some kind of emergency? But had this been so he would have been called.

Then the lights came on as the girl entered the bedroom, bringing with her the tray with the steaming teapot, the cups, the sugar bowl and the lemon slices. They sipped the hot, fragrant drink in companionable silence, their naked bodies in close contact.

She said, at last, "You pirate chiefs do yourself well, don't you?"

"Only when they have pirate molls like you to look after them. . . ."

There was a gentle tapping at the door.

Wong Lee came in. He looked at the couple in the bed with an odd combination of regret and approval; certainly there was no censoriousness.

"Your Excellency," he said, "a body of troops approaches from the city."

"Hover-tanks?" asked Grimes.

"No, Your Excellency. There are vehicles, but they seem to be personnel carriers."

"See that all weapon posts are manned. Oh—and better get the galley staff to make plenty of tea and piles of sandwiches. We may have the chance to grab a bite before the shooting starts."

"All that is already in hand, Your Excellency."

"Good man!"

Grimes jumped out of the bed, ran through to the bathroom. He made a hasty toilet, despite the fact that he was joined there by Su Lin. He even found time to depilate, knowing that a scruffy, unshaven commanding officer does not inspire the same confidence as one who looks clean and bright and on top of the Universe. He dressed again in his Far Traveler Couriers uniform, with the pistol thrust under the red sash. Followed by the girl, who was clad in form-fitting black blouse and slacks, he went up to the lookout platform.

The sun was just up.

The column of personnel carriers, led by a command car, was still a long way off, approaching slowly along the winding road from the capital.

Raoul Sanchez came to him.

He said, "I've set up the two heavy MGs to cover the drive."

"What makes you think they'll use the drive, Raoul? Those are foot soldiers. They have almost the same freedom of movement over any sort of terrain as a hover-tank."

"I had to put the guns *somewhere,* sir."

"Sorry, Raoul. And, after all, guests usually try the front door first."

He could see quite clearly now, with the aid of the powerful binoculars, the men sitting in the personnel carriers. They were wearing full battle armor. This would restrict their freedom of movement but would protect them from almost anything short of a direct hit by a heavy artillery shell. Too, a laser cannon would fry them inside their carapaces but Grimes didn't have any laser cannon, only a few pistols.

He absentmindedly munched a ham sandwich that somebody had brought him. There wasn't enough mustard.

"They're stopping," said Sanchez unnecessarily.

They were stopping, had stopped.

Two tall figures got down from the command car.

Bardon, decided Grimes. Bardon, and . . . ?

In spite of the all-concealing battle armor he knew that the other one was a woman by the way that she was moving.

So Estrelita O'Higgins was making political capital by being present at the kill.

Soldiers were disembarking from the troop carriers, forming up on the road. How many of them were there? Grimes swore under his breath. There must be at least five hundred of them. Five hundred well-armed (definitely), well-trained (possibly) professional soldiers against less than one fifth that number of rank amateurs. Even Grimes was an amateur in this sort of warfare. The Residence was not a spaceship.

Somebody must still be in the command car, using a sonic projector.

"Surrender! Come out, all of you, with your hands raised! Show a white flag to surrender!"

There was a small flagstaff on the lookout platform; so far as Grimes knew it was rarely used. But the halyards were intact. He went to them, cleared them.

"A flag . . ." he muttered. "A flag . . ."

"Sir, surely not . . ." Sanchez sounded heartbroken. "You're not showing the white flag, sir?"

"Who said anything about a *white* flag? I want something, anything, that's as unlike a white flag as possible!"

"Here!" said Su Lin, thrusting a bundle of some black cloth at him. He took it from her and suddenly realized that she had removed her shirt.

But it would do.

The black flag—the black flag of piracy, Grimes's enemies would say—rose jerkily to the masthead, stirring lazily in the light morning breeze.

Bardon put on a show.

Grimes watched it with grudging respect. There was more to the man than he had thought. He must have made a study of Australian history. Perhaps he had gotten the idea from Major Jackson's report to him on his conversation with Grimes, when Grimes had said, "You've come to the wrong shop this time, Major Johnston . . ." The New South Wales Corps, with rattling drums and squealing fifes, had marched on Bligh's Government House to place him under arrest. A drum and fife band preceded Bardon's Bullies, playing some derisory tune that Grimes could not identify.

And those musicians were unarmed, unarmored. Bardon was trading on Grimes's decency, gambling that he would not open fire on the bandsmen.

Grimes at last recognized the tune. *Lillibullero.* It had never been one of his favorites. Nonetheless, he thought wryly, the bandsmen deserved to be shot for murdering it.

But how would it look, how would it look on TV screens throughout the planet—and, eventually, on Earth—when men whose only weapons were fifes and drums were mown down by a man who had just hoisted, atop his castle, the black flag of piracy?

They were taking their time marching up the drive toward the main entrance of the Residence—the bandsmen in their colorful dress uniforms, Bardon behind them, with Estrelita O'Higgins striding, in step, beside him and, after them, the rank upon rank of robotlike troopers.

Down came the troopers, one . . . two . . . three . . .

And four, and five, and six, and . . .

Those drummers couldn't keep a tune. The beat was ragged, becoming more so. Men were having trouble keeping in step. But was that arhythmic throbbing coming from ground level? It was not. It was surging down from the sky in ragged waves.

Whistles shrilled.

The approaching army halted. Men looked upwards. Weapons were deployed to sweep the sky—but not fired. There was a ship there. A civilian ship, not a warship. An *Epsilon* Class star tramp. It would not be the first time in history that neutral onlookers had been present at a battle, as sensation-hungry voyeurs.

The spaceship steadily lost altitude. Was she going to land? Did Captain Agatha Prinn intend to rescue her one-time Commodore? *Keep out of this, you silly bitch!* Grimes was thinking, was saying aloud. *Keep out of it! If you do land you'll get shot up, and Bardon's story will be that you were caught in the crossfire . . .*

But *Agatha's Ark* was not landing. She hovered there, the cacophony of her inertial drive deafening. And was that a cargo hatch opening in her dull, pitted side? It was. Things were falling out, tumbling earthwards, bursting as they hit the ground. Bardon's men stumbled through the stifling, white cloud, the machinery of their armor clogged by the fine particles. They looked like men caught in a sudden blizzard. Grimes was reminded of pictures he had seen of Napoleon's Retreat from Moscow.

There was a lull in the bombardment.

Grimes, accompanied by Su Lin and a half dozen of the Residence's domestic staff, ran out over the flour-caked lawn and grabbed the dazed Bardon and Estrelita O'Higgins, hustled them inside the building. Sanchez, with another party, captured Bardon's command car without firing a shot. In it was the TV equipment that would be covering the taking of the Residence.

It was covering, now, the ignominious defeat of Bardon's Bullies.

Very shortly afterward other TV units, in the city, were covering the riots that immobilized the remainder of the Terran garrison and drove the members of Estrelita O'Higgins's police into hiding. Those who were lucky.

Forty-six

"I didn't think of it myself," admitted Agatha Prinn. "It was my agent, actually, Mr. Dennison of Starr, Dunleavy and Bowkett . . ."

"Dennison," said Su Lin, "is one of us. But go on, Captain Prinn."

"Mr. Dennison's idea was that I lift off as scheduled and then just sort of drift over the Residence, make a landing and snatch Grimes to safety. I said that I didn't fancy landing on anybody's lawn, no matter how big. I like to have something solid under my tail vanes when I set down. Why, I asked him, couldn't I, sort of accidentally, drop something on Bardon's boys? 'But you don't have any bombs,' he told me. 'You're just a star tramp, not a warship. And, in any case, if you play any active part in a battle, no matter on whose side, you'll be as big a pirate as your pal Grimes.'

" 'I've a cargo of flour,' I told him. 'In bags. And, while it was being loaded, some ill-intentioned person planted an incendiary device in the middle of it. Luckily this will be discovered while I'm hovering over the Residence, to pay my last respects to my old Commodore. So I will have to jettison cargo . . .' "

"Which you did," said Grimes. "I'm eternally grateful to you."

"Gratitude isn't enough, Commodore. Who's going to pay for the delay while I load a fresh cargo? Who's going to pay for the cargo that's been destroyed?"

"Lloyd's of London," Grimes told her. "I imagine that the jettison will come under the heading of General Average."

"But as the owner of *Agatha's Ark* I shall still be held liable for my share of the expense involved."

"I'm sure that Rear Admiral Damien will see you right."

"Eventually. But the tide runs very slowly through official channels."

"Then, Agatha, would you accept a job on this world, a sinecure, for a very short time and at a *very* high salary? Terms to be negotiated."

"What is it?" she asked suspiciously.

"I'm the ruler of this world until things get sorted out. A new president has to be elected and approved. Until it's done I'm the only one with legal power.

Liberia has no Examiner of Interstellar Masters and Mates. Yet. Do you want thc post?"

"What's the catch?"

"There's no catch. All you have to do is supervise just one examination. Mine. As I read the law, a Liberian Master's Certificate of Competency will be good anywhere in the Galaxy. My real Certificate, issued at Port Woomera, was suspended by that Court of Inquiry.

"So . . ."

"You're an opportunistic bastard, Grimes," she said.

"Too right," he agreed smugly.

"So we have a farce of an examination, after which I issue a Certificate of Competency, autographed by myself. Are you sure that you wouldn't like to sign it too, as Governor? And then, just to oblige you still further, I put young Sanchez on my books as Fourth Mate so he can start getting in Deep Space time for *his* certificates. Is there anything else?"

"At the moment, no. But if there is, I'll let you know."

"Do just that." She grinned. "Well, Commodore, it was all an exciting break from the usual tramping routine, just as the privateering expedition was. But I have to get back to the spaceport to see what's happening to the *Ark.* I have a strong suspicion that Lloyd's surveyors will be sniffing around the hold, trying to find evidence of a fire. . . ."

"And will there be?" asked Grimes.

"Surely, Commodore, you would not expect me to defraud an insurance company?"

She finished her drink, got up and strode out of the Governor's sitting room. (Its windows repaired, the Residence was habitable again.) Grimes and Su Lin watched her go.

Agatha Prinn, thought Grimes, was one of the women whom he would always remember with affection. Just as—he looked at her, lounging gracefully in her chair—Su Lin would be.

"What will you do now?" she asked suddenly.

"I . . . I was thinking of resigning. As soon as they can arrange a relief for me. Once I have a valid Certificate of Competency I can take over command of my ship again. But . . . I'm not so sure. Suppose I don't resign. Suppose I stay here, as Governor . . ."

"If they let you."

He ignored this.

"Being Governor's Lady wouldn't be a bad life for a woman, Su Lin. And I'd need somebody like you, who knows the planet better than I do."

"I'm sorry," she told him. "Genuinely sorry. But PAT will be reassigning me. Dennison is arranging for my passage off Liberia now. But cheer up. We'll meet again some time. There's bound to be some complicated mess somewhere that will take the two of us to clear up. And I could never settle down on one world for keeps, any more than you could.

"You're lucky. Admit it. You'll soon be getting your precious *Sister Sue* back."

But I lost Fat Susie, he thought, *and even that lopsided apology for a balloon,* Little Susie. *And it will not be long before I lose Su Lin.*

Somehow, suddenly, his memories of the girl were more vivid, more real than her flesh and blood actuality. Their lovemaking in the wrecked airship . . . She standing beside him, proudly bare-breasted, while he hoisted the piratical black flag on the flagstaff on the roof of the Residence . . .

Damn it all, he would even miss having her lighting his pipe for him.

Was he, after all, so lucky?